VANESSA

A NOVEL

VANESSA
A NOVEL

BY
HUGH WALPOLE

with an introduction by
ERIC ROBSON

FRANCES LINCOLN LIMITED
PUBLISHERS

FOR

ERIK PALMSTIERNA

IN

FRIENDSHIP

Frances Lincoln Ltd
4 Torriano Mews
Torriano Avenue
London NW5 2RZ
www.franceslincoln.com

Vanessa
First published 1933
Text copyright © The Estate of Hugh Walpole, 1933
Introduction copyright © Eric Robson, 2008

First Frances Lincoln edition: 2008
PUBLISHERS NOTE
In order to accomodate binding limitations it has been necessary
to omit six blank (but numbered) pages from this edition.
They are pages 257-8, 472-3 and 664-5.
The text is complete.

A catalogue record for this book is available from the British Library.

ISBN 978-0-7112-2892-4

Printed in the UK by CPI Bookmarque, Croydon, CR0 4TD

1 3 5 7 9 8 6 4 2

INTRODUCTION

WHEN *Rogue Herries* was first published in March 1930 John Buchan said it was the best novel published in English since *Jude the Obscure*. Hugh Walpole would probably have preferred him to say that it was the best novel in English since *Redgauntlet* because, on the whole, he felt more at home with Scott than Hardy (he had after all taken the Herries name from *Redgauntlet* as something of a homage to the master), but even so *Jude* would do very nicely.

Walpole was 46 years old and already accepted in most quarters as a novelist of the first rank. He counted among his friends and admirers Arnold Bennett, Henry James, John Galsworthy, J.B. Priestley and Virginia Woolf. He was almost as well known in America as in Britain. It was said that his stately progress through the United States outdid even that of Charles Dickens 80 years earlier. Hugh made several small fortunes from his American lecture tours and spent those fortunes filling his 'little paradise on Catbells', his house at Brackenburn overlooking Derwentwater, with fine books and exquisite pictures. He would soon be given a knighthood. The critics who had sniped at him over the years for being cosy and domestic; for being the homosexual author incapable of treating the subject of sex with any semblance of honesty, for being hopelessly romantic and for adding nothing new to the novel form, seemed to have been silenced.

Walpole had great hopes for *The Herries Chronicle*. 'These four books shall *clinch* my reputation or I'll die in the attempt' as he wrote in his journal. Thumbing his nose at any critic still lurking in the shrubbery he described *Rogue Herries* as 'a fine, queer book in the big manner'. When *Judith Paris* was published the following year it sold out of its first printing of twenty thousand copies in less than a fortnight. In 1932 *The Fortress* was greeted by reviews which said it was even better than the first two books in the series and in 1933 Hugh recorded in his journal that *Vanessa* had received 'nearly sixty reviews now and not one spiteful one'. $12,500 for the film rights from Metro-Goldwyn-Mayer was the icing on Walpole's fantastical cake.

But just as Walpole was beginning to enjoy the success of this, the grandest of his projects, a book appeared which would cast a shadow over his later years. 'A stab in the back', as he described it at the time. The book was *Cakes and Ale* by a man he'd considered a friend, Somerset Maugham, and included the character Alroy Kear, a self-serving social and literary snob who so desperately wanted to be; who connived and trampled to be the grand old man of letters. Walpole was convinced that Maugham had modelled the character on him. Maugham denied it (and, indeed, others thought it was an attack on Thomas Hardy) but Hugh, always ready to imagine enemies, would have none of it. When Maugham wrote a placatory letter Hugh petulantly replied signing himself 'Alroy Maugham Walpole'.

The anger didn't last because Hugh Walpole simply couldn't keep his boundless generosity down.

He confided in his journal that *Cakes and Ale* could only do him harm if his character was really like that. 'And if it is like that the sooner I pass out the better'. When a few years later an anonymous American author published a book there called *Gin and Bitters* which was a vicious attack on Maugham (some muttered behind their hands that Walpole had written it in revenge for *Cakes and Ale*) Hugh leapt to his friend's defence. 'I am not writing this from hysteria or any motive but one of real and true affection for yourself'. But if the generosity of spirit that allowed Hugh to write that and to help so many young writers throughout his lifetime was his greatest strength of character, his main weakness was that he had always been thin-skinned; had always worried about his legacy. Would memory of his books fade as it had with so many once famous, once feted Victorian novelists? In an essay on reading published in 1926 Walpole wrote, 'There is at the present time a superstition far too general among clever people that if a book has any large sale it cannot be good literature, and it is amusing for an onlooker to perceive how an author who has been a hero of a clever critic only yesterday may go down in his estimation as soon as a book by him wins a wide public appreciation'.

Hugh Walpole was right to worry. When he 'passed out' in 1941 at the tragically early age of 57 his critics and detractors were quick to emerge from the literary undergrowth. A particularly vitriolic obituary in The Times belittled his achievements and described him as a 'sentimental egotist' who was unpopular with his fellow writers. Many of those writers sprang to his defence. T.S. Eliot and J.B. Priestley sent indignant letters of protest but the damage had been done. He had written almost fifty books but they are all out of print save for this revival of *The Herries Chronicle.*

The irony about Sir Hugh Walpole's unwarranted loss of popularity is that for some decades he'd been his publisher's favourite author. He'd arrived on the literary scene, not as a shooting star that quickly burned out but as a hard working writer who steadily built a popular following as one novel followed another and each attracted a bigger, more appreciative audience. And there were several nibs to Walpole's prolific pen. Essentially a romantic he had a taste for the macabre and wrote psychological thrillers. One of them, *The Prelude to Adventure* attracted the attention of Carl Jung who described it as a psychological masterpiece. He wrote books for and about children, books about politics, war and religion, studies of Joseph Conrad and Anthony Trollope, drama and short stories.

When Walpole was at work he was superstitious and spontaneous. Many of his novels were started on Christmas Eve at his sister's house in Edinburgh which he believed would bring the book good luck. He dreamed the plots of many of his novels. But when he started to put those dreams to paper he worked at a frantically businesslike pace, writing in a stream of consciousness, scarcely ever revising. His critics described him as sloppy, not taking sufficient care to pick and choose his way through the perfections of language, but the sheer energy of his writing explains why books such as the *Herries* novels are still so vibrant.

There's no doubt that in some ways he was sloppy. His grasp of spelling, punctuation, consistency and historical research left a lot to be desired. He once received more than fifty letters from readers pointing out that a lady in one of his novels had a moustache on one page and none at all on another. He called his second novel *Marradick at Forty* but spelt it *Fourty* throughout the manuscript. Fortunately, at his publishers, Macmillans, there was an editor called Thomas Mark who quietly and unobtrusively sorted most things out. As Walpole's biographer Rupert Hart-Davis says, 'No one who has not compared manuscript with printed book will ever know what Hugh Walpole, particularly in the *Herries* novels, owed to Thomas Mark; but Hugh knew'.

Hugh recognised another debt, too. The debt he owed to Cumberland. He writes of his discovery of the Lake District in a rare volume of reminiscences, *Apple Trees*, published in a limited edition at Christmas 1932, just after he had completed *Vanessa*.

'I sat with my mother in a field above Ullswater. It was a perfect summer evening. They were bringing in the hay, with singing and laughter, and light – spinning as with the murmurous flash of a million golden insects – sparkled upon Ullswater... This was in fact recovered country, for as children we had been brought – my sister, brother and I – year after year to Sower Myre Farm near Gosforth – a village between Wastwater and Seascale. The years of our childhood are of course the foundation of all our life. We never altogether emerge from them.'

Restless, uncertain, at times neurotic, Hugh drew a sort of strength from memories of childhood innocence. He once wrote in his journal 'Dickens never grew up. I believe the best authors never do'. And of all the places he visited on his extensive travels nowhere captured that spirit of innocence more clearly than the Lakeland that had captivated a little boy all those years before. Standing there within sight of the Wasdale Screes and with Black Combe on the horizon it was a revelation as powerful as Alfred Wainwright's on Orrest Head. 'I stood on the pebbly path that bordered the garden behind Sower Myre farm and drank in the scene. That moment was my initiation. That little windy garden, smelling of cow-dung, carnations, snapdragons and – in some mysterious spiritual fashion – hens' feathers, looked straight out to sea.'

It was the enduring power of those memories that led directly to the *Herries* novels. From Hugh's diary on the 28th of August, 1925. 'I'm now pinning all my hopes to two or three Lakeland novels, which will at least do something for this adorable place. I feel a longing desire to pay it back for some of its goodness to me.'

Walpole the brave incomer, Walpole the alchemist set about mingling the particles of person and place that would be the dust from which grew his 200 year saga. To do justice to these powerful ingredients he created a new sort of romanticism. Not the make-believe armour of Arthurian legend; not the fragrant superficialities of the pre-Raphaelites. Instead, a style at once simple but also shot through with flashes of sensuous beauty. A style of romanticism that encourages a revolt against materialism and which, beyond the world of the senses espouses the emotional and the spiritual. A style that would be mocked by some modern novelists who thought Walpole altogether too plain, too 'real'.

But perhaps the verdict should come from the people amongst whom he was writing and about whom he was writing. As Marguerite Steen put it in her study of Walpole published just after *Herries* was completed, 'the North has accepted Hugh Walpole...it has accepted him as its interpreter: not that it cares particularly whether "foreigners" understand it or not. But it feels that through him it will be truly and justly represented in the eyes of the world: without sentimentality – which it abhors – but with due regard to that curious blend of common sense and romance which is the birthright of the Lakeland dweller.'

Walpole was, above all else, a traditional novelist and proud of it. A traditional novelist that told old truths in new ways and new truths in old ways. In 1932 he allowed himself the luxury of a little side swipe at 'modern' novelists in a monograph produced by Leonard and Virginia Woolf's Hogarth Press. In it he pointed out that, ancient or modern, all novelists are bound by the same creative rules. 'A creator works first for himself – he gives his notion of the universe through the shape and colour of his personality. He can, poor devil, do none other. Afterwards his work collects around it the citizens of the same world as himself. Be they deaf and blind, halt and maim, it is no matter. He must not be disturbed. He can do only what he can.'

ERIC ROBSON

A PREFATORY LETTER

My dear Erik,

      I take the greatest pleasure in dedicating this final novel in the Herries series to yourself because during those last years our friendship has been one of the best things I possess.

      With that pleasure I must contrast a very real sense of loss. I am, as I write the last lines of *Vanessa*, saying good-bye to work that has been, for the last six years, my constant preoccupation. It cannot interest my readers that Judith, Benjie, Vanessa and the others have appeared to me such real and constant friends, but now, as they vanish down the wind, I feel a true and personal loneliness.

      But I should like to thank those readers who have also found them friends, and to urge upon one or two critics that long novels are no new thing, and have been always in the tradition of the English novel.

      Yet more boldly I would say that in this present case these four Herries novels are intended to be read as one novel, and I hope that some day there will be a reader who will both live long enough and be idle enough to read them so ?

VANESSA

But one ambition of mine is, I find, already realised. Some of those who love and know Cumberland have found in these pages a tribute to that country which has pleased them.

Affectionately,

Hugh Walpole

'Therefore, like as May month flowereth and flourisheth in many gardens, so in like wise let every man of worship flourish his heart in this world, first unto God, and next unto the joy of them that he promised his faith unto; for there was never worshipful man nor worshipful woman, but they loved one better than another : and worship in arms may never be foiled, but first reserve the honour to God, and secondly the quarrel must come of thy lady : and such love I call virtuous love.'

SIR THOMAS MALORY

CONTENTS

PART I

PART II

VANESSA

PART III

PART IV

PART I

THE RASCAL

THE HUNDREDTH BIRTHDAY

At the sight of her son Judith's eyes and mouth broke into the loveliest smile that any member of the Herries family, there present, had ever seen. It was Judith Paris' hundredth birthday. The Family was making a Presentation.

Adam bent down and kissed her. Her tiny, trembling hand rested on the velvet collar of his coat, then lay against his cheek. Her triumph was complete; her exceeding happiness over-flowed so that, laughing though she was, tears rolled down her cheeks.

Afterwards, at the luncheon downstairs, Adam was to make the speech, but when the time came, the one that he made was very feeble. Everyone (except of course Adam's wife, Margaret, and Adam's young daughter, Vanessa) agreed that he was no speaker; the speech of the occasion came, oddly enough, from Amery Herries, of whom no one had expected very much. There were more speeches at the dinner later in the day—Timothy, Barney Newmark, Carey Rockage, Captain Will Herries, all spoke—but it was Amery who was afterwards recalled.

'Damned good speech, d'you remember?'

years later one Herries would say to another.
'At old Madame's Hundredth Birthday party up
in Cumberland. . . . Best speech ever I heard in
my life.'

Adam was a failure. He never could say
anything in public, even long ago in his Chartist
days. More than that, he was thinking of his
mother, the old lady upstairs, all the time. And
more than that again, he couldn't sound the
right Herries note. He was only *quarter* Herries
anyway, and he simply wasn't able to think of
them in the grand historical light that all the
family, expectant round the luncheon table,
desired.

But Amery could. He thought of them all
(including himself) in precisely the grand manner.

All Adam said was:

'I am sure we are all very happy to be here
to-day for my mother's hundredth birthday.
You'll forgive me, I know, if I don't say very
much. Not very good at expressing my feelings.
Yes—well—I know what you're all feeling.
We're all very proud of my mother and we all
ought to be. She's like the Queen—nothing can
beat her. I don't need to tell you how good she
is. Of course I know that better than the rest
of you—naturally I would. There's no one
like her anywhere. I ask you all to drink her
health.'

And so they did—with the greatest enthusiasm.
Nevertheless there was a feeling of disappointment, for he had said nothing about the Family
—not a word. It was expected of him. After

all, even though he *was* illegitimate, his father had been of Herries blood. They knew, they had always known, that Adam Paris failed at anything that he tried. What could you expect of a fellow who had once been a Chartist and approved of these Trades Unions, was always on the wrong side, against Disraeli, in favour of tiresome agitators like Mr. Plimsoll? (They disliked any and every agitator. They disapproved of agitation.)

But Amery made everything right again with *his* speech. He didn't look his sixty-five years, so spare of figure and straight in the back; he had not run to seed like poor Garth, who led, it was feared, a most improvident and dissolute life. Amery's speech was short but entirely to the point:

'Only a word. I won't take more than a minute. But I do want to say that my friend Adam is quite right—this *is* a great occasion for all of us! There is not, I venture to say, another family in England with so remarkable a lady at the head of it as Madame whom we are gathered together to honour. It is not only that she has reached her hundredth year—although that is an achievement in itself—but that she has reached it with such vigour, such health, such courage! It is interesting to remember that nearly a hundred and fifty years ago her father, as a young man, rode pack-horse into this district, a stranger and almost you might say homeless. There were, I suppose, members of our family scattered about England at that time, but no one, I fear, had ever heard of any of them. Now, sitting round this

table to-day we have one of England's most famous
novelists—spare your blushes, Barney Newmark
—the widow of one of England's most prominent
financiers—I bow to you, Lady Herries—whose
son is following worthily in his father's footsteps
—I drink to the City, Ellis—the son of one of
England's leading Divines, the gallant Captain here
—one of the most active members, I'm told, of the
House of Peers—never been there myself, but that's
what they tell me, Carey, my son—and one of the
loveliest women in the whole of England, Mrs.
Robert Forster—I bow towards you, Veronica!

' I promised that I would be short, so I will not
point out to you how unusual a family ours is.
You know it already (loud and happily complacent
laughter). We *are* a remarkable family. Why
should we not say so? We have done, we are
doing something for England. England, glorious England, Mistress of the World as she deserves to be.' (He was going on to say something
about foreigners but remembered just in time that
Madame's husband had been a Frenchman and
that Adam had married a German.) ' So here's
to Madame and here's to England and here's to
the Herries family! May they all three live,
prosper, and help the world along the way that it
should go! '

What cheers, what enthusiasm, what excitement! He had said exactly what they were all
longing for someone to say — the one thing
needed to make the day a perfect success!

Judith's granddaughter, Adam's daughter,

little Vanessa Paris, aged fifteen, sat between her
mother and father and was so happily excited that
she found it difficult to keep still.　Some of the
ladies thought that it was not quite correct that
she should be there.　In 1874 the golden rule was
that children should be seen (at intervals) and
never heard.　She was Madame's granddaughter
and it was proper that she should have been present at the moving ceremony when the presentation was made to the old lady, but the right thing
then was for her mother to send her back to Cat
Bells where she lived.　Nevertheless Lady Herries
agreed with Emily Newmark that the child was
tall for her age, was certainly pretty in her blue
dress, and behaved with decorum.　' It's only to
be hoped,' Lady Herries said with foreboding,
' that indulgence like this won't spoil her.　But
what can you expect?　Her mother's a German.
Adam Paris can have no idea of how to bring up
a child.　I never allowed,' Lady Herries added,
' Ellis any liberties, and no mother could wish for
a more perfect son.'

Vanessa, of course, neither knew nor cared what
anyone was saying.　She trusted the whole world
and everything and everyone in it.　She loved
everybody and especially her mother, her father,
her grandmother, Aunt Jane Bellairs, Benjamin,
Will Leathwaite (how she wished that he was
here and could see all that was going on!　She
was storing everything up to tell him when she
was home again).

From where she sat she could watch everything
that Benjamin did and said.　For the rest she was

sharply observant. She noticed the large and very hideous yellow brooch that Lady Herries wore on her meagre bosom, the beautiful colour of Aunt Elizabeth's hair (many of the ladies were her aunts, although not strictly so in chronology), the way that fat Garth Herries swallowed his wine and smacked his lips at intervals, the funny way that Aunt Jane (who had just come down from upstairs and reported that Madame was doing *splendidly* —not the *least* tired by all the fuss) made little pellets of her bread, Aunt Amabel's suspicious manner of eating as though she suspected poison in every mouthful, and the shy frightened air of Ellis. (She supposed that *that* was because his mother was watching him!)

Of them all there were two who especially interested her. One was Benjamin, whom she loved with all her heart, and the other was a lady whose name she did not know, whom she had never seen before, who appeared to her the perfection of grace and beauty.

First Benjamin, whom she knew so well that he was like part of herself. She had loved him from the first moment of seeing him when, himself between six and seven, and she somewhere about two, he had made her first sticky and afterward sick with toffee that he had made against orders at the kitchen fire. Her first memory of him was connected with disobedience; so she had known him ever after, always against the law, always doing things of which she shouldn't approve, but she kept sacred to the death every secret confided to her. She would never betray him; she would always love him for ever and ever. It was as simple as that. She knew with that intuitive quickness given to children that her mother did not approve of him. She knew more—that no one approved of him. He lived up at the Fortress with his mother, the lovely Elizabeth, and his grandfather, old broken-down Sir Walter, and it was supposed that Benjamin looked after the estate. In a way, as Vanessa knew, he did. In his own way. He would work like a saint and a hero for a week, really work and with good solid common sense. Then he would have a mad spell, disappear for days to the sorrow and grief of his mama. He told Vanessa that he simply couldn't help it. 'Must breathe fresh air,' he said. He never told anyone where he went. He was already, as Vanessa knew, 'suspect' by the Family. He had been a failure at Rugby: there were stories of scandalous doings in Town. 'He's going to be no good.' 'The makings of a fine Rascal,' and, as always with the Herries family when speaking of someone of whom they disapproved, their voices took on a sort of ceremonial ring, a kind of chanting sound. 'But what can you expect? His grandfather shot himself, and his uncle murdered his father. What an inheritance! And look at his other grandfather!—up at the Fortress—what a life he's led! Nothing better now than an idiot!'

No, poor Benjie has no chance at all, they decide with satisfaction. Nevertheless they could not help but like him—when they were with him. Of course it was different when their backs were turned. But in his company it was difficult not to smile. He was so merry, so gay, always laughing. So generous too. ' No one's enemy but his own,' Barney Newmark, who liked him greatly, said—and poor old Garth Herries, who had been no one's enemy but his own to such an extent that he was a complete wreck and ruin, sighed sadly in reply.

Vanessa was aware of much of this, although no one had ever told her. She was always hot in Benjie's defence, no matter what the charge might be. When someone accused him it was as though she herself were accused; she was conscious at such times of a strange pain in her heart—a feeling of tenderness, sympathy and apprehension. Now, as she looked across the table at him, she knew that he had no need of her sympathy. He was at his very gayest. He was not large—he would be rather a small man—but his shoulders were broad, his head round, bullet-shaped, his colour red and brown like a healthy pippin, his nose snub, his blue eyes bright and sparkling. If all the Herries were like horses, as someone had said, then Benjie was like a racy little pony, ready for anything and especially mischief. ' He's wild and, I'm sure, wicked. In fact I *know* he's wicked,' Lady Herries said. ' And Ellis doesn't like him at all. But what can you expect with such a family history? ' Then dropping her voice and looking into Emily Newmark's eyes with that intimate confidence felt by one upright woman for another: ' Women! Of course—I hear that already. . . .'

Nevertheless he was happy, he loved his beautiful mother, he feared no man, he was generous, almost everything—even the tiniest things—gave him pleasure. What if he did find women enchanting, forgot to pay his debts, possessed no sense of class at all so that a tramp was exactly the same to him as a Herries, found it difficult to work at a thing for more than a week at a time, took no thought for the morrow, saw a joke in everything? —there he was, enjoying life to the uttermost, which was more than could be said for some of the other Herries seated round the table.

As to the very beautiful lady whom Vanessa so greatly admired, her name was Rose Ormerod.

After the luncheon Vanessa flung her arms round her father and kissed him.

'Happy, my darling?'

'Oh yes. Oh yes, I've never been so happy——'

'That's right. I didn't make much of a speech, did I, my pet?'

'Oh yes, Papa! It was much better than the other one because you were thinking of Grandmama.'

'Thank you, darling. So I was. But I'm not good at speeches. That's a fact.'

She laid her cheek against his. Then, remembering, straightened up.

'Papa, may I go for a walk with Benjie? He's asked me to.'

Adam hesitated. Then, taking her small white hand between his, he said:

'All right.'

He could trust her with Benjamin. And
yet—

She clapped her hands and ran off, crying:
' Yes, Benjie, I can. Papa says I can.' She ran
into Ellis Herries and looked up laughing. ' I
beg your pardon.' She put her hand for a
moment on his sleeve.

His thin anxious face looked down at her.

' My fault, I'm sure. It's—it's a nice day,
isn't it?'

' Yes, it is.' She stood there, waiting, but
longing to get off to Benjie. It was good manners,
though, if a gentleman wished to talk to you, to
wait while he did so.

Ellis Herries was tall, thin and pale. She
noticed that he had a little brown mole in the
middle of his left cheek.

' A very happy party we're having,' he said
in his stiff anxious voice. He always spoke as
though he were afraid that the words he used
would betray him, laugh at him behind his back,
as it were.

' Oh, it *is* nice! ' She smiled, felt that she had
done her duty, and ran off.

When they walked out on to the road they
saw that they had but an hour before dark. Frost
was sharpening the air. They mounted straight
on to the moor and moved swiftly through a moth-
grey world where mountains were gigantic and
the turf was crisping under their feet. The house
stood behind them like a lighted ship. The
candles were burning in every room. Vanessa
had sometimes to run to keep up with Benjamin,

but in any case she ran because she was so happy, deeply excited and enchanted to be alone with him. Soon they slowed down, stood on a hillock and looked over to Scotland.

'There's Criffel,' he said, pointing.

'I can't see it,' Vanessa said.

'No, but it's there all the same.' He took her hand. 'I approve of you in that fine hat. Where did you find the feather?'

'Mama bought the hat in Keswick.'

He stood close to her.

'You are almost as tall as I am, Vanessa. You are going to be very tall.'

'Papa says I am. Will you never be taller, Benjie?'

'No, I hope not. You see, it's very useful to be short.'

'Useful?'

'Yes—if there's a row you can crawl under tables or hide behind a curtain or creep into the clock. I remember once in London——' He stopped.

Vanessa's innocence must be protected.

'Oh, do tell me about London!'

'One day, when you've been there. It wouldn't mean anything to you if you don't know the places.'

They walked on. They were both strong, sturdy, filled with health and excitement.

Benjamin flung out his arms.

'Don't you love this country? But of course you do. We belong to it. There'll never be any other country for either of us. Your father

once told me that when he was a boy he had a
tutor called Rackstraw who knew more about this
country than anyone. He said it was all stones
and clouds. One stone wall running up a hill,
one sky with the clouds pouring over it, and
you're happy. It's so old. There are Romans'
bones under your foot. It's so strong—Border
fights and Picts and Scots. It's so wide and
smells so good. Don't you like the smell of dry
bracken, of the trees, of the stream-water when
you lie flat and drink it? Which hill do you like
best?'

'Cat Bells,' said Vanessa promptly.

'Oh, I mean a real hill. Skiddaw has wings,
Saddleback's like a shark, Gable is a helmet . . .'
He stopped suddenly, put his arms round her and
kissed her. 'Oh, Vanessa, I do love you!'

'And I love you,' she said, a little breathless.

'Will you marry me when you grow up?'

'Of course I will,' she said, laughing.

They walked on, more slowly, he keeping his
arm around her.

'Well, you'd better not. Everyone disapproves
of me.'

'What does that matter?'

Her trust touched him most deeply.

'Would you marry me if your father and
mother forbade it?'

That was an awful question. She stopped to
consider it.

'Yes,' she said.

'Oh, you darling! But I won't allow you

to marry me. Ask anyone. No woman ought to marry me. I couldn't be faithful.'

'You would be,' said Vanessa, 'if we had children.'

'Will you like to have children?' he asked her, wondering what she would say.

'Of course. But you can't help it. God brings you a baby. You wake up in the morning and find it lying there beside you. That must be wonderful. Mama says that God knows just when you want one.'

'So you believe in God?'

Vanessa laughed. 'Why, of course. What a silly question, Benjie! Everybody does.'

'Everybody doesn't——' He pulled up. He must not disturb her.

'Of course everyone does!' she answered indignantly. 'Why, who made everything if God didn't? God's everywhere. Will Leathwaite says that when he has been swearing too much God gives him the rheumatism just to remind him.'

Benjie thought some other topic wiser.

'Well—but if I was in disgrace with everyone, had done something shameful and no one would speak to me, would you still marry me?'

'Of course I would.'

'But if you yourself thought it shameful?'

'I shouldn't think anything *you* did shameful,' she answered.

'If I killed someone as my uncle killed my father?'

She stood, puzzled, staring into the grey cold landscape.

'Yes,' she said, nodding her head. 'I would know why you did it. There would be *some* reason that I should understand.'

He caught her hands in his.

'Will you promise me that whatever happens you will always stand by me?'

'Yes, I promise.'

'Always and for ever?'

'Yes.'

'Whatever I did?'

'Yes.'

'I'll remind you of that one day.' He turned round. 'Now we'll go back to all the cats and monkeys,' he said.

They were both quiet returning. They had to go arm-in-arm, very close together, because it was growing dark. For a brief while there was a faint orange glow over Skiddaw like the reflection of a distant fire; the air grew with every moment more frosty.

Once as they were nearing the house he said:

'Don't you hate Ellis? I do. *And* his old pig of a mother.'

In the hall, standing for a moment to accustom herself to the lights and splendour after the half-dark, Vanessa found her father. He had been standing there, waiting for her, hearing the voices and laughter all over the house, the distant click of billiard-balls, someone singing to the piano sentimental songs like *Drink to me only* and *My hero, my Troubadour*, Elizabeth coming back from the Fortress where she had deposited poor old Walter, quite in pieces. She had put him to

bed. He had fallen almost at once to sleep; all
he had said, she told Adam, just before he went off
to sleep, was: 'Wake me when Uhland comes
in.' Very touching, but, as she said, a comfort for
him to think that Uhland was still alive. Sometimes, Elizabeth confessed, she thought that he
was and she could hear the tap-tap of his lame
leg mounting to his tower. . . . Then along the
passage from the kitchen came bursting Barney
Newmark and Garth and Timothy, stout, noisy
and triumphant. Why triumphant? Had they
been kissing the maids? But the Herries men got
like that very easily if things were going well and
there were no ghosts about.

In the middle of all this Adam waited anxiously
for his little daughter. His wife, Margaret,
was sitting in the parlour trying to be on terms
with Lady Herries and that fascinating Rose
Ormerod from Harrogate (she wasn't beautiful,
Adam decided—not to be compared with Elizabeth or Veronica—her nose was a little crooked, she
had a faint, a very faint moustache on her upper
lip. It was her colour, dark, black, crimson, like
a gipsy: and then she was silent—she spoke very
rarely, only smiled and used her eyes). Poor
Margaret would not be happy in there; he knew
how anxious *she* was about Vanessa! When he
told her that the child had gone for a walk with
Benjamin she gave a little cry of dismay.

'Oh, Adam! You should not have allowed her!'

'Pooh, my dear! Benjamin's safe!'

'No, he isn't! You know he isn't! And
Vanessa's growing!'

' She is only fifteen.'

He had calmed her a little, but his own fears had increased. What was he to do about this? He knew that Vanessa loved Benjamin with all the fire, loyalty, ignorance of an adoring child. Benjamin's reputation was bad, very bad. And yet he liked him. He could not help it. He had always had a weakness for sinners. . . . But Benjamin and his own child! No, no!

As the darkness strengthened about the house his alarm grew. He was about to get his coat and go after them when in they came, Vanessa glowing with colour, her eyes shining, her body so alive that it could not keep still.

He told her that she was to come up and say good-night to her grandmother.

' We must not stay for more than a moment. She is in bed and tired, of course, after such a fatiguing day. It's something to be a hundred, you know! '

Vanessa was at once subdued and still. She lived so entirely, at present, in her interest in other people that, in a moment, she became what they wanted her to be. That is if she loved them. She was quite otherwise, it is to be feared, with one or two—Aunt Amabel, for instance, whom she couldn't abide, and Timothy's fiancée, who had aggravated her by talking to her in baby language.

Judith's bedroom seemed now a mysterious place, quite different from the bright sunlit room of the morning, crowded with happy faces, and the old lady sitting so erect in her chair, smiling as they brought her their presents.

The curtains were drawn now, the room dark save for the fire and the dim lamplight beside the bed. That old four-poster with its dark hangings appeared like a little room in itself. Aunt Jane was moving softly about. When Adam and Vanessa appeared in the doorway she put her finger to her lips.

She went over to the bed, leant over.

' Aunt Judith! Aunt Judith! '

' Yes, my dear,' said a very lively voice. ' What is it? '

' Adam and Vanessa are here to say good-night.'

' Turn up the lamp.' Judith sat up, put out her hand for her spectacles, and, her eyes as sharp behind them as a bird's, said: ' That's right. Very kind of you, Adam. Come over here, my dears.'

They crossed the room, and Jane put the crimson armchair for Adam. Vanessa stood close to him, her hand on his shoulder.

The old lady seemed a little breathless. She was wearing a cap as white as snow with the sun on it, and over her shoulders Jane laid a thick white cashmere shawl. Her little face was drawn and lined, waxen in the lamplight. It was her eyes and hands that were alive, and her enchanting, humorous, slightly ironical smile.

' So I'm a hundred at last! ' she said with a sigh of satisfaction. ' That's something, Adam, isn't it? '

' Indeed it is, mother.'

' Yes, and a *very* nice day it's been.'

' You're not tired? '

' Well—a little. Yes, a little tired. My heart '—she put her hand to her breast—'jumps. There's nothing odd about that though. It's been jumping for a hundred years. It was never so steady as it ought to be.'

Vanessa smiled.

' Have you had a happy day, my darling? ' She put her hand out and took Vanessa's. How hot and dry it was, Vanessa thought—burning bones under parchment, and at the touch of it the child had a moment's realisation of what it was to be old, to be a hundred years old, to be burnt up with life and all the things that you had seen and done!

' It was nice,' Judith said, ' poor old Walter coming. Very nice. He's sadly broken up, I'm afraid. Sadly aged.' She spoke with tenderness, satisfaction and triumph. She had beaten Walter at last. She was older than he and yet here she was as lively as you like and he a poor old man who had to be led about, weak in the head, uncertain where he was!

Yet she herself was suddenly weary. She lay back on her pillow, her spectacles falling to the edge of her nose.

' I hope everyone is happy,' she murmured.

' Very happy, mother dearest,' Adam answered, catching a command from Jane's watchful eye. ' You must go to sleep now. You will be fresh as anything to-morrow.'

' Yes, dear,' Judith murmured.

Vanessa bent forward and kissed her. Then Adam, moved by the deepest emotion, tears rising to his eyes, kissed her, felt her hand lift for a moment and touch his cheek in the old familiar way.

Before they had stolen from the room she was, it seemed, asleep.

The first Ball of Vanessa's life!

Was Ball too grand a word to give to it? There was for orchestra Mrs. Blader from Troutbeck at the piano; Mr. Murdy of Keswick, violin; old Mr. Bayliss of Keswick, 'cello. There were perhaps in all thirty couples, and the dining-room, cleared, within the hour following dinner, miraculously of its table and chairs, had a perfect floor. It had often been tested. The room looked lovely, Vanessa thought, with the gleaming, glittering candelabra, the candles in their silver candlesticks, the coloured paper streamers slung from corner to corner against the ceiling. It was colours everywhere, dresses—pink, white, blue, orange—billowing and surging as the dancers moved, necks and shoulders bare, jewels sparkling; almost everyone to Vanessa seemed beautiful— even old Lady Herries, although she was absurdly painted and had a neck like a writhing chicken, had diamonds in her hair that must, Vanessa thought, be worth a fortune.

Three of the women were beautiful beyond compare—Elizabeth Herries who was fifty-nine years of age but had the arms and shoulders of a girl; and Veronica, now proudly Mrs. Forster, ' a queen of a woman, by Gad,' Will Herries murmured somewhat unwisely to his wife, who was a good woman but no beauty. The third was

Ruth Cards, who went shortly after this to live
in the wilds of Northumberland and but seldom
left them.

At first Vanessa had felt a devastating shyness.
At dinner she had been very quiet. She was
wearing her first grand evening dress and only
she and her mother knew what consultations there
had been with Miss Kew of Keswick, how often
they had paid visits to Miss Kew's stuffy little
room near St. John's, how important it had been
that it should be *half* grown-up—Miss Kew had
been alarmed: girls of fifteen did not go to Balls,
but then of course this was a family affair, a little
different . . . nevertheless, as Miss Kew confided to her brother, Mrs. Paris was a German
woman—' Such things might be well in Germany ' just as though she had said Shanghai!

So they had planned between them something
very original, the neck and shoulders bare—' Miss
Vanessa has such beautiful shoulders '—the skirt
full, but not *too* full. A pale pink silk and round
her slender neck her only piece of jewelry, a necklace of crystal beads that her father had brought
her from London.

At dinner she was certain that they must *all*
be saying: ' And what is *this* child doing here? '
All day she had been so happy that she had not
given herself a thought, but at dinner Garth
Herries had been on the one side of her and Ellis
on the other.

Rose Ormerod was Garth's other companion
and very quickly he surrendered to her as apparently all men did. He did not speak to Vanessa

once. And Ellis! Well, Ellis was very strange.
He stared at her in the oddest way. He spoke
to her confusedly as though he were afraid of her.
He said: ' I hope you are enjoying yourself,' and
then later: ' I do hope, most sincerely, that you
are enjoying yourself.' He made her embarrassed.
It was he perhaps who made her self-conscious.
He looked at her shoulders and hands, and once
he said, in a strangled fashion as though food were
choking him: ' I hope you will give me a dance.'
Very bravely she asked him once whether he
liked to live in London. ' Oh yes, indeed yes.
Very pleasant. Lived there all my life, you know.'

She coloured; she felt that it had been a very
silly question; she looked about her to find her
father, but he was sitting on the same side of the
table as herself.

Then, at first, no one asked her to dance. She
sat on a little sofa with her mother, feeling that
everyone must be looking at her bare shoulders,
not very far, if the truth must be known, from
tears. It had been a lovely day, but she had no
right to be here. She thought that, in a little
while, she would whisper something to her mother
and slip away to bed. . . .

It was Benjie who came to her rescue. The
most beautiful valse had just begun and he charged
down upon them, had her on her feet before she
knew, and then they were lost in Paradise.

She was a lovely dancer. She had danced all
her life, danced up and down the parlour at Cat
Bells while her father whistled the tunes, danced
by the Lake in Manesty, danced in the kitchen

with Will, had had dancing lessons in Keswick at
Mr. Kew's (brother to Miss Kew) dancing class.
She was a dancer by all the light of her nature.

'That child dances well,' said Lady Herries to
Rose Ormerod. 'Very pretty.'

'That child will be a beautiful woman,' said
Miss Ormerod. The two were passing them at
the moment. Miss Ormerod's intense gaze followed them round the room. In a second of time
Vanessa's misery had been changed to timeless,
priceless delight. They did not speak. Benjamin
also loved dancing. He knew at once whether his
partner was worthy of him. Already many a
young woman had found herself, after a round or
two, sitting to her own surprise on the sofa, and
Benjie beside her, charming but static.

'You dance better than anyone else in the room,
Vanessa.'

'Oh, do I?' Vanessa whispered. 'Oh, Benjie,
do I really?'

He did not tell her that he had said that to
many a partner in the past. He knew that he
would say it to thousands in the future. But to-
night he meant every word of it. When the dance
was over and they were sitting on the stairs she
confided to him how unhappy she had been at
dinner.

'You will often be unhappy again,' he in-
structed her. 'Everyone is so. Dinners are the
devil. You never know whom you will get. It's
a game, you see, Vanessa, and the worse ninny
you have beside you the better the game is.
Flatter them. That's the way. Everyone likes

to be flattered. You can't put it on too thick.
And do it as though you meant it. Then you'll
discover you *do* mean it, for the moment anyway.'

' What do you flatter them about? ' she asked.

' Oh, you'll soon discover their weak point.
Everyone has them. Ask them first what they
like best—games or travelling or adding up sums
in a stuffy office as Ellis does. After that, all
you've got to do is listen. Nobody wants you to
do anything but listen, no men anyway. Women
are different. They like you to tell them that they
are beautiful or clever. And why shouldn't they?
We all get enough of the other thing. Parties are
meant to cheer you up and make you feel for a
moment that all the things the people who know
you best think about you aren't true.'

' Well,' said Vanessa, ' whatever happens now
it won't matter. I've had one lovely dance.'

But she need not have been afraid. Soon
Amery came to ask her, then Will Herries, then
young Richard Cards, then Carey Rockage and,
at last, Ellis.

She gave them all places on her flowery programme. She swung round the room in an ecstasy.
' Isn't this lovely? ' she murmured to Amery.

Amery, who was anxious about his brother
Garth, now rather drunk and quarrelsome in the
parlour, answered at first absent-mindedly, then
realised that he was moving with a grace and charm
that he hadn't known for years. ' By Gad,' he
thought, ' I'm more of a dancer than I knew I
was,' and wondered whether if he had been more
gay in his past and his brother less gay, it wouldn't

have been better for both of them! ' Poor Sylvia! '
he thought, seeing Garth's wife, painted, raddled
and weary as she bumped round with Rockage,
who was no dancer. ' She's had a rotten life! '
He was suddenly charitable to everyone. This
charming child, light as a fairy—by Jove, she was
bewitching! Why had he known nothing like
this? He had married late, and it hadn't lasted
long. There had been others, of course—Doris,
whom he had had to keep so long after he was
tired of her, and Alice Mason, who'd smashed all
his china one night in a fit of temper, and the
Frenchwoman, Marguerite Calvin, whose father's
debts he had paid. Had he had much in return?
No, not very much. As he felt Vanessa's hand on
his arm he sighed. What was the use? He would
be just the same to-morrow.

Vanessa, to her own great amusement, began
at once to put Benjie's advice into practice with
all these gentlemen. It worked like a miracle.
Amery talked to her about money, horses, and
the Family. Will Herries talked to her about
the Navy, the sea, the West Indies, Glebeshire,
dogs, Polchester, the sea, the Family. Young
Richard (whom she liked greatly) talked about
books (*Middlemarch*, Mrs. Browning, Hawley
Smart), gardening, riding, and the Family, and
Carey talked about the place in Wiltshire, the
weather, the weather, the weather, the place in
Wiltshire, and the Family. She found that they
soon forgot that they were talking to a child.
She found that they all wanted comforting, consoling, reassuring, and so learnt one very useful

never-to-be-forgotten lesson about Men. She discovered too that all of them, except young Richard, felt that in one way or another an injustice had been done. They hadn't had fair treatment. Someone was to blame. Carey Rockage in especial was like a blinded bewildered animal whom unseen persecutors were prodding with pitchforks.

'Oh, I *am* so sorry!' she found herself saying over and over again.

And Ellis? Ellis was another matter. She had noticed that he watched her. Often, feeling that someone's eye was upon her, she saw that it was his. When their dance came it was 'Sir Roger,' and he asked her whether she would mind sitting with him instead. She *did* mind because she loved 'Sir Roger' and something in her was afraid of a long talk with Ellis, but she followed him meekly out into the hall and to a top corner of the stairs.

Here the sounds of the music were very dim, the house was still, and she thought of her darling grandmother, not far away, deep in sleep. It was as though for a moment something drew her into that bedroom. She stood there, looking at the dim light by the bed.

'Are you asleep, Grandmamma?' she seemed to say.

'Yes, dear. I'm sleeping beautifully,' the answer came. She put her hand on Ellis' thin arm. 'Did you hear anything? Anyone call?'

'No,' he said.

There seemed to her a sound of light steps

along the passage above them. Then she was compelled to give all her attention to Ellis. He forced her to do so. She did not know how old he was (he was in fact close on thirty-two), but he seemed to her both very old and very young.

He was unhappy, she was sure, and, like her grandmother, she could not bear that anyone should be unhappy. So, wanting to console him, she felt older than he. He was not exactly plain; he was distinguished in his thin, pale, quiet way; very serious; he scarcely ever smiled. But when he did his smile was rather beautiful. It lit up his thin face and his colourless eyes. It was as though he were pleading to be liked. He wants feeding up, she thought. His eyes were sometimes a little mad.

For a while he could do nothing but stammer out disconnected sentences. Then, following Benjie's advice, she asked him questions, about London, the City, theatres, and what he did in his spare time.

' I haven't any spare time,' he assured her. ' You see, my father had so many affairs in the City, and it all devolves upon me. I like it, you know. The City is a very agreeable place, it is indeed. Yes.' Then he said, staring at her with all his eyes: ' You must come one day, Cousin Vanessa, and stay with my mother and myself in Hill Street.'

' Thank you,' she said. ' I should love to go to London. I have never been to a theatre or a circus, and oh! how I should like to see the Queen!'

' The Queen is very much in retirement,' he said solemnly, as though he kept her in his pocket, ' but the Prince of Wales and the Princess are often to be seen driving.'

Then there was another awkward pause, until he broke out:

' I do hope you will come, Cousin Vanessa. Our house is not very gay, but if you came it would be——' He choked in his throat. ' Will you, please, not forget me? Will you think of me sometimes? '

' Of course I will think of you, Cousin Ellis,' she answered, laughing because she felt, for some strange reason, uncomfortable.

' Will you indeed? That will make me very happy. . . . I have not many friends,' he added. ' My own fault of course. I am shy. You may not have guessed it, but I am very shy indeed.'

She certainly *had* guessed it—not only was he shy but he made others who were with him shy too. Then the music, to her relief, began again.

' Oh, we must go! ' she cried, jumping up.

' You promise to think of me? ' he asked again urgently. ' I shall think of you often—very often indeed.'

When she was with them all again she sat for a while among the ladies and was aware of something that she had never thought of before (she was making so many discoveries to-night!), namely, that this family to which she belonged contained the real benefactors of the human race. Dorothy Bellairs, Veronica, Emily Newmark, even Sylvia

Herries—they were all the same! If it were not
for them the Poor, the Unprotected, almost everyone in fact who wasn't Herries, would perish.
Vanessa had a strange picture of all the cottage
women of England seeing through their window
the arrival in a carriage and pair of Dorothy,
Veronica, Emily, Sylvia. These ladies were
armed magnificently against the cold, their hands
were in muffs, the high collars of their coats
reached to their bonnets. Majestically they
moved down the cottage path, John, James,
William following behind with basket on arm.
Then the cottage woman hastens, straightens her
apron, puts the children in their places, arranges
grandfather by the fire, hurries to the door.

'Good afternoon, my lady.'

'Oh, good afternoon, Mrs. Cottage Woman.
How are you this afternoon?' The seat of the
chair is dusted, even the cottage clock, the cottage
cat, the cottage table are deferential. Glory has
descended upon the cottage woman!

Vanessa had never thought of this before. The
life that they enjoyed at Cat Bells was so very
different; she had never had on every side of her
so many Herries women. She had never, never
realised that were it not for the Ladies of England
the Poorer Classes would fade away. She had never
known that there *were* any Poorer Classes.

Even Veronica! Beautiful, lovely Aunt Veronica!

'Oh, well, I told her . . . that if she didn't
drink the soup . . . *would* give it to her worthless
old father. . . .'

And Rockage's wife: ' They complained about the drains, but Carey explained to them. . . . '

She turned it all over in her mind while she was dancing with young Richard.

Afterwards, when they were talking, she asked him:

' Are you glad you're partly a Herries? '

' Glad? ' he said, turning round and smiling.

' Yes. Is it better being a Herries than being a Jones or Smith? '

(While she spoke she thought: What *is* happening to me? I've never thought of these things before.)

' Well, don'tcherknow,' said Richard slowly, ' there *is* something fine in being one of the oldest families——'

' But *are* we one of the oldest? I mean, aren't the Jones and the Smiths just as old really? '

' I suppose they are. It's being English that counts.'

' Is it better to be English than German or French? '

Richard, who had no notion that Vanessa's mother was a German, answered with no hesitation at all:

' By Gad, yes—I should jolly well think it is.' So that settled it.

As the evening went on she was aware that she had seen but little of Benjamin. She went to look for him and found him in the billiard-room dancing solemnly up and down with Barney Newmark, both of them swaying a little as they moved.

Vanessa—quite suddenly a child again—stood

hesitating in the doorway, and Benjamin, looking
up, saw two Vanessas, both lovely, both darlings,
both the beloved of his heart.   But he was never
so much a gentleman as when he had drunk too
much, so he disengaged himself from Barney and
gave a courtly bow.

'Sit down, Vanessa, and I will fetch you some
lemonade.'

She stood there, bitterly disappointed.   She
had often seen gentlemen who drank too much,
but never Benjamin.   She saw that his hair was
ruffled, his eyes shining, and that he swayed on
his feet, but she knew also that she loved him as
dearly as ever, that her impulse was to go to him,
smooth his hair, straighten his tie. . . .

'No, thank you,' she said.

He came up to her and took her hand.   He
saw that she was frightened.

'Come and we'll dance, Vanessa,' he said.

'I am afraid that this one is engaged,' she
answered, looking over his shoulder at Barney
Newmark, who was gently singing to himself.
She hurried away, leaving Benjamin staring after
her.

In the dining-room again she danced once
more with Amery and soon she was happy.   How
could she help it?   Everyone was so happy around
her.   The musicians played like mad, the candles
shone like stars, the noise filled the room so that
it was like a paper-bag on the point of bursting.
The valse was a lovely tune.   They began to sing
to it.   The 'Blue Danube.'   Oh!   the 'Blue
Danube'!   How lovely!   One was not on earth

but swinging, swaying in an azure heaven, limitless, lit with radiance. The wide, full dresses eddied and billowed, the naked shoulders and arms were gleaming, there was that gentle undertone of music rocking, rocking. . . .

Wait! What's the matter? The music has stopped! With a surge the room has reasserted itself, the candles have lost their radiance, everyone is silent, standing looking. . . .

Vanessa, near to the door, saw that Aunt Jane, white-faced, shaking, Rockage's arm around her, was speaking. Amery turned to the child.

'How sad! How tragic! Madame! . . . dead!' Then realising that it was Vanessa: 'Your grandmother. . . .'

The silence that followed was so strange. Life had fled from the house.

'Yes, in her sleep. . . . Jane went up five minutes ago. . . . Quite quietly . . . in her sleep. . . . They have sent for Doctor Bettany.'

As they stared, conscious, every one of them, of the precariousness of this moment of existence, of the folly of their pretences of safety, thinking at the same time of the figure of the morning, so upright, so grand in her pleasure and happiness, all this only a moment ago, they themselves, perhaps, before the morning. . . .

But she was A Hundred! She had reached her Hundred! Nothing could deprive her of that. A great age. Best of all to go quietly in your sleep. . . . A wonderful woman!

But beyond the windows the snow has begun to fall. Are there figures there on the frosty road?

Old Herries, with the scar on his cheek, upright on his horse as when, so many many years ago, he had ridden up to that same gate to tell his son that his wife had run away; stout David, young again, riding on the wind to his beloved hills; Georges, waiting now for Judith who had been, in spite of his many infidelities, his only love; Charlie Watson waiting too, after so long an uncomplaining patience; poor Warren with that one hour of happiness to remember—and for those silent motionless watchers was there a sudden opening of the gates, a running out of a little figure, happy, daring, triumphant, a moment's stare up and down the road, and then a cry?

'Georges! Georges! . . . Charlie! Warren! . . . Father!'

Vanessa felt an arm around her as Adam drew her away with him, murmuring:

'Don't cry, my darling. It was the happiest way. Quietly, without any fuss—while we were all dancing.'

FOUNTAIN AT THE ROADSIDE

Walter Herries died in April 1880.

For the last five years of his life he was unaware of all that was happening in the world and perfectly happy. His daughter Elizabeth nursed him with infinite kindness and care and he was an infant in her hands. The Fortress, during those years, was a very quiet place. Benjamin, Elizabeth's son, managed the estate, which was not now large in extent—two farms and a cottage or two in Lower Ireby were the full extent of it.

He managed it, that is to say, when he was there. For much of that period he was away; he visited the East, was said to have left his young mark on Shanghai and to have invaded the sanctities of Indian temples, to have assisted pirates in the South Seas and to have been knifed within an inch of his life in Sarawak: it was whispered even that he had five Chinese wives, numberless Asiatic concubines. He returned, however, looking very much as he went—brown, stubby, solid, cheerful and without a conscience. ' I care for nobody, no, not I, and nobody cares for me ' was said, by all his friends and relations, to be his daily song.

He did, however, care for his mother, and after his third return in '79 swore that he would

35

settle down and become the Cumberland squire. He loved Cumberland with passion and he had a good head on his shoulders, so that, for a while, he was successful. Everyone liked him; for a brief time it seemed that he might be the most popular man in Cumberland. But soon stories were everywhere. He could not, it appeared, see a woman without kissing her, could not tell the truth (was it possible that his acquaintances had no humour?), had no social sense at all, so that he invited farmers' wives to meet Mrs. Osmaston and took a shepherd with him to supper at Uldale. He was also, it was said, an atheist and openly defended Bradlaugh. He visited London frequently and never returned thence without a scandal hanging to his tail. It was said that the lowest ground in that city was *his* ground, that he drank, gambled, spent a fortune over horses and cheeked his relations. How many of these stories came from Hill Street, from old Lady Herries and her son Ellis, who both hated him, no one could say, but certain it was that he was himself responsible for many of them because he never denied anything and never admitted anything, cherished no grudges, accused no one and told anyone who asked him that yes, it must be true if everyone said so; he had no morals, he supposed; he would like to have some; they must be useful things, but he simply didn't know where they were to be found.

On the other hand everyone was forced to admit that, as he grew older, he did not look dissipated. His colour was of the healthiest, his body of the toughest, his eyes bright and glowing. When he bathed in the Lake or a mountain stream in the summer with young Osmaston or Timothy Bellairs or Robert Forster it could be seen that his limbs were brown and supple as though he lived for ever in the open air.   He was never drunk now as many of his neighbours were; smutty stories never appealed to him in the least, and if girls were the worse for his friendliness nobody knew of it for a fact.   It was said that he walked vast distances over the hills and alone.   Nobody ever saw him out of spirits or out of temper.   He was generous to a fault.   With all this nobody really knew him and nobody trusted him.   'He's a rascal,' said the Herries in London, in Bournemouth, in Harrogate, in Manchester, in Carlisle, ' and he'll come to no good.'   In fact they longed, many of them, that he *should* come to no good as quickly as possible.

His only friends among his relations were Aunt Jane at Uldale, Adam Paris and his daughter Vanessa, Barney Newmark, and Rose Ormerod at Harrogate, who always said she'd marry him to-morrow if he asked her.

His one saving grace, they all said, was that he loved his mother—loved her, they added, quite selfishly because he left her whenever he pleased and for months she had not a line from him.   It was not hard, they added, for him to love his mother, for she was the sweetest and gentlest of ladies and gave him everything that he wanted.

It was also added that he possessed that strange

and mysterious quality known as 'charm'—
which meant that when you were with him you
could not help but like him and that, as soon as his
back was turned, you wondered whether he had
meant a word that he said.

He happened to be at home when his grandfather died. Walter was sleeping late on a spring
afternoon, and his room was bathed in sunshine.
Wrapped in a padded crimson dressing-gown, his
long white hair falling over his face as he slept, he
seemed a bundle of clothes topped by a wig.
Then he looked up, blinked at the sunlight, called
for his son Uhland, saw him come slowly tap-
tapping with his stick across the floor to him,
grinned joyfully at the long-expected sight, and
died—or, if you prefer it, went from the room,
leaning on his son's arm, happy as he had not been
for many a day.

That night, when the old man had been
decently laid out on the four-poster in the room
upstairs, Elizabeth and her son sat in the little
parlour off the hall and talked. The evening was
very warm and a window was open. The trees
faintly rustled; there came the occasional late
fluting of a bird; the scent of early spring flowers,
dim and cool with the night, hung about the room.

Benjamin sat opposite his mother, his legs
stretched wide, and thought how beautiful she still
was, how dearly he loved her, how selfish and restless he was, how quiet and unselfish was she!
Elizabeth's beauty had always been shy, delicately
coloured, fragile. She was a Herries only in her
strength of will and a certain opposition to new

ideas. She had never cared for ideas but always
for persons—and then for very few persons. As
she looked across at her son she thought: ' He is
all that I have left. I know that he loves me and
I know that I have no power over him.' Then
she raised her hand ever so slightly as though she
were touching someone who bent above her chair.
John Herries, her husband, had been dead for
more than twenty years to everyone but herself.
It was not sentiment nor vague superstition nor
longing that made her aware that he was always
alive at her side. It was plain fact—and as it was
her own concern, her own experience, it was of no
importance that others should say that this was
absurd, or weak, or against facts. She worried
no one else about the matter, not even her
son.

Benjamin loved her so dearly that evening,
thought she looked so lovely in her full black dress,
felt so intensely how lonely she would be, that he
was ready to do anything for her—except sacrifice
anything that threatened his liberty. Everything
threatened his liberty.

' So your long service is over, Mother. How
wonderful you were to him! Everyone marvelled
at it. I'm terribly proud of you.'

She looked at him, smiled (and with perhaps
a touch of affectionate irony):

' And now, Benjie, I suppose you'll go away
again?'

' Oh no, Mother. Of course not! Leave you
now!'

' Well, perhaps not just now—but soon. Jane

is coming to stay later. And Vanessa. Vanessa
is coming to-morrow for a week.'

He looked up sharply.

' Vanessa! '

' Yes. You didn't know that she was here this
evening? It was quite by chance. She had ridden
over to Uldale. She had stayed the night with
the Grigsbys. She came up to ask how everyone
was. I told her the news, and like the darling she
is she said that she would come to-morrow. Adam
is away at Kendal, so it suits very well.'

' Oh, I'm glad! ' He drummed his heels into
the carpet.

' You know, of course, that she loves you? '

' And I love her.'

Elizabeth smiled. ' You say that very easily,
Benjie.'

' Well, you know how it is.' He got up and
stood in front of the fireplace. ' We've loved one
another all our lives. Whatever else happens she
always comes first. There's no one in the world
to put beside her. But she's too fine for me to
marry her. You know she is. No one knows it
better than you do.'

He came and sat at her feet, his hand resting
on her knee.

' How too fine? '

' You know what everyone says of me; that
I'm no good, that I spoil everything I touch—a
rascal, a vagabond, all the rest. And it's true, I
suppose. I'm no man to marry anyone.'

She stroked his hair gently.

' Is it true what they say? '

' You know me better than anyone else, Mother
—or rather you and Vanessa do. I don't think
about myself. I take myself as I am. But I know
that I can't stick—to anyone or anything. It
grows worse as I'm older. I want to do a thing—
and I do it! '

' Is there any harm in that—if you don't do
bad things? '

' But perhaps I do—things that you'd call bad.
I can't tell. I don't think that I know the difference between right and wrong. Or rather my ideas
of right and wrong are different from other
people's. I'm too interested in everything to stop
and think. I think when it's too late.'

He laughed and looked up into her face.

' I'm a bad lot—but I love you and Vanessa
with all my heart.'

' Yes—but not enough to do things for us? '

' Anything you like. Tell me to fetch you
something from Pekin now and I'll go and get it.
But I can't be tied, I can't be told what to do, I
can't be preached at by anybody.'

' Perhaps,' Elizabeth said quietly, ' if you
married Vanessa that would steady you.'

He shook his head vehemently.

' Vanessa is so good and so fine. She isn't
strait-laced. She's wise and tolerant, but she's
high-minded. She believes in God, you know,
Mother.'

' And don't you? '

' You know that I don't. Not as she does. Not
as she does. I may be wrong. I dare say I am.
But I must be honest. I don't see things that way.

C 2

I'm ignorant. I don't know any more than the
next fellow and I want the next fellow to believe
as he sees, but I must be allowed to see for myself.
I can't *see* God anywhere. The things that people
believe are fine for them but nonsense to me. To
me as I am now. I've got all my life in front of
me and everything to learn. God may be proved
to me yet. I hope He will be.'

' Proved! ' Elizabeth laid her cheek for a
moment against his. ' God can't be proved,
Benjie. He must be felt.'

' Yes, I suppose so. That may come to me
one day. Meanwhile—a heathen and a vagabond
can't marry Vanessa.'

She thought for a little and then said: ' Have
you talked of these things to Vanessa? '

' No. I don't want to hurt her.'

' I don't think you would hurt her. She's very
wise and very tolerant. She doesn't want everyone's experience to be hers. Her father isn't
religious in her way, but she understands him
perfectly. So she may you.'

' Oh, she understands me, as much as she
knows of me. But I know things about myself
that I'd be ashamed for *her* to know. I'm not
ashamed of *myself*, Mother. I'd like to be different—settled, noble, unselfish. Or would I? I
can't tell. I'm not proud of myself, but I'm not
ashamed of myself either. I'm simply what I am.
All the same I don't see why I should burden
someone else with the care of me. That at least
I can do. Save others from troubling about
me.'

'Yes,' said Elizabeth. 'But if someone loves
you they want to trouble. They can't help but
trouble.'

He flung his arms around her and kissed her.

'Funny I should be your son. The luck's all
with me.'

Next day Vanessa came. She was now nearly
twenty-one years of age. Her beauty had a
quality of surprise in it. She was tall and slender.
Her face was young for her age, much younger
than her carriage, which was mature and controlled. She moved with such grace that you
thought, as you watched her, that she was fully
assured. Then when you saw her eyes and
mouth, her perpetual gaiety, the sudden change
of mood, the constant excitement, her stirred animation, you felt that life had not yet touched her.
She was like her father in sweetness of expression
but unlike him in her alertness, so that she seemed
to miss nothing that went on around her. She
was immensely kind, but could be sharp and irritated by slowness and stupidity and most of all by
any pomposity or show of self-conceit. That is,
except in the case of those whom she loved, when
she simply could not criticise. For example, she
loved Timothy Bellairs at Uldale and he *was* a
trifle pompous.

Her hair was very dark but her colouring
rather pale, unless she were excited by something.
She blushed very easily, which exasperated her.
When she moved she was like a queen, but often
when she talked or joined with others in a game

or a sport she was childish and impetuous. She
was intensely loyal, obstinate, forgiving, so warm-
hearted that her father often feared for her, but
of late she had been learning many things about
human nature. She was no fool where people
were concerned.

Her mother had died in the autumn of '77 and
since then she had lived with her father and Will
on Cat Bells. They had been always devoted
friends, she and her father, but now, after losing
both his mother and his wife, Adam seemed to
turn to Vanessa with an urgency that had something almost desperate about it. He remained
always humorous, kindly, a little cynical, half in
his fairy stories (he tried his hand at a number of
things—books for boys, biographies of Nelson
and Walter Raleigh, even two novels, but they
were all fairy stories), half in the wild, loose,
stormy Cumberland life that was in his blood and
bones. Everyone liked him, nobody knew him.
Many people laughed at him in an easy generous
fashion. Vanessa alone understood him. She
understood him because she had (although as yet
she did not realise it) very much of her grandmother's character. Adam, of course, knew that.
He saw his mother in his daughter again and
again: her kindness, generosity, sudden flashes of
temper and irritation and a constant exasperation
at belonging to the Herries family.

'We don't belong, my dear,' he said one day.

'We belong enough,' she answered in a flash
of prophetic perception, 'to have to fight them for
the rest of our lives.'

Another thing. He knew that Vanessa loved
Benjamin. It made Adam unhappy whenever
he thought of it. He was himself fond of
Benjie, but oh! he did not want him to marry
Vanessa! Margaret's last words had been:
'Adam, you mustn't let Vanessa marry Ben-
jamin,' and he had answered: 'She must be
free.'

But oh no! oh no! he did not want her to
marry Benjamin! They never discussed it. That
was their one silence.

Walter was buried in Ireby churchyard and,
ironically, not far from the grave of Jennifer
Herries, into which he once so long ago had
terrified her. At the funeral, besides Elizabeth,
Benjie and Vanessa, there were Adam, Veronica
and her husband, Timothy and his wife, and dear
Aunt Janc. Also a few neighbours.

It was a cold windy day, one of those days
when you realise how true it is that Cumberland
is composed only of cloud and stone: lovely iridescent stone with green and rosy shadows but rising
in pillars of smoke to meet the cloud, and the
cloud coming down to settle like blocks and
boulders of stone on the soil until, with the wind
in your ears, you do not know which is stone and
which is cloud. The little church tugged at the
wind like a cloud striving to be free, and the clouds
rolled in the sky as though some giant hurled
rocks at his enemy.

They all stood, blown about, in the little churchyard, and poor old Walter, a capital example of the

waste of energy that hatred involves, was dropped
into the ground.

That same evening Vanessa and Elizabeth had
a talk. Elizabeth had done all she could with the
house. Her taste had never been aesthetic and
she had dressed the cold bare bones of the place
with heavy, very heavy, material. The big bleak
rooms she had filled with large sofas, heavy car-
pets, big chairs, all in the manner of their period,
which, if it was not a very beautiful manner, was
comfortable.

She had crowds of things partly because everyone she knew did the same, partly because she
hoped thus to escape the stoniness, the melancholy, the ghostliness of the place. She could not
escape it. The rooms that were empty and shut
up—the rooms in the two towers for instance—
were heavy with ghosts. Not only she knew it.
Everyone in the countryside knew it. Voices and
steps were heard. Pale faces looked from behind
windows, dogs barked and parrots screeched.
The Fortress, in fact, was not to surrender to a
confusion of cornucopias, steel and brass fire-irons,
japanned coal-boxes, tables covered with bead-
work, satin walnut chairs, and wax flowers under
glass shades. Nevertheless in the few rooms that
she herself inhabited her presence warmed and
comforted. There were fires, Cumberland servants who adored her, flowers and books.

But Vanessa, in spite of the flowers, shivered.
She had her father's taste, her grandmother's passion for order and arrangement. How, thought

Vanessa, can Elizabeth, who is so beautiful, endure
this hideous place? She did not realise that
Elizabeth could endure anywhere so long as John,
her husband, was with her.

Benjamin had gone that evening to see a farmer
in Braithwaite. He would not be back until the
following afternoon, so the two women had the
house to themselves. They sat close together
over a roaring fire and tried not to listen to the
wind, which found the Fortress the happiest
hunting-ground it knew. Although Elizabeth was
sixty-five and Vanessa only twenty-one they understood one another very well. They believed very
much in the same things and they both loved the
same man.

That evening, in fact, was a crisis for Vanessa,
and in the course of it she set her feet resolutely
along the path that was to lead her so very far.

'What are you going to do, Elizabeth, now?'
Vanessa asked.

'Do, my dear? Why, go on as before.'

'Won't this house be very lonely for you?'

'I am used to it, you know. I'm an old
woman now and like a quiet life.'

'Benjamin will be with you. That's one good
thing.'

'Oh no, he won't!' Elizabeth smiled. 'He'll
come and go as he's always done.'

'Oh, but he must,' Vanessa answered vigorously. 'He can't leave you all alone here. He
has plenty to do, loves the country. He has
wandered enough.'

'You know that he has not,' Elizabeth an-

swered. ' He will never have wandered enough.
He might settle down if you married him.
Otherwise, never.'

She had spoken quietly but, as both women
knew, it was a challenge of the deepest import.

There was a long silence, then Vanessa said
slowly:

' Benjie has not asked me to marry him.'

' No. That is because he is afraid—afraid
of himself. He loves you more than anyone in
the world and does not want to make you unhappy.'

' Yes,' Vanessa said at last. ' He might make
me unhappy, but I would not mind, I think.'
After a pause she went on: ' You see, Elizabeth,
I have Benjie in my blood. I have always had.
I'm quite shameless about it—to myself, I mean.
What is the use of being otherwise? I would rather
be miserable with Benjie than happy with anyone
else. And perhaps I should not be miserable. I
understand him very well.'

She waited, but Elizabeth said nothing.

' We are very alike in some ways. I want
my liberty quite as much as he does his. My
great-grandmother was a gipsy, my great-grandfather a vagabond, my father illegitimate. And
Benjie——' She broke off.

' Thinks he is a vagabond too,' Elizabeth
went on, ' because of his father. You needn't
fear, Vanessa darling, to talk about it. Here we
are in the house that is filled with it. Sometimes
I wake in my bed and hear the tap of Uhland's
stick on the floor. I was impetuous, too, once,

my dear. I ran away and married John. I had courage for anything in those days; but I know now that every impetuous step, every blow in anger, can mean tragedy for the next generation. There is no end to the consequences. They are never done.'

' Perhaps it isn't what we do,' said Vanessa, ' but something in ourselves. A strain that won't let us alone. You know, Elizabeth, that when I go over and stay with Veronica there's so much Herries stolidness and convention that I feel, I'm sure, just as Judith did when she ran away to Paris. That's where I understand Benjie. And sometimes when I'm with Timothy, although I'm very fond of him, I could whip him. I could really. He won't see things and is proud of not seeing them. He believes in Gladstone but has never heard of Rossetti.'

' Rossetti, dear? ' asked Elizabeth.

' Yes—well, never mind. He writes poetry and paints.'

' Oh yes,' said Elizabeth. ' I'm sure I've heard the name——'

' I expect you have. But that doesn't matter. The point is that I would understand if Benjie wanted to go away by himself. I think it's silly of married people always to be together.'

' And then there's religion,' Elizabeth said. ' Benjie declares that he doesn't believe in God, foolish boy.'

' Many people say they don't believe in God,' Vanessa answered, speaking as though she were sixty and Elizabeth twenty. ' I don't think father

does, not as I do.   But if you love someone those
things settle themselves.   I could never be as
Timothy and Violet are, keeping the children in
awe of them, never allowing them an idea of their
own.   Why, they have to come to the dining-room
and bow, poor little things, after every meal!
And Tim's only three, but I know he's going to
be an artist.   He's always drawing things.   And
when I spoke of it to his father the other day he
was as shocked as if I'd said Tim was going to be
an actor.'

'Well,' said Elizabeth, 'that wouldn't be a
nice thing for little Tim to grow up into.'

'I don't know,' said Vanessa.   'There are the
Bancrofts anyway.   They have luncheon with the
Prince of Wales.'

'Come here, dear, and give me a kiss,' Elizabeth said.   'I'd rather have you for a daughter
than anyone in the world.'

Then came the last day of April, the day before
Vanessa returned to Cat Bells.   After dinner that
night there was a large full moon.   The air was
warm and the moonlight filled all the garden with
silver dust so that one seemed to walk on white
powdery surf, now rising on a wave of quicksilver,
then passing into an ebb of luminous grey.   The
hills were thin like silver tissue.   Benjie, governed
as ever by his mood, by the food that he had eaten,
the wine that he had drunk, thinking Vanessa
perfect in her dark dress that below the narrow
waist broke out into bows and frills and trimmings,
swearing that no neck and arms in all the world
were so lovely as hers, seemed to see her as though

this were for the first time, a new Vanessa to whom
he had but just been introduced, so that under his
breath he must murmur: 'This is the loveliest in all
the world. All my life I have been waiting for this.'

At first she would not go out with him, as
though something warned her. She stood by the
fire, laughing, talking about anything, nothing.
She had had a letter from Rose Ormerod, who was
having a gay time in London.

'No, but you must listen to this, Benjie.'

'I don't want to listen. I don't like her. I
can't think why she is your friend.'

'But she likes *you*! In this letter she says:
"If you see Benjie give him my love, my *love*,
mind." And she means it.'

'Oh, she gives everyone her love—far too
many people.'

'She has been having a beautiful visit. Lady
Herries gave a dinner-party. Very sticky, she
says. And she went to the Haymarket Theatre
and saw *Money*. A silly old play, she says, but
Marion Terry was lovely as Clara Douglas, and
Mr. Bancroft was Sir Frederick, and Mrs. Bancroft Lady Franklyn, and——'

'What *do* I care who they were? This is the
last night of April. To-morrow is the first of
May. It is as warm as summer—silly to have a
fire—and the moon is the largest——'

'Oh yes, and she went to Mr. Alma-Tadema's
studio to see the pictures he's sending to the
Academy, and one is called "Fredegonda," and
it shows an angry Queen looking out of window
at her husband——'

' Please, Vanessa.'

She looked at him and saw that he was unhappy. She nodded.

' All right. I'll come out.'

She went upstairs to fetch a shawl. Benjie,
while he waited, wondered what he was going
to do. This was the moment that for years he
had determined to avoid. He must not marry
Vanessa. He must not marry anyone. At the
thought of marriage something within him
warned him. But Vanessa—Vanessa . . . He
shivered. Outside in the garden it was warmer
than in the firelit room. That house was always
cold, do what you would with it. Vanessa—
Vanessa . . . Why had he been such a fool as
to stay? He had an impulse to go round to the
stable, fetch his horse and ride off. Ride off
anywhere—not seeing her again until she was
safely married to someone else. But would that
end it? All his life, however far away he had been,
he had been tied to her, tied by her goodness, her
beauty, her love for himself—and by all that was
best in him. His best? A very poor thing. He
had never thought so humbly of himself as at that
moment when she came towards him, saying:
' I'm ready. How lovely the moonlight is! '

They walked into the garden arm in arm.
Originally Walter Herries had planned a series of
garden-walks and a succession of little waterfalls,
dropping stage after stage into a lily-covered pond.
Now there were the sad ruins of these things,
tangled shrubberies, little winding and melancholy
paths, the doubtful splash of water and a weedy

pool. Over the ruins the moon rode throwing its silver in a conceited largesse, penetrating the uttermost tangle of the trees.

'I have just finished a very amusing book,' said Vanessa, who felt as though the moon were scornfully wishing her a disastrous destiny, like the old witches her great-grandfather had known.

'What is it called?' asked Benjamin, wondering for how long he could resist to kiss Vanessa.

'*Travels with a Donkey*.'

'What a silly name!' The muscle of his arm suddenly jumped at the touch of Vanessa's hand. 'Who wrote it?'

'His name is Stevenson. I have never heard of him before, have you?'

'No. Never.'

'He writes well.' Vanessa almost whispered as they stepped into a pool of moonlight. 'Very precious, as though he'd licked every word on his tongue first before he stuck it down. Oh, look at the moon insulting Blencathra. There! Stand here! You can just see it between the trees.'

Benjie took her in his arms and kissed her with a ferocity that Ouida—a novel by whom Vanessa had recently been enjoying—describes somewhere ' as the lovely tiger's grandeur and the abandoned wildness of the jungle.' Benjie had never kissed Vanessa before save almost as a brother. This was the first time in her life that Vanessa had ever been passionately kissed. She found it entrancing. They stayed for a long while without moving. The shawl fell from Vanessa's shoulders, but she felt no cold. The pressure of Benjie's strong hand on her shoulder was surely the thing that since the day of her birth she had longed for. Her hand touched Benjie's hair as though he were her child. He kissed her eyes, which was another thing that no one had ever done to her before. They separated. He bent down and picked up her shawl.

'This is something,' he said breathlessly, 'that I have been longing to do for years. And now we'll talk if you don't mind.'

They walked hand in hand.

'I am going away to-morrow morning and will not see you again until someone has married you.'

'I can wait,' she answered confidently. 'I will marry you any time.'

'You are not like the modern maiden, are you, Vanessa? If their young man proposes to them they faint with astonishment although they have planned nothing else all their lives.'

'No. Why should I be astonished? I always knew that we would be married one day.'

'We are not going to be married,' Benjie answered, taking his hand from hers and walking by himself. 'I ought not to have kissed you. After to-night we shall not be alone together again until you are safe. I love you as truly as any man ever loved anyone, and that is why we are not going to be married.'

Vanessa laughed and took his hand again.

'I am not a child, Benjie. I know that you are afraid of marriage—and perhaps you would be right if it were anyone else, but we are different.

We know one another so well. I shall never marry anyone else.'

'Now listen.' He put his arm around her and drew her close to him. 'You must not try to shake me, Vanessa. Really you must not. You say you know me, but it isn't true. You don't know me. Everyone is right about me. I'm no good by any standards but my own. I should make you terribly unhappy, and that I won't do. No, I will not. I will not. Other women— well, that's their affair. But you—you've got to have a wonderful life, be a Queen, have everyone worship you, adore you, have splendid children, a husband whom everyone looks up to . . .'

She interrupted him, laughing.

'But I don't want that kind of husband! I don't want to be a Queen! I don't want to be admired. I want to be free quite as much as you do. You talk as though it were my ambition to be head of the Herries family, live in Hill Street and give parties like old Lady Herries. Of course I *enjoy* parties and it will be fun to go to London one day, but without you I don't want *anything*!'

'Oh Lord! How can I get you to understand? Don't you see, Vanessa, that I'm no good? Really no good. One day I'm this, another day I'm that. If I see a pretty woman I want to kiss her. If I want to gamble I gamble. I'm no sooner in a place than I want to go somewhere else. My mother and yourself are the only two people I love. I have hurt my mother many times already, but you I won't hurt——'

'But, Benjie,' she broke in, 'I don't think you *could* hurt me! I should understand whatever you did.'

'You don't know.' He spoke angrily, breaking again away from her. 'You don't know *anything* about life, Vanessa. You don't know the things I've done, the company I've kept. If I could say to you, "Vanessa, I've sown my wild oats and now I'm going to settle down, go to church on Sunday, read Tennyson with you in the evening——"'

'But, Benjie, how absurd you are! I don't *want* to read Tennyson, and if you don't wish to go to church you needn't! Father never goes to church. And as to the rest, what you have done is no business of mine. I'm sure I'm no saint myself. I know that Timothy and Violet think me often disgraceful and are afraid that I shall harm the children. Look at Grandmother! *She* wasn't a saint although she was one of the finest women who ever lived *and* one of the bravest. And her father! He's a kind of legend for lawlessness and roguery. I think we should suit one another very well. And as to the relations and all they say about you—what do they matter? A stuffy lot! That's what they are!'

He shook his head. 'That's not the point, Vanessa. You may say what you like, but you are good and I'm not—that is by all that anyone means by good. You talk of Judith's father. I expect he was a fine fellow. I often think of him and wish I'd known him. I like that man. I could have been his friend, I know. But the truth is he made everyone unhappy who trusted him. And so shall I. I can't help it. It's something inside me. And I won't make you unhappy. I love you too much. It would be the one sin for me. I don't care about the rest, but *that* I'll avoid, so help me God! '

They had walked down to the weeded pool which lay now, like a foolish white face, dirtied and soiled, at their feet.

Vanessa spoke, but more gravely because she was feeling that her whole future life was to depend on the next ten minutes. What did she see? The man as he was? Perhaps. . . . But herself in relation to all that he might be? She did not yet know life enough for that.

'Benjie, listen. I am not asking you against your will to marry me. I don't *want* you to marry me. We have been friends all our lives and we can go on as we are. But if you want to marry somebody, then it had better be me. I'm sure you will never meet anyone again who knows you so well.' She put her hand again in his. 'Do you remember that time—Grandmother's hundredth birthday—the day she died? '

' Yes, of course I remember.'

' We went for a walk, and I told you that I would never marry anyone but you and that I would wait as long as you liked. I was only a child then. I'm a woman now. But it is the same. It hasn't changed. I don't see how it can. No one can ever be to either of us what we are to one another. As to risks, life's made for them. I'm not afraid.'

She felt his hand tremble as it clutched hers.

'Listen, Vanessa. You *must* listen. If I don't make you understand now you never will. You say you are not afraid of life, but that is because you don't know. How can you? You have been sheltered always. Your father worships you as he ought to. Everyone loves you. You have never been treated unkindly, never had to put up with slights, never made an enemy. You hear people say: "Oh, Benjamin Herries, he's a bad lot, he's a rascal!" But they are only words. You've never seen me *do* the things, *say* the things that they mean. I am at my best—a poor best but still my best—when I'm with you because I love you and I'm not a bad fellow if I'm in a good temper, not bored, able to get away when I want to. We've seen one another at long intervals. We've loved to be together and they have been grand times because we were free. But to *live* with me—that's another thing. I'm no man's good company for long. I've got old Rogue Herries' devil in me, I think. Sometimes I fancy I'm the old Rogue himself come again. And if that's nonsense—and I'm sure I don't know what's nonsense and what isn't in this ridiculous world— at least I'm like him in that I'm my own worst enemy, can see what's right to do and never do it, curse my best friend and all the rest. Oh, mind you, I'm not pitying myself or even condemning myself. I'm not bad as men go. I enjoy every minute of the day unless I've got the toothache or lose money at cards or some woman won't look at

me. And even those things are interesting. But
I'm not the man for you. You're as far above me
as that moon is above this silly-faced pond and, do
me justice, I've always known it.'

He had spoken swiftly, the words pouring out,
his face serious, mature, almost grim, as though
he were resolving that this once in his life at least
the honest truth should come from him.

'All that you have said, Benjie, I know,' Vanessa answered. 'I may be a fool as you say, protected from harm and all the rest. But Father
has never treated me as a child. We've been
companions for years and talked freely about
everything. When I stay with Veronica and
Robert Forster's drunk, as he is sometimes, I can
see some of the things marriage can be. You
may be nasty when you're drunk, but not half as
nasty as Robert is. Of course I know that marriage isn't all fun. It isn't for anybody. Only I
think that you and I would be often happy together if we were married because we know one
another so well. We'd be unhappy too, but I
don't always want to be happy. That would be
dull. When we fought we'd know that we still
loved one another. If you left me I'd know that
you would come back.'

'No, I might not,' he said in a low voice. 'I
might never come back. Loving you as much as
I do now, I might still say: "No, I can't stand
this." And I'd be off—and perhaps never return.'

'Oh, Benjie, would you?'

They were standing now by the gate that led
into the road. The road stretched in front of

them, and beyond it the country fell to the valley
like a sheet of shadowed snow.

'Oh, would you?' She was thinking. She
turned, as though she had resolved a problem, and
looked up at him, smiling. 'Then I'd be a grass
widow. They say that they have a glorious life.'

Both laughing, they walked out into the road
and at once were encompassed by a field of
dazzling stars above them, sparkling and dancing
as though they knew that to-morrow was the first
of May and the beginning of a new summer world.

'You know, Vanessa,' Benjie said, looking
over to Skiddaw, 'that I have an odd fancy. It
isn't really mine. Some old shepherd told me
some tale once. There's Skiddaw Forest where
—where my father died. Of course it's often in
my thoughts. When you stand below Skiddaw
House and look over to Skiddaw you can see sometimes, just before the hill rises, a dark patch that
looks like the opening of a cave. It is only a trick
of light. There's no cave there, but when I was a
boy I often walked there and I used to fancy that
it was the opening to a great subterranean hall, a
gigantic place, you know, that ran right under the
mountain. I told myself tales about it. I fancied
that all the men who had loved this place returned
there, had great feasts there, jolly splendid affairs,
with singing and drinking, everything that was
fine. All of them grand comrades, whoever they
were, farmers and shepherds, huntsmen, squires
and parsons—any man to whom this piece of
country is the best in the world. Perhaps on a
night like this there they all are singing and laugh-

ing, happy as grigs—old Rogue Herries and my grandfather, my father and my uncle, John Peel and Wordsworth and Southey, little Hartley, " auld Will " Ritson of Wasdale, James Jackson of Whitehaven, Ewan Clark, John Rooke, thousands on thousands more—I used to fancy on a still day that I could hear them laughing and singing. A great hall, you know, Vanessa, where they could wrestle and run, ride their horses, shout their songs, tell their stories. . . . That's where I'd like to be, Vanessa. I could do without women there. I wouldn't want to roam the world. I'd need no other company——' He broke off. ' Yes, I'd want you, I think. Wherever I was, whatever I'd be doing.'

They turned up the road and stopped at a little water-trough where from a rudely carved dolphin's head water trickled into a small basin. The thin drip of the water was the only sound.

' Why don't you say,' he murmured, ' " Benjie, you're a bad lot. We'll meet no more "? It would be better for you.'

' I can't say that,' she answered, leaning close to him, ' because I love you.'

The pause that followed marked both their lives. It had a sanctity, an intimacy that went beyond all their experience. They kissed again, but quietly now, gently, meeting in complete oneness.

At last he said:

' Be kind to me, Vanessa. I've tried to do the best. Maybe I'll change. Mother said that loving you might do it for me. Give me a chance.'

He waited, then went on,

' My darling—let us be engaged, here and now, for two years.   This is the last day of April 1880.   In April 1882 I'll come to you and ask you if you are still of the same mind.   If you are —if I can trust myself—we'll be married.   If, before then, you think otherwise you shall tell me. And in the two years we will tell nobody, not a word to a soul.   I shall be twenty-seven then, and if I'm no good at that age I shall never be any good.   Give me that chance.'

Vanessa looked in front of her, then at last turned on him, smiling.

' Yes, if that's what you'd like, Benjie.'

' Not a word to anyone.'

She waited again.

' I have always told Father everything——'

' No.   Even your father.   I'm on probation. If he knew he might not understand.'

' Very well.   Here's my hand on it.'

They held hands, looking one another in the eyes.

' It's a poor bargain for you,' he said.   ' Mind, if ever you want to be free of me you have only to tell me——'

' I shall never want to be free,' Vanessa said proudly.

' All the men under Skiddaw heard you say that,' he answered.   ' And they think me a poor lot for asking you.'

' Ah, they don't know you as I do,' she answered.

As they walked up to the house she held her head high, feeling the proudest woman in England.

And Benjie, for once in his life, was humble.

HERRIES DRAWING-ROOM

VANESSA paid the first visit of her life to London in the spring of 1882.

Old Lady Herries had, during the last two years, invited her repeatedly to stay in Hill Street, but the trouble had been that her father refused to go with her and Vanessa would not leave him.

Adam was obdurate and Vanessa was obdurate.

'No, my dear, I won't go. I hope never to see London again. I am sixty-six and entitled at last to my own way. London would upset me. I know I'm nothing at all, but London would make me feel less than nothing. I'm quite contented where I am. But of course you must go. It's time that they saw you and fell down before you. It's always been the custom that the family in London should see the Cumberland branch once and again and realise how superior it is. Your grandmother took me up when I was a boy and they all fell flat before her—so they shall before you.'

Vanessa refused. She did not want to go, she did not wish to see London, they would all think her an absurd country cousin and mock at her. With her father at her side she could mock back at them, but alone she would not dare to open her

mouth. (None of these were, of course, real
reasons. She longed to see London and she was
afraid of no one.) He wished her to go because
he was afraid that they were growing, as he described it, ' inside one another.'

For the last two years Vanessa had been strange.
She was, it seemed, quite content to be alone with
her father and, except for visits to Elizabeth at the
Fortress and to Uldale, saw nobody. She seemed
happy enough, but there were times when she
appeared abstracted, lost, far away. Once or
twice he wondered whether Benjie Herries had
anything to do with this. Benjie had been out of
England for most of the two years, deserting,
everyone said, his mother most shamefully. Could
it be that Vanessa still cared for him? Adam put
the thought violently away from him. He had an
affection for Benjie, but the fellow was a wanderer,
a wastrel, would come, Adam very much feared,
to no kind of good. And yet some wildness that
there was in Adam attracted him to the man. He
might have been, had things gone otherwise, just
such himself. And Vanessa had some wildness in
her too. Was it that that kept the men of the
county away from her? No one doubted that she
was better-looking than any other girl in the North
of England. And she was gentle with them, gave
herself no airs. But she was alone. Save for her
father, Elizabeth, and little Jane Bellairs at Uldale,
she had no friends. Oh yes, and the children at
Uldale—she adored *them*, especially young Tim.

But there it was: she had no friends of her own
age, had no gaieties, did not appear to wish for

any. It was not good for her. She must go to
London.

And at last she yielded. He could not tell the
reason. A letter came from Lady Herries. She
looked across the table at Adam and said: ' Very
well, Papa; I'll go."

Then, when it was all arranged, he did not want
her to go. He realised that he would be most
damnably lonely. He was sure that, after this
visit, she would never be the same again. She
was still, in spite of her twenty-three years, very
much of a child. She could be surprisingly naïve
and impetuous. She seemed at one moment to
judge human nature most wisely and then she
would trust someone for no reason at all. She
reminded him constantly of her grandmother in
her simple directness to everyone, her lack of all
affectation, her complete ignoring of class differences, her generosity and warmth both of heart
and temper. But she was unlike Judith in that
she had many reserves and no wish to dominate
anybody. In those things she resembled himself. Oh, he would be all right, he supposed.
There was plenty to do—his writing, his garden,
the hills of which he never wearied; he was still,
in spite of his sixty-six years, strong enough to
walk over Stye Head into Eskdale and so to the
sea, or over Watendlath to Grasmere. He had
old Will Leathwaite for company. But he would
miss her—miss her damnably. There was no one
else he cared for now but Will. He was growing
old. He continued to write—he could not help
himself—but it was poor, secondary stuff. Not

D

at all what he had meant once to do. Why,
Dickens had told him once that he would be the
equal of them all. But Dickens was warm-
hearted, generous, with his variegated waistcoats
and passion for theatricals. A great man: no
one like him now. Him and Wordsworth, that
arrogant but child-hearted little man whose genius
seemed now to cover all the country like a soft
sunny cloud, impregnating the air, calling the
scent from the flowers, echoed in the birds' call.
Dickens and Wordsworth—simple men both of
them—while to-day these Merediths and Swin-
burnes and Rossettis . . . He picked up the
Poems and Ballads from the table, read a line or
two, turned away with a sigh. Very clever.
You could not call Wordsworth clever, thank
God.

And so she went. It was arranged very
easily, because Mrs. Osmaston was travelling to
London at the same time. Mrs. Osmaston was
a good serious woman who would bore Vanessa
considerably. That would teach her, Adam
thought quite fiercely, to leave her old father!

She went: and Adam discovered, not for the
first time in his history, the tactful beauties in
Will Leathwaite's character. Will had all the
Cumbrian gift of showing his affection without
mentioning it. He scolded and grumbled and
protested as he had always done. In the evening they played backgammon together, and Will
invariably won.

'You have the most damnable luck,', Adam
swore at him.

'Aye,' said Will, 'I have.   And I play nicely too.'

Four days after her departure Adam received a letter, the first that he had ever had from his dear daughter.

'My dearest Papa,' it began.

'A letter from my daughter,' he said to Will, who was sprawling against the door-post, his hands in his pockets.   He was fat now, red in the face and grizzled in the hair.   It was in his eyes that you saw his youth, for their blue was as clear, gay and sparkling as though they were fresh from their Maker.

'Aye,' he said.   'That's grand.   Hope she's enjoying herself.   Not too much, you know. She's better than anything London can give her.'

Adam, after glancing through, read Will her letter.   Will never stirred.   His eyes, shining, luminous, and in some fashion rather sardonic, were fixed on his friend—as though he said: 'Yes.   She's spreading her wings.   You'll find I'm the only stay-by.   We're a pair of left-overs. And who cares?'

The letter was:

MY DEAREST PAPA—I don't know how to begin I've so much to tell you.   The journey was very long of course, the carriage smelt of escaping gas and oh, it was cold the last part!   My feet were frozen.   We couldn't see to read but it would not have been so bad had Mrs. Osmaston not chattered so!   She is *so* contented, *so* fortunate, has so perfect a husband, such *lovely* children (you know little Mary and James Osmaston— not lovely at all!) but the worst is that she loves all the

world. Her charity is too general to be personal. We
are all God's children in a kind of celestial nursery. Well,
I must get on.

Here I am two days in Hill Street and I *must* say that
I am enjoying it. I find them very kind. Do you know
that Lady Herries is seventy-eight? She is immensely
proud of it and all our relations are proud of it too. If
you live long enough in our family you are always looked
up to whatever you may be or do. It is when you are
young that you must be careful. She paints of course
prodigiously and wears the brightest colours. Bustles have
come in again you know, and she likes a sash and a bow
at the waist! But I must not mock for she is really kind
and wants me to be happy. So does Ellis. He is grave
and nervous. He is dreadfully afraid of doing the wrong
thing. He is exceedingly wealthy everyone tells me and
ought to be married. I am very sorry for him because
he does not know how to be careless and happy. Rose
Ormerod says that he is always his own Governess and
that no sooner does he do a thing than the Governess tells
him he should not. Hill Street is a kind of Temple for
the family. They come here and worship the god of the
clan—a three-faced god, one face Queen Victoria, one
face Commerce and one face the Herries features, high
cheek-bones, noble foreheads and a cold eye. They are
very different though. Barney Newmark, old Amery and
his son Alfred, Rose and her brother Horace, Emily
Newmark. These are the principal ones who come to
the house. Captain Will Herries and his wife are in town.
Also the Rockages. I think they like me. I amuse them
and perhaps shock them. I like Barney the best. He
laughs at everyone. The house is very large and very
cold, but of course you know it and I should imagine that
it has not altered at all in thirty years. Very cold, full of
noises from pipes and cisterns, masses of furniture, statues
and little fires that burn up the chimney. There is the
great Charles, too. Charles is the butler and he is so
large that it is always warmer when he is in the room

with one. He is very gracious and would be perfect if his eyes were not so glassy.

Just imagine! We have been to the theatre both nights! The first night was *Romeo and Juliet* with Mr. Irving and Miss Ellen Terry. Shall I whisper to you, dear Papa, that I was a little disappointed? Mr. Irving is better when he is not making love. In the balcony scene he stood behind such a ridiculous little tree that it was difficult not to laugh. When he makes love it is not the *real thing*. He has thought it all out beforehand. Miss Terry is *lovely*. Oh, how beautiful and charming! But she too acts better when she is *not* with Mr. Irving. With the *Nurse* she is perfection. I liked Mr. Terriss as Mercutio but the best of all is Mrs. Stirling as the Nurse although propriety makes them cut out all her *best* lines. The scenery is almost too good to be true I think. You admire the moonlight when you ought to be *lost* with the lovers. At least that is what I felt.

Will you be very ashamed of me when I tell you that I enjoyed the second evening more? The piece was *The Manager* at the Court Theatre. This was Barney's party and I think Ellis was a little ashamed at *laughing* at a Farce. But he could not help himself. There is an actress in this piece called Lottie Venne who is *perfect* and Mr. Clayton *splendid*! I laughed so much that Rose, who was with us, said Mr. Clayton played twice as well as usual!

Of course I have not seen very much of London yet. Rose and I are to have a morning's shopping to-morrow. There is to be a grand party in Hill Street next week and Madame Trebelli of the Opera is to sing. I have ridden in a hansom cab and found it very exciting.

And now I must go to bed. I have been writing this in my room and I am so cold that there is an icicle on the end of my nose! Do you miss me? I do hope so, but also I hope that you are not lonely. Give Will my love and the children at Uldale if you see them. If I *allow* myself I shall be homesick, but that will never do. Last night

I dreamt that you and I walked to Robinson and met five
sheep who turned into the five Miss Clewers from Troutbeck! Have you seen Elizabeth? Is her cold quite gone
now? I am hoping there will be a letter from you to-
morrow.—Your very loving daughter,   VANESSA.

' That's grand,' said Will and went off to his
work.

No one could guess from Vanessa's letter, nor
indeed from anything that she herself said or
thought, that her arrival in London was the sensation of the year for her relations. Afterwards
among them all 1882 was remembered as the year
' when Vanessa first came to town.' And this for
two reasons. One was the natural astonishment
at her beauty, for which they were quite unpre-
pared, although some of them recollected that
' she had been a damned pretty child at old
Madame's Hundredth Birthday.'
By chance it happened that the fashion of the
moment suited Vanessa: the dresses looped up
behind, crossed with fringed draperies rather in
the manner of the heavy window curtains of the
time, the waists very narrow (and Vanessa had,
all her life, a marvellous waist), the top portion of
the costume following as closely as possible the
lines of the corset, flaring out below the hips
in frills and bows and trimmings. The violent
colours just then popular also suited her dark
hair and soft skin. The dress that she wore at her
first Herries party, dark blue with an edging of
scarlet, white lace frills at the throat and wrists,
was long remembered. She arrived with only a

dress or two and they of Keswick make, but Adam
had insisted that she must 'dress like a peacock
in London' and gave her money to do it with.
They were the first grand costumes of her life,
and Rose Ormerod saw to it that they were fine.
Her beauty staggered them all, the more that she
seemed to be perfectly unaware of it. And they
saw immediately that here was a family asset.

This raw naïve girl from Cumberland might
marry anybody. There was no limit to the possibilities. Old Amery said to his son Alfred
(Amery had married late in life a parson's infant
fresh from the schoolroom: she presented him
with Alfred in '62 and incontinently died) after
his first sight of Vanessa in the Hill Street
drawing-room: 'That girl will be a Duchess—
bet you a " monkey." ' These possibilities gave
her at once a great importance in their eyes—one
more factor in the rise of Herries power!

And here that queer old Lady Herries, known
familiarly as 'the witch of Hill Street,' comes into
the story. No one in London knew anything
about that old woman save that she was useful as
an entertainer and adored her son. When Will
Herries had married her she had been a buxom,
silly, empty-headed woman of no character and less
common sense. She had given Will a son, and
that was the only sensible thing she'd ever been
known to do. But as Ellis grew to manhood her
love for him created in her a kind of personality.
People must always admire in this world any
strong, undeviating, unfaltering devotion: for one
thing it is rare, for another it appears unselfish

although it may have all its roots in selfishness. This example was the more admired because Ellis was, most certainly, not everybody's money. Only was anybody's money, in fact, because he had himself such a profusion of that admirable commodity. They led, those two, in the Hill Street house a life of extraordinary loneliness. In spite of the dinners, receptions, conversaziones, balls and theatre-parties, they had no friends, nor did they communicate, so far as anyone could see, with one another. Old Lady Herries broke into frequent rages with her son and to these he listened with a grave and unaccommodating silence. Abroad she talked of him incessantly, his brilliance in the City, his nobility, his love for his fellow-men. At home she often told him he was stupid, ungrateful and cold. Her extravagances grew with her age, her paint, gay colours, fantastic screams of laughter. She was a sight with her trimmings, fichus, shawls, her little hats perched high on her old head, her fingers covered with rings, bands and twists of hair, dyed, and interwoven with strands of ribbon and sprays of foliage. It remained, however, that she won respect because it was known that, selfish in everything else, clinging to life like a tigress, she would die for her son at any moment if the call came.

On the night of Vanessa's arrival, when the house was as silent as the moon, Ellis visited his mother in her bedroom. Sitting up in bed she looked the old, shrivelled, lonely, exhausted monkey that she really was. Ellis stood gravely beside her bed and said:

'Well, Mama, it is as I thought. Vanessa is the only woman whom I will ever marry.'

Lady Herries blinked her eyes. For eight years now, ever since the Hundredth Birthday in Cumberland, he had told her this. She did not care for Vanessa; she had thought Adam a country yokel, old Judith a mountebank. Moreover the girl's mother was a German. But if Ellis wanted anything he was to have it. God, she thought—she believed in a God made exactly in the image of herself—must be of the same opinion.

She could not deny that she had been struck by the girl's beauty. She had both the scorn and jealousy of beauty felt by many women who have fought life's battle without that great advantage. But this girl was exceptional. Raw, untrained, straight from the country: nevertheless with care and attention the girl could undoubtedly be turned into something. She had long made it a practice to refuse, at first, any request that Ellis might make of her, because she never lost hope that he might one day become more urgent in his prayers. She knew, in her heart, that this was one of the many hopes that would never be fulfilled.

So now she said: 'Nonsense. The girl's straight from a farm or a dairy or whatever it is. She's got no breeding.'

'She has perfect breeding,' Ellis said, and left her.

Next morning, considering the matter, she determined to make the girl devoted to her. Assum-

ing, as do many old people, that she would live
for ever, it was important that when Ellis married
his wife they should continue to live in Hill Street.
To lose Ellis was, of course, not to be thought of,
but Vanessa might influence him.　In her grinning, chattering way she did her best to be charming.　It was not difficult to win Vanessa's affections if sincerity was there, and Lady Herries was,
in this, sincere.　Before three days were out the
old woman felt that for the first time in her life
someone cared for her.　For the first time in her
life she herself cared for someone other than her
son.　But truly everything was enchantment to
Vanessa.　She never saw London again as she
saw it in those early days.

Everything about London was a miracle.　The
first morning she walked out she saw an old
crossing-sweeper who stood at the corner of
Berkeley Square and Charles Street dressed in
an old faded scarlet hunting-coat, given him,
Barney told her, by Lord Cork, Master of the
Buckhounds.　That old man, with his broom, in
his scarlet coat, seemed to her delighted eyes the
very symbol of London, its incongruity, unexpected romance, humanity and pathos.　There
was an Indian crossing-sweeper, too, who stood
with his broom outside the Naval and Military
Club.　There were the many Punch and Judy
shows, the poor, dark, melancholy Italian sellers
of cheap statuettes, and the old hurdy-gurdy man
with his monkey.

Hyde Park was her chief delight.　Lady
Herries liked to drive in the afternoon, and so

they paraded in a grand victoria, the old woman sitting with a back like a poker, gay as the rainbow, while Simon the coachman, in a multi-coloured livery, in figure like a sea-lion, drove, as though he were acting in a pageant, his magnificent horses.

But it was all like a pageant, the small phaetons with their high-stepping horses, the pony chaises conveying ladies of fashion, the victorias, the smart buggies driven by men about town, and the quiet-looking little broughams containing, it was supposed, all sorts of mysterious occupants!

This was a fine and warm April, and in the evening, between five and seven, everyone took the air in the Park. It was, it seemed, a world of infinite leisure where no one had anything to do but to see and be seen. On the other hand, there was nothing extravagant or forced in the display. No one, it appeared, wished to stagger anyone else. Everyone's position was too sure and certain. Rotten Row was, in fact, for more sophisticated eyes than Vanessa's, a superb affair.

In every way London was a magnificent show. The omnibuses alone gave it an air, for painted red or royal blue or green they were always handsome and individual with their strong horses and their swaggering accomplished drivers who had, with the flick of their whips, the air of conjurers about to produce rabbits out of their greatcoats.

The horses indeed were wonderful, Vanessa thought, never needing the whip, the drivers' cheerful hiss all the encouragement they wanted.

They were, she thought, both fiery and gentle, a glorious combination. The doors, the straw on the floor, these things were gone. The omnibuses were now the final word in the modern science of travel. But best of all were the hansom-cabs, the splendid horses driven by the most elegant cabmen who wore glossy hats and had flowers in their button-holes. On the first day that Barney took Vanessa down Piccadilly and Westminster in a hansom-cab, she sat, her hands clasped, her eyes shining, her smart little hat perched on her dark hair, Queen, it seemed to her, of all Fairyland.

Finally London then was a town of constant surprises. You never knew what at any moment would turn up. Every building had life and character of its own, little crooked houses next to big straight ones, sudden little streets—dark, twisted and eccentric—leading to calm dignified squares, fantastic statues, glittering fountains, shops blazing with splendour, hostelries that had not altered for hundreds of years. Everywhere colour, leisure, and, in this first superficial view, light-hearted happiness.

In that first week she spent her days with Lady Herries (Ellis was in the City all day), Rose Ormerod and her brother Horace. The power that Rose had over Vanessa from the beginning came from her jollity, her kindness, her humour, her warm-heartedness. Rose had also other qualities which appeared later in their friendship. Horace, her brother, had a job as secretary to some big benevolent society. He was rosy-

cheeked, square-shouldered, spoke well of everyone, was the friend of all the world. He was
a little naïve. He talked frankly about himself.
He was modest.

' I'm nothing exceptional, you know, Vanessa.
I don't suppose you think I am. What I say is—
why not see the best in everyone? It's easy
enough if you try. People have a hard enough
time. Why shouldn't we all make it pleasant
for one another? I must confess that I find life
a good thing.'

He was very jolly, had a hearty laugh, seemed
generous and genial to everyone. There was
something faintly episcopal about him as though
he were in training to be a bishop. Rose was
sometimes a little sarcastic about her brother, but
then she was sarcastic about everyone.

Vanessa was happy, but underneath this exciting London adventure one consuming thought
possessed her. Where was Benjie?

This was April 1882. The time had come
when Benjie would demand the conclusion to the
vow that they had made by the water-dolphin of
Ireby. Perhaps because she had seen him so seldom in these two years the thought of him by now
completely possessed her. If she had loved him
two years ago it was by this time as though he
were part of her very flesh. She was neither
romantic nor sentimental in her idea of him. She
saw him as he was just as she saw herself as she
was. Would he come? Where was he? He
had written to her, on some dozen occasions, little
letters, from Burma, China, India, North America.

In these he had not said much, and yet she knew that he needed her, that he was thinking of her as she of him. Would he come? London brought him nearer. When the first sharp excitement of her visit paled a little she began to look for him, in the Park, the streets, the theatre. Often she thought that she saw his small stocky figure, dark face, often fancied that she recognised the quick determined step with which he walked. Would he come, and, if April passed without him, what would she do? Was he faithless, volatile, careless, as they all said of him? Could she trust that he was faithful at least to her? Would he, oh, would he come? She spoke of him, of course, to no one, not even to Rose.

And then, in the second week of her visit, she began to be embarrassed by Ellis. She liked Ellis. She understood him better than others did. Most of all she was sorry for him. She wanted, as she so often wanted with people, to make him happy. There was something about his spare, grave figure that touched her heart. He was so *alone*. He wanted, she was sure, to be jolly with everyone but did not know how to set about it. She saw in him sometimes an eagerness as though he said: ' Now this time I shall be lucky and find touch.' But always his shyness, his fear of a rebuff, checked him. As Lady Herries became more confidential the old lady poured out to Vanessa the truth about Ellis as she saw it, his goodness, kindliness of heart, diffidence. ' He can't chatter away,' Lady Herries

said indignantly, ' like Barney Newmark or
Horace Ormerod; but he has ten times their
brains.'

Vanessa supposed that he had. He must be
very clever to remain so silent for so long.

As the days passed she had an odd impression
that he was approaching her ever nearer and nearer.
He was not in reality; he always sat at a distance
from her and when he walked with her seemed deliberately to take care that he should not by accident touch her. And yet she was ever more and
more conscious of his body, his high cheek-bones,
the pale skin pulled tightly over them, his sharp-
pointed nose, very Herries, with nostrils open,
slightly raw, sensitive; his thin mouth, his high
shoulder-blades, his spare slim hands, his long
legs that seemed always so lonely and desolate inside his over-official London clothes. He was
very tall and walked as though he had a poker
down his back. He was distinguished certainly
with his top-hat, his shining black tie, collar and
cuffs almost too starched and gleaming, his pale
gloves, his neatly rolled umbrella with its gold
top. People looked after him and wondered
who he might be, just as once they had wondered
about his father. His pale thin face peered out
anxiously at the world over his high collar. When
he spoke you felt that his words were important although they seldom were so. He had a nervous
little cough and often he blinked with his
eyes.

One fine spring day he took a holiday from the
City and in the company of Horace and Rose and

Vanessa walked in the Park.   Very soon Vanessa
found herself sitting alone with him while Rose
and Horace talked to friends.   She was wearing
her most beautiful frock, rose and white, the
pleated and flounced skirt with tucked panniers
over the hips, the bodice cut high in the neck, long
and pointed at the waist-line.   The wide skirt,
the modified bustle, the little hat with roses, the
different shades of rose in the dress itself, all these
things were remembered by her when many times
afterwards she recalled that costume as one of the
loveliest of her life and the one that she was
wearing when Ellis first proposed marriage.

He plunged at once like a man flinging himself with the courage of despair into icy water.

'Vanessa, I must tell you.   I can avoid it no
longer.   I love you with all my soul.   Please—
please—will you marry me?'

It was then, although his seat was apart from
hers, that she felt as if the moment, which for
days had been approaching, had arrived.   He
seemed to have flung his body on to hers; she
felt his thin hands at her neck, his bony cheek
against hers, she could feel his heart wildly, furiously beating.   She looked and saw that he had
not moved.   He was sitting, staring in front of
him at the carriages, the riders, the colours, the
sun; his gloved hands were folded on the gold
knob of his umbrella.

She wanted then, as never before in her life, to
be kind.

'Ellis!   Marry you!   But I don't want to
marry anybody!'

(That was untrue. She wanted, oh, how she wanted, to marry Benjie!)

He had recovered himself a little.

'I know that it must be a shock to you, dear Vanessa. I recognise that. I must give you time. But you must not think that it is any sudden idea of mine. I have had no other thought since I first saw you, years ago, in Cumberland. That time—we were downstairs at Uldale. From that moment I knew that only you of everyone in the world could be my wife.'

She laid her hand for a moment on his knee.

'I am proud that you should think of me like that,' she said slowly, 'but I'm afraid I can't. Ellis, I like you very much, but I don't want to be married—really I don't. I couldn't leave my father. It wouldn't be kind to him now he is all alone.'

(How stupid and stiff her words were! She wanted to be good to him, to say something that would take that wistful, forlorn look from his eyes.)

'Your father could come and live with us.'

'I'm afraid he could never live in London. He is miserable now if he is away from Cumberland.'

'If you could—if you could—love me a little, Vanessa. I would wait. I would be very patient. Perhaps you could love me a little——'

She must be honest.

'No. I don't love you, Ellis. Love is very rare, isn't it? I like you so much——'

'Well, then,' he caught her up eagerly, 'that

will perhaps turn into love. If you stay with us a little while. My mother likes you so much. I have never known her like anyone so much before. I can be very patient. I will give you as much time as you like——'

' I am afraid time will not alter it,' she answered gently. ' Friendship and love are so different——'

But he did not seem to hear. He went on eagerly.

' I will give you everything you can want. There's nothing you can ask for that you shan't have. I will never interfere with you. Only let me love you and serve you. I am not a man who has many friends. You have noticed that perhaps. I have been always shy in company, but with you beside me I feel that I could do anything. You are so good, so beautiful——'

Now the little scene was becoming dreadful to her. His intensity, his earnestness shamed her as though she had been caught in some misconduct.

' Ellis, dear. Listen. I don't love you. I'm afraid I never shall. We would be both of us most unhappy. Let us be friends, better and better friends, and you will find someone who *will* love you, who will make you so very happy——'

Words that every lady has used to every disconsolate lover! She knew it. She had not conceived that she could be so stupid. But, it seemed, he had not heard her. Rose and Horace gaily approached them, Horace laughing, greeting all the world as a jolly brother.

' Never mind, Vanessa,' Ellis said quietly. ' I

will ask you again. It is a shock, of course. I am afraid that I was very sudden.'

'We do apologise,' cried Rose. 'That was Colonel Norton. I haven't seen him for an age. We were only gone a minute.'

It seemed to Vanessa that they had been an hour away.

When, alone in her room that night, she was dressing for dinner, she most unexpectedly had a fit of crying. She did not often cry, although young ladies thought nothing of it. But now, sitting in front of the glass, twisting her hair into ringlets, she found that the tears made ridiculous splashes on the pincushion, which was fat and round like a large white toad with a bright pink eye. She was crying, she discovered, because that Ellis should love her made her want Benjie so terribly. Oh, if it had been Benjie who had said those words in the Park! But it was not. It was Ellis. Then she found that she was crying because she felt, for the first time in her life, lonely and needed her father. She seemed to see him in the glass facing her, his brown beard, his soft rather ironical, rather sleepy eyes, his broad shoulders, rough coat. . . . She thought that to-morrow morning, as early as possible, she would take the train to Cumberland. . . .

Her tears very quickly dried because she was, she saw in the glass, so long and lanky. Now Rose might cry very prettily because she was slight and delicate in spite of her dark colour. But Vanessa was too tall for tears. She stood up

in her skirt, all flounces and frills, raised her arms,
threw up her head.   Because Ellis had proposed
to her was no reason for tears!

Then she laughed.   The day before she had
paid a visit with Rose to one of Rose's friends, a
Mrs. Pettinger.   Mrs. Pettinger's husband was
an artist, and their little house in Pimlico had
shone with the new aestheticism.   The walls had
Morris wallpapers, everywhere there were Japanese fans, bamboo tables, lilies in tall thin glasses,
Japanese prints.   Also two drawings by Mr.
Whistler which, privately, Vanessa had thought
very beautiful.   Privately, because Rose had confided to her that she found them absurd.

'Why, anyone could do that!' she said.   'I
could.   Just take your pencil and draw a few
lines up and down.   You have to stand a mile
away to see what they're about.'

What made her laugh was the contrast between
the room that she was in now and Mrs. Pettinger's
house.   It seemed symbolically to be the contrast
that she felt between her love for Benjie and Ellis'
proposal.   Her large cold bedroom had not, she
supposed, been changed in detail for thirty years.
Especially did she notice, as though seeing them
for the first time, two armchairs of light oak carved
with floral decorations and upholstered with dark
green velvet having a floral pattern.   When you
sat down in one of them it clung to you as though
asserting its righteousness.   Then the frame of
Tonbridge-ware that contained a picture of a
little girl outside a church made in seaweed, the
Coalport toilet service, the dressing-table and

mirror trimmed with glazed linen and muslin, the mahogany bedstead, the needlework bell-pulls. Yes, she thought, sitting down on the green-velvet armchair, there were two worlds, as her father had always told her. Sitting there, without moving, staring before her, thinking of her mother, her father, Benjie, all those whom she loved, she moved naturally, simply into another world that had been, all her life, as real to her as the plush chair on which she was sitting. There was no effort, no conscious act of the will. An inner life flowed like a strong stream beneath all external things. This life had its own history, its own progress, its own destiny. She never spoke of it nor tried to explain it. It needed no explanation. Sometimes the two lives met, the two streams flowed together, but whereas the external life had its checks, its alarms, its vanities and empty disappointments, this inner life flowed steadily, was always there. Yes, two worlds in everything. How to connect them? The Saints, she supposed, were those who had learnt the answer, men and women in whose lives one life always interpenetrated the other. But she, Vanessa, was no saint. She could only, at certain moments, be conscious of an awareness, an illumination, that irradiated everything so that in that brilliant light both things and people had suddenly their proper values.

Sitting on her plush chair she had now such a moment. . . .

In the days that followed, Ellis behaved to her

exactly as he had always done. It was as though their little conversation in the Park had never been. She obtained increasingly from the Herries family both instruction and amusement. Old Amery greatly amused her with his intimate stories of high places, of the adventures, for example, of King William of the Netherlands, one of whose ladies broke all the crockery in his palace during one of her tempers, of some Italian prince in Paris who disguised himself as an organ-grinder for a whole month that he might station himself outside his lady-love's door, of young Lord So-and-so who, rejected by his mistress, put a large black band on his hat, went to his rooms, and committed suicide by cutting his wrist open with a razor, remembering first to place a slop-pail by the chair that there might be no mess. Young Alfred amused her because he would tolerate any-one who promised to be notable. She liked Captain Will with his breezy manner of finding the sea the only possible place, and yet now he never went there. The Rockages were redolent of the country. Carey himself, although he was tidy enough, seemed to carry good Wiltshire mud on his boots, and little Lady Rockage walked as though she were ready to spring on to a horse's back at any moment. She soon knew them all and liked them all with the single exception of Emily, Barney's sister, who was pious but not charitable, prudish with an unpleasant inquisitive-ness, and a mischief-maker for the best of motives.

She found them all most strangely alike in some basic way. They had no pose, made no attempts to assert themselves, took everything for granted.   For them all the Herries were the backbone of England, and England was the only country in the world that mattered at all.   It was Barney Newmark, however, who best explained the family position to her, sitting beside her on the occasion of the splendid Herries party in Hill Street when Mme. Trebelli sang and Signor Pesto played so enthusiastically the violin.

Vanessa liked Barney best of them all.   Rose, of course, excepted.   Barney was now fifty-two, stout, fresh-coloured and carelessly dressed but not untidy.   He looked a little Bohemian but not very; you would not know that he was a writer, said Vanessa.   That was a period when writers *looked* like writers.   He took life very lightly, laughed at everyone and everything, but behind that was, she thought, a disappointed man.   He had published a dozen novels and lived comfortably on the proceeds.   She had read several of them.   They were not very good and not very bad.   They were like the books of other authors. But he never spoke of his novels, laughed scornfully when they were mentioned to him.   She felt, however, that he would like it very much if someone else praised them.   At their first meeting in London she said what she could.   At once he stopped her.

' Dear Vanessa.   Thank you very much.   And now we need never mention them again, need we? No friends of mine can read my novels.   That is a sign of their friendship.'   Very different, had she but known it, from the man who once at a prize-fight had clasped Mortimer Collins by the shoulder!

They sat now in a corner of the big drawing-room and watched the splendid affair. The room was very crowded. It looked for the first time alive, for the heavy furniture was gone and, save for the palms, ferns and flowers packed into the corners, round the piano, in front of the great marble fireplace, only human beings filled it. The ladies wore their jewels, their shoulders gleamed under the gaslight, everyone was splendid, digni-fied, assured and, it appeared, happy. Vanessa would never have had courage to penetrate the throng, but almost at once she saw Barney, who carried her off into a corner, saying: 'Now I shall be the proudest man here for five minutes, before you are discovered, you know. Soon there will be so many proud men that you won't be able to breathe.'

She was very happy alone with him. She would like to stay thus throughout the evening.

'Tell me who everyone is, Barney dear,' she said.

He pointed out a few. 'That dignified cleric is the Bishop of London. That fine fellow there is Mr. Bancroft.'

'And oh, who is that darling old man?'

That darling old man looked like a ship's cap-tain. He had a grey beard, grey hair erect and curly through which he often ran his hands, a florid complexion, clear eyes. He was the finest man in the room.

'That is Mr. Madox Brown,' said Barney.

' And that lovely lady? '

' That lovely lady is Mrs. Samuel Maguire, and her husband gives her a diamond every morning with her coffee.'

' And that very dark man? '

' That is Isaac Lowenfeld, the financier. He once blacked gentlemen's shoes in Constantinople. Jews are coming in. The Prince of Wales likes them, and why should he not? I like them myself. They have the best hearts, the best brains and the staunchest religion in London.'

She noticed two young men with high white foreheads, long pale hair and a very languishing manner.

' And those? '

' Those are the aesthetes. They look at a lily for breakfast, worship china teacups, and lisp in poetry. I don't like 'em myself. They are not my kind. But they have their uses.'

' Everyone is here then? Lady Herries will be pleased.'

' Yes, it is a success because soon the room will be so crowded that no one can move, so noisy that no one will hear anyone else, and so hot that several young ladies will faint.'

She soon found members of the Herries family here and there.

' There is Emily. How nice and healthy Captain Will looks! I think Alfred is over-dressed.'

' Yes, we are all here,' said Barney. ' A great satisfaction to all of us. A fine family. And yet we are not of the first rank. Oh, I don't mean in history. We are, I suppose, as old as any family

in England. But we are not, and never shall be,
like the Chichesters, the Medleys. Nor like the
Beaminsters, the Cecils, the Howards. Although
in fact we *are* a kind of relation of the Howards.
But we're not like the new democrats either, people
like the Ruddards, the Denisons. All very poor
kind of talk this, but it's important, the social
history of England, partly because it's history,
partly because in another fifty years' time there
won't be any social history. There, do you see
that little woman in black with that jade pendant—
with the hard mouth and the small nose? That's
the Duchess of Wrexe. That's her daughter,
Adela Beaminster, with her. Well, she walks as
though she owned the world, every scrap of it.
Contrast her with Lady Herries. Oh, I know
she isn't a Herries really, but she's acquired *all* the
Herries characteristics. The wives of Herries
men always do. That's what I mean. We are
upper middle-class. We belong in the country,
small Squires, maiden ladies in places like Bournemouth and Harrogate, houses like Uldale for
example. That's where *we* are. For the last
hundred years we've been rising or seeming to.
Will made a heap of money and Ellis is making
more. Then there are the Rockages, a small
pocket-nobility. But we are not first-class in anything. We write—well, as I do. We are parsons and one of us becomes an Archdeacon. We
make money in the City but can't *touch* Lowenfeld.
We entertain, but when we bring off a party like
this it's a kind of accident. Not that we see ourselves like that. We think there's nobody to

touch us, but that's because we have no imagination. That's why we are of real importance in
the country. If there's ever a revolution in England it's the Herries and others like them who
will save us all. Even as we begin to die out the
lower ranks take our places and become just like
us. We are filled up from below, but we never
rise any higher. We have our good points—we
are not acquisitive, we are not greedy, we are kind
if we are not attacked, generous even; we never
lose our heads, we adore our country although we
criticise it. We never have to speak foreign
languages, we revel in our abominable climate, on
the whole we are contented.'

'But———?' asked Vanessa.

'We have one great weakness. We are terrified of anything out of the normal. If we see it
we fight and slay it. Unhappily there is a strain
of the artist in our family. It breaks out again
and again. Then we are shamed, disgraced,
humiliated. We have never learnt how to assimilate it. That is why if we breed an artist he is
always second-rate. The family is too strong for
him. That is why we fight among ourselves and
why some of us, if we are courageous enough not
to come to terms, are so unhappy. Oh, you
needn't look at me, my dear. I *have* come to
terms. I couldn't fight it out. That is why I am
what I am. I am always hoping that we shall
breed an artist who because he is forced to fight
becomes a *great* artist. Why have the English
the finest poets in the world? Because the other
members of the family have always done their

best to kill them.   Why was your grandmother so
splendid?   Because she never capitulated.'
    ' Father always says that she declared that she
did capitulate,' said Vanessa.
    ' Capitulate? She? Think of her! Capitulate?
Not she!   If she were in this room to-night she'd
blow out the Duchess of Wrexe like a farthing
dip!'
    ' And have you altogether capitulated, Barney?'
    ' Yes, my dear.   Entirely.   I'm no good at all.
But I tell you who *hasn't* capitulated.   That's
Benjie!'
    At the unexpected sound of his name the lights
blurred, the voices faded.
    ' No,' said Barney, ' but if he doesn't they'll
drum him out of the field.   You watch them.   It
will be a fight worth beholding!'
    And now the room was crammed indeed.
The roar of conversation, like the break of the
tide on shingle with here a whisper, here a grating
clatter of pebbles, here a resounding hiss, made
private talk impossible, so Barney, pleased with
his analysis of his relations, stood up and looked
about him while Vanessa watched Mr. Madox
Brown roaring at the Bishop of London, and the
lovely Mrs. Williamson (who was reputed to
bathe in milk every morning) listening kindly to
one of the young aesthetes, who twisted and bent
like a reed in a gale.
    She caught fragments of conversation.   ' I
heard Trebelli at Sims Reeves' concert in February.   No, he couldn't appear, so we had Trebelli
and Santley instead.   Oh, of course Trebelli's

the best contralto in the world. But to tell
you the honest truth I enjoyed better Santley's
" Vicar of Bray "—irresistible. Quite irresistible. . . .'

' Oh, but Bradlaugh . . .! '

' And then, my love, *what* do you think? She
went to the pastrycook's round the corner and
herself fetched a dozen cream buns in a paper
bag. . . .'

' Yes, but what *I* say is that they could keep
Jumbo here perfectly well, doncherknow, if they
wanted to—really wanted to. What I mean is,
that Jumbo is important for the country, for the
Tourists, doncherknow—something for them to go
to the Zoo and look at. What I mean is, we all
feel it *personally*. . . .'

' Very *unkind* of *Punch*, I think. Poor Mr.
Irving—to print his picture and then quote
" Romeo! Romeo! Wherefore are *thou* Romeo? "
That's too personal in my opinion. All the same
he is *not* the young, ardent lover . . .'

' Yes, but what Russell wants is to buy out the
Irish landlords and present the holdings to the
tenants! Simple! I should think so! If Gladstone would only say what he means . . .'

' And so, darling, Henry said to him, " That
lady is intended evidently for a Chinese "—trying
to be witty, poor man, and the large man with
the teeth whom he'd *never* seen before said furiously " And why, pray? That lady is my sister."
And oh, wasn't Henry clever? He answered at
once, " Why, because she has such exquisitely
small feet." '

It was Vanessa's first London party, and, standing there, waiting before she should be drawn into
the middle of it, she knew, as her grandmother
had known on just such another occasion, that
something in her responded to this with excitement and eagerness.   It was as though, a vagabond
and wanderer, peering in through a window at a
splendid feast, she exclaimed to herself: ' I can do
this as well as anyone.   I know all the tricks.'
She would never truly belong to it, but it was a
part that she could play as well as anyone there.
The personal drama had seized her.   The drama
of London, the Park with the brilliant sunlit
figures, the old crossing-sweeper with the scarlet
coat, Ellen Terry laughing into the wicked eyes
of old Mrs. Stirling, Mr. Conway rebuking his
errant daughter, Gladstone in his high collar thundering at the House, old Lady Herries fixing,
with trembling hands, the jewels about her throat,
the melancholy wail of the hurdy-gurdy two
streets away, the Prince of Wales talking to Mr.
Lowenfeld, the ' greenery-yallery ' young men
yearning over a Japanese print, the carts packed
with flowers arriving in the early morning at
Covent Garden, Gambetta drinking his morning
coffee in Paris, and that picturesque brigand
Arabi ordering an execution in Egypt, an account
that she had read only last week in a paper of a
Professor who had invented ' little electric lamps
of wires of platinum inside glass bulbs,' Ellis
loving her and Horace Ormerod's friendliness,
and Rose's adventurousness, Barney's kindness,
and, behind it all, sitting in the hut at the top of

the Cat Bells garden, watching the thin spidery rain veil the Lake in webs of lawn while fragments of blue sky, as bright as speedwells, flashed and vanished and flashed again.   Her mind was a jumble of this kind; at the back of the jumble was the deep unceasing preoccupation.   Would Benjie come before the month was out?   Would he keep his word?   Was there nothing that could still this burning ceaseless preoccupation of hers?   And, if he cared no longer for her, could she make her life without him?   She could!   She could!   She was not so weak, so helpless!   But her throat was dry at the thought!   Her hand touched her breast to check the wild beating of her heart.

She was discovered.   Rose and Horace discovered her.   They led her into the throng and at once her own life was broken into little scattered fragments.   She had no life.   She was nothing but a laughing, smiling, murmuring adjunct to all the other laughs, smiles, murmurs.

She was introduced to Mr. Madox Brown. They sat down together near the piano.   At first he said nothing, pushing his strong brown hand through his curly hair, muttering a little, looking as though he wanted to escape.   Then something happened.   *She* did not know what it was.   In actual fact it was his sudden realisation of her beauty.   He never saw her again, but many times after he would growl:

' One night at one of those damned musical parties I came on a girl . . . you never saw anyone so lovely.   Quite unconscious of it too.'

He became gentle and most friendly.   He told

her about his son. ' He died seven years ago.
There never *was* anyone so talented. Only nineteen when he died. One day when he was dying
and I sitting at his bedside he smiled and said I
smelt of tobacco. I said, "All right. I'll not
smoke again until you're better." I never *shall*
smoke again. Never. Paint? Write? He could
do anything. And sweet-natured. Oliver was
the only genius I've known. No one else. Not
genius. Genius is something from another world.
Nothing to do with this shabby one.'

He asked her where she came from.

She told him, Cumberland.

' Oh yes, Wordsworth and all that.'

Looking at her he said:

' You have beautiful eyes. Forgive an old
painter's impertinence, my dear. I always begin
with the eyes, you know. Paint the eyes of the
central figure first and that gives tone to the
picture. I begin at the top left hand of the canvas
and go straight down to the bottom. And what
do *you* do?'

' I can't paint,' she answered, laughing. ' I
can't do anything.'

' You don't need to,' he told her.

They could have become great friends had life
arranged it.

Then she was alone with Rose, sitting behind
a gigantic pessimistic palm. They were clearing
the space about the piano. Trebelli was going
to sing. What, she thought, was Rose's power
over her? Why was she so fond of her? Rose
was like a carnation, set deep in colour, slight,

with a wine-dark air. Not beautiful, for her eyes were too large for her small face, her nose a little snub, and her mouth, Vanessa must confess, rather hard. Her eyes laughed, danced, sparkled, but her mouth was always a little cold, a little cruel. If you judged people by their eyes, then Rose was a dear sweet girl, but if by their mouth, then Rose was nothing of the kind. She said once to Vanessa:

' Horace and I are both completely hard and self-seeking! '

' Oh no! ' protested Vanessa.

' Oh yes, we are! The only difference between us is that I look at myself in the glass and know *exactly* what I am. Horace looks greedily into other people's faces for his reflection and woe betide you if it isn't a pleasant one.' She added: ' We are both adventurers. We have scarcely a penny to our name. I'm the Becky Sharp in Thackeray's stupid novel except that I'm sometimes sentimental. After I've been sentimental I'm so angry with everyone that I could commit murder. I dare say I shall one day. Probably my husband. First I must get one. I'm twenty-seven, you know.'

She talked a great deal about herself, and this Vanessa found delightful, but Rose's real attraction for her was that she knew life so thoroughly. Girls who were Vanessa's contemporaries knew nothing about life at all. They were not supposed to know and, what was more, they really did not know. Most of them married without the slightest idea of what came next, with the simple

E

result that, for the rest of their days, they were a little melancholy and looked at all men, except clergymen, with a faint distrust. The women on the other hand, like Rose, for whom life (including men) had no secrets were like gipsies who pitch their caravans at their own risk. The female world looked on them with suspicion, and the male world frequently presumed farther than slight acquaintance warranted.

Rose had by this time told Vanessa everything she knew, and Vanessa, because she possessed certain beliefs, fidelities and a strong sense of humour, was not at all shocked. She hoped nevertheless that Rose would be married soon. It would be wiser.

Rose, on her side, loved Vanessa. She might be herself a lost angel—and she was a great deal more lost than Vanessa realised—but she adored a good angel with a sense of humour. She admired passionately in Vanessa all the qualities that she did not herself possess. She was no fool about human nature. She knew quite well that even from her mercenary point of view the virtues pay better in the end than the vices.

So they sat together behind the pessimistic palm and talked about those present. Rose knew something about everyone. She knew just what to tell Vanessa, amusing things but not cruel ones. She kept her cruel ones for other audiences.

Then, touching Vanessa's hand, she said: 'There, I think, is the man I am going to marry.'

'Oh, where?' cried Vanessa. 'Rose dear, do you mean it?'

' I *think* that I mean it. That man with the eyeglass, the pale whiskers, the beautiful figure.'

Vanessa looked. He was certainly very handsome.

' Oh, who is he? '

' He is Captain Fred Wycherley. He is in the Army and is very rich.'

' Oh, Rose dear, I am so glad! Has he proposed to you? Do you love him very much? '

' No, he has not proposed, but I think within the week he will. I don't love him, of course. It would never do for me to love my husband: it would give him too much power over me. But he is agreeable, amusing. I think we shall understand one another.'

Before they could say any more Trebelli began to sing. She had an extremely powerful voice and sang as though she were commanding a regiment. She was made, it appeared, of brass from head to foot.

After the singing everyone began to move about again and Vanessa was introduced to a number of people. Among them was a stout, round gentleman with fair hair and the face of a very good-natured pig, whose eyes beamed with kindliness. This, she discovered, was Lord John Beaminster, a son of the Duchess of Wrexe. He spoke in jerks, smiling upon her as though he had known her all her life.

' Very hot, these parties,' he said.

' Yes,' she said, copying Barney. ' The hotter they are the more successful they are.'

' Do you care for music? '

' Yes, sometimes.'

' That woman has deafened my ear-drum. All
the opera women shout. Do you like the opera? '

' I've never been in my life,' said Vanessa. ' I
live in the country.'

' Oh, in the country, do you? Wouldn't want
to live there. All right for a day or two. What
part? '

' Up in Cumberland.'

' Doesn't it rain there?

' Yes, when it wants to, but nobody minds the
rain.'

' I do, unless I'm shooting or hunting, you
know.' He smiled as though they had reached
the most delightful intimacy. ' Oh, that damned
feller's going to play the fiddle.'

It was then that as she looked beyond him
towards the door, as though something had compelled her, the miracle of her whole life occurred.
Beaminster was saying something to her. The
violin began to wail. The shining shoulders of
some woman at her side spread, as it appeared,
into an infinite distance.

In the doorway, looking about him with a
friendly grin, stood Benjie Herries.

She did not move. Beaminster, seeing a
friend, said, with a bow: ' Excuse me one
moment.'

Then Benjie seemed to drive, like a swimmer
breasting the tide, straight towards her. She saw
people greet him. She heard (for he was very
near to her now) Will Herries exclaim:

' Hullo, Benjie! Where have you come from? '

She did not move until his hand was on her sleeve. She heard him say: ' Come out of this. Outside.'

She went with him down the room. In the passage above the stairs there was no one. From the room within, the violin went on and on like a voice speaking only for them.

She stood up against the wall, staring at him, feeling that at any moment she might cry, unable to speak because her heart beat so fiercely, hammering her body as though it must throw her down. But there was no need to speak, no time for it.

' You thought that I wasn't coming back. Didn't you? You thought that I had forgotten. Quick, Vanessa, tell me—do you love me? Do you love me as much as two years ago? Is there anyone else? If so, where is he? I'll kill him. Quick. Tell me. I have run all the way from Brindisi. If you knew how I've run! Tell me. Tell me. Do you love me? Are you going to marry me? Can I go in there now and tell them all? Quick. Don't waste a moment! Do you love me?'

' Benjie, wait! Of course I do. I thought you'd never come! I've been longing——'

But she did not finish her sentence. He kissed her, patting her shoulder, her arm, laying his cheek against hers. Then he caught her hand in his.

' Now come! At once! We must tell everyone! We mustn't lose a moment!'

He pulled her with him to the door. The

voice of the violin came towards them, dancing over the crowd, the flowers, the palms.

Seated by the door was an old lady, blazing with diamonds, listening to the music through an ear-trumpet.

' Excuse me———' said Benjie.

' Hush! hush! ' said everyone near the door. The violin rose into a thin, long, vibrating note. Then ceased.

The old lady, turning to a man beside her, said:

' And *now* it ought to be time for supper.' Then, looking up: ' Why, it's Benjamin Herries! I thought you were in China, young man.'

Benjie wrung her hand as though she were the friend of his heart.

' I was, Lady Mullion. I was—only yesterday. Let me introduce you to Miss Vanessa Paris. We are going to be married———'

' Going to be what? ' she asked, her round red face ignorantly beaming.

He took the ear-trumpet and, in a voice loud enough for all the world to hear, shouted: ' We are going to be married.'

' Oh, is that all? ' said the old lady. ' I thought there'd been an accident. And now I do *hope* we are going down to supper.'

THE SEASHORE

TIMOTHY BELLAIRS took his wife and family that summer to an old house, Low Dene, in the village of Gosforth, which was situated ten miles from Wastwater and a little more than three miles from Seascale on the coast.

Young Tim, now aged five, had not lately been very well; one cold had followed the other. Sea air would do the children good, and he would have found some place *on* the sea had it not been for Mrs. Bellairs, who disliked the sea and all its works. So a compromise was effected.

Low Dene was one of those large rambling untidy houses of which at that time the country offered many examples. They were especially suited to the large families that good English parents thought it proper to create. The house was in a hollow under the hill to the right of the village; fields ran to the edge of the big scrambling garden; there was a croquet-lawn, a wood, shrubberies, a stream, everything that children desired. The place belonged to a retired Indian colonel whose children were now grown. He had gone with his wife and four daughters to Brighton, where he hoped to marry the daughters and recapture some of his own youth. It was one of

those houses which here are furnished and there are
not. The drawing-room, some of the bedrooms,
were crowded with large and small impedimenta,
so crowded that you could scarcely move without
disabling a china figure, upsetting an Indian idol
or flinging a wool mat to the floor. On the other
hand most of the passages, some of the bedrooms,
the bathroom, had no covering to the bare boards,
the wind whistled through the thin faded wallpapers, the piano was altogether out of tune, every
fireplace smoked, the gas hissed, the cistern
groaned, there was an odd smell of dog in every
room, and draughts played in every corner. In
spite of these things the house had an air of cosi-
ness and comfort—why, it would be difficult to
say. It was, maybe, because a large family had
grown up in it and their games, quarrels, intimacies, pleasures had sunk into the brick, per-
meated the boards of the passages, helped to
stain curtains and wallpapers into their faded
homely colours.

Timothy, his wife and children were well
pleased. Fell House, Uldale, was the joy and
boast of Timothy's heart, but it was pleasant for a
while to escape its responsibilities. Timothy was
lazy although he disguised the laziness with true
English aplomb. As to the children, this was the
happiest summer of their young lives. Discipline
was relaxed; their father condescended to walk
with them, there was the Farm at the top of the
hill, the fields with the haymaking, the mysterious
wood, the sea, and above all Vanessa.

It was Timothy who had invited Vanessa to

stay with them.   Mrs. Bellairs had objected, although in her sleepy, limited fashion she rather
liked Vanessa.   They had both been deeply
shocked—as had Herries up and down the country
—when they heard of her engagement to Benjamin Herries.   They had thought at first that
they would never speak to Vanessa again.   But
Timothy had as true an affection for her as he had
for anyone in the world.   In his stout slow body
there was little rancour, no spitefulness, temper
only with his own children.   He was negative in
all his emotions except his family pride.   He
thought that he had the finest house, the finest
wife, the finest children in the world, and perhaps,
deep in his heart, he loved his children and had an
affection for his wife.   But it was not the fashion
for either husbands or parents to be demon-
strative.   He was now forty-five years of age,
laziness and corpulency made him virtuous, but
he had still an eye for a pretty woman, and
Vanessa's beauty, although he might not speak of
it (for Mrs. Bellairs could be a jealous woman),
gave him the greatest pleasure to look upon.   He
would stare and stare at her with something of the
same emotion with which he would gaze upon
a fine shoulder of mutton freshly come to table.
Nevertheless he cared for Vanessa.   He would, at
a push, do more for her than for anyone.

Discussing the tragic Vanessa-Benjie affair in
the large family bed at Uldale, he declared that
Vanessa should be invited to come with them to
Gosforth.   Mrs. Bellairs groaned and lamented,
but knew that if he had decided on something it

was decided. They were both lazy people, but she was lazier than he. His point was that they might influence Vanessa. She had been carried off her feet by the London atmosphere. (He had the greatest contempt for London. He knew that he would not shine if he went there.) Let her spend a week or two with them in the country and they would soon show her her silly mistake.

' And her father? ' murmured Mrs. Bellairs.

' Let him come too,' said Timothy, who tolerated Adam but scorned him because he did nothing with his time but write books. ' The house is big enough.'

However, Adam refused. He might come over for a day or two.

Timothy, his wife, his sister Jane, now an old maid of forty-two, the children, Mrs. Clopton the nurse, Agnes the young maid, Jim Wilson the coachman, Peter the dog, all moved over to Low Dene in the large family chariot.

Vanessa arrived there two days later.

The real reason of Vanessa's visit was that she wished to escape from Benjie, whom she had been seeing almost every day for the last three months.

It was not that she loved Benjie less: it was that she loved him more, and this love had plunged her into a turmoil of problems, excitements and distresses not only about him but about herself as well.

She had never, until now, known any very close and intimate relation with anyone save her

father and mother. Her life had always moved on
certain fixed and stable laws. Her own faults and
failings, which were many — impetuous feeling,
hasty temper, neglect of obvious duties—had all,
when tested by a few principles, been clearly faults
and failings. There had never been any question
about what she *ought* to do. Simply she had been
wicked and failed.

But she was as honest as anyone alive, both
with herself and everyone else, and, after a week
with Benjie, she saw that neither right nor wrong
conduct would ever be so clear and simple again.

That she had been carried off her feet by
Benjie's return and proposal did not at all blind
her to the fact that no one else had. She
realised immediately at the first half-hour in the
party at Hill Street that no one anywhere was
going to approve of the engagement—no, not even
Rose. ' She is throwing herself away,' she could
hear everyone saying. Benjie's charm and light-
heartedness when he was happy affected many
when he was with them, and during that final
week in London he was very charming indeed,
but, returning to Cumberland, she found that even
Elizabeth was doubtful. ' It is what I have always wanted,' Elizabeth said. ' And oh, my dear,
I do hope he will make you happy! '

And her father? He kissed her and told her
that her happiness was dearer to him than anything
else on earth. She was a woman now. She knew
where her happiness lay.

She simply said: ' I have loved him all my
life.' He said no more, but she noticed in him

after this a constant anxiety, an extra tenderness, and, in herself, a certain reticence that had not been there before. Their relationship was for the first time in their lives a little clouded.

Benjie came up to the Fortress and lived there quietly with his mother. At first he was happy with an exuberance, a generosity to all the world, that showed him at his very best. Everyone noticed the change in him.

' I think,' Elizabeth confided to Vanessa after a week or two, ' that it will be as I hoped. You are going to change him altogether.' He told her again and again how, during those last months abroad, her image, his adoration of her, obsessed him more and more completely. On his journey home his impatience was a fever. At the sight of her at last in that silly drawing-room he nearly died! They must be married immediately. She was quite ready. She did not want to wait. Let them be married to-morrow!

Then it was he, Benjie, who postponed it. One afternoon, walking again in the garden at the Fortress, all the old doubts came forward. He was not good enough for her. Everyone was right. He would only make her unhappy. When she knew him better she would hate him. She calmed him. She laughed at him. She told him once again that she had known him all her life, that she was not blind nor ignorant about men, that they must trust one another and take what came. She was so certain of her own deep unchangeable love that they need have no fear. He asked her, in a kind of despair, why did she love

him as she did.   Soon against her will she was
asking herself that question.   What was Benjie's
power over her?   She loved him because he alone
in all the world drew everything out of her: she
loved him as a woman, as a mother, as a sister, as
a friend and a companion.   He was honest, generous, gay, independent, brave.   He was also careless, selfish, casual, forgetful, always surrendering
to the mood of the moment, hating to be tied.
But that he adored her no one could doubt.   He
knew, his mother knew, even the men and women
about the place knew that, with all his faults, this
love for Vanessa was true, staunch, unyielding.
Had his character been as fine as his love they
would be happy for evermore!

The wildness in him was quite untamed.   She
knew that and reckoned with it, but to watch it
working at a distance and to have it in close daily
communion with herself were two quite different
things.

He could conceal nothing that was in his mind,
and soon he attacked what he called her ' childishness.'   He attacked her religion.   He told her
again and again that he did not want her to change
in the least and tried to change her.   ' You know
that there can't be a God, Vanessa.   In your heart
you must know it.   You are a wise woman.   You
read and think.   Well, then, ask yourself.   How
can there be a God and life be as it is?   If there is
one He ought to be deuced ashamed of Himself,
that's all I can say.'

She disliked intensely to talk about her religion.
She had never done so with anyone save her

mother and Elizabeth. Her father had always
respected that reticence. But quietly and with
humour she answered Benjie's indignation. 'We
go by our experience, I suppose, Benjie dear. God
is as real to me as you are. Of course I don't know
why life is as it is. I am a very ignorant woman,
and Mr. Darwin's monkeys are beyond my scope.
But a hundred thousand monkeys wouldn't alter
the truth that I love you, nor would they change
my love of God either. Don't worry about it,
Benjie. Let us be what we are.'

Then soon there was another thing. She had
never known before what physical love was. She
had never been close to Benjie so constantly. She
had never conceived her own weakness. One fine
day they had ridden out to Borrowdale and, sitting
in the sun under some trees above Rosthwaite,
they had talked. She knew that everyone thought
it very disgraceful that they went about together
without a chaperon. Even her father had shyly
spoken to her of it. She had laughed and said that
he need have no fears. But now, quite suddenly,
she realised that he was right to be afraid. It was
as though she and Benjie were caught up into a
hot burning cloud of light. The world turned so
that both sound and vision were obliterated. For
a fearful dumb blind moment she was almost lost.
Then by the grace of God she escaped into sight
and sound again.

Next day she said

' Benjie, why should we wait? Let us marry
soon.'

But there was her father. She could not endure

to leave him. It is true that she would be at the
Fortress, not far away, but the thought of his
lonely days, his sitting at his table writing, looking
up out of window, thinking of her, wanting her,
was intolerable. He told her with a smile that
he would be quite happy. He had Will, he had
his work and garden. She knew that he was doing
his best. He did not take her in at all. Then in
June he fell ill. He caught a cold, suffered from
rheumatism, had to go to bed for a while. When
he was better Benjie, who had been wonderful
during Adam's sickness, coming constantly to
visit him, laughing, cheering him up, reading to
him, suffered from all his old scruples again.

'Vanessa, give me up! I'll go away and never
come back! I'm not worth all your sacrifice. I'm
not worth anyone's sacrifice.'

But he loved her more than ever and he was
more charming than ever. He was, during those
weeks in July, unselfish, thoughtful, considered
her in everything. But they decided that they
would wait until the spring. 'You will know then
finally, once and for all, whether I am worth it.'

'I know it now,' she said gently. 'Nothing
can change.'

But she perceived by now that, beyond any
doubt, it was something he knew about himself
that stirred all his self-depreciation. That, because
he knew himself so well and loved her so dearly,
he was determined to do this one decent honest
thing—not to ruin her life.

But what was it that he knew about himself?
He was not, in his attitude to anyone else, self-

depreciatory. Far from it. ' Take me as I am; as I take you,' was his attitude to the world. Only he would not spoil Vanessa's life for her.

' But of course you will not spoil it.'

' You don't know me.'

' I take the risk,' she answered.

By the end of July she felt that she must, for a little while, be at a distance from him. This indecision and hesitation could not go on. It was making them both sensitive, moody, self-conscious. So she went to Gosforth.

When she had been a day there her spirit was quieted, her gaiety returned.

Gosforth itself, small quiet village that it was, contained all the past. In the churchyard there was a cross of red sandstone which represented a figure chained beneath a serpent dropping upon him poison. This was a Christian cross and yet it had on it a heathen symbol. No one could tell its age, but many Vikings, she understood, had been half Christian, half heathen. She liked to think that this had been a Viking cross. Then there was Gosforth Hall near the church, the very house where Bishop Nicolson in the seventeenth century, as a young archdeacon, courted Barbara Copley. Near the Hall was a holy well where there had been once a mediaeval chapel, and half a mile from the Hall was the Dane's Camp, and farther from that again the King's Camp at Laconby. Many of the old houses in the neighbourhood like Ponsonby Hall and Sella Park were packed with history, while not far away was Calder Abbey.

In the middle of all this concentration of Time

slept the perfect English countryside. There was often sunshine that August and sweeping shafts of it fell across the cornfields, warming the colours into red gold, falling at the feet of the dark shadows of the woods. It was pastoral everywhere, while on windless days the silence, made more musical by the creaking of a cart, dogs barking, the call of the farmer to his horse, seemed to carry all the summer scents of flowers and corn and trees and pile them about you so that on the hot lawn you need not stir but gather, without motion, everything into your heart.

Yet how strangely even in this country of cornfield, wood and hedgerow still the mountains dominated. At every point, from every rise, Black Combe, thrusting its head like a lazy friendly whale into the sea, held your eye. From Black Combe's top you could hold in your grasp the Isle of Man, the Scottish and Welsh coasts with Snowdon greeting you, while landwards were Lancashire and the Yorkshire Fells.

To the right from a little hill above the house you could salute the Screes and in your mind's eye follow them as they rushed with all their power to bury their foundations deep in the heart of the black lake. Standing on her hill Vanessa would watch the clouds hurrying like smoke to invade the serried tops, then to spill themselves in storm or to break into pavilions snow-white or crimson with fire, or to shred and scatter into strands of gold and crimson. And she liked to sense, as she felt the motionless peace of the cornfields below them, catching the sun and throwing it up to her

again, that above those hills the wind was raging
and that their shining, slanting surface glistened
with hardness, and the stone walls, straight as a
sword, ran to the skyline over ground that was
rough and peaty and free. All history was in
this small patch of ground, and all nature too,
shadowed by the triumphant wing of the great
Eagle to whose kingly progress History was but
a day.

In the house and out of it there were the
children. They were sternly disciplined. Mrs.
Clopton, a tall dark woman with heavy eyebrows
and a faint moustache, was a Tartar. She was not
unkind, but she thrived on her despair of human
nature. She hoped for the best but gloried in her
constant disappointment. Her God—she was a
deeply religious woman—was the real God of the
Israelites, revengeful, on the watch for every
blunder, cruel in His punishments. Oddly the
children liked her; they were proud of her. She
had no need to punish; a look, a word from her
was sufficient. Not that they were perfect children. They made their own lives in their world
of perpetual discipline. They learnt their Collects
on Sunday, said 'Yes, Mama' and 'No, Mama,'
never spoke when with their elders unless spoken
to, but, once by themselves, the official eye removed from them, they were free, natural and
often naughty. It was as though they understood
the terms under which they lived and made their
plans accordingly. Violet was delicate—fair-
haired, slender, blue-eyed—and was already making her poor health her pleasant advantage.

But Tim was Vanessa's darling. He was fair
and slender like Violet, but strong and wiry. She
saw that he was an artist born and that nothing
would stop him. He drew unconsciously without
any deliberate awareness. He noticed the shapes
and colours of clouds, the patterns of leaves, the
path that the wind made through the corn, a
snail's shiny track on the lawn, the purple shadows
on the flanks of Black Combe. He was already
at odds with Herries common sense.

His father would darken the doorway.

' Tim, what are you doing? '

' Making a picture, Papa.'

' Let me see.'

Then after a pause:

' Now what is this? '

' A ship with pirates, Papa.'

' Pirates! Pirates! What do you know about
pirates? '

' Aunt Essie told us, Papa.'

' And you call this a ship? '

' I don't know ships very well and——'

' Well, wait until you do. Wasting your time
like this! What have I often told you? '

' Not to waste my time, Papa.'

' Exactly. Now put away that rubbish.'

The children worshipped Vanessa. For half
an hour before they went to bed she was allowed
to tell them stories. Mrs. Clopton listened in
stern astonishment. There was nothing of which
she disapproved so thoroughly as stories, but,
while her needles clicked, she found herself attending: fairy palaces rose above her head, the Crystal

Lake was at her feet and a White Horse of incomparable splendour strode the ice-bound hills.

' Time for their bed, Miss Vanessa.'

But, over her solitary supper, she wondered, against her will: ' What did the Princess find behind the secret door? Did the dwarf climb out of the cellar? Why was the Green Necklace the King's most treasured possession? '

Best of all there was the sea. On fine days they drove there in the victoria. The sand stretched in a floor of mother-of-pearl to the line of trembling white. On the horizon the Isle of Man hung between sea and sky. Timothy slept, Mrs. Bellairs talked, the children were busy with their fantasies, Mrs. Clopton read her Bible, Vanessa thought of Benjamin.

On a sunny afternoon, staring dreamily at the incoming tide, she saw him coming towards her.

At first she was delighted, then she was angry, then delighted again. She wanted *not* to be pleased! He was for ever breaking his word. They had agreed that they would not meet for three weeks. And why had he not written to her to tell her that he was coming? Or had he perhaps ridden over and to-morrow was returning? Or did he intend . . .? The children had seen him and began to run towards him, then stopped, remembering their elders. They loved, however, Benjie better than anyone else in the world—far better indeed. No one, not even Aunt Vanessa nor Aunt Jane nor any other, could create for

them a world and then live contentedly inside it
as Benjie could.

'Uncle Benjie! Uncle Benjie!' Tim cried
and woke up his father. Mrs. Bellairs disapproved of Benjamin completely. She was terrified
lest he should contaminate the children. She *said*
this, but in actual fact when he was in her company
she always surrendered to him. Had she been
honest with herself she would have acknowledged
that to be so vicious and yet so amiable touched
the adventurous woman in her. Although stout
and forty, completely the British matron, there
hid somewhere within her a girl who longed to
see what the other half of the world was like.
This girl was slowly starving to death. Once and
again she received sustenance: Benjie more than
any other kept her alive.

Nevertheless he *was* dangerous to the children
with all the horrible things he had seen and done,
the dreadful women he must know. Moreover,
had they not invited Vanessa to stay for the sole
purpose of showing her how shocking, how impossible Benjie was?

But what were you to do when in a moment he
was down on his knees in the sand helping Tim
with his castle, which the child had already decorated with a pink shell, the green stopper of a ginger-
beer bottle, and a piece of red rag tied to a stick?

And *what* were you to do when, smiling all
over his face, sand on his trousers, waving a child's
spade, he came over to you crying:

'Just think, Violet, I've come all the way from
the Fortress on a bicycle,'

' On a bicycle! ' She sat up, settled her bustle, arranged the large yellow brooch neatly on her bosom and stared with what she trusted was a mixture of disapprobation and dignity.

' Now don't look like that, Violet! You know you are glad I have come. One might think I was Cetewayo by your disapproval. I'm not going to poison the children or tell them naughty stories. I *may* tell you a few later on, but to be honest with you I've come to see Vanessa, the lady to whom I'm engaged, and nobody else. . . . Yes, I've come on a bicycle! I bought it in Carlisle last week.'

' Where is it? ' asked Mrs. Bellairs, speaking as though he had brought with him the late-lamented Jumbo from the Zoo.

' It is at my lodging.'

' Your lodging? Then you are going to stay here? '

' For a day or two—as long as Vanessa will put up with me.'

' Well, we can't offer you a bed at Low Dene if that's what you want. There are rooms enough but no servants. I'm sorry, but you should have told us you were coming.'

Benjie laughed. ' But, my dear Violet, why will you not understand? I have not come to see *you*. Of course if you appear sometimes I shall be glad to talk to you and to listen to what you have to say. If you are *very* good I will tell you a story or two about Port Said. But I have not the slightest interest in either yourself or Low Dene just now. I prefer the company of Mrs. Halliday and Rosemary Cottage.'

'And *who* is Mrs. Halliday?'

'A retired gentlewoman with a beautiful daughter, who, an hour ago, lured me with a card in the window which said that a bedroom was to let on moderate terms. Rosemary Cottage has a sea view, the beautiful daughter was in the parlour tending the plants. Within five minutes terms were arranged, and my bicycle is now occupying all the space in the front hall.'

'Very well. If you are satisfied. But I'm sure you might leave Vanessa alone for a little. You do not mean to say that you've come thirty miles to-day on that bicycle?'

'No. I stayed last night in Whitehaven and transacted a little piece of business.'

'I see.' She rose with great dignity, patted her bosom, shook her dress so that the frills and ruches settled in their proper places, and said:

'Timothy, it is time we were returning. Come, children. The air is chill.'

But the victoria had to be ordered, and Benjie was able to secure a moment alone with Vanessa.

'Why have you come?' Vanessa asked him. 'Three weeks was our bargain.'

'I know. I could not help it. I had to show you the bicycle.'

'No, but I am angry. Really I am. You should not have come.'

'You haven't written, Vanessa.'

'I have only been here four days.'

'Yes, but *four days*! An intolerable time. But see how tactful I am. I am here at Rosemary

Cottage. There is Mrs. Halliday's beautiful
daughter. I am quite happy, and we need not
meet at all.'

' You know that we shall meet.'

' Let the others go in front.' He caught her
hand. ' Vanessa. We must stop this nonsense.
We must be married immediately. I mean it. I
cannot live even four days without you.'

' To-morrow you will say something quite
different. I cannot trust you from one day to
another.'

' No, I know. That is why we must be married
immediately. Next month. I have told my
mother. There is nothing against it.'

' There has never been anything against it,'
she answered. ' Only your own indecision.'
Then she laughed. ' Oh, Benjie, I am so glad to
see you! I have been wanting you every minute
I have been here!'

' If,' he said, ' we walk up through those sand-
dunes no one can see us.'

Between the sand-dunes they kissed as though
they had been parted for years.

When he had seen them all drive off in the
victoria he walked to his lodging, singing. Everything was settled at last. His own indecision was
ended. After all, was he not changed? Did he
not adore Vanessa? He knew that he did! How
beautiful, how very, very beautiful she had looked
in the simple blue dress with the high dark collar,
the white frill at the throat, the little gold brooch
that he had given her, her hair brushed from her
splendid forehead, she kneeling there on the sand

watching Tim's castle. No one was so lovely, no one so good and true, no one loved him so dearly! The wildness was gone from his nature. They would settle at the Fortress, soon there would be children, boys like Tim, girls better than Violet; the garden should blossom with the rose, the Fortress should burn with light and heat. . . .

He was approaching Rosemary Cottage. It stood by itself, its feet almost in the sand-dunes, a small wind-blown desolate garden looking on to the sandy track. As he approached it he ceased to sing. The sun was setting: shadows crept over the sea and a mist veiled the little moon.

Before he entered he hesitated. Something about this place checked his high spirits. Vanessa seemed far away. A little wind, suddenly rising, blew the sand in thin spirals among the strong tufted grass.

In the sitting-room the lamp was already lit and a meal spread on the table—a ham, a dish of stewed fruit, cheese.

Mrs. Halliday appeared in the doorway.

' Shall I bring the eggs and tea now?' she asked. She was a spare desolate woman in a black silk dress. He noticed that she had no eyebrows and wore mittens on her hands.

' Thank you,' he said. He pulled off his boots, changing them for slippers, found in his bag a novel by Ouida, pulled out his pipe. She re-appeared with the tea and eggs.

' I trust you have no objection to smoking in here?' he asked, looking up at her with a smile.

' Oh, none at all, Mr.——' She paused. ' I

beg your pardon. I did not catch your name before. Pray forgive me.'

' Oh, certainly. My name is Herries.'

' Thank you. I am a little deaf in one ear.' She waited as though she expected him to speak.

' That tea looks splendid.' He moved to the table. ' I am exceedingly hungry.'

' I am very glad, I am sure.' She waited, then went on. ' I do hope we shall satisfy you. My daughter and I are not accustomed to having lodgers. We have been in this place barely a month.'

' Oh yes? ' He cut the bread.

' Yes. We come from Warwickshire. My husband was a gentleman of means. He was carried off with a severe fever six months ago.'

' Oh, I *am* sorry,' said Benjie. ' What brought you, then, to this district? '

' I have a son who has taken a farm in the Buttermere direction. He always was fond of the country, but was of course in very different circumstances when my poor husband was alive.' She paused, gave a dry little cough. ' He passed away with great suddenness. His affairs were sadly involved. He was ruined by one whom he thought his friend.'

' Oh dear, I *am* sorry,' Benjie said. But he had been startled by the extreme vindictiveness of that last sentence. Up to then she had spoken so very quietly.

' Yes, and so after that my daughter and I have had to do what we can. . . . Thank you, Mr. Herries. I hope that you have everything that you need.'

' Oh yes, thank you.'

She left the room. What an extremely quiet woman she was! It was not only that she spoke quietly, the words coming from between her thin lips reluctantly, but her movements were quiet, almost stealthy. She had been in the room before he noticed it. Had he been anyone but Benjie he would have said at once that he did not like her, but his charity was all-embracing, at any rate until he had full and sufficient reason for a stern decision. But as he ate his ham and his eggs he felt uncomfortable. He thought that perhaps tomorrow he would make a move. He had half an impulse to get up and see whether his bicycle were safe in the hall. At any rate it was stuffy in here. The room was too full of things, china dogs, pale yellow daguerreotypes, large sea-shells, little tables covered with plush fastened with bright gilt nails. There was a smell in the room as though the windows had not been opened for a very long time—a smell, was it of seaweed, of stale scent, musty and clinging? Ah well, he was an ancient mariner, he had travelled the world over and known every discomfort. He would not be disturbed by a musty smell and a china dog or two. Nevertheless he disliked intensely a large daguerreotype of a pale severe gentleman in black cloth whose cold eyes followed him wherever he moved. Possibly Mrs. Halliday would not object to moving *that* picture in the morning!

There was a knock on the door; he said ' Come in! ' and the daughter entered.

' Mother wished me to see whether you needed anything,' she said.

'Not at all,' he answered. 'Everything is excellent, thank you.'

The girl stood against the table looking at him.

She was certainly not beautiful, not even pretty. She was thin like her mother and very fair. Her colour was so pale as to be almost white; her large eyes were blue-grey. She looked at him and smiled faintly. No, she was not pretty but there was something striking about her. It was true that she was thin, but her very fragility seemed to claim your protection.

He smiled back at her.

'Do you like it here?' he asked her.

'No,' she said. 'I do not.' She came nearer to him and laid her hand on the cloth. He noticed at once what a beautiful hand she had, finely formed, with slender fingers. Her hand moved towards the teapot while still she looked at him.

He had a mad impulse to put out his hand towards hers.

He jumped up from the table.

'I shan't want anything else to-night, thank you,' he said, turning his back to her abruptly as he filled his pipe.

The world does not grow less mysterious as it grows older, and it is one of its more striking but less incalculable secrets that human love when it is strong enough defies physical distance. This was not the first time nor the last in their history that Vanessa, as now, riding in the victoria through the dark summer hedges to Low Dene, was quite suddenly aware that Benjie was in danger. Benjie

was so often in danger, whether spiritual, mental
or physical, that there must have been many occasions when Vanessa was unaware. There is also
the perfectly plausible theory that Victorian women
were exceptionally sensible to chills because they
wrapped up so much. In any case Vanessa, sitting
in the victoria, perfectly happy, feeling that at last
she was on a relationship with Benjie that was safe
and secure, began to shiver. They were turning
into the long straggling Gosforth street. The sky
in front of them was a pale translucent green in
whose bright waters some trembling silver stars
were glittering.

'Why! you are shivering, my dear!' said
Mrs. Bellairs. 'Wrap this round you! I do
trust that you haven't caught a chill!'

Young Tim was sitting beside her, and his hot
damp fist was enclosed in her gloved hand. In
his fist, as she knew, were several shells and a
piece of golden seaweed. She had the obscure
and unreasonable fancy that it was through his
hot little fist that she caught the sense that Benjie
was in danger. How could he be in danger? He
had left her only half an hour before to walk,
happy and singing, to his lodging. Rosemary
Cottage! There *could* be nothing wrong about
Rosemary Cottage. Nevertheless they were both
of a strange ancestry, she and Benjie. Francis
Herries fighting in the frosty air, Mirabell bending over her lover's body on the Carlisle stones,
Francis Herries looking at a picture on the wall
in a London lodging for the last time, John—his
son—calling through the mist in Skiddaw Forest:

'Is anyone there?', Judith, released at last, running into the road joyfully to greet her friends—these are only moments in a contemporary history where facts are important only as pointers, and where the significance is only externally material, and where Time has no significance at all.

'Thank you, Violet,' said Vanessa, gratefully accepting the Shetland shawl. 'It *is* cold after the sun sets.' At the same moment she had a most incongruous thought—that it was so *like* Timothy and Violet to christen their children with their own names!

She was uneasy all that evening and, next morning, a little talk that she had with Aunt Jane only increased that uneasiness.

It was a blazing summer day and they sat out on the lawn while the children, under the stern eye of Mrs. Clopton, knocked the croquet-balls about. Vanessa had on her knee a novel by Rhoda Broughton, and Aunt Jane had on hers a novel by Mrs. Alexander. Aunt Jane had a dear little face that would soon be covered with wrinkles. Her ringlets, her shawl (even in this warm weather), the spectacles that she used when reading, her little apprehensive starts as though she expected that at any moment a bear would jump out on her from the shrubbery, a round silver biscuit tin from which she would produce suddenly sweet biscuits for the children when Mrs. Clopton wasn't looking, her extreme delicacy about other people's feelings, her willing slavery to the wishes of other people, her single-hearted devotion to those whom

she loved, none of these attributes concealed from
Vanessa the fact that, in spite of her modesty,
reserve and deep religious beliefs, she knew a great
deal more about life and men and women than did
either Timothy or Violet.

Vanessa had not often an opportunity of being
alone with her. She was constantly busy on other
people's business. Timothy especially was always
providing her with occupations. She was, when
others were present, very silent, and her brother
and sister-in-law would have been amazed had they
realised the things that she perceived and pon-
dered. They were certain that she adored them
and considered them perfect human beings. In
the first of these they were correct or nearly
correct (she loved people in her own way, which
was not at all theirs), in the second they were
altogether wrong.

The little conversation that Vanessa now had
with her was punctuated with Mrs. Clopton's
sharp: 'Now, Master Tim, don't dirty your
stockings!' and 'Let your brother have the ball
now, Miss Violet,' and 'What did I tell you?
You must look where you are going.'

From the field above the garden came the
voices of the haymakers.

'Benjie has come to stay in Seascale, Aunt
Jane,' said Vanessa.

'Yes, dear, I know. That's very nice for
you.'

'And we are going to be married in the
autumn.'

Aunt Jane took off her spectacles.

' I'm glad of that too. I think you have been engaged quite long enough.'

' Why do you think that?' Vanessa asked quietly.

' Oh, my dear, I know nothing about marriage of course, but Benjie, I always say, is not at all an ordinary man. I would never expect *you* to marry an ordinary man, Vanessa dear. You have too much of your grandmother in you. But when a man is *not* an ordinary man I always say that it is better that he should be married.'

' Of course Benjie's not an ordinary man. But then nobody is ordinary if you know them well enough.'

' Quite so. That's what Mrs. Alexander, whose book I am finding it extremely difficult to read, does not appear to have discovered. All her characters are so *very* ordinary.'

Vanessa hesitated. Then she went on:

' Aunt Jane, I am going to ask you something. You are so very wise. You have known both Benjie and me since we were babies. Why is it, do you think, that when we are together we so often misunderstand one another?'

' That is just what I mean about marriage,' said Jane. 'People always misunderstand one another. But the point about marriage is that if you go on long enough together you arrive at an understanding. Once you are married you are bound together. I believe all married people find the connection very irritating for a long while, and if they were not married they would separate. But being married they cannot, and so, at last, the understanding arrives. I put it very badly of course. I am not clever as your grandmother was. But there it is. That's what marriage does.'

' We must not be engaged too long, Benjie and I,' Vanessa said, as though she were speaking to herself. ' There is something dangerous about waiting.'

' There is something dangerous, my dear, about every human relationship. That is God's intention. People would never learn anything if there were not plenty of danger about. That is what your grandmother always said.'

' Oh, how I wish she were still alive! ' Vanessa cried. ' She would have helped me. I know nothing about life at all—nothing about Benjie either, I sometimes think, although I've been with him all my life. How can we know anything about men? We are never alone with them; all they do is concealed from us; when they are with us they never tell us the truth.'

' Yes, dear, you are quite right,' said Jane. ' I often think that women to-day are far too sheltered. Not that I like the girls that your Miss Broughton writes about. That is surely going *too* far. But when your grandmother was a girl, as she often told me, women were far more free. I dare say they will be again one day, but as it is just now they have to spend all their time guessing.'

' Aunt Jane,' Vanessa said, staring at the rising field, the sunlight that soaked the lawn, ' I'm frightened. I feel that one wrong slip and Benjie will be carried away into some place where I can't reach him. I love him so terribly, but I am only

close to him at moments.   He's here.   He's gone.
And when he is gone I am so helpless. . . .'

Jane smiled.   'Don't be frightened, my dear.
Trust God.   He knows so very much more than
we do.   Remember always that Benjie has a tragic
history behind him, his father, his grandfather.
. . . You know, don't you, that I was the last
person to talk to his father on that dreadful day?
He was leading his horse from the stable.   Of
course I was only a little girl then, but I have
always thought that perhaps I could have stopped
him if I had known what to do or say.   I loved
him when I was a child more than I loved anyone,
and I have been haunted all my life since by the
thought that I failed him.   But what I say is,' she
went on more cheerfully, ' that if we do right as
far as we can it's all we can do.   Life's a dangerous
thing, my dear, and you can't escape the danger
by staying in bed all day or making other people
act *for* you.   Don't expect things to be easy.   Why
should they be?   God doesn't arrange the universe only for me—nor for you either.   To listen
to the way the people talk in this novel of Mrs.
Alexander's you'd think that every time they have
a toothache God ought to be ashamed of Himself. . . .'   She nodded to herself, picked up her
book.   ' I'm at page one hundred and fifty-three
and that's as far as I shall go.   I always like to
finish a book if I can; when the writer's taken so
much trouble it seems only right; but *this* time
I simply can't be bothered.   Mrs. Alexander will
never know, so there's no harm done.'

For one reason or another this little talk left

Vanessa—who as a rule was sensible enough and level-headed—in a kind of panic.   That was the quality that Aunt Jane had, that when she *did* talk she always suggested so much more than she said. Her honesty forbade her to offer false consolations. If people did not inquire what she thought she was too thorough a lady to tell them, but if they *did* ask her they must accept the consequences. Vanessa now had the conviction that Aunt Jane thought her love for Benjie a disaster!

She endured three days of a distress and apprehension altogether new to her experience.   For much of this the child that she still was was responsible.   These were perhaps the last days of immaturity, those days when persons and events have still the size and colours of nursery hours, moments when we are left alone in a room where the flickering firelight throws gigantic shadows on the wall, when the clock's tick is a menace, and the twig tapping on the window-sill threatens the approach of some dreadful stranger!

She had three days of nightmare—and was transported into Paradise!

Timothy, as befitted a Bellairs, liked society if it was proper enough, and at the houses in the neighbourhood—Muncaster and Ponsonby and others—there was plenty.   It was still the fashion, if you went out to dinner, to take a footman with you to assist at the meal, there were elaborate croquet-parties and magnificent picnics.

So one fine day Timothy and his wife set off to Muncaster, and Vanessa went with the nurse and children to the sea.   They had not been settled on the shore five minutes before Benjie was with them.   He and Vanessa started to walk across the long, shining sands.

It was a day of perfect peace.   Chroniclers may define that moment as the final peaceful one in English country life—a moment of historic tranquillity when the cornfields lay placid beneath the sun, the hedgerows slept, woods were untrodden, and every village sheltered under its immemorial elm while the villagers slumbered off their beer on the parochial bench.   At the final moment, then, before the trumpet of the new world sounded, Benjamin and Vanessa crossed Seascale sands!

She knew at once that he was disturbed.   There had been something, then, in her own unrest.

She said at once: ' Benjie, what is it? '

He caught her arm with his hand and pressed her against his side so that they might walk like one man.   She was taller than he.   She was wearing a small, rather masculine hat ornamented with blue flowers.   She held her parasol high over her head.   She was smiling, she was happy.   She could feel his hand within her arm against her heart.   All her fears were fled.

' There is nothing the matter except that I love you.   And that *is* the matter, for we must be married in a month's time.   I can wait no longer. I am bad through and through.   I am without a redeeming point, but I have told you all that so often that I shall never mention it again.'

' Certainly we will be married in a month's time.   To-morrow if you like!   I have been

dreadfully unhappy these three days.   I can't tell
you why, but as I was driving back the other evening I had a sudden fear that something had happened to you.   That cottage—what did you call
it?   Where you are staying.   I have been dreaming of it, crawling with spiders and earwigs.   I
have been thinking that if we are not married at
once we never will be married.   And Aunt Jane
frightened me.'

'What has Aunt Jane been saying?' he asked
quickly.

'Oh, nothing—dear Aunt Jane!   She loves
us both, I know.   But she is afraid for us.   I
know she is.   She thinks there is dangerous blood
in our veins.   She wants to see us *safe*.'

'She's right!' he said fiercely.   'We must be
safe—or someone will part us, something will
happen!'

They were standing at the sea-edge on a floor
of mother-of-pearl.   The incoming tide drew thin
lines of white as with a pencil on the shore and
beyond the line the sea heaved without breaking,
as gently as a sigh.

'No,' she said.   'I think that *nothing* can part
us.   I don't mean because we love one another.
I can imagine that you might come to hate me or
I would be so proud that I would never see you
again, but still we would not be parted.   It has
been like that all our lives.'

Then she added, as though to herself: 'That
is my worst fault, my pride.'

He turned and looked at her as though he were
seeing her newly.

' What do you mean, Vanessa—your pride? '

' I would endure anything, I think,' she answered, ' or so I feel. I would show what I was suffering to nobody, but it would remain inside me. I could not let it out. I cannot let things go—words that someone said years ago, little things that people have done. No one knows that I remember them, but I never forget. They do something to me. I hate my pride. I would like to be free as you are, Benjie—every day a new day——'

' No, Vanessa darling,' he broke in. ' Not like me. If there were two of us, both like me, oh, what a time we would have! You are the only one in all the world who influences me! That is why you are to marry me, teach me, change me.'

' I don't think I can teach anyone.' She sighed. ' I don't know why it is, but I would rather leave people alone, leave them as they are. Father is like that too. Mother used to be constantly distressed at how bad people were. Not that she blamed them. She was too kind. But it bewildered her. Right was so right and wrong was so wrong. I have no conscience for other people, I think—not even for you, Benjie.'

He asked her again for the thousandth time: ' Why do you love me, Vanessa? Everyone tells you not to.'

' I love you,' she answered, ' as I shall always love you, because you are part of me, because you are all that I have in the world, because without you I am always lonely, because I am not alive without you. There! ' she said, turning round

and laughing, looking at him too with infinite
tenderness, with a kind of brooding devotion as
though she could not look at him enough, could
not have him close enough to her. ' Now—are
you satisfied? '

For a moment he was silent, then he took her
hand and kissed it.

' God helping me,' he said, ' you shall not regret it.' Then, characteristically, added as they
turned to walk back: ' Although I don't believe
in Him, I expect Him to help me, you see.'

They discussed details. He had written to
Elizabeth the night before. They would be
married in Ireby church, a very quiet wedding.

' There is only Adam,' Benjie said. ' I hate
to think how he will miss you. We will do everything we can. You can go and stay with him
whenever you wish, and he shall stay with us.'

' He will be happy if I am,' she answered.
' And he is well now—stronger than for a long
while.' But nevertheless she knew leaving him
would be terrible. They must think of a plan
. . . some way. . . .

As they neared the children two women passed
them. Benjie raised his hat.

' Do you know them? ' she asked.

' Yes,' he said, laughing. ' That is the en-
chantress of Rosemary Cottage. Two enchant-
resses. Mrs. Halliday and her lovely daughter
Marion.'

Driving home, with Violet on her lap while
Mrs. Clopton told her stories of the heathen in
Africa and all that was being done to improve

their minds, she was thinking in an ecstasy of happiness:

'We are safe! We are safe! In a month we shall be married. Nothing can touch us now.'

In the morning the old postman, bent and twisted like a gnome, brought her a letter. It was from her father.

DEAREST VAN—I am not very well—nothing serious —but I think perhaps you had better come home.—Your loving   FATHER.

FALL OF THE HOUSE OF ULDALE

ADAM PARIS hovered through the whole of that autumn between life and death. His sickness began, it appeared, with some mysterious poisoning, was followed by pneumonia, and left him with a heart so weak that every excitement, every sudden movement, was a danger.

So he was told not to move, not to suffer excitement. In the early days of January he was permitted to walk a little, supported on Will Leathwaite's stout arm, in the garden. During those months Vanessa scarcely left his side; even Benjamin was almost forgotten by her.

Whatever else Adam might be, he was always a philosopher. By January 1883 he was sixty-seven years of age—sixty-seven was three years from three score and ten. To die at that age was no very terrible misfortune. He did not want to die. He did not want to leave Cumberland, nor Will, nor Vanessa. Every day held some adventure, some charm, some beauty. But he most certainly did not care to linger on an invalid, a trouble and anxiety to everyone about him. He knew that had it not been for his illness Vanessa would now be married, and although he did not wish, had never wished, that Benjamin should marry her, he wanted to see her settled before he went. Moreover, he had now perceived that it was Benjamin and Benjamin alone whom she must have, and he made the best of it.

If anybody could make anything settled and secure out of Benjamin, it was Vanessa. So great an opinion had he of her wisdom, common sense and fidelity that he thought that she might.

During those long trying days of convalescence he kept a Journal—not a very regular one, not a very original one, but he put into it his honest opinions, some of his experience. These were some pages of it:

. . . A long and dangerous illness is an odd enough thing, I find. It is a commonplace that it seems to you, when you are in good health, incredible that you should ever die, and that when you are very ill you do not care a hang whether you die or no. Nature has arranged that very cleverly. But now that I am growing stronger again I find that I want to live for the smallest, most insignificant reasons. I have, for example, a new dog that Benjie gave me the other day, a rough clumsy kind of terrier. I have called him Tux after Rousseau's animal—the one that the Duchess of Luxembourg gave him. I have always liked Prince de Conti and the Luxembourg for their niceness to Rousseau, who must have been, just then, as tiresome and sensitive a creature as God ever made—but the queer thing and the enduring thing about Rousseau is that he had in him something of Everyman. He would have felt, I

am sure, just as I did yesterday when Timothy
and Violet came up from Uldale to pay me a visit.
So very well-meaning, so extremely irritating!
However, in one thing I am luckier than he. I
have no Thérèse for them to patronise! But I felt
just as he did about presents. Timothy gave me
a shawl ' to keep my knees warm ' as though the
whole of the Herries family were presenting me
with a medal. However, it is quite natural that
he should think me a fool who all his life has
wasted his time over nothing! And I had my
ambitions once, too, but ambitions when you get
to my age are cheap affairs. Would I have been a
happier man had I been Gladstone or Dizzy or
Dickens? Sour grapes perhaps to say that I would
not. It is natural that I should like now to clap
my hand on the table and say: ' Yes, I have added
that to the world's achievements, a law or a poem,
a picture or a character.' But my illness has left
me altogether indifferent. My dear mother, I
suppose, went the wrong way for both of us when
she stayed at Uldale instead of escaping the family
and going to Watendlath. She always said that
it was the mistake of her life. Had she gone I
would have been a farmer, never seen a relation,
never lived in London, never married Margaret,
never had Vanessa for a daughter. What I would
have missed! But I might, I fancy, have been a
stronger man, a more determined character, and
I would certainly have had more of this country,
the sight and smell and sound of it. But I would
have been always a dreamer who never pursued
his dreams far enough. There can be no man

but is dissatisfied with his life when he looks back
on it. What a confusion of shreds and patches,
of starting first here and then there, of one blind
move after another—walking at night along a
dark road and thinking every tree a hobgoblin!
But I was never much of an adventurer, too easily
disheartened, too ready to be an idealist without
suffering for my ideals, far too ready to shrink
away into myself if I met a rebuff. A failure, I
suppose, trying to conceal my failure with a certain
cynicism, and yet on the whole what a happy life
I have had. I have known three glorious women
—my wife, my daughter and my mother—one
or two magnificent men—Dickens, Caesar Kraft,
Will, and in my babyhood, Reuben Sunwood. I
have been given the perception of beauty in art
and in nature and, although my own writing has
been less than nothing in its result, I have had, in
the pursuit of it, some glorious visions. Best of
all, I have never been betrayed by my own failure
into thinking man a poor affair. I have never
come to thinking human nature a bad blunder,
although in my Chartist days I met some poor
specimens. Nor, thank God, have I ever suffered
a fool gladly, least of all myself.

The whole pageant of life has been, and is, of
an extraordinary interest. I can see now clearly
enough that Time is nothing, that each and every
man is tested with the same tests and rises or falls
according to what he learns. Learning is everything. But for what? I have never been sure
of any kind of personal immortality. As my
mother used to say: ' I don't *feel* it and so I don't

believe it.' But Margaret was sure and Vanessa is sure and they are both wiser than I. There is a great deal of the pagan in me, as there was in my mother. We inherit that, I suppose. But even with my paganism I wonder that the world should be so beautiful and men often so fine and courageous if there is nothing more than this brief experience. I have touched some grand moments too: my first sight of Margaret in that little room off the Seven Dials, Dickens' hand on my shoulder, the day when I finished my first story, walks with Will, the day when in a kind of panic I ran away from Margaret up Cat Bells here, hours with books, sunrises and sunsets, even yesterday when looking from this window I saw the hills rosy and the Lake a misty blue. Do these moments of perception mean nothing at all? I don't know, and up to a week or so ago in all those months of illness I certainly did not care. One night in September I was sure I would be dead before morning and everyone else was sure too. I was quite clear-headed and quite indifferent—yes, even to Will and Vanessa. But I remember that I felt intolerably wise, that I thought that I had discovered the secret. Will turned me over in bed that I might lie easier and I muttered: ' Well, *that's* it. Why didn't I discover that before? ' But what I had discovered I haven't now the least idea. Nothing is certain except love, love of anything or anybody that takes you beyond yourself. This may be, for all I know, a proof of God. It's as good a one as anything the parsons can give you. ' For what we have received let us be truly thankful. . . .'

January 9, 1883.

Benjie came up yesterday afternoon and we had a talk. I never saw a man look so healthy. He is a gipsy for colour and hard as iron. Nothing seems to fatigue him and nothing bores him. What is best about him is that he is an individual. He is like no one else at all: you never know where you have him, or at least I don't. If you think him happy he isn't. Behind his merriment (and I must say I like it when he throws his head back and laughs as a boy laughs) there is a strain of melancholy. That he loves Vanessa there is no mistaking, but I am certain that he has misgivings about their marriage. He is right when he says he can't stick to anything. He is always against the law, whatever the law happens to be, and in that he is, I suppose, like my romantic grandfather and the Frenchman my mother married. He is of their world and so all against the Herries world, which is altogether anti-individualist. I couldn't help thinking yesterday as I listened to him that that may be the fight the whole earth is slipping into—the type against the individual. All the troubles in our family have come from the individual refusing to conform. Do I want Vanessa to be engaged in that kind of battle? No, indeed I do not. Nor do I want her to marry a type-Herries either. The truth is, I suppose, that I love her so much that I shall never find anyone good enough for her!

Benjie yesterday was in a queer state of in-

decision. He came, I fancy, that I should make
his mind up for him, but about what? He never
said. He asked me the absurdest questions all
covering something deeper that he never owned
up to. Should he go to a Ball at Greystoke?
Yes, I said, if he wanted to. Oh, he'd be sick of
it in half an hour and do something outrageous.
There's some woman and her daughter whom he
met in the summer at Seascale have come to live
in Keswick. Should he go and call on them?
Why, yes, I said, if he liked them. But he didn't
like them. Well, then, don't go. They had been
friendly to him in Seascale and so on and so on.
Vanessa had gone to Uldale, and I could see that
he was deeply disappointed and yet was relieved.
Nevertheless how charming he can be! I never
knew anyone better with Will. He gets behind
that man's defences in a moment. He knows by
instinct what are Will's reticences. He is on a
level with him completely, no patronage and no
sycophancy either. His heart is good, but he is
so restless and so impulsive that he is in trouble
before he knows where he is. He is like a wild
man who has never been tamed, and then, in a
flash, a perfect courteous gentleman. Can Vanessa
tame him? I believe that he fears himself that
she cannot, and trembles lest he should do her a
wrong. Like him I must, and fear for the future
I must too. How I wish that my mother were
alive! She would understand him as no other.
She was the daughter of one wild man and tamed
another—but my mother was unique. There
will never be anyone like her again.

When he was gone I was tired enough and Will helped me to bed. That pain just over my heart returned like an old familiar friend. Odd how a pain, to which you are accustomed, seems in a fashion friendly. I could feel its fingers pinching my flesh, then pressing heavily, constricting the muscles, and as I laboured for breath I could almost hear its voice: ' Now we are together again, you and I. Is not our intimacy pleasant?' I could not altogether own that it was, and yet I could have almost replied: ' Yes, but don't press too hard, old fellow. Spare me what you can.'

And now this morning, this bright frosted January morning, I am well and the pain is forgotten. How quickly the past is over! How dim the pain of five minutes before! Yes, and the pleasure too! I can remember how often on a fine day, walking or sitting lazily in my boat on the Lake, the beauty has been so intense that I have longed to catch it in my fingers, hold it, wrap it up, put it away for safety. And in a moment it is gone. A rosy cloud turns grey, there is a whisper on the water, the shadow envelops the hill and *that* beauty is lost! But the intensity of the realisation is caught at least. My friend Jean-Jacques, of whom for some reason I have been thinking much in these last weeks, speaks of that. I haven't the *Confessions* with me but the passage goes a little like this: ' The movement and the counter-movement of the water, the stirrings, rising, falling, gave me pleasure in mere existence. No need to think, to live at that moment was enough! Letting my boat go where

it would, I would abandon myself to reverie.
I was completely under Thy power, Nature! No
wicked men to interpose themselves between us!
Yes, all is a perpetual movement on earth. Nothing is constant. Our affections change and
alter. Everything is in front or behind. We
recall the past to which we are now indifferent or
anticipate a future that may never come. Nothing solid for our hearts! But the soul may find
a state solid enough on which it may repose with
no thought of the past, no fear for the future—
and so long as such a state endures he who
experiences it may speak of bliss. . . .'

Once on a day I knew that passage by heart,
I think: now it comes to me only in fragments.
Poor Rousseau, demon-haunted, finding no spot
where his foot might rest. How in those days
when the *Confessions* were so actual to me, I hated
Voltaire and the vile Grimm and the false Madame
d'Épinay!

But after all I suppose that his troubles were
of his own making. There would have been no
genius had there been no sickness. But I think
at my age I hate most in this life the jealousy and
rage of men against one another. How trivial and
worthless our plottings when we are here for so
short a time. How easy, you would say, for Man
to tolerate his brother. And yet how I myself
detested old Walter, so that I would lie awake
and think how I might injure him. And then at
the last that poor, weak, crying old man to be fed
with a spoon and have his mouth wiped! I swear
that if I recover from this I will never be angry

again. And yet it has been, I dare say, that I have not been angry enough in life, have not known indignation enough. I have hated injustice, but men are too often like birds in a cage. They would not be there if they could escape, and the cage is not of their own designing. This wandering along on paper has passed an hour—and now for *The Story of an African Farm* that they are all praising. New militant woman eager for her rights! If the world is to be full of them, as I suspect it will be, I shall not be sorry to have gone. . . .

FELL HOUSE, ULDALE,
    April 3, 1883.

. . . so three days ago Vanessa and I moved to Fell House for a week or two. I am a very great deal better, can take a walk by myself and am not so utterly dependent on Will as I have been—how patient, tolerant and sensible he's been no words can say, but I recognise sufficiently that two moments in my life have been supremely lucky —one when as a small boy I watched Will win a race through Keswick, the other when as Victoria returned crowned from Westminster I tumbled up against Caesar Kraft. The love of one man for another is an odd thing: it is bare of sex and yet does in certain moods surpass the love of woman. Maybe I have never been a sexual man. Looking back now I can see that it was not virtue kept me free in my youth but a certain fastidiousness that I got, as I got so much else, from my

mother. I sometimes think that had I been the
child of a street-woman and, say, a card-sharper,
I could have been something of a writer. But no
matter now. Never was anything of less importance. All the same, being what I am, I doubt
whether any relationship could be finer than mine
with Will. And it has been his fineness, not mine.
Complete unselfishness, unsparing devotion and
a deep, always by me perceptible, emotion under
it all. With all that it has been always humorous,
mixed with plenty of plain speaking. I cannot see
that it has had any falseness in it anywhere. And,
although I have no belief in immortality, it is hard
for me, I confess, to imagine a state when Will and
I will not be together and consciously together.
Such a relationship as ours goes far beyond the
body and, maybe, survives the body. There
is this at least about it that it makes you think
well of your fellow-men. It makes me wonder
sometimes whether any country but England (and
sometimes I wonder any county but Cumberland) could produce such a man as Will. He is
altogether Cumbrian in his honesty, reticence,
obstinacy. But this of course is nonsense. There
are men like him, I don't doubt, all the world
over. My grandfather had such a one. Quixote
found one, Montaigne had one; thank God the
world is full of them.

Well, after this sentiment which no eye will
ever see but my own, here is the other side of the
shield. The only other visitor here but ourselves
is Phyllis Newmark's boy, Philip Rochester.
Rochester, whom she married some thirty years

ago, has something, I fancy, to do with railways
and has amassed a nice fortune. Barney, I know,
dislikes him and always calls him a humbug. As
for Master Philip, I have seldom disliked a young
man so much. He is thin and willowy, talks in a
piping voice about the ' Inevitability of Sin ' and
that 'Art is the only Moralist.' It happens that
in this very week's *Punch* there is a little piece
which I shall have great pleasure in showing him.
It is apt enough to copy into this Journal:

TO BE SOLD, the whole of the Stock-in-Trade,
Appliances, and Inventions of a Successful Aesthete, who
is retiring from business. This will include a large stock
of faded lilies, dilapidated sunflowers, and shabby pea-
cocks' feathers, several long-haired wigs, a collection of
incomprehensible poems, and a number of impossible
pictures. Also, a valuable Manuscript Work, entitled
Instruction to Aesthetes, containing a list of aesthetic catch-
words, drawings of aesthetic attitudes and many choice
secrets of the craft. Also, a number of well-used dadoes,
sad-coloured draperies, blue and white china, and brass
fenders. To shallow-pated young men with no education,
who are anxious to embark in a profitable business which
requires no capital but impudence, and involves no pre-
vious knowledge of anything, this presents an unusual
opportunity. No reasonable offer refused. Apply in the
first instance to Messrs. SUCKLEMORE and SALLOWACK,
Solicitors, Chancery Lane.

A trifle sledge-hammer but it has got Mr.
Philip exactly. I wouldn't mind the young man's
effeminacy, his ridiculous clothes and his languor,
were it not that he considers himself the Prince
of the World. The scorn that he feels *and* ex-
presses for everyone in this house is nauseating.

Everyone but Vanessa, whom he condescends to admire, and talks of ' a perfect du Maurier ' and how he wishes that Whistler could paint her. He would apparently make the attempt himself (for he paints the most atrocious daubs) ' had he the time.' Had he the time! When he never gets up before ten, wanders about the house like a misplanted lily, pecks at the piano and studies himself in the looking-glass. His morals would be, I have no doubt, revolting had he any blood in his poor body. He speaks of ' soul-mates and the tyranny of the marriage laws ' and such disgusting nonsense. I should shudder whenever the children approached him, but they, unlike their elders, find him a kind of clown. Amazingly, Timothy and Violet are both rather impressed, and Vanessa, in her goodness of heart, is kind to him. How my mother would have dealt with him!

April 8.

It is perhaps my illness, but whatever the reason I cling to this old house as never before. My mother's presence is everywhere, but, beyond that, the house itself for ever speaks to me as though this were the last time it would ever shelter me, as though I were the last human link it will ever have with all the life that is gone. And that is true enough. There is no one else alive but myself who knew it as it was. When I first came here Francis and Jennifer were living, David and Sarah were remembered and had seen old Rogue Herries himself ride up, looking for his wandering wife. David, Jennifer, my own mother died under its roof. Violet has done all she can to ruin it, as the house very well knows. How easy and pleasant to have left some of it as it was—at least the little parlour that my mother so dearly loved. I can yet see it as it was when I was a child—the old spinet with the roses painted on the lid, the famous music-box that was played for me when I was good, with the King in his amber-coloured coat and the Queen in her green dress. Then the carpet, upon which I sprawled with John, that had the pictures of the great Battle, cannons firing and horses rising on their haunches; the Chinese wallpaper with pagodas of blue and white, temples, bridges and flowers. Best of all the sofa, the stuff of which was decorated with apple-trees and red apples. How well I remember that room and the way the clock with the gold mandarin would strike the hour, coughing a little between the strokes.

All gone now and also the things from my mother's bedroom, the red chairs, the four-poster bed. All gone, all gone, the house to-night seems to echo around me. And instead so many ugly things, mahogany wardrobes like coffins set up on end, attempts here and there to be in the fashion with imitation Morris wallpapers, sham Burne-Jones tapestry in the drawing-room—but the dining-room how awful with its circular cellar-ette, the vast Sheffield soup-tureen, the side-board with its malignant and obscene carved ends, the lacquered knife-tray, the needlework bell-pulls that Timothy tugs at so furiously when he

is impatient, the sheep-faced mahogany clock—
and all these things both Violet and Timothy
think so handsome! Yes, I can hear the old
house groaning through all its brickwork. I
am the only one who knows how deeply ashamed
it feels!

April 15.

I must write to-night to banish some of this
intolerable melancholy that has seized me. There
is a real Cumberland wind wailing about the house,
as though it had lost a thousand children. How
sharp and strong it must be on the Tops! Almost
impossible to keep your feet with the black heavy
clouds driving furiously like chariots above you,
and all the streams preparing for rain. . . . I
have not been so well these last days and I have
an assurance in my breast that my time now is
short. I had my evening meal in my room and
Vanessa came up to talk to me. I was allowed
a fire and by the light of two candles we chatted,
comfortably, easily, like the old friends we are.
Why was it that I had so dreary a sense that this
was to be our last talk? Nonsense, of course, and
in the morning, as has happened so often before,
feeling well again I shall laugh at my past terrors.
But as I sat opposite over the fire I put out my
hand to touch her dress as though I were frightened
to lose her, and she drew her chair over to mine.
She was cheerful and nonsensical as she often is,
laughing at Phil Rochester who had been reading
her some of his poems, one called ' The Lovers'

Last Cry' which was, I gathered, especially comical. Benjie is staying in Keswick. She is sure that he has some attraction there and takes it quite calmly. All she said about *that* was:

'When we marry and are together, I'll make him happy, I know.'

And to that *I* said:

'You'll have to beat him once a week. He says so himself.'

How I hate to leave her no one knows but me! She talked about herself, a thing that she very seldom does.

'I find that I'm intolerant, Papa. Intolerant and impatient.'

'Very well,' I said. 'Those are not bad things to be.'

'I was so angry with Timothy to-night that I could have smacked him. He was so extremely self-satisfied. I think all men are except yourself. Why should he talk as though he had *made* England?'

'That's a Herries habit,' I answered.

'Yes, but it's also something masculine. We were talking about Moody and Sankey and the Salvation Army and he said that such things weren't English. Englishmen never show their emotions, he said, and *that*'s why England is what it is. What he meant was, "*I* never show my emotions and *that*'s why England is what it is."'

'There's something in what he says,' I answered.

'Oh, well, I wanted to scream and beat that

hideous Indian gong in the hall.   Then he said
that *The Story of an African Farm* is a disgusting
book and ought to be burnt.   When I asked him
about it I discovered that he had only read the
first chapter.   And then after that he was going
to say something about Benjie, but Violet stopped
him.'
  ' Altogether a very pleasant meal,' I said.
  ' But why are we so different, you and I, from
Timothy and Violet? '
  ' Two halves of the whole,' I told her.   ' Life
isn't complete without both of us.'
  I could see that in reality she was deeply dissatisfied with herself.   She is maturing, and I
am sure that this long uncertain time with Benjie
is affecting her seriously, although she is too
proud to say anything about it.
  She sat close to me, holding my hand, her
splendid noble head raised high, looking into the
fire.
  ' Well, I'm a perverse creature,' she said,
nodding.   ' I seem to have no control over myself at all.'
  ' But you *have*,' I assured her.   ' You see you
didn't bang the table and you didn't beat the gong.'
  ' No, but I can't be rational, the thing that all
nice women ought to be.   I laugh when I should
be serious, I'm angry when there's nothing at all
to be angry about.   I'm not at all proper in
my feelings either.   Violet thinks it dreadful to
mention the word adultery.   She positively said
the other day that the Commandments in church
made her quite shy.   She thinks it dreadful to

be seen with a French novel. Oh! I do hope
I'm not going to be a prig! '

I laughed at that.

' Why, no, I should say the very opposite.'

' No, but, Papa, virtuous about other people
being *not* virtuous! . . . In fact I hate myself
to-night. Everything is wrong but you.'

She kissed me, laid her cheek against mine,
made a fuss of me, told me again and again how
she loved me, asked me to forgive her for all the
trouble that she had been to me. Never was she
more sweet, never more my friend and companion.
Before she went she turned at the door and blew
me a kiss with her hand, laughing and saying:
' And now I'm going to the drawing-room to
listen to Timothy telling us out of *The Times* what
he would do if he were Gladstone.'

To-morrow we are going for a drive.

This is the end of Adam's Journal. They
were the last words that he ever wrote. . . .

He lay in bed for a while, rather wide-awake,
watching the shadows from the fire leap on the
wall, hearing the wind scream about the house,
tug at the window-panes, belabour the trees and
hammer the tendrils of the vines against the glass.
He thought of the cottage at Cat Bells, how cosy,
warm with life and human affections. He had
brought there many of his mother's things, her
books, some pictures, the account she dictated to
Jane of her early days, bound in a fat green leather
volume, the presentation that they made her on
that fatal Hundredth Birthday. Vanessa would

have these things and would pass them on, pass
them on to her children and Benjie's, and they to
theirs, and so it would go on and on, until at
length it might be that it would only be through
Judith's green book that anyone knew that once
a man sold a woman at a Fair or fought for his
beloved on Stye Head. . . . He was growing
sleepy. He laid his hand on his breast inside his
shirt as though to say good-night to his heart and
request it, as a favour, to keep quiet for an hour
or two. He did not want to wake sharply to
that grinding pain, that squeezing of the muscles
between two inhuman fingers, that beating and
struggling for breath. . . . He was falling asleep
and a stout man was riding on a horse and he a
little boy as bare as your hand danced to annoy
him and the stout man raised his whip . . .

He awoke. What had roused him he did not
know. He sat up, resting on his arm. He was
so deeply accustomed now to find himself woken
at night by pain that that was his first thought:
' Where is the pain this time? Which part of me
is misbehaving?' But there was no pain. His
heart beat calmly and his back did not ache. He
had no neuralgia across his forehead. The room
was intensely dark. Many hours must have
passed since he fell asleep, for the fire had been
strong. Now there was no glimmer of dying log
or fading coal. The wind was roaring like a
beating lively voice in the darkness but, listening,
he heard something beyond the wind—a small
chattering whispering voice. Was there someone in the room? No, it sounded like several

voices, human and yet not human. He raised his head, sniffing. A moment later he was out of bed. Somewhere something was on fire. He opened the door and a belly of smoke blew towards him. He cried out: 'Fire! Fire!' and ran back into the room. It was then that the strange stillness of everything struck him. The house slept like the dead, he heard clocks ticking and somewhere a snore.

He pulled on a dressing-gown, and again, calling out 'Fire! Fire!', ran into the passage. His first thought was of Vanessa. He knew that her room was on the floor above his and, covering his mouth with his arm, turned towards the stairs, but even as he did so the passage to the left leading to the servants' quarters began—as it seemed to his excited imagination—to tremble, and a moment later through the green-baize door there shot a tongue of fire exactly like a vindictive criminal struggling to be free. A second later the flame shot upwards and little tongues began to lick the green baize, and a thin line of light, clear as day, shone between the hinges and the wall. At the same time the smoke rising in the same direction began to roll in thick grey waves, and the voices that it contained grew louder and angrier. What was strange was that the rest of the house, his room, the staircase from the hall, was cold, quiet, aloof, and even as he turned to the stair leading to the other floor he heard the cuckoo-clock that was at the corner of the hall below begin to sound the ridiculous bird's voice: 'Cuckoo! Cuckoo! Cuckoo!'

Still calling out and wondering in a mad irritation why nobody had been aroused by all this commotion, he stumbled up the stairs but, half-way up them, was met by another curling strand of smoke that seemed to issue from the wall on his left. For some reason that smoke bewildered him. It increased very rapidly, seeming to come from below him and to encircle him, to beat about his head, to come even from within himself, from his heart and lungs. He should now have been outside Vanessa's door, but he did not know where he was, for his eyes were blinded and weeping with the bitter and acrid thickness that now began to fill his mouth and heart and lungs.

He knocked his knees against a box or a chair, heard something fall somewhere and, turning his head, saw below him spurts and whirls of flame and a light that had a ferocity in it and a gigantic sense of power. He called out again and thought that some voice answered him, but he spoke against a wall, almost as though some enemy held a cloth over his mouth to deaden his cries. He thought: ' But this is absurd! Where are they all? What are they doing? ' Called again and again: ' Vanessa! Vanessa! Wake up! Fire! Fire! ' He moved to the right where he thought that her room must be, but now was caught in a perfect fog of smoke. His feet struck some more stairs and he remembered that above this floor were the attics. If he could reach those he could fling open the windows, for even his mad anxiety for Vanessa was countered by his agony for

breath. His lungs were choked, he could not
see and, although his brain was clear, his limbs
refused to obey him. At that same moment pain
leapt on to him, pain moving in the centre of the
smoke. An iron hand crushed his breast. The
fingers pressed and pressed. He fell on to his
knees. 'A moment,' he thought. 'This pain
will pass and I shall be able to move again.' But
it did not. The giant hand turned and turned,
so that he could see his poor heart crushed,
screwed round and then squeezed until the pain
seemed to draw his very eyeballs down into his
stomach.

His last conscious thought was of Vanessa.
'Vanessa,' he murmured, 'Vanessa.' He rolled
over and lay there, prone, while the eddies of
smoke—strong, careless, singing a song—rose,
saluted the wind, filling every cranny.

Vanessa had been long in a dreamless sleep
when she awoke to the sound of a loud banging
on her door. Even as she opened her eyes
Violet and Timothy rushed in, behind them a
strange glare and everywhere in the air a crackling,
murmuring, buzzing frenzy.

She did not need their cry: 'Vanessa! Get
up! The whole house is on fire!'

In an instant everything was visible and clear
to her. She seemed in that moment of springing
out of bed to have time to notice everything—the
calm undisturbed paraphernalia of the bedroom,
her clothes across the chair, the yellow sofa that
she always thought so ugly, the long looking-glass

in which were reflected Timothy and Violet,
Timothy with a riding-coat over his nightshirt,
Violet in a bright blue dressing-gown, and behind them that sinister glitter veiled with sudden
mists. The air stank of smoke. She heard a
dog bark.

Violet pulled at her arm.

'It's terrible! It's terrible!' she continued
to cry. 'The whole house is on fire!'

And Timothy, running back, called:

'The children! The children! Get the
children!'

But her own thought was at once for her father.
She thought of nothing and nobody else. She
put on her dressing-gown and slippers with a
single gesture and ran out. She saw them flock-
ing down the stairs—Philip, Timothy, Violet, the
children. The stairs were still untouched. You
seemed from the lower stairs to plunge into darkness while on the first floor the baize door was a
sheet of flame and all around her the smoke rose
like water, flooding forward, eddying back again.
She ran down the first flight and crossed at once
into her father's room. It was empty. At that
same moment she thought that through the crackle
of the fire she heard a cry from above her:
'Vanessa!' She listened, and even as she did
so saw Timothy's head and shoulders above the
lower banister.

'Father!' she cried. 'He is not in his
room!'

Timothy shouted back. 'Come down! The
whole place is falling down. It's all right—every-

one's out. Yes, Adam too. He is on the lawn!'

She turned back once more into his room, saw the bed disordered, caught—without knowing what she did, obeying some blind instinct—things from the table, his Journal, a book, his gold watch; then ran out to meet in full force a towering column of smoke that rose in front of her like some genie. Gasping, her hand over her face, she ran forward, was down the stairs, through the door and, in an instant, in a wild, chill, blowing world, the wind screaming above her, voices everywhere, shouts and cries, some child's wail, the neighing of horses, and faces white like paste in the blinding light of the fire.

She ran from figure to figure, not recognising them at all as persons, for they also seemed to be running, moving in some kind of dance through the wind.

She called again and again:

'Father! Father! Where are you?' She pulled at some man's arm: 'My father! Is he here? Have you seen him?' and some figure that she did not know, someone holding a clock and a picture, cried, as though in an ecstasy, 'The house! The house! The roof will be in!'

Then she ran into Leathwaite. He cried before she could speak:

'Miss Vanessa! The master! He's not here!'

They turned together and ran towards the house which was now all bright with flame and alive in every part, while from its heart there came a beat like a drum and above it arms of fire strained up to the ebony sky, starred with the pigeons from the loft, flying into the light as though splashed with bright water, then vanishing into darkness.

Will dashed through the door. She would have gone after him but some man's hand held her, gripping her shoulder. 'You mustn't go, Miss Vanessa,' someone shouted in her ear as though she were deaf. 'It's not safe——' and then called, 'Will! Will! Come back! Everyone's out!'

She struggled. 'Let me go! What do you mean? They are not all out. My father is there——'

A moment later Will's face, strangely unreal, appeared at a window. He shouted to them.

'He's not here! I'm in his room!' And then, after looking into the room again: 'I can't go back! The fire's too strong!'

'Jump!' several voices cried, and a woman screamed. He climbed out on to the window-sill, let his legs dangle, caught his arm in something and fell.

And, at once, as things happen in dreams, inconsequent, without reason, Vanessa saw that Benjie was beside her. She heard his voice, as from an infinite distance, explaining that he had come back from Keswick that evening, been roused and at once ridden down. 'Oh, thank God you're safe, Vanessa,' he said, hurried from her as figures do in dreams, was back again, his arm round her, crying, 'It's all right. Will's broken a leg. No one else is harmed. Everyone's safe.'

G

She tore herself away from him.

' No, no, Benjie! Don't you see? Father's in there! Father's there! '

She ran forward. He pulled her back.

' Don't be mad. No one can live in there! The roof is falling! '

She fought him, she struck his face.

' Let me go! Let me go! We must find him!'

He held her with all his strength, pressing her against him. The ground was covered with people; the horses that they had taken from the stable trampled and neighed. With a great gesture, as though in a frenzy of exultation, the flames flung up their arms, the roof crashed.

The house gave up its life.

WILD NIGHT IN THE HILLS

THERE was at that time in the hills between Derwentwater and Crummock a very lonely farm called Hatchett's Fosse.

To this farm Benjamin Herries rode some three days after Adam Paris' burial at Ireby.

Adam's charred and almost unrecognisable body had been found when at last the fire had died sufficiently for safe search to be made. The red brick walls of Fell House still stood, blackened and scorched but enduring. But these walls were a shell. Nothing else remained. The wind that night had been so ferocious that in any circumstances there could have been small hope of saving the house, but everything had contributed to aggravating the disaster: the ancient fire-engine at Braithwaite broke down on the road. There was nothing at the house itself, no protection of any kind. The horses and animals were saved. No life was lost but Adam's. A little furniture, some pictures, were rescued. That was all. Fell House, Uldale, was no more.

The death of Adam Paris shocked the whole countryside. He had not been widely known. He was held to be a ' shy sort of man ' but he was liked. He was said to be kindly, friendly, generous. No one had anything against him. He

was old Madame's son, even though he had been
born on the wrong side of the blanket, and he
wrote books.   But more than any of these, he
was the father of Vanessa, whose beauty was re-
nowned from Silloth to Kendal.   Everyone knew
how she had loved him, and there was something
deeply real and true in the sympathy that rose
now on every side of her.   Cumberland people
are reputed by those who know them little to
be too blunt of tongue for complacent comfort,
but any man in trouble will be lucky if he has
Cumbrian friends near to him.   They have not
been masters of their own soil for hundreds of
years without learning what courtesy means, and
courtesy is not in this part of England another
name for heartlessness.

But Vanessa was stricken down in these first
days beyond any possibility of help.   With Jane
Bellairs and Will she went back to Cat Bells and
there she stayed, seeing nobody.   On the day
before the funeral she saw Benjie.   He knew at
once that she could not just then bear either to see
him or talk to him.

She spoke in a low voice, looking beyond him
at the door as though she expected someone to
come in.

' I don't blame you, Benjie.   You did what
you thought right, but you should not have held
me back.'

' Vanessa, *how* could I have let you go?   The
roof fell in a moment later.   You would have been
killed as well as Adam.   What good would that
have been? '

'I had rather have been killed. To think that he was alone in there! That nobody but myself and Will thought of him!'

He saw that at present there was nothing to be done. He kissed her. She made no movement, no response. She said in a low voice:

'The awful thing is that I heard him calling me. From some other part of the house. But Timothy told me he was out. I will never forgive Timothy and I will never forgive myself.'

When he went home things were no better. His mother had been unwell for some months, and the night of the fire with its tragic consequences was a shock from which it was unlikely that she would recover. The destruction of Fell House was a dreadful thing to her. She had been there so often. John, her husband, had been born there; he had walked out of there to his death. More than that, this appeared to her to be a revenge from the past. Her father had built the Fortress to triumph over Fell House. It had seemed at his death that he was defeated: but he had *not* been defeated. This was the last unexpected triumph of the Fortress, a house that she had always hated and now detested. She seemed to hear her brother Uhland tapping with his stick night and day about the passages. How satisfied he must be! These vindictive people were stronger in death than they had been in life and there was no end to their malevolence. She had loved Adam, and her heart ached now for Vanessa. She was old, alone with ghosts. No one could help her.

Benjie, her son, it seemed, least of all. She had been very patient with his selfishness, but now at last she was exasperated. He seemed to her hard and callous. For once her intuition failed her. She did not know that he was suffering more deeply than she. On the day after Adam's funeral he came into her bedroom and said:

' I can't bear this, Mother. I must go away for a day or two.'

' What can't you bear? ' she asked him quietly.

' Vanessa,' he broke out in a kind of storm of indignation, ' thinks that I was responsible for Adam's death.'

She thought that he was indignant with Vanessa, but had she been well and strong she would have known that the indignation was with himself.

' She is suffering from shock,' she answered. ' You must be patient and wait.'

' Wait! Wait! ' he burst out. ' For what? Everything is changed, Mother. It will never be the same again.'

The farmer at Hatchett's Fosse was Fred Halliday, the son of the woman with whom Benjie had stayed at Seascale.

Some months back Benjie, riding along Main Street, saw Mrs. Halliday and her daughter Marion looking at him from across the street. His first impulse had been to move on, but something had prevented him. He did not like them, he did not wish to see them again; nevertheless he rode over and spoke to them.

They were to stay in Keswick for a while.   Mrs.
Halliday had notions of opening a boarding-
house there.   Still with that strange mingling
of attraction and repulsion, he had met them a
number of times.   Mrs. Halliday was definitely
repugnant to him: she whined, she crept, she was
genteel, she was vindictive.   The girl spoke little,
had little colour in her voice or movements,
but she had some power over him.   He kissed
her and hated himself for doing so.   She appeared to expect his distaste; indeed she said to
him once:

'How you dislike me!'

But she did not seem at all to resent this except that, in her still, motionless way, she resented
everything.   Her pale skin, thin anaemic body,
quiet, almost stealthy movements, stirred him as
though he were attracted by his own exact opposite.   She did not speak to his mind nor his heart,
but his senses.   When he touched her—and
always it seemed that it was by her volition and
not his—he felt no tenderness nor affection, but
a sensual inquisitiveness as though something
persuaded him to explore further—as though
some sensual secret were hidden there which
would, when discovered, excite and surprise him.

He did not know—and he did not care—
whether she liked him or no.   She appeared to like
no one, to have no life beside that of sudden
little movements, unexpected advances and with-
drawals.   One evening he met her in the dusk
walking down the hill behind St. John's Church.
He talked to her and then embraced her passion-

ately. She eagerly returned his embraces. He went home in a mood of bitter revulsion against himself. He had met her brother several times in Keswick. Fred Halliday was a big, broad, red-faced hearty man, quite unlike his mother and sister, who laughed at everything, drank a good deal and was friend of all the world. And yet it was true that nobody in Keswick liked him. He was not trusted, and it was said that when drunk he was very quarrelsome and abusive.

Not a very worthy family for Benjie to be friendly with, but then it was always like that with him. When he was jolly, as at most times he was, anyone would do to be jolly with. At this period of his life almost anyone was good enough to pass the time of day with. Who was he to be a judge? Except for his mother and Vanessa no one alive mattered. He was proud of not caring. Life was not important and one man resembled another. He loved Vanessa, who was much too good for him, and if women liked to be kissed, why, he liked to kiss them! In spite of his escapades he had never yet got any woman into trouble. His luck in that had held. He would not hurt anyone for the world.

But as he rode out to Hatchett's Fosse he was not sure that he did not want to hurt everybody. Fred Halliday had often invited him to come and see the farm; he had never thought that he would really go. But now anywhere would do, anywhere away from his own unhappiness, his sense that he had lost Vanessa for ever and that he deserved to have lost her.

The morbid side of his character had grown
stronger during this past year. Although he loved
the place, this Cumberland country always increased the strain of superstition so deeply in-
grained in his character. Away from his home
he was as other men and could consort with them
on equal terms, but at the Fortress and in the
country around him he felt sometimes like a man
caught in a trap. On the one hand was the small
lonely house in Skiddaw Forest where his father
had been murdered; on the other—and only a
step away—the great cavern beneath Skiddaw
where all the spirits of the true men lived and
rejoiced for ever. Surely fantastic nonsense as
food for a healthy man's brain! But in this Benjie
was not healthy, nor are most imaginative men
free of certain dreams, omens and apprehensions.
These two contrasted things were for him perhaps
only symbols, but they brought with them a conviction that, whenever he returned to this country,
he was not his own free master. And yet he must
return! He could not keep away from it. He
could not remain in it when he was there. And
were his instincts altogether wrong? Had he not,
in this last year, been twice prevented from marrying Vanessa, once by her father's illness and now
by this cursed fire? The Men under Skiddaw
would receive him in their company *if* he could
reach them, but, like a man in a dream, he was
held back. Who could dare to deny that the past
was more powerful than the present and that you
must fight like the devil or the moment you were
born you were done for! That old ancestor of his,

Francis Herries, might still have something to say!

All this was, of course, only a part of Benjie's mind. None of the men who knew him as he roamed the world would credit him with *this* kind of imagination! But he was compounded of stiff incongruities—proud and yet humble, faithful and yet most unfaithful, wandering but steadfast—and at this time he was still young with most of his soul-making ahead of him.

So as he rode down Bassenthwaite and on towards Braithwaite he felt only an urgent need of escape: escape from the senseless waste of Adam's death, from all the grief that that was causing (he had an eager sensitiveness to the unhappiness of others); escape from his mother, whom he knew that he should not be leaving; but above all escape from Vanessa, whom he loved now when he was sure that he had lost her, with a deeper sense of frustration than ever before.

Then he raised his head, looked up at the stormy sky and swore. 'Well, *this* has settled the business. She is better, far better, without me. She'll know that at last.'

But even while he said this he felt that they were inseparable, that however their lives went they would be bound together for ever—yes, even when he was secure and singing with the Men under Skiddaw he would be thinking of her!

As he began slowly to climb Whinlatter he felt the wind tugging at him. On the day following the fire the wind had folded its arms and stolen away as though the purpose of its coming were

accomplished. Then, as is often the case in the late
spring, it sprang up again and rushed about the
country in flurries of excitement, blowing the daffodils silly, making the young leaves tremble and the
young sheep skip, and flashing quivers of light
like turning glass across the streams. The colours
were all delicate—faint shadowed plum, a gold so
pale that it was almost white under cloud, a wet
virginal green of the young bracken. And field
after field, up and up the hillsides, was silver-grey.

This afternoon, though, quite another mood
was in the air, spring was forgotten. It happens
sometimes here that the hills, as though an order
had been given, suddenly dominate all the scene.
The pastoral fields, the farms, the roads, towns,
villages shrink together into nothingness and the
hills step forward, spread their shoulders, swell
their chests out, raise their heads and begin to
march. If you listen you can almost hear the
tramping. It is at such times that you can understand Benjie's fantasy of his men under the
mountain, for it is no fantasy just then. Lie
down on the turf and listen with your ear to the
ground and you can catch the echo of the voices,
a rumble of a drinking song and laughter like the
cracking of a drum's skin. At such a moment
when the hills take power there is a sense of
menace in the air. The sky is disturbed with a
furious confusion, great sweeps of cloud smoking
along with a wind behind them that is personal
in its strength. The old pictures of Aeolus blowing the four winds from his mouth is true now.
You can see him standing behind the hills, his

strong legs spread across the sea, his broad naked
shoulders stretched above his vigorous lungs.
The wind and the hills act in unison. The hills,
that are in actual measurement so slight, take on
themselves additional properties that belong to
the great mountains of the world. With white
mist flanking them and black funnels of cloud
eddying above their heads, they seem as powerful
as Everest. Their power is menacing. They
seem to crowd together in conclave: 'Now shall
we step forward and crush out of existence these
little fields, cowering hamlets, tiny midgets of
humans?' You can watch them as they bend
their heads together and twitch their shoulders
with the impatience of a group of boys waiting
for the word of release. The wind is enchanted
with the sport promised. It goes swinging from
arm to arm of the hills, crying: 'Now let us go!
Now we are off!' and it sweeps whirlwinds of rain
now here, now there, making it sting the earth
like a hail of small shot, then raising it again in
sheets of steel as though all the heavens were
letting down their defensive gates. A great game
that leads to no ill because the power here is
friendly. They have not learnt any deep vindictiveness. This square of earth is kind to the men
who settle, for a moment, upon its surface. The
Genius here is benevolent.

Such a storm of wind without rain rose about
Benjie as he climbed Whinlatter. The water of
Bassenthwaite below him that had been a field of
grey shadows as he rode beside it was now, when
he looked down upon it, trembling with white

waves that gleamed with an almost phosphorescent glow under the blackness of Skiddaw. The clouds were so low that when he was at the highest point of the Pass they skirted him on every side, shifting from place to place with long sweeps of spidery grey. It was bitterly cold and he had to lower his head, pulling up the collar of his riding-coat.

He knew that with Lorton Fell on his right, before he turned off down to Swinside, his path branched away to the left. The farm was just here somewhere, in a hollow between Grisedale Pike and Hobcarton. He directed his horse across the rough turf, moving very slowly under the sting of the wind. To his right he looked down on to the flat plain that stretched to the Border with fields like squares of a chessboard and trees and houses like dolls' furniture. The wind raced over this flat country with a shrill whistling exultation; thin patches of white broke the grey sky above the sea. It was raining above St. Bees.

It would be difficult to find this place, and if the mist came down, impossible. He might wander here for hours. He cursed himself for coming, and had an impulse to turn back. In certain moods this driving wind and cold sharp air would have exalted him, but not to-day, for he was sick with his own self-distrust and dis-approval. Nothing grand about him to-day to answer the grandeur of the elements. Why should he not turn back and wait patiently for Vanessa to recover? How impulsive he had been to have taken her present mood as permanent! And how selfish he had been to ride away from her at the

very moment when, in her heart, she needed him!
He half turned his horse's head.   He would go
back.   Then, as he looked round him, he saw the
farm, a little to his right in the fold of the hill,
a bare meagre place with a few bent trees and
a stone wall.   The first drops of rain stung his
cheek.   He rode on.

When he reached the farm two dogs ran out,
wildly barking: he heard Fred's voice cursing
them and then saw the big stout man filling the
doorway.

He gave a shout when he saw who it was.

' Hullo, Herries!   What a surprise! '

He came to meet him, his face beaming.

' You've come for the night, I hope? '

' Yes,' said Benjie.   ' If you'll have me.'

' Of course I'll have you.   Couldn't be better.'

They led the horse round to the stable at the
back of the house, Halliday talking all the time.

' My mother and sister are staying here and
some friends of ours are coming up from Lorton
this evening, so you've struck the right moment.
It's going to be a wild night.   The wind's blowing
great guns.   Come along in and get warm.'

Benjie went in, hung up his hat and coat,
passed into an inner room that seemed half kitchen,
half living-room.   Sitting beside a roaring fire
were Mrs. Halliday and her daughter.

At the moment when he saw them, the large
smoke-stained fireplace, the window that looked
out on to a little scrambling path where a cluster
of primroses was hiding, two canaries in a cage,
and a large sheep-dog lying in front of the fire

with his nose on his paws, his mood changed.
This was jolly, cheerful, friendly. They were all
friends of his. Other friends were coming. They
would make a night of it. He had closed a door,
a heavy silent-swinging door like one that guards
a cathedral, upon all that other world where his
friends were burnt, those whom he loved blamed
him and, worst of all, where he blamed himself.
Here he loved no one and no one loved him. It
was not a world of hurting, haunting intimacies.
He would be happy. So, as always when he was
happy, he wanted to do things for everybody,
drew a chair to the fire and chattered like a boy,
threw back his head and roared with laughter, his
rather ugly face with friendliness and generosity
in all its wrinkles. And the two women quietly
answered or asked questions while Fred Halliday
leaned his bulk against the kitchen dresser and,
with a smile on his face, watched them.

Benjie had all the London gossip: of the
success that *Iolanthe* was and the other piece that
the German Reeds were running, *The Mountain
Heiress*, where Corney Grain was a solicitor and
sang a wonderful song called 'Our Mess,' and
that Goring Thomas' *Esmeralda* at the Lane, where
Mr. Carl Rosa had a month's opera season, contained, they say, some pretty songs but that Mme.
Georgina Burns couldn't act for toffee.

Mrs. Halliday said that the matter with the
London theatre to-day was that it was too expensive, not comfortable enough, and that most
of the plays were silly. In fact, with a few well-
chosen words, she demolished the London theatre.

And Benjie said, oh, he didn't know. That was
a little severe, wasn't it, and that one went to the
theatre to be jolly, didn't one, and that he'd go a
long way to hear Corney Grain sing ' Our Mess.'
Then they discussed the Budget, which had been
introduced a week or two before by Mr. Childers.
Certainly had forestalled the Conservatives, who
had been intending to come out as Champions of
Economy, but Gladstone knew two of that. Everyone talking of Economy now. Yes, said Mrs. Halliday, the great thing was of course to *be* economical,
but easier to say than to do. Benjie, nodding his
head profoundly, agreed that that *was* the problem!

Then they discussed books, and Benjie said
that he did hope that Miss Marion didn't read
French novels, and Miss Marion said that she
sometimes did and thought them very amusing,
much nearer to real life than silly writers like
Rhoda Broughton and Ouida. She liked poetry,
though. Did Mr. Herries read poetry? No,
Mr. Herries didn't. A writer like Tennyson
took such a long time to say what he wanted to.
No, Miss Halliday did *not* agree. Poetry could
do something that nothing else could do. Wouldn't
Mr. Herries agree to that? And, yes, he thought
on the whole that he *did* agree to that!

So they talked in the pleasantest fashion and
the time flew by while the wind roared outside
and the rain that had swept up from the sea beat
against the window-frames. Fred Halliday had
some excellent beer and Benjie drank plenty of
it. The fire, the beer, the pleasant easy talk all
comforted and reassured him. Yes, the door,

with its heavy leather curtain, had swung to; all
sounds from the outer world were deadened.
Mrs. Halliday, he thought, was a more agreeable
woman than he supposed. She sat there knitting
a stocking most domestically. Her face was
grave, but after all, not repellent at all. The
glow from the fire softened her rather gaunt
features.

Once and again she smiled, baring her teeth
with her upper lip, almost as though she were
about to whistle.

And as to the girl he felt once more, and increasingly as the beer warmed him, that he would
like to touch her. He must be kind to her, poor
child, for she could not have much happiness in her
life. He began to wonder whether she had not finer
feelings, more sensitive tastes than her mother and
brother could satisfy. She read French, she liked
poetry. Not that she had any pride. No one could
be quieter about her accomplishments. Once or
twice he caught her looking at him, her pale eyes
staring at him, and he felt then a little embarrass-
ment, as though he should be ashamed of his
brown face and strong body when she herself was
so delicate. At the thought of her delicacy some
sensuous nerve in him was touched. She was so
slight, so fragile, that in his arms she would be
powerless, must submit to anything that he
wished. Not that he would hurt her. He would
not hurt anybody in the world.

The shrill clock on the mantelpiece struck
seven and, a moment later, the door was flung open
and Halliday came in, bringing three men with

him. These men had taken their coats off in the passage; two of them were youngish, had rough corduroy trousers with long black coats containing deep pockets. One of the two was little and wiry, with bright red hair and a small shaggy red beard; the other was broad, strong, very dark with bright, glancing, restless eyes and a close-clipped black moustache. He was a handsome fellow. These two men might be both between thirty and forty in age. The third, as Benjie immediately learned, was the father of these two. He was tall and thin, dressed in a long black coat with wide tails and black trousers. His hair was grey and sparse; he had little eyes and above them a very high domed forehead. He looked something like a schoolmaster.

Halliday introduced them to Benjie. Their name, he discovered, was Endicott; Thomas the elder one, George and Robert the two sons. They all sat down by the fire. Thomas Endicott had rather a shrill piercing voice, small in compass and high-pitched. He spoke with care as though, with difficulty, he had learned how to be cultured. The voices of the two younger men were rough. Robert, the little red-haired fellow, spoke with an effeminate note; he was restless and given to gestures. George's voice was deep but without any Cumbrian accent. They seemed friendly. They knew the two women and were old acquaintances, it appeared, of Halliday. Endicott the elder talked to Benjie, a little pompously and always with that slow carefulness as though he would choose the right word and never on any

account drop an ' h '. Oh no, they did not live
at Lorton. He himself resided in Whitehaven.
Yes, oh yes, his wife and her sister lived with him.
This boy George here, oh! he was a rascal, could
settle to nothing, had been in the Army for a bit,
hadn't he, George? Could put his hand to anything, a fine boxer; oh yes, a splendid footballer
if he kept in condition—but a rascal. Wouldn't
settle to anything, would he, George? They all
laughed, and George smiled at Benjie in friendly
fashion, as much as to say: ' I like you. I've
taken to you. We shall be friends.'

Oh yes, and Robert was a wanderer too. He
would go from place to place selling things, go
round Fairs, you know, all over the country.
What you would call a pedlar in the old days.
Didn't mind what he did any more than George.

Oh, they were a wandering family. That's
what his wife always complained of. Yes, an old
Border family. Nothing much to boast of a
hundred years ago—smugglers and worse, so he
heard.

' As a matter of fact, Mr. Herries,' he said,
' I have been wanting to meet you. We're
almost related in a kind of a way. There was a
girl in our family years ago married one of your
ancestors, well known in the Borrowdale district.
Rogue Herries he was called.'

' What! ' cried Benjie. ' Rogue Herries!
Why——! '

' Aye, there were two brothers, George and
Anthony Endicott, mad Tony they called him.
Their sister married a man called Starr and these

two had a daughter. It was her old Herries married.'

Why, that was Judith's mother! Benjie was indeed amazed; what with the beer and the warmth of the kitchen everything seemed to him now wonderful and jolly and all that it should be. Here they were, these three nice fellows, and their ancestress was Judith's mother. Judith's mother, Vanessa's great-grandmother—but at that thought the leather-curtained door, that had for a moment swung back, was closed again. No thought of Vanessa. Vanessa was far away.

' Aye,' said Thomas Endicott. ' Funny how small the world is. I've often thought I'd like to meet one of you, although maybe those ancestors of ours are nothing to be proud of.'

' Proud of them! ' cried Benjie. ' I should think I am! Francis Herries you're speaking of, was a great man, a grand fighter and a man of his hands.'

' Aye,' said Thomas Endicott slowly. ' There are plenty of stories of him in Borrowdale. He sold his woman at a Fair once, they tell.'

' And a good thing too! ' Benjie cried. ' What do you say, Mrs. Halliday? If you're tired of a woman and someone else wants her? Why not sell her? Fair exchange, you know.'

But Mrs. Halliday only smiled and went on knitting.

Then they had supper, a very good supper too, ham and beef and chicken, a big apple tart, rum butter and cheese and plenty of cakes. Halliday produced a wine, a good warming Burgundy,

and while they ate and chattered and laughed the
wind tore at the house as though it would tumble
it over. But the house was strong, very old,
Halliday told them.

'There was a man murdered here once,' Halliday said. 'In the 'forties it was. His wife and
daughter murdered him for his money. Cut his
head open with a hatchet and he bled all over this
very floor.'

After supper they all helped to clear the table
and then they sang songs. There was an old
piano there, not strictly in tune but what did that
matter? They roared out the songs and banged
the piano and laughed and stood with their arms
round one another's shoulders.

Soon Benjie knew that he was very merry, very
merry indeed. Not drunk; oh no, not drunk at
all, but as happy as a grig. He had never had
a better evening. What splendid fellows they
were, and especially George! His hand rested
on George's shoulder. He must see George
again, must see George often. This was the kind
of evening he enjoyed. Yes, he would like to do
something for him, put George in the way of a
job if he wanted one. And George looked at
him as though he liked him. He didn't say much,
but he smiled and pushed out his chest when he
sang and poured the beer down his throat.

The ladies said good-night. It was time for
them to retire.

'We shall see you in the morning,' said Mrs.
Halliday. 'What a wild night it is, to be sure!'

Some time later Benjie thought that he must

go to the door for a moment to cool his head. He slipped out, opened the front door and was almost tumbled off his feet by the wind. The world was raging outside, the rain sweeping through the air in whipping fury. With great difficulty he closed the door again and turned back to see the girl standing there quite close to him. There was a dim reflection of light from the upper floor. The voices of the men singing came raucously from the inner room.

' Why, Marion ! ' he said.

' I am just going up to bed.'

' It was so hot in there I came out for a breath of air.'

' Yes, I know. I was hot too.'

Her hand was touching his. He caught it, then, putting his arms round her, kissed her. She kissed him passionately in return, her lips clinging to his as though they would never leave them. When he held her in his arms, so slight and slender was she that he was afraid of hurting her.

' I'm hurting you,' he whispered.

' I like you to hurt me,' she whispered back, then gently freeing herself, said ' Good night ' and ran up the stairs.

Oh, well, he shouldn't have done that. But she was so close to him. She was in his arms before he realised it. Kissing a girl—nothing in it. It was natural to kiss a girl. There was something about her . . . not that he liked her. . . . He stood for a moment leaning against the wall in the dark passage, and felt an odd chagrin, an almost desperate loneliness, an impulse to

leave the house at once, fetch his horse from the
stable and ride home. . . .

But he went back into the room, joining the
chorus with them as he entered it.

Now that the women were gone, gaiety and
friendliness rose a note higher. This was what
life should be, men together with care thrown out
of the window, plenty to drink, a wild night
outside, all friends together. They might have
known one another all their lives. Father Endicott was not such a schoolmaster as you might
suppose. He possessed, in fact, a grand fund
of bawdy stories. Very funny they were. That
one about the old farmer's wife of Esthwaite and
the two simple young men and the lady from
London. There was nothing about old Cumberland life that he didn't know, the life that was
going now so fast with all the tourists in the
summer and the railways everywhere. A pity,
a pity! Those were the good old days when
Lizzie O'Branton the witch jumped out of her
coffin at her funeral and rode away on a broom-
stick, and Mrs. Machell of Penrith would drive
her ghostly carriage whenever a ' helm ' wind was
blowing, when the ' need fire ' charmed the cattle,
when the song was sung at the shearing. Here
they broke out all together:

> Heigh O! Heigh O! Heigh O!
> And he that doth this health deny,
> Before his face I him defy.
> He's fit for no good company,
> So let this health go round.

Good fun, too, when they had the public

whippings, or the hangings in Carlisle or the
witch-drownings.

' Changed times,' said old Endicott sadly.
' All the fine spirit gone.'

But *their* spirit was not gone. It increased
with every drop they drank. The table was
pushed aside and George and Benjie tried a
' wrastle.' They took off their coats, waistcoats
and shoes and went to it. Solemnly they circled
round and round trying for a hold. But Benjie
was no very great wrestler and soon George had
' buttocked' him and, throwing him, tumbled
over him. They crashed to the floor and then
lay there, panting, one on the other. For they
were not drunk, oh no, not drunk at all, but it was
comfortable there on the floor and Benjie had his
arm round George's neck, looked up at the whitewashed ceiling, pulled George's hair, said, laughing, ' I like you, George. We're friends, we are,'
and George's hand rested on Benjie's back and
he said nothing at all. Old Endicott played a
polka on the piano and they danced heavily,
clumsily, staggering about the room, and Benjie
cried:

' There's a fine place under Skiddaw, George,
where we'll go when we're dead and we'll dance
and sing for ever and ever.'

' Aye,' said George. ' Aye. That'll be
grand.'

In all the merry evening there was only one
unpleasant incident, which Benjie could never after
properly recall.

He said something to little red-bearded Robert,

and Robert took offence. The little man was
dancing with rage and screaming out:

'You're a liar, I tell you. A damned bloody
liar!'

'Call me a liar?' shouted Benjie.

'Aye, and I will too. Who do you think
I am?'

'Why!' cried Benjie. 'I'll tell you who you
are. You're a funny little man, that's who you
are!'

'I was here in this country before any of
you were born. Aye, and I was too, selling laces
and silver boxes, visiting the witches in Borrowdale——'

'Shut your mouth, Robert,' cried George.
'Who wants to listen to your lies? Why,
man——'

'Lies, are they?' The little man was screaming, dancing up and down until to Benjie's dazzled
eyes he seemed a dozen little men with peaked
caps on their heads, riding through the kitchen
on the wind and rain. But the little man wanted
to fight, and the others, roaring with laughter,
held his arms and they knocked the lamp over.
The room was dark save for the firelight. Oh,
but the little man's red beard shone and he was
angry! And Benjie embraced him, pulled his
beard, gave him a friendly kick on the pants, and
he went and sat in a corner by the fireplace, waving
his hands and making shadows of rabbits on the
wall with his fingers.

Later, Benjie found himself with a candle
wandering on his way to bed. Halliday showed

him where his room was, a little whitewashed room
at the top of the house.   Halliday helped him
into bed.

And later than that, as he lay looking at the
ceiling and smiling, the door opened.   The girl
stood there, a candle in her hand, wearing a dressing-gown with a wool collar over her night-dress.
He sat up on his elbow and looked at her.
She closed the door very softly and came over to
him.   She smiled and said:
    ' The wind's died down.   Everyone's sleep-
ing.'
He could only stare at her.   She took off her
dressing-gown and carefully laid it on the chair.
Then she blew out the candle, climbed into bed
and lay down beside him.

INSIDE THE FORTRESS

It was early in the wet and stormy weather of that year when Vanessa came to stay with Elizabeth at the Fortress.

Elizabeth had been seriously ill ever since the fire at Fell House in April. No one could say exactly where the trouble was. It was what was known as a 'decline.' She was weak, instantly tired by any exertion; her features now had the delicacy of a thin rose-tinted shell. Her hair was snow-white, her figure still slim and erect, but ghost-like in its fragility. She walked a little from room to room: although she leaned on a stick she was still tall. She was kind and gracious to everyone, but most of her, as Mrs. Harwen, the cook-housekeeper, said, was 'otherwhither.'

'It's my opinion,' John Harwen, the handyman about the place and Mrs. Harwen's little hostler-like spouse, remarked, 'that the difference between her living and her dead is so slight that you'll not notice it. After she's gone she'll still be here, so to speak.'

'We've enough ghosts in this house already,' said Mrs. Harwen.

Benjie had not been home since June. No one knew where he was. No one had heard from him.

Elizabeth had through many years practised herself to be patient about these absences, but now it was another matter. For she knew that she had not long to live and she had only one desire in her heart—that Benjie and Vanessa should be married before she went.

She had not seen very much of Vanessa. The girl had stayed first with Timothy in Eskdale, where he had thoughts of buying a house (for he had decided not to rebuild Fell House), then had returned to Cat Bells, where Will and the old cook had looked after her.

In July she visited Elizabeth, who saw at once that here now was a woman of self-command, deep reserves and a very fine courage. Vanessa was cheerful, talked freely about her father, seemed indeed to wish to talk of him, recalling days and moments and words and phrases; saying: ' Papa always felt that ' or ' Papa never troubled to be angry—he said it was waste of time.' But his death, Elizabeth saw, had made a fundamental change in Vanessa, had brought out certain qualities that were latent before, and had checked others.

She was not so impetuous: her heart was as warm but it was guarded now against shock.

Just before she went she said:
' And what about Benjie? '

Elizabeth told her that she had not heard, that she had no idea where he was.

' It's a shame! ' Vanessa cried indignantly.
' You wanting him—— '

' Yes,' said Elizabeth quietly. ' I am not

going to live much longer, my dear, and I *must* see him. But no one knows where he is.'

' I think,' said Vanessa slowly, ' that perhaps I am partly to blame. He came to see me— after the fire. I was not myself. I didn't want Benjie or anyone. I wanted to be left alone. So he went away.'

' We'll be independent of him,' said Elizabeth gently.

Then Vanessa asked if she might come and stay. Elizabeth's pale cheek flushed.

' Oh, Vanessa dearest, do you mean it? Will you really come? How happy I shall be!'

Early in September Vanessa came. No one knew what that was to her, the first time that she looked from the long windows of the Fortress down to the valley where, very clearly, in the pale colourless moving air, the walls of Fell House were still standing. She had been dreading this moment from the instant when she made her proposal of a visit to Elizabeth. She had not seen the place since the day of the funeral. But she knew that it had to be faced, that everything had to be faced. She had learnt many things since April and one of them was that the only way to make anything of life was to fit, resolutely, with courage, into the patterns that life, in change after change, presented. To attempt to force life into *your* pattern was to challenge disaster. You must accept *everything* and turn it to good.

So she stood there that morning in her black dress, her hands clenched at her sides, the house silent about her with that dull brooding silence

that seemed the Fortress' special property.   In
the valley the four bare walls stood, the moors
climbing above them as though they already
recognised that here was a spot that now they
would soon reclaim, as, one day, they would
reclaim everything.

Tears rolled down Vanessa's cheeks, but she
made no sound.   For a moment she cried within
herself: ' Oh, I cannot endure this!   I *cannot*
endure it!' and this was followed by the strong
response: ' I *can* endure it!   I can endure anything!'

The hardest thing to bear was that she had not
at present recovered her father for herself.   When
someone dearly loved passes away there is a period
when everything is blurred.   The personality
has broken up into a thousand pieces, something
here, something there, but the radiant heart is
absent.   Slowly the friend returns, never—if
feeling has been true—to be lost again.

Elizabeth, watching her, felt at first the girl's
deep loneliness.   There they were alike.   She
too was lonely, had been for years, but that is a
lesson that women learn and it is one of the principal bonds between them.   Vanessa was only
setting out on a road that Elizabeth knew by heart,
of which she was even proud.   At the same time
they were not a gloomy pair.   They laughed,
drove out in the landau, had visitors, read together, played piquet and backgammon.   Elizabeth's extreme weakness was what Vanessa needed.
She needed, more than she had ever conceived that
she would, someone to care for.   It was the

strongest need of her nature and would always be, as it had been her grandmother's. That was why she wanted Benjie more with every day that passed. Now that Adam was gone she had nobody else but Benjie. And, as Elizabeth needed him too, these two, although they seldom mentioned him, thought of him all the time.

But there were other things growing in Vanessa, as Elizabeth one day discovered.

A Mrs. Marrable from Rosthwaite called. Now the Marrable family, its colour, personality and circumstances, would make a very fit subject of study for anyone interested in English family life in the 'eighties. Mr. John Marrable had interests in China. He was now retired, wore a black beard, smoked a kind of Oriental hookah, and was to be seen for the most part in green-and-red worsted carpet slippers walking up and down the glass-covered passage on the outside of his Rosthwaite house. Mrs. Marrable was round, stout, full-bosomed, and her skirt so beflounced and beribboned that she was all bits and pieces. John Marrable was severe and extremely self-satisfied. Mrs. Marrable very talkative, serious-minded but gay with that nervous gaiety peculiar to wives who expect their husbands to enter at any moment in the worst of all possible tempers. The Marrables had five children, four girls and a boy; they lived entirely up to the later caricatured notion of Victorian manners in that the four Miss Marrables had been completely sacrificed to their brother Edward, for whom everything had been done. The result of doing everything for Edward

was that he had turned out very badly indeed,
being sent down from Cambridge for grossly insulting a Proctor and then, while supposedly following his father's Chinese interests in London,
mixing in the lowest society and incurring a
multitude of debts.   Meanwhile the four Miss
Marrables, who were not beauties, waited patiently
at home for someone to marry them, were bullied
by their father and grew ever more plain of feature.
One of them, the third in age, Lettice, Vanessa
had liked, been kind to; the result of this was that
Lettice Marrable worshipped her with a passion
that was made up of religion, sexual hunger and a
devastating loneliness.   Lettice Marrable's adoration for Vanessa had its consequences.

In any case for the moment here Mrs. Marrable was, taking tea with Elizabeth and Vanessa
in the drawing-room of the Fortress.   She chattered on for a long time in the eager, apprehensive, incoherent manner that was especially
hers, and as she talked a large locket jumped about
on her stout bosom like a thing imprisoned and
mad for freedom.

' Yes, thank you, we have heard from Ned.
His present enthusiasm is for Miss Mary Anderson.   He goes to see her every evening in *Ingomar*,
although every evening is of course the dear
fellow's exaggeration.   The play is a failure, he
tells us, but Miss Anderson is lovelier than ever.'

' Why don't you take the girls up to London,
Mrs. Marrable, for a jaunt, and go and see her? '

' Take the girls up to London!   My dear Miss
Paris!   With things in China as bad as they are!

No.   Mr. Marrable says we must economise in
every possible direction, and we are thinking of
cutting down the landau.   He tells the girls that
we must all make sacrifices and he is quite right.
Ned went with some friends to Hurlingham last
week-end and seems really to have enjoyed himself, and he actually saw the Duke of Cambridge
riding down a side-street on a bicycle the other
day!   I agree with Mr. Marrable that our Royal
Family should keep up their position.   Do not
you, Mrs. Herries?   And Mr. Marrable says that
with all this odd behaviour of France in China
there is no knowing where we shall all be and we
look to the Royal Family to keep us all together.
Although Ned writes in his letter that the Prince
of Wales really *does* encourage some very light-
hearted behaviour.   Now is it right?   What I
mean, Miss Paris, is that we all look up to the
Royal Family.   What kind of example is he setting
our girls?   And that reminds me.   They tell me
that Miss Nettleship, the daughter of Doctor
Nettleship, is going up to Girton.   Now I don't
know what *you* think, Miss Paris, but my opinion
is—and Mr. Marrable's too—that all these things
that girls are wanting to do are the *greatest* mistake.
More than that, they are unwomanly—the very
word that Mr. Marrable used this morning.'
   ' What things? ' asked Vanessa, smiling.
   Now it happened that that smile which Vanessa
had intended in all friendliness irritated Mrs.
Marrable.   She had had a trying day.   John
Marrable had come down to breakfast with a cold
and had been very severe with everyone.   She was

H

anxious about Ned's doings in London, and Mrs.
Martin of Keswick had asked for her bill (a thing
that nobody in Keswick ever dreamt of doing unless seized by some sudden insanity).   Moreover,
neither she nor Mr. Marrable really approved of
Vanessa.   It was true, of course, that she was a
great beauty, but was she quite nice?   It was said
of her that she had some very odd opinions, and
unusual she certainly must be to engage herself
to that rascal of a son of Mrs. Herries, who, poor
woman, was popular with everyone, partly because
she did no harm and partly because everyone had
the luxury of pitying her.

Mrs. Marrable did not approve of Vanessa
although she could not deny but that black suited
her, she was a very lovely girl, she was kind to
Lettice, and belonged to one of the best families
in Cumberland.   This smile, however, hinted at
broad views, was patronising, and the drive back
to Rosthwaite would be very long.   She wished
now that she had brought one of the girls to bear
her company. . . .

'What things?' cried Mrs. Marrable, a little
sharply.   'Why, anything that takes a woman
away from the home where she belongs.   All this
gadding about, doing as men do—it isn't natural
and you know it isn't, Miss Paris.'

'Why isn't it natural?' asked Vanessa.   She
was suddenly weary of Mrs. Marrable.   She
wished that she would go.   Mrs. Marrable's
bright green dress was most unsuited to her figure.

'Why isn't it natural?' Mrs. Marrable had a
maddening habit of repeating everything that the

last speaker had said. 'Why, my dear Miss Paris, what did Nature intend women for? Marriage and the home. Marriage and the home.'

'But if they don't get married?' Vanessa continued, not very wisely. 'There are more women than men in this country. Many more. What are they to do? What do they do? Sit at home, twiddle their thumbs, and look out of window for a husband.'

This was unwise of her because it was exactly what the Miss Marrables spent their time in doing, as Mrs. Marrable very well knew. She bridled in every limb.

'Well, if they do sit at home it is better in my opinion than that they should unsex themselves. Why, they are actually doctors, some of them! It is *my* opinion, Miss Paris, that that Doctor Garrett Anderson they are always talking about should be put in prison!'

Elizabeth, who was watching Vanessa rather anxiously, saw her straighten her tall body and throw back her head.

'Another cup, Mrs. Marrable?'

'Oh no, thank you, Mrs. Herries. I positively must be going.'

'Why should she be put in prison?' asked Vanessa.

'Well, really, Miss Paris,' Mrs. Marrable said, patting her locket and smiling rather nervously, 'I wonder you can ask such a question! But you, of course, are of the younger generation. We older ones wonder sometimes where the world is going to!'

' No, but, Mrs. Marrable,' Vanessa persisted,
' I truly want to know. *Why* should Doctor
Garrett Anderson be put in prison? '

This was plainly intended as a challenge and
Mrs. Marrable took it as such.

' I consider her a wicked woman and a dangerous influence. I read an article about her only
the other day. Do you know that she once
actually read a paper on " The Limits of Parental
Authority "? Do you happen to know, Miss
Paris, that she actually supports the fantastic idea
that women should have a vote? A vote indeed!
If that is not against Nature I don't know what is!
And do you know,' and here Mrs. Marrable
dropped her voice to an awful trembling hush,
' that she took the part of the fallen women in
opposing an excellent Act of Parliament demanding their supervision?—yes, and she and her
friends positively succeeded in having the Act
repealed.'

' If women do not protect fallen women I
scarcely see who will. Certainly not men.'

' Protect! Protect! My dear Miss Paris!
And you quite a young girl! One naturally dislikes discussing such a matter at all, but people
seem to discuss everything nowadays. All I can
say is that if you approve this condonation of gross
immorality I—I—I'm most surprised! '

' Let that be as it may, Mrs. Marrable,'
Vanessa said. ' I know a few things also about
Doctor Anderson. She is one of the bravest and
finest women alive in the world to-day. In fact
with the exception of Florence Nightingale there

is not a finer.   I also could tell you one or two
things about her that perhaps you don't know.
Have you ever thought of the conditions women
lived under when Doctor Anderson was a girl?   A
married woman was scarcely a human being.   She
had no rights, no property, nothing.   Did you
ever read Miss Leigh Smith's *Brief Summary of
the Most Important Laws Concerning Women*? '

'No, indeed I have not,' said Mrs. Marrable,
panting with nervousness and annoyance.

'Well then, you should.   It was written long
ago and is still excellent reading.   Do you know
that when Elizabeth Garrett wanted to be a doctor
she could not find a physician in England to whom
she could be apprenticed?   Do you know that she
worked all day at the Middlesex Hospital, where
there were no antiseptics and anaesthetic was
scarcely used?   That needed some courage, did
it not?   Do you know that the whole medical
profession tried to stop her, that they got up a
memorial against her, that London University
when she tried to matriculate was closed to women?
Do you know that she had to fight every step of the
way and that when at last with Sophia Jex-Blake
she started the School of Medicine for Women
a howl went up through the whole of England?
And all for why?   Because, Mrs. Marrable, at
last women in England have grown tired of sitting
still and looking out of the window for husbands!
They want to have a life of their own, they want
to be independent, as one day, please God, they
shall be! '

Elizabeth had never seen Vanessa like this

before.   Her voice rang across the room as though
she challenged the world.   With her shoulders
back and her eyes flashing she looked as though
she would like to crush Mrs. Marrable to powder.
In fact at that moment she hated that good,
kindly, and quite unoffending woman.

Unoffending but not unoffended!   She was
so deeply offended that she would never forget—
never forget and never forgive.   She was not, in
her life and circumstance, a happy enough woman
to forgive.   Like all women who have a grievance
which they refuse to admit, she made her friends
take the blame.   Vanessa was to be blamed for
ever and ever.

The lady got up to go, smoothing her bosom
and arranging her wide and voluminous skirt.

'Thank you, Mrs. Herries, for a most delightful afternoon.'

'I am so glad that you came, Mrs. Marrable.'

She carried it off.   She shook her fingers playfully at Vanessa.   'When you are my age, Miss
Paris,' she said, 'you will see the danger of these
things.'

'Oh dear,' said Vanessa after her departure.
'How intolerable of me!   And how unexpected!
It was the very last thing I thought of doing.   And
in your house too.'

'You were rather vehement,' said Elizabeth.
'I have never seen you like that before.'

'No, but I am afraid you will see me like
that again.   I have a terrible temper and it
flies up before I know that it's there.   You

are wise, Elizabeth. Tell me what I shall do about it.'

' No. I don't think you lost your temper, dear. You were indignant. That's all. And I agreed with every word that you said.'

Nevertheless, going to bed that night, Vanessa was very unhappy. Something was wrong, and what was wrong was that her spirit was weighed down with an intolerable loneliness. With every day that passed she realised more bitterly the agony of her father's loss. She had been wrong, perhaps, to build her life so entirely around him. It was the caring for him, the watching that he should be happy, the comfort of knowing that they loved one another—these things, gone, left in her utter desolation. Dear Elizabeth . . . but Elizabeth was now almost out of the world and did not need her. Nobody needed her, nobody anywhere.

And at that she faced the other trouble besides her father's loss. She wanted Benjie: she wanted to be married to Benjie, to care for him, understand him, comfort him, make him happy. And Benjie was away, would perhaps never return.

' That's amusing,' she thought as she lay down in bed. ' Here was I railing at Mrs. Marrable about women's independence and I myself the least independent woman in the world! '

Two days later a telegram came:

' Arriving to-night. Benjie.'

Elizabeth ran to the door, flung it open, called out ' Vanessa! Vanessa! ' and Vanessa came running down the stairs, thinking that Elizabeth was ill.

' Oh, what is it? '

But Elizabeth caught her hand.

' He's coming——to-night. That's all he says. It's sent from Liverpool.'

Vanessa took the telegram.

' To-night! Oh, Elizabeth, I am so glad! He'll take the train to Carlisle, I shouldn't wonder, and then drive. He says nothing about being met.'

All day preparations were made, roses in his bedroom, Mrs. Harwen roasting two ducks, the silver polished, the garden paths brushed, and everything at the end of it as dead around the house as it was at the beginning.

It was four in the afternoon. Tea had been just brought in. The hills beyond the windows lay like dark purple prehistoric animals bathing in a sea of orange mist. You could see them sprawling, burying their snouts, heaving their scaly backs, while below, all about the valley, the mist, like bales of wool, rolled from field to field.

Vanessa, holding Elizabeth close to her, stared at the hills.

' Benjie thinks there are men under Skiddaw,' she said. ' Dead men. A kind of Cumbrian Valhalla.'

But Elizabeth had not heard. She looked exceedingly frail to-day. Excitement was bad for her heart. She trembled a little, leaning against Vanessa's strong side.

' This house,' she said, ' whatever you do to it, it refuses to live. It was conceived in hatred, my

dear. It has always hated everybody and everything just as poor Uhland did. It is this place
should have been burnt, not Fell House. Look
at this room. Look at the roses! I have put
them here, there, everywhere. They are drooping
with uneasiness. Nothing good will ever happen
in this place. Benjie is bringing some bad news.
I know it.'

Vanessa led her back to the sofa.

' Now lie down, Elizabeth darling. I'll bring
you your tea. Don't *think* about Benjie until he's
here. What bad news *could* there be? '

She was herself triumphant. She felt that she
was able to deal with *any* situation that Benjie
might offer. Were he in trouble through some
foolishness she would stand by him. There was
nothing that he could confess, as she had told him
years ago, that she would not share with him.
And then at last, after all these postponements,
they would be married. There was nothing now
to prevent it save the old obstacle of Benjie's
scruples, which came, as she knew well, because
he loved her so much. Now when he saw that
her sorrow had only made her the more resolved,
he would be as eager as she.

She went about the house, singing. She petted
Mrs. Harwen, who in any case adored her, went
several times to Benjie's room to see that everything was right, put Elizabeth to bed.

' He will be late. He has thirty miles to drive,
you know. He shall come up to you the moment
he arrives.'

It was after ten when he came. She was stand-

ing at her window and saw the lights of the
carriage, heard the crunch of the wheels on the
road, heard the driver shout 'Whoa!' to his
horses, then, with a recognition that drove her
heart against her ribs, the well-known timbre of
Benjie's voice.

'All right, driver. I'll get someone to help
you with the box.'

He came up the path, saw the light in her
window, and looked up.

'Hulloa, Vanessa. Is that you?' he called
out.

'Yes. I'll come down.'

As their hands clasped she knew that he loved
her as dearly as ever. She was so happy that she
could have flung her arms around his neck, but
all she did was to say, smiling her quiet steady
smile:

'Elizabeth has gone to bed. She's longing
to see you.'

Old Harwen helped the driver in with the
luggage. Benjie took off his coat, nodded to her,
and saying, 'I'll see Mother a moment and come
down,' he ran up the stairs.

It was something in his voice and look that
frightened her. *What* was it? He did not look
well, but he would be tired, of course, after his
journey. It was not that. As he spoke, he had
avoided her eyes.

She went into the dining-room where some
supper was laid out for him. She told Mrs.
Harwen to bring in the soup in ten minutes.
Then she stood there under the gas that hissed

very faintly above her head and tried to calm her fear.

Something was the matter. Had she not said that nothing that he could tell her would alarm her? Now, face to face with him, she was not sure. She felt herself quite inexperienced. She had thought that she could deal with him, but what did she *really* know about men? Perhaps he was going to tell her that he did not love her any more. No, she knew that it was not that. That first gaze into one another's eyes had told her that they still belonged to one another just as they had always done. What else could it be? Had he done anything disgraceful? She would share that with him, whatever it might be. She moved restlessly about the room, moving the things upon the table, seeing that the bowl of red and yellow roses was in the centre, arranging knives and forks.

Mrs. Harwen came in with the soup tureen.

'Yes, Mrs. Harwen, I think he'll be down in a minute now.'

'And you'll ring for the meat and vegetables, Miss Vanessa?'

'Yes. He must be hungry.'

'Yes, Miss. It's a couple of ducks—and an apple tart to follow.'

She walked to the window. Why did this house always fill her with apprehension? Her anxiety was needless. He was tired after his journey. After five minutes with her he would be his old self.

The door opened and he came in. He smiled

at her, sat down and began to eat: she drew a chair
to the table near to him.

'How well you are looking, Vanessa.'

He had not seen her since the week of the fire.
They were both conscious of that, she thought.
That is why he is uneasy and will not look at me;
but her fear increased.

'Where have you been, Benjie, all this time?
Are you hungry? Is the toast dry? I told Mrs.
Harwen not to make it before she heard you
arriving.'

'I've come from Liverpool.' He looked at
her and smiled, a pathetic smile as though he
longed to be friends with her and for some reason
must not be. The childlikeness so often apparent
in him—one of his strongest appeals to women
because he was quite unconscious of it—caught
her heart, making her ache to take him in her
arms and comfort him.

He was terribly unhappy: that was certain.

'And where have you been besides Liverpool?'

'Oh, abroad. In June I went to Germany.
I thought that I'd like to see Bismarck. Not to
speak to him, of course—simply to have a sight
of the old man. And I did. He was driving one
day in Berlin in an open carriage. It was strange,
you know, Vanessa, because when I was a boy at
Rugby in 1870 I hated the Prussians—I would
have done anything to help the French—nearly
ran away to Paris to share in the Siege. But when
I saw the old boy riding through Berlin I cheered
like the others.'

'What did he look like?'

'Oh, just an old man. But he sat up straight and bowed. Very striking eyes.'

Mrs. Harwen came in with the ducks.

'Hulloa! Mrs. Harwen! How are you?'

'Very well, thank you, sir, and I hope you're the same?'

'Oh, I'm well enough! Two ducks! I can't eat two ducks!'

'I thought if one wasn't tender you could try the other, sir.'

'Thanks. But I'm not hungry.'

'There's an apple tart to follow, sir.'

'No. Not for me to-night. I'll have it cold to-morrow.'

He carved the duck, ate a little of it, then pushed his plate aside.

'I'm not hungry, Vanessa.'

'Oh, you ought to be after that long journey.'

'No, I'm not. . . . Mother's not very well, I'm afraid.'

'No, she has grown much weaker lately. I'm afraid she can't live much longer, Benjie.'

His face seemed to be shadowed. The constraint between them grew deeper with every moment.

'No, I can't eat.' He got up. 'Let's go into the other room. There's something I must say to you.'

He opened the door for her and she went out, crossing the passage, down the stairs, into the little room off the hall that had been poor old Walter's sanctum.

There was a fire there and yet the room was cheerless. They sat down in the old leather armchairs opposite one another.

' Don't you hate this house? ' he asked her.

' I don't like it. It is impossible to make it comfortable.'

' Old Walter sees to that,' he answered grimly. There followed an awful pause. At last she could endure it no longer.

' Benjie, what's the matter? '

' Nothing. Oh yes, there is. Of course there is.'

' Well, tell me. Don't be a coward about it.' She hesitated. ' Is it that you don't love me any longer? '

He too hesitated. Then he answered, looking her at last straight in the face:

' I love you more than ever.'

A wave of joy, burning with splendid warmth, swept over her. She was, for an instant, submerged by it, blind, deaf, conscious of her joy as though she were alone in space, the beautiful glass-green wave arching above her head.

' I'm glad of that,' she said at last, ' because I also love you more than ever.' She went on: ' Father's death has left me with only you. I have no one else to care for, no one else to care for *me*. When you were away so long I thought I could not endure it—not if it went on much longer. I find that I cannot live without someone to love, and as there is only you, Benjie——'

' Don't! ' he broke in with a cry. ' Vanessa, don't! '

He had sprung to his feet.   A panic of apprehension caught her.   Something terrible had
happened.   She held the arm of the chair with
her hand.

'What is it?'

'It's this.   We can't be married.   We can
never be married.'

She waited for the next word.

'We can't be married because—because'—he
turned away from her, staring at the window—
'because I was married last week.'

He had rehearsed this moment to himself all
day, and for many days past.   He had not known
what he would do, nor what she would do either.
He had thought of everything—every possibility
but one.

He had not thought that, after what seemed
to him an age of silence, she would murmur:

'Oh, poor Benjie.   Oh, what a dreadful
thing!'

She had thought first of himself.   She had
guessed instantly that he was in some bad, in-
escapable tangle.   He could have fallen at her
feet and kissed her hands for her perception.

'We should have married last year,' she said.
'That would have saved both of us.'

He turned and looked at her with a deep
sombre gaze as though he were fixing her for ever
in his mind, just as she was, now that he had lost
her.   Then he knelt down at her feet, bowed his
head: she held his hand.   Neither of them spoke
for a long time.

He got up and sat in the chair again.

' I must tell you about it,' he said.   ' You must know everything.'

' Yes, tell me,' she answered.

' After the fire when I came to see you, you were upset.   I thought that you blamed me for your father's death.   I'm so ready to be blamed. I'm blamed so often.   But I don't care.   I don't care perhaps enough—unless it is you who blame me.   So I rode off in a temper.   You remember that in Seascale last year I stayed in rooms with a widow and her daughter? '

Vanessa, looking at him with eyes that were so unhappy but so resolutely determined not to flinch that he could not face them, nodded.

' Yes, I remember.   I saw them walking one day on the beach.'

' Yes.   Well—a mother and daughter called Halliday—I didn't like them—not either of them. I was thinking only of you, Vanessa, that summer —you were obsessing me.   Nevertheless I kissed the girl, disliked her more than ever, and kissed her again.'

He flashed a look at her, then dropped his glance and went on, looking at the floor.

' You and I would have been married, of course, that autumn, had it not been for Adam's illness. Fate.   Call it what you like.   Perhaps really the best thing.   In any case the widow and her daughter came to live in Keswick.'

' Tell me,' Vanessa said, ' what she looks like. I saw her only for a moment at Seascale.   Is she beautiful?   *What* is she? '

' No, she is not. She is not beautiful, she is
not clever. My eyes have been open from the
first. She held me like one of one's pet cheap
temptations—those you are always ashamed of,
never resist, never confess to anyone. . . . I must
be fair to her, Vanessa. Whatever happens I must
be fair. But you will see in a moment what she
is like.'

Vanessa drew a deep, trembling breath. Her
hands were folded in her lap. Benjie stared at
them as though hypnotised, noticing how white
they were against the black dress. He thought
that he could tell the rest of the story better were
he holding her hand, but he did not move.

' Yes, I must be fair to her. She knew that
she had some attraction for me. She was, I think,
determined from the very beginning that I should
marry her, but really because, I am afraid, she
loved—loves—me.'

' Yes,' said Vanessa.

' Thinking of you always, loving you more
every day, yet I went to see the two of them in
Keswick. I must speak of something difficult,
Vanessa. It is this. The more I saw you the
more I loved you—and with my body as well as
the rest of me. I have always wanted my body
to have power. I have liked to see it travelling
about the world, getting experience, eating, drinking, strong, vigorous. I have always thought
that most people do not give their bodies all the
chances. Well, that spring you were occupied
with Adam, of course, and I would leave you,
restless and unsatisfied. Both of us were, I think.

But I was doubly unsatisfied—because I wanted you so badly and because I was so unworthy of you.'

She murmured: ' That has been where the mistake was.'

' Oh, don't misunderstand me, Vanessa. I don't go about the world thinking I am unworthy of people. Of nobody else. Only you. But the one thing I must not do, I tell myself, is to spoil your life. I mustn't. I mustn't, I tell myself— and then—I do. . . .

' So I went to see them. Then a day or two after the fire I rode out to Halliday's farm—the brother, you know. I stayed there the night. I drank too much. The girl slept with me.'

He waited. There was a mouse scratching somewhere. They both raised their heads together, and Vanessa thought, as she had often done before, that she heard one of the dogs that Uhland used to keep in his room howling from the Tower. Somewhere a dog *was* howling, and at that same moment she realised a hatred for that girl such as she had never felt before for anyone.

' Next day,' Benjie went on, ' I came back to the Fortress. I stayed for a while, then I went off with Halliday and two of his friends called Endicott shooting. I met the girl again. She was quiet, most respectable, as though now she had got what she wanted. I am sure her mother knew. I think her brother knew too. I was extremely unhappy. I wanted to come to you and ask that we might be married at once, but I was ashamed and afraid—you are the only human being

I have ever been afraid of, Vanessa. I went
abroad to Germany.

'When I came back the girl, her mother and
brother were in London. The girl came to see
me and told me that she was going to have a child
—my child, she said. I don't know now whether
that was the truth or no. That was a month ago.
Will you believe me, Vanessa, when I tell you
that I loved you during all this time more than
ever?'

'Yes,' said Vanessa. 'I believe you.'

'The girl said that of course now I would
marry her. The mother said the same. The
brother the same. I was not frightened of them
in the least. I have never been afraid of anyone
or anything except your despising me or doing
you harm. But also, in spite of all that I have
done, I have never got a woman into trouble. I tell
you that I didn't know, I don't know now, whether
I was responsible in this case. I want to be fair
to her in every way, but I cannot be certain of her
virtue. They were all three quite friendly and
quite frank. The girl said that she had always
loved me, always meant to marry me. The
brother said that of course it would not be pleasant
for my mother if she knew of this. I agreed with
that. Ill as she was it would probably kill her.
But I think that my mind was entirely on you.
Although I loved you so dearly I might do this
again. I have never had any trust in myself. It
is only myself that I blame, but from my birth, as
I have always told you, there has been some strain
in me that I could never trust, as there was in my

father, my grandfather.   And I have always been
honest with you.   I would have had to tell you
of this, and when you knew that this was to be
my child—would you marry me?   Would you,
Vanessa?   Would you have married me knowing
this? '

He waited with passionate eagerness for her
answer, leaning forward, looking into her face.

At last she said:

' No.   Perhaps I would not.'

He nodded his head. ' I thought not. " This
ends it," I thought.   All this struggle about you
that I have had for years.   You will be free.
Perhaps you will hate me and so be clear of me,
then after a while you will marry somebody
splendid.   One day, long after, you will acknow-
ledge that I was right.   That's what I thought.
So I married her—last week in Liverpool.'

A long, long silence followed.

At last Vanessa said:

' Do you care for her?   Are you fond of her
in any way at all? '

' No—not in any way at all.'

Then she said: •

' Thank you for telling me so honestly.'   And
then again, after another pause: ' This will be
terrible for Elizabeth.'

' Yes,' he answered.

She got up and went over to him and laid her
hand against his cheek.

' You must do all you can for her.'

He caught her hand fiercely; kissed it again
and again.

' What are we to do? I can't live without seeing you.'

She shook her head.

' No. Of course we must not meet. That would be too difficult for both of us.'

She bent down and kissed him.

' How foolish we both have been, Benjie dear.' She held him close to her like a mother her son. At that moment, with his head against her breast, she realised with the utmost clarity the desolation of her loneliness. She kissed him again, then drew herself from his grasp.

' Good night, Benjie darling. I'll go back to Cat Bells in the morning. You won't write or anything, will you? It will be much better.'

' I'll do anything you say.'

At the door she turned back.

' I don't know whether it's right. Very wrong perhaps. But although we mustn't meet or write, if you're in trouble— real, serious trouble—you must tell me.'

' I'll tell you,' he said.

Then she went out.

THE DUCHESS OF WREXE'S BALL

ONE day in November 1884 Barney Newmark went in to drink a cup of tea with his sister, Phyllis Rochester, in her pleasant little house in Eaton Place.

He chose this afternoon because he knew that his brother-in-law, Clarence Rochester, was at Brighton. He did not like Clarence at all—he thought him a humbug. And Clarence did not like Barney—he thought him an obscene, conceited libertine. Phyllis, who cared deeply for Barney and had grown accustomed to Clarence, kept the balance between them.

Phyllis, who was now a buxom woman of sixty-three (all the Newmarks of this generation were stout), loved her comforts and adored her eccentric son Philip. So long as she had plenty of the little cakes, jams and preserved fruits that she preferred and so long as Philip lived with her in Eaton Place she had no alarms. She had a charming complexion, and Clarence was away as often as not. Her one fear had been lest Philip should marry. But now it did not seem likely. Philip did not like women.

Barney to-day was in an excellent temper. He had that morning finished his novel, a novel in

which Newmarket, Boulogne and Scottish shoot-
ing-parties were his principal backgrounds, where
everything was very light and careless and the
principal scene was a baccarat-cheating scandal.
Like the majority of novelists he enjoyed, for a day
or two following a novel's conclusion, an extraordinary sense of freedom and light-heartedness.
Unlike most novelists these happy days were not
followed by an intense gloom. He knew the
thing was of no value at all. He told everybody
so. He wrote to make money. He was none
of your Merediths, Zolas or Shorthouses. He
couldn't write a novel like—what was its name?—
that *John Inglesant* to save his life. Nor did he
want to. So long as a fellow or two got his novel
from a library he was perfectly satisfied—and so
were his publishers.

Between the brother and sister sitting together
having tea in the pleasant little drawing-room
there was a strong resemblance. They were both
stout, jolly and easily amused. Barney was the
best of fellows when alone with his sister. They
were both glad that Clarence was at Brighton.
The room was very warm, heavily curtained and
crammed with knick-knacks. There were china
dogs, china shepherds and shepherdesses, china
mandarins. There was even a large china copy
of a Chinese temple with little bells that tinkled
when there was a draught, and of this Phyllis
was inordinately proud. There were photographs
everywhere. Four photographs of Mary Anderson, two of Ellen Terry, three of Mr. Terriss,
photographs of Ellis and Garth and Emily New-

mark (very forbidding) and Barney (riding a horse) and Vanessa and Carey Rockage. There were numberless little tables, all heavily loaded, a great many little chairs and a basket near the fire in which a fat pug called Charles was now wheezing. The two round tea-tables were covered with cakes, pastries, muffins, piles of buttered toast.

'Good heavens, Phil,' Barney cried, 'how many people are you expecting?'

'Nobody except you.'

'Why all the food?'

'Oh, I like to have plenty to eat. And Philip may come in.'

'Oh, may he? And what is he doing to-day?'

'He has gone to an Art Exhibition with Samuel Roscoe.'

'Oh, has he?'

To change the subject—which might be an unpleasant one—Phyllis asked:

'And what's the news?'

'I finished my novel this morning.'

'Oh, did you? What is it called?'

'*Neck or Nothing*.'

'What a clever title! I don't know how you think of all these things.'

'No, nor do I. I have been helping John Beaminster to choose a horse.'

'Oh, have you?' Phyllis was greatly interested. The Beaminsters were always exciting. 'Did he tell you anything about his mother?'

'No. What should he tell me?'

'Oh, I don't know, but I do think it is so

extraordinary her being shut up in that Portland Place house all these years. Do you remember when she came to that party that Ellis gave a year or two ago?'

'Of course I remember.'

'Well, they say she hadn't been out of doors for years before that. Then for a week or two she was seen everywhere. Then she went back again and has shut herself up ever since.'

'That was the party,' said Barney slowly, 'when Benjie suddenly appeared. Do you remember? And that night he was engaged to Vanessa.'

Phyllis, shaking her head, choosing with great care the richest of several little cakes, answered indignantly:

'Oh, don't mention Benjie to me! I have finished with him for ever and so has everybody! I consider him a murderer!'

'Oh, come now,' said Barney, smiling.

'Well, isn't he? He killed his mother by throwing Vanessa over and marrying that horrible woman.'

'You don't know that she's horrible. You've never seen her.'

'No, but other people have. Alfred was up that way with a friend the other day and thought he'd call. They had the most dreadful visit. Benjie would do nothing but swear, and the house was a pig-sty and the baby howling. Alfred said that the woman was awful! As thin as a pole and cross-eyed.'

'Oh no, not that!' said Barney, laughing.

'Well, there was something odd about her
eyes, Alfred said.   And she hardly spoke a word.'
'I like Benjie,' Barney said.   'I always have
and I always will.   There was something behind
that business we don't know.'
'Nothing to Benjie's credit, you can be sure,'
said Phyllis.   'Poor Vanessa.   So beautiful and
buried up there.   She's only been to London once
since it happened.   She stayed with Rose for a
week, you remember, and I never saw anyone
more lovely.   Very nice she was too.   Philip was
in a passion over her.'
'You needn't pity Vanessa,' said Barney
sharply.   'She needs no one's pity.'
'Oh no, of course not!'   Here again seemed
a dangerous subject, so Phyllis, finding safety in
general affairs, asked:
'And what do they say about General Gordon?'
'There is little news since Stewart's murder.
Wolseley is moving up the Nile.'
'Do you think Gladstone has made a mistake?'
'Possibly.   He'll hear of it if he has.'
'Some people say that Gordon is mad.'
'Mad people do most of the things in this
world.   That, my dear Phil, is what our family
will never learn.'
'I sometimes think Emily is mad.   What do
you think she came in here raging about yester-
day?'
'I *never* think about Emily.'
'She wants to close the Alhambra and have all
the women who go there put in prison.'
'Emily will be improperly assaulted one day

by a Salvation Army worker. Then she will learn something.'

The maid opened the door and said: ' Miss Ormerod and Mr. Ormerod.'

Rose and Horace came in and were eagerly welcomed.

Rose looked charming indeed, in one of the Scottish plaid costumes that were then most fashionable, and her hat tilted over her hair arranged in a bun was so small as to be almost invisible. 'Where,' thought Phyllis, ' *does* she get the money to buy her clothes from? '

Horace, red-faced, amiable and enthusiastic, was like a successful clergyman on holiday. His vibrating enthusiasm made Barncy very cynical. ' I always believe well of human nature,' Barncy said, ' until Horace Ormerod comes along.'

Horace rubbed his hands together, beamed, pushed his spectacles (he had been wearing spectacles for a year or two) back on to his short nose and cried: ' Well, this is splendid indeed! Rose and I were walking in the Park and I said to her, " We'll take a hansom and see if Phil has some tea for us! " Splendid day! Fresh and bright! I never felt better in my life! '

Barney said: ' I'm glad of that, Horace. We need cheering, with so many of our fellows without employment and the City in a scare and Egypt in a muddle! '

' Nonsense! Nonsense! You *will* look on the black side of things! I have it on the best of authority that the City is doing very well indeed. And as to Egypt, you trust Gladstone. He did the right thing in sending Gordon. You can take it from me! '

' I don't take it from you! ' said Barney. ' How do you know? '

' What I always say,' said Horace, ' is that you can trust Old England. She always does the right thing in the end. I hate this pessimism. It's men like you, Barney, who do all the harm. But of course you're a novelist, live in your imagination and that sort of thing.'

' Now, Horace,' Rose interrupted, ' don't be tiresome. Barney knows more about everything than you do. But I know something that *he* doesn't know! '

They were eager for information.

' Vanessa arrived at Hill Street this morning for a long visit! '

' No! ' cried Barney. ' Vanessa? How splendid! '

' Yes. I saw Alfred in the Park, and *he* had seen Ellis in the City. Our dear Vanessa is with us again, and it shan't be our fault if she doesn't stay for months.'

Phyllis nodded.

' Ellis will be glad,' she said.

' And Ellis's ma will be glad,' Rose went on. ' And I have come in only for a moment because I am going to Hill Street to see her.'

An hour later Rose was in Hill Street.

' I will tell Miss Paris,' the butler said, leaving her alone in the big cold drawing-room.

Old Lady Herries was now eighty years of age

and spent most of her time in bed where, rumour
had it, she arranged her pearls, rubies and diamonds on the counterpane, played games with
them and counted them over and over again.
But because she was in bed and Ellis for most of
the day in the City, the house was more like a
mortuary than a living-place. The drawing-room
was decorated in mustard yellow, the curtains had
heavy folds of it, the chairs and sofas were wrapped
in it. On the mantelpiece was a clock of yellow-
and-white marble. The marble statues that had
been there ever since Will Herries first bought
the house glimmered whitely under the gas.
Rose shivered.

'*What* a house! But now that Vanessa has
come they will entertain again. Now that Benjie
is out of the way they will think there is hope for
Ellis. Is there? Vanessa is lonely enough, poor
darling, to try anything, and she has always had a
kind of maternal feeling for Ellis.'

Ellis came in.

Rose did not dislike Ellis. She thought him
absurd and pathetic. She was also blind neither
to his baronetcy nor to his wealth. At one time
she had thought that she might herself marry him,
but her clear common sense soon showed her that
she did not attract him in the least.

'He has no eyes for anyone but Vanessa.'

Now when he came in she was compelled to
admit that he looked distinguished, and not really
his forty-two years. Or rather he might be any
age. His body was slim and erect. His closely
fitting black clothes and high sharp-pointed collar

gave him distinction. He was Sir Ellis Herries, Bart., all right and a ridiculous physical copy of his father. A very hideous painting of his father hung on the left side of the fireplace. Yes, ludicrously alike, but the real Ellis, Rose (who was no poor judge of character) well knew, was nervous, highly strung, sensitive, unbalanced as his father had never been.

But now as she shook hands Rose liked him, for to-day he was radiant with happiness. When Ellis was happy you were touched because his hold on his joy seemed so precarious. He was like a man who, to his own surprise, looks to be, for once, winning a game. In the end he will in all probability lose it, but this unusual, unexpected chance gains you to his side.

' I came in only for a moment,' Rose said. ' Alfred told me that Vanessa had arrived. I couldn't wait to see her.'

' Vanessa,' said Ellis, speaking in his precise careful voice, ' is, I am happy to say, under our roof again. She will be delighted to see you.'

' But this is splendid. None of us knew that she was coming.'

' No. *We* did not know until last week. She has been staying with Carey in Wiltshire.'

' How is she looking? '

' Oh, very well. Very well indeed. But here she is. Vanessa, my dear, here is Rose to see you.'

They flung themselves into one another's arms while Ellis stood benevolently by, stroking his chin and smiling.

'But, *dear* Rose! How sweet of you to come so soon!'

'Well, of course! But why not a line to anyone that you were coming?'

'I truly did not know, did I, Ellis? You see Carey and May quite suddenly were invited to Panshanger and they thought they should go. They wanted me to stay on until they returned, but—well, I fancied a little London gaiety.'

They sat down on the sofa together.

'And now, young ladies,' said Ellis in his best paternal fashion, 'I shall leave you. I am sure you have a great deal to talk over. Dinner at seven, Vanessa.'

'Oh Lord!' Rose cried, looking at her watch. 'And it is six now.'

'No, no,' said Vanessa eagerly. 'Come up with me when I dress. It is so *lovely* to see you. And are you not engaged yet to Captain What's-his-name and what other gentlemen are there and have you seen dear Barney? How is Horace? How, in fact, are all the Herries?'

They noticed at once changes in one another, as was natural after a year's separation. The difference that Vanessa saw in Rose was the same difference that her grandmother had once noticed in this same room years ago in Sylvia Herries— a slight, oh, so very slight, fading of the natural bloom, a heightening of the artificial colour, a little hardening of the voice, the eye a trifle more anxious. The Scottish plaid was extremely pretty, with its red and grey, and the little hat was a beauty — very expensive clothes. Rose looked

altogether very expensive.   Upon what in reality
did she and her brother live?

And Rose saw at once that Vanessa was a girl
no longer.   She was even for a moment or two
afraid of her.   Had she lost her?   But very soon
she realised the thing that she would realise again
so often—that once Vanessa was your friend it was
not easy to lose her.

Vanessa's dress was dove-grey, her dark hair
brushed back from her forehead. Her hand
caught Rose's and held it.

'Rose, I want to have *fun*! I want to see
people, plenty and plenty.   I want to go to the
theatre.   There is Mary Anderson as Juliet,
isn't there? and Mr. Wilson Barrett as Hamlet, and
Gilbert and Sullivan and Mrs. John Wood.   I've
been studying the papers.   Lady Herries has
asked May and Carey to come and stay so that
May can chaperon me.   They are coming from
Panshanger the day after to-morrow.   I want to
see everybody and do everything.'

'And everyone wants to see you.   You are
much the most beautiful woman in London.   Mrs.
Langtry is nothing at all in comparison.'

Vanessa smiled, very happy.

' I want to be beautiful just for a week or two—
after that I don't care in the least.   I want everyone to think me lovely, to say, " Oh, who is *that*
lovely girl? "   In fact, Rose dear, I want some
encouragement.   I've been fighting things by
myself—without any help from anyone.'

' I know, dear, I know,' Rose said, stroking
her hand.   There was something feverish, she

thought, in Vanessa's tone, something unlike her natural restraint.

'Yes, Timothy and Violet have been very good to me. I stayed there for months in the house they've bought in Eskdale. Lovely. Not far from the sea, with the mountains behind them. But of course I couldn't *talk* to them. And there was another thing——'

She broke off, then, holding Rose's hand more tightly, went on:

'This is something I want to say and then we will never mention it again. About Benjie. I know that everyone is against him, that they all think he treated me badly, that he made a wretched mess of everything, which is what they have always hoped for. Now, Rose dear, I want you to make them understand—*all* of them—that I will not hear one word against Benjie. That I will never speak again to anyone who attacks him when I'm there. Barney is the only one I'll talk to about him. Barney is his friend, I know. Will you make them all understand that?'

'Of course,' Rose hesitated. 'Vanessa, what is it? What happened? What made him do it?'

'No, Rose, I can't tell even you. It's his affair. We don't meet. We don't write. But I understand what he did. I'm his friend, and not one word shall be said against him in my presence.'

Rose felt her hand tremble, she saw that her eyes were misty. She put her arms round her and kissed her.

'And now, Rose darling,' said Vanessa cheer-

fully, ' tell me about yourself? How are you?
When are you to be married? That hat and
costume are lovely! '

' Yes, very nice,' said Rose. ' But not paid
for, my dear. Never mind me. Horace and I
live in a little house in Shepherd Market. Well,
to tell you the truth they are four rooms over a
grocer's. We got them cheap from old Lady
Martindale, who lost her money at cards and had
to decamp at a moment's notice. They are the
very best address and are cosy even if they are
small. For the rest I have debts, and gentlemen
who admire me and ladies who don't, just like any
other lady—and I shall marry the first decent man
who proposes to me, whoever he is.'

' And Horace? '

' Oh, Horace is getting along fast on the simple
plan of refusing to know anyone save those who
will be useful to him. He smiles on everyone and
has a genius for not seeing those he doesn't want
to see. And now, dear, let us go to your room. I
am longing to know what you are going to wear.'

So they went upstairs.

Vanessa dined alone with Ellis and Miss Mabel
Fortescue, the lady who now ' ran ' the Hill Street
house. Miss Fortescue reminded Vanessa at once
of Miss Murdstone, and she herself would have
felt not unlike David Copperfield had she not
quickly seen that the situation was serious and
she must rather be Betsey Trotwood. So from the
very beginning she was firm with Miss Fortescue.
Really remarkable, her resemblance to Miss

Murdstone. She had the stiff poker back, the dark complexion and black hair, the heavy eyebrows that nearly met over a large nose, and Vanessa was certain that in her bedroom were the ' two uncompromising hard black boxes, with her initials on the lids in hard brass nails.'

Ellis thought the world of her—' Most efficient woman, Vanessa. Excellently behaved. Knows just how to treat my mother.' Then waking in the early morning hours to hear the London sparrows cheep beyond the window, Vanessa discovered two other things.

' Miss Fortescue hated me at sight. And hopes to marry Ellis.'

The dinner was a very agreeable one: Ellis was so happy and when he was happy he was childlike. Vanessa knew too that he was happy because she was there, and it was so long since she had been cared for in this way. Timothy and Violet took her for granted. Aunt Jane loved her but thought her still ten years old. So also Will Leathwaite. Carey and May were fond of her, but liked their dogs and horses still better. She was, she discovered, *hungering* for affection, and placing her foot in London had as it were set all her world alight. That afternoon, going for a walk, the window of a florist in Piccadilly had been ablaze with chrysanthemums; down Bond Street into Piccadilly had come the carriages, shining in the November sun, the coachmen stout and splendid, the horses sleek, the harness glittering, and from a distance, through the walls of the houses, the echo of a barrel-organ, heard as it

always should be, a street or two away. She had
thrown up her head and sniffed the air, sharp and
horsy and honied with the sun. London! She
adored London! She could manage without
Cumberland, clouded with unhappy memories,
for a while. Then against this background there
was first Rose, who loved her, and now Ellis, who
loved her too. Ellis was improved. He was intelligent. He talked about Gladstone and Gordon,
about the ' New Radicalism ' that was interesting
itself in the conditions of housing and the happiness of the poorer classes, about the Trades
Unions, about the abolishing of the Income Tax,
about the provisions of the Electric Lighting Act,
about the Redistribution Bill, about all these
serious things, sensibly, with inside knowledge.
His tact with her was extraordinary, for he was
not by nature a tactful man. He studied her without appearing to. He was affectionate, but with
the affection of a brother. She knew of course
that he loved her, but he did not embarrass her
with any implied emotion.

After dinner she went upstairs to visit Lady
Herries. She saw at once a great change in her.
Some of the stories they told about her were true,
for she was sitting up in bed and on a white shawl
on her lap were rings, bracelets and necklaces.
She played with them like a child, holding them
up to the light, rubbing them with her fingers,
laying one against the other.

Nevertheless she appeared quite sensible. She
was enchanted to see Vanessa.

Her great pleasure was to talk about people.

Staying in her room as she did, she brought the world around her, speculating, gathering stories, chuckling over scandals and foibles.

'You will find London very much changed, my dear. Money is the only thing, getting it and losing it. If you have money you can go anywhere. That is why London is much more amusing and not nearly so remarkable as it used to be.'

She talked about the family.

'Alfred, Amery's boy, will make a fortune. He's in with all the Jews. His nose gets sharper every day. Dora, old Rodney's daughter, has such a pretty child, Cynthia. Dora married Freddie Beauchamp. Do you remember him? A thin man with a long nose. They live in London now, and Cynthia will marry well. Very well, I shouldn't wonder. Then Barney has made quite a name for himself—amusing books he writes—but he has some very odd friends. However, that doesn't matter if he's a success. Then Phyllis' boy, Philip—you remember him?—a little affected but very clever. He's quite a friend of Mr. Oscar Wilde. I'm glad Carey and May are coming. Their two girls, Maud and Helen, are *very* plain, poor things, but of course they have never done anything but ride horses, so what can you expect? They will improve as they grow older.'

She chattered on, moving the jewels about on the white shawl, sometimes talking to herself:

'Now *that* won't do! If Carey and May come on Friday I must put off Miss Blades. She comes

and reads to me, my dear. A very nice woman
with the funniest stories about everyone. . . . I
will not have that fish three days running. I must
tell Miss Fortescue.'

Then quite unexpectedly she fell asleep, letting her head, with its tousled white hair, fall on
the pillow, opening her mouth and snoring.

Vanessa soon discovered that she was to be a
gathering-point for all the family. They had
been longing for something of the kind. Hill
Street sprang to life, and Ellis was rejuvenated.
May Rockage was a simple creature whose heart
was in the country with her horses, her dogs and
her two girls. But she had a hearty power of
enjoyment and, although she dressed badly,
laughed like a man and was extremely innocent
of the world, she became very quickly an excellent
companion for Vanessa.

Vanessa threw herself into the family interests.
Soon she knew all their secrets, their fears, their
ambitions and their odd little ways.

First of all there was Rose, who, she declared
to Vanessa, was going ' the primrose path.' She
had two or three gentlemen friends, a Captain
Rackrent, horsy and raffish, a Mr. Marchbanks,
who was some sort of a publisher and encouraged
young men to write as much like the French as
possible, and a Mr. Easy, who was like a Jew but
said he was not one, Assyrian, purple-bearded and,
Rose said, very rich. He had something to do
with the Theatre. Rose said that he proposed
marriage to her every week—and she added, ' One
day when the bailiffs are drinking beer in the

parlour—the awful thing will happen—I shall marry him.'

Cynthia, Rodney's granddaughter, was the prettiest, most fairylike creature. She at once fell down at Vanessa's feet and worshipped. Her hair was spun gold, her eyes the tenderest blue, her little figure exquisite; wearing a tiny hat perched on a golden bun, her dress gathered into loops behind her, her bosom clearly defined, she was something to make men tremble. She was sweet and tender and loving but, Vanessa thought, quite ruthlessly determined to make the best marriage possible. All the girls were sweet, tender and loving, and all the girls were determined to be well married. 'You would think,' said Rose, 'to listen to these infants talk that they didn't know what men were made of. But they *do* know. They know very well indeed.'

Barney's set were writers, painters, horsy men, theatrical men and men about town. All these men—including Barney—had feminine friends who were never obtruded. Once Vanessa, going with Rose unexpectedly to Barney's rooms, found an elegant creature seated on his sofa, mending his stockings. She was delightful, and most maternal to Barney. Her name was Miss Montefiore, an actress 'resting between engagements.'

Then Vanessa was forced, against her will, to see something of Emily Newmark. Vanessa did not like Emily, but had to confess that she did good in the world. She was for ever 'rescuing' people, 'unfortunate women,' drunkards, young pickpockets and foreigners—Chinamen, negroes,

lost and strayed Scandinavians. Her only interest
in people was that they could be ' rescued.' She
lectured Vanessa, patronised her, and was sometimes unexpectedly human, bursting into tears and
saying that she was ' misjudged.'

Old Amery, tottering and bewildered, thought
only of his son Alfred. That sharp young man
was always adding up figures and subtracting
them again. He came to Ellis once a week with
schemes. Ellis said that many of these were
clever. Alfred would get on.

A very odd world, too, was that of young
Philip, Phyllis' boy. The young men, Philip's
friends, looked and were ridiculous, but they lived
up to their gospel. They wrote little stories,
painted little pictures, and treated all the Arts as
their own especial property. They arrived from
Oxford in increasing numbers. They lisped, they
languished. They thought Mr. Whistler, Mr.
Wilde, French poets and the art of Japan all ' too
utterly beautiful.'

In short the Herries were everywhere. Into
every corner of London life they drove their strong
determined wedge of common sense. Even
Philip, with his absurdities, had common sense.
England was now at the top of the world, was at
a stage of material success and triumph that exactly
suited the Herries character. No member of the
family ever boasted or wondered or explained.
They simply went everywhere, into the Beaminster
house in Portland Place, into the theatres and
restaurants, into the churches and lecture-halls,
into the Kensington drawing-rooms, into the City,

into the slums and did their good work. No
Herries was at the *top* of anything. No Herries
(with the exception of Ellis) accumulated great
wealth, cared for property, dominated politics or
the Arts or the Church or the Army. They simply
were everywhere and influenced everything.

Vanessa, however, soon discerned that her
arrival was for all of them a dramatic event. At
certain times in their history a combination of
circumstances produced an Event to which all
the family, gladly and joyfully, reacted. Their
hatred of the eccentric, the queer, the abnormal
made them respond ecstatically to anything that
allowed them to display that hatred. It had been
so in the old days of the Rogue, in the quarrels
about the famous Fan, in the dreadful scandal of
Uhland, and now it was so in the affairs of Benjamin, Vanessa and Ellis. Benjie was their rogue,
their scapegoat. Vanessa was, at this moment,
their heroine. What had happened in the North
about her engagement? No one knew. Would
she marry Ellis and become not only the most
beautiful but also one of the richest women in
London? Why had she come to Hill Street if
not to marry Ellis? Her presence made that
winter one of the most exciting in their lives.

And Vanessa let herself go. She was there to
forget all the past. She must make a world for
herself in which she could be independent—never,
never would she depend on anyone again. She
went everywhere, to balls and theatres and Hurlingham and concerts and immensely long elaborate
dinner-parties.

She and May travelled down to Brighton in the ten o'clock Pullman, lunched at Mutton's, where Barney and Alfred joined them, watched the dowagers in the carriages, the girls in the dog-carts, the invalids in the bath-chairs, the babies in the goat-chaises, men on bicycles. They went on the electric railways in Madeira Road, visited the Aquarium, listened to the band in the Bird-cage and had dinner at a fine hotel. A glorious day! Brighton in November, sunshine, sea-air. What an enchanting world!

Vanessa went to the House and heard Mr. Gladstone speak on the Maamstrasna Murders question, and when Mr. O'Connor rose and called the speech ' the lamest, weakest and most halting I have ever heard,' and young Mr. Stanhope shouted out, ' That's what the ferret said when the lion roared,' she could have clapped her hands in her delight because that was exactly what *she* thought!

She went of course to *Romeo and Juliet* at the Lyceum and thought Mary Anderson so lovely that she never troubled about the acting. She saw Mrs. John Wood in *Young Mrs. Winthrop* and laughed herself into tears. When Mrs. Wood meets her husband, from whom she has been divorced, they do nothing but wink! Oh, *what* a wink! In fact all London went to see this not very good little play because of Mrs. Wood's wink.

She was sad when Henry Fawcett died, thrilled by what Mr. Ruskin had to say to his friends at Oxford, read William Black's *Judith Shakespeare*, wanted to go to a Spiritualist meeting but could

find no one to accompany her, gazed at Mrs.
Langtry at a party, ate oysters and pheasant, drove
so often in hansoms that she thought nothing at
all about it, and enjoyed Mr. Corney Grain in
the German Reeds' entertainment. 'Nothing,' as
Emily Newmark said to her severely, ' nothing but
a life of idle pleasure.'

In that winter Vanessa caught a sense of
London that she was never after to lose, its smells
and odours, flowers and horses and fogs, its incongruities, its shabbiness, as for instance when
you passed, on the way into the Underground,
the faded photographs, smirking from the wall,
of old burlesque actresses, Planché's ghost hovering around them, or when in some of the smaller
theatres the smell of beer, the dim rose coverings
of the stalls, the dirty globes of gas, the white
spots of plaster between the flaking gilt, the past,
mournful, pathetic, strangled the struggling present. But everywhere and in every case London
was homely—homely in the clack-clack of the
horses, in the scattered rumbling of the omnibuses,
in the barrel-organs and the German bands, in
the sudden flashing splendour of the Guard riding
up St. James's from the Palace, in the gentlemen's
servants taking the air, in the elegant dandies
of the Row, in the melancholy street-singers, the
lingering notes of the church bells, in the fogs
that, yellow and sulky, crept from street to street,
in the comfortable laziness of afternoon tea, in the
high collar of Mr. Gladstone, the radiance of the
Jersey Lily, the dignity and humanity of the
Prince, and, above all, in that stout little regal

figure, never forgotten, sitting somewhere behind the walls of plain-faced Buckingham Palace or bird-haunted Windsor, receiving an Indian prince, being sharp with Mr. Gladstone or smiling at her grandchildren. All this was London and London was all this.

One further thing that winter dominated the Town: the thought of Gordon. This great victory of common sense, this triumph of plain reality—was it threatened by that figure, fanatical, heroic and alone, fearlessly erect among his enemies? Could it be—and it was a question forced again and again upon the Herries through all their history—that common sense was not enough, that there were other things, dangerous, mysterious things of the spirit that could spring upon you and defeat you did you too long disregard them? Is there another world with which we have refused to reckon?

After the disaster of Abu Hamed there was silence. On the day that Herbert Stewart started across the desert there was a message: 'Khartoum all right. 14.12.84. C. G. Gordon.'

After that, silence again.

On the 22nd of January, the day on which London learned of the battle of Abu Klea, Ellis proposed to Vanessa the second time.

They were about to go up to bed. The candles with their heavy silver snuffers stood there waiting. May Rockage had said good-night and started up the stairs, the great drawing-room with its yellow hangings stayed patiently for their departure. Ellis touched Vanessa's arm.

'Vanessa—one moment.'

She turned to him, smiling, then knew at once what he was going to say. He was very nervous, he put his hand to his throat, looked at her with a beseeching smile.

'I have been good, have I not? You have been happy during these weeks here?'

'Very happy, Ellis.'

'Your presence here has been a joy to all of us. My mother has been a different being, and I—I must tell you—I have never been so happy in all my life before.'

'I'm very glad. You have been wonderfully good to me.'

'How could one help being? But I cannot wait any longer. I must ask you once more. It is a long time, is it not, since the last occasion in the Park. Vanessa, will you marry me?'

Before she could answer he went on with a trembling eager passion that touched her and made her long to be kind to him.

'Listen. I implore you not to answer before you have thought it over. I know how much older I am. I know that you do not love me. But you like me. You are friendly, aren't you? I can feel that you are friendly.'

'Of course I am friendly, Ellis. And more than that. But——'

'Well, then, that's all I ask. Indeed it is. I ask nothing more. If you will marry me everything shall be as you wish. I know that money makes no appeal to you, but perhaps power—the power to do good, to help others, to put wrong things right—may mean a little. You are so good, you have so wonderful a character, that you *should* be able to influence your generation. I will help you to do that—under your guidance. And we are friends. We have known one another for a long time and surely can now trust one another completely. Think it over, Vanessa. Do not answer me now. Please, please not now. But think of it. . . . Good night.'

And before she could speak he was gone.

In her room that night she did indeed think of it. Ellis, during these two months, had been so kind, so unselfish and so wise—they had been such good friends—he had talked about so many things with so much understanding—that she had come to care for him as once would have appeared impossible. She did not love him. But with the impetuous certainty both of her youth and past events she was sure that love was over for her, would never return. Or, rather, she loved as she had always done. Benjie was as truly now in her heart as he had always been. But she must never think of him, neither now nor in any possible future time. So love being over was this not perhaps the next best thing?

Men had in these London weeks gathered round her. Two had proposed to her, and in the very moments of their proposal she had realised that the very thought of any man but Benjie in *that* world of romantic passion was fantastically unreal. Well, this was not romantic passion. But Ellis was the only one save Rose who belonged to her childhood and youth. She had known him

so long that he was part of all that early life.   And
he wanted to be cared for, and *she* wanted, now
more than anything else in the world, to bestow
her care on someone.

Was it also not true that she could do good in
the world with the power that his money would
give her?   She was still very young in many things
and believed that to do good to your fellows was
not so very difficult.   She did not want to make
them better, only to make them happy.   Was this
not, perhaps, her duty?   She knelt down and
prayed, passing as she always did into a world of
comfort and security.   God was more real to her
than Ellis, more real to her than Benjie. . . . But
to-night she heard no reassuring voice.   She rose
from her knees in a struggle of bewilderment, for,
coming she knew not whence, a wildness that
sometimes seized her, descended on her.   She
did not want to be here.   Her spirit was caught
away into a fantastic air of wind and rain, of
streams running wildly, of clouds tearing at the
turf, of the sea tossing at the foot of the hill.   Her
blood was not tamed.   Cold January night
though it was, she threw up her window and,
beyond the reddened haze of the gigantic town,
she saw Skiddaw's dividing lines, the serried
edge of Blencathra, and within the rhythm of a
solitary hansom's clatter was the whisper of the
running water against the shining boulder and
the bark of the dog beyond the sloping hill.
She thought of Judith.   She thought of her
father.   She thought of Will Leathwaite's slow
smile.

She closed the window. No. Oh no, she
could not marry Ellis!

A few days later came the invitation to the
Duchess of Wrexe's Ball, February 18th.

This Ball had been talked of all through the
winter. Very very seldom was there a big func-
tion at the Portland Place house, but when they
did have a show—well, it *was* a show! The old
Duchess must have some reason for this event.
Perhaps her eldest son Richard was at last to
marry. Or maybe John—or Adela. But the
Duchess herself of course would not appear.
Somewhere hidden in the dark confines of the
Portland Place house, unseen by all save a few
intimates who played cards with her, her physician
and the family, she plotted and planned. This
Ball was to be a protest, some people said, against
the new world that she detested, the Jewish
financiers, the American heiresses come to search for
titled husbands, the South Americans, the Theatre
and the rest. The Ball would be exceedingly exclusive. The Prince and Princess would be present.

It was very quickly an interesting question
as to who among the Herries had been invited.
Quite a number—Ellis, Vanessa, Carey, May,
Barney, little Cynthia and her mother. It was
characteristic of the family that so soon as it was
known that there would be several of them there,
everyone was satisfied. There was no individual
jealousy. Granted that the Herries were sufficiently represented, that was all that was necessary. There was no flavour of snobbery either.

It was important that members of the family
should be present because it would be for the
general good of English Society. Anything anywhere was better for having a mixture of Herries
in it. Barney was invited because of his friendship with Johnnie Beaminster. Little Cynthia
had achieved quite a friendship with Lady Adela.
Moreover, the Herries were the type of English
of which the Duchess approved—not Upper Ten,
of course, but good sound English stock with
practically no foreign mixture. The snobbery,
in fact, was *English*, not *Herries*. Barney commented on this. ' The English will always be
snobs because they care about caste. But it's a
fine sort of snobbery as the world is at present.
Keeps the right people at the top. One day when
the whole world is democratic and cares more for
doing things than being them, it will all seem most
ridiculous. Then England will become a third-
rate Power and everyone will be happier than
they've been for centuries.'

They were having an artistic hour at the Winter
Exhibition of the Royal Society of Painters in
Water Colours, Vanessa and Barney, Horace and
Rose. Very delightful, Vanessa thought the
pictures. Mr. Birket Foster's grand ' West High-
lands' made her feel quite sick for home, and
Sir John Gilbert's ' Retreat ' was splendid. Mr.
Watson's ' Bathers' Pool ' was enchanting, and
Du Maurier's ' Last Look at Whitby ' so very
clever. But best of all Mr. Goodwin's ' Strayed
Sheep,' so homely and English with its cawing
rooks and gentle colours.

' Oh, Horace, *do* look at the pictures! What have we come here for! '

But Horace's thoughts were on England.

' Really, Barney! England a third-rate Power! What about our Empire ? ' Everyone was beginning to beat on the word Empire as though it were the family gong.

' Our Empire! Who says it's ours? It's ours for the moment. One day it will be off on its own.'

' Politics are *so* tiresome,' said Rose. ' Doesn't that man over there look like the Claimant? He's been appearing at a music-hall. Yes, dear, I think the pictures are sweetly pretty.' She wandered off, her arm through Vanessa's. ' Vanessa darling, do you think Ellis would lend me fifty pounds if I were to ask him? '

' Oh, Rose, I shouldn't. Can't you get it in any other way? '

' Not without being under painful obligations. Oh, do look at Horace watching the door so that if anyone useful comes in he can snatch at them! '

' Rose, dear, are you in a fix? '

' Yes, I am—about ten fixes.'

' Perhaps I can help. How much do you truly need? '

' About twelve hundred pounds. But twenty would help.'

' I think I can manage that.'

' Oh, you are good to me! ' Rose was charming when she was grateful. She looked so pretty, so young, so sincere. She *was* sincere. She loved to be grateful—but to the right people.

Vanessa, thinking about this and other things, discovered that the family had come to regard her as Ellis' private conscience. When anyone wanted anything of Ellis, an opinion, an invitation, a tip from the City, Vanessa was the oracle. She could do with him, they said, anything that she liked. She knew that she could.

Then a little incident occurred. One afternoon when he had just returned from the City and they were discussing the evening plans, Ellis cut his hand. He was sharpening a pencil, the knife slipped. It was a bad gash, blood flowed, he turned ashen. She rang the bell for Buller, the butler, and helped Ellis to a chair, staunching the blood with his handkerchief, which soon was soaked. Very white, he leaned back against her, her arm around him. She thought that he would faint. Smiling very wanly he kissed her cheek. She did not move. His slender body in her arm, his confident reliance on her, his touching submission, made her feel as though he were her child. As she waited for Buller to come she thought that when Ellis depended on her for comfort she could do anything for him. At that moment she loved him. He said something, and she bent forward to catch his words. Her cheek touched his.

' I think I am going to faint.'

' Buller will be here in a moment.'

Her arm tightened about him. She just heard him sigh.

' Oh, Vanessa, how I love you! '

Then Buller came in, advancing as he always

did like a churchwarden to whom the morning's
money offerings had proved disappointing.

' Sir Ellis has cut his hand badly. Get brandy,
Buller, and something to bandage it with.'

She sat there, with Ellis in her arms. Miss
Fortescue appeared in the doorway, then hurried
forward.

' Oh, Sir Ellis, what *have* you done? '

' Only a slight cut, Miss Fortescue. Buller
has gone for some brandy.'

Miss Fortescue looked at them darkly.

' How that woman does hate me! ' Vanessa
thought.

As January drew to a close and February began
there were only two topics in the London world:
General Gordon and the Beaminster Ball. About
the first it was said on the one side that an awful
mistake had been made, on the other that exactly
the right thing had been done. About the Ball
it was said that it would be the grandest ever
given.

On the 24th of January the steamers started up
the Nile on an advance on Khartoum; on February 6th it was known that Khartoum had fallen
and the relief force had been too late. Meanwhile,
having satisfied himself that Khartoum was wholly
in the Mahdi's hands, Sir Charles Wilson had
turned his steamers and gone down stream. Then
for ten days England remained in suspense. On
the 16th of February a telegram was published
from Wolseley saying that Gordon had been killed.

Vanessa came down to breakfast on that morn-

ing to find family prayers over and Ellis standing
with *The Times* shaking in his hand.

' A crime! ' he cried, with an odd shrill voice
that she had never heard before. ' The most
monstrous crime! Gladstone will never be forgiven for this! Never! Never! Never! '

She thought for a moment that she had to do
with a madman. His pale eyes were shining, his
hands jerking the newspaper as though they would
tear it. They were alone, for Carey and May had
not yet come down and Miss Fortescue had meals
in her own fierce fastnesses.

' What is it? What has happened? '

' Gordon has been murdered! We have basely
deserted him. Left the bravest Saint and Hero to
go to his death alone! England will be shamed
before all the world! '

' Gordon murdered! Gordon killed! '

' Yes, yes; there is the telegram! '

It seemed in thousands of homes that morning
as though a veil of darkness fell over the world.
Nothing could be clearer, simpler than that splendid figure, selfless, a missionary thinking only of
his God, fearless; it was told of him how he had
gone through all the campaign in China, his only
weapon a cane, of how he had thought always of
everyone but himself in the Sudan. It seemed
now that the blackest treachery, the meanest poli-
tical chicanery had betrayed him. There were
other colours in the real picture, and it says something for the accused that, through all those weeks
of almost insane vituperation, they never attempted to dim the saintliness, the courage, the

selflessness. But Gordon's death was, perhaps, the first warning cloud on a horizon that had been now for a whole decade stainlessly blue.

That terrible news had also its private personal repercussions.

Ellis dropped the paper to the floor, sat down by the table, then, speaking now quietly, said:

' I feel as though I had myself betrayed him. Why do we all wait and trust to a kind of luck? Why are we all so cowardly? Vanessa, I am bitterly ashamed.'

His hand trembled against the tablecloth.

' I never thought that it would happen,' he said. ' I was afraid sometimes, but Gladstone was so sure. We have come to think that Gladstone always has God in his pocket. That they have intimate talks together and Gladstone tells God what to do. Well, this time God has not listened.'

Ellis was always best when he forgot himself. He had a kind of almost fanatical pure-mindedness at such times. Then something robbed him of his self-consciousness, his fears, his absurd egotisms. He would now have thrown his money, his physical cowardice, his fear of offending public opinion, even his Herries blood, out of window could he, by doing so, have saved Gordon. He had a kind of grandeur.

He and Vanessa were very close at that moment. He took her hand.

' Oh, Vanessa! ' he sighed. ' You and I—if only together we could help it to be a better world! '

Then Carey and May came in and the world

was at once a more mundane place. After breakfast Vanessa went upstairs to find old Lady Herries
in tears.

'Oh, poor General Gordon! All alone! Such
a good man! Those savages! And Gladstone
worse than any of them!'

Then as though she realised that Ellis downstairs must be very unhappy, her last word to
Vanessa was:

'Be kind to Ellis, won't you, my dear?'

We quickly forget. Two days later, although
Gordon's death was the only topic, the tragedy
had become impersonal. No one any longer
thought it was possible to have died at his side.
Not even perhaps quite desirable. What *was*
desirable was to have Mr. Gladstone's head on a
charger.

Vanessa went to the Beaminster Ball in a turmoil of varying emotions. There was, of course,
her dress, the loveliest that she had ever had. It
was a white dress, with a red rose fastened at the
narrow waist its only ornament. The bodice fitted
very tightly to the figure. She wore long white
gloves and carried a beautiful white fan of ostrich
feathers, a present from Lady Herries. Her only
ornament was a diamond brooch, bequeathed her
by Judith, fastened on her right shoulder. The
effect of her dark hair and all this cloud of dazzling
whiteness was very splendid, but, Ellis thought as
he glanced at her, it was the softness of her eyes,
the charm and kindliness of her eagerness, her
youth, her excitement, her happiness that made

her so brilliant, so unlike anyone else. For to-
night she *was* happy. She could have taken all
London into her arms and embraced it. Her
mind was set on the future, the life that she would
make for herself, the friendliness of all the world.
She was aware of her beauty and delighted that
she was beautiful. She had never *believed* that
a dress could be so marvellous a fit! She would
see the Prince and Princess! How good and
kind of Ellis to give her all this happiness! She
let her gloved hand rest on Ellis' coat as the
carriage rolled on through the lighted streets and
she heard men calling as though it were for her
that they were crying some message. She sat very
straight, her head forward, taking all this life into
her heart and intending to give it out again with
all the fullness of which she was capable. Benjie
was never out of her mind, but to-night he was
in the back of her consciousness. One day she
would be with him again, quietly, confidently, his
friend. Perhaps after all it had been for the best.
This was the safer way.

They halted. They were in a stream of
carriages that stretched down Portland Place.
Then on either side of the red carpet was a crowd
of sightseers whom a large policeman kept in
order. Vanessa and May passed up the steps,
into the hall. Looking up for a moment before
she turned to the right to the cloakroom Vanessa
saw a line of footmen in red coats and velvet knee-
breeches on either side of the great staircase.
Dimly she heard the echoes of the band.

As she arranged her hair before the looking-glass she heard May's whisper: ' Oh, you do look lovely, Vanessa darling! '

Ellis and Carey were waiting for them and slowly they mounted the staircase. At the top Adela Beaminster, blazing in diamonds, received them.

' Lord and Lady Rockage! '

' Sir Ellis Herries! '

' Miss Vanessa Paris! '

They passed on into the ballroom. It was one of the famous rooms in London with its white walls and gold ceiling, and on the white walls were hanging the Lelys, the Van Dycks, the other famous Beaminster portraits. The far end of the great room where the band played was banked with masses of white flowers. Although so many people were standing about there was plenty of dancing-space. The roar of voices rolled in waves from wall to wall.

She stood at first with May, extremely happy, quite contented to watch. Decorations were worn, the dresses of the women were superb. How ridiculous of her to have been proud of her own! She had never seen in one place so many beautiful women. The air sparkled with diamonds. A tall thin woman near her was wearing a tiara that focused all the light to itself, that made, in truth, her plain pale face shadowed like a mask. Vanessa unfolded her fan and stood, waving it slowly, smiling as though she could never have enough of this lovely scene.

She was not, however, to be left alone for long. Soon one man came up to her and then another.

During these months in London she had made
many friends and was in fact very much better
known than she had any idea of. A Captain
Verrier, who had been sending her flowers, who
had taken her and May on one occasion to
Hurlingham, asked her to dance. She adored to
waltz—surely there was no experience in life so
perfect! He talked to her, but she answered him
only in monosyllables. When the music stopped
and they had moved into a long narrow room
beyond the ballroom and sat down, he said to
her:

' I don't think you heard a word I said when
we were dancing.'

' No. I love dancing so much, it seems a pity
to talk.'

' I'm sorry, because I said some very amusing
things.'

' You can tell them me now, Captain Verrier.'

' You know, to look at you, Miss Paris, one
would imagine that you had never been to a Ball
before.'

' I never have—a Ball like this. When will
the Prince and Princess come? '

' Oh, later on. About midnight, I expect.'

' And is the Duchess sitting in her room
upstairs all this time? '

' Yes. Like a field-marshal. And her generals
deliver despatches.'

' I saw her once. She came to a party in
Hill Street.'

' Yes. She went out for a little while some
years ago. But she soon went in again. She

found that her importance was lessened as soon
as she became visible.'

Then he began to make love to her. Laughing, she stopped him.

' Are you asking me to marry you? '

He was embarrassed.

' Well, no, not exactly.   You see——'

' I should make a very bad mistress, I am
afraid.   I can imagine nothing more uncomfortable.'

' Oh no.   You misunderstand me.   I only
meant——'

' I like you very much, and I am very glad we
are friends.'

' You are not offended? '

' Oh dear, no.   Why should I be?   Only why
don't you marry?   There are so many nice girls
who are longing to be married——'

' Well, you see, I haven't a penny.   Only my
pay——'

They discussed his affairs, and Vanessa was
very maternal.

After that she was dancing all the time.   She
found everyone delightful.   Some tried to make
love to her, some confided their troubles to her,
some laughed and behaved like schoolboys, some
were extremely pompous, one asked her to go to
India with him.

' India! ' she cried.   ' What should I do in
India? '

He was not sure, except that she would make
him very happy.

Then something occurred which, on looking

back afterwards, affected, she found, strongly her
later behaviour that night. Barney appeared and
with him a charming, shy young man.

'Vanessa,' Barney said, 'here is a cousin of
yours. An unknown cousin. Be kind to him.'

The boy, who looked about nineteen, was
slender and tall with fair hair and bright, in-
genuous blue eyes.

'I'm not a good dancer,' he said, blushing
furiously. 'Shall we sit this out? I think that
you will be more comfortable that way.'

She discovered that his name was Adrian
Cards and that he was at New College, Oxford.
He was a younger brother of the Ruth and
Richard Cards who had, years ago, been present
at Judith's Hundredth Birthday. He was a great-
nephew of Jennifer Cards, Benjie's grandmother.

At first he was very shy, but no one could be
shy for long with Vanessa. He began to pour
out his heart. He had many enthusiasms. Litera-
ture. No, he did not like the Aesthetes much.
They still read Swinburne, but were not he and
Tennyson a little—well, pontifical? The earlier
Browning, but not these ' Inn Albums ' and things.
Pater, yes. The *Renaissance* was wonderful. He
had met Pater. A Society called ' The Passionate
Pilgrims ' had invited him, and there he had sat,
cross-legged, looking rather like a Chinaman.
He had seen Matthew Arnold and often Jowett.
You could see Miss Rhoda Broughton out walk-
ing. But he was all, she discovered, for phil-
anthropy! Toynbee Hall, W. T. Stead. They
had started a Mission in Bethnal Green that he

visited. Oh, Miss Paris, he did hope that she would not think him a prig. He was not that. He rowed in his College boat. He didn't like saints, he did not wish to improve people's *souls* —no, but their *bodies*! Oh, Miss Paris! Did she *know* of the distress and unemployment? Did she realise that last month four thousand men came to the Mayor in Birmingham and asked for work, that they were starving and could scarcely stand? Had she heard of the Industrial Remuneration Conference, of all the things that the Trades Unions were doing? There was a Mr. Bernard Shaw who had read a brilliant paper, and Mr. John Burns had warned them all of what England would be in another thirty years! He was burning with it all, words poured from him, while the splendour and almost fantastic pageantry of the evening passed backwards and forwards in front of them.

Then he checked himself with a most charming smile.

'You have been so sympathetic! I am ashamed of my preaching. But you are staying with Cousin Ellis, are you not? I can't help thinking of all he might do with his money if he liked! Can't you influence him, Miss Paris?'

'Don't call me Miss Paris,' she said. 'We are cousins, you know. My name is Vanessa.'

'Oh, thank you. And *my* name is Adrian.'

'Yes, Barney told me.'

'Cannot you influence him? The things he could do! If only you could persuade him just once to go to Bethnal Green.'

She told him that she had very little influence with anyone.

'Someone as beautiful as you are must have influence! Oh, I beg your pardon! Have I been impertinent?' He broke off and then with the same eagerness he asked her about Cumberland. He had never been there. Ruth had told him how lovely it was! She often spoke of Madame. What a marvellous old lady she must have been! And how sad that the house at Uldale had been burnt down!

'Oh, your father——' He was always rushing in and then out again!

'No, I like to talk of my father. He was the best man who ever lived!' She began to tell him things about Adam and Cat Bells and Uldale. She told him about Hesket and Caldbeck, of John Peel and the Herdwick sheep and the best-cured hams in the world. They had there the largest water-wheel and the smallest parish in England. Of the grand old farmers and their splendid ploughing, of an old lady she knew who had eighteen children and was ninety to-day, of how if you asked an old ploughman, strong as the horse he was leading, how old he was, he'd say 'Ah's nobbut eighty!' of how they would sing 'Old Towler' under the fellside, of Tom Pearson, the wrestler, who could dance a better step-dance than any woman, of the 'Ivinson' grey tweed, the strongest in the world—and, as she talked, all Skiddaw broke into the London house, clouds came down over the gold ceiling, and the bleating of the sheep was louder than the band!

She had missed a dance with someone or
other. She rose and held out her hand.

'You'll come and see me, Adrian? Come
to-morrow to Hill Street, tea-time.'

'Yes, I will,' he said fervently.

But when she was dancing again she knew that
something had happened to her. The wildness
was upon her again, but now it was full of fear and
warning. She must not return to Cumberland!
She must make her life in another fashion. Where
Benjie was, danger lay. That boy was right. It
was being shown to her clearly that, at the side
of Ellis, she should help the world. The two of
them together—what could they not do? Ellis
had told her that he was waiting for her to help
him. Already in these weeks in London they
had grown close together. At the thought of all
they could do for the world her cheeks burned,
her heart beat high.

She had been living without any thought of
all the unhappiness, the poverty! The things
that Ellis and she might do together. . .!

There was a pause. Everyone moved to the
right and left. The Prince and Princess had
arrived.

They walked up the room, bowing and smiling,
stopping once and again to speak to a friend,
while the women curtsied and the band blared.
It was a glorious moment. He looked so kindly
and she so beautiful. England was safe for ever
and ever: the peoples of the world were bowing.
A hero had died for his country in the Sudan.
Here and there were a ruffian or two to be taught

their place and duty! The Beaminster portraits smiled down their loyalty and patriotism, the jewels blazed, England lay like a cloak at the royal feet, and the Empire did obeisance.

' Oh! to do something splendid! ' Vanessa's heart cried.

It was Ellis who took her in to supper. He was quiet, stealing glances at her once and again. She seemed to be carried high on some wave of exaltation. She looked at him so kindly that when they moved away and sat down together in a distant corner where from the hall below they could hear them summoning the carriages, he said, now for the third time:

' Vanessa, will you marry me? '

She, staring beyond him into an imagined world, nodded her head, saying:

' Yes, Ellis dear—if you want me.'

END OF PART I

PART II

THE HUSBAND

JUBILEE

EARLY in June of the great year 1887 Ellis and Vanessa went one evening to hear Albani in *Lucia* and, waiting in the portico of the Opera House, were caught by a breeze that, in spite of the warm evening, made Ellis its victim.

In the following days he paid no attention to his chill, sternly from morn to eve pursuing his City adventures. On the eighteenth of June there was a grand party in Hill Street, a Jubilee party, with Royalty and Colonel Cody. Next day Ellis was threatened with pneumonia. On the morning of the supreme Tuesday he was as hopelessly a prisoner as any poor wretch in Vine Street.

It was a tragedy. Ellis and Vanessa had seats in the Abbey; for months Ellis had looked forward and, in his odd way, half child, half man of importance, he had come to feel (as perhaps many other Herries were feeling) that the Jubilee was created only that he should sit with the loveliest woman in London and give his approbation to his Queen's Thanksgiving.

He lay there, his cheeks mottled, his nose sharp and white, his thin body stretched like a corpse, his eyes rheumy with cold and bitter disappointment. Vanessa refused to go to the Abbey with-

out him. She would watch the Procession from
Piccadilly with Rose and Barney and young
Adrian. When she came in to say good-bye she
felt so vividly his own bitterness that she cried:
' Ellis, I won't go. I'll stay here with you. Rose
will tell me all about it, and besides the heat is
fearful or will be soon. Ellis, I'll stay.'

He longed to agree that she should. He would
not miss it so grievously if she also missed it, and
the thought that she had given this up for him
would be a salve to that intolerable unceasing
doubt, the doubt that she loved him.

But he was not so selfish; no, no, he was not so
selfish. So, in a voice thick with cold, drawing
the bedclothes close to his chin, he murmured:
' Absurd! How absurd you are, my darling!
You had better not kiss me. Go and enjoy
yourself!'

He knew that when she was gone he would
repeat to himself again and again: ' She offered
to stay. One word from me and she would have
stayed.'

How beautiful she was! He watched her
hungrily. Her dress with its full bustle, rose-
coloured, fitted her tall graceful body with exquisite symmetry. No woman in London wore
clothes as Vanessa did; the little hat, perched
on her dark hair, was wreathed with rose-buds.
The parasol that she carried was rose. Two roses,
dark and rich like the summer weather, were at
her waist. She was a Queen, he thought. Had
we gone to the Abbey she would have been
lovelier than any other woman there. ' The beauti-

ful Lady Herries . . .' and he would have been
with her, the proudest man in England.

'Give me some more of those drops, dear,
before you go.'

She thought the big bare room chill and stuffy.
Beyond the window the sun blazed on the street;
very faintly from the far distance came the sound
of a band. She could see a flag gently moving in
the morning breeze from an opposite house. She
was all impatience to be gone. She might be a
grand lady now who must never forget her dignity,
but for nothing at all she would dance down Hill
Street waving her parasol. How terrible had he
said: 'Yes, dear. Remain!' How terrible not
to see the kings and the princes, not to hear the
blare of the bands, not to see the colour and the
excited happy faces of the people, not to wave to
the Queen! She was so sorry for his disappointment that tears filled her eyes as she smoothed his
thin hair with her hand, straightened the bedclothes, laid the books and *The Times* close to
him! How old he looked when he was ill!
How old and how at the same time like an ugly
disappointed little boy! How near and how intimate to him she was, and how far-away and
separate! How kind and tender she wished to be
to him! And how her very heart contracted in
her breast when he made love to her! How
grateful for all his kindness, how deeply irritated,
against her will, by his unceasing care of her!

She sat in the chair beside his bed, holding his
hot dry hand.

'You will take care not to be in the sun.'

' Oh yes, there is a large awning over our
stand.'

He was moved by a sudden spasm of irritation
and kicked up his knees beneath the bedclothes.

' It is too bad. It is really too bad. To happen
just now! In another week I could have gone! '

' I know, I know, dear. Oh, why did we go
to that silly Opera? . . . Ellis, let me stay! I'll
go with Rose this evening and see the illuminations. . . . After all it is going to be so hot,
most uncomfortable, I expect, and a procession
is always so quickly over. . . .'

He sighed. How wonderful if it had been she
who was ill and he had been given the opportunity of sacrificing himself! At once he was
ashamed of such a thought. His love for Vanessa
prompted him to strange wicked desires. He
who would give her anything in the world, to wish
anything so wicked! He choked, coughed, drank
a little water, smiled with wan bravery.

' What you must think me! As though I could
be so selfish! Enjoy yourself, my dearest, and
tell me about it. . . .'

He picked up Walter Besant's novel, laid it
pathetically on the bedclothes. ' I shall count the
minutes until your return.'

Afterwards in the sun and splendour she felt
as though she had escaped, by a miracle, from
prison.

Early though it was, the streets were thronged
and the stands already crowded, but she had only
to slip down Berkeley Square and in at a back

door, be conducted by an extremely polite young footman through a drawing-room and so out to the stand where Rose already was.

When she settled herself and looked about her she uttered a cry of childlike delight. The sky was an unbroken blue, the full green of the trees of the Green Park was soft and deep and luminous like a sunlit cloud. From her seat she could watch the hovering flutter of the flags, the massed colour of clothes, the splashes of scarlet that broke the pearl-grey of the London stone. All this colour was translated by the sunlight into something trembling and unsubstantial as though lit by some unseen fire. There was a brooding silence scored like a sheet of music with the clatter of a horse's hoofs, the echo of distant band music rising and falling on the slight morning breeze. Above the buildings flags drifted against the blue as though under the impulse of some secret rhythm. The front of the stand was banked with flowers.

She sat there, her gloved hands clasped, her lips parted, her eyes shining. At that moment, if she had been ordered, she would have died for her country, for the Queen, for any cause that needed her. For a very little thing she would have burst into tears.

Rose, who looked very exotic with her dark colour, her red dress, was as deeply excited as Vanessa.

'This is all very foolish,' she said. 'By this afternoon I shall be ashamed of myself. No matter, I like being ashamed of myself.'

Rose read from her programme:

Her Majesty will be accompanied on horseback by the following Princes placed in the order of their relationship to Her Majesty:

Grandsons and Grandsons-in-Law of Her Majesty

H.I.H. the Grand Duke Serge of Russia

H.R.H. the Prince Henry of Prussia, G.C.B.

His Highness the Hereditary Prince of Saxe-Meiningen

H.R.H. the Prince Albert Victor of Wales, K.G.

H.R.H. the Prince George of Wales, K.G.

His Highness the Prince Christian Victor of Schleswig-Holstein

H.R.H. the Prince William of Prussia, K.G.

H.R.H. the Hereditary Grand Duke of Hesse.

His Serene Highness the Prince Louis of Battenberg, K.C.B.

Sons-in-Law of Her Majesty

H.R.H. the Prince Christian of Schleswig - Holstein, K.G.

His Imperial and Royal Highness the Crown Prince of Germany, K.G.

H.R.H. the Grand Duke of Hesse, K.G.

Sons of Her Majesty

H.R.H. the Duke of Connaught and Strathearn, K.G.

H.R.H. the Prince of Wales, K.G.

H.R.H. the Duke of Edinburgh, K.G.

She talked without ceasing, waving her hands, half rising from her seat, turning to look for friends. Did Vanessa know that people were paying twenty-five pounds for a good place? That nearly three hundred books of gold leaf had been used for decorating the State Coach, that there was still living a survivor of George III.'s Jubilee, an old lady in Gloucestershire, that the Pope is so pleased at the Jubilee that he wants

England to re-establish relations with the Vatican, that so much gas was to be used in the illuminations, that . . .?

She said:

' Oh, Vanessa, I am so happy! '

She caught Vanessa's hand, then drew away again whispering:

' No, I won't spoil your fun. Don't listen to me. It isn't true. I'm too excited to know what I am saying.'

Vanessa turned to her.

' Rose, what has happened? What have you done? '

' Nothing. Nothing. I didn't mean what I said.' Then abruptly again she broke out:

' You know that Horace is engaged? '

' No. When? To whom? '

' A few nights ago—at the Ball at the Reform Club. A Miss Lindsay. A nice little girl. With money of course. And he will treat her abominably.'

' You'll be alone, Rose. You won't like that even though Horace isn't the most——'

' No. Yes. Well, perhaps.'

' Rose, you are going to do something foolish. What is it? Tell me. I insist on your telling me.'

Their lives had been bound together. Ever since that day of Judith's Hundredth Birthday when Vanessa, looking across the luncheon table, had seen her, wanted her for a friend, loved her, there had been a bond which Rose's recklessness, her risks and mistakes and gradual descent from safety into danger, had only strengthened.

K 2

' Vanessa, you will always love me, always, always, whatever I do? '

So also Benjie had claimed. She had fulfilled her promise. She laid her hand on Rose's arm.

' Rose, don't do anything without telling me. You must not. It is not fair to me. We have been friends so long and have helped one another so often. Promise me! Promise me! '

' Look! There is someone riding up the street. He is seeing that everything is clear. Doesn't he look grand with his feathers? '

' Rose, tell me. What are you doing? Not Fred Wycherley? You told me——'

' Vanessa, darling—it is all right. Really it is. I was excited. I'm always doing something silly. Look! how the stands are filling up! Why don't Barney and Adrian come? They are missing everything——'

' But it isn't Wycherley? Promise me that it isn't Wycherley—with his wife and those two children——'

' No, of course it isn't Fred. Oh, do look at that woman in that bonnet! There, to the right! Did you ever *see* such a thing? '

At that moment Barney and Adrian Cards arrived.

Adrian, who, young as he was, was now in the Foreign Office, who wrote articles for the magazines on religion, economics, French poetry, who loved Vanessa with such open devotion that everyone thought it charming, sat on one side of her, Barney, who was now very stout, on the other.

' Here we are! ' said Barney. ' I have just

seen Timothy and Violet and their offspring.'
(Timothy had brought his family with him permanently to London.)

'I have also seen Phyllis and Rochester struggling for breath in Northumberland Avenue,
Amery, son Alfred, and the new plain wife nest-
ling under the lions in Trafalgar Square, so I have
not done so badly by the family. How is poor
Ellis?'

'Oh, Barney,' said Vanessa, ' he was crying
with disappointment. He had been *so* looking
forward——'

'Yes. It's a shame. Poor Ellis.' But he
was not thinking of poor Ellis as he leant his fat
body forward and drank in delightedly the scene,
except perhaps, without any unkindness, to relish
his own fun the more because Ellis' catastrophe
made him realise that he too might have caught
a cold and been prevented. He pushed out his
chest, stretched his stout arms a little, wondered
how little Daisy McPhail (the present lady of his
apartments) was getting on somewhere along the
Mall (he had loved her now for three months and
still found her good company), considered (as
all novelists consider) whether he would be able
to describe this heat, colour, movement, expectation on paper, looked at Vanessa and marvelled
yet once again at her beauty (' But this life with
Ellis is telling on her, and I don't wonder ');
leaned yet further forward to gaze down Piccadilly
and saw, a little to the right, only a row or two
away, Benjamin Herries.

'By Heaven——'

' What is it? ' Rose asked—and he could feel that she was trembling with some agitation deeper than any Jubilee warranted.

' Nothing.' He had pulled himself in. ' Only that everything is so jolly. *What* a day! Doesn't that old lady have luck with her weather? ' (*Was* it Benjie? Yes, certainly. He had half turned. He had seen then.) Barney suddenly was assured that Benjie had seen Vanessa from the moment of her first entry. The little man, square-backed, brown as a berry, in some fashion independent, alone like a hill-man who had come down to study, for a moment, the people of the plain, sat erect, his chin resting on the handle of his stick, the most significant thing about him his living, questing, eager eyes.

' A bandit! ' Barney thought. ' For tuppence he'd hold a gun at the lot of us! '

Benjie half turned again and gave Barney a nod, slight, humorous, secret.

' His eye never leaves Vanessa. But Vanessa must not see him. Lucky that Ellis is locked away in Hill Street! '

And again, like any novelist, he considered that here was a situation, old and hackneyed though it might be, that would make a chapter or two: Benjie, Ellis, Vanessa—all of them so much more real than anything that Barney could do on paper. And he summed up for judgment the half-written efforts of his present work, *Julia Paddock* . . . Poor thing, how she wilted and died before the sharp indifference of actual life!

' Look here, Adrian, change places with me,

will you? I'm a bit deaf in this right ear. Creeping senility, you know.'

They changed places, Adrian seated now between Vanessa and Rose. Barney's broad body would, with decent luck, hide Benjie from Vanessa.

Young Adrian talked of the People's Palace which Besant's *All Sorts and Conditions of Men* had started as popular philanthropy. Vanessa was on a Committee. Mr. Besant had come to tea in Hill Street. A nice, booming, self-confident, bustling kind of man.

'Oh, don't let's think of committees!' cried Vanessa. 'This is so much nicer. I'm not very good at committees, Adrian. My thoughts wander.'

He was only twenty-two years of age, and Vanessa was the love of his whole life. He had the imagination of the abnormal, but with it the common sense and balance of the normal. He was, in fact, closer to Will and Ellis and Timothy and old Pomfret than to Francis and John and Adam. He would never commit suicide nor dream his life away. His philanthropy, idealism, poetry, would be practical, definite things. He was the straight, normal Herries at its best. So, looking at Vanessa, he worshipped her without any thought of contact. She was the greatest lady he would ever know, the kindest, the loveliest. And how glorious to be beside her to-day when she was like a child in her pleasure! He had seen her of late so often as the hostess sitting at the end of her table at those endless dinner parties in Hill Street, curtsying to Royalty, talking to Ambassadors, moving down the room with all eyes upon her. . . . Now, for an hour, she was close to him, friend with friend. Not that she was ever affected or grand. The world in which for two years now she had moved had not touched her, but, as he had often noticed, when Ellis was not there, she was free, spontaneous, self-forgetful. . . .

'Oh! they are coming!' she cried. 'They are coming! I can hear the bands!'

Distant music broke across the heat and light as though somewhere a door had opened. All individuality was lost; colours, blue, crimson, green, hung like painted cloths about an empty room, for here in the sunlight. there was a bare space which only one figure could fill. The empty room waited for that entrance; the door would be opened and soon, for the briefest instant, a small stout old lady would be borne forward, would stay for a moment, looking about her while the colour, the music, the sunlight made a canopy over her; then, with a little bow, she would retire and all would be ended. A bell would ring, a trumpet blare, the door would close.

A kind of sanctification fell upon those people. They turned, their eyes straining down that long pathway between the banks of colour, a pathway so oddly bare. There was a fear of a last instant's frustration. Would a thunderbolt fall, the final trumpets for Judgment sound, and so—after the agonised anticipation—that royal carriage with the little bowing figure never appear? The sky, the trees, the flags, the splashes of crimson, all a painted prepared pattern for that instant of completion that even yet might not occur. Vanessa, looking upwards for a moment, saw three birds, dark and remote, slowly fly across the blue. At the sight of the first advancing soldier, glittering in the sun, his black horse moving with dignified austerity, she turned to Barney and whispered:

' My father met my mother for the first time on the Queen's Coronation Day.'

She wanted to evoke Adam. She wanted him there with his kind, sleepy smile and that touch of his hand on her arm. . . . Then she forgot everything but the Procession. Thicker and thicker they came. The pathway that had been so bare sparkled now with silver and gold. She was drawn down into a medley of colours, sounds, and, pressing close upon her, that clear clop-clop of the horses' hoofs like the ringing of little hammers on stone. Men were detached from the river of movement; a figure, the back straight as a board, the thighs stiff, one gauntleted hand raised, would become real against fantasy. You believed suddenly that it breathed, it touched its bearded cheek with its gauntlet: the rider and the horse stood out above the flood as though the trumpets had summoned it. The three Kings were in closed carriages—very disappointing of them. The cheering increased. Now, glittering with gold, an open carriage could be seen, and then, in an instant, the air broke into cheering, the caparisoned horses, the outriders, the scarlet and the gold swung into being before the green clouded trees. The Queen, her parasol raised, in a

dress of black and white, passed by. One horse-
man, in a silver helmet and shining cuirass,
seemed her especial guardian—the Crown Prince
of Germany. The door closed.

' Oh! ' said Vanessa. ' How lovely that was! '
The soldiers were still marching, the drums
and trumpets sounding, but the ordinary real
world had assumed its place again. She heard
someone behind her say: ' The twenty-sixth, remember. I'll have the carriage and we'll go
straight down.'

She sat there watching for a while, happy,
tranquil, remembering things to tell Ellis, suddenly thinking of Will Leathwaite in the cottage
on Cat Bells. He would be going out that evening
to see the bonfires and he would think of her as he
always did when anything of interest happened.

' Didn't you love that, Rose? Didn't you
think her splendid? '

But Rose was gone. How strange!

' Adrian, did you see Rose go? '

' Yes, she slipped away just after the Queen
passed. She didn't want to disturb you.'

' Oh, I wanted to tell her——' Vanessa
looked back to see whether she might yet catch
her. People were rising, moving about, already
many seats were empty.

Then, turning to the right, looking over
Barney's head, she saw Benjie.

He was staring at her, standing up in his place.
They looked at one another. He raised his hat,
bowed, gave her one more long stare; then,

turning his back, climbed up the wooden benches and disappeared.

She had invited Barney and Adrian to luncheon and they returned to the house with her, but, before she joined them, before she went in to see Ellis, she stood, without moving, in the middle of the floor of her bedroom, gazing in front of her. She had but a moment. Ellis, in the next room, knew that she had returned but, with the sunlight streaming about her, still wearing her hat and gloves, she stayed there, lost.

Benjie! She had not seen him for close on four years, but in that momentary glance it had been as it had always been. They had not separated. They *could* not separate. Marriage altered nothing, distance altered nothing; she must confess to herself what indeed she had never denied —that Benjie and herself could not be parted. He had looked as he always looked. His London clothes, his tall hat and dark coat could not change him, his apartness, his humorous defiance, his challenge to the world. He had been, apparently, alone. Had he been aware of her for a long while? Had he intended to speak to her? Was he staying in London? Was he here permanently, perhaps with his wife and boy? Or had he parted from his wife? Or was he on his way abroad? How strange that out of all the thousands who had watched the Procession they two should have been so close together. He could not have known where she would sit. Or had he perhaps met Barney the day before and asked him? Would he call at Hill Street or would he keep his part of their bargain? During these four years he had never written to her, nor sent a message. As she took off her hat and slowly drew off her gloves she knew that she would at that moment give everything—name, reputation, happiness—for one word with him.

Her body shivered. She knelt down for an instant beside her bed, pressing her hands against her eyes. Oh, how she wished that she had not seen him! Oh, how glad, how glad she was that she had! The sunlight fell hot upon her head like a caress. She bathed her face and hands and went through into Ellis' room.

Ellis lay there, his long hands with their prominent knuckles on the counterpane, and he looked at her steadily, following her with his eyes as she moved as a painted portrait does.

She came to the bed, sat down, took his hand and began to tell him all about everything. ' The colour, Ellis! You can't imagine it! The trees of the Park made everything so much brighter, and then the splashes of scarlet and the grey buildings and all the flowers. We had beautiful places, better than the Abbey. We could see both ways down Piccadilly and had a view of the Queen's carriage for ever so long. Rose was there. She was rather restless. I do hope she isn't getting into trouble again. And Barney and Adrian. Barney is really disgracefully fat. He said he'd seen Timothy and Violet and Amery and his son.'

' Did you see anyone else you knew? '

She realised at once that Ellis was hostile, that

something had happened here in her absence.
Had Benjie called? Had he written? Had
Barney been up to see Ellis already and told him?
Oh, but he would not! That was not Barney's
way. Had someone else seen Benjie about
London and told Ellis? Since their marriage
Ellis had never uttered Benjie's name. . . .

She answered quickly:

' No one to speak to. We left before the Procession was over to escape the crowd. And we
did. The Square was quite empty. Not a soul
about. But the crush in the streets was dreadful,
and what the heat must have been . . .'

He interrupted in that small cold voice always
used by him when he was offended (he was very
proud of it: he thought it was calculated to strike
terror into any heart).

' Some letters came for you while you were
away.'

So that was it! There was a letter for her in
some hand that he suspected. She had noticed
of late that he looked at the writing on the en-
velopes of her letters with an eager curiosity which
he always thought that he hid.

' Miss Fortescue brought them in,' he went on.
' She thought that you were still here.'

(' She *knew* that I was *not* here,' Vanessa
thought indignantly.)

The letters were in a little pile on a table near
the door. She went across, picked them up,
then turned and smiled at Ellis. ' Well,' she
said, ' what has disturbed you, Ellis? Something has made you unhappy.'

He said at once, his voice shaking:

'One of those letters is from Benjamin Herries.'

(Was it so? Then he had written to tell her that he was coming to London? He had written to make an appointment?)

She looked quickly. There was no letter from Benjie. One, in a man's hand, was from Keswick, but, as she knew at once, it was from a Doctor Harris there who had written asking if she would subscribe to some sports to be held in August at Threlkeld. She did not dare even glimpse at her own fierce disappointment. She was *not* disappointed. It was *much* better that Benjie should not write, should never write, never see her, never speak to her. . . .

She came quietly to the bedside and gave Ellis the letter.

'There is nothing from Benjie. This, I suppose, is the letter you meant. Read it.'

He looked quickly at the letters, then pushed them towards her.

'No, no. Of course I will not read them. I am very ashamed. Please, please forgive me. If you knew how I have been suffering!'

'It has done your cold good anyway,' she thought, 'having something else to think about.'

Her anger and indignation, of which she was always afraid because they were so strong when they were aroused, stirred in her eyes. She did not ask herself whether her disappointment assisted her anger.

' Please read them, Ellis, if you want to. I
have no secrets from you whatever.' (Had she
not?)

He looked up at her abjectly, a look that she
detested, in human beings, in animals, in anyone
or anything that should have pride.

' Please, please forgive me. The handwriting
was like. I thought that he might be coming to
London for the Jubilee. I have been lying here
all these hours longing for you. . . . You are so
beautiful to-day. . . . I love you so terribly. I
cannot grow used to it. I used to think that in
time it would become part of life, ordinary, but
it does not. It is stronger every day because it is
never satisfied. It is not your fault. But you
don't love me. You never loved me.'

That was just. That was true. At once she
felt tender towards him because of that injustice.
He was like a small son who had asked for a
present that she could not give him, and so she
put her arms around him and comforted him.
She sat down beside him and took his hand
again.

' Ellis, dear, we all care for one another in
different ways. That is everybody's trouble.
I think perhaps I am not passionate in the way
you mean. Many women are not. But we are
such splendid friends. More every day. Let
us be thankful for that. And don't begin to
suspect things. Let's trust one another. If we
do not we shall torture one another. We have
been married for over two years and have trusted
one another perfectly. Ask me always if anything

makes you uneasy; suspicion in marriage is horrible. It's worthy of neither of us.'

He moved towards her, put his thin arms round her, laid his head on her breast.

' Love me! Love me! Love me!'

She tried to comfort him; her relief when at last he moved away made her feel ashamed. To-day something new had entered their married life, something not quite new. Rather a forgotten acquaintance who unexpectedly arrives and says that now, from henceforth, he will live in the house.

She kissed him and stood up.

' I must go down to Barney and Adrian. They are waiting for luncheon. I will come up afterwards.'

He lay staring at the door long after she had left the room.

And even then this day was not done with her. When Adrian and Barney were gone she went upstairs again and read Besant's novel aloud until Ellis slept. Then she went down to the drawing-room. She had done what she could with it. There was a portrait of her by Whistler in a white dress standing against a dull gold wallpaper, holding a fan. She had not filled the room with odds and ends as many of her friends liked to do. It had now a silver-grey wallpaper, there were many flowers about, there was a deep purple Persian carpet, but the place was not alive. It would never live, it would never be home to her. The two tall windows were open—a pale blue light shadowed the houses. The sky was pale with the evening heat. There was holiday everywhere, shouts and cries, distant bands, and the flags moving lazily in the gentle summer breeze. There was that scent of burning that a very hot day in London leaves behind it, and the odour of flowers, roses, carnations, and the dry dusty fragrance of geranium leaves. She turned back into the long dusky room that was like a cool deserted cave. She walked up and down, knowing that life, after two years of comparative quiescence, had in a moment taken another turn. Everything from this hour was different. To-night there was to be a family dinner-party. Ellis had insisted that his illness should make no change. Rose and Horace, Phyllis, Clarence Rochester and Philip, Barney, Amery and his son and new daughter-in-law, Timothy and Violet and Aunt Jane, Carey and May Rockage, pretty Cynthia, Rodney's granddaughter, and her husband Peile Worcester, Adrian . . . they were all coming. No one but the Family. What an odd mixed lot they were, and yet how alike—even the wives of other stock. They moved forward in one body, not to the outer world important and yet affecting the world by their quiet insistence on normality, confidence, the domestic virtues, patriotism, deep suspicion of the foreigner, belief in the Church, Tennyson, the Houses of Parliament, the Royal Family (with reservations about the Prince of Wales, Barney's mistresses, Rose's reputation, Jews—unless they were very rich—and one or two things more).

They had been very kindly to Vanessa. Old Lady Herries before she died last year had said:

' My dear, never fight the family. I know you often want to, but it isn't worth it. They always win in the end.'

But did they? Had not Judith defeated them, and Uhland and even her own father? The battle continued. She had not, herself, surrendered. And Benjie? Oh, *where* was he? Was he quite close to her somewhere in London? She had the maddest impulse to go to Barney's rooms in Duke Street. He would know, she was sure. She went to the door, opened it, and listened. The house was as still as the inside of a drum. Only the beating of her heart seemed to thud down the passages. Then there was something else. Someone was coming up the stairs.

She went back into the drawing-room with the wildest thought that it might be Benjie. What would she do? How could she defend both herself and him? She stood, one hand pressed to her breast, staring at the door. But, when it opened, it was Finch, the new butler, a man she did not like because she was sure that he was in league with Miss Fortescue, a fat red-faced man with sandy hair.

He had a note on the salver.

' A letter for you, my lady. A boy has just left it. He said that he was told that there was no answer.'

She saw at once that it was in Rose's hand, and as soon as Finch was gone, opened it, reading it there where she stood.

DEAREST—I could not tell you this morning. I went to the Procession with a wild hope that something would occur, that I should break a leg or be strangled by the crowd. Nothing *did* occur, so by the time that you get this I shall be on my way to France with Fred. Insane. I know it. I think that we both of us know it. But I would not care if it were not for you. But you said that you would love me whatever I did. Remember—your love is all that I shall have in a year's time.

ROSE.

The note fell from her hand to the ground. She bent down and picked it up. A foreboding, dusky and cold like the room, crept to her side and touched her hand.

THE FLITTING

BENJIE HERRIES, a week or two after Jubilee Day, walked up the hill on a lovely summer evening towards the Fortress. He had been playing cricket with the young men of Ireby village. On his shoulder he was carrying his son Tom, aged three years, and beside him was Bob Rantwood, a famous poacher, drunkard and ne'er-do-well, one of Benjie's best friends. A sunny haze covered all the world. In the village there had been much motion, the long wagon drawn by its splendid team of horses, the chatter at the little inn with its coloured prints, its gay pictures of hunters and horses, and a grand flower-and-fruit piece that was the landlord's especial joy, left there by some travellers to pay a debt more than a hundred years ago, the flagged passage, and beyond the bottle-green windows the clear blue of the summer sky, Mrs. Enderby's shop with the liquorice, bull's-eyes, boot-laces and a portrait of the Prince of Wales, the long fields rising to the grey hills, the deep oaks, the bleatings of sheep, the brilliant leaves of the copper-beech, the scent of clover and bean-blossom.

He was at peace and not at peace; he had enjoyed the game, the comradeship (for they liked him), the taste and sound of Cumbrian air and soil, but Rantwood unsettled him. He had poached with him many a time, knew all about salmon and trout poaching, the ' draughting ' and ' poling.' Lovely nights he had had with Rantwood draughting a river, or, by himself, guiding his poles, knowing exactly where there is a spile or a crook. The thrill, in mild weather, to find a spot where the fish are spawning, or on a dark night to see the dawn steal over the fan-shaped hill, to hear the moorhen plunge! Or, draughting with Rantwood, trailing the net slowly down the river, stoning the water to frighten the salmon into the net—or best of all on a moonlight night, when an old coat has been soaked with paraffin, the thrill of the moment when this improvised torch is lit and the men with him, sticks in hand, plunge into the water . . .

Rantwood, like most poachers, was a discontented, cursing, but most amiable fellow. Nothing was ever right with him. He would swear at the game-laws by the hour together, ' gloweran' aboot ' like a madman, and then he would laugh, throw his thick arms around, and call Benjie, for whom he had warm friendship but no reverence, ' thoo girt daft cauf, thoo.'

He was always restless, always wanting to be somewhere where he was not—and so was Benjie. But Benjie knew what was now the matter with him. He should not have gone to London, should not have seen Vanessa . . .

Three days he had stayed there. He had not especially enjoyed his visit although he had done

all the things that would, he thought, amuse him.
He had visited Earl's Court and seen ' Buffalo
Bill' Cody's Wild West Show, had travelled on
the Underground Railway and been stifled by
the sulphur and smoke from the engine, the fumes
from the oil lamp, the reeking pipes of his fellow-
travellers. He had visited the Gaiety Bar and
talked to the magnificent ladies who served him,
had spent several hours in the Argyle Music Hall,
admired the Chairman who with such militant
authority banged the table with his gavel, and
wondered at the amount of liquor he could con-
sume.

He had wandered the streets and like any country yokel stared at the illuminations, had watched
London Society display its elegance in Hyde
Park, had been pleased with the superb procession
of curricles, landaus, victorias, the powdered footmen, the silk stockings, the yellow plush; had
found a beautiful lady at the Alhambra, gone with
her to her room in Portland Street, but once there,
after half an hour's most elegant conversation,
had politely left her. He had been, in fact, the
loneliest of men. That seat from which he had
viewed the Procession (a pretty penny he had
paid for it!) had been his ruin. He had gone to
London on a sudden impulse, resolving to visit
no member of the family. It had been the
cruellest fate (the kind of check to his virtue that
fate was for ever dealing out to him) that Vanessa
should be sitting there, almost at his side! For
two hours he had watched her. Every detail of
her dress, every movement had been absorbed by

him. It was not her loveliness that had struck him to the heart, but his intimacy with her so that he knew instantly, at the first sight of her, that nothing was altered, that his four years' exile from her had hindered nothing.

He had made no attempt to speak to her. Weak, irresolute as he was, he would keep his word—at least, for a little longer. But he returned to Cumberland a haunted man.

He shifted young Tom a little, liking to feel the warmth of those small confident fingers against his neck. A funny freak of chance that Tom should have in him some kindred blood with the second wife of Vanessa's great-grandfather. After Vanessa he loved Tom—the only two in the world whom he loved.

' All the family have cleared out of the country,' he said aloud, following his thoughts. ' I'm the last here. We were all over the County a while ago.'

' Aye,' said Rantwood, who was pursuing his own thoughts. Would Herries ask him in for a drink? He had a thirst all right. But Mrs. Herries—she didn't like him. Nor he her— whimsey-whumsey kind of female.

' My great-great-grandfather rode into Keswick one night from Doncaster. That's how it all started. We were all over the place once. Oh, I've told you before. And now we're all away again.' He looked over the hedge down the valley where the summer evening breathed tranquilly under a stainless sky. Around them the insects were humming and on the other side

of the hedge a brook sang beneath the willows.
Voices cried through the stillness with a dying
fall. As though he spoke aloud: 'I am walking
up this hill and soon I will be gone. I have done
my best. I have kept my vow, but soon I shall
be wandering again. I can neither be free of
this country nor settle in it, and when I am
away I shall remember just such an evening as
this, the meadow falling into dusk, and all the
names that I love—Blencathra, Uldale (almost
all the bricks of the house are gone now: soon
there will be nothing but the turf and the sheep
cropping it), Bassenthwaite, Ireby—beautiful
names like the words of a vow, a vow that I
have kept but can keep no longer. I hate this
house I am coming to. I have always hated it.
I hate this woman in the house. I have always
hated her, and one day soon I shall take young
Tom and we will walk away and never come back.
The last Herries . . . but the place will be
always in my bones. I shall never tread on such
turf again nor drink such running water nor see
such lithe walls running into the sky nor hear such
friendly voices. But I have lived long enough
away from Vanessa, and although I never speak
to her again I must see her once between one day
and another day.'

'That was a good catch I made to get Will
Davidson,' he said aloud.

'Aye,' said Rantwood. 'Thoo can play at
cricket a' reet.'

'Well, good night to you, Bob.' He turned
in at the gate.

'I mun slacken my thirst wi' watter,' Rantwood
thought discontentedly, starting down the hill.

Inside the house even on this summer evening
it was damp. They had come down to live only
in three rooms and the kitchen. An old woman,
Mrs. Cumming, was the present successor to all
the in-and-out females who had done service in
that place. The room at the top of the first
stair-flight that had once been the drawing-room
with the fine gilt chairs, the naked goddesses, the
rosy cupids on the ceiling, was now the general
living-room. All that remained of Walter's
splendours was the long mirror with the gilded
frame, and reflected in this Benjie now stood with
his little son. His shirt wide-open showed his
brown chest, his neck firmly set, his head like a
hard apple, the twinkling kindly eyes alive and
eager, his small restless body upon which clothes
seemed always an excrescence, Benjamin Herries,
rogue, good fellow, a 'deep' chap, a good-for-
nothing, the kindest man in the county, the
suddenest-tempered, 'a man all by himself,' a
jolly man, a man of his word, a man you couldn't
trust, a gentleman, a vagabond, a wise man, a
fool—just as your personal experience happened
to be.

And his small son stood beside him, like his
father because he had the brown colour and the
sparkling eyes, a child always laughing, filled
already with secret plans and plays of his own,
never wanting company, never afraid, never asking
anyone to help him.

The mirror also reflected the room, which was

a scramble and a confusion, littered with fishing-rods, guns, a woman's dress, a child's playthings, a table with the remains of a meal, and a sofa with a hole in it.

' Vanessa,' said Benjie, looking into the mirror.

Later, to the light of a smoking lamp, Mr. and Mrs. Herries enjoyed their evening meal together, old Mrs. Cumming clattering in on her clogs bringing the beef and gooseberry-pudding, banging them down on the table, going out with a toss of the head because she and Mrs. Herries had but now crossed swords in the kitchen.

Mrs. Herries was the thinnest woman in all Cumberland and her face was of a faintly green pallor. But she was the same reserved passive woman she had ever been. In years she was still a girl, but her features were of that ageless cast belonging to women who have matured when very young and live on their passions. Benjie was always kind to her; that he hated her was not her fault. He knew that she had been many times unfaithful to him, but she was no more personal to him than her pale reflection in the mirror might be. It was amazing to him that they had stayed together in this horrible house for three years, but his vow had kept him, he supposed. He had shown Vanessa that he could be faithful. This woman had at least done that for him; so he was kind to her, smiled across the table at her and told her he had made thirty runs in the cricket game. He ate his beef, seeing that the long gilt mirror was loose on its nail and swayed ever so slightly, so that the room rocked too a little. The two high windows were open and the place was suffused with the summer evening heat, with the odour of the roses that rioted about the garden. A moon, tip-tilted on the edge of one small cloud lit from within like cotton-wool around a lantern, drunkenly grinned through the window.

'Mrs. Cumming can't cook meat, that's one thing certain,' he said, smiling at his wife.

'No, she can't,' the late Miss Halliday agreed. 'But we never get a decent servant here.'

'We pay them plenty,' said Benjie, who from land, from money left him by Elizabeth, was not so badly off.

'They won't come here. They are afraid of you.'

'What! that I'll go to bed with them? You know that I've been faithful to you since our wedding-day.'

(He had, marvel of marvels! Or no—to put it better, he had been faithful to Vanessa.)

'That doesn't interest me,' Mrs. Herries said. 'You know you're free to do what you like. Oh, it isn't you. They would know how to deal with you if you started anything. No, it's the house.'

'Ghosts?' said Benjie.

'What you like to call them. Mrs. Cumming was talking about it to-night—steps up and down the passage, a dog whining. You've heard the dog yourself up there in the Tower. Someone tapping with a stick. And that woman in black wandering about the garden.'

'Do you believe in spirits, then?' he asked her.

'Spirits!' she answered impatiently. 'These

L

gooseberries aren't half cooked. Well, what are
you to think? Those friends of my brother's, *your*
friends, those Endicott men, they've seen things
time and again. But there's something queer
about this house.'

'Yes, from the moment the first stone was laid.
My grandfather spoilt it with his obstinacy. If
you see a thing isn't going to turn out well you
should give it up. No good going on if the signs
are against you.'

She sat leaning forward, her sharp-peaked chin
resting on her hands. He noticed that she was
regarding him with great attention to-night. He
felt that something was in the wind.

'Ghosts!' He smiled. 'I saw one in London
the other day—a beauty. She was tall like a lily,
carried herself like a queen, she was dressed like
a rose and had dark, dark hair. It makes you
think of a ghost like that when you see a room in
the mess this is in. Why don't you tidy things a
bit, Marion; keep things in order more?'

'Ah! What's the use? You're never in,
and nothing would ever stay neat in this house.
Three years I've had of it——'

'You're a strange woman.' They regarded
one another in friendly fashion. 'You've never
had any liking for the boy, and he's a fine little
chap too. It has meant nothing to you, being a
mother.'

'No, nothing at all,' she answered. 'Women
mean nothing to me, no, nor children. But men
—ah! that's another story! And you, Benjie,
more than any. I want to be in your arms as badly

as ever I did the first time I saw you. But what's
the use? Why you've stayed with me all this time
I can't imagine. . . . Well, I must wash the
dishes. I won't have that sneak of a woman in the
house after to-night. She goes to-morrow.'

'Why, what has she been doing?'

She was standing up, her hands on her hips,
staring at him as though she would never see him
again.

'I like you like that with your shirt open.
You're brown all over like a foreigner. Where
did you get that skin from?'

'Who knows where one gets anything from?
That's the mystery. Where we come from, who
made us what we are, what we make ourselves
into, where we are going to. And we've lived three
years together, Marion, and are as far apart as
ever we were.'

'Yes,' she said. 'It's all the body, what it
looks like, what its clothes are. I'm not your
beautiful ghost like a rose, tall as a lily. But see
the rose's nose crooked and give her a black eye,
and where's your love for her then?'

'I'm not so sure,' said Benjie. 'I'm not so
sure.'

'But I am! It's only because you've a brown
skin and are strong and haven't an ugly mark on
your body that I'm in love with you. But what's
the use? You don't care for me and never did.
And you're the only man I've never tired of.
Most men are the same after you've known them
once.'

She said all this in a quiet, dispassionate voice.

Was it because of her own unresting physical passion that he had once on a day been caught by her? Maybe. But that didn't matter now. It was not her fault. A pity that she didn't care about young Tom, though. That might have been something of a bond between them.

'Well, I mustn't stay talking here. That woman's stealing the spoons, I wouldn't wonder.' She went out, carrying the beef with her.

He wandered out into the garden.

Moonlight on a summer's night is a most impermanent thing. Everything is new-born, but only for a moment, and when the silvery world rises it is like a dream that, even while you are enchanted, you know that you must not trust. The flowers on such a night are ghosts that at a touch will vanish away, and water, shining under the moon, belongs to no earthly stream. This garden had never yielded to any man's will. Flowers had died when you cared for them and waxed abundant when you neglected them. The moonlight poured out now from under the trees like a flood that, at the beckoning of a cloud, would be withdrawn. Only the trees stood firm, waiting the moment when they would advance, cover the ground, swallow the house and resume their kingdom. Man had never been wanted here, especially man filled with the spirit of obstinacy, revenge, and pride.

Was there some dark figure moving under the trees? He stood there watching. It was easy to imagine, with all that you had heard, that a tall woman in black, now in moonlight, now in grey shadow, moved, hesitated, moved again. He walked forward, the plants crowding about him; then he turned to the stone steps that ran to the higher ground at the side of the house. He had always disliked these steps. His mother had told him that for some reason they had always frightened her. Uhland had tap-tapped down them with his stick, Walter's drunken friends had sprawled against them and fallen from top to bottom like the helpless fools that they were. Now they were washed white in the moonlight and you could see the tufts of grass like black bunches of fingers pressing up between the broken flagstones. Here, standing half-way up, he was exactly under Uhland's stair and he could fancy that behind that dark window Uhland was standing and behind him perhaps old Rogue Herries. The two of them watching the third in that sequence. He stretched his arms. He whistled a tune. He might be of their family, but he was not of their destinies. He was fit and well and strong; he had a son and he loved a woman, he had friends and a hundred miles of country that he would not exchange, with its clouds and stones, for all the sunny kingdoms of the world. He looked down on that moonlit garden. He could hear the water falling from one pool to another. An owl hooted. *Was* not that a woman who moved from tree to tree? He whistled his tune, kicked the loose stones from under his foot and went in to see that his child was comfortably sleeping on this hot night.

Tom slept in a corner of his own bedroom, a

room in Uhland's Tower, once used by Walter
as a guest-room. It was sparsely furnished, his
bed, Tom's small one, a large tin bath, a dressing-
table, his hunting prints and the faded painting
of the old Elizabethan Herries that had once hung
in Borrowdale. A fierce, frowning old boy with
no nonsense about him! The carpet had holes,
the cupboard where Benjie kept his clothes creaked
with every wind, but to-night it was transformed
with the moonlight and the scent of the roses.
Although the window was open the room was very
hot, and the child had thrown off the bedclothes
and lay, his nightshirt ruffled to his chest, his
little legs drawn up, one fist—clutching a small
wooden horse—still clenched.

Benjie stood there, looking at him. This was
his son, and not a bad son either. Pity he had
that Halliday blood which was no good at all in
his veins, but Benjie flattered himself that his own
Herries blood could beat the Halliday mixture.
Vanessa had as yet no child. That anaemic husband of hers would never give her one—and, perhaps, one day Tom would know her and love her
and get his idea of women from her.

Poor Benjie sighed. He was really ashamed of
himself for having a son at all. He was no sort of
father for a boy to have, and he knew already what
a man, who is no great hero and has done a
shameful thing or two in his time, can feel when
a small boy thinks him perfect. 'Well, he won't
think me perfect long, and I can teach him to shoot
and ride and not be afraid of anyone. . . . Still, he
ought to have some sort of mother to care for him.'

Then he undressed. He could not find a nightshirt so he slept naked, curling up his legs as his child had done. Father and son slept side by side and the clouds came up over the moon, drenching the room with darkness.

Tom always woke very early and came into his father's bed. He would lie, his small head against his father's chest, looking at the trees beyond the window, waiting until his father should wake. He talked to his horse, named Caesar, telling him about the things that they would do that day, bacon for breakfast, a visit to the village, and, if very lucky, a ride to Bassenthwaite. He didn't *promise* Caesar these delights. He had learnt already that it did not do to expect *anything*, that one was left alone when one least expected it, or, worst of all, handed over to Mrs. Cumming with her constant: ' Now don't be a worrit ' or ' Keep quiet, do.' He was accustomed to being without his father for days at a time and, although his mother was never unkind to him, he knew quite well that she did not care for him. Only once had she been really angry with him, and that was when, coming into a room unexpectedly, he had seen her sitting on a fat man's knee. She had slapped him severely although he did not know what wrong he had done, and then the fat man had given him sixpence. The only fear that he had was that, when his father went away, he would never come back again. He discussed this often with Caesar, and Caesar reassured him. *Of course* his father would come back. But when he was in bed with his father he clutched him very tightly, his arm on his breast or his neck. That comforted him greatly.

At last the grand moment arrived when his father opened his eyes, grinned, yawned, stretched his arms, played a game or two. Then he watched his father splash in the tin bath, after which he was himself plunged into the same. His father helped him with his clothes, fastening his buttons, brushing his hair, and tying his boots. This was a lovely morning, as fresh as a bird's wing, and between the trees you could see Blencathra's shoulder resting against the faint early summer blue. His father whistled and sang, which showed that he was happy this morning; then, hand in hand, they went down to breakfast together.

The big untidy room was bright with sunshine, but there was no breakfast; no cloth was on the table, and, although it was by now half-past eight, no sign nor sound of Mrs. Herries.

Then Mrs. Cumming came clopping in, carrying a plate of bacon in one hand and a dented silver coffee-pot in the other.

' Where's Mrs. Herries? ' asked Benjie.

' Mrs. Herries is gone,' said Mrs. Cumming, her eyes staring with a fat, half-sleepy curiosity.

' Gone? '

' Aye. Mr. Ewart's trap come and fetch her seven this morning. She told me they was driving into Carlisle and she left a letter.'

She felt in the pocket of her cotton dress and produced it; she gave him a stare and went out.

He held the letter in his hand, but, before he

opened it, settled Tom in his place, cut the bread, gave him some bacon and poured out the coffee. Tom wriggled until he was comfortable, set Caesar up on the table in front of his place and set to.

The letter was as follows:

DEAR BENJAMIN—I have gone away with Charlie Ewart and shall never return. He has been pressing me for a long time. I'd have told you last night, but what's the use? There's nothing to be said. You don't want me, you never have after the first night or two. I did a wrong thing in the first place to force you to it as I did, but mother pressed me and I was in love with you. I wonder we've stayed together as long as we have and I must say you've always been very patient, your nature being what it is. We haven't had what you could really call a cross word all these years. All the same we haven't been happy, either of us. I wish I could have felt more for the boy. I'm sure I've tried, but it isn't in my nature. I wasn't meant to have children and if I can help it shan't ever have another.

You'll be much better without me; I haven't a gift for keeping things straight and tidy. What Charlie Ewart sees in me I can't think, and I don't suppose we shall be together long although he says different. You can divorce me if you want to but I don't want any money from you and I'll never be married again. Well, good-bye, Benjie. One thing I'm glad of, that I shan't have to live in the Fortress any more. It's a place would make a cat sick.— Your sincere friend,

MARION.

Benjie read the letter through three times, then he gave his son some more bacon. 'Well, that settles it,' he said aloud. As though the sunshine penetrated his heart he felt a great joy and gladness. He was free again; he had been set free.

He had kept his vow and now, without any act on his part, he was liberated. Charlie Ewart! That thin, shanky, lop-eared farmer! Poor Marion! He was so sorry for her that had she at that moment appeared in the doorway he would, in spite of his disappointment at her return, have been kind and considerate. But, thank heaven, there was no need to be kind and considerate any more!

He went into the passage and called Mrs. Cumming.

'Mrs. Cumming, Mrs. Herries has gone to London. I am going also and I want you to order Sam Bender round with the trap in an hour's time. I'll catch the train from Carlisle. I'm taking the boy with me. I don't know when I'll be back, but I'll write from London.'

So that was the end of the Fortress. He would sell the damned place and be done with it for ever. He would be in London and Vanessa would be in London. He had done what he could, and it was not his fault that now he was free to go where he would.

Poor Marion! Charlie Ewart! Well, well . . .

He went to his room and packed a few things, Tom going hand in hand with him everywhere. He dressed Tom in his best suit and his grey summer jacket.

'We are going to London,' he said. 'You, I and Caesar.'

While he was sitting waiting for the trap, he talked to his son.

'We're going away, Tom, and I don't expect we'll ever live in this house again. Years and years ago a man rode into this country with his son and went to live in a little house the other side of Keswick.   He had a brother living in Keswick too.   And as the years went by his son had a wife, and they went and lived in a house down in the valley there which was burnt in a fire later on. There were many of our family in the country, but, one by one, they died and went away until you and I are the only ones left.   And now we're going away too.   But that's not the end of it.   You and I have got this country in our blood.   You don't know what that means now, but you will one day. Everything you ever do will be affected by this country, and however far you travel you'll never find any other country so beautiful nor any other that's in your bones as this one is.   You'll come back to it.   Be sure of that.   But I hope you won't come back to this house, because it was built in a bad temper and hasn't been any good to anybody.'

Tom seemed to understand.   'The funny thing is,' thought Benjie, 'that one remembers after the things that one was told although one was too young at the time.   I remember things that Adam told me about birds and wrestling. Very rum that.'

'You've got to be a better man than I've been, Tom,' he added.   'And I hope you'll stay in one place sometimes.   You never learn anything if you're always moving.   But you'll be all right so long as you're never afraid of anyone.   There's nothing to be afraid of really.'

It wasn't like him to preach, but the warm sun

was comforting and he felt so happy and cheerful that he had to be talking to someone.

They took a last look at the place together, the Cumberland stone, the overgrown garden, the two cross-faced towers. A dog was whining somewhere and little flakes of plaster fell from the ceiling of the living-room.

Then Sam Bender came with his trap and took them both away.

VIOLET BELLAIRS IS PREVENTED

WHEN Timothy Bellairs and Violet his wife had been established in London a year or so they became the centre of social exchange for the London members of the Herries family.

Hill Street was of course the Temple: all the splendour and sanctification were in Hill Street. Only Vanessa of all the Herries entertained the Prince and Princess to tea (although it was said that the Prince *had* paid pretty little Cynthia a visit at her pretty little house in Charles Street); only Vanessa invited Archbishop Benson to luncheon; only Vanessa was on friendly personal terms with Mr. Chamberlain.

During these years Hill Street was the Temple. But neither Ellis nor Vanessa cared for gossip. At least Vanessa enjoyed it but appeared to consider some things spiteful when they were only amusing. Now Violet Bellairs was quite different from this. A Cumberland country cousin, she had become very speedily a most entertaining London hostess. She was not, of course, very clever: you could laugh at her to her face and she seldom perceived it. She had no talent for the Arts, thought Oscar Wilde an actor, and supposed that *Robert Elsmere* was written by a clergy-

man, and had only just heard of young Mr. Kipling.
But it was not for the Arts that any Herries went
to Onslow Square. They went, quite frankly, to
hear about the other Herries. You could always
tell when any scandal was afoot because Violet,
her stout body enclosed within the brightest
colours, her red face beaming, her hat elegant
with a stuffed bird, her eager, friendly voice with
its ' Well, how are you? Haven't seen you for an
age!' was to be seen everywhere—at Charles
Street, in Barney's bachelor rooms in Duke Street,
in Phyllis' overcrowded drawing-room, even in
the cold and gloomy place in Kensington where
old Emily Newmark held her prayer-meetings.

Violet was always in the best of spirits, kind
and friendly to everyone, leaving a trail of scandal
behind her. She *did* enjoy a gossip, she freely
confessed, and liking, quite naturally, to be the
centre of any company, if she had no thrilling tale
to tell she invented one. Her husband, who was
fat and sleepy, spent his days in the Conservative
Club and his evenings at Jimmie's or the Alhambra or where you please. He was no trouble
to her at all.

Violet, like so many women who married
Herries men, became more Herries than the
Herries. She was patriotic, strictly moral and all
for the law. Nevertheless any human failing
made her happy because she was never censorious,
but treated a ' mishap ' as a town-crier treats a lost
dog—rang her bell, felt kindly towards the dog
but hoped that it would not be found before the
whole town had had time to observe that it was

lost. Her best women friends among the Herries were old Phyllis Rochester, Cynthia Worcester, Alfred's wife (Amery's daughter-in-law) and (again oddly enough) old Emily Newmark.

She had, of course, many many friends quite outside the Herries circle, but they were not of quite the same importance to her. As she often said: ' Our family holds together. There's not another family like it in England for that.'

It happened that, early in September 1889, Violet was very busy. It had not been a dull summer, for first there had been Mrs. Maybrick (dreadful woman: why was she not hung?), and then those terrible Dock Strikers who, week after week, poor abandoned creatures, went about demanding their Rights, starving and altogether behaving disgracefully. It was not, however, either Mrs. Maybrick or the Strikers who gave her so agreeable a week or two at the beginning of this September. It was a real Herries sensation—*what* was happening in Hill Street?

Two years earlier, a week or two after the Jubilee, the question had been—what *will* happen in Hill Street? for Benjamin Herries had come to Town, leading his son by the hand, and one of those family crises so greatly beloved by the Herries promised to be on the way. Then, to everyone's surprise—to the surprise of old Garth, old Amery, young Alfred, heavy Emily, dear little Cynthia, even the stout Barney himself—*nothing* occurred. Benjie called on none of them. He spent an evening or two with Barney; he never went *near* Hill Street. So far as anyone could tell, he neither wrote to Vanessa nor spoke to her. Everything had been the more dramatic in that summer of 1887 because of the dreadful (but rather delightful) Rose scandal. She had escaped to Paris with Captain Fred Wycherley, leaving Mrs. Wycherley, poor thing, and two young children in London. (' Did you expect him to take them with him? ' Barney asked ironically.) More than that, she met Carey Rockage in the Rue de Rivoli one September day and laughed and joked with him as though nothing had occurred.

Carey was in a fine way because May, his wife, and Maud, his elder daughter, were at a hotel not two streets distant. How fearful if Rose should suggest that she should call! But Rose (who was looking both young and pretty, Carey thought) suggested nothing of the kind.

' I know you have May and Maud with you, Carey. You were at the Opéra-Comique last night. If you are making a domestic parade one day and meet Fred and myself, we shall expect to be cut, you know. So don't worry. Only, if out on a little bit of evening fun on your own, Carey, remember that Fred has his spies everywhere. He'll give you a tip or two as to the best places if you ask him! He's the kindest of creatures! ' She went off, laughing, swinging her bustle. Poor Rose. She had been always a coarse woman. Horace, her brother, married last autumn and it was understood that he did not wish Rose's name to be mentioned. Simply because of the awkwardness that it caused to others.

Looking more like a Bishop than ever, he let it be understood that he was devoted to Rose. ' Which of us is above reproach? ' he inquired of Barney. ' What I mean, old fellow, is that charity is the finest of the virtues. For my part I look at the good qualities in my fellow-men. Who am I to judge? And Rose has loved Fred Wycherley for years.'

Nevertheless it could not be expected that Miss Ada Lindsay that was, a plain pale-faced girl, twenty-one years of age to Horace's thirty when he married her, coming as she did straight from a wealthy but Christian family in Kensington, would care to hear such things mentioned. What Ada herself thought of it nobody knew because she seldom spoke. No one knew what her thoughts were about anything—including Horace.

However, the really interesting side to Rose's disgrace was that it was well known in all Herries circles that there was a deep difference of opinion concerning it in Hill Street. Ellis was disgusted. Vanessa would not listen to a word against Rose. Cynthia Worcester was known to be devoted to Vanessa, to worship her in fact, but even she confessed that if Vanessa was going to ' bite her nose off like that all about nothing ' she would think twice about visiting Hill Street again. All that she had said was that Rose had got at last what she wanted, and Vanessa had turned on her, scolded her in front of Ellis as though she were ten years old.

It was plain then that Vanessa's own views on morals were a little queer. Had they not always been queer? After all, had not Judith Paris been her grandmother, Rogue Herries her great-grandfather? Had not her own father been illegitimate and her mother a German? No one meant any of this unkindly. Vanessa was so beautiful, so generous and socially so resplendent that one could forgive her almost anything; nevertheless she belonged to the quarter from which the dangerous winds were for ever blowing, those winds that had for centuries disturbed the peace and order of the right-living, right-thinking Herries.

Benjie, however, was a disappointment. He did nothing spectacular. Nobody saw him. They said that his wife in Cumberland had run away from him after he had beaten her to a jelly, that he drank like a fish and consorted with abandoned women. But these things were but rumour and Barney stoutly denied all of them. In the winter of '87 he left London for what destination no one knew.

It was in the spring of '88 that everyone began to say that things were not well in Hill Street. On the surface everything was very well indeed. Vanessa went everywhere and Ellis was often at her side, looking as proud as a peacock. Everyone *loved* Vanessa; how could you help it, so kind and generous and simple-hearted as she was? Nevertheless she made few friendships. Cynthia complained that 'there was always a barrier,' but old Phyllis Rochester said that Cynthia was 'socially jealous.' Did Vanessa give herself airs? Surely not. She was the same to everyone, knew no social distinctions, and had been seen one day by Emily Newmark sitting on the top of a 'bus and chatting to the driver.   Her only close friend was young Adrian Cards.   She certainly spoilt that young man, who, because he was in the Foreign Office, looked after a Boys' Club in the East End and wrote for Mr. Henley, thought himself quite out of the ordinary.   *Of course* no one suggested that Vanessa was in love with him, but it was agreed that he visited Hill Street a great deal more often than Ellis cared for, and he helped Vanessa with her many charities.

Ellis was, in fact, the mystery.   What went on behind that cold reserved official manner of his?   He loved Vanessa madly: ever *more* madly as the time went on.   He behaved to her in public with a really exaggerated courtesy and deference, but it began to be said that in private he was impossibly jealous.   How do these things become known?   Miss Fortescue (who, as everyone was aware, did not like Vanessa) told a thing or two, and there was that occasion when Alfred and his wife were lunching at Hill Street.   Ellis had left the table abruptly and had not appeared again. Very odd.   They all shook their heads over it. Then, in the late spring of '89, Benjie Herries once more reappeared in London.   He lived in two rooms in Soho Square with his little boy.   Poor little boy!   That was the first thing that everyone said. Benjie did not now conceal himself as he had done on the earlier occasion.   He paid calls on everyone—including Vanessa—and aroused the greatest interest.   They all surrendered to his charm while he was *with* them.   He looked peculiar, wearing clothes of a rough tweed, sometimes the new

knickerbockers, but for the most part loose baggy
trousers. His tie was generally a deep red in
colour and enclosed in a gold ring, and this colour
with his dark skin gave him the nickname of ' the
little gipsy.' They told one another, however,
with a rather reluctant satisfaction, that you could
never mistake him for anything but a gentleman.
He was always at his ease, laughed like a boy, was
worshipped by any Herries children who happened to be about. He made no effort to win
the affections of his relations: they could take him
or leave him, and for a while they certainly took
him. After June there was an exodus from
London: Cynthia and her husband went to
Ostend; Timothy and his family to Eastbourne;
Alfred and his wife to Brighton.

Old Emily of course remained, and it was from
her one must suppose that the story spread—the
story that one night at the Alhambra, Benjie was
engaged in a disgraceful scuffle, knocked a man
down and spent the night in a police station.
There *had* been a scuffle, that was certain, but
Barney said that it had been extremely creditable
to Benjie. Some drunken ruffian had insulted
the lady in Benjie's company and Benjie had
knocked him down. But what was Benjie doing
at the Alhambra with a lady and what sort of a
lady was she?

Then in August came the great news that
Benjie had paid a call at Hill Street and been for-
bidden the house for evermore by Ellis. This
was from Miss Fortescue.

Well, now, what do you think of that? Some-

body said that Ellis had slapped Benjie's face,
someone else that Vanessa had had to rush in
between the two men and separate them. No
one knew what had happened because nobody was
present. Ellis and Vanessa left town to pay a
series of visits. They stayed with the Rockages
in Wiltshire, and with Horace Newmark—
Barney's brother—now an old man of seventy,
in his grand house near Manchester.

It was reported that Vanessa was serene and
happy, but that Ellis was ' queer.' What do you
mean by queer? Well, May Rockage was bound
to confess that she didn't like the look in Ellis'
eye. He seemed unhappy if Vanessa left him
even for a moment. Pathetic to see how he adored
her, and Vanessa looked after him as though he
were her son, but he was restless and Carey confessed that ' he didn't seem normal,' the most
alarming thing that any one Herries could say
about another. All the old family scandals were
revived, the misbehaviour of the ancient Rogue,
the old quarrel at Christabel's ball, the suicide of
Francis, and of course the dreadful affair of poor
John and the crazy Uhland. Was the family
never to be allowed to sit down quietly by its fire-
side and enjoy its domesticity, serve the country
and worship its Maker? What was this crazy
spirit that refused to leave them alone? Benjie
was as bad as the old Rogue, and the sooner he
left the country for good the better.

Early in September most of the Herries were
back in London again; Vanessa was at Hill Street,
Amery and Alfred in Tavistock Square, Timothy

and Violet in Onslow Square, and Emily remained in Tutton Street, South Kensington.

So one fine September afternoon Violet thought that she would go and see what everyone was thinking. She took her son, young Timothy, aged now twelve, with her. Timothy was a beautiful boy; she refused to cut his hair, which fell in gold ringlets to his broad white collar. For parties or calls he was dressed in a black velvet suit. He was the pride of his mother's heart. It is sad to have to record that at this period of his life he detested his mother. He was not allowed to go to school, but shared his sister's governess. He was washed and dressed and brushed morning, noon and evening. He loathed his long hair, his velvet suit, the comments of his mother's friends; he was mocked at and shouted after by little street boys; he cried himself to sleep at nights because of their insults. The only thing in the world for which he cared was to draw and paint; this he must do in secret because his father, whom he rarely saw, laughed at such nonsense and his mother showed his drawings to her friends. He had to drive in an open carriage in the Park with his mama, he had to sit on a chair in ladies' drawing-rooms and be commented on as though he were something in a circus. His settled resolve was to run away as soon as the proper moment occurred. Barney Newmark was his only friend. Barney had said to Timothy: 'What the devil do you dress the poor child up like that for? It's cruelty to children, poor little beggar,' and Violet, hearing of this, never forgave him.

On this particular afternoon in Cynthia Worcester's drawing-room, he was not altogether out of place. Two young poets were present, a lady dressed in blue velvet and peacock's feathers, and Mr. Oscar Wilde. Mr. Wilde was very kind to him, sat beside him in a corner and told him a story about a young Prince who ran away from his father's kingdom and became a bell-ringer in a church with a wonderfully high tower. One day when the Prince was ringing the bells, a swallow flew into the tower and rested on his shoulder. The swallow had damaged its wing, so the Prince took it back with him to the cottage where he was living. . . .

At this point the ladies demanded that Mr. Wilde should entertain them, so the tall heavy man with the grave eyes and the beautiful voice had reluctantly to leave young Tim, who never afterwards forgot him.

Two more men and a girl came in. There was a great chatter. Violet admired Cynthia's looks but she must say she couldn't admire the way that she did her drawing-room with the pale grey wall-paper, some flowers in a white vase, a Japanese screen, one little table with some odd-looking thin books upon it—nothing else. No photographs! No cosy coverings to her room, no fans pinned to the wall, or shelves with cups and saucers and large blue plates. However, Cynthia *loved* a good talk and was just jealous enough of Vanessa to enjoy a story or two. You could not find two types more exactly opposite than Cynthia—so small and fair, with such very light-blue eyes—

and Vanessa—tall, dark, 'one of Du Maurier's women,' or as Horace Ormerod liked to say impressively, ' " A daughter of the gods divinely fair "—fair in the sense of beautiful, you know.' So that there was just enough difference between the two for Cynthia not to object to a little scandal . . . no harm, only to ask where Benjie was, had anyone seen him, did Cynthia know what Ellis, when he was staying down in Wiltshire . . .?

So that Violet was pleased when the two young men and the girl came in, because now it would be perfectly easy to have a little chat with Cynthia without disturbing the others. Smiling happily upon everyone as though she would say, ' Now I know I'm a large woman and when I move it is a little upsetting, but I like you all immensely and you must none of you be disturbed,' she drew her chair closer to Cynthia's.

' Cynthia darling—what *beautiful* tea-cups! Where did you find them? Everything you have is always so lovely. Listen, dear.' She dropped her voice. ' *Have* you heard what Benjie has been doing? They tell me that Ellis . . .'

But something was wrong. For once Cynthia did not appear to be attending.

She said: ' Yes, Violet dear, how interesting! ' but her sharp blue eyes were fastened on the heavy frock-coated man with the pale jowl, the friendly smile, the heavily lidded eyes, who, standing in front of the fireplace, talked with a self-confidence that awed Violet although privately she thought it a little vulgar.

One of the young men said something with a

titter about the Queen. All the patriotic Herries
in Violet (acquired by marriage) was affronted.
Smiling very brightly she said:

'The Queen! Surely we must be proud to
have such a Queen. Young man, you are dis-
loyal.' (Shaking her finger at him playfully.)

'Violet is really dreadful when she's coy,'
thought Cynthia, and for the first time (because
she was not interested in children) wondered
whether it was not rather a shame that that poor
child on the sofa (to whom one of the ladies was
now talking) should be dressed as a doll.

Mr. Wilde said: 'The Queen? Do you know,
madam, what Thackeray once wrote about our
Queen?'

'No,' said Violet. 'Something fine, I'm sure.'

'Very fine,' said Mr. Wilde, looking at her
with so kindly an expression that she wondered
whether she would not invite him to luncheon.
'He wrote, as nearly as I recollect, something like
this: "I salute the sovereign; the good mother;
the accomplished lady; the enlightened friend of
art."'

'How very fine—and how true!' said Violet.

'Not true at all, madam. The Queen has not
been a good mother, she is not accomplished, and
she has not been a friend to art in any fashion
whatever.'

Everyone laughed. Violet felt most uncomfortable.

'We owe to her in fact the present interest in
the Arts. An Englishman is only an artist when
those in authority despise the Arts.'

' What about Queen Elizabeth? ' said Cynthia, laughing.

' Do you imagine that Elizabeth was an artist or cared for the Arts? She wanted to be entertained and made love to, and because the Arts then were part of a man's daily life, to tempt a man to make love to you was to rouse the artist in him. The Arts to-day can only exist by separating themselves from daily life. That is why the real artists to-day are never successful lovers, live from hand to mouth and wander the streets. Very different from the life of our Queen.'

' You are forgetting Mr. Kipling,' said Violet, who had been persuaded only a week or two ago to read *Soldiers Three*.

' Mr. Kipling believes in the Empire,' said Mr. Wilde, smiling.

' Do we not all believe in the Empire? ' asked Violet, pleased that she was holding her own in this very intellectual conversation.

' Do you know what Tennyson wrote for the Jubilee? '

' A very splendid poem, I remember,' said Violet.

' He wrote:

> ' Fifty years of ever-broadening Commerce!
> Fifty years of ever-brightening Science!
> Fifty years of ever-widening Empire! '

Everyone laughed, but Violet did not see that there was anything to laugh at. Uncomfortable without knowing why, she waited a minute or two and then attempted Cynthia again:

' Do tell me, Cynthia darling.   Have you been to Hill Street since they came back from the country?   How did you think Vanessa was looking? '

' No, I haven't seen Vanessa for weeks.'

' It seems that Ellis has been behaving so very strangely—not sleeping, they say, and absurdly jealous.   Phyllis had a letter from May Rock-age . . .'

Everyone was laughing.   The young man with the flowing black tie on the sofa had been drawing a picture for Timothy, and here was Timothy actually himself drawing something!

' It's a ship!   It's a ship! ' he cried excitedly.

One of the other young men jumped up and began to recite dramatically:

' Spirit of Beauty!   Tarry still awhile.
    They are not dead, thine ancient votaries,
Some few there are to whom thy radiant smile
    Is better than a thousand victories,
Though all the nobly slain of Waterloo
Rise up in wrath against them! Tarry still, there are a few

' Who for thy sake would give their manlihood
    And consecrate their being.   I at least
Have done so, made thy lips my daily food,
    And in thy temples found a goodlier feast
Than this starved age can give me, spite of all
Its new-found creeds so sceptical and so dogmatical.'

' A very good poem,' said Mr. Wilde, ' who-ever wrote it.   Its fault is that it contains a philo-sophy.   Poetry has nothing to do with philosophy, but only with feeling.'

'You had a philosophy when you wrote it, Oscar,' said one of the young men.

'Yes, and got rid of it by writing about it. Any philosophy is foolish if you look it in the face. Christ hid His face, you remember, to cover the foolishness of His disciples. And that is why He loved John, because John had no philosophy —only feeling.'

'What very bad taste,' Violet thought, 'to talk about Christ in that ordinary fashion.'

Nevertheless it was now that she was disturbed by an odd sensation. There was something in this room that deprived her of her desire for gossip. It was not that she thought the Arts important; the young men looked most unhealthy, and Mr. Wilde's complexion was anything but hearty. Nor was she ashamed of wishing to talk about the family, but there was something here before which personalities seemed unimportant. She felt frustrated, prevented. Even Cynthia, whom she knew so well, was different. The things of which these men talked were not in Violet's mind beautiful, and yet beauty was in the air. Perhaps after all her drawing-room in Onslow Square was a little overcrowded. The flowers in the white vase were a pretty colour . . .

It was almost as though someone had laid a hand on her mouth. She was most uncomfortable and thought at the first opportunity she would make an excuse and go.

One of the young men had, it seemed, but just returned from Paris and had seen there a performance of *Othello*.

'The absurdity about *Othello*,' Cynthia said, 'is that he should be upset so easily by so trivial a matter. A magnificent general, the strongest man in the State, and a little strawberry-spotted handkerchief——'

'You are wrong, dear lady,' said Mr. Wilde. 'The tragedy of *Othello* is not Desdemona. She is only one element in his downfall. We know, when he appears before the Senate, that he is poised above an abyss. He knows, we know, the Senate knows, that this new command is his last chance. He would have been recalled from Cyprus and Cassio given his place had there been no wife, no jealousy, no murder. Before the play begins he has reached the moment that comes to every man when the journey downhill has started. I have always seen Othello played as though he were a king of men in the majesty of purple triumph, with the trumpets sounding about him. That is wrong; he has the bitter knowledge that the glory is already in the past. It is of the past that he speaks to Desdemona, not the future. He comes to the Senate, leading Desdemona by the hand, and despair is already seated in his eyes. Great success demands great failure.' He laughed, smiling at them all. 'I am already preparing for the day when I shall know St. Helena, and perhaps Calvary. I hope I shall not complain, because the only artist who can count himself fortunate is he who has learnt the value of great failure. When Othello pierced his breast with his sword and remembered Aleppo his soul cried triumphantly: "Now my experience is complete.

I thank the Gods!" For Othello was undoubtedly a great artist.'

'You are making him out to be as self-conscious as yourself, Oscar,' said one of the young men.

' Not to be self-conscious is not to be conscious at all,' Mr. Wilde answered.

' And not to be conscious at all—well, that is to be " Ruskin." '

Everyone laughed, although again Violet saw nothing funny in the remark. Mr. Ruskin, whose name was constantly in the paper, was most certainly of a greater importance than Mr. Wilde. To be important was, apparently, with these young men, to be mocked at. The Queen, Lord Tennyson, Mr. Kipling, Thackeray, Mr. Ruskin . . . it was some comfort to her to recollect that she admired them all. She wanted to remain and she wanted to go. Something stirred in her. The house in Onslow Square, Timothy, the general trend and colour of her daily life—she was suddenly dissatisfied with them all. Family gossip, for a moment, seemed stupid and worthless.

But this was absurd. She resented her disloyalty to herself. She got up to go.

' Do tell me, Mr. Wilde,' she said, ' one or two interesting new poets to read.'

He regarded her with so kindly a glance that once again she wondered whether she would not invite him to luncheon.

' I am afraid there *are* no new poets,' he answered her. ' But then there never have been. The best poets are old from the beginning. · Mr. Dowson there is a poet, and a very old one indeed, although he only left Oxford a year or so ago.' He indicated one of the young men on the sofa.

'I will remember.' She nodded graciously to the young man. 'Come, Timothy. Well, Cynthia, it has been most delightful. You must come to luncheon one day soon, dear, and perhaps you will bring Mr. Wilde with you.'

But in the carriage she was indignant. Whatever had possessed her to be affected by two or three young men who were so irreverent and common? And how stupid of her to have determined to have a word or two with Cynthia. It was a lovely afternoon; she would drive to Kensington and see old Emily, who always loved a gossip and was certain to know the latest thing about Vanessa and Ellis.

Timothy was silent as he always was when exposed in public. But he was not unhappy. He thought longingly of the large heavy man who had begun to tell him a story and the other pale-faced man who had drawn things for him, who had not laughed at his own drawing of a ship but on the contrary had liked it so well that he had shown it to his friend.

The weather brought out the bicycles. What Timothy longed for more than any of the world's treasures was a bicycle. As a very small infant at Uldale he had seen Mr. Rander, the clergyman from Ireby, ride a penny-farthing, and that glorious entrancing vehicle with its high front wheel and tiny back wheel had seemed to him the height of possible adventure. Now first Mr. Stanley and then Mr. Dunlop had provided safety and reasonableness. Everyone was beginning to bicycle. Timothy, sitting stiffly opposite his mama wishing that his hands were as large as umbrellas that they might cover his velvet suit, thought of the kind gentleman who had told him a story, and then with longing eyes looked out on the driver of the omnibus, yet more fervently on the driver of the hansom, but most passionately of all upon the bicyclist. It was the bicycle that must be—not, he hoped, so far distantly—his engine of escape!

'Now here we are at Miss Newmark's,' said Violet to her little son, speaking with some severity. She was still uncomfortable, still felt the touch of an unknown hand upon her mouth. . . .

Here at any rate there would be no hindrance to a nice heart-to-heart gossip. But, as always when she was ill at ease, she was severe with her children, and now she spoke impatiently to Timothy and told Hunter, the coachman, that she might be a long time, she might not, she did not know, she could not tell, all this in the severe irritable voice that the Herries always use when they are nervous.

She had no need to be nervous as she stood, holding Timothy's hand, outside the gloomy plague-stricken door of Miss Newmark's Kensington home. She had been here so very often before and called the door ' plague-stricken ' because the paint had faded and blistered until the surface represented a chart for one of the more sinister Oriental diseases. Above the door was

a top-hat made of iron and painted a faded green.
The lower part of the house had once belonged to
a hatter. Violet had often noticed how, when she
called upon Emily on a sunny day, there was
always a gloomy sky in Emily's street. Very odd
—as though the houses in Emily's street were
mountains! It was the same to-day. Just as
Parker, Emily's viperish maid, opened the door,
the first drop of rain fell. Parker had been with
Emily for twenty years and hated and despised
all her fellow human beings without any exception
whatever, save only her mistress. She could not
be said to love her mistress, because she was part
of her, bone of her bone and flesh of her flesh, and
both Parker and Emily were above any kind of
personal vanity. But Parker was of importance
at this moment in the Herries family affairs because she was on speaking terms with Miss
Fortescue from Hill Street. Miss Fortescue, who
as a child had lived in a family of Second Advent-
ists, visited Emily frequently and had many a chat
with Parker before she left the house. These
little social contacts have made history before now.

Violet and Timothy climbed the steep dark
stairs and heard the thunder roll beyond the walls.

'I said it was going to thunder,' said Violet.
All the way up the staircase Timothy gazed with
a terrified eye at the series of pictures from the
Bible decorating the wall. He hated to come to
this house for many reasons, but chiefly because of
these pictures, which represented all the more
dreadful scenes in Old Testament history—the
murder of Abel, the destruction of the Cities of

M

the Plain, the Flood, the Serpent in the Wilder-
ness, the Plagues of the Egyptians. He wanted
to hurry past, but his mother held him always
tightly by the hand; her movements were slow
and solemn. He wanted not to look, but was compelled. There was in one picture a fat snake with
a flicking tongue, which writhed its coils around
a shrieking woman and her child. That snake
was remembered by Timothy all his life long.

'Mrs. Bellairs and Master Bellairs, Miss
Newmark.' So Parker always announced them
in tones of the deepest dissatisfaction. She called
her mistress ' Miss Newmark ' on every occasion.
They both preferred it.

In spite of the gloomy and uncertain light of
the drawing-room, Violet saw at once that there
were other visitors. Emily, now a large and heavy
woman with hair of a steely grey, a slight grey
moustache on her upper lip, dressed always in
black and having the oddest resemblance at times
both in voice and features to her very different
brother Barney, came forward and greeted them.

' Miss Pope. Mr. Pope. Mrs. Glass,' she said,
introducing a pale young woman, a young man
and a stout round lady wearing an old-fashioned
bonnet, a very large bustle and a cashmere shawl.

On all ordinary occasions when Violet paid
Emily a visit the same procedure was followed:
first Timothy was put into a corner of a sofa
and given a large illustrated Bible to look at and
then the two ladies drew up to the fire (or the
window if it were summer) and gossiped away the
fortunes and happiness of every Herries in Eng-

land. But to-day things were different. The lady in the shawl, Mrs. Glass, said almost at once to Timothy: ' Oh, the pretty dear! Come and talk to me, my dear, and tell me where you got your lovely curls from.'

The room was littered with properties, sacred and reminiscent: Bibles, huge sea-shells, family albums, and volumes of poetry of a pious nature. These things gave the room the homely comfort which it needed. But to-day there was no homely comfort. Although the curtains were drawn and the gas lit, the thunderstorm could very distinctly be heard.

' I'll ring for some fresh tea,' said Emily.

' Oh no,' said Violet. ' I have had some tea with Cynthia '—then wished that she had not mentioned Cynthia, because Emily disapproved of her even more than she did of Vanessa. But to-day the mention of Cynthia roused no response. Emily seemed absent-minded. The three visitors were talking together, making a fuss of Timothy, who was struggling with a vast fragment of ancient and desiccated seed-cake.

Violet sighed, then patted Emily's knee.

' Well, how are you, my dear? I thought that I must just drive round and see how you were. For one thing Phyllis has had a letter from May Rockage that would, I was certain, interest you. Vanessa and Ellis have been staying with them, you know, and it seems from what May says that Ellis's jealousy is becoming *quite* abnormal. She says that if Vanessa leaves the room for a single moment he begins——'

' There you are, Miss Pope! ' Emily suddenly
interrupted. ' Just what you said! A thunderstorm! Now isn't that strange after Mr. Euclid's
sermon last Sunday evening? Did he not fore-
tell this very thing? God will thunder forth from
His Heavens that we may be warned of the Wrath
to come! Those were his very words. Violet,
I've told you again and again that you should go
to St. Hilary's of a Sunday. Yes, and bring your
husband with you. It would do him a world of
good. . . . Listen to that thunder! God speaking to us if ever He did and yet we will not listen.
. . . I beg your pardon, Violet. . . . What were
you saying about May Rockage? '

But here the pale young woman, Miss Pope,
interrupted. She had, Violet thought, a *hysterical*
face, for set like little fires in that pallor were her
large burning eyes. She had a quiet, rather
pleasing voice; her long, thin hands were clasped
together as she spoke, and her body trembled
slightly.

' Miss Newmark, you must come next time
with my brother and myself. Really you must!
You cannot imagine how affecting it was! The
dock directors are monstrous. They could not
behave as they do had they seen some of the sights
that Edward and I see every day. They refuse
to agree to the payment of sixpence an hour. Sixpence an hour! They would give a dog more!
Dr. Liddon's fund for the women and children
is being wonderfully supported and that shows
what the public feeling is! You should go down
to the docks, Miss Newmark! They are empty.

The Corn Exchange and the Coal Exchange are practically empty. You should have heard how Mr. Burns and Mr. Tillett were cheered last week, by big City men themselves. I cannot sleep, Miss Newmark, thinking of the women and children—the starving children——'

Violet thought that she was about to cry, and oh! how uncomfortable that would be!

Emily said: ' God is working for them. The day will come when these wicked oppressors will be punished as they deserve.' Her voice was gentle. She was touched as Violet had never seen her before. Really, with the thunder outside and this emotion inside, the atmosphere of the room was quite embarrassing, but soon the three on the sofa with Timothy began to talk eagerly together once more.

' Have you seen Vanessa since she returned, Emily? ' Violet asked.

' No, my dear.'

' I do hope that everything is all right in Hill Street. You know that Benjie is in London again . . .'

' We should go through the streets,' Emily cried, ' with Christ at our head and *force* the world to listen. I suggest, Miss Pope, that you go and see Mr. Euclid and suggest something of the kind to him. I know that you would find him sympathetic. We don't ask God's help enough. That's what *I* think! We try with our own feeble hands to build up His kingdom. We can do nothing of ourselves.'

' You are right, Miss Newmark,' said the

young man in a voice unexpectedly deep and manly. He got up. ' Would you mind—should we not offer up a prayer now to Almighty God and ask Him to help these poor brothers and sisters of ours? Where two or three are gathered together . . .'

He went down on his knees, almost upsetting the table as he did so. The three ladies did the same and Violet was also compelled to do so, although she felt extremely awkward.

' O Lord! ' said Mr. Pope, ' we Thy humble servants gathered by chance together speak to Thee with one voice for our unhappy brothers and sisters. We have sinned in our selfishness. We have not asked for Thy guidance. Show us, dear Lord, in Thine own good time how these, our suffering brothers and sisters, may be rightly helped and taken out of their undeserved misery, and open the hearts of the wicked taskmasters that they may incline towards mercy and know that without Thee the temple that they build rests on sand. Show us what to do, O Lord, and give us strength so that without fear we may go forward in Thy good work to Thy glory, world without end, Amen.'

' Amen,' said everyone.

Then Emily repeated the Lord's Prayer.

When they rose from their knees they showed no shyness at all, but began eagerly to talk together.

For the second time that afternoon Violet felt that a hand had been laid on her mouth.

There was nothing to do but go.

' Come, Timothy! . . . Well, Emily,' she broke in upon their talk, ' we must be on our way. Do let me know in what way I can help. I had no idea that the poor people were suffering so. It does seem too bad indeed.'

She embraced Emily, bowed to the others and departed.

In the carriage again, as she turned towards home, she felt vexed and uneasy. There had been something very queer abroad this afternoon. Now, as they drove through the streets, the lamps seemed to blow in the breeze that had sprung up, everyone was moving swiftly as though bent on some secret mission. Her mind hung about Vanessa. Vanessa was in great trouble. She was sure of it. It was as though the lights, the passers-by, the air of the September evening thickening as though with a film of thin smoke about the roofs and chimneys—all these formed a clouded mirror in whose glass she saw pictures shaping. Real trouble. Not something at a distant remove, about which it would be amusing to gossip. Her heart was moved, she could not tell why. She made Timothy sit beside her, wrapping the carriage rug round him, then put her arm about him drawing him closer to her. She would go and see Vanessa to-morrow . . .

Vanessa was in trouble. And then these poor people at the Docks . . .

' How much is there in your money-box, Timothy? '

' I don't know, Mama. About three shillings, I think.'

'Wouldn't it be nice to give it to those poor women who can't give their children enough to eat?'

'Yes, Mama.'

But he thought: 'Now it will be longer than ever to buy the bicycle.'

'We must be kind to everyone,' said his mother, kissing him.

A JOURNAL AND SOME LETTERS

BARNEY NEWMARK kept for many years a Journal. In 1896 he squeezed out of it what he felt to be some of the more interesting passages and made a volume of reminiscences which failed to attract much attention,[1] but for the purposes of a family chronicle some extracts from the original diaries are of interest. It was their misfortune, from the ordinary reader's point of view, that they dealt with private persons rather than public, family incidents rather than general affairs. He had always kept them for his own amusement and in that at least he had the advantage of some of his contemporaries.

February 4, 1890.

. . . I could not conceive what he wanted me there for. I came to the house, I'll confess, in spite of my advanced years, rather like a naughty schoolboy ordered to the headmaster's study. He has of course never liked me. That is in fact putting it mildly. I date his positive antagonism from that evening long ago when he went with me and young Benjie on an evening out, went

---

[1] *Some Memories,* by Barnabas Newmark. Hatcher and Thorburn, 1896.

reluctant and returned disgusted. With the years his dislike has grown to a kind of horror. I stand for everything that he most abominates—a writer of cheap novels, irreligious, a lover of horses and women, a gambler, a drunkard. That I have been none of these things very desperately has given him only the greater displeasure. Had I gone to the dogs he could have pitied me. As it is I have kept my head just sufficiently above water to be still a danger. Vanessa's persistent loyalty to me has only aggravated the trouble. This is the first time that he has asked to see me for at least twenty years. The odd thing is that I have always rather liked him. He has an integrity that I can admire. Then I understand so well his desire to win affection and his inability to do so, his shyness, his rectitude of conduct, his honesty. But is not his rectitude at last threatened? After yesterday I am inclined to think so.

I arrived at Hill Street punctually at four o'clock. Orders had been given that I was to be taken straight to his private Cave and I was conveyed up dark stairs and along sombre passages as though I were either a criminal or a spy—both, perhaps.

He was not there when I arrived and I had time to look about me in what is surely one of the gloomiest little rooms in London—bookcases filled with those dreary volumes of Journals and Papers marked with little white paper labels, a bald bust of some dead Roman, a large stern writing-table with silver writing things and an immaculate blotter, a grim, grizzling little fire and two leather armchairs. Poor Ellis! Many is the time, I am sure, that he has paced that little room, wondering why things are wrong when he is himself so right, shrinking from a world that he would give his soul to placate, lonely and bewildered, suspicious and uneasy.

I was not there very long. He came in, said: ' Well, Barney, how are you?' asked me to sit down, seated himself opposite me, and then, tapping his fingers together, looked all round and about him with a kind of distressed dismay on his features that was both pathetic and funny.

We hung about for a long time without coming to the point. He said that it was a long while since we had met, that it was a pity, that he understood that Allsopp's brewery was in difficulties, that the shortage of gold made separate bank reserves very difficult, that it was high time the Treasury dealt with the Coinage question, and so on and so on. He asked me whether I was writing anything just now in that tone in which people who despise novels speak to novelists—as you might inquire of a coiner whether he has been doing well lately.

I made some suitable reply and then silence fell. I had no intention of helping him out. It was his affair, not mine.

Then suddenly it came:

Would I use my influence to persuade Benjie Herries to leave England?

So that was it? I stared and said nothing. He was extremely uncomfortable. He got up and began to walk the room. I must under-

stand that he had nothing against the fellow. He
disliked him, of course. He would be perfectly
frank with me. He had always disliked him.
He dare say that he was well enough from his own
point of view, but I would have to admit that he
had never been a credit to the family—very much
the opposite in fact. His life, quite frankly, had
been something of a scandal. That was Benjie's
private affair. The last thing that Ellis wanted
to do was to interfere with anyone's private life,
but his continued residence here in London was
distressing to many of us, and he, Ellis, as head of
the family in London, had felt for a considerable
time that something ought to be done. He wished
me to understand that he brought no kind of personal charge and he hoped that I would regard
this conversation as most strictly confidential. I
broke in there that of course he understood that
I was Benjie's friend. I also asked him did he
wish me to tell Benjie that he had spoken to me?

To which he answered in great distress, Oh
no! of course not! The last thing that he wanted
was any quarrel with Benjie. It was unfortunate,
most unfortunate, that some time ago he had been
compelled to ask Benjie not to pay any more visits
in Hill Street. He regretted it, regretted it
greatly, but on his last visit he had been so outrageous in some of his views and had behaved
most insultingly to Miss Fortescue—' My wife's
lady housekeeper,' he added, poor dear, as though
he didn't know that *I* know exactly all that Miss
Fortescue is and how thoroughly Vanessa has
always detested her.

But really, he went on, the point was simply this. He did not wish to detain me. He knew that I was an extremely busy man. Did I think that I could persuade Benjie that a residence abroad would be more suitable, more suitable in every way . . . more suitable in every way . . .? While he was speaking my mind ran over past family history. How odd this perpetual desire in our family for one member to rid himself of another! Old Francis the Rogue and his brother, Jennifer and Christabel, Walter and Jennifer, John and Uhland—as though it is a law with us that one half of us shall always aggravate the other to madness! Yes, to madness! As I watched Ellis, with his pale face, long restless hands, pacing up and down the room, it seemed to me that there was a kind of insanity, born of brooding unhappiness and perhaps jealousy—born anyway of a tormented unsatisfied love—not so far away!

I replied, quietly enough, that I certainly could not ask Benjie to leave the country. I could not agree with him that Benjie was a scandal. He was sometimes in London, sometimes abroad; he had his own friends, lived his own life. I could not see that he did harm to anyone.

At that Ellis became more agitated. Oh, indeed! And what had I to say to his fight at the Alhambra and a night in Vine Street? What had I to say to . . . Here, with a great effort, he pulled himself up. He must repeat that he had no charges against Benjie. It was only for his own good, for his own good and the general good. . . . Did I think—— Here he paused,

seemed to be greatly agitated.　Did I think that
a sum of money . . . ? He was prepared to offer . . .

At that I rose from my stiff leather chair.

'Look here, Ellis,' I said.　'This goes no
further of course.　It ends here.　But you don't
know what you're saying.　You send for me and
suggest to me that I should bribe a friend of mine
for no reason whatever to leave the country, go
into exile.　He has a son, you know, a fine little
boy.　Frankly I shall forget that we ever had this
conversation.　It is not worthy of you.'

I went to the door.　He followed me and
looked at me for a moment with such malevolence
that it was a new Ellis, one I had never seen before.

'Oh, of course,' he said.　'You are his friend.
I might have known. . . . *Good* afternoon.'

And that was all.　I was out of the house
almost as soon as I was in it.　As I walked away
I thought that I had never known a queerer business.　How could he have supposed for a moment
that I would have listened to anything of the kind?
And to what a pitch of brooding and suspicion
he must have come to send for *me*, whom he has
always so greatly disliked!　At first I was so
angry that I felt like turning back and punching
his head.　Then the pathos of the man himself
came to me.　And after that real fear and anxiety
for Vanessa.　I have known for some while that
things are not going well with her, but she keeps
up so brave a front that none of us can tell what
is really happening to her.　Is she meeting
Benjie?　Does Ellis know of something hidden
from the rest of us?　Of one thing I am sure—

that she will be honest and straightforward in all
her dealings; but all last night the thought of her
enclosed behind those walls with Ellis for her
companion and Fortescue in attendance—well,
frankly it spoilt my evening. But I have put
everything concerned with this little incident down
here exactly as it occurred. The facts may be
useful one day. I am Benjie's friend, Vanessa's
friend, even—who knows?—Ellis's friend. A nuisance for an old, selfish, comfort-loving bachelor
who hates to be disturbed. All day to-day I have
been tempted to go and see Vanessa. But no.
It is better that I avoid Hill Street for a time.
The nuisance is that to-night when I should have
been getting on with my novel I haven't been able
to think of a thing. Quite impossible to get
Vanessa and Ellis out of my head!

From Vanessa Herries to Rose Ormerod at
27 Rue Montaigne, Paris.

Sept. 6, 1890.

MY DEAREST ROSE—I have the whole evening
to myself—Ellis has gone out to some meeting
and I have done what I love better than anything
else in the world, gone to bed, had some supper
on a tray and now can write you a long letter without fear of any interruption.

After you left on Wednesday I was very unhappy. We had so short a time together and said
so little although we both wanted to say so much.
I was unhappy too because I knew that you were.

You could not disguise it from me. All your brave talk about your loving to be alone and Fred's having been so generous in his settlement and your finding it such a relief to have done with men for ever—none of it deceived me in the least. The very fact that we had to meet as furtively as we did in Miss Mercer's rooms speaks volumes! You and I furtive! Doesn't that of itself show that there is something very wrong? Why not have come to Hill Street? Ellis would not have eaten you. You never used to be afraid of anyone. And although you pretended that it was for *my* sake. Well, I can deal with Ellis, you know. I haven't lived with him all these years for nothing! It struck me suddenly to-night with a kind of terror that for the first time in all our married life I have, in this one week, concealed two things from him—one my meeting with you, the other, well, I will tell you of the other in a moment.

But now, Rose, listen. Let me tell you here sitting alone in my room, loving you very dearly, something that I could not when we were together. The association with Fred Wycherley has been dreadfully bad for you. You know it better than I. I was shocked at the change and more shocked still at your own consciousness of it. You saw also a change in me. Yes, it is true. I know now this about life—that, far more than I had ever supposed, we affect one another. To live with another is to have to fight for your own integrity morning and night. I suppose if you love someone enough you lose your own integrity and find another much finer. But if you don't . . .

You know, Rose, when leaning on that hideous
mantelpiece at Miss Mercer's you looked over
your shoulder and said: 'Vanessa, men don't
mind what they turn their women into,' I knew
and you knew where you have got to in these last
years. Rose darling, oh darling darling Rose, let
this life go. Leave Paris. Settle somewhere in
England where it isn't too dull. You have some
money, you have intelligence enough not to need
the kind of life Fred gave you. I suppose you
don't hunger for Cumberland all day and every
day as I do, but why not try it for a while? Try
Eskdale or Coniston or Ullswater for a month or
two. They are lovely in the autumn. The Cumbrians are kindly uninquisitive folk. Why not
bring that Mlle. Mathieu with you whom you
like? I don't know. Making plans for others is
never any good, but if you were to tell me that I
was to have a week on Cat Bells beginning to-
morrow, I think I'd just go crazy with joy! But
Ellis is frightened of Cumberland. He thinks
I'll go wild there, leave him for a gipsy or something. Yes, after all these years of my good proper
social behaviour he still fears it. More now than
ever. Which brings me to the other thing. I
nearly told you on Wednesday. I tell you now
because you are the only one I can tell. I won't
even say that it's a secret. If Ellis asks me to-
morrow morning: 'Have you seen Benjie
Herries?' I shall say yes and tell him all (or
almost all) about it. But if he doesn't ask me . . .

This is all it is, my grand secret. Since 1887
I have seen Benjie a few times and spoken with

him, but never by arrangement. I saw him at the Jubilee Procession. I saw him once at the Theatre. On neither occasion did we exchange a word. Last week on a lovely afternoon I had been visiting Cynthia. I sent the carriage back and walked in the Park. I was wandering down one of the paths, thinking how old I was getting (I am thirty-one, you know), frightened as old married ladies will be at the way that life was passing, when I looked up and there was Benjie with his little boy walking straight into me! Well, what were we to do? We couldn't, all things considered, just pass one another with a stiff bow! I had never seen his little boy. But in any case we could not stop to reason. We have been friends since we were babies. He belongs to all my life, all of it that I love the most passionately. We—oh well, why explain anything to you? There we were and both of us so happy at meeting that we could only look at one another, without words. It was, as it always is when we are together, as though we had never parted. We sat down on a bench, the little boy beside me. We had then the happiest hour of our lives. We did not mind who saw us. People were passing all the time. If Ellis had come by, I would not have cared. What was there to be ashamed of? Even Ellis must admit that all this time we have done our duty, never tried to see one another, never written. We love one another of course. We have always loved one another. I have no doubt that if we had married as we meant to, we would have been very unhappy, but happiness and unhappiness have nothing to do with love. If Ellis asks me—as he will one day—do you love Benjie, of course I will say yes. I will never lie to him or to anyone. We thought of none of this, not of Ellis nor the family nor anyone at all but ourselves. He told me about his life, that he was lonely, that Tom his boy—who is six now—is going soon to a little day school in Bloomsbury; I told him a little about Hill Street—not everything. But we didn't talk very much as I remember. We were simply so happy to be together again. Then we walked a little way and parted. We made an arrangement to meet in Barney's rooms. He was to be there and I was to come as though by accident. But in the evening when I was home again I knew that it would not do. I wrote him a letter saying that we must not meet again and I know that I was right. Nothing stands still. At every meeting it would be harder to part and what would the end of it be? But, Rose—never forget it—Benjie has been wonderful during these years. With his character and nature to keep away as he has done, to help me by keeping away—no man has ever done anything finer.

Well, there it is. So we go on, the three of us, doing our best. The queer thing is that since that meeting, Ellis, although he can't possibly know of it, has been increasingly uneasy and suspicious. He isn't well, is working too hard and has dreadful headaches. Then there is Miss Fortescue, who hates me, of course, and would do me harm if she could. Poor Ellis—if only he would be content with what we have. All these years we have been friends. When he is happy we are *such* good friends and life goes so calmly, but lately I have been afraid. He behaved so strangely last year in Wiltshire that everyone noticed it. His love frightens me often and is becoming every week less tranquil. Can I manage all this? Of course I can. I have never been beaten by anything yet, but marriage isn't easy when it's dramatic—or perhaps it is I who hate scenes. *How* I hate them! Their childishness and extravagance . . .

Rose, darling, good night. Come away from Paris. Come home. I saw Horace yesterday and his silent wife. He was *very* cheerful and bright and breezy.—Your most loving

VANESSA.

Part of a letter from Mrs. Timothy Bellairs to Miss Lavinia Newmark, Constance Court, near Manchester.

June 25, 1891.

. . . I do hope that your father is better. Of course at his age one must expect a day in bed now and again. Timothy has been complaining of lumbago and I insisted on his staying in bed last week. As you may imagine, no one has been talking of anything but the Baccarat Case. Poor Sir William! I am quite *sure* that he did not intend cheating and I really think that some of them showed great vindictiveness. Mrs. Lycett Green is quite a friend of May Rockage's you know, and Timothy has often met Lord Coventry at his Club. Of course the Prince's appearance in the witness-box was *the* sensation and everyone

thinks that he came out of it very well and that it
was most unnecessary of the *Times* to say what it
did! It is all a great pity and very bad for the
working classes, who are inclined in any case to
be troublesome just now. Timothy says that that
man Burns is a danger to the country and ought
to be in gaol. I suppose you haven't heard of
poor Vanessa's illness. So unlike her to be ill
and nobody *quite* knows what the matter has been.
They say all sorts of things, but I refuse to listen
to gossip, especially of the family variety. . . .

Barney Newmark's Journal.

February 18, 1892.

I haven't entered anything in this Journal for
weeks, but yesterday afternoon deserves a record.
Stephen Bertrand, the novelist, came in most unexpectedly to see me. And then who should
enter directly after but dear Horace Ormerod?
It was really entertaining to see them together.
Horace I knew had come for some purpose. He
would never waste his time on me unless he wanted
something. Bertrand had met him once or twice
before and was pleased to see him again, as well
he might be, for no human alive could better
satisfy his passion for innocent copy! I could see
Bertrand's round, obese little body hurrying home
that he might not waste a moment before putting
Horace's self-revelations into his notebook! And
how Horace gratified him! He was nervous a
little, I suppose, of Bertrand's cold penetrating

eye and talked therefore twice as much as ordinary!
His healthy rosy face beamed with complacency;
his honest, clean and incipiently stout person
vibrated with energy. His friendly eyes shone
behind their glasses. With jolly deprecation
he told us how good he found life to be, how easy
it was to be generous, how simple to see the best
in everyone! ' Have you seen Valentine lately? '
Bertrand asked rather cruelly. Valentine at the
time of the success two or three years back had
been a great friend of Horace's, who liked to be
intimate with one of the most promising poets of
the day. *Then* one thought that he would be
John Lane's proudest boast, that Dowson, Lionel
Johnson and the rest were not in the race compared
with him! But alas, the bottle and the ladies
have been too much for poor Valentine! No one
is a greater adept than Horace at dropping a
failure gracefully! There were, I swear, tears
behind his glasses as he cried:

' Poor Valentine! I wish I could do something for him. He's his own worst enemy, I fear.
I did have a word with him some six months ago,
but he has become oddly embittered, poor fellow.'

This was joy indeed to Bertrand, who most
skilfully led poor Horace on until I could not bear
it any longer and had to interfere. When Bertrand was gone Horace said complacently:

' Nice fellow, Bertrand. I must invite him
to lunch at the Club. He seems to know everybody and that last novel of his had quite a success,
hadn't it? '

I told him that it had.

' What was it called? '

I told him.

' I must remember and read it before he comes to luncheon.   You novelists are all so sensitive! '

Funnily enough, on reflection, I felt a strong resemblance between Bertrand and Horace, although I must confess that I like Bertrand the better of the two.   Both are equally complacent, Horace because he is a fool and Bertrand because he is pleased with his gifts, with his penetration into human motives, with his cold, clear eye, with his horror of sentiment.   But both are sentimentalists, Bertrand perhaps the greater of the two.   Bertrand cannot understand that he is disliked (as I fear that he is) and attributes it to the fear of his fellow human beings for the naked truth.   Bertrand is the kindest of men and Horace one of the unkindest, yet Bertrand is held to be cruel and Horace, although a fool, good-natured. Bertrand means no unfriendliness when he puts his acquaintances into his books.   Indeed he thinks they are lucky fellows to be used for so fine a work of art!   ' The artist,' he says, ' thinks only of his art,' and forgets that his friends, and still more his friends' friends, think only of their reputations.   And this is odd because Bertrand himself thinks a great deal of his own reputation. But I like Bertrand and give him free leave to make any use of me that he pleases!

But now to the point, Horace's point.   Violet Bellairs and Horace have become great friends of late.   They have many things in common. Violet, it seems, often appeals to Horace for help in her

troubles.   Here is the latest!   Young Timothy
(a very decent kid who will be an artist one day)
has, it appears, been indulging a secret friendship
with Tom, Benjie's boy!   Where they first met,
or how, I don't know.   It has been a complete
and most dreadful surprise to Timothy's poor
mother!   Tim is fourteen and Tom under eight,
so you would not suppose that Tim was in great
danger!   But Tom is already—according to
Horace (who by the way has never set eyes on the
child)—a young ruffian and a moral danger to
any companion.   This letter was discovered by
Violet Bellairs in the pocket of one of her young
son's jackets.   Horace left it with me and I copy
it here verbatim, spelling and all:

DEAR TOM—Mother is going out tomorrow afternoon and it's a harfholiday.   The old cat is in bed with
inflewensa so i can meat you the same place.—Your
loving   TIM.

I at once inquired of Horace whether 'the old cat'
was Tim's mother, but it seems not.   She is apparently Violet's governess, and I at once said that
Violet deserved all she got if she wouldn't send
Tim to a decent school like any other boy.   ' Oh,
well,' said Horace, who never defends his friends
whole-heartedly unless everyone around him is
doing the same, ' Violet thinks Tim's delicate.'
    ' She only thinks he's delicate because she's
tried to make him so,' I burst out, ' with his curls
and all.   The kid's a fighter and with a will of
his own.   He'll be a grand artist one day.   But
what's the matter anyway if Tim does make a
friend of young Tom? '

Oh, then Horace broke out, forgetting all his natural caution. Benjie was a danger to everyone. They were all coming to feel it. I, poor fool, was the only one left to stand by him. He was contaminating the family reputation. Ellis had done with him long ago. Alfred hated him. Cynthia wouldn't have him in the house, and now, through his nasty little boy, Benjie was perverting Violet's child. Only I and of course Vanessa . . . and everyone knew that Vanessa was in love with him even though she *didn't* see him. . . .

At that I did gloriously what I haven't done for years. I lost my temper. I lost it so that I took Horace by his fat shoulders and shook him so that his glasses rolled on his fat nose. All my long dislike of Horace was at last expressed. I called him every name I could think of, obscene words that Horace's soul would shudder at; I told him what I thought of him, that he was false, sycophantic, mean, treacherous. (Only one side of Horace after all, for he is not a whit worse than the rest of us, only naïver.) I told him that I was Benjie's friend and that Benjie was worth all the family put together (which Benjie isn't, of course), I told him that he was not fit to breathe in Vanessa's presence and that if I ever heard him utter a word against Vanessa again I'd murder him. I'm sure he thought that I would. I never saw a man look more frightened. So I threw him out of the room, washed my face and hands and laughed a little. But it is truly no laughing matter. The thing grows. It is instinctive. Benjie is some wild half-human animal to them and Vanessa

does love him. And Ellis' brain begins to turn.
Well, God help them all, say I, and myself no less
than the rest. But how the troubles in this world
come from chatter! Fools like Horace and Violet!
—and perhaps ruin to nobler men because there
are parrots on the trees. Could we but keep
silent for a little while and let men work out their
own salvation without comment. Too much ever
to hope for!

A letter from Benjamin Herries to Vanessa Herries.

TOLEDO, Spain, *April* 6, 1893.

Vanessa, will you ever see this? For the first
time I am breaking my vow and now I shall continue to break it, for my endurance has been
tested too sharply. This goes to Barney. I have
told him to let you have it. I expect no answer
but I am hungering for one—only one line to tell
me that you understand the sort of fate that
follows me, a ridiculous fate that I cannot escape
and shall no longer try to, by God! This last
time was too much! As though it wasn't enough
that Cynthia should be there, but Alfred and his
wife as well! I had not drunk a drop that evening.
You may believe it, Vanessa. I have never lied to
you yet. I came into the place as sober as a
church. The woman who was with me was a poor
thing I used to know, hadn't seen for years, found
that afternoon longing for a meal in a decent
restaurant, quietly, with a friend. Well, the Café
Riche is decent enough, isn't it? We were having

our meal as quietly as two churchwardens all sober in our corner. I saw Cynthia come in with a man. Then a little later Alfred and his wife. We had nearly finished when Fanny Church (the girl with me) caught my arm, begged me to pay my bill and go. There was a man at the other side of the room of whom she was terrified. She had been his mistress once, it seemed, and he had treated her damnably—a heavy man with a black beard. Before I could do anything he had seen us and come to our table. He paid no attention to me, but, smiling at Fanny, said he was glad to see her again and where had she been all this time and wouldn't she tell him where she was living? She was trembling all over, poor girl, looking at me to protect her, and I, very quietly and most politely, asked him to go. He asked me who the devil I was and did I know that I was interfering with his friends, his *very* old friends. Then he put his hand on her arm. What could I do then but knock him down? Wouldn't any man have done the same? He was a big man and he fell heavily and a table went over. Of course there was a row. I waited quietly, told him that I would pay for the damage, left my card and went out with Fanny. That was all. But quite enough of course. Cynthia and Alfred had all the evidence they wanted.

But the *second* public row, Vanessa! After all these years of discipline. Was there ever anyone born more unlucky? Well, this is the end. I can do no more. I was never made for this hypocrisy nor were *you* made for that life in Hill Street.

Tom is at a good school, that's one comfort, and I
am finished for ever with London and that farce
of civilisation and the damned family and their
chatter and my trying to be what I'm not. I'm
finished for ever with everything but loving you.
I shall write sometimes and tell you how I love
you, for I am a boy no longer. If you do not
answer me it will make no difference. I cannot
believe any longer that you are happy, for I know
that you are not. I shall always let you hear where
I am, one way or another, and one day, if it is all
too much for you, come to me. In this black
town I am at peace again. The walls go sheer
down to the plain. As I look from my window I
can see the gipsies moving off along the narrow
street, and in the Cathedral it is so cool and dark
that you can stay there by the hour and hear
no man's chatter. I have a room in an inn; my
room is high up. Everything is grand here, the
gold in the Cathedral, the wind against the wall,
the sound of water falling as it does in Cumberland. One thing already makes me think of you.
In a little church at the end of my street there is a
picture painted years ago, they say—*pictor ignotus*
—of a Black Centaur pawing the ground, his head
up, while over the hill there goes a Procession
carrying the Host. I don't know its meaning,
bringing Christ to the Heathen or some such
thing, but the Centaur is noble. His head is up,
he is ready for what may come, and he made me
think of you because of that dream you used to
tell me of—the horse that strikes the mountain
with his hooves, springing from the water. I *will*

not be dismayed, Vanessa! That little London
is behind me. I have only Tom and you in the
world, but *you* know and *I* know that as long as life
lasts we will go on finding the meaning of it,
loving one another although we never meet again,
not fearing anything, not despising life until we
know that it is worthless, which it is not and never
will be. I have tried hard all these years to do as
you say. *You* know how I have tried—but I will
be tied down no longer. They think, Cynthia and
Alfred and Ellis and the rest, that life is a cow to
be milked—but it is rather the Centaur on to
whose back I will leap. One day you will ride
with me. When you see Barncy tell him to write
to me once a week about Tom. That's a good
school, they say, and I liked the man when I saw
him. There's someone playing music in the inn
room and I'm going down.

You won't despise me I know, or believe anything they say. You are part of me and the law
is we must *not* despise ourselves. Give my love to
dear Violet and Timothy and Barney's sweet sister
Emily. Oh God! but I'm glad I'm done with
London!—Your loving, loving   BENJIE.

*A letter from Vanessa Herries to Barney Newmark
in Rome.*

March 13, 1894.

MY DEAR BARNEY—The moment I received
your telegram I went down to the school. Fortunately Ellis was away on a visit to old Horace

for three days. I went down, taking Lettice
Marrable with me. You don't know who she is,
do you? She is a girl from Cumberland whom
I have brought to Hill Street as my secretary—
a kind of counter to Miss Fortescue. She is an
odd girl, would like to dress like a man, has all
this new craze for tennis, breeches, women's
freedom—all a result of the frightful way she has
been kept down all her life at home. However,
you won't want me to waste your time with *her*
except that she is the most loyal, faithful, attached
creature who ever lived and a great comfort to
me. We went by train to Salisbury and drove
over to the school. The headmaster, Mr. Collins,
was exceedingly kind. I took the greatest fancy
to him, his wild black beard, his black eyes so
lively behind his glasses, and his evident friendship
and loyalty to Benjie. He took me to the In-
firmary where Tom was. He *has* been very ill,
but is much better. He lay there as white as
paper, but he has Benjie's smile, hasn't he? I had
only ever met him once before—in the Park a long
time ago—but he remembered me and told me
about the book the nurse was reading to him—
a Talbot Baines Reed—and he was greatly
amused by Lettice's hard straw hat and the sort
of golfing-suit she wears! He likes funny things,
Mr. Collins says. He asked me had I seen Tim,
Violet's boy? He showed me a letter Tim had
written him in secret. Awkward for me, wasn't
it? He was too white-faced for me to say it was
wrong for himself and Tim to write to one another.
I said nothing. In fact, dear Barney, *all* my ideas

of the difference between right and wrong are fast
vanishing! Which brings me to this. You
must send me Benjie's address, tell me where he
is. I had a letter last year from Toledo. I did
not answer it. I have not written a line to him
since he left England, although *you* know how I
have wanted to! But I can keep it up no longer.
I must send him word about Tom, right or wrong.
He worships his father of course. He said to me
over and over again: 'When is he coming? He
hasn't been here for a long time!' For the
Easter holiday he is going, as you know, to the
Quintires again at Longbridge Deveril. He says
it is nice there, they are kind to him, pleasant girls
who tell him stories. They write them them
selves, he says, which seems to him marvellous.
They have a magazine among themselves and oh!
Tom said, wouldn't they be lucky if they could
get Tim to draw pictures for it! He is a warm-
hearted little boy. I wished, coming back in the
train, that I had one like that of my own. Lettice
slipped some money under his pillow. I saw her
do it, and it's good of her because she hasn't a
penny! But he's all right, Barney, and I like that
master. For myself what shall I tell you? Nothing. You're in Rome and London is far away.
We have been to *Charley's Aunt* and *The Second
Mrs. Tanqueray*. We have had a party. Cynthia
has had a party. I have had a letter from Will
Leathwaite, from Cat Bells. Barney, Cat Bells!
Cat Bells! Cat Bells! . . . No more of that.
Shall I tell you about clothes? Sleeves are very
wide, waists narrower than ever. Skirts are long

and trailing. My arm aches with holding mine
up. Everyone is wanting to be rich. If you are
rich enough you can go anywhere. Alfred gets
richer every day. But this is not what you want
in Rome. I have read a beautiful book by a man
called Yeats, *The Celtic Twilight.* Have you
heard of him? But of course you have. Ibsen
is the fashion. Ellis—but I will not weary you
with my silly troubles. Am I happy? No,
Barney, I am not. Is anyone happy? Possibly
no one. Are we all being gay and merry? Very
gay and merry indeed. Send me Benjie's address.
—Your loving
                                    .VANESSA.

Extracts from Barney Newmark's Journal.

April and May 1895.

COPLEY BECK, DUDDON VALLEY.

. . . This letter. What am I to do about it?
Ellis has not spoken to me for years, thinks I am
altogether on Benjie's side and must know that
Benjie is in England. I showed him the letter
at once and asked him what I should do. It is
a number of days old, forwarded with some bills
and papers from Duke Street—and we have been
walking from Seascale to Boot, from Boot here—
that's two days. Vanessa is probably in Cumberland by now. She gives a Keswick hotel as an
address. But Benjie swears that she can have no
idea that he is even in England, much less that he
is walking up here with me. But is Ellis likely

to believe that? Can I prevent them meeting, do I even want to? I put it to Benjie on his conscience. 'My conscience says that I am to see her,' he answered, and his silly brown face lit up with such happiness at the thought that I would be a thief robbing a blind man to prevent him. Why should I stop their half-hour? She has the Marrable she-male with her, she tells me, and she is surely enough for anyone as guard! Ellis need never know—*will* never know! Benjie is even now, as I write, standing out on the sward, looking at the lambs, the water jumping the rocks of Harter Fell in a thundercloud and the sun striking like a sword on the fresh green of the larch. He is standing there kicking stones with his foot, giving little leaps. For a small man, he is a packet of vitality, but it is happiness that makes him leap! To see her, out of the blue, without arrangement on his part . . . by divine accident! He will go over to the little hotel at Dungeon Ghyll for a day. Vanessa and the Marrable girl can stay the night there or drive over from Ambleside. Could anything be more discreet? And I'm tired of Ellis. He has been considerably rude to me for years and he is making Vanessa unhappy. That's enough for me. . . .

. . . Benjie and I have been talking for hours about the Wilde affair. Benjie sees her tomorrow and can think of nothing else, so I talk to divert him. But poor Oscar! What a muddle of vanity, British hypocrisy, snobbery and false judgment. As to the crime itself I say nothing. It has not, thank God, been one of my temptations, but as I have always yielded to every temptation I *have* had, if that had been one of them I might have yielded to it. How do I know? Anyway it is more mental than criminal, I suspect. But this I do know: that Oscar is always at his best with very simple childish people. He is himself a child with his vanity, heartlessness, kindness, generosities and self-confidence. I always disliked him when he was showing off, but put him with children or stupid kindly men or warm-hearted impulsive women and he is lovable indeed. Men like Whistler or Charles Brookfield or Carson really terrify him at heart, as children are frightened when, sent for by unwise parents to show off to their elders, they suddenly see the cold eye of a guest speculatively fixed upon them.

This remains at least, that never even in hypocritical England has there been such a revolting show of hypocrisy as this—and it will put Art and Letters in England back for twenty years. . . .

. . . Well, we are back again, and Benjie is out walking in the rain and dark by himself. I have had a happy afternoon walking for two and a half hours with the Marrable girl. We landed at last, after climbing Wrynose, back at Blea Tarn and sat there patiently. I never saw it more beautiful with the trees coming down black as thunder to the very edge, Wordsworth's ' Solitary's ' cottage white in the sun and the sky pale yellow behind the Pikes. I was interested too, for she told me enough about Ellis to fill a volume. Vanessa's

patience with him must be a marvellous thing, and
even Lettice Marrable who hates him, pities him
too. It must be a weird household now with the
monstrous Fortescue, Ellis half-mad with a vague
torturing jealousy that has no facts at all to justify
it, and this odd, masculine country girl who worships Vanessa. ' I would *die* for her! ' she cries,
looking into the green water of the Tarn.

' Now would you? ' I ask her cynically.
' Easily said.' Then look at her and feel that she
really would!

What will be the end of it?

Of what Vanessa and Benjie said to one another
I know nothing. I asked nothing. I was told
nothing. Vanessa is better than ever. She is
surely the grand lady. To see her walk across a
room is a benefit to humanity. But she is a child
too. When she saw Benjie there she simply
laughed, took his arm and walked off with him. I
don't think I ever before realised so sharply that,
behind all this present fuss and bother, there is the
fact that they have been friends all their lives
long. That makes a difference, of course.

I said: ' Miss Marrable, shall we take a stroll? '
And so we did. *What* a plain girl! But I can't
help liking her.

*Part of a letter from Violet Bellairs to Cynthia
Worcester.*

Sept. 9, 1896.

. . . We have been with the Rockages a week
now. I can't say that it's a comfortable house—

horses and dogs morning and night, and Carey is so far behind with the *Times*—which he intends to read every night but goes to sleep over—that he is still discussing the Jameson Raid. It has been the hottest summer ever known here and the children feel it. Timothy is being very difficult. Carey agrees with me that this painting nonsense must be knocked out of him! I never knew anyone talk so much about *Cricket* as Carey does. It's Ranjitsinhji for every meal, or whether Cambridge or Oxford bowled balls that *weren't* balls in the University Match! Men are too strange and I've simply given up trying to understand them. Timothy *will* read this nasty new paper the *Daily Mail*. I think it's the *halfpenny* that appeals to him. He always *loves* to get something for nothing. I hear that Benjie Herries is in Africa and has married a negress. Thank heaven that friendship between his boy and Timothy was nipped in the bud. Did you ever know anything so horrible as the baby-farming murder? I hear that the Dyer woman actually . . .

From Master Tom Herries to Timothy Bellairs.

LONGBRIDGE DEVERIL,
September 9, 1896.

DEAR TIM—I will bicycle over on Tuesday and be *just inside* the farm gate by Locker Wood at half-past three.—Your loving

T.

ELLIS IN PRISON

On that warm evening in July 1897 Timothy
Bellairs senior left Ellis soon after dinner and went
home. He was going to bed; he had a touch of
lumbago and would catch it in time.

' He looks a lot more than his sixty years,' Ellis
thought with some satisfaction. And he did. He
had grown terribly stout. It would have been
better for his health had he stayed in Cumberland.

The house was still as the tomb after Timothy's
departure—and why was it never really warm even
on these summer evenings? Or was it Ellis who
was never warm? After seeing Timothy off, he
stood in the hall listening to the silence. Vanessa
was at the theatre with the Worcesters, and he had
promised her to go to bed early because all day
he had had one of his terrible headaches. It was
she who had suggested that he should invite old
Timothy to have dinner with him, because Timothy
was no trouble but would chatter on and on about
anything or nothing. So he had done; about
the Jubilee, very different from the '87 affair—
not many people in the streets and the Queen so
feeble, poor old lady, that it had almost killed her;
all the same, *what* a country England was! The
Review at Spithead made you feel that: no other

country could touch us for a Navy! Still, the
country hadn't the style it used to have with
cohorts of young men on bicycles and these halfpenny papers. Fine poem, Kipling's ' Reces-
sional.' (He recited some of it as though Ellis
had never heard it before!) Made you feel proud
to be a Briton *and* a Herries! He could remember
when he was a boy in Cumberland. . . . And Salisbury had said that Africa was created to be the
plague of the Foreign Office. Some truth there!
They had better watch President Krüger. (He
spoke with scorn of Krüger as though the Herries
family had decided in conclave that Krüger was
a rat and ought to be stamped on.) Well, we are
getting on, getting on. . . . Sixty last birthday, and
yet it seemed only yesterday when old Madame—
Judith Paris—had threatened him with the cane
she always carried, for stealing gooseberries out
of the Uldale garden. Pity that place was burned
down! Fine place. And there was something
about Cumberland which . . . But Ellis did not
like to hear about Cumberland, and changed the
conversation. Well, he must be getting home.
This damnable lumbago . . . Driving with Violet
yesterday in the Park. Did Ellis know that
Alfred had bought one of these motor-cars, and
only last year, wasn't it, they had changed the law
about a man walking in front with a red flag?
Pity in his opinion they *had* changed the law.
How were you to protect the public with these
things charging all over the place? However,
they would never do away with the carriage, thank
heaven. Sensible people would always prefer the

horse to those stinking, screaming engines that nobody could control. Well, well, it was a changing world and time he went home. Violet wasn't quite the woman she had been. A bit puffy in the chest and they were not quite happy about Timothy, who was at Cambridge now and not settling down as he should. Always wanting to go to Paris and paint! Ridiculous notion for a gentleman's son.

Well, well, good night to you, Ellis. Give my love to Vanessa. Still the handsomest woman in London. . . .

Why was the house so silent? When would Vanessa be back from the theatre? It was of no use to go to bed. He never slept until she came to say good-night to him, and she knew that, and was good about returning early. Good? Was Vanessa good? As usual so soon as he began to think of her his heart thumped in his thin bony breast, and that other man, taller than he, with the handkerchief wrapped round his head, stole out of the wall and stood beside him. *Why* was the house so silent? The servants must be moving about somewhere. Miss Fortescue must be in her room. He climbed the stairs to his study, the other figure keeping pace with him. The room was cold. The bust of Cicero watched him with its blind lidless eyes. Could you watch anyone were you blind? Why, most certainly. His shadow with the handkerchief bound about its head was blind and yet, with ceaseless preoccupation, it watched him.

He began to pace the room as now so many,

many times a day he paced it. The distance that
he must cover was not of great extent *and* how
well he knew it! So far to the writing-table
where he would pause and arrange, rearrange,
arrange again the silver writing-things. Then,
half turn, four paces to the wall where there hung
an excellent engraving of that fine picture, ' Christ
Leaving the Praetorium.' Christ, so gentle, so
kindly, His hands bound in front of Him, the
crowd pressing forward, the stout muscle-swelling
guards restraining them. One guard Ellis had
come to know well, a broad, cheerful, helmeted
fellow looking over his shoulder at Ellis and, Ellis
thought, in some friendly way warning him.
Warning him of what? Well, and then, half turn
again and down the room until you reached the
door. This door, which was painted an ugly
light brown, had for a handle a round cold white
knob. Ellis always touched this knob, grasped
it indeed with his warm fingers, for its chill indifferent hardness comforted him; it stilled his
beating heart. He thought of it sometimes when
he was in the City or the Park or at the Play. That
cold white knob, so gloriously indifferent! What
did *it* care whether he were torn with jealousy,
whether Vanessa loved him? . . . But of course
Vanessa did not love him. That was the first
fact. He stopped, as a thousand times he had
stopped, in the middle of that floor, and marshalled the facts that, when seen in an ordinary
row, would make him a sensible clear-headed man.

It only needed that they should be properly
marshalled, and he saw them like little children

(cretins perhaps) with large round white heads like the door-knob, all sitting in a line, their white fishy hands folded, waiting to be marshalled.

Bald-headed Fact One. Vanessa did not love him, had never loved him, would never love him.

Bald-headed Fact Two. He loved Vanessa with a burning, devouring fire. (It was literally that. In a cavity behind his ribs this fire was burning. He could see the flames leap and fall and leap again.)

Bald-headed Fact Three. He was jealous without reason. Jealousy. Dreadful. Like catching a disease that turned your bones to water. Intermittent. It was most devilish in this—that it left you for five, ten minutes so that, within that space, you saw quite clearly and wondered how you ever could *be* jealous. See! See! No reason. Vanessa has never been faithless to you. She is honest, is fond of you, has been very, very good to you for more than a dozen years. And then, the more savage for its brief absence, the jealousy returns, just distorting everything so that the wallpaper is tinged with green and the cat moves to its platter of milk with private purpose in its eyes.

Bald-headed Fact Four. That he is no longer any good in the City. That his business powers have left him. That young Alfred who has come into the Firm is already taking his place. He must see to this. He is losing money.

Bald-headed Fact Five. His body. That he cannot sleep. That he has headaches. That he is suspicious of everyone. That he is drinking.

That his body is hot at one moment and cold the next. That he sleeps with Vanessa when she does not wish it, which is what no gentleman should do. That the Family—Violet and Cynthia and Alfred and Emily and the effeminate Philip— are watching him just as he is watching them and everyone else. Cat and Mouse. Mouse and Cat.

Bald-headed Fact Six. That he thinks much about the past. His father who wanted him to love him, but he could not; his poor old mother; his shyness and awkwardness and longing to be liked; the first moment when on old Madame's Hundredth Birthday he had seen Vanessa. Shadows, shadows of the Past. That Cumberland which he hated and feared. Always trying to lure him back to it again so that it might set its fingers about his throat and hold him there while the mocking rain poured down on his upturned face and the stone walls crowded him in and the clouds came lower and lower . . . All the ghosts of the Past. Old Herries, poor Francis who shot himself, John who was murdered, mad Uhland.

Bald-headed Fact Seven. That this beastly, threatening world had as its representative that brown, ragamuffin, dissolute gipsy whom Vanessa loved. Had always loved. They had been children together.

Bald-headed Fact Eight. That when all the Facts were seated quietly in the row he would see how unreal they were, would see that he was Sir Ellis Herries, third Baronet, a wealthy decent citizen of Queen Victoria, much honoured by his friends, thought well of in the City, possessing

the handsomest woman in London for his wife,
'the kindest, the truest, most popular. There
was, he would see, no reason at all for agitation. All was well. He had reason to be
happy. He must go about and show people
that he meant them well, that he was a likeable
good man, that the hospitality for which his house
was famous was practised because he wished them
well, because he liked them and wished them
well. . . .

Someone was in the room. He started as
though a gun had been let off in his ear. Oh! it
was Miss Fortescue.

' I beg your pardon, Sir Ellis. I thought you
had gone to bed. I came to put these papers
ready for you in the morning.'

Miss Fortescue was now, in appearance, completely the sinister remorseless figure of one of Mr.
Wilkie Collins' savage women. She was hard,
black (hair, eyes, eyebrows), efficient and humour-
less. Nevertheless she was no villainess. She
was sentimental, read with passion and admiration
the novels of Ouida, Miss Braddon, and that
comparatively new writer Mr. Hall Caine. She
was lonely and romantic and had, from the first
moment of seeing him, decided that Ellis also was
lonely and romantic. She was not in love with
him; she had loved so many times so many heroes
in fiction that no man in everyday life could satisfy
her. But she had from the first considered her
master as her child, to be protected, guarded,
aided. Vanessa's beauty had always irritated her.
She thought her kindliness a posture, for she was

convinced that she had married Ellis for his
money while in secret she had loved another—
which was quite in agreement with her reading.
She also by temperament distrusted Vanessa's
general friendliness, her high spirits, her generosities. This was not a world in which women
could let themselves go. There was danger,
as her novels told her, on every side. She kept
her romanticism and sentiment for her reading
and for one or two human beings—Ellis, her
ancient mother who lived at Canterbury, and an
ailing brother. It had, however, taken many years
for her dislike and distrust of Vanessa to grow into
hatred—that true and unalterable hatred that can
come to any human being who has never known
passion nor independence nor compliments. In
daily life she was an excellent practical woman.
She gave no joy to the house in Hill Street but she
managed it perfectly. Vanessa always admitted
that all the burdens were taken from her shoulders.
She added that she would willingly sweep the
floors and make the beds were Miss Fortescue
removed. She had never asked for her removal
because, as the years advanced, it became more
and more evident that Ellis would be a lost man
without her.

She stood now, her black dress sweeping the
floor in iron folds, the high puffs of her sleeves
made, it seemed, of steel.

Her pale cheeks might, had she been another
woman, have betrayed her excitement. The
moment for which, during many long, unjust,
weary years, she had been waiting, had arrived.

He had paused in his walk and seemed to be listening. Then he realised her.

'I thought you had gone to bed,' he said.

'Yes, Sir Ellis. I am just going. But there is one thing——'

'Yes?' he said, more at ease and comfortable now that the silence was broken and that the tall figure with the handkerchief on its head had slipped into the wall again. He sat down in one of the armchairs, picking up aimlessly a Society paper that was lying there. He opened it, turning over the pages, looking at the illustrations. There was a supplement illustrating the Spithead Review.

She stood near to him, her hands folded.

'You have often told me,' she said, 'that if there was anything that I thought you ought to know, I should tell you.'

'Certainly,' he answered. 'Yes, Miss Fortescue.'

'Something has come to my ears that I think you should know.' This was like a scene in one of Miss Braddon's novels. She recognised every step and movement. She was (a luxury seldom allowed her) herself a figure in one of her beloved stories. At the same time this was real life. The room was real; the persons concerned were real. She was the sort of woman who might poison an acquaintance, with no malice at all, simply that she might justify her own reading. Nevertheless there was malice, true revenge for beauty, wealth, power, that she had never enjoyed.

'I learnt to-day from an unquestioned source

that a little more than two years ago Lady Herries spent a whole day, practically alone, with Mr. Benjamin Herries in Cumberland. Probably she has already told you of this; if she has not, I think it right that you should know. It is exactly information of this kind that you have said to me that you *wish* to know.'

He asked her: 'Where did you learn this, Miss Fortescue?'

'A sister of Miss Marrable's is in London. She told Miss Emily Newmark, who this afternoon told me. Both Lady Herries and Mr. Herries, who are of course well known in the district, were seen in a compromising position at a hotel called the Dungeon Ghyll Hotel.'

He was shaking from head to foot, but all that Miss Fortescue saw was that his hand trembled against the paper and his foot tapped the floor.

'It is a long while ago.'

'Yes; but it can be completely substantiated by reliable witnesses if you wish it.'

Incredible that, loving Vanessa as he did, he should not have sprung from his chair and banished Miss Fortescue from the house for ever, but at her first word he had moved from the world where things are as they are, to the world, long familiar to him, where men are seen as shadows and a mist-like smoke reveals only monsters of distrust.

'Where and when do you say this occurred?'

'Just over two years ago. At a hotel called the Dungeon Ghyll Hotel in Cumberland.'

He waited a long time; then he said:

'It is of no importance.   Lady Herries, I think,
spoke to me about it.'   He looked at her.   'You
misunderstood me if you thought that I wished to
hear such things.   I know that you always wish to
help me, but I have complete confidence in Lady
Herries.'

She cleared her throat, a small, dry, mechanical
sound.

'I thought it my duty; I cannot bear to see
you deceived.   Whatever I do, I do out of loyalty
to you.   You are the only interest that I have and
you have taken me on many occasions into your
confidence.'

'Yes, yes,' he said.   'But I do not wish you to
speak of Lady Herries to me.   That is not your
province.'

'I understand,' she answered.   'If I have done
wrong, please forgive me.   I considered the matter
and thought that it was better that you should hear
of it from me than from someone—someone less
loyal.'

He took the paper and began to read.

'Good night,' she said, and went.

He read very seriously with knitted brows the
Society paper.   He read every word.

'*The sight of London divested of its boards and
bunting was too distressing to my aesthetic soul, so I
came down to Medmenham Abbey Hotel for a few
days' perfect rest, where the flags are not scarlet and
blue but violet and purple, and where they rest not
against crimson cotton, but on a tender background of
green leaves.   It is quite beautiful down here, the
only drawback to its complete charm being its distance*

from the railway station. I have a passion for flying from my fellow-creatures, so that they can flee after me; but when it is a question of a four-mile drive after an hour's journey with a change of trains at Bourne End, their pursuing ardour seems to cool. However, Mr. Playfair, whose marriage was such a blow to me last year, and who is living in the neighbourhood to write a book, offers to supply the social deficiencies of my existence, and Florrie's husband has comforted me with the loan of his punt, which looks absolutely beautiful with new blue and white cushions, so I expect I shall get on very well, and by my calm acquiescence in my solitary state excite the suspicions of my unworthy family. I have seen only two dresses worthy of the name since I came here, and they were both my own; one of light drab homespun with a mauve batiste shirt, with a turn-down linen collar and a black necktie, which does duty with a white linen skirt, crowned with a pale-green mushroom-shaped hat, trimmed with a mass of shaded green wings. Now I must go out and see if I can get Mr. Playfair to agree with me as to the charms of this latter.'

Of all of this he read every word; he read it all twice over, murmuring aloud some of the sentences: 'A tender background of green leaves' . . . 'I have a passion for flying from my fellow-creatures' . . . 'Mr. Playfair, whose marriage was such a blow to me' . . . 'Florrie's husband has comforted me' . . . 'The suspicions of my unworthy family' . . . 'A pale-green mushroom-shaped hat' . . . 'A mass of shaded green wings' . . . 'If I can get Mr. Playfair to agree with me.'

'Mr. Playfair, Mr. Playfair, Mr. Playfair,' he

repeated, looking at the shaded eyes of Cicero. Although he read the whole of this passage with such intensity and although some of the sentences from it were to remain with him for the rest of his life, he was not, at the moment, in the least aware of anything that he had been reading. He put the paper down, got his hat, and went out.

It was after ten o'clock, and the streets were quiet. Berkeley Square was very still, the leaves of the trees rustling faintly in an evening breeze, the clop-clop of a hansom's horse sounding once and again from Piccadilly. At this hour London streets and houses take on themselves a listening, watching air. They resume their own proper purposeful life which has been disguised during the day by the rushing torrent of human beings; with their lighted windows they watch the traffic of the world that moves without sound, their chimneys and doorways re-establish communication one with another. Like cats they can see in the dark.

Ellis walked, his tall body bent, his head with its high black hat a little forward, his hands clasped behind his back. He passed into the light of Piccadilly, then back again into thin-shadowed streets. His companion walked with him. It is the condition of the disease of jealousy that love, self-pity and hatred move forward together. The victim can be cured, in a moment, by a word, only to be the more diseased by another. He moves always in double form, for while he sees clearly his own madness he at the same time embraces it with eager conviction. He cries out for relief from his torture and at the same time refuses to allow himself to be relieved. Every word, every sound is a significant portent, and yet he is aware how insignificant these words can, in the final truth, prove themselves.

He accepts greedily evidence that he knows to be no evidence at all.

With Ellis this was the climax to years of unsatisfied desire—a climax, the night, the trees, the houses, the lighted windows, thundered into his ears, and yet he knew also that the facts were in themselves almost nothing. Two years ago. In all the time since then Vanessa had been kind, honest, attentive. If, at any moment, he had said to her: ' Vanessa, have you seen Benjie Herries? ' he knew that she would at once have replied: ' Yes—in Cumberland on such a day.' Thousands upon thousands of times in these twelve years he had longed to ask her this question and yet never once had he dared to do so. Since the day of the '87 Jubilee when he had spoken to her of the letter he had scarcely mentioned Herries, but in blind, secret, surreptitious ways he had spied upon her. That had been disgraceful. It had been disgraceful that he had permitted Miss Fortescue to speak to him to-night, but it is a symptom of jealousy that the noblest of men may commit disgraceful acts as a chaste woman will utter obscenities in delirium. And Ellis was not the noblest of men. He had, all his life, been lonely, mistrustful, caught in a web that he could not break.

This remained: Vanessa had spent a day with

Herries and had not told him.   She had spent
one day—why not others?   She had deceived
him in this.   Then she had deceived him often.
But she had not deceived him because he had not
asked her.   She had not lied.   She had, he knew,
never lied to him—but is it not a lie when a woman
sees her lover in secret?   Was Herries her lover?
It was at that agonising moment, a moment that
had visited him often before but never with such
tyranny as now, that he looked about him and saw
that the starlit sky, the houses, the deserted street,
were coloured a faint green.   'A tender background of green leaves.'   'A pale-green mushroom-shaped hat.'   'A mass of shaded green
wings.'   This faint green light trembled like the
mist of a cloud of green flies, touching the steps
before dark walls, the white posters of the evening
papers outside the closed and barred newspaper
shop, the bent figure of an old woman in a battered
straw hat picking something from the gutter, the
light of a gas lamp.

A hansom clattered past.   A bell from some
church sounded the hour.   Trembling with a
terrible chilling heat, Ellis turned homewards.

He was half undressed when he heard Vanessa
come in.   As though he were a man with a thousand ears he had been listening ever since he
entered his room for those sounds.   His door was
just ajar.   He knew what he would hear.   The
closing of the hall door, the soft voice of the butler,
Vanessa's softer one, a little pause.   Then ' Good
night,' the butler's ' Good night, my lady,' then

the sweep of her long dress as she climbed the
stairs. Then the opening of her own door, its
shutting.

After that he undressed feverishly, but was
extremely careful to fold his clothes, to place his
studs in their silver box, to brush his scanty hair.
Over his nightdress he drew on his dark grey
dressing-gown, went into the passage, listened,
then knocked.

She knew of course his knock. He heard her
say: ' Come in.'

She was sitting in front of her mirror, a white
wrap over her shoulders, brushing her long dark
hair which fell to her waist. As he came in she
looked at him over her shoulder, smiling.

' I thought you would be asleep. I came in
as quietly as I could.'

He stood by the door staring at her; seeing in
the lamplight with that dark flood of hair, the
white wrap over the loose white robe, her smile so
friendly and simple, he felt so furious a storm of
jealousy sweep over him that he lowered his eyes
as though, in actuality, he had been overwhelmed
by a tremendous arching wave of blinding deafen-
ing water.

At last he moved across the room and sat in a
chair near the bed. She continued to brush her
hair, talking happily. ' We went to *The Prisoner
of Zenda* after all. Peile had seen it before, but
as he never remembers anything *that* didn't
matter. It was new to the rest of us. George
Alexander and Fay Davis, you know. Miss
Davis is handsome, but *what* a stick of a part, and

Alexander never can forget the clothes he's wearing. The house was full, but of course it was
only revived last week. I saw Johnny Beaminster
and, oh yes, Alice Parlington. You remember
—you danced with her at the Devonshire Ball.
She was Isabella of Spain or something. Well,
she asked about you and wants us to go to dinner
one night. . . .'

She moved into her dressing-room. For a
long while he sat there, staring in front of him.
She returned and got into bed, giving him a light
kiss on his forehead as she passed him.

'What sort of an evening have you had? Was
old Timothy a terrible bore? I thought of you
when Alexander was an hour or more kissing
Flavia's hand. I was most dreadfully bored but
comforted myself with thinking that you were
equally bored at home. Cynthia looked so pretty,
but I am sure she is harming herself with her tiny
waist. It is smaller every time I see her. And
the smaller her waist grows the more intellectual
she becomes. Ibsen is her only wear. Elizabeth
Robins and Janet Achurch her only actresses.
She was so horrified when she found that I hadn't
read *Esther Waters* that I thought she'd fall out of
the box, and yet she puts up with Peile Worcester
who can hardly spell his own name. She loves
him, I really believe . . .' She stopped. She
was aware that he had not spoken since he had
entered the room. She sat up, resting her head
on her hand.

'What is it, Ellis? Aren't you well? Is your
head still bad?'

She put out her hand and touched his forehead.
' Why, you're in a fever.   Let me——'
' No,' he said.   ' Don't do anything.   I want
to speak to you.'

She saw then that he was trembling from head
to foot and, as always when someone near her was
suffering, she forgot everything save that distress.
She got out of bed, put on the white wrap and went
towards the door.

' You're ill.   You're shaking all over.   Wait,
while I——'

He looked across the room at her.

' No, please.   There's something I must say.
Go back to bed.'

She did so.   She knew that something had
occurred while she was at the theatre.   She had
now for so many years been prepared for some
crisis that never arrived.   How many times there
had been a preface like this: Ellis in misery, dumb
with some hidden trouble, beginning to speak,
turning away like a child afraid, and because he
was always a child to her she always comforted
him, not asking him what his trouble was, but
consoling him.   Men seemed to her completely
inarticulate in any real distress—her father, Benjie,
Ellis, they were all the same.   They could not
speak when they had something important to say,
and when there was nothing they chattered inter-
minably.   She had been tired, wearied with her
day, the gossip, the heat of the theatre, but now
she forgot herself, wondering only, as she had
wondered so often before, what she could do to
soothe him.

Then he said, not looking at her:

' I heard this evening that two years ago you were alone in Cumberland with Herries—alone for a whole day, seen in a compromising position.'

So *that* was it! Two years ago. Ridiculous. A compromising position. That angered her. She drew back into the bed like a child who has been hurt.

' It is quite true that I was with Benjie in Cumberland one afternoon two years ago. The " compromising position " part of it is insulting. You remember, I went to Cumberland for a week. I had no idea that Benjie was there, of course. When we found that we were so near, we met. If you had asked me I would have told you.'

' Then you admit it? '

' Admit what? '

' That you met him secretly, spent the day with him alone, and told me nothing afterwards.'

' I met him certainly. We were alone for part of the time. I would have told you had you asked me.'

She looked at him, forgetting very quickly her own anger because the fuss was about so little, was so unimportant. Once sure of that, her earlier sensation swept back—that here was something small, childlike, suffering, and that she must comfort him. She moved nearer to him. She put out her hand and let it rest very gently on his shoulder.

' Ellis dear, there is no mystery, no adultery, nothing sensational. Miss Fortescue, I suppose, told you—to-night while I was at the theatre.

The "compromising position" could be only hers.
Now listen, Ellis. I have seen Benjie perhaps
half a dozen times since our marriage—and we have
been married over twelve years—so that's not bad,
is it? I have spoken to him twice alone, once in
the Park, once in Cumberland. I gave no promise
not to speak to him. If you had ever asked me I
would have told you. You must remember that
Benjie and I have been friends all our lives. I
know that some of the family don't like him, that
you don't like him, but when you have known
someone always—you see them differently.'

She had broken off abruptly, the tone of her
voice had changed, her hand had withdrawn from
his shoulder, because suddenly in the middle of a
sentence she saw that he, not hearing what she was
saying to him, was staring at her and that his stare
was crazy. Two people living together with
some ill-adjustment often find that they go with
slow measured steps for a long period and that
then quite suddenly, and for no apparent cause, as
though someone caught them in the small of their
backs and jerked them forward, they are hurled
into a precipitous and often catastrophic descent.
It is only afterwards, on looking back, that they
can see that this sudden jerk forward had the
beginning of its impetus in those very first slow
steps.

It was so with Vanessa now. She looked at
Ellis and saw a grotesque. Under the shade of
the lamp a man with a high domed forehead and a
lean peaked nose was sitting. This man wore a
grey dressing-gown and a nightdress that was open

at the neck so that two protruding bones, pink in the lamplight, gave him a hen's neck. His bare ankles too were pink and sharply boned. This thin bony man with his long body looped together in the chair had two eyes that looked at Vanessa but did not see her, looked beyond her at the room but did not see that either, saw something that frightened and angered them, something that no one else saw. This separate and apart vision—which is what the sane man means when he calls his brother insane—gave the figure in the chair an aspect of loneliness, isolation. Put this man in a crowded theatre and he would be quite alone, put him in a solitary cell and he would have company.

Vanessa saw life very simply. She had some of the good sense and quiet of her father, some of the good sense and love of action of her grandmother. She was entirely sane about all things. That she was also a poet because of the country blood in her veins affected not at all her relations with her fellows. She had lived with Ellis for more than twelve years and had needed all her patience, sanity, humour and common sense. Any woman, living with a man who loves her, whom she herself does not love, needs all these things, day by day and week by week. But she had learnt that you can care for a man without loving him and obtain satisfaction of your need—so she cared for Ellis. But behind her care there had grown and grown the fear that one day the situation would be too difficult for her. As she always herself said, she hated scenes, melodramas, floods of tears, self-pityings, shrieks and beatings

of the breast. She did not know how to behave in
such a world. Her father and mother had been
quiet people and she was a quiet person, although
as with her grandmother there was a wild passionate life at the core of her nature. She had also a
strong sense of the ridiculous both in herself and
in others.

But now, looking at Ellis, she had no sense of
the ridiculous. There was something here both
real and terrible. Instinctively, as she always did
in a crisis, she thought of her father. 'Help me
through this,' she said as she had done when she
was a little child on Cat Bells.

She suspected that Ellis was going to scream.
'He will rouse the whole house.' She even
remembered that Miss Fortescue would not yet
be asleep and that her room was not far away.
However, Ellis did not scream. He said very
quietly:

'You are a liar. Herries has been your lover
for years.'

(Even as he said it he knew that it was not
true. A very quiet little animal squatting inside
his head observed rather wearily: ' *That* you know
is not true.')

'Ellis, let us talk sense.' Vanessa held her
hands tightly together under the bedclothes.
'You are fifty-four. I shall soon be thirty-eight.
We have lived together for years and you know
that I have never lied to you, not in the smallest,
most unimportant matter. I have never been
Benjie's lover nor anyone's lover. You must trust
me as I trust you, otherwise we must separate.'

He leant forward towards her: her impulse
was to shrink back, but courage in this dangerous
moment for which, she felt now, she had for years
been preparing, was of more importance than any
other quality. So she sat up, put out her hand
and picked up the white silk wrap from the chair
on the other side of the bed; then with it warmly
around her, her hair falling darkly about her,
leaning forward, her hands clasped on her raised
knees, she said, very quietly:

' Ellis, listen. We are too old not to be sensible
about this. We matter too much to one another
to have scenes. Besides, I hate scenes. You
mustn't be unhappy and there is no reason——'

' No reason! ' he broke in. His thin hand shot
forward and caught her upraised knee. ' No
reason when you have made me unhappy for
years—not loving me, pretending, taking people
in, but not me. Do you hear?—never me! Do
you hear? Do you hear? I've had enough of it.
You drive me mad with your unkindness! You—
your lover . . .'

All drama verges on the ridiculous, and especially English drama. Vanessa had once, years ago,
in the Park, felt Ellis' physical contact although
he had not touched her. When her protective
affection was aroused Ellis' body was there for
her to comfort. But when he was angry or
sexually passionate she hated his touch. One
hand had closed about her knee, the other was on
her breast; his face was close to hers, his body
stretching up to the bed. If this scene was ludicrous she was too angry to notice it.

' You are hurting me,' she said.

He threw himself on the bed, his body convulsed, trembling, thrusting against hers. He tore open her nightdress; with his knees on the bed, his arms around her body, his hands bruising her, he pushed her down into the bed. Then his hands moved to her neck: panting, murmuring unintelligible words, he twisted her head round into the pillow. His hysteria gave him great strength; she began to wonder, in a quite detached way, whether he would kill her, and she had no power at all to resist. She tried to conserve her strength, for his hands now were so tightly about her neck that she could not breathe except in little gasps of pain. A black cloud, scattered with spots of intense light, pushed against her vision.

She thought: ' This is absurd,' and anger, fear of death, pain were all mingled in the dark wavering cloud.

The pressure of his hands relaxed. His body, without moving, lay heavily on hers. He was crying. She listened, as it seemed for a long time, to his sobs. At last, very wearily, she turned. He slowly raised himself, slipped off the bed. She lifted herself painfully and saw that he was kneeling on the floor, his head bowed, hidden in the bed, his body shaken with sobs.

For a long while there was no other sound in the room. At last she rose, went into the dressing-room, bathed her face and hands, stood there for a while wondering what she would do. When she came back he was still there, his body bent low, his face buried in his hands, crying.

She touched his shoulder.

'You will catch cold, Ellis.' She took her white cloak and wrapped it round him, but as her hands came into contact with his body he trembled. She went back into bed and waited for him to recover.

THE GREAT TIMOTHY SCANDAL

'YES, that is the cruel moment, when you really begin to feel old,' said Barney, nodding his head and settling his fat body more comfortably in his chair. 'I am sixty-eight, you know, Vanessa, in this year of grace eighteen hundred and ninety-eight—close on seventy—and I had no sense of age at all until last week when Nevinson took me to a Fabian Reception. There we were all walking about, already in the New Century, and every macaroon was a hard little Fact and every cup of tea an admonition not to be silly. Well, I like to be silly. In the coming century no one is going to be silly. It will be motor-cars, telephones, and all our food will be in little pills. If it weren't for things like the Klondike madness and the German Emperor and Sarah Grand I should know that the Fairy-Tale World was gone for ever. I've lived all my life in it, you know—charming world where everything had a meaning, when we believed in Faith, Hope, and Charity, assisted by Watts, when we really meant to be good even if we were not, when our children said 'Sir' and 'Ma'am,' when we thought the Albert Memorial lovely, and were certain that it was our duty to convert every unhappy Black Man to trousers and

the worship of our Sovereign. Why, in the
coming century I wouldn't wonder if we don't
believe in the Empire any more! I wouldn't be
surprised if even adultery becomes a scientific
fact rather than a moral crime. But I liked the
old world. It was *my* world. My silly novels
amused it (or a small fragment of it). I could
lead my own life without interference so long as
I didn't shock anyone in public, I could eat and
drink as much as I liked. I remember, Vanessa,
when I was a lad going to the fight between
Sayers and Heenan, the last great fight in England
it was. It was just an adventure then, but I can
see now that it was the end of an epoch. Epochs
are always ending, I suppose; it doesn't matter
unless you're seventy. Well, I've had a good life.
I can grow as fat as I like. Nobody cares any
more.'

'I care,' said Vanessa, smiling across the table
at him. They were having tea alone together in
Hill Street.

'While I'm getting fatter you're getting
thinner.'

'Am I? I'm thirty-nine this year, you know.'

He looked at her intently. He loved her very
dearly, more now than any other woman in the
world.

'You haven't been very merry lately, Vanessa,'
he said. 'I haven't heard you laugh as you used
to do for a long time.'

'I'm not very merry,' she answered, getting
up and walking about the room, her long black-
and-white dress trailing behind her. She turned

round, came over to him and stood beside
him.

' Barney—what are the family saying? '

' The family? '

' Yes—Violet, Cynthia, Alfred—all of them.'

' Saying about what? '

' Us—Ellis. This house.'

He didn't answer at first, then he said
slowly :

' Nothing much.'

' Oh! They are! In the last few months
they've been closing in—nearer and nearer. For
one thing Miss Fortescue's going must have been
enough to start them——' She drew a chair close
to him and sat down.

' I can't keep quiet any longer. Something
must be done. I've never been beaten by anything before, and I said that *this* shouldn't beat
me either. Two other bad things have happened to me in my life—once when my father died,
once when Benjie and I—oh, well, that's past
history. Each time I held my head up and said:
" I can manage this "—and manage it I did. My
married life hasn't been easy, you know, but there
have always been all kinds of little things to help
it along. Life, I'm sure, isn't *meant* to be too
tragic and I've had great consolation in feeling
that I was dressing up—*pretending* to be a grand
hostess, you know. Grandmother had a devil of
pride inside her and so have I had, and all the
time that I was longing to run away to Cumberland and be my real self I have felt as though she
and father knew about this game that I was playing

and wanted me to do my best at it. Then there's
been Ellis. I did him a terrible injustice in
marrying him when I didn't love him. The only
thing I could do in return was to be kind to him,
protect him, be his friend. . . . I'm not boast-
ing, Barney, but I truly have played the game all
these years. Now I can play it no longer. I'm
beaten.'

Barney took her hand in his.

' What's happened, my dear? '

' Last July Ellis and I had a dreadful scene.
Miss Fortescue told him one evening that I had
been alone with Benjie two years before in
Cumberland. You know—that day at Dungeon
Ghyll. In itself that was nothing, but Ellis had
been wretchedly jealous long before, as you know.
This was the climax. I was in bed and he almost
strangled me—a ridiculous scene, and it ended
in his crying all night, imploring me to forgive
him, going to sleep at last in my arms. For weeks
after that he was abject. He dismissed Miss
Fortescue, as you know, and for a time I thought
that I could manage him. That was July. This
is February. I know now that I'll never be able
to manage him again.'

She paused. Barney felt her hand tremble in
his.

' What is it? ' he asked.

' Ellis is mad. He has been mad for months.
Oh, only at times. We have parties here, he goes
to the City. So far as I know no one except
Lettice Marrable suspects anything. The servants may. I don't know. . . . You can't think,

Barney, how pitiful it is! If I could help him neither you nor anyone else should know anything, but I *can't* help him. It is I who aggravate him. I would give him anything, anything he asks if it would help him. Nothing can help him. I don't know whether to go or stay. But one day it will be too much for me and I shall go. The worst of it is that now, although I am so sorry for him, I don't feel even kind. If I had loved him I would stay with him for ever, but the dreadful thing now . . . the dreadful thing . . .' She turned her head. ' I hate him. I fear him. I have never been afraid of anyone or anything, but now the very sound of his step . . .'

She began to cry. Barney had never seen her cry before.

' I am middle-aged. I have loved one man all my life with my whole heart and he has loved me. Why should I lose everything? What have I done?'

Very quickly she recovered herself. She walked to the window and he waited. When she returned she was quite calm again.

' Listen, Barney. You are to say nothing of this to anybody. Only . . . if it gets too difficult . . . I shall ask you to help me. It may be better soon. He has been quite normal for the last month. Very quiet. Very submissive. Poor Ellis! Listen! He's coming. . . . I know his step now, even when I don't hear it.'

Ellis came in. But he was not alone: on either side of him walked a lady, and Barney remembered afterwards with amusement that the

first sight that he had of his two relations, Miss
Vera Trent and Miss Winifred Trent, was this
entry, guarding and protecting Ellis.

For they were, it seemed, distant cousins.
Ellis, quietly and with much courtesy, explained
it. 'Henry Cards—he had a wife back in the
eighteenth century, Lucilla. I can remember,
dear Miss Trent, my father speaking of her. My
father was born in 1770—it seems odd, doesn't it?
—and Lucilla died about 1780, I think. She
painted very charming water-colours. I shouldn't
wonder if there are not one or two still about
somewhere. Henry and Lucilla had two sons.
One of them, Prosper, was Jennifer's father, my
dear Vanessa. Well, Prosper married a Miss
Amelia Trent, and our two cousins descend
from her younger brother. Now what does
that make you to us, Miss Trent? About second
cousin twice removed, does it not? Still, there's
always a strong family feeling, a very strong
family feeling. . . .'

Everyone laughed. The butler brought in
fresh tea. Who were these two ladies? Vanessa
had the sense that they had been in this house all
their lives and had known Ellis for ever. However, it appeared not. They had never visited
Hill Street. Their carriage had driven up just as
Ellis had arrived from the City. They had met
on the doorstep. Oh! they must apologise, but
the fact is that they had lived all their lives in
Bournemouth. Such a charming place, and a
hundred years ago there was nothing at all but the
sea-waves, the sand, a tree or two! Yes, they

loved Bournemouth. Vanessa interrupted. That
was where Jennifer's father and mother had lived,
was it not? Yes, indeed, Doctor Trent of those
days had been a close friend of Mr. and Mrs.
Cards. Mrs. Cards had been *so* proud of
Bournemouth, so proud that she used to speak
and write of the town as a fashionable watering-
place when it was really only a house or two.
Doctor Trent and Mr. and Mrs. Cards had been
among its earliest inhabitants. Oh yes, they remembered all about the beautiful Jennifer! At
one time it was thought that she would become
the Duchess of Wrexe. She was actually engaged
to the Duke for a brief while, they believed. . . .

They chattered on, most happily. They were
both tall and elderly women and remarkably alike.
They were slim and had soft grey hair under their
large black hats. They wore black feather boas,
black silk dresses very long in the skirts; each lady
had a big bunch of imitation Parma violets pinned
to her breast and wore a very thin gold chain.
Their faces resembled those of placid, extremely
kindly sheep, but behind the mildness, Vanessa
decided, there was a strong and possibly relentless
determination. It certainly appeared that they
had made complete appropriation of Ellis. They
sat one on either side of him and, although they
smiled at Vanessa and listened with deference to
Barney, it was Ellis whom they admired. Their
voices were soft with that comforting murmur that
belongs to a distant mowing-machine on a summer
day. They took off their gloves; each wore two
or three rings, thickly studded with diamonds, on

the fingers. They were alike in almost every
particular; the only difference perhaps being that
Miss Vera was a little the more severe and determined of the two, Miss Winifred the softer and
more melting. They were greatly interested in
all the Herries relations—Alfred and his wife,
Horace and *his* wife, Emily, Phyllis' son Philip,
old Horace in Manchester, the Rockages in Wiltshire and their girls Maud and Helen, Cynthia and
Peile Worcester. They seemed to have the fullest
information about all of them. Vanessa noticed
that they made no mention of Benjie or Rose and
that they shook their heads over Timothy at
Cambridge. Yesterday, it appeared, they had
paid a call on Violet. With all their comments
and questions they were kind and hushed. They
behaved, Vanessa thought, as though they were
nurses in a sick-room.

Barney watched all this in amazement. He
found that he could not tear himself away. How
dramatic a transition! A moment before Vanessa
had been telling him of the most awful things,
speaking, he could not doubt, with the most
absolute sincerity, and now here they were all
drinking tea together, these two old maids like
two cows in a field, and Ellis, calm, benign, dignified, smiling and courteous! Had Vanessa been
imagining her terrors? No, he knew her too
well. She was the least hysterical of women. He
would not wonder but that the tears that she had
just now shed were the first since her childhood.
As he saw her now so quiet and so lovely in her
black-and-white dress, laughing, looking after the

two old women as though they were her first care in the world, smiling up at Ellis, her broad unruffled brow, her large dark eyes that had never lost the frankness, the eagerness of her earlier simplicity, her dignity as hostess, her natural friendliness as one human being with another, he thought: ' Well, I'm damned if she can't manage this. It's not so bad as she said.'

When he got up to go, Ellis most courteously went all the way downstairs with him, bending his long neck to hear what Barney had to say, rather as an Ambassador listens with the utmost attention to a diplomatic visitor.

' Hullo! That's a new clock you've got! ' Barney said, at the turn of the stairs. It was a long thin clock of gilded red Chinese lacquer.

' Yes,' said Ellis. ' Vanessa saw it somewhere and liked it.'

' Of course he hates me,' Barney thought. ' We both know that. Still, he's behaving very well.'

Finally, in the street, he shook his head. Ellis was not mad. He, Barney, knew a madman when he saw one!

When the ladies were gone Vanessa praised them. Ellis walked about the room and praised them too. How quiet, intelligent and well-behaved! He had feared that the women in England were lost, with their clubs, their passion for ' this Bridge,' their bicycle-riding, their indecent novels, their conceit. He understood that there were in London alone thirty clubs for ladies. What did ladies want with clubs? What——

He stopped, went to a table and fidgeted with a small silver box, a paper-knife, a book. He picked up the book, put it down.

'Vanessa, I did not care for that hat you were wearing yesterday.'

The room was rather dimly lit, the fire low. Her nerves had been shaken by her little talk with Barney, and as she got up and went across to him she felt an impulse, so strong that she wondered whether she would be able to conquer it, to tell him that she could endure this no longer, that she must leave the house, London, all the life that had, so ridiculously, been built up around her . . . leave the house, at once, without a moment's delay. . . .

'What hat?' she asked.

'The one you were wearing yesterday. The one with the—green birds' wings.' He seemed to have difficulty in speaking the last words.

She was standing close to him. Her agitation fell from her because his eyes were so weary that she was suddenly filled with pity.

'Oh, Ellis, you're tired. Go and lie down until dinner. Or stay here. I'll read to you.'

'No. But you understand, Vanessa? Please don't wear that hat again.'

She laughed and was frightened. His hand was shaking against the dark stuff of his trousers.

'It's quite new. Yesterday was the first time I had worn it. I thought you would like it.'

'Then you must change its colour. You know that . . . green . . . I don't like it as a colour.'

She tried to speak easily. 'Certainly. You shall never see the hat again.'

He put his hand out and touched her forehead. All her strength was needed not to move away, so she came closer to him.

'How cool your forehead is! Mine is always burning.'

She put her hand through his arm and drew him to the sofa. She helped him to lie down, arranging the cushions, but he said, as though he were half asleep: 'No, sit here—close to me.'

She sat down and he laid his head on her lap. He closed his eyes. The creeping whisper of the fire, the steady determined tick of the large gold clock on the mantelpiece filled the long, shadowy room. She sat there without moving. Her childhood—the friendly figures of her father, Will Leathwaite, Elizabeth, Aunt Jane, her grandmother—the places, the Cat Bells garden with the little sturdy wood, the stream, the line of the hill above the cottage, lovely days at Uldale, the seashore at Seascale, the purple shadows of Skiddaw, sunlit brilliant clouds of snow on Blencathra, the main street of Keswick, someone riding by on a horse, the scarlet coach from Kendal, the friendliness, the small gardens of daffodils and primulas, the grey steeple of St. John's above the green fields running to the Lake's edge, the hillsides flaming with bracken, the Herdwicks moving their thick sturdy bodies slowly in front of the shepherd . . . her father, her father waving his hand to her from his writing-table as she passed along the garden path, her father with his soft

lazy eyes, his loving ironical glance, his hand resting on Will's shoulder . . .

Tears stole down her cheek. Without moving
yet she felt that she was hastening, against her
will, down a dark path away from everything in
life that was loving and good into a house dark
and chill, with doors that would be locked behind
her. How dearly she loved life! How hard she
had tried to do what was right, and now she was
nearly forty, frightened like a small child, and
lonely . . .! She had never known that it was
possible for anyone to be as lonely as she was.
What was she to do?

And Benjie? She had, in these hard minutes,
kept him away from her, but now, heart and mind
opened, too weak any longer to resist, she threw
out her arms, he came running, running to her.
She clasped him to her, felt his face pressed close
to hers, his heart beat against her breast.

The Chinese clock on the stairs struck. The
gold clock followed it. For an hour she had not
moved and Ellis, pallid as a dead man, lay with his
head on her lap.

Then the Great Timothy Scandal sprang upon
her. It was an excellent moment for a family
excitement. There was but little in May 1898
for anyone to discuss. A small coal strike, a war
between the United States and Spain, the death of
poor old Mr. Gladstone, the Dreyfus case, the
low spirits of the Liberal Party. In none of these
things did the Herries take a very extravagant interest. Cynthia redecorated her little house and

O 2

gave an evening party for the Ibsen enthusiasts,
Alfred introduced everywhere an astonishingly
uncouth South African who was said to be worth
millions, Emily discovered a Prophet from Shore-
ditch. The Season began and huge evening
receptions rolled from house to house. The
West End was populated with coachmen, footmen and men with grave diplomatic countenances
hired for the evening. Every kind of carriage
and every kind of horse glittered and shone.
The window-boxes blazed with geraniums. The
Opera sparkled with diamonds. There was so
much money that everyone despised it and would
do anything, invite anybody, go anywhere, to
obtain more. Morals were as loose as usual and
manners beginning to crumble. Woman was no
longer subservient to Man, and the Empire was
at its apogee.

The Herries took all this for granted as every
other English family was taking it for granted.
The Herries concluded that everything would
last for ever just as it was. Emily's Prophet
said uncomfortable things, and Cynthia, Violet,
Mrs. Alfred, went to a meeting to hear him.
They found him very sweet with his deep black
eyes and flowing black hair. Melba sang at
the Opera. Also at one of Vanessa's parties.
A man called Conrad published a book called
Tales of Unrest, but no member of the Herries
family read it. Several ladies and gentlemen rode
in electric cabs. Violet wore an evening dress with
a high collar encircled with four rows of pearls.
Lettice Marrable was seen bicycling in a pair

of knickerbockers. For some while, however,
inside this dazzling world the Herries circle had
been moving quietly. There had been no family
sensation. Something strange was happening in
Hill Street although Vanessa appeared as usual
and Ellis was stiff, courtly and boring as usual.
Rose, it was said, was drinking herself to death in
Paris. Nothing had been heard of Benjie. One
topic of interest was the career of the two Miss
Trents, who went everywhere and were constantly at Hill Street. That, however, was not
a scandal—far from it. Two quieter, gentler
ladies could not be found anywhere.

The Great Timothy Scandal, then, burst
brilliantly and, small though its cause, it brought
in its sequence changes to many people. It struck
Vanessa on a sunny May day when, coming back
after a drive in the Park with Cynthia, when they
had both been very gay and talked much nonsense,
Lettice Marrable threw the news at the quiet tea-
table. Cynthia always regarded Miss Marrable
as a kind of aboriginal savage: her little hard hats,
her man-like tunic, short skirt, her brusque masculine tone and quite extraordinary masculine attitudes, her public smoking of cigarettes, her
abilities at tennis and golf, her passionate desire
that women should sit in Parliament, all these
things filled Cynthia with a wondering amaze.
She was never weary of looking at her, although
she did not care to be seen with her in public.

Lettice Marrable now came in and said:

' Timothy Bellairs has run away to Paris with
Tom, Benjie Herries' boy. Violet has just heard.

Timothy had a letter written from Paris.   Violet is
in a terrible way and says that Tom has perverted
Timothy or some word like that.   Timothy senior
has left for Paris.   If he sees Benjie he is going
to shoot him.   They are all talking at Violet's now.
I've just come from there.   Horace and the Miss
Trents and Carey Rockage . . . Benjie Herries
is to be horsewhipped whenever he's found.   Oh,
you never saw anything so funny in your life as
Horace threatening to whip Benjie—*when* he
finds him!   And the real joke is that Tom is only
fourteen.   He must have run away from school
up to town and met Tim here.   Anyway they are
both safe in Paris.'

Cynthia said: ' I wish I was.'

Vanessa said: ' But it is ridiculous of Violet to
blame anyone but herself.   Tim has wanted to
be a painter since he was a baby.   It is nothing
to do with Benjie at all.'

After that with every hour the affair grew.   It
seemed that Benjie *was* in Paris and that the two
boys stayed with him.   Then came news of a
meeting between old Timothy and Benjie.   Old
Timothy gave it him, it was generally understood,
' hot and strong.'   What really happened no one
knew because no third person was present: it was
difficult, however, for the Herries to believe that
Timothy gave anyone anything ' hot and strong.'
He was sixty-one, suffered from his heart, was
as fat as a barrel.   Moreover he was amiably
minded.

It appeared that Benjie's attitude was that, as
regarded his own boy, if he wanted to leave school

and see the world, he should do so. Benjie was
the same at his age. As for Timothy, he was
twenty-one and ought to know his own mind. As
a matter of fact he always *had* known his own mind,
and it was only the stupid conventionality of his
parents that held him back. It was said that at
this point old Timothy called Benjie ' a damned
blackguard ' and that Benjie did not resent the
insult as any gentleman would have done, but
offered Timothy a cigarette. It was further said
that the interview between Timothy and his son
was extremely painful. Young Timothy declared
that now that he was in Paris he was going to stay
there and that Tom Herries had had nothing whatever to do with it. They had been friends all
their lives, he and Tom; Tom hated his school
and wanted to be with his father. By this time it
was generally admitted that Benjie was the Devil.
He had always been the Devil. It was time the
family were rid of him.

Would Benjie come to London and face his
accusers? It was understood that, with a shrug
of his shoulders, he said that of course he would
come to London, although he had no idea what
he was to be accused of.

He came to London.

A meeting, as famous in its own small way as
Christabel's Ball or Walter's historic visit to the
Christmas party at Uldale, took place on the
second of June at the Rockland Club between
these gentlemen: Carey Rockage, Timothy Bellairs, Alfred Herries, Horace Ormerod, Barney
Newmark and Benjamin Herries, Esquire.

The best evidence of what actually occurred is to be found in Barney's Journal (the Journals are all in the family archives at Centor Park, bound in faded red leather, behind glass, in the library. Judith Paris' book and the earlier eighteenth-century papers are in the same bookshelf, equally protected and equally unread).

DUKE STREET, W. *June* 2, 1898.

I will try to put down as briefly as possible what occurred to-day at Rockland's, a matter purely of family interest but important perhaps one day to young Tim and to Tom.

I met Benjie at the Criterion for lunch. I hadn't seen him for a considerable time, but there he was, just the same as ever, brown with health, cocky as a robin—very like a robin. He has just that bright, roguish, adventurous, don't-care-a-damn kind of eye and, although he's stocky, his lack of height (always a sore point with him) gives him a birdlike appearance. He looked, I'll confess, a bit odd because he wasn't wearing a hat; he had a soft nondescript collar with his usual dark red tie in its gold ring, and his clothes were a sort of wine-coloured tweed. He is always scrupulously clean, though. Benjie's careless but at the same time spruce, and his brown cheeks, bright eyes, stiff close-cropped wiry hair, hands that look as hard as iron, taut springy body—all these, with the very kindly wrinkles about his eyes and his extremely engaging smile, prejudice you in his favour if you're an ordinary man on two legs

and not a hypocrite like Horace or a prig like
Ellis.

Anyway there he was, saying 'Hullo, Barney! '
just as though we'd met yesterday, and walking into
the big room at the Criterion as though he owned
the place and at the same time found it very absurd.

As usual he ate very little. We didn't talk
much either. He couldn't understand what they
wanted to see him about. ' I'm not a boy, you
know. I'm forty-three. I haven't harmed the
family so far as I can see. They seem to think
that I've lured Tim to Paris and that I may ruin
him body and soul—using young Tom as a decoy.
Damnable nonsense! Tim's a fine painter. I
don't know much about it, but he's started away
at Lucien's, which is, I believe, one of the best of
those places, and old Lucien himself thinks highly
of him. Tim's crazy about these men I don't
understand—Gauguin, Van Gogh, Cézanne—but
I'm ready to tell him he's right. How do you
and I know? We may have taste but we don't
care enough really to know. You can only know
about Art if you happen both to love it and have a
trained taste. Anyway, there he is and Tom's
learning languages. He's got a passion for them
and his great idea is to train for a War Correspondent. "What'll you do if there's never a war
again?" I asked him. "Oh, there'll always be
one somewhere," he said, and I expect he's right.
He can put things down on paper pretty smartly
for his age. Well, there they are, a decent pair of
kids. What's the trouble? *I* had nothing to do
with it. What do they want *me* to do? '

' As I understand it,' I answered, ' they want
you to tell Tim to return to his parents. They
think you've got some unholy influence over him.'

' Unholy be damned! ' said Benjie. ' I've
never had the smallest influence over anyone.'

' If you refuse they'll expel you with bell, book
and candle.'

' Expel me from what? '

' The family circle.'

' A fat lot *I* care! '

So after luncheon we went along. Rockland's
is, I have always thought, the stupidest and slowest
Club in London. It is just right for elderly
Herries like Timothy and Carey Rockage and old
Horace when he comes down from Manchester.
It is small and dingy, and the room where they
waited for us smelt of whisky and stale cigar-
smoke. The windows looked as though they
hadn't been cleaned for months. Timothy and
Carey belong to grander Clubs of course, and when
they want to show off they go to them, but for a
real family bust-up Rockland's is the place. They
were all waiting for us in an upstairs card-room
which we had to ourselves. When we came in it
struck me at once how large physically we were
compared with Benjie and how physically unfit.
Carey, Timothy, Horace and myself are all stout
men and Alfred is pasty. Benjie could have
taken the lot of us on and thrown us all out of
window! However, he was not in the least
aggressive. He smiled at everyone as though he
loved them and if no one smiled back that was not
his fault! Oddly enough as I looked round the

room I felt, although I'd come there of course as
Benjie's friend and supporter, an acute sympathy
with all of them. I understood exactly how they
felt. With the exception of Horace they are all
decent men, and in my opinion the decent normal
Herries man is about as decent as any Englishman anywhere. He is brave, loyal, patriotic, God-
fearing, good to his women and generous to all
men. Simply he hasn't any imagination. A little
imagination and they would understand that
Benjie's type is permanent. You can't get rid of
it by cursing and abusing it. You've got somehow to make terms with it. Put it in gaol, exile it,
and it will always return. When men like Carey
and old Timothy have learnt how to assimilate
men like Benjie, the Herries family will rule the
world—until then it will be always second-rate.
But, of course, that assimilation will never occur.
So there will be always tales to tell, poets formed
out of rebellion, and wars between nations. But
I understood how they felt about Benjie. You
could see, as they looked at his country clothes and
his round head with its sharp little eyes and his
sturdy little legs, that he was the personification of
disorder to them! And they were right.

Old Timothy, as the principal sufferer, took
charge and, standing in front of the fireplace, with
his legs spread, he outlined the case. Unfortunately he was both lengthy and pompous. He said
the same thing over and over again. What it came
to was that he wanted his son back, that Benjie
had tempted him to Paris and must therefore bring
him back to London again. There was nothing

personal in this. He spoke as though Benjie were
the kind of man with whom he could not possibly
have any personal relations.

When Timothy had finished at last, Benjie
answered quietly that he had *not* tempted young
Tim to Paris, that Tim was of age, and that,
although of course it was a pity that he and his
father did not agree, it was nevertheless the boy's
own affair. ' In fact,' said Benjie, beaming round
on all of them, ' I cannot see what I have to do
with it or why you have asked me to meet you
here.'

At that everyone wanted to speak at once. It
was interesting to me to see the strong likeness
that springs up between the men of our family
when we are together. Alfred with his sharp
nose that is always a little shiny, his high cheek-
bones and short black curly hair can hardly be said
to resemble short-armed, short-legged, paunchy
Carey who is the perfect Country Gentleman, or
Timothy who is a kind of hundred-times-cleaned-
scrubbed-and-brushed pillow-case, or myself who
am just fat, careless and, alas, now purple-veined
about the nostrils. And yet alike we all are, alike
we always have been. Is it our English beef and
cabbage that has made us so? Or our politics?
Or the Battle of Hastings, 1066? Or insular
security?

There in any case we all were, leaning forward
like one man wanting to tell Benjie what we
thought of him. Carey, who always speaks as
though the thick Wiltshire soil had through the
years crept up and swallowed his tonsils, had his

word. He spoke as an English peer who has the
crops, the family and the British reputation among
foreigners all to protect at once.

' Why we have asked you here,' he said, ' is
because we feel, rightly or wrongly, that you are
responsible for Timothy's boy's behaviour. The
lad has caused his mother and father much pain.
He has carried on a clandestine correspondence
with your boy, it seems, for a long time past and
of that we feel that you must have been—ah—
cognisant.' (Here I caricature old Carey's style
a bit.) ' *Therefore*, therefore we have asked you
to meet us. We are representing here to-day the
family in London. I need not emphasise to you
the grief that this has caused the lad's mother,
nor the necessity we all feel that her boy—her only
boy—should be restored to her. The lad is a good
lad—fundamentally a good lad—and we feel that
he must have been under some most unfortunate
influence to persuade him——'

' Rot! ' Benjie broke in. ' Never was greater
nonsense. Tim's been pleading since he was
in that unfortunate velvet suit that his mother
always made him wear, to be allowed to be a
painter. There isn't one of us here who understands anything about Art, including Barney, even
if he does write novels. Why the devil,' he went
on, suddenly attacking Timothy, ' couldn't you
have let the boy try his hand? It's none of my
business or was none until I was dragged into it
like this, but no one is responsible for Tim's
running off to Paris except his parents—and that's
the truth! '

This was from every point of view a most unfortunate speech, and after it there was no hope
at all of saving anybody's bacon.   I had tried to
advise Benjie at luncheon that he must go slow,
placate the old boys, show them that he meant
them no harm.   But it was of course hopeless from
the start.   The very sight of their London clothes,
the air they had not only of owning the Rockland
(to which they were thoroughly welcome) but the
whole of England, annoyed him, exasperated him.
However, it might not have been so bad had it not
been for his allusion to Art.   Now none of them—
not Timothy, nor Carey, nor Alfred nor Horace
—cared a damn about pictures, but they hated to
be told that they knew nothing about them.   Carey
said to me long afterwards : ' It was the arrogance
of it, you know—telling us we don't know a picture
when we see one !   Why, damn it, a picture is a
picture, isn't it?   A feller has eyes, hasn't he?'

When Benjie had finished Carey rapped out:
' Are you going to bring young Tim back to
London or not?'

' Certainly not,' said Benjie.

Horace broke in:

' Oh, but, Benjie, I'm sure that Carey mis-
understands you !   What you mean to say is that
you will do all you can in the circumstances——'

Benjie jumped to his feet.

' I mean nothing of the sort !' (He really
loathed Horace.) ' I consider it a piece of damned-
est impertinence, all of you sitting round here
as though you were in judgment on me.   I only
came to show you that I didn't care a damn for

any of you! You can all go to hell for all I
care!'

Both Carey and Alfred, who were hot-tempered, jumped to their feet and I thought for a
moment that there would be a bit of a fight. Alfred
is tall and wiry; Carey, although his arms are so
short, has shoulders like a coal-heaver and is
strong for his sixty-odd years. Benjie stood there,
almost touching them, waiting for anything that
might come. Horace was nervously pushing at
his glasses in a way that he has when he is frightened (Rose used to imitate this very well), Timothy
threw out his stomach as a sort of vanguard of
protection.

But this was where I came in. I took Benjie
by the arm and led him out of the group.

'We're not in the Klondike,' I remarked (or
something equally cheap). 'Benjie doesn't see
that he has any responsibility for Tim's being in
Paris and I don't see that he has either. Feeling
no responsibility, he doesn't see that he can do
anything about it. And that's the end of it.'

I could see them looking at us and classing us
together. All writers are queer to men like Carey
and Timothy, and at that time with the Wilde
trial still fresh in their minds queerer than queer.
It was perhaps some feeling about the Wilde business that made them the more intolerant of Benjie
although they all knew that Benjie was normal
enough. The fact remains that the Wilde trial
made many people in England think, for a long
time, that all writers, painters, musicians, were
freaks and dangerous freaks. So there we were,

the ' little gipsy,' the rogue of the family, and the loose-living, novel-writing eccentric. We were damned together.

' That's not the end of it,' said Carey at last. ' We don't want to be unfair, Benjie, but the fact is that we've had about enough of you. For years now you've been upsetting everyone. Even as a boy you were a family scandal. You've been mixed up in two public brawls already and now there's this business. It is the feeling of all of us that we wish to have nothing more to do with you. And if you're a gentleman we trust you'll respect our feeling.'

Then it was I who figured in the scene. I lost my temper. Never mind what I said. It's of no importance. But as I once told Horace what I thought of him, so now I told Timothy, Carey and Alfred. I enjoyed myself for at least five minutes.

When, scant of breath (for I'm nearly seventy and my heart is not as good as it was), I had ended, it was Benjie who drew me away.

He smiled at them all. ' Good-bye, friends and relations,' he said. ' I shan't bother any of you again.' (He liked a little theatricality at times. It stirred his sense of colour.)

So, his arm through mine, we went out together.

VANESSA IN PRISON

HYSTERIA is the only word for the emotional state in which the Herries family now indulged. It is little exaggeration to say that as London once saw Jack the Ripper behind every area step, so now the Herries saw Benjie.

In 1898 and 1899, as afterwards in 1913 and 1914, London itself became hysterical. A mad craze for wealth and pleasure, an extravagance of display, a fantastic exhibitionism of non-morality raged everywhere. Diamonds and politics from Africa, an international plutocracy from the Holy Land, a pride and arrogance and self-confidence, a recklessness of materialism, the beginning of the breaking down of all the barriers of caste and exclusive traditions: these things marked these years, the last defiant ' Ta-ra-ra-boom-de-ay ' before the drums beat in the figures and the problems of the new world.

The Kaiser waved his theatrical arm in Potsdam, old Krüger sat in his kitchen reading his Bible, in London jumping signs for the first time illuminated the night sky and frightened the horses, *The Belle of New York* and *The Gay Lord Quex* shocked the religious, vast audiences swallowed gladly the wild tales of de Rougemont;

Kipling frightened two hemispheres by threatening to die of pneumonia; the cry was everywhere,
' Let 'em all come! '

In the week of the Rockland meeting young
Timothy caught pneumonia in Paris, nearly died
of it and refused to see either his father or
mother when they hurried over to him. But
Violet saw Benjie. She could not deny that he
was quiet and courteous. He was eager that
she should see her son: it was Timothy who
refused to allow her to enter his room. She
returned to London like an insane woman. It
was perhaps that she felt in her heart that
she had herself been to blame in the first place.
She was an old woman. She was a tiresome
woman. Her passion for chatter had grown into
a garrulousness that bored the world; her griev-
ances were so many that she was herself confused
by their number. She said that ' everything had
begun ' on an awful day when old Emily Newmark had prayed over her and Oscar Wilde had
laughed at her. Violet—her daughter—married
in 1897 a Colonel Caldecott. The house in
Onslow Square was the stiller and emptier for old
Violet's ceaseless chatter.

Bore though everyone found her, it became
the accepted fact that Benjie had stolen her son
from her and ruined her life. Respectable people
like the Rockages and the Worcesters and the
Alfred Herries were, in sober fact, terrified of what
Benjie might do next. The Worcesters and the
Alfreds now had young children—Cynthia had
two girls, Alfred a boy and a girl; who knew but

that Benjie might kidnap them and hold them for
ransom?

He was seen in London and the whole Herries
world shuddered.   The situation was developed
by the part that Adrian Cards played in it.   He
went everywhere—and he was now a man of importance in the London world, an Under-Secretary
and a writer of witty articles (' Very malicious,'
Alfred and Horace thought him)—saying that
Benjie Herries was the best of fellows and that his
relations were ridiculous people.   The Herries—
the Worcesters, Alfred, Violet and old Timothy,
the Rockages—felt that everywhere Adrian went
they were mocked.   They knew of course the
reason of his championship of Benjie.   It was, as
they assured everyone, because of his passion for
Vanessa.   He went with Vanessa everywhere.
She was, at last, after years of good behaviour, forgetting her position, her duty to Ellis.   All that
wildness that *must* be in her blood when you remember her grandmother and great-grandfather,
was at last coming out.   It was true that Ellis
must be very trying.   But could she not remember what she owed to her position?   There, too,
Benjie's influence could be traced.   After the
scene at the Rockland Club, Benjie was banished
from all decent male society, and yet Vanessa was
known to have said that all the Herries men,
except Barney, had behaved like fools in that
affair.

It was true, Vanessa was at last angry.   For
thirteen years she had behaved, both in public
and in private, as she ought to behave.   Now

she was beginning not to care whether she
behaved or no. For she was increasingly unhappy, frightened and indignant. She was moving swiftly, with a crazy husband at her side, no
close woman friend except Lettice Marrable in the
world, a sense of deep injustice burning within
her, to a climax.

The two ladies, Miss Vera and Miss Winifred
Trent, helped to precipitate it. 'What is reality?
This mirror is real because I can touch the silver
tracing on the woodwork of the frame, but I stand,
looking into it, brushing my hair, and Ellis is suddenly standing behind me. Ellis is not real.
Then is the mirror not real any longer? Ellis is
listening behind the door? I open it and the
carpet on the stairs is real, the ticking from the
Chinese clock is real, but is there not the sudden
sharp click of a closing door, the very crack of the
finger of unreality? And through all this I am
a woman who longs to love and be loved in return.
I am nearing forty and my life is more than half gone.
I have had no children, no one—since my father
died—to whom I might freely give my whole
heart. Only Benjie and Rose—both disgraced,
both exiles. . . . Is that, then, at last *my* reality,
my hunger for love, my *hunger*, my *hunger* . . .
in a woman who is nearly forty surely *that* cannot
be real . . .? The Miss Trents have called. As
they call now every day.'

'Dear Vanessa. We drove round to see how
you and dear Ellis are. *How* is Ellis? Is his
headache better?'

'Yes,' says Vanessa. 'To-night we are going

to *The Canary*. They say that it is a most amusing play.'

They look at her, inspect her with their large, soft and yet most resolute gaze. Everyone is watching her just as Ellis never ceases to watch her.

' If I don't get out of this I shall go mad, just as Ellis is. . . .'

Yet, with all this, she could not prevent herself from enjoying to the full any fun that came her way. She went out and about with Adrian, Barney, Cynthia. She had plenty of the great world, for the Duchess of Devonshire was less formidable with her than with any other woman in London, she watched Lady Londonderry's passion for power with all the more sympathy because she had never herself known the passion, and she helped Lady de Grey turn the Opera from a shabby squalling business into a splendid tiaraed pageant. Of all the grand ladies Lady Dorothy Nevill was to her taste the most delightful; she never tired of her daintiness, her humour, her anecdotes, her resolute vulgarities, and her eager curiosity about human nature. No one who came to Hill Street thought that there was anything but peace and plenty there. Only the Family knew and the Family didn't say. It was the business of the Family to inform the world in general that anything Herries was right. Vanessa was the Family public pride and of the utmost importance to them all.

Adrian was Lady Dorothy Nevill's especial pet, and he and Vanessa went together very often to the house in Charles Street.

' You're not in love with the young man, are you, my dear?' she asked.

' Not the least little bit,' said Vanessa, laughing.

' Not that it matters,' said Lady Dorothy, tossing her little head with its marvellous auburn wig, shaking her many beads and necklets and amulets. ' You're not like these modern girls with all their paintin' and powderin'. How men can kiss them *I* can't understand. What Dizzy if *he* were alive . . .'

Vanessa had friends everywhere, girls in shops, young men from the East End in whom Adrian was interested, writers famous like Henry James and Kipling, obscure like young Mr. Smith who brought her the tattered manuscript of his novel to read or Mr. Brown who had written an Epic on the Armada, actresses and actors like Irving, Ellen Terry, Forbes-Robertson and young men who walked on at the Lyceum. All were alike to her. She had no pose, no arrogances, no prejudices. So life whirled on the outside while within steadily the drama grew more intolerable.

Insanity is of all things the most pathetic, the most piteous, the most intangible. Everyone *within* the house knew that Ellis was insane. The servants nodded their heads together and watched him as children watch a strange and unaccountable animal. They developed a kind of pride in him. They marvelled that towards the outside world he was ' always all right.' Seriously, with an almost magisterial dignity, saying very little, listening to his guests with a sort of absorbed gravity (he was not listening; he was watching the figures *behind* the figures), he played his part. With Finch the butler, Mrs. Martin the cook, the two men-servants, the housemaids, Lettice Marrable, he was the master of the house, betraying himself to them only by the twitching of his fingers, the way in which he would look over their shoulders, the sudden impatient ' Very well, very well ' or a sharp ' Is that door closed? I can hear someone moving upstairs '

The servants had for both their master and mistress a new and rather touching kindliness. They were very well treated, were paid excellent wages. Vanessa they adored. (Even Finch, who, after Miss Fortescue's departure, robbed right and left, drank the best wine and so had a real friendliness to his employers.) They were kind, did their duties, but they waited. . . . Something would happen soon. . . . They might all be murdered in their beds. . . . This made them feel privileged.

Vanessa herself wondered, often enough, whether there were not two Ellises. He was very often, when alone with her, so quiet and rational that it was almost as though the old friendly days were back again. When he slept beside her he moaned in his sleep and she drew him to her, stroked his forehead, felt as though she were pro-tecting him against an evil demon. Yet, with this, she suffered an appalling fear of him that, do what she would, always increased. Perhaps one night he would kill her. She was always prepared for that. She would not, she thought, mind very greatly.   Oddly, pity and fear went hand in hand together.   She too waited for the next step. . . .

Then one day in June 1898 she received a letter saying that Will Leathwaite was dead.

She had just come in from a drive and stood in the hall, the letter in her hand.   It was from Mrs. Newson, who had looked after the cottage and Will for some years—a very decent woman.   It simply said that Will had been ailing for some time past, hadn't cared for his food, complained of his legs.   Mrs. Newson had gone to Grange to see a friend and, returning about seven of the evening, found Will dying in his chair by the fire.

' I thought you'd like to know, my lady, that it was your father's name he kept saying before he died, over and over.   I don't rightly think he was ever the same man after your father died.   But he was tranquil up to the last, and a finer-looking man not to be found anywhere I always said.   And no trouble at all, not to no one.'

She stood there, lost in the past.   Will was gone: now everyone was gone.   She remembered her father's description of Will winning the race at Keswick years and years ago, how he pounded up the hill to the Druids' Circle, and young Adam, himself only a boy, riding in front of Will's father on the family mare, yelled encouragement.   And then how Will had come up to Adam one Christmas Day and asked if he did not want a servant. Will's love for Adam had been the best that one human being can find for another: its character was paternal, protective, selfless, and also gay, simple, unsycophantic, man to man, brother to brother. It had been perhaps the finest thing in her father's life, Vanessa thought, looking back. Was there not always antagonism in every sex relation? But in this perfect charity, honesty, and—above all, best of all—equality . . .

There was no Past when you experienced a love like this, for Adam and Will would go on for ever, for ever racing up the Keswick hill, for ever meeting, the snow sun-glittering at their feet, the blue smoke rising in the silent air, for ever one waiting the other's return, for ever that exchange of glance, sure and trustful, for ever that touch of hand on hand. . . . In all this changing, bewildering, unstable world the one sure and certain proof that there is something eternal in man's soul; that, once in a lifetime, one touches, deep in the heart, evidence of immortality.

The letter fell to the ground: she heard the Chinese lacquered clock strike the half-hour with its sententious solemn purr. The clock's voice resembled Horace's. Will's death increased her loneliness. She had not seen him for so long a time and yet he had been behind her—they two together thinking of Adam.

She picked up the letter and saw that Ellis was standing near to her and looking at her. Why did she never hear his step these days?

' Oh, Ellis! ' she cried. ' Will Leathwaite is dead! '

Ridiculously, tears stole down her cheek behind her veil.

' Will Leathwaite? ' he asked.

'Yes. Father's servant. You've seen him—a big fair-haired man with blue eyes.'

She had trained herself never to mention anything in connection with Cumberland, but at this moment she was thinking of Will, not of Ellis.

He nodded, looked at her without speaking, and walked upstairs.

A few days later a very unaccountable thing occurred. He came to her in her room where she was reading and, timidly, as though he were asking a favour, said:

'Vanessa, let us go to Cumberland for a week —to your cottage on Derwentwater.'

He stood in front of her, very tall, very pale and rigid, as though she had ordered him in front of her to be scolded.

'To Cumberland?' She was so deeply astonished that she dropped the book. 'But, Ellis, you hate Cumberland!'

'No—who told you that?'

'Nobody, of course. Only yourself.'

'When have I said that I hated Cumberland?'

'Not *hated*. But disliked it. The rain—and you don't like the North——'

'Who told you that I hated Cumberland?'

She got up and walked away. His eyes frightened her. He bent down and picked up the book. 'Why do they bind books in green? It is such an ugly colour.' Then, in rather a shrill voice: 'I don't hate Cumberland. Of course not. It will be very agreeable. I need a holiday.'

She came back to him, smiling.

' That *is* good of you, Ellis. Of course I shall love to go.'

And they went. On the evening of her arrival she could not believe that she was there. In the living-room there were all her father's things just as they had always been. His books—the little blue volumes of the *Iliad* and the *Odyssey*—the tattered shilling parts of *Pickwick*, the *English Poets*, *Sir Charles Grandison* and *Tristram Shandy*, Barney's novels, *Dandy Grimmett* and the rest.

And all the old beloved things, part of her very life: the two cornucopias, Zobel's sand picture, ' The Saddle Horse,' the old water-colour, ' The Lady of the House,' the Baxter print ' Dippers and Nest,' the Peepshow of the Central Hall at the Great Exhibition, above all, the spinet from Uldale with the roses painted on the lid, and the music-box with the King in his amber coat and the Queen in her green dress.

As she stood at the window, with all these beloved things around her, she held her hands tightly together lest she should show her emotion. The last evening light touched the hills: Skiddaw's twin peaks lay like islands in a clear cold silver above bars of fleecy cloud, and the ridge of Blencathra was black against the whitewashed sky. Between the trees the water of the Lake, struck by the trail of a tiny boat, fell into darker and darker shadow. The wood-pigeons murmured from the wood. Some ghostly sheep wandered, just as they had so often done, slowly up the road. This was her home. How foolish she

P

had been to be so long an exile from it! And as she watched, the years fell away from her. Twenty of those years were suddenly gone. She raised her arms above her head and, smiling, saw herself, another very different woman, moving slowly up the staircase of some grand house, hearing the names called, the distant band—Lady Herries, a middle-aged woman with a dull, stiff husband, still beautiful but soon not to be very interesting, to be nothing more than a London hostess who knew everyone, whom everyone knew, who mattered to no one, to whom no one mattered. Her body seemed to her young again; she would hear her father call her name, Benjie would be riding over from Uldale, all life was before her. . . . All life before her? She shivered. It was behind her. She was in prison with Ellis.

But in the following days she could not keep down her joy. She had come home. What is it that makes in a certain square of ground every blade of grass, every hovering uncertain cloud, every note in a bird's song one's own? She had heard often enough, in London, scorn of this country, its rain, its ponds, its little hills, old Wordsworth and his daffodils, Coleridge and his opium, reading parties from Cambridge. She had had often to hold herself back from a ridiculous personal protest as though the scoffers had insulted herself. She had wondered why Lettice and Timothy and Violet, who had lived so long here, had had no personal feeling. She had heard Timothy thank his stars that he had done with the ' beastly climate.' She had asked Lettice whether

she did not want to go back. 'Go back? All the
unhappiest part of my life was there. I never want
to see the place again.' She knew for herself that
if her childhood had been one long misery still she
must return . . . and return . . .

There was something deeper here, some inheritance that was mingled with all the truest,
most importunate things in life. Her love of this
place was her key to the connection between the
two worlds. 'Only connect . . .' 'Only connect . . .' The whole problem for man and for
woman was here. They move as in a game of
blind-man's buff from figure to figure, turned,
twisted, bewildered. Guess rightly and the light
floods in. . . .

As she stood at the window, the world beyond
it sinking into darkness, she knew with sudden
certainty that to find the key of connection was
man's only business on this earth. All else was
folly beside it. And the key for her, as it had been
for her father, her grandmother, her great-grandfather, was here—like a pot of gold hidden in this
square of ground. For Benjie too perhaps? She
had, in that instant, one of those illuminating
flashes of revelation that once and again are granted
the Hoodman Blind. God the Invisible and man
exploring; she smiled as she thought of the ironies
of Barney or Benjie or Rose if she told them of her
naïveté.

'I looked out of the window as the world grew
dark and knew that there are two worlds, that they
are linked together, and that it is God's purpose
that we should find the connection. All beauty

is for that.   I must have courage, honesty, and
I must rid myself of my Blind Man's Hood, my
egotism. . . . I must test life by no experience
but my own.   For you, dear Barney, God is an
exploded superstition.   That is *your* experience.
You are right to hold honestly by it.   But for
myself, standing at this window, I have another
guide.   Credit my honesty and I will credit yours.
Let us be tolerant to one another.'

As she turned back into the lighted room she
had a moment of almost blinding happiness.   Her
troubles faded.   What matter if she were close on
forty, if she loved Benjie whom she could never be
with any more?   What was her fear of Ellis?   All
the values of life were for a moment altered.   She
had courage for anything.

She needed that courage in the days that
followed.

They were sitting quietly after supper, she
reading a novel, he a newspaper.   He said, still
looking at his paper:

'Vanessa, when we return to London, I shall
wish you to see a doctor.'

'A doctor?'

'Yes,' he said, leaning forward and laying his
long bony hands on his knees.   'I have been long
coming to the conclusion that you are not well.
I came up here with you that I might observe you
a little.   In London it is so difficult.   So many
people to interfere.   We do not see enough of
one another.   My suspicions—my suspicions,' he
repeated the word softly, 'are quite confirmed.'

'What suspicions? I am perfectly well, Ellis dear.'

'Ah, so you think,' he went on quietly. 'That, I fear, is part of the disease.'

'Disease?' she broke in. Her heart was hammering. She looked quickly about among the old familiar things in the room to reassure herself. 'Why, I was never better in my life, and especially since I have come up here.'

'There, there. You mustn't get excited. Excitement is bad for both of us. I have said nothing until I could be certain. I did not wish to alarm you. I have myself for some while been none too well, but now I am quite recovered— quite recovered,' he repeated, nodding his head. 'But now that I have mentioned it, you can speak to me without fear. There is no one listening. At least I think not.' He got up, went very cautiously to the door and listened, then to the windows, pulling back the curtains for a moment. He walked on tiptoe.

'Listen, Vanessa. For a long time we have not been happy. Oh, I know that it has not been altogether your fault. For a time I was accompanied everywhere by someone. Very unagreeable and difficult to account for, but now that he is gone again—and I took care not to bother you with his intrusion—I realise that your care of me during these last years, in addition to all your social duties, has been too much for your strength, your mental strength. And then it is hereditary, no doubt. Your grandmother . . . You will need great quiet in the future, and an

able doctor—perhaps retirement into the country
to some soothing place . . .' He stopped to
listen. 'You heard nothing? The country is
so noisy and restless. Always something moving.'

She picked up her book. Her hands were
trembling, but she answered quietly:

'There is nothing the matter with me, Ellis.'
Forcing herself, she looked up at him and smiled.
'We have both been tired a little by London.
That is why this week in the country was such a
good idea.'

He bent down, patted her shoulder, kissed her
forehead.

'There, there. You must not disturb yourself. I will see to it.' He straightened himself
and tiptoed to the door. He listened, looking
anxiously into the wall. 'And now I think I will
go up to bed. Don't worry. Worry is bad for
you. Quiet, quiet. We must all have quiet.'

She lay awake for hours that night, wondering
what she should do. In the large bed that they
shared he slept the peace of the insane just. He
breathed like a child, never stirring. She beat
herself into common sense. Panic was so near
that, all the night through, she kept it off only by
using her utmost strength. She could run away,
leave him never to return, but that would mean
defeat and cowardice. If she left him it would
not be long before he would be put somewhere,
in some awful, silent house, faced with dark silent
windows, inhabited by poor sufferers like himself.
She must not go until the last test of endurance

had been reached.   But this new twist of his brain
was so awful that she refused to face it.   If he,
mad though he was, thought *her* mad, might not
others also think so?   Had the strain of these last
years been too much for her?   Had there been
something hysterically unreal in her manner?   In
the darkness of the room she saw the Misses
Trent, in their large black hats, their trailing
gowns, standing close together watching her.
' Yes,' she heard one of them say to Ellis.   ' You
are right. Vanessa has been behaving very
strangely. . . .'   But then her common sense
returned.   She had never been more sane in her
life than she was now.   She could deal with this
as she had dealt with everything that preceded it.
She turned on her side and slept.

Then, after one happy hour, she realised to the
full the danger that she was in.   That day, the
seventeenth of June 1898, was stamped, in its
tiniest detail, on her memory for ever.

In the afternoon she drove to Rosthwaite.   A
lady, Mrs. Merriman, who lived in Borrowdale,
gave a party for some of the children from Grange,
Rosthwaite, Seatoller, and invited Vanessa.   They
all knew her here.   She was one of themselves
and had it not been for her silent, pale-faced,
alarming husband they would have asked her
everywhere.   They hoped, now that she had
returned to her real home, that she would often
come and, although they did not say so, without
her husband.   They knew that she was a grand
lady in London, but Cumberland people take
things naturally.   Everyone is on a level, and if

anyone behaves grandly they look foolish and are
to be pitied. Vanessa of course did not behave
grandly at all. No one could be more simple, and
on this afternoon in Rosthwaite she sat on the floor
and allowed the babies to climb all over her, played
musical chairs with breathless excitement and then,
to the cracked piano, sang songs for them and
afterwards played for them to dance. Mrs.
Merriman, who was thin and pale, had an invalid
husband and more children than she wanted, had
been inclined to be jealous at first of this woman
with her lovely clothes, her beauty, her life in the
great world. ' She has everything. How unfair
it is.' But soon she was not sure that she had
everything. There was something, she told her
husband, pathetic about Vanessa. ' She played
with the children as though she could not bear to
let them go. She told me that coming back here
was heaven to her. She went to the window and
looked out at the hill like a starving woman.
" Well, why don't you come here more often,
Lady Herries? " I asked her. " After all, it's
your home. We are all delighted to have you
here." " Oh, how I wish I could! " she said.
I wouldn't wonder if she's not happy with her
husband. I'm sure I shouldn't be. He really
frightened me, he was so stiff and solemn. I
never saw a woman carry herself so beautifully,
and such lovely dark hair as she's got and such a
kind expression. But I'm certain she's not happy.
Lovely dark hair with not a grey thread, although
she can't be far off forty. No airs at all, although
the Prince and Princess often come to her house, I

believe. You know, Philip, I felt like a mother
to her. There's something makes me feel that
she needs someone to love her. Oh, I know
you'll call me romantic. But I can't help it.
She's the most beautiful woman I've ever seen and
simply sweet with the children. You could tell
her anything, I'm sure.'

When the children were having tea Vanessa
slipped out, crossed the road, the bridge, and
looked at the solid, comfortable little Victorian
house with its sloping lawn, its trim garden, the
house built on the very spot where her great-
grandfather had once lived. She stood there,
listening to the running water, feeling the afternoon sun on her face, wondering where that old
wild man now was. He, too, had stood here,
looking at the hills, feeling the sun on his face,
waiting for his wife to return. It had been wild
then: the bare rock, the tumbling water, the valley
beyond uncouth and deserted. The sun had
shone on his purple coat and silver braid. She
felt intimately close to him. Once again time was
not. Was it fancy that a hand rested on her
shoulder, comforting her? Of course it was
fancy.

Here was the trim garden and on the lawn two
garden-chairs, a small mowing-machine, a water-
ing-pot. An old bent gardener was clipping the
roses. Two bicyclists passed down the road, and
then a scarlet coach filled with tourists. But,
after the coach was gone, silence tumbled back
again, the hills, clear and defined in the sunshine,
cut the cloudless sky. The gardener pushed the

mowing-machine, and the soft dreamy whirr filled the world with summer peace. As she turned to the bridge she whispered ' Good-bye.' Was it fancy that a figure in a purple coat watched her go?

' And now, children, we must all thank Lady Herries for helping to make our afternoon such a pleasant one.'

They all thanked her in shrill treble voices. They ran into the road to see the splendid lady in her rose-coloured coat get into the carriage, and one baby cried because it was not allowed to go with her. She kissed Mrs. Merriman.

' Come back soon,' Mrs. Merriman said.

' Yes, I will,' said Vanessa.

Ellis locked the door. Vanessa looked up from her book at the sound of the turning key. Why had he locked the door? She had thought that he had gone up to bed. The little clock with the painted moon and stars (as a baby she had been lifted again and again to count them) pointed to quarter to eleven.

Mrs. Newson and her husband slept on the far side of the cottage. They would hear nothing. She continued to read. This was a very clever book of short stories; it was written by a woman who must be simply too clever to do any of the ordinary things that ordinary women did. The stories were in the manner that was becoming popular; they had no beginning. One story called ' The Haystack ' started with this sentence: ' Oh, but dripping is so cheap . . . and it's really not bad when you get used to it.' Nor had they

any conclusion. 'The Haystack' ended: 'Yes,
but half a crown—that was altogether too much
for such a second-rate article.' They were de-
pressing stories. London in the rain, hateful
boarding-houses, shabby men making love, the
British Museum Reading-Room, someone wring-
ing a chicken's neck outside the kitchen window.
They were very feminist. Men figured as poor
creatures, mean, faithless and greedy. But oh!
what cleverness! What observation! Nothing
escaped this lady's eye; the yellow stain on the
tablecloth where mustard had been spilled at the
last meal, the tear in the cheap umbrella, the
shabby feather in the outworn hat. . . . Vanessa
knew, as she read, that one thing that was the
matter with herself was that she was not clever
at all. Neither clever nor witty. She could not
remember that she had ever said a brilliant thing in
her life. Rose, Cynthia, Lady Dorothy Nevill—
what clever things they were always saying! 'I'm
a bore,' thought Vanessa. 'The woman who wrote
this book wouldn't endure me for five minutes.'

But why had he locked the door? He came
and sat down opposite to her. The clothes that
he was wearing, a dark brown cloth intended for
the country, did not suit him nor did they look like
country clothes. Wherever he might be, he wore
always the deep sharp collar that belonged to the
Gladstone caricatures, and that did not suit him
either because his throat was so thin, his Adam's
apple so large. She noticed to-night for the first
time that the back of his pale long hand was
freckled.

He sighed, then said:

'It was not kind of you, Vanessa, to have me watched all this afternoon.'

She looked at him steadily, determining that to-night at least she would not be afraid. They were returning to London to-morrow and then something must be done. For her own safety, for his, something must be done.

'What *do* you mean, Ellis? No one was watching you.'

'Ah, come, Vanessa. Why lie to me? I don't blame you, not at all. I know that you are not yourself. But it is wrong of you to embarrass me. And such an unpleasant man. I stood here for half an hour while he watched me outside the window. He never moved until I came myself to the window; then he vanished into that green bush beyond the flower-bed. Then when I returned to the fireplace pretending not to notice him, he came to the window again. A long thin man in a green coat. I fancied that I had seen him before.'

She got up and came over to him, seeming very tall in that small room.

'Ellis dear, let's go to bed. You know that I haven't had you watched. Why should I? Now come to bed.'

'Oh, I'm not vexed, my dear. Not at all vexed. I said to myself, " If he hadn't got that green coat I really should not mind. He could watch me as long as he pleased. But I dislike green as a colour and his eyes were most unpleasant." When I went out into the garden he was gone. Then he came back again. He pressed his face to the window-pane. All the same you would dislike it if I had *you* watched, you know. You wouldn't like it at all. In fact, lately, I've had it in my mind because, being as you are, it isn't safe for you to go about alone.' He sighed, deeply, deeply as though in dreadful distress. ' The truth is that we are neither of us well. Life has been a failure for both of us. It is better for us to end it.'

She looked about the room to reassure herself with the old homely comfort of the familiar things —the spinet, the books, the music-box, the pictures. She walked to the window, then from the far side of the table said: ' Ellis, give me that key. You have locked the door. Give me that key.'

' No, my dear, certainly not. Because you had me watched this afternoon is reason enough. We have not been happy for a long time; indeed I have never been happy. I cannot remember a time when I was happy. Nor are you happy. So here, very quietly, while there is no one about, is a very good opportunity to finish all this tiresome business. I feel it my duty. I have hesitated for some time, but now my duty is quite clear.'

He fumbled in his inside coat-pocket and brought from it a large kitchen knife with a thick brown handle.

' You will feel nothing,' he said smiling. ' It will be no more than a cut on the finger. And then I will follow you. I can't possibly express to you how agreeable it will be to be tired no longer, to have no more headaches. For both of us it will be a relief, I am sure——'

He held the knife in one hand and stroked its edge, very gently, with the other. The little clock struck eleven.

'This is the silliest scene,' she thought, 'I have ever been in. So unreal that all the things in the room have become unreal too.' She thought also: 'But this ends everything. At last, thank heaven, this ends everything.'

'I have thought it all out,' he said. 'Sit in that chair, Vanessa. Close your eyes. You'll feel nothing at all.' He was very close to her now, but she did not move.

'Ellis, give me the key. Put down that knife. Go to bed. You are behaving like a baby. Put that knife down on that table.'

'Perhaps I will,' he said, looking at her very cunningly. 'Perhaps I will not. But it won't matter, because nothing you can say will alter my decision. And how absurd of you not to do as I wish! But you have never done as I wish. A pale-green mushroom hat that you are always wearing. You know that I dislike it. And yet day after day you persist in wearing it.' He murmured: 'A mass of shaded green wings. A mass of shaded green wings. That's what Mr. Playfair said.'

He threw out his hand and caught her arm.

'Come to the chair, Vanessa. Come to the chair. That is the easiest way.'

He looked up at her like a beseeching child. His eyes were filled with tears.

'Dear Vanessa. How I love you! How unhappy we are!'

His arm encircled her body. . . . His head
fell forward and rested on her breast. The knife
tumbled to the floor. She led him back to the
armchair, he submitting like a child.

'Please, Ellis, give me the key,' she said.

Tears pouring down his cheeks, he fumbled
for the key, found it, gave it her.

'Another time,' he sobbed. 'Perhaps another
time will be better. I meant it for the best. . . .'
Then, as she moved away, he caught her hand:
'Don't leave me. Don't leave me. I am afraid
of being alone.'

She knelt down beside him, comforting him as
she had done so often before. But, in her heart,
she knew that this was for the last time.

ESCAPE INTO DANGER

They had to leave very early next morning to catch the train for London. Vanessa, who had not slept at all, stood at the lawn's edge and found that the world was rolling in rosy smoke. It would be a hot day. The smoke lifted from the Lake even as she looked, as someone lifts the covers from a bed: the Lake shivered, trembling, at the touch of the sun that itself also dared as yet only to breathe upon the water, but to breathe like God, strongly, confidently (in spite of so very many disappointments) and with the very tenderness of love. The colour flew upwards from the hills and broke into petals of rose against the sky that would soon be drenched with sun. All the hills waited—Cat Bells, Robinson, Gable, Scafell, the Langdales, Helvellyn, Blencathra—they all waited for their illumination high, high above these madmen who to-day are one thing and to-morrow another.

This would be a horrible journey—and so it was.

'Perhaps,' said Ellis, when they were half-way down England, 'you would like my *Times*?' He spoke to a stout fellow in a suit of loud checks who had been, ever since Penrith, staggered by

Vanessa's beauty. For she wore a small toque, a spotted veil, her rose-coloured coat; behind the veil, the man in the checks was, with beating heart, assured, breathed the only woman for whom all his life he had been searching. He had money; he had rude health, a kind wife and a mistress in Carlisle, but he had not, he had never, never had, the Beauty for which he longed.

'Thank you, sir. Very kind of you. Hooley's bankruptcy means the end of the cycling boom. Mark my word.'

The fields rushed up to the window and all the houses bobbed and curtsied in the sun. Vanessa sat there, her clever book of stories on her lap, and fought down her terrors. She had not slept, and Ellis, who now looked like a Prime Minister, a director of a railway company or the real author of *Robert Elsmere*, had last night wished to cut her throat with a knife with a brown handle. He had, as usual, wept leaning against her breast. He would never weep against her breast again, for her duty there was ended. Once she had loved him as a mother her child, then she had pitied him because he was sick, now she was a weary, angry woman resolved on escape. Next week they were giving a Ball in Hill Street, a very grand Ball indeed, and that should be the last. That should be the end, for her, of Ellis, Hill Street, London. . . . One need not, one must not, be stuck so deep in a quagmire of ludicrous danger . . . ludicrous kitchen knives, Ellis's tears and tiptoe to the window, Ellis's man in the green bush beyond the window, Ellis's moaning in his sleep, poor Ellis. . . . ' To find some life that is neither false nor dangerous . . .' Letting her head fall, she slept at last, dreaming that the babies in Rosthwaite pulled her with eager hands up the hill to the water falling with such cool certainty down the face of the rock. Standing waiting for her there was Benjie.

At Hill Street was a letter for her from Rose. Next day she went to see her. Rose was living in two very small dingy rooms off Baker Street. She met Vanessa defiantly, as though to say: ' I know you will find me changed and you can say, if you wish, that you never want to see me again.' Yes, Rose *was* changed. Her cheeks were painted, the puffed shoulders of her dress absurdly exaggerated, her waist too small for any comfort, her eyes unhappy. Her room was untidy, clothes thrown about, a dusty piano open with a bright green hat ornamented with a bird of paradise plume flung down on the keys.

A strange thought struck Vanessa. ' This is the world into which, very shortly, I may be moving.'

But oh! it was wonderful to be loved again! She could not believe that she had endured all these years without it! She was like a woman starved as, sitting with Rose on the shabby hole-and-corner sofa, she heard what Rose chose to tell her (a sort of fairy-story in which every gentleman was kind, money sprang from the carpet, and life was one long victory).

At the end of it Vanessa said:

' I'm glad you're so happy.'

And Rose said:

' Life's hell.   Don't believe a word I've said, Vanessa.'

They discovered very quickly that life just then was bad for both of them.   Vanessa did not tell Rose that Ellis had wanted to cut her throat with a kitchen knife, but she *did* give her to understand that the end of Hill Street had arrived at last and that Rose must be prepared. . . .

There came in upon them without a word of warning the most dreadful man—Major Feather-stone-Haigh.   The Major was short, purple in the face, smelt of brandy, called Vanessa ' My dear ' and looked at Rose as though he owned her—which, at that moment, he probably did.

Vanessa went back to Hill Street.   She went back to Hill Street to find Miss Vera and Miss Winifred Trent waiting for her in the drawing-room.   Standing in her room, before she went down to them, she knew a moment of fear worse than any that had preceded it.   She stood, motion-less, her head up as though she were listening. Then with quick nervous movements she took off her white soft-feathered toque, her veil, her long gloves.   She listened again.   It was a hot thundery day and her windows were wide open. A hansom clop-clopped down Hill Street; she looked out and saw a man crying his flowers which blazed in a cloud of colour on his barrow—roses, carnations, lilies.   Below the windows of the houses the window-boxes shone with bright blue, with scarlet, with flaunting yellows.   At the end

of the street was a barrel-organ that played again
and again an old air from *Trovatore*. Light,
colour, music: but inside the house it was cold
and dark as it always was. Her dress was white
and black, the shoulders very puffed, the waist
very small. She looked at herself in the long
silver mirror. She seemed to herself hideous,
her pale face beneath the dark hair, her long white
neck, her full bosom; her height was ridiculous.
She hated the way that she carried her head, stiff,
pompous, ' as though I were for ever at the top
of the stairs, receiving. Thank heaven, it is
ended. In a week or two, in one way or another,
it will be over. I will never receive anyone any
more. Death, perhaps.' It did not seem impossible, for there was Ellis loose about the house,
and the house so still, and those two old women
in their long trailing black waiting for her in the
drawing-room.

At that moment, looking at herself in the mirror
with disgust as at someone for whom everything
was over, someone moving in a crazy house cold
as the grave, a lunatic its master, she had almost,
for the first time, lost all her courage. Rose lost,
Benjie somewhere wandering, no one else. . . .
Then also she remembered her grandmother, that
small indomitable woman with the white hair and
ivory cane who lived to be a hundred, who had
faced everything because she knew how to be
indifferent to life whilst adoring it. ' She did
—so can I.' She went down to the two ladies.

' Ah, dear Vanessa, how nice to see you again.
And how are you? '

' Very well indeed, thank you.'

They both kissed her, and as they did so it was as though they were graciously inviting her to stay for an hour or so in her own drawing-room. They were extremely quiet. When they moved, their long black dresses scarcely rustled. They appeared also to have a secret understanding. They had moreover the power to make you feel that you could not take a step without their permission. Finch brought in the tea, and it seemed likely for a moment that Miss Vera Trent would instruct him where the table should be placed. Their voices were what Barney once called ' boneless.'

' We have already seen dear Ellis,' said Miss Winifred.

' He says that his holiday has done him good,' said Miss Vera.

' But we advised him to be careful during these hot weeks in London,' said Miss Winifred. ' The worst thing possible for his headaches. How is he, do you think, Vanessa? '

' Oh, very well,' said Vanessa brightly. ' We had such lovely weather in Cumberland.'

' You did? ' said Miss Winifred. ' Now isn't that delightful? Cumberland when it is *fine* must be indeed charming.'

' And for you—to return to your old home again—how delightful!' said Miss Vera. ' There is no place quite the same as one's childhood's home.'

' And what have you been doing? ' asked Vanessa. ' What are the family scandals? Whom have you seen? '

' Oh, we lead quiet lives, you know,' said Miss Winifred. ' We had tea one day with dear Cynthia. May and her girls were in London for a week. And poor Violet—not at all well, I fear, and now that both children——' She broke off. The Misses Trent were nothing if not tactful, and, after all, Vanessa most strangely defended that horrible man who had lured poor Violet's boy——

They both looked at her together, a strange look, a look full of some knowledge that at present they would keep to themselves. Miss Vera said, smiling, raising her hand on which her diamond rings sparkled, to help herself to a little cake: ' And what is this that Ellis tells us, dear Vanessa, about your own health? Rather a sad report, I fear.'

' My health? ' said Vanessa. ' Why, it was never better.'

Miss Vera shook her finger. ' Now that is not at all what dear Ellis tells us. He insists that you see a doctor. Altogether over-fatigued, he says, and I am sure that I don't wonder with all that you do. And then this great Ball next week to which Winifred and I are so greatly looking forward. But after it Ellis thinks that a quiet time in the country——'

Her anger rose. She was suddenly aware that she hated these two women as she had never hated anyone in her life before. ' I think that I am the best judge of that,' she said quietly. ' I am perfectly well.'

The door opened and she saw that Ellis had

come in. The two ladies rose and moved to either side of him. He greeted them with a grave smile.

Surely, they must be aware of his strangeness, his eyes are never still nor do they see the things at which they are looking, and he walks now like a cat with padded feet. . . .

All three looked at her. Then Ellis said:
' A little tea, my dear. Thundery weather.'
They all sat down.

One more move needed to complete the preparation. Next day meeting Barney at Cynthia's he put in her hand a note. It was from Benjie.

18 HALF MOON STREET.

DEAR VANESSA—I am here and shall be so for some weeks. If I may not see you I may at least be happy because I am near you. **B.**

The last Ball ever given by Vanessa and Ellis in Hill Street was a brilliant success. Vanessa, in a dress of white satin and with diamonds in her hair, stood at the top of the stairs. She saw, as though it were a mechanical toy wound up for her amusement, the figures appear around the bend of the staircase—one two, one two, one two—the ladies' heads erect, bosoms thrust forward, trains draped over their arms, jewels glittering, a scent of powder and roses and the heat of the London June evening . . .

' Lord and Lady Danesborough.'
' Sir James and Lady Ford.'

' Mr. Forbes-Robertson.'
' Lady Carteris.'
' Lord John Beaminster.'
' Lady Adela Beaminster.'
' Miss Rachel Beaminster.'
' Mr. Timothy Herries.'
' Miss Vera Trent.'
' Miss Winifred Trent.'
' Lady Dorothy Nevill.'
' Sir Henry and Miss Nevill and Lady Wade.'
' Madame Sarah Bernhardt.'
' Mr. and Mrs. Peile Worcester.'
' Lord Clancarty.'
' Mr. Henry James.'
' Mr. Edmund Gosse.'
' Mr. and Mrs. Colvin.'
' Lady Sarah Meux.'
' Monsieur Felix Brun.'
' Mr. Yale Ross.'
' Lady Carloes.'
' Mr. Robert Hichens.'
' Sir Roderick Seddon.'
' The Honourable Lionel Talmache.'
' Mr. Adrian Cards.'
' Lady Lettice Forjambe.'
' Mr. and Mrs. Humphry Ward.'
' Sir Peter and Lady Thornby.'
' Miss Mary Thornby.'
' Lady Eustace.'
' Miss Pamela Eustace.'
' Mrs. Clifford.'
' Mr. Barnabas Newmark.'
' Lord and Lady Rockage.'

' Miss Veasey.'
' Mr. and Mrs. Ormerod.'
' Lady Cynthia Lamb.'
' Mr. and Mrs. Frederick Macmillan.'
' Mrs. Grant Bingham.'
' Mr. Herbert Beerbohm Tree.'
' Mr. Pendle Smith.'
' Mrs. Langtry.'
' General Fortescue and Mrs. Fortescue.'
' Mr. Max Beerbohm.'
' Miss Carlyon.'
' Mr. Ross.'
' Mr. Tumer.'
' Mrs. Fortescue Brown.'
' Mr. Brookfield.'
' Mrs. Craigie.'
' Mr. Charles Wyndham.'

She reflected: ' It must be midnight.   The
actors and actresses are arriving.'   She glanced
back and saw that the long room was now filled
to overflowing with dancers.

' Mr. Bertrand.'
' Lady Garvice.'
' Miss Garvice.'
' Mr. Galleon.'
' Lady Torring.'
' Mr. and Mrs. Frost.'

Barney, a little later, found himself in a corner
with Bertrand the novelist.

' I suppose,' Bertrand said, ' you think I'm
here to pour scorn on my fellow-creatures.'

' No, not especially,' said Barney.   ' Any more
than anyone else.'

'As a matter of fact,' said Bertrand, 'I love my fellow-creatures. I think we are all absurd, of course. And to-night I feel something sinister in the air.'

'Sinister?' asked Barney.

'Yes. I can't explain it except that I think London *is* sinister just now. Have you read Hichens' *Londoners*, or don't you read your fellow-novelists?'

'Not very often,' said Barney.

'Neither do I. But Hichens' book is clever madness—too long, but not really exaggerated. We are all mad.' He looked around him. 'Do you see that little man over there talking to Mrs. Langtry?' He pointed to a small, very dapper gentleman, with bright observant eyes, who was talking with exceeding animation and a good deal of un-English gesticulation.

'That is Felix Brun. He lives only for the social history of Europe. He knows all the moves, the undercurrents, the plots and plotters. Whenever he appears in London, you can be sure that there is a change coming. I met him a week or two ago at the Rede Gallery where he had come to look at Ross's portrait of the old Duchess of Wrexe—a very fine painting, by the way. He was very interesting. Like myself, he has no illusions.'

'You must have been a fine gloomy pair,' Barney said, laughing.

'Oh, not gloomy at all. Why be gloomy? It has been dull, this long sleepy prosperity. Brun agrees with me that things are breaking up.'

' What things? ' Barney asked. He was looking at Ellis, who, standing near to him, alone, had
in his eyes so fixed a gaze, and in his pose so odd
an air of waiting for someone, that he interested
Barney.

' What things? ' repeated Bertrand. ' Oh, all
this. The conviction that we are the finest people
in the world, superior to everything and everybody.
The conviction that we rule the world and it is
right that we should. Brun says that England's
day as ruler of the world is over.'

' That must give you great satisfaction.'

' No—why should it? We do some things
very well, but we have no taste, no subtlety, no
sensitiveness to what other people are feeling, and
our Imperial ambitions are revolting. I am going
to live in France.'

Beaminster brought up to Vanessa a very
beautiful girl.

' This is my niece Rachel, Vanessa. You
were at her Ball the other day. She has not
been out long enough yet to be *blasée*. She
thinks you are the most wonderful woman in
London.'

Vanessa looked with great pleasure at the girl
in front of her. Miss Rachel Beaminster, granddaughter of the old Duchess of Wrexe. Vanessa
had gone in May to a very grand Ball in Portland Place given for this child's coming-out.
The girl was tall and thin, with dark hair and
beautiful eyes, a little gauche and a little foreign.
Her mother had been a Russian actress, and
the old Duchess had, Vanessa was told, never

forgiven her son for his *mésalliance*. But the importance of this meeting for Vanessa was that this girl might be herself—herself twenty years ago.

'I do hope you're enjoying yourself.'

'Oh yes, Lady Herries. It's a lovely Ball.'

'Plenty of partners?'

The girl smiled and became at once transformed; her happiness took away that little awkwardness and you felt pleasure, excitement, anticipation beat through her body.

'Plenty. I could dance all night.'

'I have known your uncle a long time. He is one of my oldest friends.'

'Oh, Uncle John? Isn't he a dear? I should have been terrified of everything had it not been for him.'

Yes, and she might be, Vanessa thought, with that awful old grandmother and stiff, forbidding Adela for an aunt and prim, pompous Richard for an uncle!

'It's so wonderful,' Rachel said, 'seeing Sarah Bernhardt. Uncle John is taking me next week to one of her plays at the Lyric. She looks kinder, more simple——'

'Would you like to meet her?' asked Vanessa.

'Oh yes! Can I? You see, my mother was an actress——'

'Come along and I'll introduce you. Tell her about your mother.'

They went across to where the great woman was listening, with eyes half closed, to M. Brun.

Vanessa presented the girl and was pleased to

see with what ease and simplicity the child behaved.
She turned and for a moment before she was caught
again watched the room, swinging under the lights
to the rhythm and symmetry of the waltzes. The
music softly beat into her ears: ' The last time—
the last time—the last time . . .'

What if there should be a scene? What if
Ellis should commit some awful indiscretion?
He was looking strange to-night. Surely others
had noticed it besides herself. She talked, she
laughed, she walked with uplifted head. Many
said afterwards that she had never seemed more
splendid than at this Ball, more easily the mistress
of her world. ' And for her age still such a
beauty,' said little Brun. ' What is she? Nearly
forty? She must be.' He remarked to Bertrand: 'An interesting family, these Herries. So
typically English and yet with a strain of something——'

' " And we'll have fires out of the Grand
Duke's Wood," ' quoted Bertrand.

' Fires out of the wood? '

' Yes—a quotation from one of the other
Herries—the mad ones, you know.'

' Ah, there have been mad ones then? '

' Oh, plenty. There are several scandals at
the moment.'

' Ah,' said Brun. ' That's what makes you
English so interesting. You are madder than
any other people and yet so conventional. Impossible to understand, you turn and rend your
madmen while they are alive and yet are so proud
of them after they are dead.'

' That,' said Bertrand, who was suddenly bored
with little Brun (he tired of people very quickly—
of himself also), ' is why we are so conceited. We
have so much common sense that when our poets
have written their poetry we kill them. Except
Wordsworth and Tennyson of course. But they
were mad very young and got over it.'

After that Bertrand sat by himself for a while
and collected notes for his notebook. He watched
Madame Bernhardt act and Henry James unravel
sentences of benignity from his beard, Mrs.
Langtry raise her lovely arm, bishops grow
genial, politicians indiscreet and all the most
beautiful girls in London manœuvre for husbands.
Then he noticed his host, who listened at first with
grave intensity to a stout lady in a bright green
dress, and then, when she left him, stood as though
bewildered, staring about him.

' By Jove, the old boy's trembling from head
to foot,' he said to himself. ' He'll have a fit or
something.'

Ellis backed to the wall. He straightened
himself against it. Then Bertrand saw that he
felt the wall with the palm of his hand; he moved
his hand up and down against the surface, and in
his eyes was the most unhappy gaze that Bertrand
had ever seen in a human countenance. Then
Bertrand saw that two tall elderly ladies came up
to him, stood on either side of him, talking to him.
With his hand through the arm of one of them,
Ellis moved away. Bertrand wrote in his notebook that night:

' But the strangest thing this evening was the

terror of my host.   A very commonplace dull
man, you would say, but the dullest of us may
become interesting when, lost in the bush, he
hears the tom-toms of the approaching cannibals.'

The Ball reached its apogee.   There was a
superb and nearly riotous set of Lancers.   Everyone had had supper.   The summer morning was
breaking beyond the windows.   The carriages
drove away.   Finch, downstairs, entertained the
footmen and the maids with his splendid imita-
tions of the more important guests.

Vanessa, reaching her room at last, locked the
door.   A few minutes later there was a knock.
She stood motionless, listening.   The knock was
several times repeated.   Then silence.

As the small brown silver-faced clock that she
had brought with her from Cat Bells struck eleven,
she awoke.   She had told them not to call her;
now she rang the bell, looked at her letters, the
newspaper, drank her coffee.   Through and behind it all was a sense of crisis.   And yet why?
She had given last night one of the most successful
Balls of the season; no hitch, no misadventure.
And to-day there was no reason why anything
should happen.   Something *soon* must be done,
but immediately, to-day . . .

The sun poured into the room.   The paper
told her that there was a new successful play at the
Court—*His Excellency the Governor*—and that her
friend, Irene Vanbrugh, one of the women whom
for her generous spirit, unaffected good-nature

and cheerful courage she liked best in London, had made a great success in it. She read of a hat that sounded a miracle of loveliness:

' *A daring little toque of turquoise straw, jet pins with very big heads, white wings and a black velvet rosette in front.*' She also read: ' *The Louis Seize bow is almost ubiquitous. We meet it on hats, it is a charming head-dress for evening wear, it occurs in almost every embroidery, every appliqué of lace, it airs itself in the lace curtains, on our walls, every-where.*'

' There shall be no Louis Seize bows on *my* walls,' she thought, half asleep, and then remembered, with the sharpness of a knife cutting through tissue paper, an unexpected little incident of the evening before. Just after she had come up from supper Ellis appeared at her elbow and with him a stout roughly bearded man. All that Ellis had said was that this was a friend of his, a Doctor Playfair. She had talked with the man for five minutes. What had they discussed? Bernhardt's season at the Lyric, the Spanish-American War, Gladstone's funeral, Cecil Rhodes —anything, nothing? He had seemed a well-informed, pleasant enough man. As soon as his back was turned she had forgotten him. She had not thought of him again until now when, suddenly, she seemed to see him in the room here with her— his untidy brown beard speckled with grey, his white waistcoat that fitted ill over his paunch, his heavy bowed shoulders, but above all his thick glasses behind which his large grey eyes had stared at her without blinking. How he had stared! She had not at the time thought of it, for, by now, she was accustomed that people should stare at her. But how he had stared! She fancied now that there had been some especial emphasis in Ellis' introduction. . . .

She must get away! Oh! at once! at once! Somewhere, anywhere. Was she perhaps nervously overstrung? This trembling, this beating of the heart . . . Had people been thinking her ill and not cared to tell her? *Was* her mind affected by this last horrible year? She jumped out of bed, went to the mirror. Nothing ailed her. She was in the full vigorous possession of her brain, her will, her heart. She had never been more conscious of true bodily strength, of real and absolute sanity. She had been imagining the doctor . . . There had been nothing intended, nothing sinister—but with Ellis now from minute to minute you never knew . . . you never knew . . .

She had luncheon alone and afterwards drove to the Rede Art Gallery in Bond Street, where she had arranged to meet Barney. They had agreed that they must see Yale Ross' portrait of the Duchess of Wrexe. He was waiting for her inside the Gallery and she thought to herself: ' What a nice wide-awake amusing face he has for an old man of nearly seventy! How pleasant it is always to see him! What a friend he has always been to both Benjie and myself!'

They went together and looked at the portrait. It was certainly brilliant. The old woman sat, leaning a little forward, holding a black ebony

Q

cane, in a high carved chair. The most striking
thing in her pose was the way in which her dry
claw-like fingers clutched her cane. Her dress
was black and the only colour against it was the
dull green of a jade pendant. The colour of her
face was almost dead white and the skin was drawn
so tightly over the veins that a sigh, a breath, you
felt, would snap it. She looked indomitable, remorseless, proud, nor was there a shadow of
humour in her mouth (which was cruel) and her
eyes (which were cold). On either side of the
chair were two green and white dragons, grotesques
with large flat feet and open mouths. A tapestry
of dull figured gold filled the background.

' Theatrical, brilliant, and most uncompli-
mentary,' Vanessa said.

' She wouldn't think so,' said Barney. ' I'm
told she's delighted with the picture. And she
is theatrical—her life, I mean. She shuts herself
up in Portland Place so that she may be a figure.
If she went out and about she would be simply an
old and tiresome woman who had outlived her time.
As it is people think that she pulls all the strings.'

Vanessa thought of the young girl, Rachel,
to whom she had spoken last night.

' That girl has character,' she said. ' It
would be a tussle between the two of them if they
fought.'

They found a quiet corner. The little room
with its cool light, its gleaming pictures, its
silence, was most refreshing.

' Now tell me, Barney, quite honestly, have you
noticed anything strange in me lately? '

'No. Nothing. Of course not. I never
saw you more beautiful, more completely mistress of yourself, than last night. Everyone said
the same.'

'Thank you, my dear. And now listen.'

Vanessa told him everything; of the journey
to Cumberland, the incident of the knife, Ellis'
remarks about her health, the two old women in
the house, the few minutes with the doctor.
Barney was horrified.

'At least that settles it. Something must be
done at once—at once.'

'Yes, but what? I cannot—no, I cannot—
endure another week of this. And it is not right
for Ellis either. We are not safe and he is not
safe.'

Barney stared in front of him. 'This is dreadful. I knew that things were bad, but not like
this.'

'How much does anyone else know?'

'Well, we—the family—have realised that
something was wrong with Ellis for a long time.
But only vaguely. I have only known what you
told me and the others have guessed a little perhaps, but so long as everything was all right on
.the surface they have accepted it. They don't
want, you see, that there should be anything public.
There have been enough Herries scandals.'

Vanessa went on:

'And it is all my fault. The sin was my
marrying Ellis in the first place when it was Benjie
whom I loved. I thought of myself rather than
Ellis. But there was this strain, perhaps, in him

from the beginning. . . . I can't *deal* with it,
Barney. My courage is gone, and I thought once
that I had enough for anything. But how can I
leave him like this, defenceless, without anybody,
in that awful world of his own? If you saw how
unhappy he sometimes looks, the way that he
cries, the *bitterness* of his weeping! How lonely
one must be! '

She trembled and put one gloved hand on
Barney's knee to steady herself.

' Oh, Barney, *what* am I to do? '

' Wait,' Barney said. ' Let's be sensible about
this. Under the cold eyes of the old Duchess.
What would *she* do? Lock Ellis up in a Portland
Place cellar and feed him on bread and water.
No, my dear, I'm not laughing. This is serious
enough for anything, but forgive me if I'm thinking about you first. You have to be protected,
you know. Let's be practical. Ellis is dangerous, poor chap. And there are the two old
women. And that doctor last night.'

She asked him, dropping her voice:

' Can they do anything? I mean if they really
tried to get me away into the country. Oh, I
don't mean murder me. But shut me up, isolate
me? '

' Oh no—not while Benjie and I are about.
That is only a crazy idea of Ellis's. He honestly
believes it, I shouldn't wonder. He may have
persuaded the two old ladies that at least you are
tired, overstrung. But you *must* leave him—for
the time, anyway.'

' And precipitate everything,' she went on

quickly. 'If I go and refuse to return there will be no question about Ellis—everyone will know.'

'Will they? I wonder. You will be blamed of course.' He looked at her. 'Vanessa, will you mind blame, criticism? You have had very little in your life, haven't you? Everyone has loved you. It will be different. You won't be the splendid Lady Herries any more. . . .'

'Oh, that! That is nothing. But there is something else . . .'

Some people had come into the Gallery. She lowered her voice.

'I don't think, Barney, that I can go on any longer without seeing Benjie. I've had thirteen years of it, you know. I love him as deeply as ever I did—more deeply, I think. He is alone, has been for years. I know that it is wrong. I've no illusions about that at all. I'm very old-fashioned about God, my friends tell me, but of this I'm sure—that to live with Benjie would be a sin and that somewhere, sometime, I should suffer and rightly suffer. If I sinned it would be deliberately, one thing against another. But I think now that perhaps to sin and be punished is better than to live and die without loving anyone.'

When Vanessa talked like this she seemed to Barney so touchingly childish that he wanted to pat her hand and say: 'There! There! my dear. I'll go with you and tell them it wasn't your fault. I'll see that you're not punished.' Sin! Good heavens! What a word! And the things that

he had done, the fine times he had had, and
here he was nearing seventy and as hale and
hearty . . .

'Well, that may be, my dear—or it may not
be.   Sin seems to me a vague word.   If you're
right and there's some old tyrant waiting to see
you slip and punish you, why, then I'd defy him
and tell him to do his worst.   Let's be practical.
Go off with Benjie, well and good.   But there are
two things to consider.   One is the social part of
it.   Probably that seems unimportant to you, but
it isn't so nice in practice.   Men and women can
be very nasty when they see someone enjoying a
freedom they haven't themselves the courage for.'

'Yes,' said Vanessa, and thought of Rose.

'And there's another thing.   What about
Benjie?   How old is he now?   Forty something,
isn't he?   You aren't either of you very young any
longer.   Benjie's a rover.   He *is* a bit of the
gipsy they call him.   He loves you, I know.
That has been the finest, by far the finest, thing
in his life.   I think if you've courage enough
you can bring it off.   But you'll need all the
courage you've got.'

She stood up, pulling down her veil, standing
there in her pale dress of grey and silver, for a
moment, as desolate and lonely as he'd ever seen
her.

'I know,' she said.   'I'm in a muddle, aren't
I?   Father always used to say that I was a careless
little fool—not those words, you know, but that's
what it amounted to.   And yet for so long I've
been so careful—so absurdly careful.'

As they went out she said:

' I wish we hadn't talked under the eyes of that dreadful old woman, Barney.'

As they went down the stairs Barney caught her hand.

' Remember, Vanessa, that I'm here whenever you want me. Always, whatever you decide.'

' Yes,' she said, smiling back at him. ' You, Benjie, Rose, Adrian, Lettice. Five. In the whole world. Well, I suppose there are many people would be grateful for so many.' She added, as she got into her carriage: ' And I *am* grateful! You're a friend worth having, Barney.'

They dined alone, very late, she and Ellis, and at once she saw that the crisis was upon her. Ellis had some plan that was not to wait long for its explanation. Living with him as she had done in these last years, she had learnt something of the strange country in which he was now lodging. She knew that his brain always moved along a single path, or rather the paths lay side by side like railway tracks and he might jump at any second from one to another, but that he was conscious *only* of the one that he was, at that moment, treading. To-night she was very close to him; she could see clearly the character of the world in which he moved, its grey uncertain darkness so that you went stumbling, hitting your shins against sharp edges like razors, or of a sudden putting your hand on a cold soft substance, a gelatinous mass on whose surface spiders wove webs. And then at such contacts you screamed. What could you do other, alone as you were, wrapped in darkness, driving forward but with no knowledge of your destination?

She understood too how bewildering were the sudden flares of light—like the up-blazing in some works when, conducted around by the manager, he explains the moving of some minute wheel—both of you lit by the glare of Hell. That was Ellis' world, and these flares of hot flaming light were all he had to guide him. They might be a hat with a mass of green wings, the name of Playfair, a man looking through the window, the swinging of a mirror for no cause, the whistle of a train, a book read late at night when the house is silent—these and such as these were all he had to light his path. But pursue his path he must and would with an absorbed intensity. One track —one purpose. The burning molten substance flares to heaven, and the track and purpose are changed—changed but as intensely pursued.

She knew to-night that some intention completely absorbed him and that that intention concerned herself. Because she knew this she had a kind of prevision of what was coming. At least she was quite certain that this very evening would see the finish of all her business here. She even knew, as she smiled at Finch and said: ' No, no more asparagus, thank you, Finch,' that this was the last time that she would sit at this table, the last time at least for many a day. . . . One might return. She speculated about that. To what did one not return? The same tests were repeated again and again. She felt that there was neither time nor space to-night but that together she, her

father, grandmother, great-grandfather, Will Leathwaite, Rose, Benjie's wife, anyone you please,
all in the same moment stood up to be tested
while the Eagle flew across the sun . . .

Just before she rose from the table to lead the
way up to the drawing-room, she had the halluci-
nation, staring at the wallpaper under the candle-
light, that it would be for ever thus—she and Ellis
facing one another over the broken fruit-skins and
half-emptied glasses, her father swinging her to
and fro above the grass of the Cat Bells lawn, old
David falling at the news of the Bastille, older
Herries standing at his door waiting for his wife,
Rose and Major Featherstone-Haigh, all the
Herries, nay, all the world transfixed into immobility while God cries from His judgment-seat:
' Now! ' The candles blew in the wind, a picture
swung very, very slightly on its cord, and it was
Ellis, not God, who said ' Now! '

' Now, Vanessa, we will go upstairs. There is
something I must tell you.'

So highly pitched was her sensibility that
when they were alone together in the drawing-
room and the door closed behind them, she felt
like an animal entrapped. There was, in fact,
good reasonable common sense here, for you could
not one evening allow your husband to attempt to
cut your throat without, after that, finding other
evenings with him rather dangerous. The door
was not, this time, locked. Finch and the young
footman were within calling distance. She had
always hated this room. She had done what she
could with it, taken down the yellow hangings,

allowed Whistler to paint her portrait, spread rugs,
bought roses, carnations, lilies — but Whistlers,
rugs, roses, carnations, lilies could not prevent that
this room was still the yellow drawing-room that,
even though only last night it had swung with a
maze of happy figures under the crystal candelabra,
was dead like a mausoleum and cold as Hell must
be for those who love the warmth.

He made her sit down beside him on the sofa.
He patted her hand and his hand was warm and
dry.

' Are you tired, Vanessa? '   He spoke to her
with infinite consideration.

' Not in the least.'

' Not after last night's festivities? '

' No.   I slept until eleven.'

' What have you done to-day? '

' Oh, nothing very much.   I went to the Rede
Gallery to see Ross's portrait of the old Duchess
that everyone is talking of.'

' Did anyone go with you? '

' Yes.   Barney.'

' Ah . . . Barney. . . . Everyone agrees that
last night's was a most successful Ball.'

' I think it was.   Really Finch and the servants
did excellently.   Finch may have his faults, but
he knows his business.'

' Did you notice last night,' Ellis asked her,
' how those who were not invited came and laughed
at us?   It disturbed me greatly, but I said nothing
to anybody.   They gathered in groups.   I was
afraid at one time there would be trouble.'

' No one came who was not invited.'

'Oh yes. You are quite wrong. There were many there who had no right to be present. I thought at one time that I would have them driven out of the house. But that would have made a scene. Neither of us wished for that. Everything must be done quietly.'

She moved a little away. She looked at the clock. It was five minutes to ten. The servants would go to bed early to-night.

'Well,' he went on cheerfully, patting his knee with his hand, 'we must be thankful that all went off well. It is the last Ball that we shall give for a long time, because to-morrow I am going to send you into the country.'

'And where are you sending me?' she asked, smiling.

'There is a Doctor Playfair. At least I call him that. I am not sure at the moment whether that is his right name. He has a place—in Gloucestershire, I think. But I have it all written down. I am sure that it is Gloucestershire.'

She began to speak.

'But why——'

He put up his hand. 'Now, Vanessa, please. I have one of my headaches to-night—spiders in the brain, you know. That is exactly what Doctor Playfair said when I told him about my headaches. "Like spiders in the brain?" he asked. "Exactly," I replied, "and behind the eyes." He understood as though it had been his own experience, and when I spoke to him this morning about you—he had had five minutes' conversation with you last night——'

' I remember,' said Vanessa. ' A large heavy man with spectacles and an untidy beard.'

' Exactly. Doctor Playfair. He called to see me this morning. At this house in Gloucestershire—I *think* he said Gloucestershire—you will find every comfort. It is very quiet there. There are woods. Only the other patients——'

Vanessa laughed. ' This is all nonsense, of course, about my wanting a rest. But even if it were not, do you really suppose, Ellis, that I would leave you all alone here? '

' Ah, that is what I had intended to tell you. I shall *not* be alone. Vera and Winifred will for the future live here. This will be their home.'

So *that* was it! At the same instant as she realised with a flash of discovery that her responsibility was ended—and *how* strange *that* revelation was, liberating her, she suddenly saw, from years of bondage—a horror of being caught seized her. Those two old women! Did she not act immediately she would never escape. How they would hold her she did not know, but hold her they would! So many things came to her at the same instant and with these a new view of Ellis as though he had become twice as dangerous and twice as far removed. Through all the insanity of this last year she had thought at least that he needed her; now, with that spoken sentence, she saw that he did not need her. Those two old women had taken her place. . . . But there were three against her now instead of one.

' Vera and Winifred? To make this their

home?   But that's preposterous.   You are joking, Ellis.   You——'

'It is arranged,' he answered, smiling and patting his knee.   'Very satisfactory.   You will rest in the country and they will see that I am comfortable while you are away.   I shall shut up part of the house.   I am very tired of parties and I shall see no one—only Doctor Playfair and one or two old friends.   The house will be thoroughly cleaned, swept from top to bottom.   The windows need cleaning.   They have grown darker every day.'

He came very close to her.   He put his hand on her forehead.

'See how hot your forehead is!   You have been ill for a long, long time.   That is why I have myself been so very uneasy.   Doctor Playfair agrees that what you need is quiet.   And what *I* need is quiet.   We will have shutters on the windows and someone will see to the doors. They have been far too noisy.'

He got up.   'To-morrow afternoon,' he said, 'you shall go down to Gloucestershire.'   He stood, looking down at her.

'Poor dear, poor dear!'   He kissed her forehead.   'Go to bed now.   Rest is what you want. I shall be in my room for a while.   I have most important work—very important work indeed.'

When he was gone she sat there thinking. Her first impulse was for immediate flight.   But where?   Rose.   Yes, Rose.   Then she thought: 'No.   This will be cowardice.   And besides this may be all Ellis's imagination.   How do

I know that this absurd idea about Winifred and
Vera is not invented by him?   And this ridiculous
notion about my going into the country.   Of
course he cannot *make* me go.   I must talk to him
again.   Just now I said nothing.   I must talk
to Barney.   Perhaps *he* will see Ellis.   In any
case I can't leave him like this without knowing
the truth, the facts . . .'

Then she thought of Benjie.   She was in a
turmoil of weariness, fear, indignation.   The
appalling element in it was her own isolation, and
she saw now that, for months, she had been becoming more isolated; everything had been closing in upon her, shutting her off.

It came to her like a cry.   She would see
Benjie.   About her future now she was reckless.
She had done her utmost, she had fought battle
after battle, and now she would fight no more.
The thought that half an hour from now she
might be with Benjie, have, at last, after all this
long waiting, his love again . . . simply to see
him, to hear his voice, to escape from this fantasy
of the last years so easily . . . The room swam
before her eyes.

She ran up to her room, found a hat and cloak,
waited on the landing, listening, reached the hall
in safety (no sound in all the house but the ticking
of the clocks), opened the door and, at the end of
Hill Street, found a hansom.   She gave the man
the number in Half Moon Street.   Benjie would,
in all probability, be out.   Would she wait in his
rooms for him?   The old stock situation of the
Society melodrama . . . As the hansom turned

into Half Moon Street, which was only a minute's distance from Hill Street, she tried to think what she would do, but she could not. She was ringing the bell before she came to any decision. A grave elderly man-servant opened the door.

'Is Mr. Herries at home?' she asked.

He did not seem in the least surprised to see her.

'If you will come in a moment, madam, I will see. What name, madam?'

'Lady Herries.'

'Very good, my lady, if you would not mind waiting.'

He disappeared around the corner of the stairs. Almost at once he appeared again, saying:

'Yes, Mr. Herries is in. Will you come up, please?'

Benjie was at the door of his room. She went in and he followed her, closing the door behind him. He stared at her as though a cloud of angels had floated down to him from the ceiling.

'Vanessa!'

'Yes. This is just like a play, isn't it?' She was trembling but was determined that he should not see it. At the very sight of him she was so happy that she could only smile, stare back at him, then, with fumbling hands, take off her hat.

'Here,' he said. 'Take this chair. It is the only comfortable one. Oh, my God, Vanessa! If you knew how many times I've sat here imagining just this: saying to myself, "And now the bell will ring and Humphries will come to the door and he will say 'Lady Herries,' and I . . ."'

' That's in the play too.' She steadied her
hands, holding them tightly together. ' But there
is nothing dramatic in this, Benjie. I have come
only for five minutes. But that isn't true either.
It *is* dramatic, I suppose. You must give me
advice. Tell me what to do.'

He sat down in the chair on the other side of
the fireplace, his small body balanced forward,
staring and staring and staring.

She saw that he was looking splendid, as brown
and hard as a russet apple, spare, taut, not changed.
Oh, not changed in the least these twenty years!

' I shouldn't have done this, I suppose,' she
went on. ' At least—I don't know. There's no
shouldn't any more. The fact is, quite simply, that
Ellis is proposing to send me away to a private
asylum in the country to-morrow. . . . It has
been to-night a situation that I couldn't face by
myself any longer. You know about Ellis? You
have heard something? '

' My God! ' Benjie shouted, springing up.
' Send *you* away? Send you to an asylum? '

' Yes. Quietly, Benjie dear. We have got to
be sensible about this. The fact is that Ellis has
been out of his mind for the last year or more.
Twice he has tried to kill me, and still I held on.
It has been miserable, tragic . . . I don't want to
talk about that part of it. That is past. But I
must do something now, now, at once. You know
Winifred and Vera Trent? '

Benjie nodded.

' They have taken charge of him. I think
they intended to from the first. Oh, I don't mean

that it is they who have planned to get me out of the house. I don't think they had the least idea of it. That is only Ellis's crazy notion. But it has come to this—that to-night, an hour ago, Ellis told me that they were from now on to live in the house, I was to be sent into the country, most of the house to be shut up. I don't know how much is Ellis's fantasy, how much is truth, but I *did* know, as he went oh talking, that I could stand no more. I have been alone in this thing too long. And so—I came to see you.'

' Oh, Vanessa! ' he sighed. ' At last! '

She nodded, smiling.

' Yes—at last. I have wasted my whole life. I can't go on without you any longer.'

He came over to her, knelt down beside her and took her hand. He sat on the floor, resting his head against her, her hand pulsing against his. They stayed for a long time quietly, without speaking, feeling as at every long-separated meeting they had always done—that there had never been any parting.

Then he became practical. He asked her every sort of question and she told him everything. For the first time in all these many years she poured everything from her heart, her unresting love for himself, her increasing loneliness, the friendship that she and Ellis had had for the first few years, the influence of Miss Fortescue, Ellis' headaches, the day of the Jubilee when he had first made her uneasy, the night when he had attacked her, and then detail after detail to the last Cumberland visit.

'But now—even now—I would not go were it not for those two old women. How I hate them! Oh, Benjie, how I hate them! But it isn't that; it is that my responsibility is over.'

He nodded.

'You have always been dreadfully conscientious, Vanessa. And now you are coming to me —for ever and ever and ever, amen.'

'Yes. I talked to Barney about it this afternoon.'

'And what did *he* say?'

'He pointed out that the world would be shocked, Violet would close her doors to me, I should no more be asked to Grosset.'

'Yes, that's true. And shall you mind?'

'I don't know—a little, perhaps. What I *do* know is that I am doing wrong. I shall suffer for it in one way or another. I suppose that, without realising it, I have been thinking of this for a long time. I am not a fool about it. I know the delight—and I know the punishment.'

'Punishment!' he cried. 'There will be no punishment! We shall be happy for ever!'

She smiled, shaking her head.

'Of course nobody is happy for ever.' She put her hand under his chin, turning his face up towards hers. 'Benjie, are you *sure* you want me? Are you certain? I'm middle-aged, you know. You're middle-aged too, but for a man it is quite different. Are you *sure* that you want me—still —after all this time?'

'Sure? Sure? Why, Vanessa, I love you more than I did twenty years ago. Loving you has been the only good thing in me—that, and caring for Tom. Are *you* sure,' he went on, ' that *you* want me? I'm not much, you know, Vanessa. Apart from you I'm nothing at all. With you I may still do something.'

' Yes, I'm sure,' she said quietly.

' It is true, too, what Barney said. We shall be cut, you know. Wherever we live someone will be unkind. And as to the relations! Yet another scandal in the Herries history! '

' Oh yes.' She nodded her head. ' I understand just how things will be.' (Again, for a flashing instant, she thought of Rose.) ' I understand everything, I think,' she went on. ' I'm not a child now. I have seen how things go. Often and often I have been tempted to come to you. You must have known that! But I was wrong when I married Ellis, and his needing me— or my thinking that he did—kept me there. And then,' she added after a moment, ' to fly in the face of God. I know those are only words to you, but it is true reality to me. But if I can make you happy—isn't that something? You see, I've never made anyone happy since my father died. No one. Isn't that awful? If I had made *myself* happy it would have been a little, but not even that. Until to-night. Until now. Now I am so happy that there *must* be something right in it somewhere. Don't you think so? '

' I don't know about God. I think that's a tall word. But here and now we are going to do the best we can by one another. Until

your God separates us we'll stay together just as
years ago we meant to do.'

After a while they discussed the immediate
plan.

'To-night I'm returning to Hill Street,'
Vanessa said. 'I must see Ellis once more and
know what is fact and what isn't. I can't leave
him until I know.'

'Then I am coming back with you,' Benjie
said.

'To Hill Street?'

'Certainly. I must see that you are safe. If
Ellis has gone to bed and is asleep, well and good.
What time is it? Nearly twelve. He ought to
be asleep. If he is not, I will talk to him. Don't
be frightened. There shall be none of my famous
fights. But I don't leave you until you are safe.'

She agreed. She wished now to hide nothing.
If Ellis in reality intended to carry out his crazy
plan it was right that she should be no longer
alone. And she felt a feverish impatience that
this absurd business should be settled once and for
all. And she could not face Ellis alone again that
night.

They walked round to Hill Street. In that
clear air they heard Big Ben strike midnight as
she opened the door with her key. They went
up to the drawing-room. Ellis was standing
there in front of the big marble fireplace.

Benjie spoke at once.

'I beg your pardon, Ellis, for coming at this
impossible hour. Vanessa came round to me

to-night to tell me that you intended to send her into the country to-morrow—to some doctor's. Well, Vanessa and I are very old friends, you know. We have obeyed your wishes all these years and kept apart, but when Vanessa told me this we thought it better that we should both see you. We can talk about it to-morrow if you prefer, but in that case Vanessa will go to a hotel for the night.'

Vanessa said: ' Ellis, after our talk to-night I couldn't stay here alone. For both our sakes——'

But Ellis, without moving and very quietly, waved his hand at the door.

' Would you mind,' he said to Benjie, ' coming further into the room? They may be listening outside.'

Benjie came forward.

' Thank you.' Ellis looked at him very severely. ' I thought I told you that you were never to enter my house again?'

' Yes,' said Benjie. ' You did, and I wouldn't have come had it not been for Vanessa. Frankly, Ellis, she's frightened. You shouldn't have talked that nonsense about sending her into the country.'

' That is perfectly correct,' said Ellis. ' She is going to Doctor Playfair's.'

' Well—she is not,' said Benjie. ' Nothing of the kind. You must see, Ellis, that she can't live with you any longer after this. I didn't want her to come back here to-night at all, but she said she must know whether you *meant* what you said. It seems that you do.'

Vanessa had been standing, her hand up to the white cloak with the high white collar that she was wearing. She had been looking into Ellis' face, trying to find there some appeal to herself for help, some kindliness. If at that moment he had turned and gone to her, blindly asking her, as he used to do, that she should help him, she would, even now, have stayed . . .

But he did not seem in the least unusual. There was no sign of madness in him anywhere, and after that one sentence to Benjie about the door there was, in this scene, *no* queerness. There was no *queerness*, but there was hatred.

' You see, Ellis,' Vanessa said, ' I have realised that you don't need me any more. We haven't been happy together for a long time, have we? And as you don't need me we had better separate.'

' That is our affair,' he said. ' We can settle that to-morrow. If you were well, Vanessa, I'd have something to say to you for bringing this dirty ruffian here. As it is, Herries, get out and keep out.'

' Come on, Vanessa,' Benjie said. ' Let's go.'

She took a step forward to Ellis.

' Ellis. Don't you see how impossible it is——? '

He moved forward to her. Benjie stepped between them, then, taking her arm, he drew her away.

With quick steps Ellis followed them. He passed them as though he did not see them and ran down the stairs. In the hall he turned.

In a high, shrill, convulsed voice he cried:

' Get out, both of you!   Get out!   Get out! '
At the same moment the Chinese clock struck
the half-hour.   Benjie, half-way down the stairs,
put his hand on Vanessa's shoulder.   They
waited.   He did not know what Ellis would do.
But the scene ended very quietly.   Ellis did not
move.   Vanessa and Benjie walked out of the
house.

They found a hansom in Piccadilly.
' And now where? ' Benjie asked.
' I'll go to Rose,' Vanessa answered.
She was trembling and he put his arm round
her, holding her close to him.   Benjie gave the
address to the cabman.

END OF PART II

PART III

THE LOVER

HAPPINESS IN RAVENGLASS

One fine September afternoon of that momentous year 1899, Mrs. Runcing of Olive Bank, Ravenglass, came to tea with Mrs. Jocelyn of Sea View Cottage. It was a most beautiful day, and the sun caressed the sea, the sea caressed the shore, and the birds rising in little flocks from the island hovered against the quivering sky like blown petals, silver-grey, and as the wing turned, of glittering metal. The cry of the gulls made the lazy sky lazier.

The two ladies sat at the window of Sea View Cottage and drank their tea.

' I'm using this room,' Mrs. Jocelyn explained, ' because of my lodgers. I'm not sure that I don't like it quite as well as the other.'

A lady and a gentleman rode past on a tandem bicycle. The gentleman rang his bell.

' What's that, dear? ' an odd, croaking, half-strangled voice asked from within the room.

' Only a bicycle, mother.'

On the farther side of the fireplace, almost hidden with shawls, was old Mrs. Burgess, Mrs. Jocelyn's mother. Mrs. Burgess was ninety-two and, except that she was never warm, was a wonder for her age. She was as lively and spiteful and selfish and scandal-mongering as though she had

been a young thing of twenty. There was
nothing that happened from Barrow to Whitehaven in which she did not take an interest, and
most especially of course in anything that had to
do with love and—most particularly—illicit love.
She was a Puritan and had all the eager questing
spirit of the Puritan. Her curiosity it was that
had kept her alive and would, it seemed, keep her
alive for evermore.

Her daughter, Hester Jocelyn, was in every
way her opposite: a little, warm-blooded, impetuous, charitable, kind-hearted woman whose
husband had, ten years earlier, run away with an
actress to South America. She had not loved him
very much, but her loneliness was often worst
at three in the morning when she could not
sleep—quite terrible, yet she was cheerful, busy,
charitable and infinitely patient with her horrid old
mother. Something of a heroine perhaps.

Mrs. Runcing, her visitor, was nothing of a
heroine: a long bony woman with three daughters
whom she would sell her eyes to marry. She
threw them at the men of the district as you throw
darts at a dart-board. As with so many women of
their time, they had been trained to nothing, taught
nothing. Their father thought them too tiresome
for words, their mother hated them because no one
would have them and yet loved them because they
were hers. The poor Miss Runcings!

' Things look bad in South Africa,' said Mrs.
Runcing. ' Henry says we shall have war for
certain. It's all the fault of that wicked old
Kruger. And so you like your lodgers, Hetty

dear?' She laid rum butter thickly on her bread. She was a greedy woman.

'Like them!' said Mrs. Jocelyn. 'I should think so! No one could help it. Mr. Herries is as gay a gentleman as you'd find anywhere, always singing and laughing. No trouble at all. But Mrs. Herries is my favourite. She's a *lovely* lady —so kind and thoughtful, and so friendly. It's nice to see a married pair so happy—and not young either. I've never had visitors I've taken to so.'

There was a pause. Mrs. Jocelyn looked up.

'What is it, Cecilia? You've something on your mind.'

Mrs. Runcing paused yet longer, then, dropping her voice, said: 'Hetty, there's something you ought to know.'

Mrs. Jocelyn moved uneasily. She knew well this opening of her friend's and always it meant no good.

'Know? What ought I to know?'

'It's just like you, Hetty. The last in the place to be aware of what everyone is saying.'

'*What* is everyone saying?'

'About Mrs. Herries. She isn't Mrs. Herries at all. She's Lady Herries—and she and Mr. Herries are no more married than . . . than you and I are!'

'Cecilia, what *are* you saying?' Mrs. Jocelyn got up from the window. 'Now I won't have it! You've always got some story about someone, Cecilia. It's too bad. It's a shame.'

'Oh, is it! Always got some story, have I?

That's a nice thing to say to an old friend. I'm telling you out of kindness. It's been the talk here for days and you ought to know it.'

There was an excited movement of the shawls from the back of the room.

' I'm sure Mr. and Mrs. Herries are married. I don't care what anyone says.'

' Well, you're wrong for once. Mrs. Herries is Lady Herries, wife of Sir Ellis Herries in London. She ran away from him last year, with this Mr. Herries.'

' What's that you are saying, Cecilia? ' the old lady from the fireplace croaked. ' Not married, you say? Not married? Well, I never! Well, I never did! Not married! '

' Of course they're not married. The affair made a sensation last year in London. And more than that, they've been lovers for years and years. Everybody knows them. The Herries are Cumberland people or, anyway, they've been in Cumberland for centuries. There was an old Mr. Herries lived here in Ravenglass years ago, they say, and this Mr. Herries has a house near Bassenthwaite Lake. Lady Herries was brought up on Derwentwater. She was a great lady in London for years. I call it a piece of downright impertinence for them to come back to this part of the country where everyone knows them. Disgusting, I call it. But they say there's been one scandal after another in that family. Years and years ago there was a Mr. Herries who was a holy terror, and some fifty years back one of the Herries murdered another one somewhere by

Keswick. It's a disgrace their coming to Ravenglass. They should be ashamed to show their
faces! '

Mrs. Runcing had not intended to be so
violent, but, as often before, when denouncing
the vices of others her own virtues grew in colour
and strength. As others went down she herself
went up, and the higher she went the better she
felt.

Little Mrs. Jocelyn had turned very pale. At
last she said:

' I don't care whether they're married or not.
They shall stay here as long as they like! '

'Hetty! ' Here was a thing for a decent
Christian woman to say!

' I don't care! I mean it! '

' Think of what people will say! '

And there was a croak from the fireplace:
' Not married . . . in this house! '

Then, beyond the half-open window, they
heard a step on the gravel path. Both women
turned and looked. Vanessa was coming up
from the sea.

' All I know,' said Mrs. Jocelyn, almost sobbing with emotion, ' is that that's the finest lady
I've ever met. She's welcome to this roof as long
as she wishes.'

Vanessa was walking, her head back to the sea
breeze, her dress blown against her legs. Her
face was warm with colour. She had grown a
little stouter in this last year, her bosom fuller,
and, carrying herself thus strongly, she moved like
a woman who was happy, free and self-confident.

This seemed to Mrs. Runcing, whose own bosom, do what she would, was never what it ought to be, insulting.

'You'd think she had nothing to be ashamed of,' she said.

'Neither she has,' answered Mrs. Jocelyn indignantly. 'They're happy, aren't they? And that's more than most people manage to be. I expect her husband was horrible.'

Mrs. Runcing set her lips. 'You'll be sorry, Hetty,' she said. 'Encouraging immorality. You'll see how people will talk. . . .'

Meanwhile Vanessa had gone into the little sitting-room on the other side of the passage, taken off her straw hat, and sat down by the window to wait for Benjie. He had gone fishing. In an hour's time he would return, they would sit reading, talking, the veils of light would fall over the sea, the stars would come out, the cries of the birds would die away; after supper they would take a last walk, then, tired and happy, return, light the lamp, play chess, go up the crooked staircase to bed.

She sat there, dreaming.

More than a year had passed and still God had not let loose His thunderbolts. She had known a period of perfect unrestrained happiness. She looked back, first to the time at Eastbourne, then to the months in France, then to the wonderful glorious experience of coming home to Cumberland. What troubles had there been? In Eastbourne she had been cut by Mrs. Harbin, a friend

of Violet's.   Alfred and his wife had met her in
the hotel lounge and that had been a little uncomfortable.   On the other hand Adrian, at one time,
Rose at another, Barney at another, had stayed
with them.   The news from London had at first
been a little distressing.   The talk had been, she
understood, terrific.   The sympathy had gone,
universally, to Ellis.   Winifred and Vera Trent
had gone to live in Hill Street and, so far as
Vanessa could discover, Ellis had been quite tranquil, had enjoyed the sympathy and had allowed
it generally to be understood that he was able to
bear his misfortunes like a gentleman.   Often—
and this was perhaps her severest trouble—she
asked herself whether she had imagined all that
queerness.   But no: the scene in Cumberland,
the frenzies and tears in Hill Street had been real
enough, but how much of it had been histrionic,
an attempt on Ellis' side to catch her sympathy,
a passion for melodrama?

Strangely the question of Ellis' insanity was no
longer the main one.   She knew now, in the light
of these last months, that for years she had been
living in prison.   It was only now that she understood how solemn, how unhumorous, how dreary
that Hill Street life had been, what a *dreary*
creature she herself had become!   Everything in
it had been false, the social fuss, the hours that she
had spent with people for whom she did not care,
the shamness of her interests.   She thought of the
balls, the receptions, the silly games, the sillier
country-houses and race-meetings and baccarat;
her weak good-nature, her amiability, her own

stupidity, she told herself, had kept her there long, long after she should have left it.

And Benjie? She smiled as she lay back in her chair looking at the long dune like the back of a whale over whose brown surface little waves broke in edges of white and silver. Benjie was not perfect. She had never supposed that he would be. There had been the night at Eastbourne when she had entered their bedroom to discover him kissing the chambermaid. Twice, once at Eastbourne, once in Paris, he had left her for two days without warning. Sometimes he was out of temper, sometimes (but very seldom) he was drunk. He knew some very queer people, although he was scrupulous about the company he introduced her to. Once he had declared that he must go immediately to Italy to meet a man in Siena. Tom, who, although he was only still a boy, had much wisdom, had settled that little business. Tom, by good fortune, thought Vanessa the most wonderful woman in the world.

Vanessa, on her side, was not always perfect. Far from it. She was impatient, suffered fools badly (and some of Benjie's friends were very foolish), sometimes nagged Benjie, sometimes (as she well knew) bored him with her naïveté, her religion, her obstinacy. But they had been saved, both of them, by their splendid comradeship. Because they had been friends all their lives long that business of compromise, so difficult in the first year of marriage, had been quite natural for both of them. They loved for every kind of reason, but chiefly because they knew one another so well and admired and laughed at, for the most part, the same things. The wildness in Benjie Vanessa understood because, in her own way, she had the same wildness. They must both be free. They stayed together only because they loved one another. The troubles that they had were on the surface because the base of their relationship was firm, unshakable. They were honest, but not so honest that they were for ever challenging weaknesses. *Of course* they were weak, mistaken, faulty in this way or that. They took these things for granted. Because Benjie kissed the chambermaid it did not mean that he did not love Vanessa. He loved *only* Vanessa. He had loved Vanessa only, all his life long.

But the best of their relationship was its gaiety. Vanessa found that she had not been gay for thirteen years but now, like a language once learnt and long unpractised, living with the natives again, back it returned.

Love, if it is to be worth anything, must be honest, trusting, humorous, protective, far-seeing. With them both it was all these things.

And under its influence Vanessa grew and developed. It had been her danger always that because of her great simplicity of nature she would become tiresome company. Her mother and father had both been very simple people and it was possible that they had bored a good many persons. Vanessa, in her London years, had learnt superficial variety—that is, she had been trained to adapt herself to a great many different characters—but her lack of subtlety sometimes revealed her.

Bertrand, the novelist, whose eye was so sharp that its rather fishy, sleepy indifference often deceived the innocent, said that the only women who were interesting were the good ones who wanted to be bad, that no women were so dull as the bad women who wanted to be good.   The bad ones who were content to be bad were, he said, amusing companions, but they were all the same—know one and you knew all.

Now Vanessa had, in London, been a good woman determined to be unprejudiced and open-minded.   She defended Rose because she loved her, but also a little to show that she was above censorship.   She had never *really* known the kind of life that a woman like Rose was leading.   Her father, Barney, her husband, Lettice Marrable—from none of these did she get the real sense of it. But after a year with Benjie she knew.   They talked together like two schoolboys without any reticences whatever.   She was now *truly* aware of the humour, the generosity, the comradeship, the dirty untidy tragedy of the ' vicious ' world.   She knew that it was *not* vicious—simply a place inhabited by the uncontrolled, the needy, the weak, the greedy and, above all, the lonely.   That the very last thing that it called for was superior patronage and that those who lived in it did not wish, for the most part, for any sympathy from anybody.

So Vanessa grew wise.   She learnt now to be patient, tolerant and unpriggish.   This continuous love that burnt steadily from hour to hour, from day to day, warmed her heart so that it was impossible *not* to be generous. It is only the disappointed, starved, and robbed who are jealous and unfair.

Waiting now for Benjie she had on her lap and read from time to time Judith's old green-bound book. She had rescued it from her father's room at Uldale on the night of the fire. Judith, in her old age, had dictated it to Aunt Jane, and in Aunt Jane's clear spidery hand it was as fresh as though written last week. There was a piece about Ravenglass.

It seemed that in the spring of 1737, Judith's father, Rogue Herries, had ridden over with his son David to spend a night or two with his brother Harcourt Herries, an old bachelor who had lived for many years in Ravenglass.

'David used to tell us,' Judith's book said, ' of that visit to Ravenglass as one of the striking incidents in his life because of the quarrel that he had with his father there. He would describe to us the ride over Stye Head on horseback, how gloomy his father was on that ride, suffering from one of his " demons," how they came into Ravenglass in the evening, clattering over the cobbles, smelling the sea and hearing the gulls. Then there was Uncle Harcourt, who was a very precise old bachelor and wouldn't have a woman in his house, and he wore, David remembered, a wonderful ring on his finger with a green stone, and a rose-coloured skirted coat. After supper Uncle Harcourt talked of the London of Queen Anne, where he had been as a boy, of the Sacheverell Riots, of the Thames barge the *Folly*,

and the coffee-houses, and of how he had seen
Mrs. Rogers as Berenice.

' Uncle Harcourt was a fervent Jacobite and
gave the toast of " The King over the water,"
breaking his wine-glass after it, and he recited
to them Pope's " Elegy to the Memory of an
Unfortunate Lady." Then David's father lost
his temper, took David out to the sea and ordered
him to strip for a beating as a punishment for
some fancied misdemeanour. David refused and
said that he was no longer a child, and that was
the beginning of a new relationship between
them. This,' Judith went on, ' was one of David's
favourite stories and, as a little girl, while I
listened I could see it all as vividly as though I
had been there—the London of Queen Anne, and
the little bachelor declaiming Pope, and David
and his father standing by the sea.'

'And here I am,' thought Vanessa, 'in this same
place as though time never had been. Little
Uncle Harcourt might walk in at this door any
moment. I knew Judith so well and she lived
in the same house with the man whose uncle saw
the Sacheverell Riots. In London now they have
the telephone and there are these new " moving
pictures " and Alfred Herries has a motor-car.
Time does not separate any of us, but rather our
stupidities, selfishness and fears. Judith, if she
were here, would scold me for moralising. She
always hated it. But, on the other hand, she
would be glad that I am happy and would altogether approve of my running away from
Ellis. . . .'

She heard the hall-door open and close, a quick step, and Benjie had come in. 'They say that when you live with anyone their features become so familiar that you can't see them any more. Well, I can see Benjie all right, his bright eyes with the humorous crows'-feet at the corners, his brown hands, the part of his forehead that grows white above the brown just below his hair; I know how his arms fasten about me and how strong is his kiss on my lips. It is all as new as though it had never happened until now, and my heart beats at the sound of his step as though now for the first time he was about to tell me that he loved me.'

He went up and washed. Mrs. Jocelyn brought in the supper, and after they had eaten they sat close together by the window.

'I've been reading Judith's book, Benjie,' Vanessa said. 'The part about Ravenglass. It seemed as though time hadn't passed at all and little Harcourt Herries might be walking in on us with his green ring and rose-coloured coat. My great-grandfather was born in William III.'s reign, and Alfred has a motor-car. So soon as I am back in this part of the country time doesn't exist. We none of us die here——'

'Take a step,' Benjie said lazily, 'and you are at Gosforth; another, and it's Ennerdale. Then over the hill to Buttermere, Honister, Borrowdale. Yes, we're back in our own country, Vanessa. Bold of us, perhaps. The old boatman wasn't so friendly to-day. He knows we're living in sin.'

She did not answer. They had been living in sin for a year and she was not yet aware of it. Was it now, when she had returned to her own people, that she *would* be aware?

' I've had a letter from that man Alington. He advises me to go in for those Australian mines— at once, without losing a minute. Shall I? '

She looked at him quietly. ' No, I don't think so.' Everyone was speculating. The fever in London had spread everywhere, and Gold Mines glittered on every doorstep. ' You promised me, you know. We don't know enough about it. We have enough. We don't want to be rich, either of us.'

' Don't we? ' She saw that he was restless. ' I'm not sure that I don't. I've never been rich. I wouldn't mind the sensation.'

She put out her hand and caught his.

' You're restless—what is it? '

' It's South Africa for one thing. It looks bad —or good if you like. A war would be fun. We haven't had one for ages. Tom would go as a war correspondent if he weren't so young.'

' Well, *you're* too old to go. That's one comfort.'

' Oh no, I'm not,' he answered quickly.

' You're forty-four.'

' What's that? No age at all. And I'm as fit as a fiddle.'

' Let's not talk of it.' She stilled her fear. ' I'm so happy. Don't spoil it.'

' If there *was* a war,' he said, ' it would be only for a week or two. I'd be back in no time—with a V.C. probably and all the Family greeting me like a hero.'

He drew his chair closer to her and leant his head on her shoulder.

' Vanessa, you're not tired of me yet? '

' No, I'm not tired of you.'

' How happy we've been and are! ' He sighed. ' Why can't everyone find love like this? It seems so simple when you get it. I suppose that somewhere there's the right person for every-one—one for each—but they don't meet. Do you find there's something a little pathetic in two people of our age loving one another so? We ought to be young—we ought to be twenty—as we might have been had I not been such a fool. And I'm still a fool, Vanessa. It may break out any time.'

She laid her hand against his cheek.

' We used to say long ago that nothing could separate us. Nothing has. Nothing can now.'

' Yes—death,' he answered.

' You know that I don't think so.'

' Without our bodies? Shall we love still? You without your hair, your eyes, without the warm touch of your hand against my cheek? When I can see you smile no longer nor the way that you put your hand up to your hair, nor hear your voice. And I! I'll be a poor ghost, Vanessa——'

' What of your Valhalla under the hill, the men singing? '

' Ah, you won't be there! And I'll be such a wild ghost, flying from Top to Top, haunting

R 2

old women down the chimney, stealing the butter
from the dairy, pinching the young women. I
love you for every conceivable reason, Vanessa,
but without your body I shouldn't know you.
I'd be as restless as I used to be. I'd never find
you. I'd go searching from ghost to ghost . . .
And you'd be so good. You'd be in favour in
Heaven, one of the guardian angels. They'd
have no use for me, I'm afraid, and whatever job
they set me to do I'd do it wrong.'

She kissed him.

' I'd find you. Wherever you went I'd go
too.'

' Are you sure,' he asked her, ' that you never
miss London? Not Ellis, of course, nor Hill
Street—but all your friends and the good times
you had with all the nobs. Don't you *mind* being
a disgrace and something to make virtuous ladies
shudder over?'

' I've never been so happy in all my life,' she
said, her voice very low. ' I seem to have reached
middle-age quite emptily—as though I'd been
born yesterday. There was my childhood—that
was happy. And now there's this. Nothing
between.'

' And now there's this,' he repeated contentedly.

They were aware that the door opened. They
both turned together, thinking that it was Mrs.
Jocelyn who had come to say good-night. The
lamp was burning dimly and in the half-light they
saw the oddest figure in the doorway. It was old
Mrs. Burgess, wrapped in a multitude of shawls,

leaning on her stick; she stood there, her old brown wrinkled face pushed forward like the head of a tortoise. She stared at them, they could see, as though she could never satisfy her curiosity. Then she vanished.

'What did *she* want?' Benjie asked. He got up and went to the door. 'What cheek! To come in without knocking——'

'She's half crazy, poor old thing,' Vanessa said. 'Mrs. Jocelyn says that she ought to be in her bed, but they can't keep her there.'

'What did she want? She looked at us as though she'd never seen us before.'

They played their game of chess and went up to bed. Long after Benjie was asleep in Vanessa's arms she lay there awake. He slept like a child, his hand on her breast. She lay there, forcing herself resolutely, quite calmly, to a new courage. Instinct, light words lightly spoken, some shadow like the finger of a cloud on a sunlit hill, told her that it would be needed.

She was right. It *was* needed. Next day Benjie had moved into his savage state. That was how she always put it to herself. It was as though he reverted into some old wild existence where the rules, objects, dangers, joys of life were all quite different from this one. He seemed physically to change. He could not stay in the same spot from one tick of the clock to another. He moved about the room as though he were unclothed, his brown finely muscled body moving naked through tall grass, his eyes shiningly alert for the enemy. As often as not he did not hear what you said to him, he snapped back replies, he suddenly started walking down the road saying that he did not know when he would return.

The happy thing was that Vanessa understood this transformed state to perfection. She was aware of it often in herself but, being a woman and therefore having all her eggs in one basket (which was Benjie), Benjie could satisfy her wildest longings. She could not satisfy Benjie's. Nor did she try. When this restlessness came on him she let him go free.

But now there was more serious trouble. His words about South Africa had clutched her heart. Was there going to be war? If so, then Benjie would be off. . . . Nothing could keep him. . . . He would revel in it. He would be killed, perhaps. People were killed in wars. . . .

To-day was the eighteenth of September and it seemed that on the sixteenth the Transvaal had replied to the British proposals of starting the argument all over again by proposing to revert to a joint Commission. There was something sinister in the tone underlying the Boer phrases.

What was it all about? For a long while she had not taken it with any seriousness. It was all due, it seemed, to Krüger's fear of Rand dominion of his country. It all went back to the old Gold Rushes into the Rand. Rather naturally, Vanessa considered, Krüger thought that to give franchise to the Rand population must entirely alter Boer

rule. He was honest perhaps in wishing to keep
the Transvaal an agricultural country. On the
other hand, the British Government must protect
its subjects. But ought those subjects to be in
that country at all? Didn't it look as though a
small, resolute, independent people were to be
bullied and affronted by a big Power when all that
the little people wanted was freedom to live as
they wished on their own soil? On the other
hand, *could* Great Britain allow her own sons to
be persecuted, ill-treated, mishandled, and say
nothing?

It seemed, Vanessa thought with a sigh, one of
those questions that had so clearly two sides to
it. And the Boers were thick-headed, obstinate,
stupid, hypocritical perhaps. . . . On the other
hand, it *was* their country! Or wasn't it? She
soon, however, abandoned the wider, more public
question for the private personal one. If there
was a war, Benjie would go. . . . If Benjie went
. . . She pulled herself to her full height, clasping
her hands behind her head, staring in front of her.
The stiffest job of her whole life was approaching
her.

Then a very absurd thing occurred. Coming
into the house one morning she encountered old
Mrs. Burgess, who was shuffling along in flat
slippers, trailing shawls about her and making
that odd wheezy noise peculiarly her own. She
saw Vanessa and, thrusting her old head forward,
hissed some word. Then, with yellow convulsive
hands, drawing her shawls tightly about her, she
slip-slopped into her fastness.

Vanessa did not know what the word was, but it was evidently intended to express moral horror and indignation. She asked Mrs. Jocelyn to come and speak to her. She told her of it. She liked Mrs. Jocelyn extremely.

' Sit down, Mrs. Jocelyn,' Vanessa said. ' Let's sit together by the window.' They sat down. ' Now I'm not wrong, am I, in supposing that your mother has learnt that Mr. Herries and I are not married? '

Mrs. Jocelyn nervously rubbed her hands together.

' No, Mrs. Herries. That's correct.'

' I should have told you before. I'm not Mrs. Herries. I'm Lady Herries. I left my husband last year.'

' Oh yes . . .' said Mrs. Jocelyn nervously.

' I should have told you. I did not mean to conceal anything. I would have told you at once if you had asked me, but I really did not feel that it was anyone's business but our own. Now I suppose you would like us to go. I quite understand and I do hope you'll forgive us for putting you into this unpleasant position. We have been so happy here and you have been so very good to us.'

Mrs. Jocelyn was a sentimental and emotional little woman. Her eyes glittered with tears as she looked out of the window. Many things made her cry: the music of a band in the street, reading of a deed of heroism in the newspaper, details of a wedding, the more moving portions of almost any novel. But although she was emotional, she had the strength (and sometimes the obstinacy) of Mr. Krüger himself.

'Oh no, Lady Herries,' she said. 'Please don't think of going. A friend told us, a week or so ago. It appears that you and Mr. Herries are well known in Cumberland and Westmorland. You come from these parts, do you not? So of course the people here have talked about you. But please pay no attention. Mother is a very old lady and not always accountable. It doesn't matter at all. Really it doesn't.'

Vanessa smiled.

'Thank you, Mrs. Jocelyn, for saying that. We'll never forget it. But of course we mustn't stay here. It would be wrong for us to make it awkward for you in any way.'

'It doesn't make it awkward,' said Mrs. Jocelyn with tremendous energy. 'I hope you won't think it impertinent, but my knowing you, Lady Herries, has been the nicest thing that has ever happened to me. I don't know, of course, what reasons you had for leaving your husband, but I'm sure they were very good ones. There were times in the past when I quite easily might have left Mr. Jocelyn, although now that he isn't here I wouldn't like to say anything against him. I'm sorry, of course, that you and Mr. Herries can't be married, but as you can't you can't, and that's all there is to it.'

Vanessa was very much moved.

'I'm afraid that isn't all there is to it,' she said. 'I have done something that is wrong. I did it knowing that it was wrong, and the fact that we

are both happy doesn't make it any more right.
But I did it deliberately and I will take what comes.
All the same it's not fair that anyone else should be
involved, especially anyone as kind and good as
you are.'

' I'm neither kind nor good,' Mrs. Jocelyn
replied. ' I'm often most unkind to my mother,
I'm afraid. And as to being good, I'm too old
now, I suppose, to be anything else very much,
but when I was younger there were times when
I would have run away from Mr. Jocelyn most
gladly if there had been anyone to run away
with.'

She got up and added, smiling rather timidly:
' I've not had many friends and my life hasn't
been very exciting, but when I *have* a friend—
well, there it is. If you were to go away I should
be very unhappy. And don't mind mother. I'll
see that she doesn't worry you.'

Vanessa went with her to the door and kissed
her.

' Then we'll stay,' she said.

On October 9 the Boers delivered their
ultimatum. For three weeks after this neither
Benjie nor Vanessa spoke of the only subject in
their minds.

Under the eyes of a watchful and gossiping
Ravenglass they spent quiet days, bicycling to
Wastwater and Black Combe, seeing the shadows
turn the flanks of the Screes to purple and the
bracken flame in Eskdale. Then Vanessa had
a letter from Adrian.

DEAREST VANESSA—How are things going with you?
Here we talk nothing but the War. General opinion is
that it will be over before Christmas and everyone—except
your humble servant—is turning himself into a soldier as
quickly as possible that he may see something of the fun
before it is finished. I am not so sure. It seems to me
that we are already everywhere on the defensive. I lie low
and say nothing, for the general feeling is that it is all a
great lark—a sort of polo game in which even the poorest
may join. I listened to Chamberlain defending the
Government for three long hours and what he *did* say was
all right—but how about all the things he didn't?

What is certain is that we are now beholding the end
of the Victorian Era. Do you remember young Violet
complaining to you and me once how, when the maid was
busy. elsewhere, she must sit indoors all a fine afternoon
because she must not go out alone? Haven't you, at your
own Balls, seen the chaperons sitting in weary rows hour
after hour? I prophesy that you will never see those
chaperons again and that Alfred's girl will, in another
fifteen years or so, be smoking a cigarette as she enjoys
her luncheon alone at the Criterion.

The Family, by the way, is amusing. They take the
War of course as their own affair. Krüger is a kind of
Benjie who has insulted them all personally. It is ' *Our*
War '—Horace especially is full of club-martial ardour.
Carey is going out in some capacity or another although
he's sixty-three or so. Also Peile Worcester and—would
you believe it?—Philip is being sent out by some paper.
I am generally despised because I say that the Government
must be carried on and if *I* go who will remain?

And Benjie? What is he going to do? If he goes,
don't worry. Benjie will always survive things like wars.
They were made for him, not he for them. Write and
tell me . . .

Then Benjie had a letter from Paris. Tom,
young though he was, had hitched himself on to

some French newspaper man and was already on the sea. Tim had thrown over his painting and come home to enlist.

' You see,' Benjie said, staring at her as though he were taking her image into his very heart. ' I've got to go.'

' Yes,' said Vanessa, smiling. ' Of course you have.'

Their last night in Ravenglass they did not sleep. They lay in one another's arms while the rain lashed the windows and the wind screamed along the sea. A bird, in the early morning, beat its wings against the pane.

' You mustn't be lonely,' Benjie said over and over again. ' I shall be back almost before I've gone. I shall think of you all the time. You mustn't be lonely. You mustn't be lonely.'

As the light wove grey webs upon the wall he said, stroking her cheek:

' When I loved you a year ago, Vanessa, I didn't know what love was. This year has taught me.'

' And I love you,' she answered simply, ' more every day. I thought it couldn't grow; I didn't know . . . I didn't believe . . .'

She began to cry—a ridiculous thing, she thought, a woman of forty crying. But this once when there was no one to see . . . He kissed her tears. He had lain so often in her arms like a boy. Now he held her like a man and she was a child.

They were both very merry that morning. She would not come with him to London. She saw him drive off in the old cab; she waved her hand, laughing, while all Ravenglass watched from behind its windows.

Then she walked, her head bent to the wind, and did not return till it was dark.

THE KOPJE

SHE went back to Cat Bells.

Was not that perhaps a piece of impertinence?
Everyone in the neighbourhood thought so. But
she was not at all disturbed by the thoughts of her
neighbours. She said to Mrs. Newson on the
evening of her arrival:

' You know, Mrs. Newson, that I've left my
husband.'

' Yes—so I've heard, my lady.'

' And since that time Mr. Benjamin Herries
and I have lived as man and wife. He has gone
out to South Africa.'

' Yes, my lady. I hope he'll come back safe.'

' So do I,' said Vanessa, smiling. ' But I want
you to tell me if you and your husband would
rather get some other position. I shall be glad
to help you until you are suited.'

Mrs. Newson, who was a stout short woman
with red cheeks and grey hair, paused. Then
slowly delivered her mind.

' It's like this, my lady. It wouldn't be fair
to say that me and Robert haven't talked this over.
We have. We don't think it right in general for
a woman to live with a man she's not married to.
I wouldn't do it myself, nor would Robert. But

you see, you're different.   Folks can say what they
like, but you're our own, so to speak.   The last
thing Will Leathwaite said to me while he was
sensible enough to say anything was you was a
grand lady and I wasn't to forget it.   In Cumberland we're slow but sure, and me and Robert
think you must have had good reasons for what
you done, and there's no place can be to us what
this cottage is after being here so long, so we'll be
staying if it's all the same to you, my lady.'

After a week she could not have been more
private, she thought, had she lived in a nunnery.
No one came to see her; she went to see no one.
She walked, read, followed with passionate interest every detail of the war.   Gradually the
peace of that place stole about her and enfolded
her.   Her father, her mother, Will seemed to
keep her company.   The fell that rose above the
roof of the cottage was burnished with the dying
bracken; the herons sailed majestically against
the sky.   The little field circled with its toy-like
trees on the slope above Lodore caught the morning light with such confident tranquillity that
its curve, like the bowl of a cup, filled, emptied,
filled again as though obeying happily its com-
mander.

She bicycled over to the Fortress and looked
down into the Uldale valley.   There was a church
there now and sheep were grazing where Fell
House had been.   The Fortress, she heard, was
let to a Mr. Swanwick.   Children were playing
in the garden, a bicycle leant against the door,
two dogs ran to the gate and barked at her.

She thought day and night of Benjie. His earlier training as one of the much-bemocked Volunteers years before helped him now and he had sailed for South Africa early in November. She took a hurried journey to London, stayed there with him for two nights, seeing no one else but Barney, and returned to Cumberland. Then, some weeks later, she received her first letter.

My Darling—This must be only a short note. I shall soon have a chance, I hope, of a long letter. The worst part of the voyage was its monotony. From the moment we left London we were shut off from all news. To be without news for a fortnight at a time like this— you can imagine what hell it is! We thought we'd learn something at Madeira. Not a word. We were all inoculated against enteric and I to my shame took it badly. We had cinematograph men on board, but I don't myself think *that* will ever come to much! The machinery is so cumbrous that if they want to take anything that moves it is gone before their machines are ready. Then at last we sighted a sail and we were so close that when they put a board up with some news on it, we could read it easily. What they told us was: ' Three battles. Boers defeated ' —and then didn't we cheer? After that no more news till we sighted Robben Island. *Then* there was news all right! . . . But you will know it all by this time and much more.

What else can I tell you but that I love you, love you, my darling? I carry you with me. You are never absent from me for a single moment, your courage, your goodness, your loyalty to a poor old devil whom no one has a good word for. But haven't they? The world has changed, Vanessa. Everyone is to me like a brother. No member of the Herries family here to tell the world what I really am—all damned good fellows—and, old though I am, I'm as lively as the youngest and will make you proud of me before I'm done. So cheer up, my sweetest, and believe in me as you have always done. To-morrow, I believe, we are off again—whither I don't know. I'm as impatient as a flea on a hot plate. Impatient also for your first letter. Tell me *everything*—how the stream runs down through the garden, what you do every hour of the day, are the Newsons good to you? Have you had a look at the Fortress?

They are calling me. I must go.—Your loving and devoted and eternally faithful   B.

A fortnight passed and there was another letter, a long one. Part of it was as follows:

. . . It was a bit of a battle. How can I make you see it? Looking back I can see a green hill, kopje, almost blood colour, and then grass-green veldt. The trains stopped and poured khaki into the veldt. Funny to see the confused mass, then order forming out of it, then the line of tiny dots, then a thicker line, more and more lines, then a mass of khaki. First the dots were at the base, almost lost in the brown of the hill, then altogether lost, then suddenly against the sky-line. Away on the right the Imperial Light Horse. Then our guns thudded, and thud came the answer. Then the shells. Thin whirr, screaming cry. Ball after ball of white smoke struck the kopje, then little balloons of shrapnel from our guns; then the guns pealing faster and faster. Just as our own order to move came, down crashed the rain. You never saw anything like it, Vanessa. It drove through mackintoshes like blotting-paper. The earth underfoot melted while you looked at it into mud and the mud turned to water. Everything was blotted out in the cloud of swirling water, but the guns thundered and doggedly we pushed ahead.

Soon we were in it—my first battle, you know. What did I feel? I can't tell you—except that the ridges we must conquer seemed endless. Up one there was another! I wasn't afraid. The bugles and the pipes stirred your blood. And then I was caught into the noise.

Officers shouting, swearing, cursing; all of us stumbling, falling, jumping, killing—and then, like a maniac's desired dream there at our feet the Boer camp and the Boers galloping out of it!

As I started down the hill, though, something struck me. Don't be frightened. It turned out to be nothing— a slight scratch—but my face was buried in mud, all the world seemed to crash over my head and when at last I raised myself and wiped the mud from my eyes I seemed to be transfixed by a small kopje not far off. It stared at me, I at it. Brown-red in colour, it was shaped like a pig with horns. It seemed to move, to wriggle as though it wanted to scratch its back. I was dazed of course, and didn't rightly know for a moment where I was, but I thought it moved towards me, wagging its ears. Then the scene cleared. I stood up. I was all right and ran down the hill. . . .

Afterwards it was cold and drizzling. Some of the prisoners joined us and we were all most friendly. Decent chaps the Boers really—fine fellows with their beards and corduroys, with a grand dignity, some of them. There's been a lot of looting and you see men with the weirdest clothes. And you should watch the guns scatter at a shell. See the legs of the horses leap! You never imagined such nimbleness. . . .

And who do you think has turned up? George Endicott, a friend of my wife's brother. A wild chap but I always liked him, and now here he is in my own regiment. Small world, isn't it? Young Tom's shut up in Mafeking. Carey Rockage is in Ladysmith. Are you well, my darling, and keeping up your spirits? You seem to be always with me. Last night I talked to you. . . .

She held on, but the strain began to tell. The loneliness of her days and nights frightened her. She became restless. She wanted to be doing something, something for the war, something, through others, for Benjie.

After the Black Week, the 10th - 16th of
December: Stormberg, Magersfontein, Tugela
River, the feeling of the whole country changed.
What was this that had happened to England?
While the rest of the world looked on, jeering,
hostile, longing for our humiliation—here was the
most shameful time for us since the Indian Mutiny.
Lord Roberts was appointed to the chief command,
and Kitchener of Khartoum was to go with him.
The appointment roused a storm of new energy.
The gay, light-hearted jesting was over. This was
a job that the country must settle. The colonies
offered new contingents, a great call went out for
yeomanry, and the new infantry volunteers flamed
into being. The City of London would raise and
equip a regiment entirely at its own expense.
Everywhere there were new khaki uniforms. From
all parts of the country, shipyard-men, squires'
sons, farmers' sons, artisans and clerks poured
into the new forces. Nothing spectacular any
more. Had they but known it, that Black Week
killed spectacular warfare for ever. Nothing to
catch the eye was tolerated. Scarlet fled, never to
return to the battlefield. A new patience, a fresh
endurance, no more the reckless charge, but ' the
infinitely painful crawl through the long, long
day.'

For Vanessa those first months in the new year
became an agony. She heard now from Benjie at
the longest intervals. This country, for the first
time in her life, failed her. The old beloved names
—Skiddaw and Scafell, the running Derwent, the
ridge of Blencathra, the slow ripple of the quiet

Lake meant nothing. The valleys held no peace and the running water no music.

Her ostracism now terribly distressed her. It was a time when she wanted to have part and lot with all her fellow-beings, but on Cat Bells she was like a prisoner. Her loneliness became a horror; she could not sleep. She walked restlessly, tried to read and could not. She grew thin and pale. The Newsons heard her talking to herself, and once Mrs. Newson found her crying, her head in her hands.

'Don't cry, my lady. It will be all right. 'Twill be over soon, they all say.'

Then at the beginning of April she had a brief letter from Benjie that frightened her. He had been ill in hospital; he was better, but things moved slowly. It would be all right, of course, but the Boers were obstinate fellows and Tom in Mafeking made it anxious work. . . . But he was all right. . . . She wasn't to worry. . . . That letter was too much for her. She came to London.

She went to a little hotel called 'The Clarence,' off Baker Street. A lady in the train told her of it and she thought: 'How funny! I have never stayed by myself in a hotel before!' As soon as she was in the hansom driving to the hotel she was happy. She was nearer to Benjie; she was in touch with human beings again. She had not minded at all when Mrs. Hope of Portinscale cut her in the Keswick street, when Mrs. Merriman who had before been so kind to her in Rosthwaite gave her a sharp little bow and hurried down the Borrowdale Road. No, no, she had not minded. . . . She had been prepared for it. She had taken it gaily. Nevertheless how different these things were without Benjie! Loneliness had returned, not the old spiritual loneliness of the life at Hill Street, but physical, material loneliness, hearing no voice, touching no hand, receiving no kiss. Now she was in the middle of life again. She noticed how many motors there were now; all the traffic was speedier and pedestrians were speedier too. One good thing—these new motor-cars would soon kill that London plague, the cab-tout who had run at the side of your hansom pestering to serve you. She had a rich grand sense, after the silence of those Cumberland months, of plunging into a roaring new world ready to welcome her. Well, the Family would not be ready to welcome her. But she need not see them—only Barney and Adrian and Rose. And perhaps Cynthia— she had not, in the old days, been so violently shocked! It would be pleasant to have tea with Cynthia again in her pretty room, to hear the gossip, to ask about the theatres and to catch, even though from a distance, the tone and colour of that world to which she had once belonged! She sat upright in her hansom staring through the glass in front of her like a young girl free for the first time!

' The Clarence ' was odd enough. A very large lady, her hair puffed out over elaborate pads, her shoulders very high, her waist almost invisible beneath her swelling bosom, her costume sweeping the floor, received Vanessa in an affected manner

and directed a minute and rather shabby page-boy
to show her to her room.　This was dingy, with a
view of chimney-pots, a large portrait of Queen
Victoria and a general gurgling of water-pipes to
give it character and life.　The hotel smelt of fog
and dead geraniums.　At the head of the stairs
was a large tank in which goldfish were swimming.　The walls were everywhere very thin.　As
Vanessa changed her dress she heard from the next
room a protesting voice:

'But, Mama, why not?'

'Because mother thinks it better not, dear.'

'But, Mama——'

'Now, Cecily.　Mother knows best.　He is
not a young man who can possibly mean anything
seriously.　He has not a penny besides his Army
pay.'

'But, Mama——'

The intimacy of this conversation terrified
Vanessa, and when next afternoon Adrian came
to visit her and they sat in a room crowded with
palms and dimmed by windows with blue and red
glass, Vanessa told him that this was the most
virtuous hotel in London.　No indiscretion could
be committed without everyone in the hotel being
aware of it.

She was gay, merry, full of eagerness to enter
life again.

'I must get something to do, Adrian.　It was
dreadful in Cumberland.　I simply moped.　I
must work, help, tire myself to death until Benjie
returns.'

She was aware of a certain awkwardness in

Adrian. She remembered unexpectedly that
evening, years ago, when Adrian had been led up
to her at the Ball, his eagerness, his vitality, his
impulsive determination to help the world. He
was as kind, as affectionate as ever, but he was
now a Government servant, the *Herries* Government
servant. His clothes were exquisite, his
manner that of one who had to carry a good many
public burdens on his shoulders. Was he writing
anything? No, he had little time he was afraid.
H. D. Traill's death had distressed him greatly;
he had given him a good deal of reviewing in
Literature. Had she read Fleury's *Louis XV.
Intime?* A most interesting work with a very
striking portrait of La Pompadour. And Dr.
Barry's *Arden Massiter*, quite good as novels go.
A little over-written. And a very amusing little
book, *Lambkin's Remains*. The writer signed himself
H. B. He was the author of *The Bad Child's
Book of Beasts*. 'You remember, Vanessa.'

But Vanessa, alas, did not remember. She
had never heard of Dr. Barry and was not sure
whether she had met Mr. Traill or no.

'Perhaps he came to one of our parties.'

Oh no, Traill never went to parties. But
Vanessa was trembling for news.

'Adrian, tell me about Hill Street.'

Adrian's pale, still very youthful countenance
coloured.

'Oh, no one goes there now. Winifred and
Vera keep Ellis quite a prisoner. He likes it, I
believe. He's queer, of course. They say he
makes paper boats and has toy engines. He

doesn't go to the City any more. Alfred has everything in his hands. But they say Ellis is quite happy.'

Did Vanessa imagine it or was there a new note in Adrian's voice? Was he a little, a very little, superior? Why did he seem to patronise? Vanessa's imagination. And then he must hate this hotel.

'It's a horrid hotel, isn't it?' she said.

'Yes. Beastly. But you want it quiet, don't you? I mean—you don't want to run up against any of the family.'

'Oh no—except Barney, of course.'

'Dear old Barney—he's getting pretty aged. He plays bridge all his evenings.'

'Bridge?'

'Why, of course!' Adrian expressed surprise. 'Where *have* you been? Don't they play it in Cumberland? London's crazy about it— has been for ages.'

There was a pause. Mrs. Mont, the proprietress, came into the room and looked around. It was odd to see her balance her enormous bosom on two such very small feet! She patted her great head of hair and stared at the pair of them.

'Has she already heard about me?' Vanessa wondered.

'Oh yes—and do tell me about the others. Carey's shut up in Ladysmith, Benjie told me. And Cynthia's husband—he's in Natal, isn't he? Adrian!—Cynthia—how does she feel about me? Do you think I could go and see her? Would she mind? She used to be very broad-minded. . . .'

There was an awkward pause. Adrian coughed, stroking the side of his nose in a manner common to many of the Herries men.

At last he spoke: ' Look here, Vanessa. There's something I ought to say. You're such a sport, you're so wise, I know you'll understand perfectly. But the whole family has taken this awfully badly. They can't get over it. You see —they admired you so much and they were so proud of Hill Street. And then—if it had been anyone but Benjie, whom they've disapproved of for years! And then there have been so many family scandals! It didn't matter so much perhaps years ago when they weren't anyone particularly, but now they are respected everywhere. Alfred's a great man in the City, and Cynthia thinks herself Queen of London. She does really. You'd be amused if you saw her. Already she's bringing her two girls up most awfully carefully. They're nice little girls too. She wants them to marry Dukes. What I mean is—there's me and there's Barney—but the others—well, I'm afraid you mustn't expect them to change. They won't. They are more respectable than you've any idea of. They can't endure Benjie and they think you —they think you were unkind to Ellis.'

' I see,' said Vanessa quietly. ' Thank you for telling me, Adrian.'

' Oh, that's all right. I say, isn't there rather a queer smell in here? It may be my fancy.'

He got up.

' Well, I must be off. Got some work to do. You tell me, Vanessa, if there's anything I can do.

We'll go out one night. We'll do a play. The one at the St. James's isn't bad—*The Man of Forty*. Alexander and Fay Davis.'

'Thank you, Adrian.' She stood looking at him with a wise and rather maternal smile. She could not resist saying: 'You won't be ashamed to be seen out with me, will you, Adrian?'

He blushed, looking like a boy of eighteen.

'My God, no! Why, what do you think, Vanessa? *I* haven't any prejudices. I'll be proud!'

But, a little later, sitting in her bedroom and listening to the gurgles of the water-pipes, she was not so sure.

Then, next day, when old Barney came to see her, she learnt more about the Family. Barney was seventy, stout, rather untidy. There were pouches under the eyes, his cheeks were puffed out, giving him a childish pouting expression, but the eyes themselves were full of sparkle, humour, kindliness, and his grey hair, though it was untidy, was strong and wiry. He had a paunch, but he walked on his thick legs sturdily, his back straight, his head up, and always that slightly mocking boy-out-for-a-lark expression at his mouth's corners as though he found life more of a joke than ever. And yet you could, if you knew the Family, tell that he was old Emily's brother and pompous, long-buried Newmark's son. He found life a joke indeed because there had been originally enough of the solemn Herries there for him to see how ridiculous it could be.

Sitting again in the room with the palms and

the coloured glass, this tea-time was very different
from the one of yesterday. Vanessa was one of
Barney's *real* devotions. As he saw her now,
seated very quietly, a middle-aged woman whose
hair was turning grey, in this shabby hotel, and
thought how barely two years ago he had seen
her with her white satin and diamonds leading
the cotillion in the Hill Street drawing-room,
satin and diamonds seemed to him very vulgar
things. But did she mind this shabby hotel,
he wondered? Was she still satisfied with her
bargain?

'Adrian came to tea yesterday,' she told him.
'I thought him a little—well, a little superior.
Has he become so, or is it only with me because I'm a black sheep now, or did I imagine
it?'

'Oh, Adrian's a little more Herries than he
was—that's all. The Foreign Office might have
been invented by our family—it's so exactly what
we most approve of.'

He looked at her anxiously, rather as though he
were her father.

'You're happy, Vanessa?'

'Well, I'm rather lonely, Barney, at the
moment. I miss Benjie, you see—and I want
work, something to do. Can you find me something? I must be busy.'

'Yes, I think I can find something. There's
a Mrs. Cundlip who's a friend of mine. She has
a working party. They make things for the
soldiers three afternoons a week. She and her
friends live very quietly in Kensington. They

s

don't gossip and they are nice kind women.   I
think you'd like it.'

   ' Oh, Barney, thank you!   You *are* a dear!'

   He was touched by her gratitude.   Poor
Vanessa, she *must* have been lonely!   He told her
more of the Family.   Cynthia was now the star.
Worcester was doing very well in South Africa.
He was to join Roberts' staff.   May Rockage was
in London, doing war work and desperately trying
to find husbands for her girls.   Horace was rather
chastened.   His silent wife had developed into a
grim woman who frightened him.   Alfred's two
children were nice little things.   Richard Cards
—Adrian's older brother—was now living in
London.   He had married rather late and had
two children.   Barney gave very much the same
account of Hill Street as Adrian had done.   No
one saw Ellis and it was generally known that he
was eccentric.   Barney did not tell Vanessa the
general opinion that her flight had turned Ellis'
brain.   Winifred and Vera Trent never left him.
And that was that.   Vanessa understood quite
clearly that the Family would have nothing to do
with her. . . .

   In another day or two she went to call on Mrs.
Cundlip, found her a kindly simple woman with
a son at the Front and a plain energetic daughter
with a passion for the clergy.

   Whether Mrs. Cundlip and her friend knew
Vanessa's story or no, they gave no sign of interest
in it.   Indeed they seemed never to gossip and
had, as a group, a curiously impersonal air as
though they were part of the quiet Kensington

scene like the trees in the Gardens, the nurses
with their perambulators, the solid policeman at
the gates, the decorous shoppers in the High
Street. Vanessa found them a comfort. She
worked in the gentle Kensington drawing-room
hung with water-colours of Switzerland and Italy
and thought of Benjie and tried to be happy. As
the days passed she found that increasingly she
was afraid of a chance encounter with one of the
Family. She remained in her unpleasant hotel
because it was so safe. None of them would ever
come there. When she shopped or went to the
theatre her apprehension was always alive. It
would hurt her, she knew now, to be cut by
Cynthia or May. *Would* May cut her?—that
kind, simple countrywoman in whose house she
had so often stayed? But May had her girls now
to think of. Old Violet Bellairs was very ill and
never left her bed. The younger Violet who had
married a Colonel belonged, Vanessa heard, to a
very fast set (in revenge for her constricted youth)
who played bridge all day and all night. And
Lettice Marrable? Lettice was secretary now to
a branch in Manchester of Women's Suffrage.
She wrote very lovingly to Vanessa and said that
she would come to see her as soon as she had time
to visit London. She was very busy and talked
in her letter about The Cause as though there were
but one in all the world.

So there they all were.

Then one sunny afternoon early in May,
Vanessa tumbled almost into Horace's arms in
the Army and Navy Stores. There was no way of

avoiding it! There was Horace, red-faced, stout,
benignant behind his glasses, buying soap. He
stepped back unexpectedly, almost trod on
Vanessa, said, ' I beg your pardon ' with his
customary episcopal courtesy and saw who it was.
His plump cheeks were scarlet.

' Vanessa! ' he said.

' How are you, Horace? ' she replied, holding
out her hand and smiling.

They shook hands and she noticed that at once
he moved with her a little out of earshot.

' I'm so glad to see you, Horace. You're
looking very well.'

' Yes, I'm very well, thanks.'

' I can see you're busy. So am I.'

She smiled at him very gaily. Oh yes, it *was*
pleasant to see one of the Family even though it
were only Horace, with his high white forehead,
large spectacles and protruding chin! For the
first time in her life she *liked* Horace.

' Oh yes—indeed yes . . . very busy . . .'
he stuttered, looking nervously about him. No
one was near him, no one was looking at him. He
coughed. ' Very agreeable to see you, Vanessa.
Are you long in London? '

' Yes, for some time, I think.' She looked
him straight between the glasses. ' Benjie is in
South Africa, you know.'

' Oh yes, indeed. I had heard . . .' (Why
wasn't he a Bishop? Not that she had anything
against Bishops. Often the noblest of men, but
Horace's benevolence needed an apron.)

Now that he was assured that no one was

observing them he was more at his ease. He
began to talk with some of his old eager but, in
some odd way, calculated friendliness. He spoke
of the nobility of our men at the Front, of Britain's
showing the world, of everyone doing what they
could, of human nature being at its best in times
of stress. He became more practical, revealing
himself, as he had always liked to do, at the very
centre of affairs. He had just been lunching with
a most interesting man—name of Yerkes—the
projector of the new electric Underground. He
confidently prophesied that we should all be living
at least fifty miles out of London owing to electri-
fied trains—we should think nothing of it, nothing
of it at all; said what a nuisance half-sovereigns
were—he had nearly given one just now as a tip
instead of a sixpence; that all the best horses had
gone to South Africa, so that the omnibuses were
sadly suffering. He talked as though he were
delivering an address to a gathering of charity-
children, Vanessa thought, but he meant to be
kindly. It had always been Horace's trouble that
he meant so well, but had weaknesses, insincerities,
tempers and absent-mindedness like the rest of us.
Then he saw some ladies approaching and, raising his hat, hurried away.

' The gentleman has forgotten his soap,' the
shopman said.

' He will come back for it, I'm sure,' said
Vanessa.

She was very tired. It would have been nice
of Horace if he had invited her to take a cup of
tea. But certainly that was too much to expect.

Her arm ached. She was suffering from what was known as ' skirt wrist.'

A night or two later she had a horrible dream. She dreamt that she was on a vast green plain, bounded by hills spotted with small black patches. She had lost her way and then saw coming towards her the kopje that Benjie had mentioned in one of his first letters. It was coloured red, as Benjie had said, and shaped like a pig. It came wriggling after her, flapping large naked red ears. It covered the ground with extraordinary speed. She began to run but made no advance. It came nearer and nearer; she could smell its fetid breath and see, on its back, tufts of hair. The thing rolled in its movement. It had no face, only the flapping ears. ' This is my punishment,' she thought in her despair. ' I knew that I could not escape it.' She screamed for Benjie and woke.

After that night she seemed always to be tired. The loneliness that she had felt in Cumberland returned. Both Adrian and Barney were kind, but they were busy people; the ladies in Kensington were most pleasant, but they did not invite her to their houses; she grew no nearer in intimacy to any of them, nor did she wish to. After that dream she was haunted with fear for Benjie. It was a fortnight now since she had heard from him, and his last letter had seemed to her dispirited, disappointed. With increasing unrest she looked every day at the casualties in the newspaper. She told herself that she must be calm and brave, that thousands of other women were suffering as she was, but it became soon

impossible for her to be impersonal. There
seemed to be no one in the world but Benjie.   It
was not only that he might be killed, but that his
restlessness, his passion for liberty, must be fed by
this adventure, that the longer he was away from
her the easier it would be for him to remain away.

She suffered as all women do who love a man
but are tied to him by no official bond.   She had
no hold on him at all but his love for her, and he
might love other women as he loved her.   When
he was there she knew that he loved her, but now
she was tortured by the very indefiniteness of their
relationship, although at its heart it was anything
but indefinite.

Then, on the eighteenth of May, sitting in her
bedroom, reading, she heard a timid knock on the
door.

'Come in!' she said.

The blowzy good-natured chambermaid, Kate
by name, put her head in through the door.

'Excuse me, mum,' she said, 'but I thought
you'd like to know. They're saying as Mafeking's been relieved!'

'Oh no!' Vanessa cried, jumping up.

'Yes, mum. Ain't it grand? Relieved
yesterday, they say!'

Her first thought was for Tom. How delighted Benjie would be!   And then that it would
mean that the war would be soon ended, very soon
perhaps. And, after that, that now England
could hold her head up again, the long period of
doubt and failure was over. She was so happy
that, in a moment, all her troubles seemed to be

ended. Everyone would be happy! Everyone
was happy!

At dinner in the hotel that evening even the
old waiter in his dirty dicky could scarcely carry
the plates for joy. Two old ladies who had never
before spoken to her said: ' Isn't it excellent?
Such good news! We are so glad! ' as though
it had all been done for their especial benefit.

At the table next to hers a schoolgirl with her
mother was in a state of almost frenzied excitement. She had, it seemed, been allowed to come
down to dinner in celebration of the great event.
She was a plain little girl, wearing the hideous
khaki-coloured dress then considered patriotic
for schoolgirls. She was talking of some elder
girl who was allowed to wear a red, white and blue
costume, with a regimental clasp in front. The
' thing ' at school was to pin on to yourself many
penny buttons decorated with the heads of generals,
and one girl was the envy of all the others because
she had found somewhere a regular saucer with
the picture of Baden-Powell and went everywhere
with this pinned to her chest.

As Vanessa listened she thought, ' I'd like to
have a little girl of my own. Would it be unfair
to her that Benjie and I are not married? Father
was illegitimate and never minded. Is it worse
for a girl? Would *I* have minded? Nothing
that Father had done would have seemed to me
wrong.' Soon she would be too old to have
children. She had missed that as she had missed
other things. But she had not missed love. . . .
Benjie would soon be back now, and Tom. She

would love Tom with all her heart, be a splendid
friend to him and, in her old age, stand by him,
help his wife when he married. For Tom was
unusual like all the other unusual Herries—wild
at the heart, wanting often to be free of everyone;
hard men for a woman to understand were these
Herries!

She would go out and share in everybody's
happiness. In Baker Street she boarded an omnibus, but when they reached Oxford Circus they
could go no farther. She climbed down and
plunged into pandemonium. She stayed for a
while in a shop-door and let the crowd surge
past her. First, looking upwards it was as
though the sky itself had gone mad. From nowhere out of nothing (for there had been little
warning) the façades had created their illumination. Electric light was still rare and, at its
greatest peak of grandeur, could not have rivalled
the magic of those gas-jets. Their wonder was
that they were swayed by those little winds that
came and went, running in blue-and-gold ripples
like water against the grey surface, seeming for a
moment to be blown out and then, with a sense
of mischievous laughter, bursting into life again,
as though by their own happy agency they had
relighted themselves. They ran in waves of
trembling light, hesitated, vanished and, with
new energy, ran again. The sky was alive with
beauty.

Beneath it what a world—as though a new race
inhabited the earth! Men in evening dress, hats
on the back of their heads, cocked sideways,

evening capes flying, danced arm-in-arm with the
ladies of the East End.   These women who were
to go down in history, dressed in black satin, wore
great hats crowned with ostrich plumes; and so
they danced, their fine bosoms swelling, the
flounces of their long dresses swinging from their
tiny waists, petticoats whitely revealed and vanishing.   Their own gentlemen for that night at least
were in ' high dress ' with mother-of-pearl on their
flat caps, trousers tight to the knee, flapping round
the ankles.   They changed hats with their Donahs,
moving in the ' double-shuffle ' in an ecstasy of joy.
The East End came West that night, and the West
was glad.

And the noise!   Everyone was shouting, singing, turning rattles, blowing the coiled paper
springs, screaming down pink-and-white tuppenny
trumpets gay with silvery angels' hair.   You were
' killing Kruger with your mouth.'   You were
singing ' Duke's son, cook's son, son of a belted
Earl.'   You were shouting ' *W'ere* did you get
that 'at?', ' Wot price old Kruger! ', ' Git yer 'air
cut! '   You were singing:

> Hark! I hear the bugle calling,
> And I can no longer stay.
> Good-bye, Dolly, I must leave you.
> Good-bye, Dolly Gray!

That night the British Army was worshipped.
It was to be worshipped again, but in another
sterner spirit, when tuppenny trumpets and
mother-of-pearl could not meet a far more menacing enemy.

The soldier and the sailor were the heroes, and

the ' Little Englander ' was the villain of the piece.
Close to Vanessa a girl, waving her arms, screamed:
' Down with Lloyd George ! ' and behold his
image was flung deep under the dancing shoes of
that multitude.   And there is a god in a monocle,
with an orchid in his buttonhole—' Three cheers
for Joe ! '   ' Not for Joseph ! '   ' Good old Joe ! '
Labour?   One man named Keir Hardie has boldly
walked into the House with a cloth cap on his
head.   So much for Labour.   Squeakers and
ticklers and corncrakes have, that evening, little
consciousness of a new world that very soon will
be demanding very different instruments. . . .

Vanessa for a while was safe in her doorway,
but soon the crowd was wilder.   Hansoms appearing from the very bowels of the earth discharged
young men in evening dress;   something other
than tea is the draught of the Town;   here there is
a fight between a cabman and a fare, there a policeman has seized some gesticulating figure, raised
him above the crowd, then, as though abandoning
the hopeless charge, dropped him back into the
crowd again.

Vanessa has been swung from her doorstep.
It is best to go with the crowd.   Someone has
linked arms with her and she is swayed down
Regent Street, all the shouts, songs, cries seeming
to catch a sudden rhythm so that it is as though
the very sky itself were singing.   At the edge of
Piccadilly Circus the surge forward is arrested and
you see a rising, falling pattern of life—not individual life now but something made up of the
windy, swaying lights, tumbling bursts of sound,

the very buildings swinging, it seemed, in the uncertain glare.

A woman grasped her arm: with her other
hand she wielded a toy trumpet, her straw hat at
the back of her padded hair.   Vanessa turned and
looked.   It was Rose.

' Hooray!   Hooray! ' she cried, waving the
trumpet. ' Hooray for Joe!   Hooray—— ' She
said confidently to Vanessa: ' Come on, dear!
Let's give him a cheer! '

' Rose,' Vanessa said, bending her body sideways to avoid the pressure of a stout perspiring
gentleman with a tickler.   ' Don't you know me? '

Rose stared. ' Vanessa! ' She threw her
arms around her, scratching the back of her
neck with her trumpet. Her straw hat, falling,
disappeared. ' Oh, Vanessa—my darling! my
darling! '

Vanessa realised that Rose had been too
splendidly celebrating victory.   At the moment
she could realise nothing further, for the impulse
of the crowd swept them both off their feet.   It
appeared not unlikely that there and then they
would find death in one another's arms, bells
clanging in their ears, somewhere the trumpets of
a distant band, the smell of sweating bodies,
broadcloth, patchouli, against their nostrils and,
against the sky, grey walls like rocks on whose
surfaces flickered in the wind the jets of blue,
green, red, thrown up from the tossing dark
pool at their feet.   It was then confusion.   The
fountain of the Circus stood out above the singing waters.   Heads rose and fell like despair-

ing drowning mariners. Fastened firmly in the midst was the rock of a towering hansom up whose side figures were climbing. Beyond that again an effigy with a tangled beard, a battered high hat, jerked as though in agony against the lights— Krüger moving to his bonfire.

Then the waters parted. Waves of human beings slumped like falling walls. The effigy was moving forward, followed by a great cheering procession, men waving their hats, women screaming, and under the confusion—above it, outside and within it—the steady pulse of 'The Soldiers of the Queen,' into whose tune at last all the scattered sounds and voices were gathered.

Driven back at the corner of Shaftesbury Avenue, Vanessa suddenly discovered that, a wide porch of a restaurant protecting her, she was free. Miraculously, still holding to her arm was Rose.

'Oh, where is he?' Rose cried. 'The Captain! The Captain gone! He swore he wouldn't leave me. Oh, Vanessa, I'm lost—I don't know where he lives. He's got my little green bag, my little bag . . .'

They stood in the shelter of the porch against the wall, shoulder to shoulder. Rose cried out as though she were demented. A lock of false hair had detached itself from the disordered pile and tickled her mouth. There was a small scratch on her cheek from which blood was trickling. Altogether a battered Rose.

She looked at Vanessa, and as she looked her wildness fell from her.

'Oh, Vanessa, I've drunk too much. Take

me home.   I don't care if I never see the Captain
again.'

Very slowly they moved up Shaftesbury
Avenue; then, turning at the first opening, found
themselves in a little dark street, deserted,
melancholy, shutting off like a curtain the lights,
the singing, the press of the surging crowd.

'Where's your hat, dear?' Vanessa asked.
She took out her handkerchief and wiped Rose's
cheek.   Rose began to cry.

'Oh, you must think me dreadful.   Fancy
your meeting me like this after all this time.   But
it was all the Captain's fault, and my bag had all
my money in it.'

Vanessa, her hand through Rose's arm, led
her from little street to little street.   Near Oxford
Street they found a hansom.

'Now, Rose, where are you living?'

Rose stared.   'I don't know. . . . Oh yes,
Three Orcutt Street.   That's where I was living
three days ago, before I met the Captain.'

'Well—is that where you want to go?'

'Yes.   You'll come with me, Vanessa?   I'm
not drunk really.   I only had a drop in the Captain's room.'

In the hansom Rose leant her head against
Vanessa's bosom and sobbed.

'Mafeking!   Mafeking!   I wish to God I
had never heard of Mafeking or the Captain
either.'

In a grim little street they stopped at a grim
little house.

'No.   Don't come in.   My room isn't very

grand.' She was quite sober now, looking like a dishevelled child afraid of a scolding. 'But you'll come and see me to-morrow? Or I'll come and see *you*. May I?'

Vanessa told her the address of the hotel. Once more Rose flung her arms about her neck and passionately kissed her.

'It all feels different, meeting you. Like old times.' She wiped her eyes. 'I've lost my hat. I don't know what Mrs. Blaker will think if she sees me. She doesn't think much of me anyway. Good night, darling.'

Later up to Vanessa's bedroom came the shouts and cries of a city madly rejoicing. Some kind of a triumph. A passionate impulse of compassion caught her heart, compassion for the world, for Rose, for all lonely and misguided creatures. The kopje could not frighten her now.

Indeed, indeed it could not. Two weeks later there was a telegram forwarded from Cumberland. Benjie had lost an arm and was being sent home at once.

She sat, with the telegram in her hand, staring in front of her. She was so happy that she could scarcely breathe lest the telegram should prove unreal. Then she knelt down by her bed and thanked God.

YOUNG TOM IN NEWLANDS

Young Tom Herries, sitting one summer evening on a slope below Dale Head, the peak which closes the Newlands Valley, watched the sky. It had for some while fascinated him and distracted him from the second volume of Hardy's *Woodlanders*, which lay on the turf beside him. He was always known as Young Tom, but even in years he was not so young any longer, for he was now seventeen years of age, but in character, in a subtle intuition of motive and feeling, in self-command, he had never been young. In looks he was something like his father, dark, short and thick with a round hard head and short wiry hair. He had also some of his father's geniality and all of his warmth of heart.

But he was different from him altogether in his self-control, in his patience, in his consideration for others. His early flight to Paris with Timothy, the free life there spent always in the company of his elders, his experiences in South Africa, his acquaintance with all the ways of humankind, bad, good, sensual, virtuous, foolish, wise, had helped him to come to terms with real life long before the common time. But, with this, there was something young in him that made folk, the country

people, the townspeople, all who knew him, speak
of him as Young Tom. He *was* young in this:
that unlike his father he took all his responsibilities with extreme seriousness. His principal responsibility was to his father and to Vanessa. He
loved them both, but he knew his father too well
to think him in any way wonderful. He felt to
his father as he would to a younger brother whose
faults he knew by heart but whom he loved and
guarded the more for those faults, but Vanessa he
worshipped.

He had been living with them now in this little
house in the Vale of Newlands for six months, and
the longer he lived with them the deeper did his
devotion to Vanessa grow. He was thinking of
her now as he lay on his back, his arms behind his
head, looking at the sky. She seemed to him of
another kind altogether from any women he had
ever known, and he had known some very strange
ones. Her love for him, which she had felt since
she had visited him a little boy ill at school, made
her more natural with him, perhaps, than she was
with anyone else. They were very often alone
together and then she talked to him as though she
were a girl of his own age. She poured out all
her heart to him: she told him more than she had
ever told Benjie. She told him everything: of
her childhood, her love for her father, her life in
London with Ellis, her love for Tom's father—and
they discussed, for hours together, Benjie's character, his sweetness, irresponsibility, restlessness,
honesty, infidelities. When Benjie was drunk
(rare occasions but unfortunate) Tom managed

him to a marvel.   When Benjie disappeared, Tom
reassured Vanessa until he appeared again.   Tom
sometimes rated his father as though their positions
were reversed.   Benjie never resented it.   He
was as proud of his son as he could be.   Tom
himself of course was far from perfect.   He was
obstinate and sometimes sulked.   He was given
to fits of melancholy that he inherited from his
own Herries strain, and then he would go away by
himself and brood.   There were many causes for
these, but the chief of them was that he had always
meant, since he was a tiny boy, to be a great writer
and he thought now that he would never be even a
good one.   His early devotion to Timothy had
been stirred the more by his saying to himself that
Tim would be a great painter and he would be a
great writer.   Now Tim was, if not a great painter,
a very good one.   He was in Paris selling his
pictures.   He was known everywhere as a promising and unusual artist.   But Tom, although he
was a fair journalist, was no more.   He talked to
Vanessa again and again about this; he showed
her his attempts.   She was too honest and knew
the value that he put on her honesty too well to
encourage him.

'What is it,' he said to her in despair, ' that
I can't get? '

' It is something, I suppose, that doesn't come
by asking for it.   Never mind, Tom.   You began
so young.   You're only seventeen now!   There are
so many writers.   You will do something better
in another way.'

Now, thinking of *The Woodlanders*, he felt a

sort of rage against fate.   Yes, he was only seventeen—there was plenty of time—and yet he did
not lie to himself.   *This* thing would never be his.
And *what* was it?   Hardy, Tom thought, was a
peasant, he had scarcely moved from his countryside: he already knew far more about the wide
world than Hardy could know. Hardy often made
his characters talk in stilted, unnatural sentences;
his books were filled with ridiculous coincidences
—but here in these pages was life, the life that so
many polished sophisticated writers missed altogether.   Tom looked at the scene around him
and his spirits fell into quiet.

For the last fortnight there had been perfect
weather in Cumberland. By day the sun had
shone, veiled with mist sufficient to give hill and
water their rightful size.   It was a late year and
so the larch still stood in patterns of green flame
against the smoky shadows of yew and fir, the
stems of the young bracken were pellucid as are
the throats of pale-green glasses.   And with the
sunny mist, over the green flats, up the stony
sides of the fells, above the glittering chattering
runnels of water, there was now thin shadow, now
a breadth of light, all warm, kindly, beneficent;
as a generous man's hand strokes his dog's
shoulder, so God bent down from His cloud and
caressed His world.

Tom, lying on his back, wondered that now the
sky could be so quiet and so pure when so often he
had watched clouds battling in armies for suprem-
acy, seen one fierce cloud-captain drag another
by his hair, watched the surge upward, from the

hinder-parts of the Tops, of whirling frenzied clouds, angrily purple, and the thick grey sullen banks of storm mount and spread until all the world was covered with them and rain fell in spears of steel upon the earth. Now the sky was pale like the inside of a pearl-shell; light was translucent and softer than down. Cat Bells and Dale Head, Robinson and Maiden Moor were bathed in a peace that seemed eternal, and towards the dip where Lobstone Band hid its rocky tors, a carpet of purple shadow hung above the little fields that welcomed the evening.

Near him Herdwick sheep were browsing— the bravest little sheep in England and the most adaptable. Their wool may be harsh, but so faithful in spirit are they that all their lives they will not move far from the place where they were born, not because they are unenterprising, but because here for generations their ancestors have been and here, like proper Cumbrians, their heart is set. So, with the old forest trees, the fir, the oak, the birch, with the stones and boulders that they can, if they will, so closely resemble, with the running water and the flying clouds, they obey the law.

Soon the stars would come out, breaking the green of the evening sky, and a young crescent moon would rise, and all night long the light would last, paler than ivory, quieter than sleep. The air was scented with the newly cut hay from a field near by, with the first honey-suckle, with the summer heat drawn from grass and fern. Birds winged slowly, making the silence vocal.   The line of the hills grew with every moment sharper as the shining sky paled.

Tom's thoughts turned to his own future. This had been a fine holiday, but it could not last for ever.   He loved this country as he loved none other, but soon he must go back into the world again.   He had for so long now been a man— ever since he was fourteen—that he had not a boy's light indifference of waiting until life should begin for him.   He had been kicked about in Paris, he had endured a historic siege like the other men with him, and time would not wait. For six months too he had been ostracised.   No one came to see them at Cold Fell.   His mother's cottage was only ten minutes away over the hill. It was let to a painter and his family, but that long slow slope of Cat Bells cut the three of them from the world as though they were on a separate planet.   Sometimes, when he rode into Keswick, he was looked at almost as though he had a de- formity.   He minded in spite of himself.   What did it matter that his father and Vanessa were not married?   They *would* be married if only that crazy old lunatic in London would die.   They loved one another more faithfully than many a married pair, and, stroking the back of *The Wood- landers* with his hand, he thought to himself that the writer of that book would understand if he were here and would come to see them and be their friend.   There was something terribly wrong with the world when people as good as his father and Vanessa could be exiled simply because some old clergyman had not blessed them.   He knew, though, that it all went farther than this, that people thought it impertinent of his father to come back and live with his woman here in the very spot where they were so well known, and that there had been scandals before, old scandals of a hundred and fifty years ago that everyone in these valleys knew, scandals that had lost nothing in constant telling.

His young heart was passionately in sympathy with all the outlaws. It was enough for someone to be in disgrace for Tom to be on his side so long as the outlaw was not cruel nor mean nor a coward. At his age it seemed very easy for the world to be wrong and for all the good men to be outlaws. And he was, like his father, a born champion of lost causes.

He heard voices and, sitting up, saw his father coming towards him and with him a large rough untidy-looking man. Benjie, when he saw his son, waved his one arm and, as they came up, introduced his companion.

' Tom, this is Mr. George Endicott, an old friend of mine.' Then, reaching his hand up to the big man's shoulder, he said: ' George, this is my boy, Tom. I don't think you've seen him before. Tom, Endicott was with me in Africa. This boy, you know, George, was all through the Mafeking siege.'

The man, Tom thought, was one of the strongest and wildest he had ever seen. He looked like part of the countryside, belonging to the stones and bracken like the Herdwick sheep. He wore no hat, his face was of a brick-red

colour, and his shirt was wide open, showing a
brown chest with a pelt of black hair. His body
was solid like a stone, but he moved lightly on his
feet, making no sound. He had only nodded at
Tom and then passed straight up the fell, swinging his arms.

'Tom, look here. I'm glad I saw you. When
you go down tell them I shan't be back to-night.'

'When will you be back?'

'Oh, to-morrow likely. Endicott has come
over from Whitehaven. We're going for a
tramp.'

Benjie looked shamefaced. He knew that
Tom knew that he had gone from the house without telling Vanessa.

'All right,' Tom said shortly, and without
another word, picking up his book, he started
down the hill. He hated it when his father was
ashamed, when Vanessa was disappointed, when
rough ill-looking men from God-knows-where
took his father off to drink and fool with girls and
not to return for days perhaps. His father was
fine, his father was the best man he knew—but
why must he make Vanessa unhappy?

Cold Fell had changed not at all in the last
hundred years, with its whitewashed front, its
narrow passages and low-ceilinged rooms, the
rough cobbling before the door, the slope down
the hill where the hens were and the broad fields
that crossed the stream and the valley, the cows
now clustered for the cool under a large oak, the
sheep browsing on the fell-slope. Great sweeping
shadows of gold covered the valley, and the sun,

low now above the hill, struck through the thick
leafage of the oak. The river, shrunk though it was
now, could be heard very clearly chattering over
its stones, so still was the air.

Vanessa was standing in the doorway when
Tom came up.

'Have you seen your father, Tom?'

'Yes.' Tom put his arm round her and
kissed her. He did not kiss anyone easily, but he
liked to kiss Vanessa—her skin was so cool and so
firm. Her hair was greying but her cheek had
a girl's freshness. 'Yes. He's away for the
night.'

She said nothing but went in.

Later they had their supper in the porch. An
old woman called Mrs. Williams came every day
and 'did' for them. But Benjie and Vanessa
cooked, and they, all three of them, did the house,
looked after the piece of garden at the back. Tom
went into Keswick for the shopping. For six
months Vanessa had scarcely stirred from the
valley. She looked now like a woman who had
always lived in the country, her hair very simply
brushed back, parted in the middle, leaving her
fine brow clear and broad. She wore a plain blue
cotton dress, shorter by a great deal than the
prevailing fashion. Her waist was not pinched
nor were her shoulders puffed. She looked her
age, but her body had strengthened. With her
height, her broad shoulders, her firm big breasts,
she was a woman who would be noticed anywhere,
and all her life she had carried herself superbly.

They had cold chicken and Cumberland ham,

a salad, a cold apple tart and a cheese.   A fine
supper on a summer evening with the murmur of
the river coming up to them and the air as sweet as
honey.

Vanessa, leaning her arms on the table, looked
out to the valley.

'You know, Tom, I think Benjie might have
told me.'

'He was afraid to.   He had a man with him.'

'A man?—what man?'

'His name was Enderby, or Enderley—something like that.'

'Endicott.   George Endicott.   I know him.
He is an old friend of Benjie's.   He met him first
when he met your mother.   He was a friend of
your uncle's.'

'What kind of man is he?'

'Oh, all right, I dare say.   Rough, wild,
always on the tramp.'

'Father said he was with him in Africa.'

'I wouldn't mind,' she went on, after a pause,
'if only he'd tell me when he's going, but he slips
out of the house as though he were ashamed.'

'He *is* ashamed,' said Tom.

'The trouble is that each time I say to myself:
"Perhaps this time he won't come back."   Judith,
my grandmother, used to talk to me sometimes
when I was a girl about *her* married life.   She's
often told me that her husband—he was a Frenchman—would go off just like that, only he would
be away for months.   The difference was, though,
that Judith was married.   I'm not.   I've no hold
on your father except that we love one another.

That's the only hold any woman ought to want, but women are funny. I've never known a woman, Tom, who was really sure of a man. Men belong to a different world, and you can't be sure, from minute to minute, that they won't have a new idea in their heads. Women are too serious about everything. They can't take things lightly. It isn't that I doubt your father. We've loved one another all our lives—but I've nothing else now. I've put all my eggs in one basket.'

' You've got me,' Tom said proudly.

' Yes. You're very faithful. You'll make a splendid husband one day.'

Tom saw that she was struggling not to be unhappy; he saw how deeply disappointed she was and, with an intuition wonderful for a boy, knew that she was dreading the long lonely summer night. He wanted terribly to help her.

' I know what it is in father,' he said. ' It isn't anything to do with you and me. He wants to be free sometimes. He told me once that there's bad blood in us. My great-uncle killed my grandfather in Skiddaw Forest and my great-grandfather killed himself. You know all that. And I think sometimes it all comes over my father —a kind of superstition about the past. Of course the past can't do anything to you *really*, can it? But you have to fight it sometimes perhaps. So he goes away and fights and then comes back to you again. That's *how* I explain it!' he ended.

She got up and kissed him.

' The truth is, Tom dear, that I've never been a very sensible woman. I haven't enough humour.

If I could only see how funny things are it would
be a lot easier. When the Queen died I was unhappy for weeks. Why should I have been? I'd
never known her, but I couldn't get used to her
not being there. It's always been the same if I've
loved anyone. You take life lightly, Tom, and
people easily. It's the only way.'

' I'm rather serious-minded too, I expect,' said
Tom. ' Tim's always said so. Tim used to say
that I ought to have been an old nurse with
families of other people's children to look after.'
He laughed. ' Don't you worry. Father will be
back to-morrow.' He got up and patted her on
the shoulder, then moved about taking the plates
and dishes into the house.

Vanessa sat there, her chin propped on her
hands, staring in front of her.

Three days passed and Benjie had not returned
nor had any word come from him. This was the
longest time that he had ever been away from
Vanessa since her flight from Hill Street. The
hours were quiet, stealthy and packed with a
secret significance. She did not know that time
could be so long and on the third day she found
herself walking down the valley towards the hills,
standing and looking about her, starting with an
agitated excitement at the figure of a shepherd,
thinking that stones were men and that every
sound in the air was Benjie's voice. Tom's care
of her, which he tried to make unconcerned and
indifferent, irritated her. She came back to the
house on the afternoon of the fourth day, driven
by absurd fear. Benjie had been planning this

for months past; he was weary of her and had not
the courage to tell her so. Some woman somewhere had entrapped him and, as he had always
been faithless, so now he proved it to her for ever.
She was intensely humiliated. ' I have never been
able to hold anyone to myself; there is something
in me charmless, dull, wearying; everything that
I touch falls away from me.' She was even
haunted by the dazzling dominating figure of her
grandmother who, with her head up, stamping
her ivory cane, could rule the world if she wished,
but she, Vanessa, who had had beauty and all the
world to charm, had been able to hold no one.
Women between thirty and forty often know an
especial terror and apprehension, for youth has
gone; if they have had children they are being
abandoned by them, men are searching for
younger faces, and old age, that demands more
wisdom for the subduing of its terrors from
women than from men, already leers, like a cock-
sure arrogant old man, over the fence. Women
have greater courage wherewith to meet spiritual
loneliness than men have, but their capacity for
spiritual experience is also greater.

She came back to the house, its floors flooded
with the June sun as though to taunt her, and said
passionately to Tom: ' He is never coming back.
I can make my mind up to it.'

Tom said something. She turned on him
furiously with one of her old tempers. ' What
do you know about it? You are only a boy! '

Then she burst out of the house again and
walked swiftly away from the hills. She was in

a mood for anything. That old, scared, irrational Herries blood for ever mixing in the personal Herries history beat now in her brain. Why not end it? Her life had been a failure from beginning to end. Her father had died when she might have saved him, she had married a man without loving him and he had gone crazy from it, she had risked everything for another Herries who was notorious for his instability and lightness. But even now, in this passion of fear and unhappiness, she would not blame Benjie. No, it was herself—her dullness and heaviness of spirit. 'Why have I not managed life better? What is lacking, has always been lacking in me?' She came to the little church and, scarcely knowing that she did so, finding the door open, entered.

She had often, in the last six months, visited this little place and had grown to love it. Behind its wall, guarded by its trees, hills mounting to every side of it and one of the loveliest small rivers in England at its back, quiet, restrained and confident, it held something in its heart greater than change or fashion. Everything was simple, the whitewashed walls, the altar, the pews, the birds that nested in its roof, the scents that filled it from the summer fields, and the unceasing rhythm of the river.

Very unhappy, Vanessa knelt and prayed: 'God, in this quiet place, help me to find my courage again. I knew, when I did wrong, that I would suffer, but if it be possible allow me not to suffer without anyone to help me. It is not right that I should ask You anything, for I have not yet repented of the wrong that I did. I know that You ask me to be honest, and so I say that if there was that wrong to do again I would do it again. I feel that I acted against a law and against my conscience, but I did it deliberately. God, don't take Benjie away from me. Let me care for him and watch over him and share his life later when he will need somebody. If You are my Father as, in this quiet place, I feel You to be, do as my own father would have done, and let me be good to someone I love. Don't take Benjie from me. I know him better than anyone else does. I can care for him more than anyone else can. Let me be punished in any other way, but not by losing Benjie. You have placed this church here that we should make our requests in it. This is my only prayer—let me keep Benjie. . . .'

She found that she was saying aloud, her hands clenched, her eyes staring at the little altar on which was a glass bowl filled with red and white roses: ' Don't take Benjie away from me! Don't take Benjie away from me! '

The strain of her intensity snapped. She rose from her knees and sat on the hard bench. She heard a bird singing, the water swinging by, and the voice of a shepherd as he crossed the grass by the church wall, talking to another.

' Well, good night.'

' Good night.'

She knew the man by his voice and with that familiarity all the outer world swung in. She heard Barney in London saying: ' Why, no,

Vanessa dear, if it makes you happy to believe in such things . . .'

She saw the Prince and Princess entering in procession into the Hill Street drawing-room. . . . She was in a theatre and Bernhardt was speaking. . . . Then, someone saying: 'God? Oh, God died long ago. Didn't you know?'

But the church filled with light. She heard the sheep with their gentle sleepy rustle pass beyond the wall. A fragrance of flowers and new-mown hay seemed to be carried, by the sweet, persistent note of the bird, into the church again. She knew with a sudden delighted conviction that for herself at least this presence was true. Some wise power entered into her and, falling on her knees again and hiding her face in her hands, she was pervaded, through and through, with intimate kindliness. That intimacy! To be lonely no more! 'Only connect . . .' The connection was there, her hands were held, her bent head blessed. Time was lost. The bird continued its song as the shadows came down upon the mountains.

When she came into the house again Tom was there in the passage.

'It's all right,' he said (a little shyly, for she had been angry when she went away). 'Father's back. He's upstairs and he's awfully tired, for he's walked miles.'

She went up into the low-ceilinged bedroom and there was Benjie, lying, stripped to his trousers, on the bed, his arm behind his head.

He grinned but didn't move. She saw the stump of his arm where the flesh had been joined in a sharp red line, the deep brown of his bare chest, taut and spare as a boy's, his hair tumbled over his forehead, his impudent ashamed grin, and she was drowned in a wave of triumphant happiness. But she must not show it. She must be calm, sarcastically humorous as a wise woman would be, indifferent as though whether he went or came meant little to her. So she stood where she was and looked at him.

' So you're back? '

' Yes.' Then as she still didn't move, with his bright eyes fastened on her face he said: ' Haven't you a kiss for me? '

' No, I haven't. Why did you go off without telling me? '

' Oh, I don't know. That man Endicott came over from Whitehaven. He wanted a walk.'

' I see. You never thought, I suppose, how anxious Tom and I would be.'

' Why should you be anxious? You knew I'd come back.'

' Four days is a long time without a word from you.' She gave him one long look, then turned to the door. ' I suppose I'd better get you something to eat. You'll be hungry.'

' Yes—famished.' He looked at her, smiling. He put out his arm. ' Here, Vanessa. Come here. Don't be so cross with me. I haven't seen you for four days.'

' I'm not cross.' She came over to the bed and stood there. He put his bare arm round her

waist, then drew her down.   She knelt by the bed
and they embraced.   Then she rested her head on
his body, he stroking her hair.

'Benjie, it wasn't kind . . . four whole days
. . . I was in a panic.   Tom and I are all alone
here.   Nobody comes, and if you're away the
days drag.   I've been watching the hills all day.'

He turned on his side, drew her on to the bed,
put his hand inside her cotton dress that it might
rest on her heart.   Her hand stroked his back,
rejoicing in the strong muscles, the smooth skin
warm and fresh like the summer evening.   Through
the open window she could hear the bird singing
and the running water as she had done in the
church.   He settled himself comfortably against
her.

'Now I'll tell you all about it.   Quite truthfully.   George Endicott turned up and as soon as
I saw him I wanted to go off.   He wasn't here
more than a minute.   You were in the back of the
house.   I said " Hullo, George," and he said,
" Hullo."   I asked him where he had come from
and he said " Whitehaven."   I asked him whether
he wanted a walk and he said " Yes " and there we
were.   I *had* to go off when I saw him, Vanessa.
I *had* to.   I'd have told you, only I knew you'd
want to know *where* I was going and how long I'd
be, and I didn't know where and I didn't know
how long.'

'I wouldn't,' she murmured.   (But she knew
that she would.)

'Then we went up the Fell and saw young
Tom and I told him.   It was pretty late by then,

but we got on to Robinson and then at dusk on
Honister. It isn't dusk, you know—there's a
white light in the sky. There was a new moon
too. We found a cave on the other side of
Honister. Endicott said that in the old days,
years ago, his great-grandfather used the cave
when they were smuggling. They were bad lots,
you know—as bad as they make 'em. When we
came to the cave there were two others there—a
man and a girl. The girl had red hair and was
pretty in a way. They didn't say much, but they
were cooking a hare and they let us share their
meal.

' Then we all curled up and went to sleep and
I was as happy, Vanessa, as I've ever been in my
life. I didn't care for you or Tom or anybody or
anything. It was just like that—I'm telling you
honestly. I was free and the air was fine and
warm. I'd drunk their whisky and eaten their
meat and beyond the cave there was the misty
moonlight over the hills. I was a free man and I
didn't want ever to be tied again. Well, I went
to sleep and, after a time, I woke to find the girl
had come over and was lying close to me, right up
against me she was, with her arm around me.
There she lay all night. I didn't do a thing to her.
I didn't even kiss her. I'm telling you honestly,
mind. I'd tell you just the same if there'd been
anything, I'm not being virtuous about it. I
might have done a lot of things but I just didn't.
In the morning we set off again, the four of us.
We were together the next three days. We went
down into Eskdale, then over to Coniston, on to

Helvellyn, along to Saddleback. This morning
we separated, and here I am. It was grand, I tell
you, Vanessa—lovely days and fine nights, not
saying much, any of us. George wanted me to
come back to Whitehaven and stay with him a
bit, but by this morning you'd all come over me
again, Vanessa. I *had* to see you. I didn't feel
free any longer. I didn't *want* to be free. So I
kissed the red-haired girl for the first time, gave
George a kick, and here I am. I know I did
wrong not to tell you, but if I'd told you I wouldn't
have had such a good time somehow. You've got
to forgive me and believe me too. I've never told
you a lie yet.'

She sat up on the bed, her arm around him.
This was something of a crisis between them and
she wanted to say what was best and wisest.

' Yes, Benjie, that's all right. I know you
must be free. Haven't I always said so? '

' Yes, you've always *said* so,' he answered,
laughing and stroking her cheek.

' Have I prevented you? Have I ever stopped
you? ' she asked.

' Don't be so serious, darling. Take it lightly.
I've only been for a walk—and here I am.'

' That's easy to say,' she answered. ' Does no
man *ever* understand these things? Every time
you go off I can't be sure you'll ever come back
again. Oh yes, I feel safe enough now—now
that you are here and close to me—but when you
are gone I say to myself, why should he come
back? I've no hold on him. He may be tired
of me, hiding it from me.'

'Tired of you? I love you more than I ever did. Why, Vanessa, I've loved you all my life! How could I *not* come back? I'll always return——'

'Ah yes, you think so!' she answered quickly. 'But I've seen you change your mind so often about so many things! If I were younger, gayer! But sometimes I seem to myself so dull, so heavy! Women are faithful if they're given a chance—it's the thing they like best to be! But men—when they've got what they want, they want something else. Then,' she went on, 'it's lonely when you're away. For six months here we've seen nobody. When you're with me I don't *want* to see anyone, but when you're away every minute is an hour. It wouldn't be if I knew you'd be back at such and such a time. But when you haven't said a word——'

He sat up. 'Look here, Vanessa. Let's have a child! Then you wouldn't doubt any more——'

'Oh no,' she answered slowly. 'That would be wrong——'

'Why wrong? Your father didn't mind because he was illegitimate.'

'I think he did. It made a difference to his life.'

'If only Ellis would die!' He beat the bed with his hand. 'Now don't be hypocritical about that, Vanessa. You know it would be much better if he should die. He's old, he's crazy. Life can't be any fun for him.'

But he was afraid of alluding to Ellis. A

shadow crept into her eyes. He hated that she should think of the past.

'Look, Vanessa! I have to go off sometimes. Sometimes I'm restless beyond bearing. I think of my father, my mad uncle, my grandfather. There are days when I hate myself, my ancestry, all the past and the present together. Then you can't help me—nobody can. But never doubt that you're the love of my whole life, Vanessa. If ever any man in the world loved anyone, I love you! Why, even now I couldn't be away three days from you without running back! But there's this country, every fell-side, every stream, every stone wall, is in my blood! Why, you know that as well as I! Wasn't it crazy of us to come back here where everyone knows us and all our family history? But could we help it? Of course not! No man escapes the past, nor the fields where he was as a boy if that poison is in his blood. With some of us it is, with some of us it isn't. What do Timothy or Violet or Ellis care for this country? That's why they'll never understand us nor why we do what we do! We are the gipsies, with the smell of the ground always in our nostrils. That's our history, mixed up with the country, with Cumberland, with England.'

He stretched himself and yawned.

'Lord! I'm a poet! And I'm famished too! I could eat a whole sheep!'

He held her tightly in his arm, kissing her again and again.

'Darling, don't be sad, don't be too serious.

I'm yours for ever and ever. You're the one thing I'll never leave. You and this country here. And I'll be good next time—I'll tell you before I go. And I didn't make love to the red-haired girl. Remember that! Vanessa, sweetheart, darling sweetheart, don't you *know* that you've got me for ever and ever? Have you no sense? Can't you *tell* a thing like that? '

A little later, going down to prepare the food, she found Tom making, very seriously, an omelette.

' Father's frightfully hungry,' he said. Then he saw how happy she was. He sighed as though a great burden were lifted from him. She kissed him.

' I'm sorry I was angry this afternoon,' she said. Then, as she began to make the meal, she added: ' I'm afraid, Tom dear, that we both take life too seriously.'

An hour later, in front of the cottage, the moon, cherry-tinted in a white sky, rising above the hill, they had the best meal of their lives.

STORM COMING UP

'TIME, of course,' said Mr. Benbow who was, during September, taking the work of the Vicar of Newlands, ' docs not exist. There *is* no time.' He was, he had always been, of a mathematical mind, but he did not know, as he said this, raising his glass of beer and looking at the charming sun through its smoky depths, the strange things that his simple sentence provoked.

Here, in the September sunshine, sitting with Benjie and Vanessa outside their white house (he was a man who cared nothing for social conventions), he killed history. There was no past. Upon this square of ground, over which the Eagle was magnificently sailing, even as he spoke, across the spine of hill that rose in front of them, Francis Herries, his small son tight against his breast, rode over the wild land, not pastured now, sweeping in unchecked confusion down Borrowdale to the small house under the moon, with its shining suits of armour. ' Take me to the Fair with you,' Mrs. Press cried. ' No, I will not,' he answered, while Margaret his wife lay sick in the room above.

Keswick waited basking in the sun while the coach rolled in from Kendal, and old Pomfret, a little drunken, looked out of his study window.

At the same moment David, at Uldale, heard of the fall of the Bastille and cursed his son, Jennifer walked tapping with her slippers up the road to the Fortress, and Judith's boy, naked by the Tarn, mocked the big man on the white horse. In his London rooms Francis, David's son, sick of life, blew his brains out while young Tom Macaulay talked with old Rogers in Hatchard's bookshop. Judith saw the big woman count the lumps of sugar in the Paris café, and young Will raced up to the Druids' Circle while Adam cheered him on. 'It's war then,' said Judith, nodding her bonnet at Walter, and, even as she spoke, the flames leapt upon Uldale and her son fell fighting the choking fumes. The carriages moved slowly at Will's funeral, and Sayers with a broken arm faced unflinchingly the blinded Heenan.

'Thank you very much, Miss Martineau,' said Judith, shouting down the ear-trumpet, one eye on the tea tent, and John called through the mists of Skiddaw for his enemy. 'Yes, it's too late,' said Benjie, bowing his head; 'I'm married already,' and Vanessa turned, in the long drawing-room, thinking that she heard Ellis' step on the stair. The Chinese clock strikes, and old Emily has offered up a prayer while young Tom, his hand for a moment on Vanessa's shoulder, says: 'He'll be back soon. He'll be back soon, Vanessa.'

Behind these figures, mingling with them, giving them their meaning and sharing in their destinies, fog swallows up Carlisle to hide Prince Charlie's men, Keswick receives Mr. Gray and the

young gentlemen from Cambridge who hope to
have a word with Mr. Southey while on their
reading-party, the Reform Bill rides in with a
cheering mob behind it, trees fall, the roads are
bound with stone walls, figures from here, there,
everywhere, buy lead pencils, picnic on Skiddaw,
whose green slopes young Mr. Keats and sturdy
Sir Walter find adventurous. A Macclesfield
paper advertises for workers: ' Wanted, between
4000 and 5000 persons between the ages of 7 and
21 years.' Thick bellies of smoke veil the Mid-
land sky. Disraeli sees the war of the two
nations; Mr. Joseph Hebergam, aged seventeen,
works from five in the morning until eight at night
with a break of thirty minutes at noon. ' Bravo!
Bravo! ' cry Will and Horace and the Vicar of
Little Rodney-on-the-Marsh, ' England rules the
world,' while a man or two, with pens in their
hands—Shelley, Carlyle, Dickens, Ruskin, Morris,
—speak of 'a Golgotha of souls and bodies buried
alive.' The Herries are rising, the lights of
London grow brighter, the fields of middle England are lost in smoke, slowly, slowly men are
pushing up from under ground, are meeting, are
banding together, demanding their share, pulling
down the Park railings, putting up bright little
red houses, chasing the Squire's wife out of the
cottages, pushing into Westminster Hall, driving
the South African millionaires out of Park Lane,
running here, running there from coast to coast
with their children behind them, dancing on
Primrose Hill, standing in rows of shiny black as,
at last, the old Queen passes . . .

And still on that square of ground, over which the Eagle is hovering, nothing has changed. The coach rolls in to Keswick square, the shepherd searches the mist under Helvellyn for his wandering sheep, the sun falls from Seatoller on to the silent blue of Buttermere and, under Gable, the Tarn sleeps like a rusted shield.

'There is no time,' said Mr. Benbow. 'Time is an anachronism. At this moment Caesar falls on the steps of the Capitol and David challenges his giant enemy.'

At this moment, too, Cynthia Worcester brought her two little girls on a visit to Cumberland. Strange how the Herries were drawn back, again and again, to this patch of ground. But in Cynthia's case it was perhaps Vanessa rather than Cumberland that drew her. Cynthia had never set an eye on Vanessa since the flight from Hill Street. She had not seen her but had stepped into her place—or very nearly. Peile Worcester was not of course as rich as Ellis; they could not, in their house in Charles Street, entertain as Vanessa had done in Hill Street. On the other hand, they were cleverer than Vanessa. Vanessa had not been clever—kind, gentle, generous, most beautiful to look upon, but *not*, oh, most certainly not clever.

Cynthia was as pretty as a rosebud (a flower to which she had been often compared) and *also* as clever as a monkey. She had always been *inside* the Arts as Vanessa had never attempted to be. Indeed, so far was Cynthia now inside that her set embalmed her like a fly in amber. But everyone

came to her afternoons, her evenings — Mr.
Bernard Shaw, the Sidney Webbs and Mr. H. G.
Wells; while on the other side there were the
aesthetes, Mr. Sidney Colvin at the Museum,
young Mr. Binyon, a wild young man who had
sailed before the mast and swept the floor in a bar,
Mr. Masefield, and, above all, the Homer, the
Milton (who knew, perhaps the Shakespeare of
our day ?), honey-voiced Mr. Stephen Phillips.
The politicians came too—Cynthia had no party
politics: Sir Henry Campbell-Bannerman dined
at her table as well as Mr. Balfour. Even the
new Labour candidate for Barnard Castle, Mr.
Arthur Henderson, came to tea. . . .

Cynthia had taken Vanessa's place. She was
the social head of the family now, and the
younger generation, Alfred's children, Maurice
and Clara, Carey's girls, cousins from Manchester
and cousins from Bournemouth, Philip and his
odd effeminate friends, young Violet and her
stupid husband—they recognised it and submitted
to it.

Nevertheless (as is always the case in every
family history) some things were not quite right.
Cynthia was not as happy as she ought to be.
She possessed just enough imagination to wish her
position a little different. *Her* struggle between
Prose and Poetry was, of course, all on the side of
Prose. There was never any doubt as to which
party she belonged to. Of the world of Judith,
of Rose, of Vanessa she would never even glimpse
the borders: nevertheless the world where she was
was not quite good enough. Peile Worcester was

not quite good enough, their income was not quite good enough, their two lovely obedient little girls were not quite good enough. In fact, in this September of 1903 Cynthia was supremely discontented, her rosebud mouth curled down at the ends; she, one afternoon, startled Mr. Phillips almost out of his life by saying that to-day she really didn't want to listen to *Marpessa*, and she lost her temper altogether with Horace when he informed her that ' in his own small way he grew with every increasing year more and more of an optimist.' She could not *abide* Horace, she decided, with his high domed forehead, his mild eyes naked of eyebrows, his plump rosy cheeks and his way of being able to help anyone in the world out of any trouble so long as he personally got the glory of it.

After her rudeness to Horace (for which she was sincerely sorry, for she was a kind-hearted little thing) she took herself in hand. What was the matter with her? Two things. One, her husband. The other, that she longed to see Vanessa again. She must get away from Peile for a while and she must see Vanessa, if only for a moment. With a start of surprise, staring into her mirror, she discovered that, in all probability, she cared for and admired Vanessa more than anyone else in the world. Vanessa had of course done a dreadful thing. Had she run away with anyone but Benjie Herries! Nevertheless Cynthia, feeling as she did at the moment about Peile, thought that running away from one's husband was not so extraordinary a business. Only it was

a thing that a Herries must never do, because the
eyes of the world were on the Herries family,
they stood for domesticity, patriotism and virtuous
common sense. That was why Vanessa's affair
had been so truly awful!

The matter with Peile was that he never
changed. He was exactly the same as he had
been when she married him, *exactly* the same, and
all the things for which she had loved him then
were precisely the things that exasperated her
now!

He had not changed in looks; he was as good-
looking as ever. He did not appear a day older
(how she wished he did!) with his crinkly fair hair,
his fair short moustache, his splendid figure, his
immaculate clothes. He was an English Gentleman *in excelsis*. He had to-day precisely the same
complaints against the English middle classes that
he had had when he married her. *Then* they had
seemed to her charming, and she had agreed with
every one of them, for the Herries belonged to
the Upper Middle Classes and thought therefore
that almost everything that the Middle Middle
Classes did was a pity. Peile's complaints and
sarcasms now were just what they had always been
but were more, far more, vehemently expressed,
because he was older now and had all the Englishman's touching faith that the older you grew the
more important your opinions were.

At this particular moment there were a number
of things that made the Middle Middle Classes
especially offensive to Peile. Business was bad.
The country had not yet recovered from the effects

of that stupid mismanaged war. How ironical to
remember the cheering crowds lining the streets
as the C.I.V.s marched past, or the shocking
vulgar manifestations of Mafeking night! Then
there was the Whitaker-Wright affair that had
been dragging on for years, and only in March
had the Public Prosecutor seen fit to prosecute.
There was Chamberlain's absurd loan of thirty-
five million pounds to South Africa. *There* was
a nice burden for the Upper Middle Class (on
whom now *all* the taxes were falling!) to pay!
There were the unemployed walking about the
streets with their collecting-boxes. There was
Brodrick's ridiculous ' Phantom Army Corps '
of which young Winston Churchill so rightly
made fun. There was this demand on the part
of the Lower Middle Classes for cheap food—and
they were getting it too, mostly in tins, of course,
but nevertheless eating lobster and asparagus,
peas and apricots, as though these things were
their right instead of a luxury. There was the
horrible ' Art and Craft ' furniture with which the
Lower Middle Classes were encumbering their
homes, dreadful cheap confusions of memories
of William Morris and vulgar German *Kunst*. A
typist whom Alfred had engaged actually owned
a mechanical piano-player, bought of course on
hire-purchase. There was this new passion on
the part of the Lower Middle Classes for learning
things, for buying cheap books about atheism and
how to put a bicycle together. There were their
odd forms of entertainment and exercise—walking
races to Brighton. There had been the other day

a race to Brighton for waitresses! There was a
sudden craze for swimming the Channel, and
schools for quite inferior children were mad about
hockey teams, just like the school attended by his
own girls. There was this crazy ugly music by
Richard Strauss that had not a tune in it, and this
vulgar new halfpenny paper, the *Daily Mirror*, for
women. There was the sordid excitement over
the Moat Farm Murder, and there was this fearful
increase in motor vehicles, so that a law was to be
passed ordering them to be numbered and some
' test of efficiency ' for the driver . . .

It was not that Peile was a snob. He did not
think himself better than anyone else, or only so
very, very little better, but anyone could see that
this new power in the Lower Middle Classes,
their crazy desire for the best of things and intolerable fashion of making themselves heard
through the daily Press, through Leagues and
Unions and meetings and speeches was doing Old
England no good, was in fact fast dragging her
down from her grand position as Mistress of the
World. Something must be done about it, and
the Upper Middle Classes were the people to do
it: it was their right and their duty. Peile did
not know *what* everyone was about! The country
going to wrack and ruin and nobody cared. What
was Alfred doing, and old Barney and older
Horace in Manchester? Why, simply nothing
at all!

It was after Cynthia had endured months and
months of this at every meal and for an hour or
so every night in the quiet of the matrimonial

chamber that she decided to take the girls for a holiday to Cumberland.

She simply told Peile one evening and, next morning, departed.

Arrived in Keswick, she looked for rooms, preferring these to a hotel, and found them—most charming ones—on the right side of the road that ran down to the Lake. She spent half an hour putting the rooms' things away into a cupboard —trays from India, china figures from Manchester, bead mats, two large coloured portraits and three huge sea-shells. Mrs. Colbourne the landlady was a little astonished, but there was something about Cynthia, so tiny but so charming, with such lovely hair, such lovely eyes, and a manner that had just the right mixture of kindliness and authority. Mrs. Colbourne, who was a widow and came from near Liverpool (had she been a Cumbrian she would not have been so quickly melted), surrendered to Cynthia entirely, giving the governess special food (for she had a delicate stomach), sitting up one night when Rosalind had a cough that might become pneumonia (you never can tell), and hiring a pony-trap from her friend Mr. Lewthwaite at especial terms for Cynthia's especial use. In those few days she used it in fact a great deal. She became a familiar sight in Keswick, sitting up driving, her little back like a ramrod, and a veil concealing her lovely features. The citizens of Keswick are not very easily impressed—they have too many visitors—but the Hon. Mrs. Peile Worcester, driving her pony-

cart, her two lovely little girls sitting as stiff
as Royalty behind with their governess, Miss
King, was a sight that they did not for a while
forget.

Then, after four extremely happy days, there
came a peremptory letter from Peile. He was
not well. He had been in bed all day. He had
a temperature. The doctor thought that it might
be serious. He demanded her instant return.

She did not return instantly, however. She
waited a day. She went with her two little girls
and called on Vanessa. The pony-trap arrived at
the church. There they all three dismounted and
walked across the meadows to the white house.
Having tea by the house door were Vanessa,
Benjie and Tom. At first Cynthia thought it was
the farmer and his wife. It was one of those
lovely September days when above the turning
bracken the sun lies in happy content from shoulder
to shoulder of the hills and all the little streams
flash with light. Perhaps one small cloud, dark
as a mulberry, hangs motionless like a hawk above
the glittering valley and, for a moment, the sun
slips behind its shelter. Then at that instant all
is sombre—the hill, the streams, the little running
walls, as though a vast curving wing from the
protecting Eagle shadowed the world. Then the
sun is free of the cloud, and light leaps up from
the heart of the soil.

It was such a day, but very warm: Benjie was
in his shirt sleeves, the sleeve of his one arm rolled
up; his neck was bare. He was wearing corduroy
riding-breeches, and Vanessa in a sun-bonnet

had a cotton dress—white scattered with blue flowers.

After another look Cynthia saw that it was indeed Vanessa: she ran forward with a little cry. The two women embraced.

Two days after her return to London, Cynthia wrote to May Rockage. This is part of the letter:

. . . But of course I wasn't going to miss Vanessa, the very thing I'd come up there for. So we drove over, the girls and I, to the funny little valley where they live. Peile was very annoyed when he heard that I took the girls. Very annoyed indeed, especially as he has a sore throat and thinks himself on the point of death. (He's better to-night. Nothing but a bad cold. Aren't husbands absurd?) But the girls enjoyed themselves. They went off quite alone with Benjie's boy, Tom. He's nineteen now, Vanessa told me, and *most* serious as though he was eighty. But of course he had all that time in Paris and South Africa, which makes him more grown-up. Anyway I knew the children were quite safe with him. I think both of them have fallen in love with him. They've talked of nothing else since. Benjie was nice. I should say Vanessa's calmed him down. Of course he *looks* rough. He might have been a tramp or gipsy or anything, and he's brown as a berry. But he's always a gentleman even if he hasn't always behaved like one.

But, May dear, here's the great news. Vanessa is going to have a baby. Any time. It might have come while we were there having tea! She doesn't attempt to conceal it. Really I was rather afraid what the girls would think, but they're too young, thank heaven, to know anything about it. Miss King is *excellent* at answering awkward questions. When I went up with Vanessa to her room (*such* a small room, with whitewashed walls and smelling of hay), she told me that they hadn't meant to have one—a baby I mean—but there it is, and of course

it will be illegitimate, which is a pity.   Isn't it funny how
we *can't* keep illegitimacy out of the family, and yet I'm
sure most of us are as proper as can be?   When I was
with Vanessa I couldn't help feeling I'd made a mistake
and it would have been much better to have run away in
a caravan with a gipsy instead of all these silly London
parties.   Benjie and Vanessa seemed so *very* happy.   But
of course as soon as I was in London again I knew it would
never have done.   I'd *never* be happy in a caravan roasting
hedgehogs and telling people's fortunes.   But what *is* there
about Vanessa?   Of course she's still beautiful even as she
is and dressed like a cottage woman with a sun-bonnet.
But her features are lovely, so *noble* without being a bit
superior.   She has the grandest eyes, the finest forehead,
the kindest mouth of any woman I've ever seen.   I've
always adored her, even though I *was* a little jealous of
her in London.   She's just as quiet as she always was.
She sits there, her hands on her lap, and you feel you could
tell her anything.   She isn't clever of course—I mean she
never *says* anything that's clever—but you can trust her
absolutely, which you can't do with many women.   She
asked about Ellis, but I couldn't tell her much except that
he's quite happy looked after by those two awful old
women.   I asked her whether she were happy and she
said she was.   I think she is—part of the time.   But I
caught her looking at Benjie as though she expected him
to go off any moment.   Not that she lets *him* see that.
She's too wise.   She knows that men want to *feel* they're
free even though they're not really.   I asked her whether
she were anxious about the baby. She's forty-four you
know and it's her first.   But she said no.   She said she
didn't mind dying so long as Benjie was there.   But I
don't know *what* he'd do without her.   He may be wild
and all the rest, but if any man ever loved a woman Benjie
loves Vanessa.   And it was all so quiet there, with the
sun on the fields and the sheep grazing and the noise of
running water.   If Maud and Helen are coming up next
week to town do let me know.   Peile says . . .

'A storm's coming up,' said Benjie, looking back towards Keskadale and Buttermere Hause. The sky was a stainless blue, but over Whiteless Pike little shreds of cloud like tags of cotton wool floated and gathered. A low whispering wind stirred the dying bracken.

'I'm coming with you,' Vanessa said. As she said it she thought: 'Now this is foolish of me. This is what I determined not to do—not to force myself on him. He doesn't want me. He will be so much happier by himself. And yet I'm determined. What is it? Is it the child? I can't bear these days to let him out of my sight.'

'Better not,' Benjie said. 'There's a storm coming. And I'm out for a long walk—Hindscarth, Robinson, over Red Pike to Ennerdale. You'll never do it, Van, as you are. It wouldn't be safe.'

How well she knew him when he thought that someone was laying a hand on him to constrain him—herself, anyone—like a hare who, with ears pricked, hears the hunter treading the long grass. But she was determined. All her cautious ways of dealing with him were gone. She could not *endure* a whole day and night just now without him. If she had asked him to stay he would have stayed—but reluctantly, behaving all day as though she had tethered him with a rope to a stone! How well she knew him! As though it were herself who was resenting it.

'I can't help it,' she said, smiling, her head up, her hands on her broad hips. 'I must come,

Benjie. It will be all right. Wenlock says that it won't be yet. I never felt better in my life.'

He looked at her and she knew what he was thinking: 'This big broad woman stands over me like a gaoler. Why did I tie myself up? Can't even go off for a walk by myself!'

And yet, all these months, since they had known that there was to be a child, he had been exquisitely tender for her, taking every trouble, thinking of her, watching over her as he never would have done for anyone five years ago. Oh! he had grown. Living with her, loving her, had taught him something. Had taught *her* something too—should have taught her not to worry him, to let him go off free! But he ought not to want to go for a night and a day now, when, in spite of what the doctor had said, he knew that the child *might* be born . . . and she alone with Tom in the house. The child *might* be born . . . it was mad of her to insist that she must go with him. And yet she *did* insist.

' I'm coming,' she said obstinately.

' Look here.' He did not look at her, but slanted his eyes, bright, lively, shining in his brown face, away from her, looking at the walls of the house, the sheep cropping, the wind stirring in the bracken. ' Look here, I've told you. There's a storm coming. I must have a walk. I've been cooped up for weeks. (' Oh no, you haven't,' Vanessa thought. ' Last week you were away for two nights.') I'll be back to-morrow morning. It's madness for you to think of coming. Look

here.   Walk to the end of the lane with me.   Then
come back.'

'No, I'm coming,' she answered obstinately.
She went in to get some things.   As she was
collecting them she thought: 'What is making
me do this?   And why, at moments like this, do
we almost hate one another?   I would give him
anything, anything in the world.   I would die for
him.   It wouldn't be hard at all.   But now the
more he wants me not to come with him the
more I'm coming.   And when it's like this it
seems as though we had always been fighting
one another, all our lives long.   And yet soon—
when we are agreed again—it will seem as though
we had never had a fight in our lives worth mentioning.'

When she came down in her short skirt and
with her stick and rucksack she looked in at the
lower room to say good-bye to Tom.   He was
seated at the table, his square arm firmly planted,
his honest determined eyes bent on a book.   He
sprang up.

'Why, where are you going?'

'I'm going with Benjie for a walk.'

The look came into his eyes that she knew so
well—of fear and love and motherly anxiety.

'Oh, but you shouldn't!   Not now.   What's
father doing to let you——?'

She smiled the old ironical mischievous smile
that she had had as a child, a smile just like
Adam's.

'He doesn't want me to.   He's very cross
about it, in fact.'

'Well, of course he is. Oh, Van, you mustn't.'
She caught him to her and kissed him.

'Dear Tom! You're going to have an awful
life—always upsetting yourself about other people.'

She went outside. Benjie never said a word,
but he was as sulky as a scolded schoolboy. They
set off. She waved to Tom who was watching at
the window, who would be, she knew, anxious
and miserable all day.

'I don't care,' she thought defiantly. 'They're
only men. They haven't the least idea what a
woman wants. It will be good for me, this
exercise. I never felt better in my life.' She
walked, her head up, striding, a smile on her lips,
and Benjie stepped along at her side, whistling,
kicking pebbles. Only as they crossed the beck
and she jumped from a stone to the bank he
said:

'You're a fool, Van, you know. But on your
own head be it.' Then he seemed better. He
could never be sulky for long. Any little thing
interrupted his mood. 'Look, Van! Look at
that hawk! Like a stone on the sky! Ah! it's
dropped—a field-mouse, I expect. Here. Take
my hand. This fence is a bit steep.'

Then all was well again; they were as close
together as though they were one body, moving
through the air, treading the turf so lightly, brushing the bracken as they began to climb. She
looked back on the little stream before they left it.
It played lingeringly about its gleaming stones
as though loath to leave them, and the stones too
seemed to cling to the water, stopping it, having

excited murmurous chats with it, then, as though
trying a last strategy, exercising in a tiny dance
with flurries of silver lines and circles.   All about
the stream the scene was ' calm as a resting wheel '
and the air so clean that trees and hill-lines seemed
stamped on the atmosphere like a seal on blue
paper.   The September day was exceptionally
warm, but everywhere was the finger of decay, the
leaves gold and dun and then of a sudden brightly
green as though defiant of approaching death.
At a cottage above the right bank of the stream a
woman called to a shepherd striding uphill, two
dogs at his heel: ' Well, anudder time . . .' Her
voice rang out in the still air like a cry.

' Oh, how happy I am! ' Vanessa thought, ' and
ten minutes back I was nervous, uncertain, anxious.
I only want Benjie to be happy and then everything
in me is tranquil.'   She remembered, as they pressed
past a big boulder and began to tread the turf and
to feel the wind, touched with the salt of the sea,
in their faces, her London life.   How dead and
gone that seemed!   But Cynthia's visit had stirred
her strangely.   She had accepted her ostracism
almost gladly—she had suffered so little—but
she had been moved, deeply moved that Cynthia
had brought her children.   Yes, and had allowed
Tom to take them off across the valley.   Tom had
thought little Mary the most beautiful creature he
had ever beheld.   He had spoken of her again
and again.   He was to go shortly to London.   He
was to be given a trial on the *Standard* newspaper,
a job that dear old Barney had found for him.
How would the Family receive him?   Peile and

Alfred and Horace. . . . Would May and Carey
invite him to Wiltshire? After all, it was not
his fault, poor boy, that his father had disgraced
himself! And Society was more tolerant now.
Every kind of queer person was admitted. When
she had married Ellis the conventions had been
rigid, as though you belonged to a Regiment,
and any social or moral offence was as bad as
desertion. She did not care for herself—*her* case
was socially hopeless and would be more so after
the birth of a child—but she *did* want Tom to
have a good time!

Benjie took her arm to help her up a steep
place. At his touch warmth poured through her
body. It was always so. She had had, in her
life, so little experience, but she had always heard
that, when passion was gone, the best that a
married pair could hope for was a kind of compromising friendship. But still, after all these
years, Benjie's body was lovely to her. She would
lie awake at night, while he slept, her hand on his
thigh, and know that his vigour, his warmth, the
freshness of his skin, the strength of his bones was
unique for her and always would be. Now she
understood fidelity—spiritual fidelity. Yes, that
she had always understood, but when it was aided
by the body how undefeated it must be! She
understood now the tragedy of the marriage in
which physical things were disharmonised. Easy
for others to argue that it must be endured, but
the touch, the kiss, the stroke of the hand, the
meeting of cheek against cheek, the personal
flavour of the flesh, how much of spiritual contact

went with these physical things—they were the
very gateway of the spirit!

So, on the brow of the hill, she said that they
would sit down for a moment and they did so.
He put his arm around her and she drew his head
to her breast.   She felt almost a faintness of
ecstasy, here in this high air, with the smell of
bracken and short stiff grass and the sea-wind.
Far below them she saw a little figure of a man
leading his horse, and she thought of him, the year
going past him, rousing his horses, driving his
plough through flint and marl, the peewits wheel-
ing above him, kestrels soaring, his eyes always
so patient, so wise about so many things, walking
as his forefathers had done in all the old ways.
The child leapt in her womb, and with that lovely
sense of new life, her eyes grew bright with comfort and she smiled.

They moved on again.   She asked Benjie:

' I suppose now you think you know me better
than anyone else in the world? '

' Yes, I think I do.'

' Yes, now.   Father knew me; Rose—poor
Rose—knew me. . . . Don't you know me so
well, Benjie, that it's dull? '

' Dull? '

' Yes.   I never can surprise you any more.
You always know what I'm going to do.'

' I know you as though you were part of myself
—the better part.   You *are* part of myself.   You
always have been.'

' A part you often want to be rid of.'

' No, not often.   Sometimes.   Every man is

like that.' He stopped and looked at her. ' Sure
you're all right? Not tired? '

' Splendid. I could walk a hundred miles.'

' You know, when you said you were coming
with me I hated you for a moment. I could have
run off and never come back. That's what I felt
like.'

' Yes, I knew you did.'

' Aren't you wise? You resent nothing. You
forgive everything.'

' Yes,' she said, laughing. ' I'm placid—like
a cow.'

' No. Oh no! ' He struck his stick against
a stone. ' You've a fearful temper. You can be
so angry that the air quivers. But you never
resent. You forgive and pass on. Every day
you're finer.'

' Am I? That's because I love you.'

' Yes, and I love *you*! I love you! I love
you! I love you! ' he called. ' Do you hear the
echo? It comes from that rift of rock.' Then,
looking about him, sniffing the air, he went on:
' I was right about the storm, Van. It's coming.
Do you see those clouds? '

Over Newlands a fleet of small, ragged clouds
were slowly gathering, as though with purpose, as
though marshalled. The sun shone brightly, but
the air was colder and the wind now was busy along
the ground, whistling in an undertone.

She didn't care about the storm. It would be
nothing. She took her last look at the valley, so
small but packed with history. In the time of
Elizabeth the German company had worked the

mines in Newlands: there had been the Goldscope
lead mines worked at the beginning of the nine-
teenth century. At Stair there had been the
woollen mills—all that energy and human life,
love-making and child-bearing, foreign tongues,
and Elizabeth's sharp eye fixed on her profits—
and now the little valley bathed in silence, the
small farms, the enclosed fields, the hawks and
kestrels, the shepherd calling his dogs, the farmer
ploughing the stiff field . . .

'Benjie, this is the only place in the world for
us! The only spot . . . and for my father, my
grandmother, her father . . .'

'Yes,' he answered. 'I can't tear away from
it. Try as I may I can't. Everything passes—
on the surface everything passes. But underneath, Van, you land on the rock, you give a cry of
delight, you defend yourself against attack, and
then, in a moment, you're gone to join the others
under Skiddaw perhaps. We *seem* to change but
we don't.'

She stopped, leaning on her stick.

'Yes, God gives you your moment of experience—to overcome fear.'

'Oh, you and your God!' he said, laughing.
'Hasn't science taught you anything yet, Vanessa?'

'Science—I don't know. . . .'

He looked at her curiously. 'Then God does
exist for you, Van? Just as I do?'

'Yes, if one's brave enough to believe in Him,'
she said shyly. 'It needs courage like everything
else. We never talk about Him, Benjie. Why?

Because I'm afraid that you'll laugh, and *you're* afraid—what are you afraid of? Of looking too far. What does everyone say? That Huxley and Darwin have settled the whole question, so why argue? And they leave it like that because it's easier, because it's dangerous to look any further. I shouldn't have the courage if I were not driven to it, but I think God has tormented me all my life. Tormented isn't the right word perhaps. Moved restlessly in and around me. *You* say that that is superstition. *I* say that there's no other choice for me. I *have* to be aware that you are there; I know your step, your voice, your frown. So I'm aware that God is there. I didn't ask for it. I'm not better or worse than you or anyone else because of it. It's simply a fact.'

She had not for a very long time discussed such things with him. He knew that she prayed, that much of the tranquillity that was always increasing in her came from some inner experience, the only thing that she did not share with him. Once he had been jealous of it, angry with her because of it. Now he loved her so much that he only wanted her to be happy. Perhaps . . .? Who knows . . .?

'It's a great thing to conquer fear,' he said. 'Anyone who does that is a kind of god.'

Even as he spoke the storm broke on them. Benjie knew the dangers of this piece of country. Robinson and Hindscarth had rough faces with much scree, and the ghylls into Buttermere had loose and falling rock with water suddenly, and sodden turf on the fell-side. A nasty ground for mist. But, at the moment, he could think of nothing but the wind which, quite suddenly, leapt from the ground, rushed forward from the hillside and tore up the valley. The clouds boiled from behind the hill, and the sun was obscured. The moss, heather, bracken that had been so brightly lit lost all colour.

' Are you all right? ' he shouted to Vanessa.

' Yes, yes, I'm all right,' she answered.

Could they reach the bend of the hill they would have shelter. The storm was so furious that it could not last, he thought, but how strange was this sudden roaring of waters! The rain had begun to fall in slanting whips of steel, but the becks and mountain rivulets had not had time to absorb it; yet in his ears it was as though all the thundering waters of the world had been unloosed! It was as though a spirit with inky hair strode the fell and passed, blowing a great horn summoning his army! They could see the rain sweeping from the farthest horizon in curtains of gauze, blowing, bending, but never breaking.

' Turn your back to it! ' he cried to Vanessa. ' Get your breath! There'll be a rock soon that we can shelter against.'

She turned, her skirts blown against her legs, her hair in her eyes and, at that same moment, with a little gasp of pain, felt a strong hand clutch her vitals, squeeze them, let them go. She bent her head. The stab of pain passed. She hurried, pressing through the storm so swiftly that Benjie cried:

' Come on! That's the spirit! We'll find shelter beyond the brow.'

They were both soaked through their coats, but a sort of ecstasy seized Benjie. This was what he loved, all the hills bared by the wind, all the streams exulting because they would be strong and vehement again, rain and wind at their full power and the sky black with cloud. If Vanessa were not beaten by it! But there she was, her head up, striding forward, striking the earth with her stick! He ran, he jumped the stones, he sang! Then, through the rain, the mist surged forward. It rose, broke to show dark fell and shining rock, closed again with its fingers on your eyes, lifted from the ground a little to reveal the short grass tugging to escape the soil. . . .

Vanessa was gone. . . . He shouted.

'Van! Van! Vanessa! Where are you?'

The mist broke and he saw one jet-black cloud, and toward it everything, fell and gleaming stone and line of hill, seemed to strain.

He saw Vanessa standing, her hand to her heart. He caught up with her.

'Are you all right?'

Her face was grey in that half-light, but as she answered him the mist came down again, hiding her.

But she was glad that he could not see her, for she was about to die. She knew it as certainly as though the tall figure, grey-cloaked with grave assured eyes, stood in the mist, his curving silver-gleaming scythe in his hand. Her knees bent, her head was bowed on her breast. So appalling was the pain that death held no terrors, nor her loneliness. Strange that her one thought about death for years had been that Benjie must be with her when it came. And now it was here, and she hoped that Benjie would not see her, but would pass on, striking his iron-tipped stick on the stone, and she would drop there where she was and die, alone, hidden in mist. . . . She did not want anyone to see her die.

So fearful was the pain that she could not keep back a moan, and then another. But only her own heart heard. The wind screamed in her ear, and the mist, wet like a thin soaked towel, pressed on her eyes and nose and mouth. Dimly through her pain she thought how silly it had been that, only ten minutes before, she had been talking so confidently about God. God was not here. She was animal, only fighting for endurance and to die without cowardice. . . .

Then the pain was so fierce that she thought of nothing, neither the storm nor any company. She knelt on the sodden turf, her head back, her teeth set, hands clenched. She fancied that, from a great distance, she heard Benjie calling, and a sudden warming thought as though it were the very last that she would have in this world came to her of his sweetness, jollity, kindliness. Nothing in this world mattered so much as kindliness . . . that men should be kind to one another because they suffered, one and all, and life was short. . . .

The pain passed. It withdrew as though a figure that had been bending over her had moved away.

She looked up and saw that the mist had broken,

leaving a round cup like a room suddenly revealed, a room furnished with a gleaming rock like a ship's stern. The pain was gone: she would not die yet. The child should be born. Not rain nor wind should defeat her, and she rose from her knees and breasted the wind, moving forward. The mist cleared still further and she saw Benjie moving back to her.

' It's all right,' he shouted. ' There's a farm here just on the bend. Where the trees are.'

She took his arm.

' Isn't the wind strong? It almost beat me to my knees.'

He had noticed nothing, and she now brought all her resources to the business of meeting the pain again when it returned. For return it would. She could hear it afar off as though faintly the thin warning of a distant horn.

When they came to the trees they were rocking and groaning like mad things. The mist was shredded now, blowing in crazy tears and tatters over a landscape that was all fell scattered with stone and rock. The scene was immemorial and had changed in nothing since, maybe, Roman trumpets had echoed there from distance to distance.

It was a little white farmhouse, very simple, with a small beck rushing furiously at its side, the whole world filled with wind and rain. Benjie knocked on the door, two dogs barked, then a woman opened it and looked out. The wind rushed in and they followed it, coming into a clean and bright kitchen. It was low-roofed; there were

U

legs of cured mutton and hams hanging from the
smoky rafters.   On a shelf near by there were
pots and jars, little yellow cheeses, dried herbs.
By the ingle there was an old white-haired man,
another younger man with broad shoulders and
a bull-neck standing up, the woman who had
opened the door, and a pretty girl in a blue gown
busy at the table.

They were very cordial and friendly, made
Vanessa and Benjie come to the fire to dry themselves.   Yes, they had a spare room for the night
if the storm kept on.   The old man was loqua-
cious; he had light blue eyes like flowers.

'Aye,' he said.   'We're verra oot o't warld—
seven mile fra a shop, eight mile fra a church—
an' hard roads.'

He was proud of their isolation.   The house-
wife asked them if they were hungry.   Benjie said
indeed he was.   She began to be busy cooking
eggs and Cumberland ham.

Vanessa sat there, her knees close together,
looking into the fire, waiting for the next pain to
come.   She wondered how soon she might go up
to the bed, take her things off: Benjie had noticed
nothing.   He was exceedingly happy, had taken
off his boots and stockings, coat and waistcoat, and
sat there, smiling at them all.   He told them how
he had lost his arm in Africa in the war.   The old
man had a long story to tell about sheep—' terrible
wark ' sometimes.   The young man had a newspaper a week old.   'A newspaper!   Aye—we
mun gang a lang ways to get yan o' thame here.'
And Benjie laughed and chattered, loving the

sound of the storm beyond the house, the smell of
the frying eggs and ham. His twinkling eyes
rested on the girl. *What* a pretty girl! Dark,
slim and a cheeky upturned nose such as he preferred. He smiled at her and she shyly smiled
back again. . . .

Later Vanessa said: 'Benjie, I am tired. I
think I'll go to bed.'

'Supper's nearly ready. You must be starved.
I know I am.'

'I'm not hungry,' she answered. 'I think I'll
go up.'

She stood, her hand pressed to her side. He
looked at her anxiously but she smiled back at
him. The girl went up with her to show her the
room.

The storm died down. Benjie had his supper,
the woman and girl waiting on him. It was now,
in a place like this with simple, friendly people,
that he felt at his best. In his shirt and trousers
he sat there, eating, drinking big cups of tea,
laughing, telling them about South Africa and
other parts of the world where he had been. Once
and again he smiled at the girl and she glanced back
at him, their eyes meeting, holding one another,
parting quickly. The storm had died away and
beyond the kitchen window a flood of primrose
light laced with the tree-branches spread above
the bare fell.

'Hurray! The storm is over!' Benjie said.

The girl had gone. He could hear her moving
on the floor above. He got up.

' I'll go and see how my wife is,' he said. But, even as he spoke, the wind came again, raging in a fury about the house, banging at the house-door, rattling the windows. All the trees screamed and the colour ebbed from the sky, leaving it white.

' That was sudden,' he said, turning round. ' I thought it had died.'

He saw a scurry of leaves blow against the pane and flatten. Some stayed, pressed against the window.

' 'Twill be a wild neet,' the old man said calmly.

Benjie climbed the crooked stairs that smelt of mice and whitewash. At the top was the girl just coming down. There was a ghostly light from the passage window. He caught the girl with his arm and she surrendered to him at once, pressing closely against him as though she were hungry to be loved, which indeed she was. He held her tight, kissing her eyes, her cheeks, her mouth. Then, behind the pleasure and strength and warm happiness that wrapped him in, he heard a deep breath as of someone close at his elbow. Looking past the girl he saw Vanessa at the doorway. Her hair fell about her shoulders and she had caught a patchwork quilt around her; the colours were bizarre—blue, crimson, orange, green—and above it her eyes, fixed as though fastened on some desperate resolution, stared at him. She said something, but the wind was shaking the window. All the house seemed to be quivering. The girl was as though she had never been, and as he reached Vanessa's side he said:

' Vanessa, it was nothing. . . . Vanessa darling . . .'

She looked at him, tried to smile, but her mouth
shook. He heard her murmur, ' I'm very ill. . . .
Tell the woman to come. . . .'

So, as nearly ninety years ago Judith Paris, her
grandmother, had borne an illegitimate child in
the heart of storm and confusion, did Vanessa now.

Sally, daughter of Benjamin Herries and
Vanessa Herries, was born at eleven-thirty on the
night of September 21st, 1903, at Randle Farm in
Cumberland.

PERFECT LOVE

Vanessa sat on the slope of the hill behind the white farm watching for Tom's coming.

Sally, now nearly three years of age, sprawled beside her. Vanessa had a book on her lap but she was not reading. It was a cold sunny May afternoon. The scene was so still that it was like a painted canvas—or a bowl with flowers, for the hills circled her in but flowers were everywhere—crab blossom, speedwell blue as a jewel, anemones. In the garden behind the farm the primroses were still in yellow clumps, violets, celandines and pansies. Soon the blue hyacinths would be full-blown. But the bowl that held the flowers was harsh with the tang of winter. The higher hills were thinly powdered with snow and the rocks so black that they glittered in the May sun like steel, and the little coppice beyond the stream yet seemed to tremble as though it could not be sure that winter was truly over.

Sally was not a pretty child but she too was a flower. She was small, spare, taut. Her hair had a red shadow in its brown, and she was always pale, but not with the pallor of ill-health. She was the strongest child. Nothing ever ailed her. When she cried it was from ill-temper. She had a most determined will, hated to be frustrated, knew her own way and intention always. But she never sulked, loved where she loved, hated where she hated, stood no nonsense, refused to be either flattered or petted and thought her mother the beginning and end of all things.

The love of this baby for her mother was astonishing. It had been so from the very beginning, and Vanessa, sitting there in the sun, felt a supreme content. Three human beings loved her—Benjie, Tom and Sally. They would not love her for ever perhaps. Benjie still moved towards her and then away from her again. Tom, although he was the most faithful of men, had his own life now and much of it she could not share. Sally would grow up and leave her. But at this moment, in this pellucid air, happy in this bowl of flowers, she thanked God for all that He had given her.

'Am I still frightened?' she asked herself. For, since her childhood, she had had to battle with fear. She had, all her life, given her heart to someone of whom she could not be certain and that was perhaps the reason that she loved him so dearly. Would the time ever come when she would be *certain* of Benjie? He was fifty-one now, she nearing forty-seven, but the old alarms returned, day after day, as they had always done. When he went would he return?

Nevertheless in the years since Sally's birth she had known greater happiness than ever before. They had been shut off from all the world; the friends they had made had been farmers, shep-

herds, wandering men. They had had almost
no communication with London. An occasional
letter from old Barney, Adrian, once from Cynthia.
Benjie had been twice abroad, once to Italy, once
to Spain, but had not stayed in London on either
occasion. Anything that they knew of the outer
life was from Tom. When he came he told them
all the news, journalistic, social, family. He was
happy on his newspaper; the family were kind
to him, and he was deeply, hopelessly in love with
Mary, Cynthia's girl, who was still only a child
but, Tom said (he confessed only to Vanessa), the
love of his life. . . .

Time had passed with incredible swiftness.
They were forgotten, Vanessa said, not only by
the world but by time as well. They were contented.

But for how long would this endure? Still
she never woke of a morning without wondering
whether before night Benjie would not leave her.
He loved her—of course he loved her—but the
restlessness was there in his blood as it had ever
been. One day he would go, and he would be
lured further and further, always intending to
return, never returning. . . . What she had
suffered during his two adventures out of England
no one would ever know. She had, by now,
trained herself to the complete hiding of her fear.
She gave him no sign. . . .

Somewhere a dog barked and at the same
moment she saw that a trap had drawn up at the
gate behind the church. Someone climbed out.
It was Tom.

' Sally! Sally! ' she cried. ' It's Tom! ' She was as excited as a child.

Sally screamed: ' Tom! Tom! Tom! '

She picked Sally up and ran down the slope to the farm.

They hurried along the green sward, she carrying the child in the crook of her arm. She waved with the other hand. Tom waved back. A moment later they were all together.

Tom was short and sturdy. He had Adam's figure before he became stout and he had Adam's quietness and certainty. You knew always exactly where you were with him. Some people would think him dull as they had thought Adam. Other people found that he was to be trusted beyond most men and that, once his loyalty and affection were engaged, nothing could cause them to waver again. A dull quality, loyalty, and an unimaginative! But valuable to some people who believe in knowing where they are.

He was not dull to Vanessa. For one thing he loved her, as he showed with every look, every movement. For another he was their herald from the outer world. As they sat that evening round the table he had a thousand things to tell them. He had taken Adrian to one of these wrestling matches, now so popular. There had been a dinner-party at Cynthia's. He had met Edmund Gosse, who had told funny stories about George Eliot.

' I haven't the least notion who Edmund Gosse is, darling,' Vanessa said.

Barney had been ill with rheumatism. But

the most sensational piece of news was that Maud
and Helen, Carey's girls, had become desperate
Suffragettes. Really desperate. They wanted
to break into the Houses of Parliament. They
had marched in a procession carrying banners.
Their mother was dreadfully distressed.

About journalism there were many exciting
things. It was rumoured that Harmsworth, now
Lord Northcliffe, intended to purchase *The Times*.
Everything in Fleet Street was changing. Men
were dismissed from their jobs at a moment's
notice. No one was safe any longer.

' Oh, it's nice here! ' he said at last. ' It's so
quiet. There's such a good smell.'

' How long have you got? ' Benjie asked.

' A fortnight.' He wanted to walk. He
wanted to go over to Haweswater and spend two
days in Eskdale.

' I'll go with you,' said Benjie.

' Oh, that will be grand! ' Tom said.

But Vanessa was sure that he wanted to go
alone. There was something not quite intimate
between himself and his father—something a little
uneasy.

And that night as Benjie was undressing he
said to Vanessa:

' Tom doesn't want me with him.'

He was pulling off his shirt, a little awkwardly
with his one arm. His face flushed, his hair
tousled, looking at her over the top of his shirt
before he dragged it over his head, he seemed to
her suddenly pathetic a little, and her love went
out to him with an unexpected fierce rush of

emotion. She was sitting before the glass brushing her hair. She turned, the brush in her hand. He, standing bare to the waist, looked back at her. They exchanged a long deep gaze. The room was lit with candles that blew in the breeze from the open window, and their shadows were gigantic on the white wall.

They stayed, transfixed, looking at one another. Then at last, with a deep breath as though he were experiencing some extraordinary new emotion, he came over to her. He put his hand on her shoulder, then moved it to her neck and so held her, her gaze still upon him. Her eyes filled with tears; her heart was hammering. It was as though he had never made love to her before, as though at last he were about to say to her the words for which she had so long been aching.

He knelt down and enfolded her with his arm, his head on her breast. With light gentle fingers she stroked his hair, staring in front of her, all the room dimmed because her eyes were dim. A ridiculous clock that had a note, Benjie always said, like an angry parrot, told the hour, but the sound was an infinite distance away. What had happened? What was then this tumultuous fiery rush of joy at her heart?

'What is it?' she said at last. 'Benjie—darling—tell me. Are you unhappy about Tom?'

He did not answer. He held her only the more tightly. At last he said:

'It's like this, Van. . . . It's as though I had never seen you before.'

He got up and stood there, looking at her.

' You'll catch cold with the window open.'

But he did not move; only stood there staring at her.

' Isn't it odd, Van? I'm falling in love with you all over again.'

She finished brushing her hair, although it was difficult because her hands trembled. She slipped on her nightdress and got into bed.

He always wore at night an open shirt that came no further than the knees. For a moment he was naked and, looking at him in the candle-light, she thought how wonderfully he had pre-served his body. For a man of past fifty he had an astonishing spareness and hardness. No fat. Nothing slack. And, as always, he looked as though he never wore clothes, as though his flesh were always exposed to the wind and sun. He stretched himself like an animal, raised his arm above his head, swelled out his brown chest. But he never took his bright, blue, fearless eyes from her face. She had never seen such eyes in any other man. They were so childlike, honest, dependable. But he was not a child and he was not dependable. . . .

She expected that her own emotion would recede. It had been but a moment, born perhaps of her maternal longing over him because he was disappointed in Tom. But the emotion did not recede. She clasped her hands under the bed-clothes and tried to beat down her joy. Like many another woman she was afraid of it lest it should lead her to expect too much and bring soon some disappointment that would be almost un-

bearably bitter—that she would remember afterwards, when the joy was forgotten.

' I mustn't love him too much,' she told herself,
as so many, many times she had told herself before.
He blew out the candles and lay down beside her.
She knew at once by his touch on her breast that
to-night he was very gentle.   He scarcely touched
her and yet she was thrilled by his proximity as she
had never been before.   They kissed and it was a
kiss far deeper than passion.   They did not stir,
only their two hearts beating the one against the
other, but this kiss was different from any other
that they had ever exchanged.   It was radiant
with awe and wonder and reverence at something
quite beyond and outside themselves.

At last he said: ' What has happened, Van?
I have never loved anyone as I do you to-night.'
His hand found hers and now they lay, very
quietly, side by side, hand in hand.   She turned
on her side, laying her cheek against his.

' How still it is!   Only the running water! '

He stroked her arm with his hand, very gently,
as though he were afraid lest he should hurt her.

' Van, this is heaven.   I have never loved you
before as I do to-night.'

' Nor I you, Benjie.'

' We'll never forget this.'

' No.   Never, never.'

' I seem to understand at this moment what
life ought to be.'   She sighed with a deep, yearning happiness.   ' I'm not afraid any more.   I
don't care now what happens.   We have never
been together like this before. . . .'

' No.   Never.   I wonder why. . . . '

They turned to meet one another in a passionate embrace.

And, with the morning, nothing was changed.
She knew immediately that he was still moving in
this new relationship.   She saw that Tom was at
once aware of it and that he came in an instant
more closely to his father.   Benjie was quiet.   In
ordinary he conveyed a sense of restlessness, of
wanting to move from the place where he was to
some other place.   But this morning after they
had breakfasted he stood in front of the farm
looking at the green field, the hills, the flowers, as
though he had never seen them before.

' Come for a stroll,' he said to Vanessa, and
they went.   But, as they walked, they scarcely
spoke.   They went side by side, and for Vanessa
it was as though they were not walking but rather
were held, in some burning cloud, alone, away
from man and time and destiny.   What had
happened?   Was it not impossible that at their
age, after they had lived so long together, known
one another so intimately, there could be a new
relationship between them?   Friendship, comradeship, yes; but a new emotion, a new passion?
Surely it was impossible?

Only at the end of this walk, before they
went into the house, he turned to her and said
again:

' Vanessa, what has happened to us?   Are we
in love for the first time? '

Day followed day, week followed week; the
summer passed and autumn was smoke and flame,

smoke of the clouds, flame of the bracken.   With
November the rains fell.   There was clouded
light over the dales and the wind-currents were as
vexed and troubled as the twists and turns of a
stream.   A black whirlwind of cloud would rush
across the tops, discharging its waters as though
from a gigantic tub impatiently overset by a
celestial housemaid: you would wake to a morning
of universal dark; the very fire burnt dimly and
the rain fell with the tramp of armies; or the wet
mists would blow from Robinson, from Cat Bells,
thin and airy, carrying with them all the scene, a
bare hillside lit by a sudden splash of shining rock,
a herd of sheep stalwart under the chill stone walls,
houses of stone raised into air by the web of vapour.
Or it would rain quite solemnly like a clergyman
of the old school preaching into eternity or a
writer of stories for whom two hundred years are
but as a day, and then nothing lovelier in the
world could be seen than that quick break before
dusk when a pulse of gold beats through the dark
and the sun creeps from under the blanket of
cloud and everything is lit with radiance for a short
breathless while.   In these valleys and hills rain
is as beautiful as fair weather and more various,
and it is rain always broken by sudden breath-
taking surprises.   Only in this weather and perhaps only in this country can you see what the
ebon flank of a cloud may be above a misty hill, or
how purple—richer than grape-bloom—can cover
a fell after tempest, or the white shadow, whiter
than ivory and thin like glass, that strokes the field
under a pale young stormy moon.

Men who write of these things are always
defeated by them, so rare and strange is their
beauty, but in their hearts an eternal home-sickness
is created so that they are never either safe or
happy again in any land where it is dry and the
sun is for ever shining.

Throughout the summer, the autumn, the
winter, this miracle remained for Benjie and
Vanessa. Many writers for hundreds of years
have written about first love, and some writers
(but not so very many) have spoken of the
happiness of married comradeship. But life is
never settled nor arranged nor does it behave
as it ought, by the laws of the written word, to
do. Many men and women would behave nobly
were they given the perfect conditions and circumstances, but there is always toothache, a broken
promise, a jealousy, an unreasonable desire. Only
once in a lifetime perhaps a Beethoven Symphony
arrives punctually and, in a lighted room, two
friends forget that there is such a tyranny as Time.
And, even then, sentiment may steal the prize.

Vanessa and Benjie had good fortune. Not by
their own desire, and, in any case, they did not
know where to look for it. It came to them and
they knew what perfect love can be.

During that winter they were never parted.
Their happiness was too deep and soundless for
them to fear it. For Vanessa it was as though
God kept them in continual company. Her ideas
of God were, of course, very simple; she felt His
radiance as though she moved from morning to
night in sunlight. For Benjie it was simpler still.

He wanted to be near Vanessa; he did not know why she irritated him no more, why he was restless no longer. He did not search for reasons. He only knew that body, soul, and spirit, he was complete.

One starlit night after Christmas they climbed the hill and sat down together. The sky was quite clear. It was as though they were wrapped in star-dust. A little way above them the snow began. It was bitterly cold, but he wrapped his large shepherd's cloak around both of them and, because there was no wind, they took no hurt.

'It would not be bad, Van,' he said, 'if we were to die now, both of us together.'

Then, as she did not answer, he went on: 'That is what all lovers have always said. But *young* lovers. Lovers in their first ecstasy. We are very *old* lovers.'

'I don't feel old,' she answered at last. 'When shall we begin to feel old?'

'Oh, I suppose—with sickness, separation...'

'We will never be separated now,' she said quickly.

He held her to him, under the cloak, more closely.

'I don't trust life even now. I think you're the only thing in the whole world I trust. There never was anyone so trustworthy as you are.'

She laughed. 'Yes, that's why I'm dull—for everyone except you and Tom.'

'No. You're not dull. They didn't think you dull in London. But you're shy. You can't

show people what you are. You're courageous
enough about *things*. You'd stand up to anything. But you're shy of human beings. Only
in these last months have even I known what
you are.'

'For the first time since my father died,' she
said, ' I'm not afraid.'

Five weeks later the letter came.

It came, as catastrophic letters often come, with
an almost maidenly quietness. Vanessa opened
it, looking over the table to Benjie, and laughing
at something that he had just said. This was the
letter:

> HILL STREET, LONDON, W.
> *February* 8, 1907.

DEAR VANESSA—You will, I am sure, be extremely
surprised to receive a letter from me—surprised and not
altogether pleased, I fear, but Vera and I have, for some
weeks now, discussed the matter and have at last decided
that this letter must be written. The matter is quite
simply this. For some while now—ever since last summer
in fact—Ellis has been seriously ailing. He has not of
course been strong mentally for a very long time past.
That you know. But his bodily conditions have been
surprisingly good: he has eaten and slept well, and, within
his own mental world, has really lived with content under
our care. We have done our best. It has not always been
easy, but of that I wish here to say nothing. Last summer
we took Ellis to Harrogate as perhaps you heard at the
time. We found a small and comfortable house where
we could enjoy privacy and where at the same time my
sister (whose rheumatism has for some time been trying)
and Ellis could receive medical attention.

It was during our stay in Harrogate that the change
took place. He has long been given, as you must have

heard, to childish pursuits. He enjoys playing with dolls,
soldiers and trains. We have always, under excellent
Doctor Lancaster's advice, humoured him in this and one
day in Harrogate Vera bought him a doll to give him
pleasure. So soon as he saw it it reminded him of you.
I must tell you that he had not, so far as my sister and I
were aware, once mentioned your name during all these
years. But on this occasion, on Vera's presenting him
with the doll, he said at once: ' Why, this is Vanessa come
back again! ' At first he seemed extremely happy at his
fancy, but my sister and I noticed that from this moment
he began to be less well. His headaches, which you will
perhaps remember, returned. His temperature was often
above normal. He was restless. Many of the things that
had amused him seemed to amuse him no longer. He is
of course not young any more—sixty-four years of age—
and his recurrent fever made us anxious. Whatever you
may feel about my sister and myself you must remember,
Vanessa, that we have both for a very long time now been
most deeply and sincerely attached to your husband.
Throughout this last winter he has been most unwell and
now for several weeks has not left his bed. Doctor
Lancaster says that it is difficult to say that there is anything organically wrong, but he fears that he has not long
to live. We feel, Vera and I, that if this is indeed so, we
must do everything to make the last months of his life
happy. We are two childless women and in these years
at Hill Street we have come to feel for Ellis as though he
were our son. I hope you will forgive my saying this, but
the whole situation is—and has always been—so very
strange!
     And now to come to the point of this letter (it has not
been an easy one to write). It is that, continually, during
these last weeks Ellis has begged for your return. He has,
it seems, a clear memory of the events that led up to your
departure, but his mental decay has wiped from his recol-
lection all bitterness and anger. He is as gentle and submissive as the child that so often he seems to be. ' I want

Vanessa!' he cries and, again and again: 'When is
Vanessa coming? Why does Vanessa not come?'

In these circumstances my sister and I feel it right that
you should know how things stand. It is not easy for us
to take this step. We cannot pretend that we approved,
or now approve, of the action that you took. But it is not
for us to judge and we can only assure you that if you
return to Hill Street for the few remaining weeks of Ellis'
life (Doctor Lancaster tells us that it cannot be much more)
you will hear no single word of reproach from us and we
will regard you as the mistress of this house in every way.
Your place just now, Vanessa, is with your husband,
whatever the past has been. You have it in your power to
give him this last happiness. We feel that we would never
forgive ourselves if we did not acquaint you with the facts.
—Yours sincerely,

                                        WINIFRED TRENT.

Vanessa read the letter. Benjie, watching her
from the other side of the table, saw at once
that something of the uttermost seriousness had
occurred.

'What is it?' he asked, coming across to her.

She gave him the letter. He read it slowly,
sometimes repeating some of the words aloud.

'But this is monstrous!' he said at last. His
face was flushed with anger, and also with the
beginning of a terrible fear.

She sat down, staring in front of her, then held
out her hand for the letter and read it through
again.

'Yes,' she said. 'I have always known that
the punishment would come. It *had* to come—to
make things just.'

'Now—look, Van.' He sat down beside her.

' You are not to consider this for a moment; what the old witch suggests, I mean. Go to London. I'll come with you. Go to Hill Street. Pay him a visit. We'll stay in London if you like and you shall go often and see him—anything else is preposterous.'

She shook her head.

' He wants me back. I never would have left him if he had wanted me. But he didn't. Now he does. He's dying.'

Benjie with an effort to be calm—one of the hardest things he had attempted for many a day (for this *was* preposterous; this was a plot, Hill Street all madmen and witches)—put his hand on hers, which was trembling, and summoned all his wisdom:

' Listen, Van. He doesn't want you. He can't. He doesn't know what he wants. It's some plot to get you back there again. The two old women are tired of their job, I shouldn't wonder. They think it would be a fine thing for you to take it on again. He *can't* want you with his dolls and his trains.'

' No. I don't like Vera and Winifred—but they're honest. They have no imagination and no humour, but they're honest and they've been angels to Ellis. When I wrote to Vera three years ago—you remember—to ask her to persuade Ellis to divorce me, her letter wasn't kind but it was honest and plucky. I don't like them, but there are no lies in this letter.'

She turned round and stared at him. She looked, he thought, quite suddenly an ageing woman. Her confidence and happiness had left her.

'This is awful,' she said at last. 'Terrible. The worst thing that could happen. To go back to that house, that life . . . to leave you. Oh!' she cried, her hand on her breast. 'I don't think I can! I don't think I can!'

'Of course you can't—and, I tell you, there's no need to. We'll go to London. We'll see Ellis. . . .'

But she shook her head. She had recovered her courage.

'Of course I must go—and you know it, Benjie. There can be no other way. What would I feel now if, after that letter, I didn't go? How could I go on living with you as we have been living? Oh, I knew it was too good to last! Something *had* to happen . . . these last six months—we've had a new life—and it was too fine, too wonderful to be allowed much of. It's unfair, it's unfair. That one mistake I made so long ago, to be punished for it so many times!' Then she cried out in a kind of agony: 'That house, Benjie! I can't *stand* that house!'

Then he was really frightened and because he was frightened he was angry. He got up roughly, knocking his chair over.

'Look here, Van—if you leave me now because two crazy old women write a letter—if you leave me after all that has happened to us these last months—you'll lose me. I can't keep up without you now. I'm not young any more. I could have done without you once, perhaps, but not now. . . . You owe me more than you owe Ellis.'

'No, I don't,' she interrupted. 'I ruined Ellis's life. I've made you happy, I made him unhappy.'

'It was his own fault. He made you marry him.' (He did not remember that it had been *his* fault.)

'No, he did not. I need not have married him. . . .' Then she turned and caught his arm. 'Benjie, there's Sally! There's Sally!'

'You see,' he cried triumphantly. 'You see how impossible it is. Of course you can't leave Sally. She's your child, isn't she?'

'No. . . . No. . . . Of course, I would have to have Sally with me. I would insist on that. I would make my terms——'

Then he swore at her. 'Damn you, Vanessa, am *I* nothing? What about me? You think of your crazy husband, you think of your baby. But I'm to be left out of it. Anything can happen to me——' He was not going to plead for himself. He looked at her and saw that her mind was made up. This was the law: Vanessa's character being what it was, this was fate.

He saw that and saw, also, for himself a future so intolerable that he closed his eyes and bowed his head.

Then they drew together and clung together, without a word. Both knew that in this there was no alternative.

OLD Barney Newmark died quite suddenly in his sleep in the autumn of 1909. The Family were sorry because they had approved of Barney's fame as a novelist. It was not perhaps very great and he belonged to a very different generation from the present. The obituaries were kind; he had been a genial fellow, always in London, friendly and cheerful with everyone. He was spoken of as the ' Hawley Smart of his period.' The *Referee* wrote: ' Mr. Newmark could write of horses and pretty women with a grace and humour that exceeded any of his contemporaries.' But the paragraph that pleased the Family was one in the *Daily Telegraph*: ' Mr. Newmark, whose loss was so widely deplored last week, was of course a member of the famous Herries family, so well known in so many directions. Lord Rockage, who owns in Wiltshire one of the finest houses in England, is a member of it; Mr. Alfred Herries, the well-known financier, another; Mr. Timothy Bellairs, whose picture " Mme. Rochambert " created a sensation in last year's Salon, another. The Hon. Mrs. Peile Worcester, whose parties in Charles Street have long been famous, is a member of the family, and another member, Mr. Horace

Newmark, who died not so long ago, was known
for many years as " the Monarch of Manchester."
The Herries family is very well known in the
North of England, most especially in Cumberland
and the Border country.   One of the most remarkable women of an earlier generation in the North
was Madame Paris, also a member of the famous
family.   She has become almost a legend in
Cumberland and Westmorland, I believe.   Mr.
Newmark's delightful friendly, easy, and merry
novels belonged to a time when the art of fiction was scarcely as seriously considered as it is
to-day.   This has been a sad year for English
letters, mourning as we do both Meredith and
Swinburne.   Mr. Newmark would have been the
first to deprecate any comparison between two
such giants and his own agreeable novels.   Nevertheless he will be missed and for a long time to
come.'

This was very pleasant.   It had been for the
Herries family a year of definite accomplishment.
They had lived down the misadventures of the
South African War and the disgrace of Vanessa's
elopement (both events, in their view, of equal
family importance).   The Edwardian period, with
its gracious (if materially minded) monarch, its
common sense, its proper appreciation of money,
its fostering of the upper middle class (even though
the lower orders *were* behaving immodestly), its
enthusiasm for Empire, its general applause for
the solider English virtues, exactly suited the
Herries: wildness, immorality, gambling, these
things, when they appeared, became almost at once

socially rationalised. The Family had no objection to immorality when it was photographed at a
week-end house-party during the shooting season.
Private behaviour was no matter so long as it
appeared publicly decent, and this was not
hypocrisy on the Herries' part. It was simply that
they cared for England, guarded her reputation
most zealously. And this was natural, for England was Herries and Herries were England. . . .

At last they could sit back for a moment and
see that all was well. Family feuds (ridiculous,
all about nothing—a fan, a green vase, a house
on a hill) were things of the past. One possible
scandal, the unspeakable Rose—poor Horace
Ormerod's sister—had, luckily, been hidden by
the grime of mean streets. Vanessa was living
once again most properly with her husband; even
Barney's death was not so bad a thing, for he had
outlived his reputation and had been inclined at
times to say oddly sarcastic things about the Family.

England had never seemed more secure, more
prosperous, more certain of the grandeur of her
great destiny—and as England was, so were the
Herries.

It happened that Timothy Bellairs, the painter,
came over to London for Barney's funeral. The
old boy had been good to him in times past.
Barney and Benjie (and of course young Tom)
were the only members of the Family for whom he
cared. He had lived so long in Paris that he did
not feel Herries any longer. Or did he? He
came over to London to find out.

He was a tall thin man with very light blue eyes and hair the colour of pale corn. He wore a small pointed beard. He had a way of watching you while you talked, of agreeing with you but causing you to wonder whether he did not think you a terrible fool. His voice was gentle and he had a charming smile. He appeared detached and impersonal. He had in fact only two passions —one was for painting, the other for one or two individuals. He was capable of iron fidelity. Benjie and Tom were two of his devotions, although he had not seen either of them for a very long time. Another was a stout and extremely cynical lady who shared his bed and board in Paris.

Attending Barney's funeral he observed the Family.

Vanessa was there. He had not seen her for many years but, knowing her story and of her return to Ellis nearly three years ago, he watched her with especial interest. Her grey hair under the black hat, the pale face beneath the veil—these gave her a greater appearance of age than he had expected. But her carriage (he watched her as, attended by a little thin woman, she walked up the aisle to her seat) was very fine. She was a big woman, full-breasted, large-shouldered and, he thought, as he saw her before she turned into her seat, apart from everyone else there. ' She has learnt how to play her rôle.'

Tom was with him and whispered some names. That was Horace, that stout fellow in glasses, with plump cheeks, the full Herries chin and an air of self-conscious benevolence. ' Barney hated him,' Tom whispered. Cynthia swept up, Peile Worcester in attendance. Very smart, Timothy thought, with her beautifully fitting black and Parma violets—not thinking about Barney, though.

An extremely thin tall gentleman, wearing pince-nez, his black clothes rigid as though cut from wood, ' very Herries ' in feature, moved to his seat as though he were taking his place as chairman of a board meeting.

' That's Alfred.'

A fat cheerful gentleman and a very fat cheerful lady hurried up the aisle, showering benevolence on all around them. ' Sidney and Mary—Horace's son from Manchester.'

Then old Carey Rockage, bent with rheumatism, May thin and short-sighted, with the two suffragette daughters who strode forward looking about them with an air of resentment.

Timothy's sister, who had married a Colonel and lived in Surbiton, was not present. Vanessa was by far the most interesting person in that church to Timothy. He thought of Barney.

' Good old boy. He had a fine life. Did what he wanted, enjoyed every moment of it.' When he remembered Barney's mistresses it amused him that the Family should come, in such numbers, to pay him the last compliments. ' They wouldn't do the same for Benjie,' he thought, feeling the touch of Tom's shoulder against his. But Barney, in some clever fashion of his own, had never openly outraged the conventions. No member of the Family had ever been brought face

to face with his mistresses, while in poor Benjie's
case every rebellion had been as open as it could
be! And then, just as the service was about to
start, Benjie walked up the aisle. He walked
slowly, his brown face and bright blue eyes unconcerned, the empty sleeve of his jacket pinned
to his breast. He was wearing a loose dark suit
—so far he had submitted to convention—but he
looked, as he always looked in public, apart, as
though he were of another country, an exile and a
rebellious one. 'He looks more than that,' Tim
thought. 'He looks worn and strained. He's
too thin.'

Had he seen Tom and Timothy he would
undoubtedly have stopped and sat with them, but,
his head up, seeing nobody, he walked straight
ahead. 'He said he wasn't coming,' Tom
whispered.

He passed the seat where Vanessa was. Some
instinct seemed to tell him. He stopped for a
moment, then turned and found a place on the
other side of the aisle beside stout Sidney and
Mary Newmark. It amused Timothy to observe
the startled and frightened look that they gave him.

So old Barney Newmark, accorded by the
Family full honours, joined (perhaps thankfully)
the Rogue and David, Judith and young John, and
was, beyond question, glad of their company.

Timothy had not as yet paid Benjie a proper
visit. Tom, who shared lodgings with his father
in Tite Street, told Tim that Benjie was in one of
his bad moods.

' He'll tell you all about it when you go.　He's
very unhappy—but he'll tell you.　Only you'd
better wait till he chooses his day.'

Meanwhile Timothy was painting Mary Worcester's picture.　He had seen, at once, that this
was a thing that he had to do.　She was the
loveliest child he had ever beheld.　She was going
to be a real beauty.　The modelling of her face
was exquisite, her colour perfect, everything
delicate, gentle, dark hair, dark eyes, already a
sense of poise and movement.　But, he decided
very quickly, she was stupid and dull.　Her
voice was lovely in tone, soft and resonant,
but she had nothing to say.　Her eyes were large
and full; she had a way of using them so that they
rested on you as though they found you enchanting.　But she did not find you enchanting.　She
was not thinking about you at all.　She was only
sixteen and had been kept, at home, closely
guarded, but even then Timothy thought, she
surely had *some* ideas about something!　It
seemed that she had not.

Her mother, whose little figure was still perfect
but was betrayed by her too bony neck and eyes
that were older than her complexion allowed for,
said about her beautiful daughter that: ' You've
no idea how intelligent that child is!　Now
Rosalind says just what's in her head and nine
times out of ten it's nonsense, as I tell her—but
Mary!　No one knows what that child's thinking!'

Cynthia also unburdened herself to Timothy
about Vanessa:

' Of course it's awful for her.　We all realise

that. She came back nearly three years ago
thinking that Ellis had only a week or two to live.
And now there he is quite strong and hearty!
Of course he's mad as a hatter, but quite nice and
gentle, I believe. He's simply Vanessa's slave,
poor thing. And isn't it odd? Vera and Winifred
Trent used to hate her, but since Vera died last
year Winifred adores her. I must say Vanessa
always had the power of making people fond of
her. I always have loved her in spite of what she
did. What is it about Vanessa? Perhaps you'll
find out, Timothy. Because she's really dull and
has no sense of humour at all. I must say she's
very sporting. Right or wrong, Benjie's the love
of her life and there they both are, eating their
hearts out. Between you and me I wonder Benjie
doesn't creep into Hill Street and poison Ellis.
What's the good of his living? He's quite hopeless mentally, you know. Of course Vanessa's
got Sally with her. She insisted on that. Her
little girl and Benjie's. It always seems funny to
me when Ellis, poor thing, has always been so
proper and moral, that Vanessa's illegitimate child
should be in his house under his roof. And I
believe he's passionately fond of the child. Altogether very queer. Vanessa doesn't go out into
society at all, but she likes people to go and see
her. I go sometimes although Peile doesn't much
like my doing it and I confess the place gives me
the shudders.'

' Does she see Benjie? ' Timothy asked.

' Oh yes, sometimes. There's nothing im-
proper of course. The fact is, Timothy, they are

the only example I know anywhere of real love.
It's gone on all their lives and they're as much in
love as ever they were. She's quite tamed Benjie.
He used to be as wild as anything. It's a bit
hard on him, isn't it? Separated from his child,
too, but I believe he thinks it the right thing for
Vanessa to do. They're an odd pair altogether.'

It happened that on the afternoon following the
funeral Cynthia was giving a small children's party.
For a brief while Timothy observed the ceremony;
not for long—he detested children unless they
were paintable. He was extremely sharp at
catching character from face, voice and movement.
He had a number of young Herries under his eye
(the coming upholders of the Herries tradition)
and quickly decided that only one of them was
beautiful (Mary Worcester of course) and only
one charming—little Sally, Vanessa's daughter.
He wondered for a moment that ' a little bastard '
should be allowed in among all the true-born offspring, but decided that this was the Herries
way of showing Vanessa that they had forgiven
her.

The Herries children were: first Mary and
Rosalind Worcester (Mary a gracious and lovely
hostess, Rosalind clutching her friend little Ada
Newmark—Horace's grandchild, the daughter of
stout Sidney and stout Mary—and going off with
her into a corner), the aforesaid Ada and her
brother Gordon, Maurice and Clara, Alfred's
children, plain, with good manners, but wanting
the best for themselves. Mary, Rosalind, Ada,
Gordon, Maurice and Clara: little ordinary

Herries, all that they should be. It was amusing, he thought, as he watched, to notice the way in which these Herries children took command of the other children who were not Herries. Took command quite confidently, without arrogance or tiresome conceit, but quite as though it must be. And yet, with the notable exception of Mary, they were not very beautiful nor certainly were they brilliant. The Herries, he reflected, were never first-class unless they were mad. ' I am not first-class because I am not mad. Benjie, although he has never done anything with his life except love Vanessa, has something first-class about him. A first-class passion for something outside one-self can make one first-class. I have a passion for my Art. Why am I not first-class? Because there is just enough Herries in me to prevent my escape from myself.'

Then he saw little Sally and went and talked to her. She was an odd-looking child, small with straight uncurling brown hair and a pale face. But she was all alive. She sat on a sofa and her eyes were everywhere, eager, merry and very in-telligent. She did not join in anything until she was invited, but she suffered from no self-con-sciousness. Little coloured balloons were handed round (they were to be blown across a tablecloth). Clara, Alfred's child, preferred the colour of Sally's balloon to her own and said so. Sally at once gave her hers, but Tim thought that she, at the same time, looked at her with a little baby irony as much as to say: ' You're like that, are you, even at your age?'— a very elderly look for a child of six. ' But then,' thought Timothy, ' it will be odd if she isn't queer, born as she was and brought up in Hill Street.'

Next day he went and visited Benjie. London was very interesting to him. It was so long since he had stayed here. This was a great year for mechanical progress. The virtue of single planes advanced in a sudden leap the history of flying. In July, Blériot had crossed the Channel. In October there was a flying week at Blackpool and Mr. Farman surprised everyone by flying for half an hour in wild and gusty weather.

But the great change in London was the advance of motor-cabs. Hitherto motoring had been mainly for the well-to-do. Now it was discovered that cabs could be made both cheaply and strongly. The new cabs, fitted with taximeters, were comfortable, safe, and the old uncertainty of the proper fare for the tiresome and truculent old cabby was gone. Only a little while before, motors had been the property of the rich: now, quite suddenly, they were everywhere. The whole aspect of the London streets was changed. It signified perhaps the final advent to assured power and importance of the middle classes.

Timothy felt this most emphatically during his evening expeditions about the town. He went everywhere: to the White City, to a first-night at Wyndham's, or the Haymarket, or the St. James's, to a dinner at the Savage Club, to the National Sporting Club, to the London Sketch Club, to a Sunday night at the New Lyric, and everywhere it was the same—the English Middle Class was now

triumphant, subservient to nothing and nobody.
The reign of the Autocrats in England was
over. Sargent painted his Jew millionaires, Wells
and Bennett invigorated the novel with their
portraits of lower middle-class life. The word
'respectable' had no longer any especial significance in English life. The ordinary man ruled
England and he was determined to find pleasure
where he could and hold to it. The ordinary
man ruled England, and Herries were the ordinary man.

He found Benjie in three rooms of the upper
part of a house in Tite Street, Chelsea. When he
came in, Benjie was walking up and down. He
was wearing an old grey jacket, grey flannel
trousers and a faded red tie. Tim was struck,
more than ever, by his spareness, the fierceness
of his blue eyes. He noticed that his hair was
turning grey at the temples. He looked as
though he had been lost in the desert and rescued
in the nick of time. After half an hour's talk
Tim felt that Benjie would, on the whole, have
preferred that the rescue had not taken place.

The room was very bare, but it had a broad
bright window filled with scurrying clouds and a
cold blue sky. Very shortly it would be dark.
In the window was a long deal table with Vanessa's
photograph (a very old one), a book which Tim
picked up and found to be Hudson's *Purple Land*,
some writing paper, a pen and a long truculent-
looking ruler. On the walls there was nothing save
over the fireplace two grinning masks made of some
dark wood. There were two shabby armchairs.

Tim knew Benjie well. In the very old days
when he had gone over to Paris with Tom, Benjie
had been his saviour. He had protected him
against the Family. Tim, who was faithful, would
stick to Benjie always because of that, were there
no other reason. But there *were* other reasons,
plenty of them. He liked Benjie because he was
honest, generous, courageous, and his own worst
enemy. Benjie had one charming quality, and a
very rare one it is. He always, whatever his own
personal melodramas, wanted to hear about the
adventures of his friends. This was not from
self-conscious duty nor from a desire to be kind.
He was truly interested.

So Timothy told him—about Mlle. Thérèse,
his stout but charming mistress, about his new
flat, about the portrait he was painting of the two
little girls of the Minister of Finance, about his
picking up a charming Berthe Morisot for almost
nothing, of English writers whom he had met in
Paris—Somerset Maugham and Arnold Bennett
(' both interested in painting—very odd '), about
this and about that.

' And you? ' he asked at last.

' Oh—I? ' Benjie sat on the deal table,
swinging his legs. ' I go on—as you see.'

Tim was aware, at that moment, just as a rather
slatternly white-haired woman brought in the tea,
that he was encountering some experience so deep
and poignant that he was frightened of it. He
was frightened of very little; he was certainly not
frightened of Benjie. But there was something
here that belonged to that rarest of all worlds—

the world of absolute and positive experience.
'Because,' he thought, ' we all live one skin deep
at the most.   We do not, most of us, know that
we can go deeper.'

So to ease things he himself talked.

' I've been observing the Family.   I haven't
seen it, you know, for a long time.   Coming along
very nicely, I should say.   It ostracised me once
and now it welcomes me because I'm a moderate
success.   I'm not exactly prejudiced in its favour.
But we've settled down.   All the quarrels are
over.   All the same there are a few rebels left, but
they're not so grand as they used to be.'   Then
he said an incautious thing.   ' But I tell you what,
Benjie—your daughter's going to be a rebel.   You
should have seen her with the rest of them.   It
persists, the divine strain.   How I wish I had
more of it! '

Benjie jumped to the floor.

' You've seen Sally—where? when? '

' Oh, yesterday—at a children's party at
Cynthia's.'

' Did you talk to her?   She's remarkable, isn't
she?   Unusual? '

' Yes, I talked to her a little.   I loathe children's
parties, you know.   Certainly she's unusual.   I
was saying so.'

' I see her, you know.'   Benjie came and sat
down close to him, bending eagerly forward.
' Quite often.   In fact I can see her as often as I
like so long as I never go to the house.   Odd
situation, isn't it? '

' Very,' said Timothy, terribly touched by his

friend's emotion, thinking too of the old Benjie
who had been a wandering kind of rascal with no
very constant attachment.

'Have you been to see Vanessa, Tim?'

'No, not yet. Do you think she would like
to see me?'

'Of course she would. And you must go
soon. Then come and tell me about it.'

'Tell you about it?'

'Yes. Vanessa and I meet sometimes. Not
too often or it would be unbearable. But I never
enter the house of course. And I don't ask her
about the house. When we are together in fact
we don't talk very much. Talking seems to waste
the time. The only one who told me much about
what it was like inside was old Barney. And now
he's gone. Adrian goes there, but Adrian's a
prig. The rest of the family don't see much of
me, you know.'

'I see,' said Timothy. 'Of course I'll go if
she won't think it impertinent.'

'Oh no, she'll love it. Especially if you tell
her you've been here. You'll have to repeat every
word of our conversation, you know.'

Tim said slowly: 'It's all damned hard on
you.'

Benjie answered quickly: 'It's far worse for
her. You see, the bad part of it is that we were
having such a marvellous time just before he
wanted her. And we thought it was only for a
month or two. Now it's been close on three
years, and God knows how much longer!'

'Well, if you want my opinion,' Timothy

broke out, ' I think the whole thing's preposterous!
There are you, two people in the prime of life,
loving one another, and on the other side Ellis
who's too mad to know whether she's there or no.'

' You're wrong,' Benjie said quietly. ' Know?
Why, she's his very life! He worships her. If
she left him it would be like leaving a helpless
child, and worse than that, because she married
him. She only left him because he *didn't* want
her. No, there's no other way—until Ellis dies.
She would never be happy for a moment if she
came away. Not that she's happy as it is, but
she's got Sally.'

' And you?' Tim asked.

' Oh, I? Don't mind about me. Don't think
I'm being noble either. I'm not. I curse like
hell. I'd hate him if—if he were normal. As it
is one can't hate anyone in the affair, more's the
pity. Oh, I'm all right. I go abroad sometimes.
There's Tom here for company and he's so kind
that I could kill him. I'm working at a job too.
I go to a travel agency every day and advise people
about foreign parts. Sometimes I go wild for a
day or two. I've got some awful friends, you
know. But I'm never wild for long nor away for
long. I come slinking back because Vanessa's
here.'

' I'm glad you love her so much,' Tim said.
' Anyone's in luck to have the chance of the real
thing.'

' Love her?' He threw his head back. ' Did
you ever know our real story, Tim? No. Well,
I'm not going to bore you with it. But we loved

one another from childhood. We meant to marry.
First her father died—was burnt in the fire at
Uldale. That stopped it. Then—imagine it!—
I married someone else! Fantastic? Not at all.
My cursed imbecility that has made me do the
wrong thing at the wrong time all my life. But
listen. However wild I've been, however caught
she's been—caught in a trap, because that's what
her marriage to Ellis was—we've never ceased to
love one another for a single moment. At the
very instant of making love to another woman
I've always known it was only Vanessa I loved.
And the best time we ever had was just before
we parted. And now we'll never be free of one
another—I doubt if death can part us. And yet
when I say that, how ridiculous, how sentimental!
Hasn't every lover always said the same? But
we are such *old* lovers! It goes far beyond the
body—beyond—into what? Is it simply association, all that we have been through together?
Vanessa isn't very clever. She isn't any longer
very beautiful. But she's *lovely*, Tim. She never
falters, she never lets you down, she has a childish
pleasure in tiny things, she's generous, loyal, and
although she thinks she's a coward, she never
flinches at anything. And yet it's only a little for
her character that I love her. One doesn't love
people for their character, does one? Or only a
little. Why? Why? Why are Vanessa and I
bound together? Is she right, do you think? Is
there a spiritual life that outlasts the bodily? Will
Vanessa and I go on together, never apart, loving
one another . . .? Sometimes when I sit alone in

here at night, hearing the mouse in the wall and seeing those masks grin, knowing that she's there and I here—such a little distance—I begin to believe that I can pull her spirit in here with me, her body there in Hill Street. I could swear that she comes in, sits with her head against my knee as she used to do in Cumberland—Is this mad, Tim, do you think? Am I going queer a bit? Do I *look* queer? '

' No, Benjie, not in the least. Only it's bad for both of you, I should think, separated like this and yet so near to one another. Lord! I wish I loved someone like that, though! Or do I? It's a terrible strain. One can't work if one's always wanting someone. . . . '

He waited a while, then he said abruptly:

' Do you ever read history, Benjie? '

' History? No. Oh, I've read Macaulay and a bit of Froude——'

' You *should* read history. There's nothing so interesting. History or biography. A nation or a family or an individual—it's all the same. The point is that men's values are all wrong. The things that they *think* are happening aren't happening at all. Do you remember Tolstoi's *Anna Karénina* and the racecourse scene? Everyone *thought* that the racing was the important thing. It wasn't in the least. It was the struggle in the hearts of Anna and Karénin and Vronsky. Yes, and in thousands of other souls that day. Little temptations to meanness, lusts, sacrifices. Small tests, tests as small as a pin—but soul-histories are the only histories. Write an account of a

family or a county and find out where the crises
of the human spirit lie. See how it meets all the
tests, is beaten, is victorious, encounters its two
chief enemies, greed and fear, is encouraged to
extend into something wider, grander, nobler than
itself. Shakespeare knew that that was the only
kind of history. What are the stories of his six
great kings but soul-histories? What does he care
for national history? It is Richard in his tent,
Henry praying before the battle, the old king
dying in Westminster. . . . I'm not religious,
you know. I can't swear to heaven. I don't
know whether there are pearly gates. And I'm
not given to preaching. But I do know that you've
got the only thing that matters, Benjie. You can
feed your soul with an unselfish passion. You're
not starving it. You should see old Monet painting. He's like an eagle beating his wings for joy
that he's free, gross, fat old man that he is! To
escape beyond oneself! To lose one's soul because one's beyond fear, and so to save it. That's
the history of the endeavour of every man and
woman born on this earth. The only thing that
gives us grandeur, fleas on a cinder as we are! '

Benjie smiled.

' I've never heard you talk like that before.'

' No. I'm growing old. I've faced up to the
fact that I shall never be the painter I hoped to be,
never meet the woman I hoped to meet. We all
do. I'm just of the age. I hold my tongue. I
haven't talked like this for an age. The French
are a cynical people, you know. All the same it's
a marvel to me that men can refuse so obstinately

to think of the only things that really matter.
We'll suffer for it. We're bound to. Well, I
must go.'

He raised his long thin body, pulled at his
pale corn-coloured beard, stretched his arms and
yawned.

' You're going to see Vanessa, aren't you? '

' Yes—to-morrow.'

' And you'll come and see me again? '

' I'll come and see you again.'

When he was gone Benjie sat down and wrote
to Vanessa.

Next day Tim went to Hill Street. An old
butler with a face like a muffin, plump, boneless,
without shape, received him and led him upstairs.
In the long drawing-room Vanessa was entertaining Mary Newmark, wife of Sidney, old Horace's
son. Mary Newmark was fat in a bright, cheerful way. She wore a dress of shining blue and
she had a large hat with blue feathers. Under
the hat her face, like a gigantic strawberry,
beamed on the world. Beside her Vanessa, who
was dressed in black, looked very quiet. But
Tim was surprised. He had expected her to be
grave and a little ceremonious. Not at all. She
was extremely human. He could see that she
was bored with Mary Newmark, who quite clearly
had no idea of it. Mary was one of those women
who, without any arrogance, feel that their presence is a benefit to all concerned. She was also
convinced that any statement, any opinion on her
part, was of the first importance.

Tim saw that Vanessa was surprised to see
him and greatly pleased. Mary Newmark was
flustered a little; artists were to her strange
creatures: moreover Timothy lived in Paris. She
was plainly determined to be kind to him whatever he might have done.

' No, don't send for more tea,' he said. ' This
is splendid. If it's stewed I like it stewed.'

' I was telling Vanessa,' Mary Newmark began, ' that Sidney and I disapprove totally of the
Suffragettes.'

' Why? ' asked Timothy.

' The proper place for women is the home. I
don't want a vote. What would I do with one?'

As Timothy was about to speak she shook a
finger at him.

' Now, Mr. Bellairs, I know you're an artist
and have, I'm sure, all sorts of queer ideas. But
if women don't look after their homes, who
will? '

' Perhaps the men will,' said Timothy.

' Men! ' said Mary Newmark gaily. ' Would
you like to know what I think about men? '

' Very much,' said Timothy.

' Men are children. Nothing but children.
They never grow up. Once learn that about a
man and you never have any more trouble.'

' Well, then, isn't it wrong if men are only
children that they should have all the say in
governing the country? If women are so much
wiser——'

' Ah, that's just it,' said Mary Newmark with
complete self - confidence. ' Women *are* much

cleverer, but their proper place is behind the scenes, influencing the men. Sidney doesn't know it, but there's not a thought in his head that doesn't come from me.' She beamed on the world. ' I've no use at all for all this modern nonsense, nor has Sidney. Modern books, modern pictures, modern women—I don't mean anything personal, Mr. Bellairs. I'm sure you paint very nice pictures—very pleasant, I'm sure, but what was good enough for my mother is good enough for me. What modern writer have we to compare with Charles Dickens? Answer me that now.'

' It would be a great pity, wouldn't it,' said Timothy, ' if we had Dickens over and over again? One Dickens, yes — but a hundred Dickenses ! '

' Well, I don't know, I'm sure. I've certainly read *David Copperfield* over and over—my favourite bits, you know. Sidney reads aloud to me in the evenings in Manchester.'

The door opened and Sally came in. She stood for a moment, hesitating and smiling. Then she came forward.

' Say how do you do to Mrs. Newmark, darling.'

' How do you do? ' said Sally.

' And to Mr. Bellairs. You met him the other day, you know.'

' How do you do? ' said Sally, grinning.

Mary Newmark drew Sally forward and spoke to her in the voice she considered suitable to children, a voice she also used for little dogs.

'Well, darling? And what have you been doing to-day?'

'I've done my lessons and I've been for a walk.'

'That's a good little girl. And where did you go for a walk?'

'I went in Kensington Gardens.'

'And what did you see there?'

'Oh, nothing particular.'

Mrs. Newmark pinched her cheek, a thing that she considered children adored.

'And what lessons have you done to-day?'

This was frightful. Vanessa intervened.

'At present she has lessons with me. I'm not a very good teacher, I'm afraid.'

There was silence. Sally was looking at Mrs. Newmark with a smile that in some undefined way she felt to be sarcastic. A strange child, with her peaked face and dark brown hair. She was suddenly uncomfortable. The house was so very silent and the painter not very friendly. Moreover, there was Ellis somewhere and at any moment he might break in. How unpleasant that would be! Whenever she was uncomfortable she moved on. She moved on now.

'I'm afraid I must be going, Vanessa dear. It *has* been delightful. You must come and see us before we go back to Manchester. Good-bye, Mr. Bellairs. Don't become *too* modern in your painting!' She kissed Sally and sailed away. Half-way down the stairs she stopped a moment to listen whether she could hear Ellis moving about. There was no sound anywhere.

After she had gone they all three sat on the sofa together. Timothy had at once noticed that there was a strong and deep alliance between the mother and the child. When Sally moved and spoke it was as though Vanessa moved and spoke with her. Now Sally sat beside her mother; they sat hand in hand. They made no allusion at all to Mrs. Newmark. Their feelings about her were identical. They were all three very happy and confidential together.

'Now, darling, you must go to bed.'

Sally got up from the sofa. She sighed.

'Don't you wish you hadn't to go to bed?' she asked Timothy.

'I love my bed,' he answered. 'It's the best place there is.'

She looked at him sharply to see whether he were speaking the truth. She decided that he was.

'When I'm older I shall go to bed only once a week—every Friday.'

'Why Friday?'

'Because Saturday's a nice day and Thursday's a nice day, but Friday's horrid.'

She lifted up her face to be kissed.

'I'll come up and see you, darling,' Vanessa said.

She walked away rather sadly. At the door she looked back and smiled.

Vanessa looked at the door for a moment after it closed. Then she turned back.

'It was extraordinarily nice of you to come and see me.'

There was something young about her, Timothy thought, and eager. She was not dull as he had half expected to find her. She had lived, he knew, for years in lonely country but she was not dowdy. Her wide clear forehead, her grey hair parted in the middle, the severity of her black dress, her breadth and height, gave her massiveness, but he had an unexpected conviction that she was younger than he, years and years younger.

'It's very strange,' Vanessa said, 'but I've never set eyes on you since you were a small boy. I can see you now sitting up in an open carriage dressed like little Lord Fauntleroy and hating it.'

'Yes, I did hate it. And I'm afraid I hated my mother too for making a show of me.'

'No—but when you were such wonderful friends with Tom and Benjie . . . it's absurd that we should never have met! You were with Benjie yesterday!' she added quickly.

'Yes. How did you know?'

'I had a letter from him this morning, telling me about your visit. He writes and tells me if anything especially nice has happened. How was he? How was he looking?'

'Rather thin, I thought. No spare flesh.'

'No. I saw him last a fortnight ago. I wish he'd eat more. He doesn't look after himself.'

And then, in front of him, her face in a moment aged. She was sitting quietly, her hands folded on her lap, but he felt that behind her serenity she was enduring to the limit of everything: one burden more and she would break. He was a man who found life in general amusing and absurd rather than dramatic, but he was very sharply aware of the drama now being played in front of him—this long chill room, the house beyond it where Ellis was playing at soldiers or nursing a doll, Benjie in Tite Street, and all the Family moving like figures in a wavering tapestry as a frame to the scene. Vanessa, he thought, must be fifty or more and yet he had, at that moment, as urgent a longing to help her to escape to her lover as though she were a lovely girl of twenty!

' Benjie tells me,' she went on, ' that he talked about me—about us. Do—do you think—— Do you think that it is all getting to be more than he can stand? I mean—oughtn't I perhaps to *make* him go away, to insist on it? Perhaps, away from me, he would find someone——'

' There's nothing you can do. He will never be able to go away. He will never find someone else.'

' I don't want him to go away, you know.' She smiled again. ' I think I'd die if he did. Oh, don't fancy that I'm pitying myself. I have him and Tom—and Sally of course. Don't you like Sally? '

' I do indeed. She's very unusual.'

' Yes, she is, isn't she? And—I'm telling you everything because you have been Benjie's friend so long and of course that makes you mine. Ellis . . . I have grown fond of him. No one could help it. He needs me, and he is so docile and so affectionate. So different from what he was. But of course it's not a good house for Sally to grow up in. It's not healthy here, although she's too young to understand things and behaves to Ellis as though he were her brother. I thought at first that I would keep them apart, but Sally made that impossible. She goes to him quite naturally, never seems to think it strange that an old man of sixty-six should play with dolls and soldiers. Perhaps she knows more than we think. Children may be much wiser than we suppose.'

' You are all, it seems to me,' said Timothy, ' behaving very finely.'

' Oh no, we're not! I don't see how we could behave otherwise. And I myself am not fine at all. Often I long for Ellis to die. Sometimes I feel that I *cannot* keep away from Benjie any longer. You see, we thought that it would only be for a month or two. Already it has been nearly three years . . .' She hesitated, looking down at her lap. ' The hardest part of it has been that in Cumberland, just before we separated, Benjie and I were happier than ever before.'

' I know. Benjie told me.'

' Oh, did he tell you? I'm so very glad.' She went on: ' You must think this all very senti-mental, Timothy. Two old people like Benjie and me both pouring out our hearts to you.'

' Only false things are sentimental,' Timothy said. 'And this isn't false, Vanessa. Your grand-mother, Judith Paris, wouldn't have thought so. I gather that she was anything but sentimental.'

' No—she wouldn't have thought it false. I so often think of her and sometimes feel as if she were here helping us both. I still have a tiny tea-set she gave me when I was a little girl, and it seems only yesterday that I climbed on to her bed and kissed her.'

There was a pause.   He got up to go.

' I must be moving on.   I'm so glad that we have met, and if there is anything I can do, Vanessa, I always will.   You can count on me. I've got every weakness except infidelity.'

' Yes; Benjie always says that you are one of the most faithful people in the world.'

Before he went he said, rather shyly:

' Look here!   Don't let this be too much of a strain on you.   One can only stand so much, you know.   Oughtn't you to go out more? '

' Go out? '

' Yes, be gay a little—go to theatres and see the sights.'

' Oh, I do go out.   And I've had so much of that in the past.   But it's all right.   I'm perfectly happy.'

With that brave challenge in his ears he left the house, but for several days he could not get her out of his mind.

When he had gone, Vanessa went up to say good-night to Sally.   She was in bed waiting. Vanessa sat on the bed and Sally lay within her arm, very contentedly, her eyes smiling.

' Mummy, Mrs. Newmark *is* a funny lady! ' (It was like Sally to have the surname quite clearly and accurately.)

' In what way funny, darling? '

' She thinks children silly.   They aren't, are they? '

' Sometimes.'

'Well, not like *that*, anyway.'

Soon she was asleep.

Then Vanessa went to Ellis. The upper part of the house had now been made into a suite for him. He had a sitting-room, bedroom and bathroom of his own. The sitting-room was large, with high windows looking out on to chimney-pots and sky. On the table was a large bowl with chrysanthemums (he loved flowers). Near the flowers was a big wooden fort with guns and soldiers. In one armchair an elaborate doll, dressed in blue silk, was lolling.

Ellis himself was sitting, when she came in, very busy with one of those puzzles the point of which is that little black balls should roll into little silver holes. He was bending over this, shaking it, holding it very still, shaking it again. He looked very old. His thin hair was white now, his shoulders very bent. He had the almost waxen cleanliness of a patient who is constantly washed and brushed by others.

'Oh, Vanessa!' he cried, when he saw her. 'I'm so glad you've come. I've been trying to do this for ever so long. As soon as one's in another rolls out.'

She sat down beside him and took the puzzle. He watched her as she manipulated it, with the eager attention of a dog who is waiting for you to throw a ball.

Soon all the little black balls were in the little silver holes. He clapped his hands.

'Oh, that's lovely! Now shake it! Now I'll see if I can do it!'

She sat there quietly beside him.

He put the puzzle down.

' I'm very hungry,' he said.

' Your dinner will be coming very soon, dear.'

' What do you think it will be? '

' I don't know.   Something nice.'

' Marmalade pudding? '

' Perhaps.'

' Oh, I hope so.'   He sighed, laying his head against his hand.   She put her arm around him.

' Did you have a nice drive? ' she asked him.

' We saw some soldiers.'

' Was there a band? '

' No.   There wasn't a band.   I wish we could have a band—here in this room.   Wouldn't it make a fine noise? '   He sighed again.   ' My head aches.'

' It's the weather, Ellis dear.   It's been very close all day.   My head's been aching all day.'

' Has it? '   He put his hand up and stroked her forehead and then her cheek.   He loved to do that.   At first she had shrunk from it.   His hand was dry and hot and his finger-nails very white, like a dead man's nails.   But now it moved her strangely when he made any demonstration. And once, years and years ago, he had wanted to kill her!   How queer!

With the abrupt restlessness that was characteristic of him he got up and fetched the doll from the chair.

' I've dressed and undressed her three times

to-day,' he said. ' She doesn't seem to mind.' He gave her to Vanessa. ' Will you play for me to-night, Vanessa? '

In the corner of the room was a small piano. Vanessa did not play very well—only old and simple things, old songs, hymn tunes, waltzes. He loved her to play. He could sit for hours watching her.

' Yes, of course, dear. I'll come up when I've had my dinner.'

He was delighted.

' Oh, how nice! Play the one with mice in the can.'

' Yes, I'll play that one.'

' And the one with armies marching.'

' Yes, dear.'

She put her arm around him and he lay back against her with his eyes closed.

After a while Winifred Trent came in. She was very thin and her pale long face was covered with wrinkles.

' I think dinner is ready, Vanessa. I'll stay with Ellis while he has his.'

A gong sounded from below. Winifred Trent said every evening this same sentence.

' Thank you, Winifred.' Vanessa got up. She kissed Ellis and went downstairs.

The dining-room seemed very large and empty. Rodd, the butler with a face like a muffin, waited on her.

' Sole, my lady? '

' Thank you, Rodd.'

She sat staring in front of her. Suddenly she

smiled. Benjie had enjoyed Timothy's visit. He would be happier to-day.

'Brussels sprouts, my lady?'

'Thank you, Rodd.'

After Ellis was in bed she would write to Benjie and tell him about Timothy's visit.

WHITE WITH SWANS

ONE night, early in 1912, Vanessa woke and was assured that she was about to die. She was conscious of no especial pain, only a scantness of breath and a general faintness. Dimly, as though she were many miles away, she realised that the early morning light, very cold and thin, laid ghostly shadows on the floor. She heard a sparrow twitter.

But so certain was she that the end had come that she felt that she must write something to Benjie, saying good-bye, telling him to be good to Sally . . . but she found that she had no wish to make the slightest movement. She lay there, her eyes fixed on the ceiling upon whose dark surface some strange light, thin and bright like a lustre bowl, seemed to hover. Her brain was quite clear. For months past she had known that her energy was leaving her as water trickles from a cistern. Until less than three years ago (she could fix the time exactly, for the change had come when Timothy Bellairs, the painter, had paid her a visit and, turning to her, had said: 'Don't let this be too much of a strain on you') her resistance had been equal to the struggle. But after that day (she remembered that when Timothy had gone she had been up and said good-night to Sally, had visited Ellis, had dined downstairs alone, and Rodd had said ' Brussels sprouts, my lady? ') something had snapped. Her nobility had gone, she supposed. Lying now, about to pass away altogether from this silly business, she could summarise the past clearly and without sentiment. Her nobility had gone. She no longer, after that day, wanted to play her part. What she wanted was for Ellis to die and then, for herself, that she should go to Benjie and never again, for one single moment, night or day, leave him.

She seemed after this (it was as though she were now speaking to God Himself, for life was over and He would understand) to be without scruples and yet to be tied with scruples. She was now quite shameless and, in intention, had already left Ellis and was somewhere safe in Cumberland with Benjie, but in fact of course she did nothing of the kind.

For three more years she did as she had already done; nursed Ellis, played her part, ached (oh God, how her heart had ached!) for Benjie, and there it was. But whereas in the first three years she had acted as she did because she thought it right, in the second three she acted as she did because she had to. She could not leave Ellis because he was so helpless, but her heart became a strange confusion of disgust and misery and longing and sheer exhausted weariness.

The effort was becoming always more frightful, and not only for herself but also for Benjie. For

one whole year he went abroad. They wrote
and met when he was in London. They poured
their very souls into their letters. But the longing became too great. He returned, thin as a
stick, new lines of age and perhaps of bitterness
in his face. During this last year they met more
and more often, but always as though, at the very
moment of meeting, they must part. As for
Ellis, nothing ailed him, and Vanessa was his very
life. Then Winifred Trent died. Six months
ago a chill had carried her off. Before she died
she said to Vanessa: ' You've been wonderful,'
and Vanessa, although she had grown to be fond
of Winifred Trent, had a terrible impulse to tell
Winifred Trent a number of coarse truths. . . .

After that strength had ebbed from her. She
woke weary; she went to bed too tired to sleep.
And Ellis grew stronger and stronger in the body.
He liked her to play to him on the little piano by
the hour. Well, now she was going to die and
the whole thing would be over. She thought of
Benjie and Sally and Tom, and summoned them
to her side.

To Benjie she said: ' My darling, my beloved,
this can't separate. . . .'

To Tom: ' Thank you for looking after me,
Tom dear. Mary Worcester isn't worth it. . . .'

And to Sally: ' Don't forget me. Have a
good life, darling. . . .'

Then it seemed to her that her heart ceased to
beat. She thought of God as very near to her.
She clasped her hands and began the Lord's
Prayer. . . .

A moment later apparently Janet, the maid, came in, carrying the tea, drawing the blinds. So she had not died!

She lay there, drank her tea.

' What kind of day is it, Janet? '

' Nice and bright, my lady.'

Then Janet said:

' You don't look very well this morning, my lady. Have your breakfast in bed. Do now.'

(Janet had from the first, two years ago, been very friendly, maternal and comforting.)

' Oh no, Janet. I must get up. I didn't sleep very well.'

' What a shame! I should stay the morning in bed, my lady.'

And she did. She was surprised at herself. Sally came in to say good-bye to her before departing to her school in Kensington. She had her luncheon with Ellis in his room.

But, after this, the obsession remained with her that she had not long to live.

One evening she was gay: that is, she went with Cynthia, Philip Rochester and Horace Ormerod to the first-night of a new play. It was Tuesday, March 5 — Cynthia's birthday — and they had a very charming dinner first at Claridge's. Cynthia was very coy about her age, Horace hearty and hopeful, and Philip—who painted his face so cleverly that you wouldn't notice it unless you were a woman—was most witty at the expense of all his nearest and dearest.

' But I thought you liked Humphrey Bell! '

Cynthia said, when Philip had just intimated that
Humphrey cheated at cards and beat his mistresses.

'Oh, so I do! I *adore* Humphrey! He's a
perfect pet! I know he wouldn't mind a *word*
I've been saying!'

'Well, I'm not so sure,' observed Cynthia.

How very old, Vanessa thought, Philip was!
He was all Dowsonish and Wildeish. And how
long ago was that buried age with its glittering
surface and tinkling music-box echoes! The time
when she had been a hostess and driven in the
Park, had tea with Mrs. Langtry in that extraordinarily cosy drawing-room, breathing that lovely
lady's good-nature and kindness of heart. It had
been a cosy, good-natured time—yes, and an enter-
prising one too! Now—what was the matter?—
everyone was restless, uneasy; nothing seemed
secure. She herself felt shabby, an old owl not
used to the light. She sat in the back of the
box with Horace, feeling a little faint, longing
for Cumberland and Benjie and the Newlands
farm. . . .

The play seemed to answer some of her questions. It was called *Milestones* and was by Arnold
Bennett and Edward Knoblock. The little
Royalty Theatre contained that night many celebrated persons. The customary first-night remark was made that if a bomb were dropped on
the theatre . . . In fact, all the customary first-
night remarks were made. Mr. Knoblock was
discerned sitting in a box with his sister. Famous
persons were observed, commented upon. But

it was not, as it happened, a first-night quite like
other first-nights. It was, in itself, a Milestone.
This passing of time, this blindness of each
generation to the significant things, the battle
between the helpless imaginative and the confident unimaginative.

'Why, these are Herries!' Vanessa thought.
'These are our very selves!'

And then Haidée Wright's brilliant passionate Aunt was simply Judith Paris come to
life. She seemed to Vanessa to be living there on
the stage in front of her. She was eternal, im-
mortal, as Judith was. That little figure, her voice
trembling with her vitality and courage, dominated not only the theatre but the world beyond
it. 'So Judith still dominates us all.' In the
last Act an actress made a great success. She
was extremely beautiful, and Vanessa, who had
never seen her before, searched her programme.
Her name was Gladys Cooper. There was something in her self-confidence and scorn of sentiment that spoke of the future. 'Will Sally be
like that? Not so beautiful of course, but
brave, scornful of anything that seems to her unreal?' Everyone in the theatre that night was
thinking a little as Vanessa. How time passes and
we don't know it! We are at the mercy of forces
greater than ourselves. What if these forces
grow stronger than we? What if we become
their slaves? A wind of insecurity blew through
the theatre that night. The actors seemed like
figures in a Morality.

In the second interval, Cynthia and Philip

went out to greet some friends. In the back of
the box, Vanessa and Horace talked. Vanessa
had never liked Horace before, but to-night he
touched her sympathy. His wife had died in the
preceding year. He said that he was very lonely.
This big heavy man with the protruding chin,
the shining forehead, the gleaming glasses, was
suddenly a small and very unprotected schoolboy.

' I suppose it's my own fault,' he said. ' I'm
sure I've always done my best, looked on the
bright side, been cheerful very often when I really
didn't feel it, but people don't want you to be
cheerful and kind and jolly. They like you much
better if you're sour and cynical. The fact is, I
know it, people get bored with me. There was
a woman once, Vanessa, whom I loved to distrac-
tion. I'd have done anything for her. For a
month or so it was like heaven—it was really. I
thought she loved me passionately. One week-
end she went to Eastbourne and wrote me two of
the most wonderful letters. Beautiful they were.
And then, one night, she was to dine with me in
my flat. I was all ready and waiting. I'd ordered
the most beautiful little dinner. But instead of
coming herself she sent a letter—a short, curt note
saying that she was afraid she couldn't see me any
more. She was very sorry. She had thought
about it and decided that it wasn't right her
seeing me and so on. But I knew that *that*
wasn't the reason. It was simply that she was
bored with me. And yet I'd always done my
best.'

' You'd spoilt her, I expect,' said Vanessa.

' No. I'd done what any other man would have done. She found me a bore. Yes, it's very strange. People like you if you're cruel and malicious. I've never been cruel in my life to anyone.'

' Would you mind, Horace,' Vanessa said, ' getting me a glass of water? I feel rather faint.'

When he returned with one he had something he wanted to say. It was about Rose. He had seen Rose that very afternoon.

' Oh, Rose!' Vanessa exclaimed. ' Quick, Horace, tell me! I have written to her and had no answer. Once a letter from Madrid, a short one, telling me nothing.'

' I've seen her from time to time,' Horace said. ' Of course it's been very painful. But she was always determined that you shouldn't see her. It's been the one thing that she resolved. She was ashamed. . . .'

' Oh no,' Vanessa cried. ' She shouldn't have been. I'm her friend. Quick, Horace, they're coming back. Where is she now? Is she in London?'

' Yes, that's why I told you. She's very ill. She's going to have a serious operation. This is her address. I've written it down.'

(Poor old Horace. Not such a bad fellow—or at any rate not so bad in old age and loneliness, much more bearable in misfortune.)

Cynthia and Philip came into the box. Vanessa had the address. She thought, as the curtain went up—' They've forgiven me. They consider me respectable again. But Rose they have pushed down and down . . .'

On the following afternoon she found her way to the street in Bloomsbury. It was a fine March day with gay light clouds hurrying like ballerinas across the chimney-pots. The pigeons fluttered on the steps of the Museum, and there was a sniff of spring in the air.

Rose's room was at the very top of the thin grey house and, half-way up, Vanessa felt once more her faintness, had to pause while the stairs slowly rose and fell and a grimy window bent anxiously towards her. At last she was there. She knocked on the door and went in. Rose was sitting, a shawl over her shoulders, before a grumbling, sulky fire. The room was stuffy and had the smell of a not very clean blanket.

' Oh! Vanessa! ' Rose cried out.

Vanessa bent down and they embraced as though they would never let one another go. Rose cried a little, wiping her eyes with a rather soiled handkerchief. Then she brightened. She was fearfully thin and her complexion was a pale and dry yellow. She was wearing a shabby blue skirt and faded silver slippers. She held Vanessa's hand.

' At last I told Horace that you might come and see me. I wouldn't hear of it before. But my number's up at last and I had to have one last glimpse of you before I met St. Peter.'

' I've tried to see you——'

' Yes, I know. I've been abroad. Here, let's have a look at you! '

She took Vanessa by the shoulder and held her off so that she might see her.

' This bloody gas! It isn't very gay, is it? But we don't run to electric light here yet. Well, my dear, you don't look any too grand yourself, if I may say so. You're a fine big woman, of course —always were. But you look as though you hadn't had any sleep for a month.'

' I haven't been sleeping very well, but never mind me. What about yourself? What's the matter, Rose darling? '

' Oh, the wages of sin. As a matter of fact it's cancer and that's the plain truth. Old Furry-Face the doctor says, " Only a little internal trouble. We'll have you right in no time." But *I* know. You can't cheat me. I'm starving to death and I'm sick of it. Horace has been a brick, though. He's paying for the nursing-home, insists on it although I tell him any old ditch will do to die in.'

' But, Rose, you're wrong. I'm sure you are! After all, they know—— '

' Wrong my foot! You can't kid me. Now look here, my dear, now you *are* here! I want to know everything. How *are* you? How's Benjie? How much longer are you going on in this ridiculous way? '

Vanessa told her something of her life, ending up : ' You see, we thought that it wouldn't be so long. It's been five years.'

' And Benjie and you eating your hearts out! Well, I think it's a bit of sentimental tosh! Giving

Y

yourself up heart, soul and body to someone who'd be just as happy with any nurse——'

' No,' Vanessa said. ' You're wrong there. I might have left him, perhaps, if he hadn't needed me. Because it hasn't been fair on Benjie. But he *does* need me. Every year it has been more impossible to leave him.'

'And now you're killing yourself! Oh, I know! It's draining all the strength out of you. I can see it. And here we are, the two of us! You've done the virtuous thing. I've done the other! Not much to choose . . .'

They talked about old times. Rose never let Vanessa's hand go. Her clutch was hot and feverish.

' You needn't be afraid, Vanessa. It's all over. There's no drunken Major coming in. Even my taste for drink has gone. I was in Madrid three years. Yes, a Professor kept me—a very nice little man he was, with a curly black beard and a wife he couldn't stand the sight of. I was fond of him. I truly was. That's a funny thing. In spite of the life I've led I haven't got tired of wanting to be fond of men—really fond of them, mend their clothes, put their buttons on, that sort of thing. Then I get tired of them. Domestic one minute, restless the next. But virtue's got nothing to do with it. I've never felt more virtuous than when I've been doing my worst. . . . There was a young fellow from College once went off with me. Pretty well broke his mother's heart, too. We went on a trip to Scotland. We stopped at Keswick. I wanted to have a look at it, and there it was, same as ever—St. John's spire and the square with the clock. We went down to the Lake the night we arrived and I can hear the water lapping against the jetty now. And Friar's Crag. We went on to Friar's Crag and the boy talked about Ruskin. Well, you never saw a more virtuous pair than we were that trip, reading Shelley and wondering whether there was a God and picking flowers . . . and I suppose I never did a wickeder thing than taking that young man away. Funny, isn't it? This morality! Very vexed question, if you ask me!'

After a while she asked Vanessa:

'Why do you love Benjie so, Vanessa? I've never loved anyone like that. You're the only one I've loved all my life long and you're a woman. Why do you love him so?'

'Oh, I don't know,' said Vanessa. 'He's everything I want in a man. You should ask rather why he loves me. I often tell him he should have a gay, lively woman, witty, and quick to see things. There's *one* reason I love him, I think. I can see his jokes. It used to be terrible in the old days in Hill Street when I didn't see a joke and had to pretend I did. But Benjie and I find one another amusing. We're comic to one another. That's a good reason for love.'

They fell into silence. Vanessa thought that Rose had fallen asleep. At last it was time for her to go.

'Rose darling—are you looked after here? Is there anyone to care for you?'

'Oh yes, it isn't so bad. The woman's quite

decent. And I'm going to the nursing-home to-morrow. You'll come and see me there, won't you?'

Vanessa promised. She looked back at the door and saw Rose's eyes — hungry, shining, feverish—fixed upon her. She went slowly away.

She visited Rose every day in the nursing-home. A week later Rose had her operation and three days after that she died. She was worn out, the doctor said. Injudicious living in the past . . . yes . . . sad . . . but, as a matter of fact, there would have been no hope. She could not have recovered.

Vanessa was happy for her sake. That was the way that she would have wished it.

Meanwhile the Family watched Vanessa with curiosity. She went round paying visits on everybody exactly as though she were going away somewhere.

Cynthia and May Rockage (who was in London just then) and stout Mary Newmark, putting their heads together, decided that she was going off with Benjie again. She was gay, light-hearted and extraordinarily kind. She said some odd things. She said to Cynthia: 'I can't get that play *Milestones* out of my head. Do you remember the girl in the last Act saying, " Please remember that we're in the year 1912 "? Isn't it funny to think that for Sally one day 1912 will be as old-fashioned as 1812? Doesn't it make you feel queer?'

'Not in the least,' said Cynthia.

'Oh, well, then—doesn't it seem odd to you that my grandmother probably said, "Please remember that we're in the year 1812"?'

'Not in the least. Your grandmother lived to be a hundred.'

'Oh, I know. That isn't what I mean. What I mean is that people are more important than time. What I mean is that my father, who was a darling, once said in his garden on Cat Bells: "Look, Vanessa! There's the squirrel again!" That, my relationship to him, our love for one another, all of it comes back as I think of that sentence: it isn't dead, it isn't gone. He's alive because we loved one another. 1812, 1912 doesn't mean anything at all. What we think is life is nothing—the secret life has quite another history. Am I being very stupid?'

'No, dear,' said Cynthia, who was only half listening, because there were some new and extremely beautiful photographs of her daughter Mary that she was examining. 'You're being very clever—too clever for me, I'm afraid.'

('One half of our family will *never* understand what the other half is after—never, never, never!' Vanessa thought.)

'Aren't these good?' said Cynthia. 'I don't want to be the fond mother, but really Mary is going to be a beauty.'

'Yes, she is,' said Vanessa eagerly, glad that Cynthia was happy and at the same time wishing, in spite of herself, that Sally was taller and had a brighter complexion.

'Do you think, Cynthia, that there is something

true in what the old man said at the end of *Mile-stones*?'

'What did he say, dear?' asked Cynthia, hold-ing one of the photographs at an odd angle and smiling at it.

'Don't you remember? He said women of to-day aren't what they used to be. They're hard. They've none of the old charm. They're un-sexed. Are Sally and Mary going to be hard? They *are* different from us. I've noticed it. Sally isn't afraid of anything and she doesn't like to show her feelings. She's rather like a boy sometimes. Won't it be dreadful if all the women are like men and all the men——'

'Like Philip,' Cynthia concluded. 'Why do you think so much about the future, Vanessa? The present is so very agreeable. Peile hasn't been in a bad temper for weeks. Everything is so comfortable and settled.'

'Settled? Do you think so?' said Vanessa.

Later, the Family recalled the strangeness of Vanessa during these weeks. They had, perhaps, none of them ever really known her. She became again rather beautiful. Her pallor suited her grey hair, and her eyes were still lovely, soft, gentle and generous. No, they had none of them really known her. There was something wild in the middle of her gentleness. You might call her timid because she disliked quarrelling, high words. Yet she had a temper, she could be most cour-ageous. She had been, by all Herries standards, grossly immoral, living for years with a man to whom she was not married, and yet she was re-

ligious as none of them were. She had succeeded
in holding a man's devotion for a whole lifetime,
and a most difficult man too. And yet she was
not a woman of the type, you would suppose, for
Benjie. For five years she had performed a task
that was, they all admitted, an exceedingly hard
one. They admired her now although they had
once criticised her so severely. But she was outside them all—a stranger in the end. 'There
have been always odd ones in the family,' Mary
Newmark said complacently. 'As Sidney says,
" We're different from ordinary families." '

Vanessa meanwhile paid a visit to her doctor.

' Is there anything wrong with me? I'd like
to know.'

He examined her.

' You have been under a great strain. You're
very tired. Can't you go abroad for a while and
have a proper rest? '

' No,' said Vanessa. ' I can't, I'm afraid.'

' Well, you aren't looking after yourself
properly——'

' Is anything organically wrong? '

' No. You're nearly fifty-three, though, and
should take care of yourself. A chill or an extra
strain—any little thing—might be serious.'

She smiled. They were very old friends.

' Thank you. I'll try and take care.'

Then the day came (she had known that it was
coming) when she could not leave Benjie. They
had been having tea in his room, as they did about
once a fortnight. (' How old we're getting! ' she
said to Benjie once. ' No one thinks it immoral for

us to be alone any more.') She got up to go. She
could not. She stared at him helplessly.

'What is it?' he asked, getting up and coming
to her.

'Oh, I don't know!' She tried to smile, but
her mouth trembled. 'Suppose that this should
be the last time!'

'What do you mean—the last time?'

'It's always been like that lately—harder to
part.' She drew away from him. 'Oh, I was
forgetting! I brought you something.'

She went to the deal table and picked something up. 'I thought I'd like you to have this.'

'What is it? You're always giving me things.'

She undid the paper wrapper.

'This is Judith's book. You know, the one
we used to read out of in Cumberland.' She held
it up, with its faded green cover. 'I thought I'd
like *you* to have it now.'

'Why? But you are so fond of it!'

'Yes—but if anything happened. . . . You
know, Benjie, I've always thought it such a pity
that someone shouldn't publish it; it's so lively
and amusing.'

'People aren't interested. We aren't a very
remarkable family.'

'Aren't we?' said Vanessa. 'I think we are.'

He kissed her. 'All right. I'll look after it
for you. Write your name in it—your name and
mine.'

She went to the table and sat down. She wrote:
'For Benjie with love from Vanessa Herries and
Judith Paris. March 29, 1912.'

' I feel as though she were in the room with us now.'

He laughed. He was standing behind her, his hand on her shoulder.

' Ghosts! What a child you are, Van! Once we're gone we're gone! '

He felt her shiver.

' What's the matter? ' he asked. ' Are you cold? '

' No.' She turned round, looked up into his face, her hands on his chest. ' Don't say that, Benjie. I can't endure to think that death—physical death—can separate us. After all—who knows?—it may be only after that that we're really together. When two people have loved one another so long and so truly as we have, isn't it absurd to think that a little thing—a cold, a stumble in the street, oh! anything—can separate us for ever? '

' Well,' he said, looking down at her with great tenderness, ' life *is* absurd, my darling—absurd, meaningless, cruel.'

She lowered her eyes. He felt her tremble again.

' Perhaps I'm wrong,' he said, putting his arm round her, holding her to him. ' I don't know any more than the next fellow. It's ridiculous to dogmatise. But if there's a God and He's kept us apart for five years as a cat tortures a mouse, why, then I say as many a man has said before me—— '

He stopped. She was crying. He knelt down beside her.

' Oh, my darling, don't cry! After all, we've got one another. We've had years of one another. That's something. And this can't go on for ever. It mustn't. It shan't. It gets harder every day. It's killing both of us. . . . Darling, look up! Think of the happy times! Think of the night in Newlands when Tom arrived from London! And even now—the hours we have, the way our love grows stronger and stronger. . . .'

He knelt, holding her, while she sobbed against his shoulder. He caught some words.

' I'm so tired . . . I love you so much . . .'

She rose, wiping her eyes. ' There! At my age! Wait. I'll wash my face in your bedroom!'

While she was gone he stood there in perplexity. To-night he could not endure that she should leave him and return to that house, to that dark house, that insane house. . . .

This could not go on as it was. They had both endured it too long. He must think of some way.

She came back smiling, but he saw that she was dreadfully weary.

' Come with me to the King's Road until I get a cab.'

At the door they embraced, clinging to one another with an almost dreadful desperation.

' I wish I'd seen Tom,' she said. ' Say good-bye to him for me.'

' Of course. But you'll be seeing him next week.'

' Oh yes. It was so good of him to take Sally out the other day. She *did* enjoy it so!'

They went down the long stairs hand in hand.

He walked beside her with the defiant boyish adventurous air that was so especially his, his hat cocked a little to the side, his empty sleeve, a flower in his coat.

In the King's Road they saw a cab, but she said:

'Let's walk a little farther. There'll be another.' The only other thing that she said was: 'What do you think? Carey and May are going to America in April. Adventurous for old things like them, isn't it? They're going in this wonderful new ship, the *Titanic*.'

'We'll go to America one day!' he said.

In Sloane Square she found a cab and got in. He stood looking after it until it turned the corner.

It was a quiet, still evening with little clouds of peach blossom floating serenely across a gentle sky. The traffic moved as in a dream and she stopped the cab by the Ritz (she wanted to go to Hatchard's bookshop), got out and walked. Influenced as she always was by the world about her, all humankind seemed, in this evening hush, to be amiable and friendly. She thought of the Family, that they had all been good to her after their lights, Cynthia and Mary and May and Alfred, Horace and Adrian; two old bachelor brothers, George and Stephen Cards, who, having come to live in London, had been especially good to her, leaving flowers at Hill Street and inviting her to their funny little dinners. All the feuds were over. Into what kind of world would Sally, Mary and Rosalind and Maurice grow up? The Family had risen now above the old jealousies

and causeless rivalries. She felt that she herself
had done her part in the mysterious weaving of
God's shuttle by her return to Ellis. Her love
and Benjie's had not been wasted. Nothing was
wasted, no goodness, no kindness, no little un-
heeded courtesy.

She lost, for a moment, under that peach-
blossom sky, consciousness of her own small personal history and so was happy. But she was
tired. She sat down on one of Mr. Hatchard's
chairs as they fastened up for her a book, *Carnival*,
by some new young man. Adrian had told her
that she must certainly read it. Then, as she went
out into the street again, she was conscious of a
small, stabbing pain in her side. As she was
aware of it she knew also a sudden mysterious
foreboding as though someone had whispered in
her ear: ' This is what you have been waiting
for. You will need now all your courage.' She
put her hand to her side as though to reassure
herself.

At home again she went up to Sally's room and
found her sitting at her table biting her pencil over
arithmetic. She sprawled over the table, the
perfect schoolgirl in her dark blue dress, ink on
her cheek and her hair ruffled, drumming her
heels on the floor.

' I'm no good at sums, darling,' Vanessa said,
sitting down beside her and loving her with a
passionate desire to draw her into her arms and
never let her go again. But she knew well that
Sally did not care for demonstrations.

' Oh, that's all right, Mummy,' Sally said.

' I'll do the beastly things. It's in our blood, I expect, not to be good at sums.' Then she added casually: ' I'm playing for the First at Hockey on Saturday.'

Vanessa knew that this had been, during the last two months, Sally's besetting ambition, but she only said:

' Oh, are you, darling? I'm so glad.'

' Yes.' Sally pushed the book away and looked at her mother. ' You *do* look sweet! Who gave you the violets? '

' Your father.'

' Good.' She thought a moment. Then she went on: ' Mummy, ought I to mind about being illegitimate? '

' Why, dear? '

' Well, Mabel Staines said to-day that she wouldn't be illegitimate for anything, and that her mother wanted to ask me to tea but wouldn't when Mabel told her.'

' I shouldn't worry about it, Sally dear,' Vanessa said.

' Oh, *I* don't worry! ' Sally said cheerfully. ' I told her that her mother could keep her old tea. I rather like being illegitimate. I'm different from the other girls.'

' Do most of the girls know? ' asked Vanessa.

' I don't think so. They're all quite decent anyway.' Then she looked at her mother again. ' Mummy, you're tired. You want some tea. I'll get some.'

' No, dear, thank you. I've had some.'

Then Sally did what was rare with her. She

threw her arms round Vanessa's neck and hugged
her.   She rubbed her cheek against her mother's.

' I'll look after you when you're older, and
you're the only one I *will* look after.'

' Will you, darling? '

' Yes, you shall have everything you want.
I'll make money for you and keep you.'

' What'll you make money with? '

' Oh, I don't know—be a secretary or a market-
gardener or something.'

' Perhaps you'll marry? '

' Indeed I shan't.   I think boys and men are
awful.   All except Tom and Daddy and Ellis.'
Then she dropped her voice confidentially.
' Ellis came in here crying a little while ago.
He'd broken a green vase they put flowers in.   I
told him not to worry.'

(Extraordinary, Vanessa thought, how Sally
takes everything for granted!)

' I must go up to him.'

Sally gave her a long and very wet kiss.

' Darling Mummy, I do love you so!' she
murmured.

' And I love you,' Vanessa said.

She went up to Ellis and found him, quite
contented, playing cards.   There was a very simple
Patience that Vanessa had taught him.   As he
played he murmured to himself.   ' That's the Red
Queen.   Now where's the next one.   What comes
after nine, Vanessa? ' he asked as she came in.

' Ten,' she said.

' No, the other way.'

' Eight comes before nine.'

' Eight.   Eight.   Eight,' he said.

He had grown, in the last few weeks, to look very old.   His face was wizened, very wrinkled.   He looked like a pathetic old monkey.

' Play the piano,' he said, smiling at her.

She sat down at the piano, and as she played ' Annie Laurie ' and ' Drink to me only ' she felt the pain at her side like a knife.   He came and stood beside her, humming out the tune.   Then he drew a chair and sat there, all huddled up, nursing his knees.

He was like a little gnome, and with his dead white finger-nails he tapped on his knee.

Soon she stopped.

' I'm tired to-night,' she said.

' Yes, I'm tired too,' he said and laid his head on her lap.   She stroked his white hair as he liked her to do.   Poor Ellis!   Would it not be kinder . . .?   Then, at the thought which some-times came to her like a messenger falsely tempt-ing her, she put her arms round his thin body and held him close to her.

But she was too weary to go on.   She kissed him and left him, he looking after her with his pathetic wondering eyes.

She went to bed.   She was brought some food, but could not eat it.   When, at last, to her great relief, she was left alone, she propped her pillows up and wrote a letter to Benjie.   Then she lay down to sleep.   She could not sleep.   Out of a cave of darkness where a dragon slumbered, she moved (carefully lest she should rouse the dragon).   She thought that she would read, and she opened

a book that was on the little table.   It was a volume
of Rossetti's poems and, to pain now stabbing her
with every breath, she read some verses:

> Although the lattice had dropped loose
>   There was no wind; the heat
> Being so at rest that Amelotte
> Heard far beneath the plunge and float
> Of a hound swimming in the moat.
>
> Some minutes since, two rooks had toiled
>   Home to the nests that crowned
> Ancestral ash-trees.   Through the glare
> Beating again, they seemed to tear
> With that thick caw the woof o' the air.
>
> But else, 'twas at the dead of noon
>   Absolute silence: all
> From the raised bridge and guarded sconce
> To green-clad places of pleasaunce
> Where the long lake was white with swans.

She let the book fall and lay back that she
might struggle the better with her painful breathing.   What was the matter with her?   She was ill.
She felt the heat rising, as in dry dusty wafts from
the desert, through her body, and this heat seemed
to be mingled with the clear, sharp picture in the
poem that she had just been reading.   She herself
leant out from some high window on a day of
fierce heat and in the general stillness she could
hear the sudden cool splash of the hound, and
then the caw of the rooks tearing the still air, and
then, turning her weary head, she saw the lake,
like a mirror in a green wall, and over its glassy
green-reflected light the swans, whiter than sunny

snow, floated. Ah, this heat and this coldness!
This stillness behind whose surface heat beat like
a drum! And the swans became horses, great
white horses struggling through the lake that now
was black; out of the icy water the horses struggled
up on to the flank of the frozen hills and their
hoofs rang against the ice! As the splendid white
horses drew breath with pain, so she fought for
hers. Everything moved and shifted. She was
a child running across the Cat Bells lawn to greet
her father, the house was burning, flames rose
mountain-high, as high as Skiddaw, and she was
burning too.

But Benjie came and caught her up with his
one arm and they rode on the white horse over
Skiddaw, Blencathra, over Helvellyn and the
Pikes, sailed above Scafell and so out to sea, to
the magical island on the horizon, and below them
all Wastwater was a lake set in a green wall, and
the white swans, with a grand remote dignity,
floated on its surface. . . .

At some moment, she could not tell when, she
saw the crumpled face of Rodd, the butler, bending over her.

' No, Rodd,' she whispered from an infinite
distance. ' I'm not very well. I don't think I'll
get up to-day.'

Rodd went upstairs to see the nurse who tended
Ellis. She was a big bony woman with a serious
kindly face. She had a faint moustache and grey
eyes that were both practical and gentle. Her
name was Milligan.

'Nurse, her ladyship is very unwell. I don't like the look of her at all.'

The nurse went down. Vanessa recognised her and smiled at her.

'I'm not very well,' she said. 'I have a bad pain in my side. I don't think I'll get up, if you don't mind.'

'It's pneumonia,' Milligan said to Rodd. 'I'll get Doctor Lancaster at once.'

Doctor Lancaster came. Vanessa was very ill.

Later in the morning Rodd telephoned to Cynthia. Cynthia had, a moment before, been telephoning about bridge and she was annoyed because she could not, that afternoon, secure the four that she wanted. It was stupid of Anne Fellowes to bother, on that afternoon of all afternoons, about her old husband just because he had only been home from China a week. 'When he's been home another fortnight she won't bother,' she thought. She put down the receiver and wondered whom she should ask. The bell rang.

'Well,' she said in that little voice exactly like ice knocking against glass, a voice that was warning enough to anyone who was sensitive. 'Oh, is that you, Rodd?' she said.

'Yes, madam,' said Rodd, who was not at all sensitive. 'It's her ladyship, madam. She's very ill. Pneumonia, Doctor Lancaster said. We were wondering whether you could come to Hill Street.'

Half an hour later she was in Hill Street. As she came into the room she heard a strange sound of recurrent short breaths, something inhuman and cruel. Vanessa did not recognise her, but murmured: ' The white swans. Benjie! Benjie! Look at the swans! '

On the following morning Benjie was roused, at about half-past seven, from a deep sleep by the ringing of the telephone. When he went to it he heard to his surprise Cynthia's voice:

' Benjie, is that you? '

' Yes,' he said, shivering a little in his pyjamas.

' I'm at Hill Street. I think you'd better come as soon as possible.'

' Hill Street? ' he repeated, bewildered.

' Yes. It's Vanessa. She's terribly ill. Double pneumonia.'

' I'll come at once,' he answered quietly.

He was aware that Tom was in the room.

' Father, what is it? '

' It's Vanessa. She's very ill. Double pneumonia.'

' Oh no! Oh no! ' Tom cried.

' Yes. I must go at once.'

He felt nothing except that he must get to Vanessa. He must get to Vanessa and save her.

He found a cab, rang in a frenzy the bell, rushed into the house and up the stairs. On the first landing he saw Cynthia.

' Oh, Benjie! ' she cried and stopped. Then, the tears streaming down her face, she said: ' Vanessa's dead! '

He did not see her. He stood in the long drawing-room like a man lost, his eyes

wandering from wall to wall. He was not thinking at all.

He felt a touch on his arm and, turning, saw
at his side an old, wizened, bent, and wrinkle-faced
man who looked up at him with questioning eyes.
Moving from some infinite cold distance he came
close to this strange figure. Then, with no shock
of surprise, he realised that it was Ellis. From
this same room Ellis had once driven him out.
Now he said, in a trembling voice:

'Where is Vanessa?'

Benjie led him to the sofa and the old man sat
down beside him, close to him, shivering a little.

'Vanessa's all right,' he said.

'No. But why isn't she here? Why hasn't she
come upstairs? I want her to play the piano.'

He put his arm round the old man. 'We must
both be patient,' he said.

'Yes, I'll be patient,' Ellis said and sat there,
staring in front of him, waiting. . . .

Afterwards Cynthia gave him a letter.

'It is for you, Benjie. Vanessa had written
on the envelope that it was to be given to you after
she was gone.' Cynthia, who had loved Vanessa,
looked at him as though she would like to achieve
with him some new and affectionate relation, but
she discovered at once that she did not know him
at all, that he looked 'foreign,' and that he scarcely
saw her. He took the letter and walked out of
the house.

He read it in his own room.

My Darling—I'm writing this in bed. Perhaps you
will never read it, but I am writing because I feel unwell

to-night and for weeks now have had a foreboding that I
might die without seeing you. This is probably nothing
except my being very tired, as I have been now for a
long time. But in any case it is like talking to you,
and is better than that in some ways because I can say
some things that I might be shy to say to your face, well
though I know you—or perhaps because I do know you
so well.

What I want most to say is that if I were to die very
suddenly and you not see me, you are never to feel afterwards that our love has been wasted. It has been the most
wonderful and glorious thing in both our lives, hasn't it?
It has been everything to me, not only because of our love,
but because it has shown me that there is something in life
far deeper than anything physical or material. I have
sometimes thought that the separation of these last years
has been the best thing that could have happened, because
we have been separated and yet in every important way
have been closer together than ever we were. I have
wished so often that I could have been a different kind of
woman for you—I suppose every woman wishes that for
the man she loves. I would have liked to be brilliant,
witty, the kind of woman clever men describe in their
books. I have been unfortunate, I sometimes think, because I have been a woman between two periods. Forty
years ago women knew what they were supposed to be
and do. In fact there was no choice for most of them.
In times to come when Sally is grown up, women, I expect,
will be free, equal with men, afraid of nothing. I have
not, I'm sure, made a success of my life, and yet I feel that
I have, because I won and *kept* your love, and Sally and
Tom love me too. I won't say anything about religion,
because I know that it bores you, but think sometimes
of me that I had no more doubt that God exists than I
have of your love for me. People nowadays seem to
think that anyone who believes in God is a hypocrite,
trying to believe because it is more comfortable, but it
isn't so. There are many people who are not stupid

nor false who feel God close to them quite as practically as they feel the people they know close to them. I express this very badly and I don't want you to think I am influencing you—only when I am gone remember that this was the greatest *true* fact in my life. Perhaps you will come to feel one day that there may be some other life that goes on side by side with, or rather *inside*, the physical one. I feel that just now everyone is bewildered, unhappy and restless. It wasn't always so, I am sure. People will understand God one day perhaps in a new fashion when they have been unsatisfied and restless long enough.

But I didn't mean this letter to be a sermon. I only meant to thank you, again and again, for loving me so much and so long. Don't be sad if I go. Perhaps I shall be more with you than I have been. Who knows? Do you really think that our love, after all it has been through, can be killed by physical death? I am sure that it cannot. Think often of all the happy times we have had, especially in Newlands. That is our country. That is where I will always be closest to you. It has been our country for nearly two hundred years and perhaps before that. Every stone and tree there is a witness that life is worth living, however hard it is, beautiful and terrible and comic and disappointing and rewarding. Go and climb Robinson or stand by the Watendlath Tarn and think of Judith and remember old Herries in Borrowdale. I *know* that nothing is lost, that everything lives, that there is no death, whatever people say.

You will care for Sally, won't you? She is very high-spirited and determined, and I sometimes think that she is the first *fearless* Herries, the first one to rise above all the jealousy and fear and greediness that there has been so long. Perhaps the world that is coming will be full of Sallies! And give Tom all the love that you can. He will miss me, I think, more than anyone. He has such a warm heart and all his happiness is bound up in other people. Forgive me for all the times that you have thought me sentimental and stupid and slow to see things. But I know you have and will. Remember that our love isn't ended, that it will never end, that nothing can destroy it now.—Your most loving and devoted VANESSA.

If you have a chance, see poor Ellis sometimes.

END OF PART III

KALEIDOSCOPE

I

THE FLAME

THREE weeks after the outbreak of war several of the Herries family dined at Alfred's fine house in Drummond Street.

It was a kind of farewell dinner, because Tom, Maurice—Alfred's son—and Gordon—the son of Sidney and Mary Newmark—would be shortly departing for the Front. There were present Alfred himself, Benjie (who, in two days' time, was leaving for Russia), Tom, Mary Worcester (now twenty-one years of age and a frantic beauty), Rosalind (her sister), Maurice and Clara (Alfred's children), Gordon and Ada, with Sidney and Mary Newmark (their parents)—and Sally, who was not quite eleven, but was allowed to stay up on this one occasion because it might be a long time before she had dinner with Benjie and Tom again.

There were twelve of the family in all.

Dinner was finished. Tom, Maurice and Gordon, looking very young and innocent in uniform, were sipping Alfred's brandy with the quiet air of practised connoisseurs.

Alfred got up to make a speech. The Herries

family had always been rather fond of making
speeches. Alfred especially enjoyed it. He was
a practised hand at making speeches in the City
and proving in his cold, restrained voice that
everything was absolutely for the best so long as
he and his fellow-directors were in charge.

To-night, however, his voice was not quite
cold, not quite restrained. His long nose and
thin horse-like face looked down at them with a
kind of anxious tenderness, and he looked especially at Maurice, his son, whose face was round and
rosy, whose tastes were for the Arts rather than
figures, who was unlike him in everything.

And he was doing for the first time in his life,
perhaps, an artistic thing. He held in one long,
bony hand a thin, beautifully chased silver candle-
stick. Up its slender stem ran a pattern of leaves
and branches.

' I'm not going to make a long speech,' he said.
' But I must say something. Here we all are as
a family, all together, wishing one another well.
It hasn't always been so, you may remember. At
one time, in the days of our grandfathers and
grandmothers, there was some trouble, as I dare
say you know. But now we are all united, a
symbol, I like to think, of England itself—all
united to fight the greatest enemy the world has
ever known—Prussian militarism. Whatever else
you may say about our family, no one can deny
that, on the whole, we have always stood for
England's best interests. One of our ancestors
helped to defend Carlisle against Prince Charlie
and the Scots. Benjie here lost an arm in South

Africa, and in countless other ways we have backed our country. And now we are doing it again. She has never needed us as she needs us now, but because we believe she is in the right we are giving all we have, our sons, our money, our lives. Ahem! yes . . . well . . . It was Maurice's idea that we should do some little thing to-night that we should all remember when we are separated later on, and that when we remember it we should remember one another. . . . Yes . . . I have, left me by my father, a pair of old candlesticks. They belonged, I believe, to an ancestor of ours, Harcourt Herries, who lived in Cumberland in the eighteenth century, and before him to an old Elizabethan Herries who had something to do with the mines in Keswick. Well, that's past history and this is present history, and it was Maurice's idea that we should link up past and present, that we should pass this candle round, each one of us standing up in his or her turn, holding the lighted candle and wishing the rest of us good luck.

'Well . . . ahem . . . that's all, I think. Except that Sally here, the youngest, shall be the one to light it.'

It was done as he said. Sally—standing on a chair because she was so small—lit it and round it went. The electric light was switched out and round the little flame went, very clear and bright and steady. Everyone wished everyone else good luck.

It was a frosty, sparkling morning and the guns were still. Two hours after midnight there had been a fearful bombardment. On and on went that shattering malignant thunder. Then it ended. There was a perfect cloud of silence everywhere over the desolate country. Tom was ordered to see how the land, now remorselessly altered, might look. New mounds, new pits. Four or five of the raiders lay stretched out, abandoned and desolate; one a stout officer with a snub nose and part of his face gone, another a dark squat-shaped boy who lay, his head on his arm, his wide dark eyes staring at the sky. The raid had been well planned. Tom returned. The light was strengthening, but the air was thin like stretched paper and most bitterly cold. He looked out over a land that might have been trampled by dinosaurs. The country was quite deserted save for one or two snipers at the saphead. No sound anywhere, but he knew that all about him thousands of men were concealed. Desolation and silence. . . .

He went into his dug-out and began a letter to Sally.

DARLING LITTLE SALLY—I've got half an hour to myself and everything's as quiet as the top of Cat Bells. They raided us last night and for an hour or two there was a terrible din. We lost some men, I'm afraid. It's a cold and frosty morning, which is heaps better than the mud and the rain. I'm all right, feeling very well in fact. Do you remember the dinner at Alfred's when you lit the candle, and do you remember his saying that we were proud, as proper, right-minded Herries, of defending the world against Prussian Militarism? I suppose we were right at the time to feel like that, and it's still nice to think of that lighted candle going round the table, isn't it? But how long ago that all seems now, and how our point of view has altered!

I haven't had any sleep for twenty-four hours, but last time I *did* sleep I dreamt of Vanessa. It was scarcely like a dream. She seemed to be sitting beside me holding my hand and wearing the clothes she used to wear in Newlands—just as I would wake sometimes in the morning and find her sitting on my bed. Doesn't she seem *peaceful* now in all this trouble? Do you remember how calm she used to be when something went wrong, and the way she smiled? . . .

He broke off and stared in front of him, smiling at the thought of Vanessa. Then he went on:

The thing I hate most here is being sent out to reconnoitre positions and getting lost. It's awful. Perhaps it's raining, and through the mist you see lights trembling on the horizon, or you think you do. Then, out of nowhere, someone says, as though they were fearfully angry, ' Get down! ' and you find yourself in a barrage. Then you run for your life, the wet clay clinging to your legs like hands. Then you're lost again—in darkness. You go up and you go down, not knowing what is hill and what isn't. Perhaps some rifles suddenly open on you. You run and crouch, and slip and crouch and run—always lost, always alone and dirty and cold, like a nightmare after we'd eaten too much as kids.

How are you? Are you doing well at school? Remember there are the three of us—you and I and father— or four with Vanessa. Never forget Vanessa, darling, will you? Of course I know you won't. Have you heard from father in Russia? I haven't for ages. Have you seen Mary? Did you ask her to write to me? She promised to but she hasn't yet. *Don't forget this*. It's very important. Do you write to father regularly? You must, even though he seems so far away. I think he's in Galicia somewhere. Isn't this funny? It's lying on the table beside me. Someone left it:

PLEASE!

Will you help your lad at the Front and all other lads, in a very simple way, and will you give your friends the chance to help as well?

Do it Thus!

Fill in THIS POSTCARD with your name and address, and post it back to us. We will then send you a number of bookmarkers . . .

Bookmarkers! You don't know how funny that sounds here. And lads! Don't you hate the word ' lads '?

Well, darling, keep up your spirits and behave just as though everything were all right. I'm fine myself and perhaps I'll get a spot of leave soon. Don't forget to write to father and don't forget to ask Mary to write to me. Tell me what she was wearing when you saw her last. That's important.—Your most loving brother,

TOM.

The candle, stuck in a bottle with a collar of grease, flared up. The flame was bright, pure, steady, of gold.

' There's a flame! ' cried Benjie.

The Retreat had begun and with the rest of the Otriad he had been flung into the little town of O———. It was a place of dust, whirling clouds of dust, dust in your eyes and mouth and nose. This dust was blown by the wind and behind the thin spirals of it a hot sun blazed. Everywhere there was the Russian soldier, the Russian soldier apathetic like a cow but humorous and touching also. He was everywhere, in the streets, on the dirty staircases, crowding the tumbled untidy rooms; the Russian soldier and the dust.

' I never want to see either of them again,' thought Benjie.

But he had cried out at the sudden flame. It was evening and, after the dust-storms and the hot malignant sun, the pale blue of the sky and the cool air were friendly. The members of the Otriad were lying or walking or sitting in the half-ruined building into which Molozov, their chief, had turned them. Benjie found this place intolerable. It was a long room with a naked gleaming floor and an apparently endless succession of looking-glasses. This gleaming empty reflection was broken with an infernal clatter through the open window of horses, soldiers and carts that rattled on the cobbles. There was a smell everywhere of dust and dung.

He went to see if he could be of any use with the wounded. Going out originally in August 1914 with two journalists who were friends of his, he kicked his heels in Moscow for some weary months and at last only found adventure by joining, after a week or two in a Moscow hospital, a Red Cross unit attached to the Ninth Army. They had been sent to Galicia and, after some apparent victories, had begun a retreat. He would never forget the moment of that change of fortune. He and several soldiers had gone, under the charge of a rather feckless Englishman called Trenchard, to the forest to bury the dead. This was not his own Otriad. He had come over

z

with two of his own unit to pay this Otriad a visit.
It had been pleasant to find another Englishman
here, although no two men could have been found
more different than Benjie with his short thick
figure, his off-hand but commanding independent
personality, and this untidy, seemingly foolish
Englishman who would wander about singing
' Early One Morning ' in a cracked voice or,
quite unexpectedly, looking so wretched that you
thought he would burst into tears.   Benjie was
told that he had been engaged to a pretty, charming nurse in his Otriad who had thrown him over.

Benjie was to return that same evening to his
own Otriad.   But he did not.   Under the trees
of the forest he was looking at a dead man—a man
who had been dead some three weeks perhaps.
This man was all right until you came to his face.
His strong blue-grey trousers were in splendid
condition and he had good stout boots.   Out of
the top of one boot a tin spoon protruded.   But he
had no face, only a grinning skull, and in and out
of the mouth and eye-sockets little black creatures
like ants were crawling.   It was all very peaceful
there.   The sanitars began to dig a grave.   Some
quietly smoked cigarettes.   Then a sanitar observed
that the bursting of the shrapnel that had been
dim and distant all day now sounded much closer.
That was the beginning of the Retreat. . . .

But it was at the town of O—— that he saw
the sudden flame.   He had been for nearly a
week now with this Otriad that was not his own.
He had begun to know them all—Molozov, the
stocky square-shouldered Chief who would say

over and over again: ' There's no method . . .
no system . . . nothing at all. . . . By God,
there's a pretty girl! ' Nikitin, a doctor who had
a charming intellectual face; a surgeon, Alexei
Petrovitch Semyonov, a striking-looking fellow,
very thick-set and muscular with a strange square-
cut beard of so fair a colour that in some lights
it seemed almost white. A man of very strong
personality and great self-confidence. There was
the pretty Sister, Marie Ivanovna, and the feckless
untidy Englishman, Trenchard. He made friends
with them and liked them, but they were nevertheless all shadows on a screen to him who had
his constant, secret preoccupations.

He found work to do in the vast room at
O——. This was a strange place. It had been
the theatre of the town. It was lit now with
candles stuck into bottles, and in this dim and
wavering light the doctors did their work. The
busy silence was broken with patient plaintive
cries of ' *Oh, Steritza! Oh, Steritza!* ' or ' *Borjé
moi! Borjé moi!* ' and then the sharp official
questions, ' What regiment? What division?
Shrapnel or bullet? '

And across the stage at the back of the room
was still hanging, wavering in the draught, the
painted backcloth of some old play. This amused
Benjie by its incongruity, for there was a picture
of a market-place in a town all very gaily painted,
and down the marble stairs flower-girls with legs
like bolsters came merrily tripping while soldiers
in scarlet and blue drank with their girls at little
tables.

Meanwhile the real soldiers cried out in their agony ' Oh! Oh! Oh! . . . *Oh! Borjé moi . . . Borjé moi!* ' as Nikitin and Semyonov probed for bullets under the uncertain flame of the candles, and a soldier in delirium sang a song about gathering the corn, in a shrill broken voice.

The dominating square-bearded man, Semyonov, had stopped his work for a moment and stood, his arms folded, looking on, beside Benjie.

' You seem to stand this pretty well,' he said. ' If it isn't impertinent—how old are you? '

' Just gone sixty,' said Benjie.

' Yes.   You look fit.   Lose your arm in this War? '

' No.   In the Boer War.'

' Bad luck.'

' Oh, I'm used to it.'

' What do you think of us—the Russians, I mean? ' Semyonov asked.

' Oh, you're plucky — marvellous.   I never saw such courage.   But you're a bit muddled high up, aren't you? '

' Yes.   Hopeless.   Everyone's robbing and cheating and spying and betraying.   It's a mess of a war altogether.   When do you think it will end? '

' Never, I should think,' said Benjie.

' I agree.   Why don't you people do something on the other Front? '

' We're doing our best, I believe,' said Benjie.

' I believe you are.   But they're beginning to be impatient over here.'   He turned angrily, and Benjie thought he had never seen a more de-

termined aggressive profile. ' There's that bloody
fellow-countryman of yours messing things up
again. Never saw a more useless fellow in my
life.'

' Oh, you mean Trenchard,' Benjie said.

' Yes. I wish to God he'd get back to his own
country.'

It was then that a candle, close at Benjie's
elbow, flared. It was low down in its socket. In
the spurt of light Benjie thought that he saw
Vanessa. She stood quietly there, smiling at
Trenchard, who was nervously bandaging the
knee of a large patient-eyed soldier. She smiled
at him, then turned her eyes to Benjie's. They
drank in one another's happiness. Oh! how glad
he was to see her again! But she was not there.
Only the flame, bright, pure, steady.

And Sally, seeing it, said to Mary Worcester:
' Look, Mary! That light in the sky! '

Sally and Mary were looking out from behind
the blinds in Cynthia's house in Eaton Place.
Cynthia had taken the house six months ago. It
was small, compact, could be worked with four
servants. Everyone must make sacrifices now.

Ellis had died two months after Vanessa. He
had been lost, bewildered; he had cried a great
deal and would sit for hours, his knees hunched
up, staring like an old sick monkey at the closed
piano. They had found him there one morning
huddled up in the chair dead. So had passed away
the son of Will's old age and great hopes.

After his death Sally had gone to live with her

father and Tom, and then, when war broke out,
Cynthia had taken her. Although she was now,
at the beginning of 1916, over twelve years of age,
she did not grow. She did not herself mind.

' I'm like my great-grandmother. She didn't
grow, but nobody cared.'

She never worried in the least about her own
personal appearance, as, in fact, her great-grandmother had done. How many, many times Judith
Paris had wished that her legs were longer, but
Sally Herries didn't care a damn!

She was, Mary thought, regrettably tomboyish.
She didn't care how she looked, how she sat, what
clothes she wore. She might be made to look
rather striking with her brown hair and pale
face. She said she simply could not bother.
She was, at her present stage, direct and honest
to a terrible degree. Loyal and warm-hearted,
if she liked anyone. Unfortunately she did
not like Mary nor did Mary like her. Mary
considered that Sally was envious of her great
beauty and, further, that she was jealous of her
because her adored Tom thought Mary a queen
and a goddess.

In the first of these there was no truth at all.
Sally *did* think Mary the most beautiful woman
in the world. She also thought her the coldest
and most selfish, and for this last reason she resented Tom's quite hopeless passion. For Mary
would never dream of marrying a poor journalist
like Tom. She was extremely ambitious. On
the other hand, she was neither so cold nor so
hard-hearted as Sally supposed her. The true

basic reason for Sally's dislike of Mary, however, was that Mary had no feeling about Vanessa. Vanessa was the principal abiding fact in Sally's life. There never had been, there never would be again, anyone like Sally's mother. Sally was neither sentimental nor gushing, but deep in her nature lived intense emotion. All this, as yet, was given to the memory of her mother. She adored Tom, she liked her father, but they also were part of Vanessa.

Now, for Mary, when someone was dead someone was dead. Moreover, she had not seen Vanessa very often and remembered her only as a large rather calm lady with a broad white forehead and grey hair parted in an old-fashioned way. Also Vanessa had lived with a man not her husband and of this Sally was the result. Mary was conventional. She liked people to do the proper things. So why *should* she be passionate about Vanessa? Twice she had spoken rather slightingly to Sally about her mother—only in joke of course, but Mary's sense of humour was not very delicate. She was neither witty nor quick-witted. Like other beautiful women, her beauty was all she needed.

But, ironically, she had, if she had known it, something of the beauty that Vanessa had had as a young woman. She was tall, dark, full-breasted. She had been told that she carried herself like a queen and never forgot it. It was her tragedy, perhaps, that she was moving into an age when carrying yourself like a queen would be no longer an asset.

Sally knelt on a chair beside Mary and stared, from behind the blind, at a dark and dead London. No light showed anywhere. Only on the horizon there had flashed a sudden finger of light.

' A flame in the sky! ' Sally cried.

' It's a searchlight,' said Mary.

Rosalind, a plain-faced, good-natured girl, was seated at the table within the room, knitting. They had all been knitting, making chest-pro-tectors. The Ladies' Committee for which they worked wanted body-belts, Warleigh leggings, gas-masks, pneumonia-jackets and operation-shirts. Sally hated to knit and so did Mary. Rosalind enjoyed it.

' Take care you don't show any light,' she said mildly, for the penalty of failing to conform was actually One Hundred Pounds or six months' imprisonment. People were making blinds from old curtains and women's skirts.

' Oh, that's all right! ' Sally came back to the table. ' I suppose I must do my beastly algebra. Oh dear, there's never any peace these days! '

At first the War had been fun, then it had been a bore, now it was rather terrible. Many girls at school had lost their fathers and brothers, and when it came to your best friend (whose name was Charlotte Greene) having to leave because her father was killed and there was no money in the family any more — why, then you positively realised it. Tom had been home on leave twice, and last time he had been pale-faced, nervous and oddly silent. But the worst was Maurice, Alfred's son, who, two nights before he went back, alone with Sally in his father's dining-room had, quite unexpectedly, burst into tears. He had been joking but a moment before.

'I don't want to go back! I don't want to go back!' he had cried.

Sally had plenty of common sense. She never lost her head, but if at that moment it had been suggested that she should return to France instead of Maurice, she would at once have agreed to go.

She stood by the table thinking of her father (so far away in Russia, with only his one arm), of Tom who wrote her such splendid letters, of poor Maurice and of Gordon Newmark, who did not seem to mind a bit and had won the D.S.O. Standing there, thinking, it seemed to Sally as though, across a dark stretch of water, there was a black marshy land and down its length spread a vast scaly dragon, flame issuing from its jaws.

'You funny little thing!' said Mary, who, drawn to her full height, was looking very beautiful in front of the blind. 'What are you thinking about?'

But Sally pushed past her and, on the other side of the blind, stared into the dark. Even as she looked a flame of light shot up into the sky.

'*That* was a flash!' said Maurice Herries.

This was from one of the gas-projectors from the hill behind them. They were hurling opened cylinders of gas on to the enemy position some thousand yards away. Maurice shivered. Time

was short. He ordered the morning rum issue
to be taken round the platoons.   Then suddenly
there began a procession of ' whizz-bangs.'

Maurice stood there wishing that he might
' stop one ' before he had to go over the top.   It
was that cold, terrifying moment half an hour
before the dawn when everything is clear and un-
mistakable like hell.   ' In another forty minutes
I may be dead.   In another forty minutes I may
be sticking my bayonet into a Boche's belly, deep,
deep, as though into butter.   In forty minutes
I may be mad with pain, my sight gone, my body
crippled for life. . . .'

Many men did not think of those things.
Maurice was a poet.   He thought Shakespeare,
Blake and Gerard Manley Hopkins the three
greatest men in the world.   He loathed the mud
and the filth and the smells and Berkley Cannon,
his best friend, dying in his arms, and he loved
the comradeship, the good-humour, the courage,
the friendly simplicity of common men, the
moments of ecstasy . . . and he hated this pause
before action, hated it as he had never hated anything in his life before.

He wondered whether a Boche attack had
forestalled their own.   ' Perhaps they have learned
our plans and will shatter our huddled groups
before we leave our lines.'

Then the flame!   It stabbed the sky.   First
the roar was one blow as on a great sheet of iron,
then after a pause another, then a pause again and
another.   Then one continuous throbbing thunder.
The shells screamed and a pillar of fire leaned up

the wall of the dim uncertain sky. ' Our barrage,'
Maurice thought.   ' Zero hour.'

Maurice shouted to his little group, they
jumped out of the trench and stumbled forward.   Now came the moment that he always
dreaded, when the group broke and one straggled
forward singly, one little mannikin in a world of
malignant danger.   Through the noise as of
cannon-balls rolling down sheets of iron, there
was the phut! phut! of rifle bullets.   And there
to the right are heads of Boches in a shell-hole
shooting.   Trotter, a giant of a man, one of the
jolliest, most care-free and kindest, staggers, seems
to leap on his feet, crashes down.   ' No, there is
no chance for us tumbling through this mud with
those fellows shooting at us,' and he and Conklin,
Bush and two others have slithered down into a
shell-hole and are firing over the top of it.   Conklin's face is smashed in.   We have got two of the
Boches but more are running up.   The sky is
lightening, and the roar of the guns, and now the
German guns, thunders on—but by this time it
is familiar, belonging to a world that one knows,
that is part of one, that is almost friendly.

Then Maurice ' stopped one.'   There was an
impact on his right shoulder as though a big stone
had hit him.   No pain.   He slipped down into
the bottom of the shell-hole and, staring upwards,
was aware now that the sky was much lighter and,
to his great surprise, that he was alone there except for Conklin who, his smashed face in the
mud, huddled at his feet.   His shoulder, his arm,
his hand were soaking wet, but still there was no

pain. He did not want to move. He was quite happy. A faint, a very faint blue was stealing into the sky, and some small clouds, like rosy petals, seemed to his eye to be dancing, gently and carefully, against the blue.

The thundering noise withdrew, and in front of his eyes, which he soon must close, a small and delicate flame wavered. The flame of the candle that Sally had lit! He smiled. He would write a poem about it, this small candle-flame that neither the wind of the great guns nor the delicate fleeciness of the morning clouds could put out. Pity that his father hated him to write poetry, thought all books a mistake, wanted him to add up sums in the City. He would never add up sums, but he would write poems to the glory of England as Rupert Brooke had done, or about old ships like Flecker. . . . He would carry on the glory of the Family, would go and live in Cumberland, near the sea, in the valleys of which old Benjie Herries had told him. A face bent close to his. Someone moved him and a flame of pain licked his heart. He cried out and the flame moved up, spreading, glorious, golden, blotting out, with its light, the whole world. There were two flames. . . .

The two flames burnt steadily, illuminating the mirror, lighting the dressing-table, the pictures on the walls, of ' Queen Victoria receiving the News of her Accession ' and ' Dignity and Impudence,' the narrow bed and the small shining table beside it.

'The electric light's fused,' said Gordon Newmark, looking in at the door.

'I know,' said Tom. 'I've found some candles.' He sat in front of the mirror, brushing his hair with his two old battered silver brushes.

'Hurry up, you blighter,' Gordon said.

'All right. I won't be a minute.'

Gordon Newmark was broad and tall and the pink of self-confidence. Tom seemed gentle, small, submissive beside him. Tom was thirty-two and Gordon twenty-one, but Gordon had won the D.S.O., loved the War—'best time I'm ever likely to have, old boy'—and was home now on leave as a kind of conqueror, patronising, in a jolly friendly way, all the family, especially his old father and mother and his sister Ada, who all adored him. He was, if he had known it, the re-current Herries type, the type of old Pomfret, of Prosper—Jennifer's father, of Rodney—Cynthia's grandfather, and especially of Walter—Tom's great-grandfather. But he didn't know it. He didn't care. He was the triumphant, riding, roughshod, bullying Herries. But the type had softened, emasculated a bit. He thought old Benjie a dissolute old rogue and Tom a 'soft 'un' and Maurice Herries 'a decent sort of ass who writes poems'; his type was as far from the other as ever, in the family history, it had been, but the two did not quarrel any more. Life was beginning to move too swiftly: you had too much to do to bother about quarrels. The Herries didn't fight any more. But Gordon felt, all the same, a sort

of friendly scorn as he saw Tom struggling into
his clothes. Under the light of the candles Tom's
face was serious, careworn, too kindly to be aggressive. ' That's all he'll ever be,' Gordon thought,
' a sort of second-rate journalist. Thinks too
much about other people. Almost a woman—
about his old father, his kid sister, his father's
mistress who died. I'd worry! ' thought Gordon,
who hoped that night to pick up a pretty girl
somewhere . . . you needn't be too particular
these days when you'd be returning in a week's
time to be killed maybe. . . . But Tom didn't
want a girl. He was sweet on Mary Worcester.
Poor old Tom! He hadn't a dog's chance with
that beautiful swollen-headed female!

Tom blew out the candles. They groped their
way down the dark staircase. Tom still stuck to
the rooms in Tite Street. In the dark King's
Road they found a taxi, and through a town of
pitch they plunged until the friendly arms of the
Carlton Grill received them. Then they went to
the Alhambra to see *The Bing Boys* for the twentieth
time, sang ' If you were the only girl in the world '
with other of their slightly intoxicated fellows and
roared at George Robey whenever he lifted his
eyebrows.

Afterwards they found a dingy door in Soho
and behind it a yet dingier night-club known as
' The Five Pennies.' Tom had not wanted to go.
' Leave ' was offering no attractions. He wanted
to be back in France, although he didn't like that
either. Mary tortured him. She liked him, he
thought. Sometimes he fancied that she more

than liked him, but he knew in his heart that he
had no chance with her, and knowing it loved her
only the more desperately. He had loved her
always. He was chaste, having had no sexual experience whatever, and this chastity seemed, just
now, to separate him from everybody. Men, all
men, seemed to be caught into a passionate longing for sexual intercourse—any intercourse with
anyone. . . . It was a hunger, the only solace
for the filth, the fear, the cold, the wounds, the
long-drawn-out tension of this fantastic trial. And
he? He thought always of Vanessa and of Mary.
Of his father and Sally and his friends as well,
but Vanessa and Mary were always with him,
one the kindest, gentlest, most understanding of
mothers, the other the loveliest, divinest of goddesses. And he could touch neither: one was a
ghost, the other a dream. . . .

As he sat in the small, fearfully hot and in-
decently smelling room of ' The Five Pennies '
he screwed his courage to the sticking-point. His
life seemed just now to be running on hard lines,
but it was worse for others. Worse for poor
Maurice, for instance, who had lost his arm,
worse for hundreds, for thousands of fine men.
He would stick it, but he wished that he had
Gordon's hardy indifference—Gordon who was,
at this moment, talking to two women with a care-
free gaiety that made him seem the only really
happy person in the room. A girl came and sat
beside Tom. He ordered her a drink; drink
was being served in coffee-cups. He watched
Gordon a little anxiously. He knew that these

places just now were haunted by ' crows,' women who made their men friends drunk, took them on somewhere and robbed them of everything they had. But Gordon was no fool. He knew a thing or two.

The girl at Tom's table was tired. She complained, through the raucous jazz music, in a weary little voice, of the violence and callousness of men. Men didn't seem to care. They weren't kind any more. Generous, yes, but not kind. Life wasn't really gay, although everyone pretended that it was. Food was awful. Why, fancy, eggs were a luxury food. Fancy eggs being a luxury! Butter was half a crown a pound and a chicken cost thirteen bob! Why, fancy a chicken costing . . . So she went on, repeating everything twice.

Suddenly, into the middle of the jazz, the laughter, the movement of the dancers, a voice broke. A tall swaying officer had pushed into the middle of the floor, he was brushing the dancers aside. He was drunk, of course. And he cried out in a shrill scream:

' Blast this bloody war! Blast this bloody war! To hell with it! Blast this bloody war! To hell with the bloody war! To hell . . .'

Two waiters caught hold of him and led him away. People laughed.

' You see,' said the girl. ' That's just what I say. What I mean to say is that nobody really enjoys things much. And they aren't kind any more. If you were a woman you'd agree with me. And the women aren't kind either. What

I mean to say is, it's affected everybody, and how we're ever to get back to the way we were——'

'We'll never get back,' said Tom.

He was watching a man near him who held up, with a rather unsteady hand, a lighter. He pushed at his cigarette with it. The little flame burnt bravely, with a fine uprightness. Then it went out.

KALEIDOSCOPE

II

Triumphal Arch

In the early days of 1917 Sally Herries had a strange experience. It was at Cynthia's house in Eaton Place.

Altogether life was strange at this time, strange and yet familiar. Sally was over thirteen years of age, went to school every day, did on the whole what she was told, was calm and quiet and collected, but suffered, at unexpected moments, extraordinary and poignant longings for her mother—also, but less poignantly, for her father and for Tom.

She had only a few friends, but in this dark uncertain world that now surrounded everyone friendships were not important. Some of the girls at school she liked, but they had all now their own especial interests—the ways in which they were helping the War, brothers, fathers at the Front, food that had become important because it was rationed, the personal experiences of air-raids or the second-hand experiences of emotionalists, rumour and story and gossip; it seemed that all these things kept one apart from the ordinary relationships of

ordinary life. Sally did not care. At Eaton
Place she was quite alone. Mary and Rosalind
were too old, Peile a silly (but kindly) old man,
Cynthia infinitely distant.

But *how* fantastic a world it was! That
moment after dusk when all the world was dark,
the first experience of an air-raid with the alarm,
the silence, the distant firing, the expectancy (not
at all frightening—pleasurable, like being at the
theatre just before the curtain went up), the
rumours, the stories that people told, the anxieties
about Tom, about Gordon, the many women
wearing black, the tales that reached even her
ears of the funny ways that soldiers and their girl-
friends had in places like Trafalgar Square after
dark. . . .

She was aware that her family was behaving
very finely. She herself caught some of the
family pride. It was really true, she felt, that but
for her family England and the War would be lost.
When she went to other people's houses—the
houses of the parents of her friends—she heard
many very despairing remarks. It would make
no difference, they said, that America had severed
diplomatic relations with Germany. America
would not be able to be in time, we would all
be defeated before America could do anything.
Someone told a story about going into a tear-shell
factory and weeping tears enough to fill a jug.
People recounted horrible details of wounds and
suffering and lonely agonies. Sally tried not to
listen but she *had* to. . . . Her imagination was
vivid. She saw these dreadful things as though

they were happening in front of her.   She grew
older very quickly.   People said that we were
bound to be beaten.   All the glory was gone.   We
were led by idiotic Generals, our politicians were
impossible fools.   People said that it would be
better if we made terms with the Germans.   Let
them have the glory!

'Oh no!' Sally cried out in the house of kind
Mrs. Mickleham, the mother of Connie Mickleham who was so clever at algebra.   'That would
be wicked!'   And for once she burst into tears
and ran from the room.

But *inside* the family it was *all* quite different.
No one dreamt of anything but complete victory.
We would go on for ever and ever but victory
must certainly be ours.

It was now that the Herries were seen at their
very best.   Their normality, their common sense,
the absence of *grab* in their natures, their non-
property qualities, so to speak, their courage, their
indifference to facts that they refused to realise,
enabled them to become completely patriotic.
They loved their country because their country
depended on them and while *they* were there all
must be well.

Maurice came home without an arm and sat,
with a white face, staring into distance.   They
were sorry for him but disregarded him.   Gordon
came home, filled with the War.   It was glorious.
When the Americans came in we would soon
sweep the dirty Boche back to Berlin.   He
had extraordinary stories about the dirtiness of
the Boche, his meanness, cruelty, cowardice and

savagery. The Herries on one side, the Germans on the other. Who could doubt of the result?

It was on one March evening that Sally had her funny little adventure.

She had been doing her school work in her cold little room at the top of the house and remembered that her geography book was in the dining-room. She came downstairs for it. The house was still and plunged into that eerie dusk that seemed now to be always the atmosphere of rooms and passages. She reached the hall that had only a light at the farthest end, near the kitchen stairs. She walked forward to the dining-room door and saw that a man was hiding, close up against the wall, behind the umbrella-stand. He was a little man with spectacles, a rather dirty face, and he was in uniform. As she saw him he whispered, but without moving from the wall to which he seemed to be fastened, ' If yer say a word I'll throttle yer.'

It was all part of the general strangeness, the half-light, the silent streets, the sense of the War, prowling like a large cat almost at one's very door, of Benjie somewhere in Russia, of Tom underground in France eating plum and apple jam to the light of a single candle, of that man weeping a bucket of tears in the factory, of Maurice without an arm, that this little man should be pinned against the wall of the house in Eaton Place.

She saw that he was very frightened and she wanted to give him something. She gave him half a crown that she was saving to buy something for Tom with.

He said, 'Gawd bless yer, Miss,' and in another moment had opened the hall-door and slipped away, letting into the house a blast of cold biting air before the door closed. She stood there wondering. What had he wanted? Had he come to steal? He looked very unhappy. He was a piece of the War. She had encountered the War. She continued quickly to grow up.

Her father, crossing a small snow-covered square in Petrograd, heard a strange sound. He was walking with a little black-bearded Jew, Konrad Mathias. Mathias had just said: 'It is between personality and non-personality. Everything comes down to that. Am I, Konrad Mathias, an individual with a history, an important history like no one else's, or am I a little gas, a little acid, a little water, dissipated at the prick of a pin . . .? Do you see? Am I Konrad Mathias? Am I? Am I?'

'I should think you probably are,' Benjie had said, looking at a church dome, a brilliant green against the burning blue of the sky. The snow sparkled at his feet. 'I like this,' he said. 'The green, the blue, the sparkling snow. It stirs me— not the acid and water in me, I think. Or is it?'

'No, no!' Little Mathias, in his black woolly fur cap, jumped on the snow.

'Well, I don't know,' Benjie said. 'The individual can't be very important. If the world goes topsy-turvy the individual starves and is very

quickly gas and water again. There's a revolution in South America and Mr. Smith in London
loses his job. His child dies because it hasn't
enough nourishment. It's the revolution that
matters. Certainly not Mr. Smith.'

' Oh, you're wrong,' Mathias cried. ' What if
he does lose his job? He's losing it or gaining it
all the time. Everyone in a lifetime meets his
personal crisis whether there's a revolution or not.
Birth, love, death, economic struggle, falling out
of love with one's wife, seeing a pretty girl round
the corner, having a suspicion there's a God, then
deciding there isn't. Always the same crisis turning up for everybody. The hoops of the circus—
you must jump through them. That's fate. The
way you jump. That's free-will and is the only
thing that matters. It's the individual who is
always different. How will you meet this? A
toothache, syphilis, cancer, a sudden bit of success.
That's history.'

' Then you believe in God? '

' Of course I do. Only He doesn't interfere.
He sets the scene. You play your part. I've
been about the world a lot. It's everywhere the
same. Are you a realist or a romantic? If you're
the first it will be the dates, the scientific facts, the
large movements, the cold truth that will seem to
you to be important. If you're the second it will
be the things behind the facts—what each man
does with his soul.'

' You think man has a soul? '

' A spiritual life? Of course. It's the only
thing that squares the facts.'

' Is there a life after death, do you think? '
Benjie asked more eagerly than he had intended.

' Life? Death? There's always death. Every
man is living and dying all the time. But *physical*
death—that's not important. Men are so thought-
less. And they worry about the wrong things.'

' So you think the old world is finished? '

' Of course it is. And the new one will take
a long while settling itself. But that doesn't
matter. Men will have their personal histories
just the same. Why, take myself! I'm fifty-
five—a Jew of no importance whatever. But I
was afraid for years, afraid of everything and
everyone. Thought people despised me. And
I was greedy too. Now I'm not often afraid and
not greedy. That's more important than a
revolution. Not because I'm important, mind
you—no more and no less than the next man—
but it's important to God that I should get a move
on. More important than that Napoleon should
win Austerlitz or Rasputin be murdered.'

' But Rasputin's death has affected millions.'

' No. Only provided situations for men to
meet. They'd meet them in one fashion or
another in any case.'

It was then that Benjie heard the noise. It
was like the sharp cracking of twigs. The scene
was very peaceful. At the end of the square was
the canal and along the side of it a cab was slowly
crawling, the *isvostchik*, in his fat clothes, bunched
up on the seat. Some birds flew slowly across
the blue. Some church bells were ringing. It
was about three in the afternoon.

A moment later it was as though the blue sky had burst and poured confusion on to the earth. Down the path by the canal a mob of people, shouting, crying, came pouring, and on to the square from the other end rolled a lorry, piled high with soldiers, bristling with rifles. The lorry stayed still. A man came running from the canal. He ran a little way into the square, outlined very sharply against the snow. He stopped and looked back at the people. Then from the lorry there came a noise like the clearing of a throat, and the man ran a step, stood, crumpled at the knees, fell, raised himself, fell flat, wriggled like a worm and lay still.

Benjie had known many bad moments in his life but none so bad as this one—for there he was, isolated, alone in all that gleaming, glittering colour. He must run for miles, it seemed, before he could reach security. But Mathias was already running. An absurd notion came to Benjie that it would be undignified to run. He walked slowly, his hand in his pocket. But now many people were running into the square, and as they did so a red light rose like a fan above the houses and spread into the blue.

He walked slowly and as he went repeated to himself like a man in a dream, aloud: ' This is Revolution. This is Revolution.' Then he saw the square flooded with people. They were shouting: ' To the Nevski!' ' No, no, to the Duma!' He was carried with the crowd. . . .

And it was now September. Tom on leave,

walking down Piccadilly, heard the air-raid warning. Instinctively he hurried his step and then slowed down again. For what did it matter?

He had come from half an hour with the lovely Mary. On his way there he had thought: ' Well, now, to-night I'll ask her. She will be sorry for me, perhaps, moved because next week I return to France. She will think " Oh, poor boy." And she will be kind.' As he had walked towards Eaton Place his love—that had been part of him for so long now, that had gained so terribly in intensity out there where every homeward vision shone with a mystical light—his love had dried and constricted his heart so that it was a shrivelling little ball in his body. Away, beyond the houses, not far distant, somewhere hanging in the pale September sky was his hope. He would say:

' Mary, I have loved you so long. Let me go back with just this to remember! I may not return. Be kind to me.' A weak, cowardly sort of prayer, but he was beyond all pride now. He wanted her so. His thoughts were lascivious and pure, of the body and the soul, all things together. Oh! if she would only be kind!

And she had been kind—kind and abstracted. Her eyes had rested on him without seeing him, and then she had been suddenly aware that she must do something about this poor man who had loved her since she was a child and was so good and patient and so tiresome. And next week he would return to France and would suffer horrors, perhaps, would be frightened and tired and lonely.

Comprehension came into her eyes. She saw

Tom. She wanted to be good to him. She asked him questions about the Front.

But he knew that it was only kindness. He refused a second cup of tea and went.

So he did not mind now if there were an air-raid. The omnibuses seemed to hasten, and soon, as he neared the Circus, the streets were quite empty. This was the week when there were almost daily air-raids. They said that people's nerves were beginning to go, and Tom remembered how a friend had told him that, two nights ago, he had walked down a street in Pimlico during a raid and that it had been naked, empty, shining, but that behind every window people were playing pianos.

No pianos here. Nothing but the Circus, bare as though set for a scene in a theatre. The firing came nearer and flashes lit the sky. Light hit the Circus and sprang away. But nothing happened. The all-clear sounded. He went on a bus back to Chelsea.

During the remaining days of his leave he found that he could endure no one but Sally. For the first time he was afraid that his nerve was breaking. He was so *tired* of it—sick to death of it all, he was. And worst was the chatter. He lunched with Alfred and listened to Gordon. He lunched with Cynthia and listened to poor old Peile. He heard that Sir Henry Wilson was sold to the French, that £100,000,000 had been spent on gas, that German cruisers were lying off Harwich, that . . . Oh, what did it matter? Everything was unreal now. Life itself was unreal, the physical processes of the body, the putting on of a collar, brushing one's teeth. . . .

He went to entertainments, heard Beecham conduct *Figaro*, saw a farce, was made miserable by a musical comedy. All these were unreal.

But Sally was real. He had always loved her with that patient, unchanging, unfaltering devotion that was so especially his. He delighted in the growth that he saw in her. Although she was so young she had great common sense, courage and much humour. And, in one way or another, she constantly reminded him of Vanessa. She had Vanessa's integrity.

On the last evening before his return they talked.

' I wish I was going with you, Tom,' Sally said.

' Do you? ' he laughed. ' You wouldn't like it.'

' No, of course I shouldn't. The girls at school all wanted to go once, were dying for the time when they'd be grown-up enough to be nurses or something, but now they're not so keen. I don't want to go for any adventurous reason. Only to help.'

' You do help,' he said, ' by staying quietly here and being good-humoured and patient.'

' How long do you think it will last, Tom? '

' Oh, I don't know.' He was holding her small but strong hand in his. ' I've given up prophesying.'

' Do you think that after all we may be beaten? ' Her voice sank into an awed whisper.

' No. The Germans won't last as long as we will—not now the Americans have come in.'

' Yes—but the Russians won't fight any more now, will they? '   She seemed to be looking into great distances.   ' I wonder how Daddy is? '

' Oh, he'll be all right wherever he is,' said Tom.

· ' When I grow up I hope I shan't forget all I feel now. Don't you, Tom? It would be awful if when we're older we all forgot how horrid it all is and let there be another war.'

She sat on the edge of his chair and put her arms round his neck.

She produced a present, a scarf that she had knitted.

' It isn't very good.   I'm not clever with my fingers and, to tell you the truth, I'd have hated the bother if it had been for anyone else.'

So he went back again, trying not to think of Mary. But he didn't think of anyone much. He was terribly tired, not in the body but in the head. And he dreaded the noise. It would be almost better to be dead, because then at least there would be quiet.

And Maurice, the son of Alfred, the son of Amery (thin-legged, dyspeptic, high-stocked, over-large Adam's apple), the son of Durward (of Rocklington Hall; stout, plethoric, fine calves), the son of Pelham (stubborn, hot-tempered), the son of Grandison (exceedingly stout, dewlapped like a bull, intimate with St. John), son of Robert (stout, good-natured sot, gambler and humorist, a friend of Charles II.), son of Robert who first brought distinction on the family by breeding bullocks in

Wiltshire and marrying a Scottish heiress—(he was son of the Herries who came to watch German miners in Borrowdale in his Queen's service, that cross-grained bitter fellow whose portrait hung in the Herries house in Rosthwaite and later at the Fortress)—well, what of Maurice?

Not very much. ' A poor reward for all the trouble I've taken,' his father would think, looking at him. ' What if he *has* lost an arm? So have lots of other fellows, and worse, blinded, tubes in their stomach, mice in the brain—and there he sits, doing nothing but stare or read or listen to high-class music on the gramophone. Can hardly believe he's my son. Rotten pessimist too. No patriotism. I believe he likes the Germans better than the English.'

So Alfred told him one day at lunch:

' My God, Maurice, I believe you'd rather be a German than an Englishman.'

Maurice gave him a queer look.

' I'd rather be anything than a Herries,' he said.

For by this time in the spring of 1918 he was very, very tired of his family. It was May and the Billing-Maud Allan case was amusing everyone at the Courts. That the case was poisonously hysterical startled nobody. The Family—Alfred, Gordon, Cynthia—alluded darkly to perversion. ' We must sweep these abnormalities from our national life,' wheezed old Horace. ' It's a splendid thing for England that this cancer should be revealed.' But he confided privately to Maurice: ' I know what you're feeling, my boy. To tell you

the truth, I'm not as optimistic as I used to be.
But one has to put a brave face on things.'

' Why? ' asked Maurice.

Horace didn't exactly know. He supposed
that he had always been determined to see the
bright side of things. All his life it had been the
same. After all it wasn't life that was important
but the way that you dealt with it. Some writer
had said that somewhere, and he thought that it
was very true. He wheezed in his chair (his
heart was bad) and looked bravely, through
rheumy eyes, into Maurice's face.

' I've been laughed at all my life,' he said.
' I've wanted people to like me and they've only
laughed at me. I've thought I've done my best,
but I can see now that I've failed. My sister
went on the streets and died there, and everyone's
found me a bore.' He sat there; a thick heavy
tear trickled on to his fat cheek and stayed there.
He brushed it away.

' All the same,' he said, ' even if I've made a
mess of things, what I say is true all the same.
It's better to be cheerful and it needs a lot of
obstinacy. Cheer up, Maurice. You might have
lost both your legs, you know.'

But Maurice couldn't cheer up. His father,
his sister, all the Herries save little Sally, drove
him mad. He thought perhaps that he was going
mad. There were times when the guns sounded
so loudly in his ears that he could hear nothing
else. He would sit in his bedroom and try to
read Joyce or T. S. Eliot or D. H. Lawrence.
Beautiful, wonderful things their books had in

them. They told the truth at last. For centuries writers had been lying about life, but now no honest writer need ever deceive again. Lawrence seemed to him a kind of young god, fighting all the hypocrisies, the prejudices, the falsities of mankind, and fighting all alone, his back to the wall. He had been persecuted by the damned interfering authorities simply because he protested against this bloody war. And then, when Maurice thought of the authorities (he saw them as a fat, red-tabbed crimson-faced officer screaming at some trembling private . . .), he would get up and walk about his room, and the stump of his arm would ache and the guns would sound in his ears and strange fierce lights would flash over the dressing-table and crimson the eiderdown on his bed.

There came a night when he thought that he would end it. He woke at an early hour of grey dawn and a voice said, quite clearly, in his ear: ' Come on. Put an end to this. You've had enough of it. You're never going to be any good at anything. Never. Life is endless.'

So, as though obedient to a command, he got out of bed and wondered what he would do. Should he go down to the kitchen and turn on the gas? That seemed a long business and would need a lot of arranging. He had a pen-knife. Should he cut an artery? A messy affair. Should he throw himself from his bedroom window? That might not finish him. He walked up and down, followed, it seemed to him, by this persuasive voice.

' Go on, you're no good. You're spoilt and finished. Better get out of it. . . .'

At last he sat down in the chair by the ash-strewn fire and burst into tears. He cried and cried as though he never would stop. Then he fell asleep in the chair where he was.

A poor affair. Nothing fine about it anywhere. He had a job those last months in the Ministry of Information and so he walked, alone and unattended save by his private demon, from one place to another. . . .

About half-past ten on Monday morning, November 11, Benjie went into Hatchard's bookshop. While waiting there he was accosted by a stout pale-faced gentleman who said to him: ' I say—the Armistice is signed.'

' Oh, is it? ' said Benjie, bought his book and walked into Piccadilly. There was no sign anywhere of excitement—the buses rolled along, people passed on their business, a young man stood with his eyes seriously fixed on Mr. Jackson's appetising window.

Benjie had moved from Chelsea after his return from Russia and had rooms now in Ryder Street. As he was about to turn into Jermyn Street he spoke to an old man with newspapers.

' Is it true,' he asked, ' that the Armistice is signed? '

' Can't say, sir, I'm sure,' the old man answered, rubbing his nose with the back of his hand.

' Very strange,' Benjie thought. ' This is the

moment for which we have all been passionately waiting and no one cares, no one cares at all.'

Entering his flat he saw Sally and Tom sitting together on the sofa.

' Hullo! ' he said. ' What are you two doing here? '

' Tom found me in Piccadilly,' Sally explained.

' Why aren't you at school? '

' There's mumps. We were all sent off this morning.' Then she added: ' Tom says the Armistice is signed.'

The valet of the flats came out of Benjie's bedroom with a suit over his arm.

' Bailey,' Benjie said, ' the Armistice is signed.'

' Indeed, sir,' said Bailey. ' I'm very glad, I'm sure. A great relief to everyone. Will you be in to luncheon? '

' Yes—no. Look here, we'll go and celebrate somewhere.'

He looked at both of them.

' Are you sure it's true? ' he asked Tom.

' Oh yes—quite true. The paper had it in an hour ago.'

' This is all wrong,' Benjie thought. He went to the window and glanced down into Ryder Street. No one was stirring.

He looked back at them. ' One day in Russia,' he said, ' about a week after the March Revolution, I got caught in the crowd. We all marched singing through the streets. Everybody was singing. It was the most marvellous thing. . . . Well, why aren't we singing? The greatest and most horrible war in history is over.'

'I suppose we can't realise it,' said Tom.
' And we're all rather tired.'

'Yes, we're all rather tired,' Benjie thought, 'and
we're going to be tired for years and years. Perhaps nobody will have the energy to sing again.'

' All the same,' he added aloud, ' it's something
that men aren't going to be killed any more.
That's something.'

At that moment they heard the maroons going
off and the silver clock on the mantelpiece struck
in its thin surprised tone eleven o'clock. They all
went to the window and saw people pouring into
the street. From every door they seemed to be
coming. Men, without hats, rushed out, waving
their arms. Flinging the window open, Benjie
could hear distant shouting.

' Come on,' he said. ' Let's go out and see
the sights.'

After that they were part of a vast, wild, cheering and yet oddly unexcited crowd. That at least
was what Benjie felt, as though all these people said
to him with one voice (not a loud voice—almost a
whisper): ' It is right for us to be excited. We've
won a great war, but life is changed. We can
never be quite so light-hearted and careless again.
Once, not so very long ago, on Mafeking night,
we all went mad. But we shan't go mad now.
We have to behave as though we were gloriously
happy. But we are not. By to-night we may
be drunk a little and make a noise, but it doesn't
mean anything.'

Nevertheless, with Sally close at his side, he
could not but feel that something was accom-

plished. Another phase of history, another phase of his own life, was closed. His adventurous days were over and so too, maybe, were the adventurous days of the world. It would be all cold mechanism now—mechanism, science, a remorseless progress.

He had a sudden longing for Vanessa and at that same moment Sally said: "How I wish that mother was here! ' He pressed her arm close to him. So long as Sally was alive things would not be mechanical. She was too individual for that.

They had pushed their way to Trafalgar Square, but here they were brought to a standstill. A thick unbroken mass of humanity. Men were shouting and singing, girls waving. But Benjie felt that everyone was waiting for something. That moment of singing in Petrograd would not be recovered here. It would never be recovered. It had been a moment of extravagant idealistic hope.

' There should be a Triumphal Arch,' he thought. ' Here in front of the lions. And everyone should march away under it, swearing as they passed beneath it that never again would men hate, plunder, be greedy. . . . Never again! ' He smiled. Not bad nonsense for an old cynic like himself. That was the sort of thing that old Horace would say. Alfred and Gordon and the others would have a fine time to-night. They at least would be happy, for they had won the War and were Lords of the Earth.

But not perhaps for long. The battle was not over yet between the Maurices and the Gordons, the Cynthias and the Vanessas.

'Come on,' he said.   'We'll go to the
Berkeley and have a feed.'

A thin rain had begun to fall.   There was no
Triumphal Arch.   As they pushed their way
slowly Benjie saw a soldier, motionless, staring,
unshifted by the crowd.   'Perhaps he's thinking
that now he won't be killed.   He won't have to go
back to that hell.   That's something anyway.'

He thought constantly of Vanessa.   If she were
here how happy she would be that he was safe
now, and that Tom was safe.   She would be
happy for all the women all over the world.

All the women!   Yes, that was something.

But there was no Triumphal Arch.

SALLY AND TOM

Cynthia gave Gordon Newmark a theatre-party on his thirtieth birthday (he was thirty on February 4, 1925) and Sally and old Horace Ormerod and Rosalind and Adrian came too. Cynthia (who was now over sixty, although you would never think it unless you looked at her neck), had a weakness for Gordon and hoped that, with judicious management, he might be induced to marry her daughter Rosalind. Rosalind was a good girl, had the best character in the world, and, although she was on the plain side and was now over thirty, would make a good wife for Gordon. Gordon once might have married her, for he was just the kind of man to appreciate good solid wearing qualities in a wife, but after the deaths of old Sidney and Mary Newmark (they died within a week or two of one another) it was discovered that their children, Gordon and Ada, would have large fortunes. Gordon was of course in his grandfather's business but made his headquarters in London. He was of another generation from old Horace Newmark, who thought that there was no city in the world to equal Manchester. Gordon was good-looking, with clear-cut features (a little too clear-cut perhaps) and that fashion that cropped up again and again in Herries business men of wearing clothes that looked too immaculate to be human. He was an agreeable well-mannered fellow, proud of his own looks, his D.S.O., his business ability, his family and his ' I like a man with no nonsense about him '—one of his favourite sayings. He intended a little later to go into politics and he would have a peerage before he finished. But first he must marry, and Cynthia hoped that in spite of his money, his profile and his self-confidence he might marry Rosalind.

For alas, neither Mary nor Rosalind was yet married. It was too extraordinary! Mary was still lovely, but for some reason young men didn't propose to her. They came up to her, looked at her with wonder in their eyes and went away again. The fact was that, thirty years earlier, when Vanessa ruled Hill Street, Mary would have been exactly what everyone wanted—beautiful, dignified, graceful, and not too clever. Now the young men (who after all had served their country) wanted something more lively.

So Cynthia had her troubles. Peile was aged and, although his figure was still good, this new post-War world appeared to have struck him dumb with amazement. It had been, at one time, the middle classes that had seemed to him astonishing. He had appealed to his Herries relations to save the country. But the job had been, it seemed, altogether too much for his relatives. So now, standing on his thin aristocratic legs, looking at the Income Tax and the closing of the great houses of England and the young women who looked like boys and the young men who looked like girls, he could only stare and stutter and gasp.

So he was not of very much use to Cynthia, who, from the house in Eaton Place, did what she could, looking now like a rather pretty little pig, with her hair a little too yellow, her cheeks a little too pink, her skirts a little too short, and her neck (in spite of all she could do) a little too wrinkled.

She had invited Sally to the theatre-party because she had invited old Horace. She had had no intention of asking Horace, but one afternoon when he had called on her and had sat there looking so old and pathetic, her heart (which was still kindly when she gave it an opportunity) was moved to say: 'Well, Horace, you must come to the theatre with us. Come next week. We are going to that play that everyone is talking about—by a new young man whose name I forget. They say he's extraordinarily clever and only left school last year.' Horace, who was now nearing seventy, had purple streaks on either side of his nose, an unwieldy stomach, and a cheery smile that was habit rather than intention (and so seemed to Cynthia terribly pathetic), said eagerly that he'd love to come. He was free practically any night next week.

('What a bore!' thought Cynthia. 'Whatever did I ask him for?')

Having done so she must also invite Sally, for the strange thing was (one of the many strange

things about Sally) that she was attached to
Horace; she was kind to him and never showed
him that sharp tongue and penetrating criticism
only too apparent with others. Sally would look
after Horace. It was a pity that Gordon did not
like Sally. That, however, would throw Gordon
all the more into Rosalind's company, and she,
Cynthia, could be amused by Adrian, who was
elegant, witty, drily cynical, and knew the private
behaviour of everyone.

So they went to *The Vortex*. They met at the
theatre because the play began early, and instead
of dinner before they would have supper at the
Savoy Grill afterwards. Sally was the first to
arrive and Gordon the second. Each was annoyed
at seeing the other.

'Who else is coming?' asked Gordon.

'Horace.'

'Horace? Oh Lord, what a bore!'

'Why?' said Sally.

'Oh, well, he's a bit comic,' said Gordon.

'Comic?' said Sally. 'So's everyone. I am
—you are.'

Gordon said nothing but he was greatly annoyed. *He* comic? You might call him anything
you like—everyone with personality has detractors
—but comic? He looked at Sally with great distaste. Her hair, which had now lost its carroty
shade and was a plain dark brown, was bobbed in
the new fashion. With a few more inches and a
little more colour she would not have been so bad.
She was slim, her eyes and mouth were bright,
alive—too alive, perhaps, for he hated young girls

to look sarcastic. She was unlike other girls and
that he also disliked. The height of good form,
he thought, was that you should not attract attention in a crowd. Of course if you were a *beautiful*
woman, that was another matter. No one could
call Sally Herries beautiful, and there she was,
thinking no end of herself, secretary to some old
Jew (she worked because she liked it, not because
she had to), living in the most independent manner
with another girl, illegitimate (although of course
in these days no one minded that) and, worst of all,
Benjie Herries' daughter. Now that Gordon considered himself the head of the Herries family and
responsible for its good behaviour, he greatly regretted Benjie, who, in spite of his being seventy
and having only one arm, often behaved out-
rageously and had some dreadful friends.

So Gordon (' Who *is* that handsome man? '
someone, standing near him in the foyer, asked
her companion. ' What splendid features! He
looks like an actor.') and Sally stood there dis-
liking one another exceedingly. The others
arrived and they all went in. Soon the curtain
went up, and the young author of the play, himself playing the lead, began to tell the other
characters exactly what he thought of them.

Cynthia, as she listened, became more and more
uncomfortable. What a *very* queer collection of
people! The mother, with her cropped hair, her
painted face, her passion for cigarettes and cock-
tails, was of course nothing like Cynthia, and it
made it all the queerer that the part should be
acted by nice Miss Lilian Braithwaite, whom

Cynthia knew well, a charming woman with nothing very modern about her. No, the mother on the stage was nothing like Cynthia, who was received everywhere, and by the young people especially, with the greatest warmth. She so often said: ' I don't feel a day more than thirty,' and it was true, she did not, unless her neuritis bothered, or chance had forced upon her a succession of late nights. No, she did not resemble this woman in any way nor did any of the friends of Mary or Rosalind resemble the girl with the Eton crop, played by Miss Molly Kerr, or the dreadful young man whom Noel Coward presented so vigorously. When the curtain went down she turned to Adrian.

' Well I never—what an extraordinary lot of people! '

Adrian, whose eyelids were always a little weary like Mr. Pater's Monna Lisa's, said: ' Oh, do you think so? There are lots like them nowadays! '

' Surely not! '

He waited a little. Then he said:

' When I see this sort of thing, I think of Vanessa. I never forget her as I saw her first at a ball. She was dressed in white, with her dark hair piled on the top of her head. I have never seen anything so beautiful before or since.'

' Poor Vanessa! ' said Cynthia. ' How terrible she would think all of this! '

' Not at all,' Adrian said sharply. ' She was too simple to be frightened off by external differences. She would be shy, of course, and think that she was being stupid, but she would make friends with that boy and girl in no time. There's been nobody like her since she died.'

' Oh, do you think so? Well, if you come to that, nobody's like anybody, are they? But I can't agree with you, Adrian. Vanessa would be miserable in a world like this. She wouldn't know how to adapt herself.'

' She wouldn't try to,' said Adrian rather crossly. ' She'd just be natural. Of course some people would find her dull. Some people always did. But others—she'd be just what they are always looking for now and can't find.'

(' Adrian's getting a bore,' Cynthia thought. ' And old—a fussy old Foreign Office bachelor.')

Sally took Horace for a stroll.

' Are you enjoying yourself, Horace dear? ' she asked him.

' Oh, I should just think I am! ' he answered her in his full philanthropic voice. ' I enjoy everything. When you get to my age, my dear, you'll realise how true it is what Stevenson once said: " We all ought to be as happy as kings." '

' Your tie's up at the back of your collar,' Sally said critically. ' What a whacking lie if Stevenson ever did say that. And you know you don't mean it, Horace. Even though you've been pretending to be jolly all your life you needn't pretend it now with me.'

' But I *am* enjoying the play,' he said a little sheepishly. ' I don't go so often to the theatre nowadays, you know. I like a jaunt. I'm a lonely old widower and a bit of fun does me good.'

Behind his red cheeks and large round glasses

and protruding chin there was fear: fear of illness, fear of being laughed at, fear of solitude at
the last and, above all, fear of being left behind.
Sally knew that it was true, that the world found
Horace a dreadful bore, that men at the Club
slipped away as he approached, that young men
laughed at him and that all his relations despised
him.   She was fond of him because she knew all
these things.

'Lonely!   Of course you're not!' she said
cheerfully.   'Look here, come and have tea with
Margaret and me to-morrow afternoon.   I've got
an afternoon off.   My old Jew's going down to
Brighton.'

'Oh, thank you, my dear.'   Horace's glasses
beamed.   'I should enjoy it immensely.   I like
your friend Margaret.'

'Margaret's a pet,' said Sally.

'And when is your father returning from
South Africa?'

'Oh, any day now.'

'And Tom—how's Tom getting on?'

'Very well indeed.   He writes some of the
leaders now.'

'That's fine,' said Horace, looking proudly
about him.   Here he was with a splendid girl—a
true representative of the young generation—and
she had asked him to tea, and Cynthia, one of the
smartest women in London, had invited him to
the theatre, and he belonged to one of the most
prominent families in England.   He forgot, in
his sudden exuberance, the faded gloom of his
rooms in Jermyn Street, the surly indifference of

his man-servant, and the rude manner with which
Alfred had turned his back on him a few days
ago.

He had always said: ' I don't know what it is,
but there's a sort of inner happiness in me which
nothing can destroy.' It wasn't quite true any
longer and he had never realised that his consciousness of it had been, in the past, one of the
principal reasons for his unpopularity, but it was
true enough at the moment for him to look at
all the men near him with a certain kindly con-
descension as though they had all just fallen into
the water and he was there, with a strong manly
hand, ready to pull them out again.

Cynthia and Adrian joined them.

(' Why is it,' Sally had once asked Tom, ' that
all the members of our family move about as
though they had just opened public buildings? ')

' I think the play's absurd,' said Cynthia. ' I
never saw such people! '

' Oh, do you? ' said Sally. ' There are lots
of them about. I'm rather like it myself.'

She wasn't and she knew that she wasn't, but
it pleased her to irritate Cynthia.

At that moment Adrian brought up a man.
' Cynthia, this is a friend of mine at the Foreign
Office—Arnold Young.'

The man was perhaps about five-and-twenty,
slim, tall, fair-haired. He had a weak chin, a
mouth with humour and bright blue eyes. He
looked weak and amiable, as though he needed
caring for and would be charming if you cared
for him.

Sally looked at him and her heart was moved. He instantly smiled. ' You were rather like a choir-boy,' he told her afterwards, ' who was bored to death with the sermon.'

The bell rang and they turned into the passage.

' Do you like this play? ' the young man asked Sally.

' Oh, frightfully! '

' Isn't Noel Coward marvellous? '

' Simply marvellous.'

And just as they reached the stalls he said to her:

' I say—I hope we meet again somewhere.'

They must have met somewhere again very shortly after this, because, about a week later, Sally had this conversation with Tom.

Tom, who was a concrete Conservative, still inhabited the rooms in Tite Street.

Tom was now forty-one years of age. He was heavily built but not stout, short and square-shouldered, with a pale, anxious, extremely kindly face. Many years of journalism had not changed him. He was dressed in a black coat, black tie, striped dark trousers always. He played golf a little, and in the summer tennis a little. He liked his work but was not enthusiastic about it. He had only two passions—Cumberland and the few people he loved—Vanessa, his father, Mary and Sally. Over these four (Vanessa's ghost was certainly one of them) he watched and worried until they would sometimes scream with annoyance. He knew this and now did all he could to hide his care of them. He pretended to be quite indifferent as to whether they came or went. He was even a little afraid of letting Vanessa's ghost know how often he thought of her! Because he cared for his father less than for the others he irritated him the least. Besides, in these days, Benjie was often abroad. But Mary and Sally were simply his whole world. When they snapped at him, as they frequently did, he would slowly flush and blame himself for being so tiresome. Curiously, in relation to the rest of the world he was rather indifferent. Men in Fleet Street both respected and liked him. He was not clever enough to rouse their jealousy and he was always ready to do someone a turn, not from sentiment but simply because he was good-natured.

But that world hardly existed for him. He would have been a better journalist if it had. When he could snatch a night or two he would hurry up to Cumberland. There was a farm between Grange and Cat Bells where he always had a bedroom. Then he would walk, generally alone. He knew the Tops like his London bedroom wallpaper.

Sally loved him and bullied him. It exasperated her that year after year he should long for Mary Worcester who would never marry him. With glee she told him one day that people said that she was going to marry the young Duke of Wrexe.

'Funny, isn't it? History repeats itself. Our great-grandmother was engaged for a while to the Duke of Wrexe of her day. The lovely Jennifer—lovely and stupid like Mary.'

However, the young Duke of Wrexe married an American girl.

'Why do you tease me about Mary, Sally?' Tom asked her once. 'I never mention her.'

'Why do you go on year after year when it's hopeless? I want you to marry a nice good girl and make me an aunt.'

'You wouldn't like it if I did,' he said truthfully.

On this particular day when Sally had tea with him in Tite Street she did not tease him. She was very affectionate. He loved her dearly when she was kind. All the best in her came out. Her eternal qualities of courage and honesty were transmuted when she was kind into a true nobility. When she was not kind she seemed sometimes hard and selfish.

But to-day she looked at him with eyes of love. She sat on the edge of his armchair, swinging her legs, his arm round her.

'When's Father coming home?'

'Any time now.'

'I wonder what he's been doing in South Africa. I hope he's been behaving himself. Every year I think he's getting too old to misbehave any more, but he doesn't. Vanessa managed him, but no one else ever has.' She waved her arms. 'I love him! He's such a pet with his little ruddy face and his sharp eyes and his one arm and his eagerness to fall into any scrap that's coming! He'll startle us all yet and shock the family once again before he's done.'

She looked at Tom meditatively.

'Tom, I'm going to tell you something. You'll probably hate it. I'm in love—for the first time in my life.'

His arm clutched her a little more tightly. His heart began to hammer and he told himself: 'Now be careful. Don't show her that you mind. Don't show her that you're anxious. She's a modern girl. She won't stand being warned or advised.' He was able to say very quietly:

'Who with, Sally darling?'

She stroked his head.

'That's right, my pet. You're taking it well. He's a man in the Foreign Office. He's a friend of Adrian's and his name is Arnold Young.'

'Oh yes? I don't think I've met him.'

(Inside he was saying to himself: 'Now I shall have to protect Sally without her knowing it and see that he treats her right. She thinks she knows everything about life, like all girls now, but she doesn't.')

'No, you wouldn't have. Well, he's tall and got a lovely figure and he's very fair with blue eyes. On the other hand, he has no chin and wants looking after. He has a mother who plays bridge, morning, noon and night.'

'Does he know you're in love with him? Where did you meet him?'

'I met him when I went to *The Vortex* with Cynthia   I don't think he knows I'm in love with him. We've only met twice. I'm very rude to him. I've never been in love before and it's a funny feeling.'

'Would you like to marry him?'

' Yes, I think so—if he asked me. Of course all Margaret's friends think marriage is rot nowadays. As long as you don't have a baby there's no point about marriage, they say. But I don't quite agree. It's all very well going away with a man for a week-end, but I think it would be nice to *look after* Arnold, run his home for him and everything. I expect I'm old-fashioned. Margaret says I am.'

' Is he a decent fellow? ' Tom asked. ' I mean has he got a mistress somewhere or anything like that? '

' Oh no,' said Sally. ' He doesn't seem to care for girls. He's terribly under his mother's influence. That's the worst thing about him. But he isn't one of those, you know, or anything like that. Not a bit nancy. I don't say he's very fine or grand or wonderful. I'm just in love with him, that's all—here in the pit of the stomach! '

Then to Tom's astonishment she put her arms round his neck, kissed him and laid her cheek against his. She hardly ever kissed him.

' Do you know,' she said, ' we're all by ourselves—Vanessa, Father, you and I. Misfits. Still, we don't have a bad time.'

She began to roam round the room. Looking up, on a shelf above her head she saw an old green book. She stood on her toes and brought it down. She looked into it. It was a large fat book filled with rather faded writing in an old-fashioned female hand.

' What's this? ' she asked.

' Oh, don't you know? That's some recollec-

tions Judith Paris wrote when she was an old lady
—or rather she dictated them.'

' How marvellous! May I read them? '

' You'd better not take them away. Father
asked me to take care of them for him.'

' Why—are they shocking? '

' Not in the least. But Judith gave them to
Adam, Vanessa's father, and Vanessa gave them
to Father.'

' Oh, but listen, Tom! They go back ever so
far—almost to the beginning of the eighteenth
century.'

' Yes; Judith lived to be a hundred, you know.'

' Oh, let me take them! I'll be frightfully
careful.'

He hesitated. ' Well, if you're *fearfully* careful——'

' Of course I will. I must go now.' She came
to him and kissed him. ' Dear old Tom. I don't
want to be sloppy, but you *are* a darling.'

He held her with his hand on her arm.

' Sally. Look here. I know you hate my
being serious, but—well, what I mean is you
haven't got anyone but me, in a way. Father isn't
here and he wouldn't be much use. Vanessa told
me to look after you.'

She smiled.

' Well—what is it? '

' You will be careful, won't you? I know girls
know everything these days. Since the War they
don't care *what* they do. But—you'll be careful,
won't you? Tell me if you want any help about
anything. Are you sure he's a decent fellow? '

' Of course he is. I can look after myself.'

After she was gone Tom walked about the room sighing. She looked such a baby. She was such a good sort. He loved her so dearly. But there you were. It wasn't the thing now to show your feelings. He had such a lot. Had he only been able to write! He sat down and soon was lost in a book of Santayana's. Now *there* was a writer!

On a day in April Adrian gave a luncheon-party at his rooms in Lincoln's Inn. He invited Sally, Maurice, Maurice's young woman, Arnold Young, Miss Culloden, the well-known novelist, and her friend Miss James.

Sally hadn't known that Arnold was to be there. She had not seen him for three weeks. Adrian had asked her very casually and she had thought that very possibly she would be the only guest besides Maurice and Emily Tempest, to whom he was engaged. When she saw Miss Culloden she was afflicted with the shyness that she inherited from her mother. She was always sorry when she was shy, because shyness made her rude and abrupt in self-defence. Sally had read none of Miss Culloden's books. She read very little and for the most part the authors whom her friend Margaret admired— Lawrence and Aldous Huxley. She had attempted *Women in Love* and *Ulysses* and found them very tiresome. Then one evening she had found an old faded copy of Rider Haggard's *She* tucked away on a shelf. Scornfully she had begun it, and Margaret, coming in at one in the morning, had found her, curled up in a corner of the sofa, entranced.

'Whatever are you reading?' said Margaret. And then, when she saw, all she said was: 'My God!'

So Sally did not know what her real taste in books was. But she did know that she had read nothing by Miss Culloden.

Miss Culloden was a large cheerful friendly woman who reminded Sally of one of those broad-backed white horses at the circus, who go patiently round and round while ladies spring on to them and off them again. Miss James was her little friend who went with her everywhere and 'brought her out' on the subject of her works. Sally could not conceive why Adrian had invited her, for Adrian's taste in the Arts was severe, but it afterwards appeared that Miss Culloden had met him somewhere and had insisted on being invited. That was why the party to-day was mainly 'Family.' No celebrated persons. Miss Culloden was the life and soul. She was one of those fortunate writers (very rare) who are completely satisfied with every-thing—their own works, their publishers, their public and everything concerning them.

'You remember, Molly,' said Miss James, 'there was that chapter about Venice in *Grapes and Thistles*—one of your best bits, I always thought.'

Adrian changed the conversation to Sargent, who was recently dead.

'Everyone said at the time,' said Miss James

' that the artist in *Models for Sale* was intended for
Sargent.'

' Well, he wasn't,' said Miss Culloden very
firmly. ' He was a composite portrait.'

' I remember you were very anxious at the
time,' said Miss James.

' Well, I'd have hated Sargent's feelings to be
hurt. People are terribly sensitive. They're hurt
if they think they're *in* a book and they're hurt if
they're not.'

After a while Miss Culloden surveyed the
table. ' You're quite a family party, aren't you?
Netta and I feel honoured at being made one of
you like this. Oh yes, I know what I wanted to
say. I was hearing about a marvellous member
of your family the other day, an old lady who
lived to be a hundred. And she'd actually seen
Napoleon just before Waterloo, and knew Disraeli
and all sorts of famous people. Wouldn't she be
wonderful for a novel? I wonder if you'd all
mind if I wrote a book about her one day?'

' I don't think she actually *saw* Napoleon,'
Adrian said. ' She was Sally's great-grandmother——'

' Was she *really*? ' Miss Culloden beamed upon
Sally. ' Oh, how splendid! Now do tell me! '

' If you ever *dare* to put her in a book,' Sally
said, her voice trembling, ' I'll bring an action.'

Everyone was uncomfortable. That was just
like the girl, Adrian thought, to take the old fool
seriously. You never knew what she *would* be
serious over! But of course with Benjie for a
father . . .

However, Miss Culloden didn't mind in the
least, but thought: ' What a strange, unusual little
girl!   I'll see more of her.'

Adrian changed the conversation yet once
again and asked Miss Culloden whether she had
been to the theatre.   Had she seen *No, No,
Nanette*?

' Yes, indeed—and it's simply splendid——'
she began.

But Sally was miserable.   There she was,
making a fool of herself before Arnold.   She could
remember when she was seven or six or some
absurd age that Vanessa had warned her about
her tempers.   She could see Vanessa standing by
the window in the room at Hill Street, the room
with the two yellow globes and the picture with
' Miss Muffet and the Spider.'   Yes, Vanessa was
there, wanting not to laugh, wanting to be stern
and severe, but Sally had made a face and Vanessa
had laughed. . . .

'—and if Miss Herries *ever* forgives me,' Miss
Culloden was saying, ' I shall ask her one day——'

Everyone was looking at Sally as though they
expected her to do something, so she smiled at
Miss Culloden, hating herself, one of those horrible smiles that you fastened on to your mouth
as a dentist fastens on a gag.

And not only was Vanessa standing there, but
now also Judith Paris, for, in the last weeks, Sally
had absorbed that old green book into her very
blood and bones.   She knew it almost by heart
and it was agony to her when it stopped, stopped
at one of its most thrilling moments when Judith

was remembering the terrible quarrel about the
fan at Christabel's Ball. Why, conceive it! Here
was Sally and there at her very elbow was Judith
who, going on a jaunt with her French husband
to the ' Elephant and Castle,' had worn a dress—
' a jaquette of pale silver-coloured silk and the
bodice and underdress were of dark wine colour:
I wore a hat of light straw and my shoes had
silver buckles.' There was Judith in her old age
dictating to her great-great-niece Jane Bellairs,
who, a sweet old maiden lady with ringlets, had
died as recently as 1905, and here was she, Sally,
in 1925, feeling that Judith was in the very room
with her, the hat of light straw perched on her
red hair . . .

' I'm sure you are wrong, dear,' Miss James
was saying in her firm even voice that was like a
ruler drawing lines on a piece of white paper. ' It
wasn't until *Love in a Garret* that America really
took you to its heart. I remember so well your
telling me that the Americans were fickle and that
you were not going to allow yourself to be persuaded by the success of one book into thinking
that it would last. You told me, I remember,
that Sir Philip Gibbs said———'

' Oh, God! this is awful!' Adrian thought.
He looked at Maurice, who was one of the discontented members of the family. ' A legacy of
the War,' Cynthia called Maurice, and it was
certainly true that he had lost an arm and written
a little book about Blake and got himself engaged,
when he had no money at all, to a young woman
who painted ladies with green hair and the oddest

legs, all things—in the opinion of Cynthia and
Alfred and Gordon—that might be classed together as a ' pity.'

' Oh, these awful women! ' thought Adrian.
' What *can* Maurice be thinking of them? '

He had a high opinion of Maurice, who had
bought a Matisse in Paris very cheap, and had
had tea with James Joyce. But he was wrong
about Maurice, who liked Miss Culloden very
much. She reassured him. Obviously to her the
world was not a bloody, menacing place in which
everything and everybody was going to hell. He
liked her, whereas he loathed Gordon, who also
believed in life. But then Gordon believed in life
because Gordon was such a wonderful fellow, and
Miss Culloden believed in life because she was
naturally happy, like a lark in the sky. . . .

When the party was breaking up, Arnold said
to Sally: ' Can I take you anywhere? I've got
a car.'

Sally's heart leapt for joy.

' Yes, you can,' she said. ' Anywhere you
like. I haven't got to be at the office till four.'
She was so happy that, on bidding farewell, she
looked up at Miss Culloden and said, smiling (this
time with real if rather childlike sincerity):

' Please forgive me if I was rude.'

' Rude, my dear! ' cried Miss Culloden.
' Why, you're too sweet for anything! Now you
must come and have lunch with me, you really
must—and I promise not to say a word about
your great-aunt or whatever she was. Now what
day can you come? ' She produced a small silver-

edged notebook. ' I'm talking to the Sorop-
timists on Tuesday and there's Marie Lowndes on
Wednesday. Thursday I'm going out to Surbiton. Now what about Friday? Friday's quite
all right. There's only the Tallboys Club Committee in the afternoon. . . . Now *what* about
Friday? '

So Sally was engaged for Friday.

In the little car (which was bright red in colour
and *very* smart) Sally said: ' Where are we going? '

' Anywhere you like.'

' Haven't you any work or anything? '

' Oh yes, but I *must* talk to you.'

' Well, let's go to the National Gallery and
look at the Sargents.'

Side by side on a settee alone in the room,
looking at one lovely woman after another, Sally
said:

' I like Mrs. Charles Hunter's hat.' Then
she added: ' They're all quite unreal, aren't
they? '

' Yes,' said Arnold. ' He despised women.
The only thing he admired about them was their
clothes. You can see how he hated his sitters.
His hatred is real in the pictures even if nothing
else is.'

' Yes,' said Sally, who, sitting there very
meekly, wishing that her legs were a little longer
and that altogether she was built on a larger scale,
was nevertheless a great deal happier than any girl
of her generation thought it fitting to be.

' Will you marry me? ' Arnold said suddenly.

' Yes,' Sally said. ' I'd love to.'

' I'm terribly glad,' Arnold said. ' I loved you from the first moment I saw you.'

As he said this Sally thought that he'd never wanted looking after so badly as now. She longed to put her arm round him. All she said was:

' You know I'm illegitimate.'

' What on earth does that matter? '

' Have you any money, Arnold darling? '

' Well, not a lot. There's what I get in the Foreign Office and my mother makes me an allowance.'

' Your mother doesn't like me,' Sally said quickly.

' She will when she knows you, darling.'

' No, she never will. She thinks I'm Bohemian and she's heard things about father. She knows father and mother weren't married. These things matter to *her* and always will.'

A shadow seemed to pass very swiftly over Arnold's face. (Poor dear! he certainly *did* need looking after!)

' She wants you to marry a fine girl of a noble family. Her generation are *like* that.'

' Well, your family's all right. It's one of the best in England.'

' I know, dear—but don't let's be snobbish. The point about our family is that there are the right ones and the wrong ones. There always have been. Cynthia Worcester and Alfred and Gordon are the right ones—but my father and I are the wrong ones, I'm afraid.'

' What nonsense you're talking, Sally darling. You're splendid! You're wonderful! And my

mother isn't going to say whom I'm going to
marry! It's my life, not hers!' It was the
bravest thing Arnold had ever said.

'Well, you go and talk to her,' Sally said,
laying her hand for a moment on his. 'I won't
be engaged until you've talked to her, but I do
love you frightfully and I think I always will.'

There, in that public room, in front of all the
Sargent ladies, they kissed, and as he felt Sally's
small body tremble against his he swore to himself
that he would defy a thousand mothers. . . .

'Oh, of course,' young Mr. Elton was saying,
'if you prefer to read people like Galsworthy and
Barrie——'

'Why shouldn't I?' said Mary Worcester,
'I don't, if you want to know. But why shouldn't
I?'

'Because they're false as hell,' said young Mr.
Elton. Then he saw that his audience was de-
spicable, made his adieus and departed.

'I suppose I'd better be going too,' said Tom.
'I don't think mother will be in now. She's
playing bridge and *said* she'd be back, but with
bridge you never know . . .'

Tom stood in the middle of the charming little
drawing-room, which in the fashion of the moment
had only one French picture on its walls—a late
and not-at-all-good Utrillo—a bronze by Dobson
on the mantelpiece, and very little else.

Then, hiding his fear, he spoke the words that,
for almost all his life, had been trembling on his
lips. Why now? Was it less hopeless than ever?

Certainly not. Mary, who in these days was often depressed, was very depressed indeed at the moment. An extremely agreeable handsome young man who would have been an excellent escort to all kinds of places, had found her, like all the other agreeable young men, most appallingly dull. She didn't *want* to be dull. She was ready to admire their painters, their poets, their morals, their cynicism, their atheism, although in her heart she found all these things unpleasant, but it was of no use. They found her a bore and practically said so. She was thirty-two. Life was ghastly.

Nevertheless the words came pouring from Tom's lips.

' Mary, I can't help it. I've wanted to say this so often. You know I have. Won't you marry me? I've loved you all my life. It mightn't turn out so badly. I've got a rise. I'm doing leaders on the paper now, and there are articles too I write for the weeklies. It isn't such a bad income and, if you married me, I believe I could do ever so much better still. I would look after you—I would care for you——'

He stopped because the words choked him. He looked away from her at the Dobson bronze, a figure with thighs so enormous and a head so small that it filled him, at this moment, with terror.

Mary looked at him with great kindness. She patted the grey sofa with her hand.

' Tom, come and sit down.' He came and sat down. ' You know I can't.'

' Why not? No one has loved you so long nor
so faithfully——'

' Yes, I know. But there are other things
beside fidelity. One thing is that I don't love
you. You know that I don't. That isn't my fault
or yours. Another is that I'm frightfully stupid.
If I lived with you I'd bore you terribly. Another
is that I must marry someone with money. And
another—perhaps the most important—is that I
never would marry any member of our family.'

He came closer to her and she allowed him to
take her hand.

' Then there's another. You're *too* good,
you're *too* faithful. I couldn't bear anyone who
loved me as you do. I know I'm not worth it,
but it isn't that. No one's worth it. But I like
people who are independent of me, who don't give
a damn whether I'm nice to them or no. If I snap
at you it's as though I struck you. You wince.
But I *do* like you. I don't mean that. Only to
live with you—never, dear Tom.'

She hesitated, then went on:

' You see, you're old-fashioned. You believe
in God and kindness and charity and all the old
things. How you can, I can't think! It's a
rotten world run by stupid people. It may come
right again one day, although not in our time, I
expect. You're like old Horace in that, except
that you really *do* believe in the things you say.
You're like Vanessa, who was, I'm sure, the finest
woman who ever lived, but she simply doesn't
belong to our time.'

' You're not to say a word——' began Tom.

' There you are, you see? You won't face the facts. You never do. I didn't know Vanessa very well, but I *do* think she was splendid—much finer than any of us are! But she seems old-fashioned now—she was Victorian—and you're a bit Victorian too.'

There was a long pause. Then he said:

' What do you mean—you wouldn't marry one of our family? '

' Just what I say! I hate and loathe our family! Either we're prigs or we're mad. We are so damnably English whatever we are. Mother's all right, I suppose, but look at father and Rosalind and Alfred and Gordon—and poor Maurice who's as cracked as can be; and there was Ellis who was mad for years; and Rose, Horace's sister, who died in the gutter. And if you go back it's just the same. Your grandfather was murdered by your great-uncle, and before that there was a Herries shot himself in London, and there was the crazy Herries in the eighteenth century. And in between the others have all been dull and self-satisfied and self-righteous. I shall marry someone or other just to get away. But I won't marry to stay.'

Tom answered slowly: ' You're wrong, Mary. Whether we've been mad or sane we've been alive. You may laugh at England, but it's the finest——Oh, don't let's talk about the family! What does it matter? I'm only half Herries! The family can't make any difference! And I won't fuss over you, Mary, really I won't. You shall have your own life. You shan't see

more of me than you want to! We get on together. We have for years. You like being
with me. . If you married me——'

She sighed. ' It's a shame,' she said at last.
' I'm glad you've told me, though, because—now
that you see that it's hopeless perhaps you'll find
someone else. I've wanted for years to tell you
how hopeless it is. Of course I like you and like
being with you—sometimes. But I'm not worth
it—not worth your kind of devotion, Tom. And
you'd regret it like anything. I shall get fat and
plain and peevish. I haven't an idea in my head,
only scraps of other people's ideas. And I want
money. It's the only thing that can save me.
With money I can make things do, perhaps.
Without it——'

' If you loved me,' he said at last, ' would any
of these other things have mattered? '

' Once they wouldn't. But now—it isn't love
I want but money and comfort and safety.'

He got up. She liked him at that moment very
much. She got up and held out her hand.

' Good-bye, Tom dear,' she said.

' Good-bye,' he answered and left her.

He went back to Tite Street, sat in his room,
his head between his hands, thinking. This was
awful. Mary's refusal had made no difference to
his love for her. How could it when it was part
of his very being? But now he had got to make
terms with it, he thought. He must manage his
life henceforth so that this dead hope did not
spread like a cancer into all his energies. For,
until to-day, there had always been a hope—for

years and years that hope had been a light in his
room.   Now he must manage without it.

He was so desperately tired that he slept in his
chair, his head forward on his breast.

He woke to find that the light had been switched
on and his father was standing there.   He rubbed
his eyes, for he was only half awake, and Benjie
was like a figure in a dream, standing in a rough
heather-coloured overcoat and holding on a chain
a very alert, eye-shining, panting rough-haired
terrier.

' Good God! ' Tom cried, jumping up.

' Yes,' said Benjie, smiling.   ' Here I am.'

' Why didn't you send a wire? '

' Well, you see, Tom, I didn't know when I'd
arrive.   As it is I've been in the New Forest a
whole week wandering about.   That's where I
bought this.'

The dog, its tongue out and its brilliant deep
brown eyes almost jumping from its head, strained
at the hold.   The colour of its coat was black
and tan, with a fine rough white patch across the
neck.

' Why didn't you write from the New Forest? '
asked Tom.

' Oh Lord, I don't know!   Don't badger me.
My bags are in the other room.   Isn't this a nice
overcoat?   I won it in a bet on the boat.   Luckily
the other fellow was just my size.   Heavens! but
I'm tired! '

He took his coat off.   He was thinner and
browner than ever, thought Tom, and his eyes had
the same desperate brightness as the dog's.   He

went and poured himself out a whisky and soda.
He sat on the edge of the deal table, swinging his
thin legs, his little animal-like face cocked a bit
over his glass.   Tom had noticed that the very
first thing he had looked at across the room was a
large photograph of Vanessa.
' Any news? '
' Sally's engaged.'
' What! ' Benjie sprang off the table.   ' Sally!
My little Sally!   Heavens!   Who to? '
' A fellow called Young — Arnold Young.
He's in the Foreign Office.'
Benjie was excited.   He came over to Tom,
holding up his glass with his one hand.
' What's he like? '
' Oh, he's all right, I suppose.   Sally thinks
so.   But he's just the sort of chap Sally would pick
up—a bit weak, I should think, and wants looking
after.'
' Any money? '
' Got a rich mother, and I should think she's
bloody from what Sally says.   Nor does she like
Sally.   She goes about everywhere, I believe,
saying that there's no engagement and it's pre-
posterous and so on.'
' Why, what has she got against my Sally? '
' Oh, I don't know.'
' Born out of wedlock, scamp of a father—that
sort of thing? '
' I don't know.   I haven't seen her.'
Then, very like Benjie, he drove the thing right
out of his mind.   He had released the dog, who
now bounded all over the room, sometimes pran-

cing on four legs at once like a young lamb, and examining everything.

' What's its name? '

' Sam.'

' It's a shame to keep a dog like that in London.'

' I shan't keep it in London.   I'm going up to Cumberland.'

' Oh, I say, are you really! ' Tom's eyes shone.

Benjie put his glass down and rested his hand on Tom's shoulder.

' Like to come too? '

' Wouldn't I, though! '

' Could you get off? '

' Yes, for a bit, I think.'

Benjie looked at him critically, then drew him closer until shoulder touched shoulder.

' You're not looking any too fine.'

' Oh, I'm all right.'

Father and son gave one another a glance and each smiled.

' What's the matter?   Mary turned you down? '

' Yes.   How did you know? '

' Oh, I guessed.   I'm a bit lonely too.   South Africa was all right—interesting seeing it again after all these years.   But it would have been better if Vanessa had been there.'   Then he added cheerfully: ' I say — Mary's damned dull, you know.'

Tom shook his head.

' You don't understand how it is.'

' Oh, don't I? '   He laughed.   ' You bet I do! I've been in love with the same woman fifty years.

How about that?' For a brief moment he held Tom closely to him.

'Come on and eat.'

'What about the dog?' asked Tom.

'Oh, he'll come too. I know a place where they don't mind dogs.'

Meanwhile on that same evening another member of the family was carrying on the Herries history a further stage. Arnold had taken Sally out to the theatre—to Mr. Lonsdale's play *Spring Cleaning*. Sally enjoyed the play, although she thought it old-fashioned. They were having supper at 'The Gargoyle,' they were dancing a little, talking a little. They were, both of them, terribly in love.

'Yes,' said Sally. 'I think all these plays about how wicked we are seem very Victorian— *East Lynne*, you know. There's *The Vortex* and *Fallen Angels* and the one to-night. All the young men are—well, you know, and the young women have monocles and Eton crops. Everyone drinks and they go to bed with one another in the bathroom. Just as they did in Mrs. Henry Wood's day——'

'Well, aren't we all like that just now? Look round you, my pet, and observe.'

'There are just about forty million people,' said Sally, 'who've never heard of "The Gargoyle" or Noel Coward. They don't sleep together in the bathroom nor do their young men powder their faces.'

'What do they do then?' asked Arnold.

' They go to football matches, read the *News of the World* and sleep cosily with their wives and husbands.'

He drove her to her door. Then he asked her whether he might come in for a moment. She hesitated, for Margaret was away. But then she nodded. The sitting-room that she shared with Margaret had a very comfortable sofa, a long well-filled bookcase, a gas stove, and posters by Mr. McKnight Kauffer pinned to the walls. Over the mantelpiece there was a water-colour by Charles Holmes of a black hill with a shaft of sunlight breaking on it and illuminating a field that shone with the brilliance of a missal.

' That's nice,' said Arnold. ' Where is it? '

' It's Stonethwaite Valley in Cumberland.'

There was also an old photograph of Vanessa. She was standing, her hand on a chair; her dress had the puffed sleeves and the small waist of the period. But she did not look absurd. She looked very charming indeed.

' Who's that? ' Arnold asked.

' That's my mother.'

' By Jove, she was a beauty.'

' Yes, wasn't she? '

On the sofa she gathered him into her thin childish arms.

' Oh, Arnold,' she said. ' I want you to be happy! '

(She was not aware that more than a hundred years before in a ragged deserted house in Borrowdale, Judith Paris had said the same words. But Judith had not loved Vanessa's grandfather.)

He strained up to her, putting his arm up to hold her round boyish head as in a cup.

'And so do I you.' He kissed her, holding her so closely to him that their two hearts seemed to beat as one.

'Well, you can make me happy—frightfully happy——'

'Yes, darling?' Sally said, stroking his hair.

'Let me stay here to-night.'

She drew away from him, placing her hand firmly on his arm. She sat back against the corner of the sofa and looked at him.

'Well, really, Arnold!' She was suddenly frightened, frightened in a way that a modern girl with all her knowledge of life should never be.

He began to speak eagerly:

'See here, Sally. There's nothing so very dreadful. I know how to look after you. Why shouldn't we have a good time? Everyone else does. You don't believe in God or hell-fire or any of that old junk, do you?' He laughed rather nervously. He was not a practised seducer. He had never seduced anyone before. He did not feel that he was trying to seduce Sally. He simply, he thought, loved her so madly that he wanted to be as close to her as possible.

'I don't believe in hell-fire,' she said slowly. 'But I'm not sure about God. My mother believed in God.'

'Of course. So does mine. All their generation did, but ours doesn't. We're simply some sort of chemical mixture. There's no future or past or anything, so why shouldn't we enjoy our-

selves? We'll only be young once, and perhaps
before we're much older there'll be another war
like the last and we'll all be blown to bits.'

' I think it would be nicer,' Sally said slowly,
' to wait till we're married. If we have everything
now there won't be anything new to experience
later on.'

' Yes, but don't you see, Sally? As we are
going to be married it doesn't matter anticipating
it a bit, does it? '

She knelt on the sofa, turning her little body
towards him, holding his head between her hands,
looking at him very seriously.

' Arnold—we *are* going to be married, aren't
we? '

' But of course we are! ' He moved his soft
cheek against her hand.

' Yes, but what if your mother goes on hating
me? '

' She doesn't hate you. She doesn't know
you.'

' No, she *won't* know me! Now tell me—it's
true, isn't it?—she told you that our engagement
is absurd, that I'm no good and my father's no
good and that she won't have her darling wee pet
of an Arnold marrying a little bastard.'

' No, of course not, darling. How absurd you
are! '

She jumped back from him, sprang to her feet.
She stood there, small, pale-faced, but dominating.

' Now listen, Arnold! She *does* say that. You
know it and I know it! And I'll tell you something—I'm as good as anyone in England, as

proud, as independent. I had the grandest mother anyone ever had. There never has been, and there never will be again, anyone as fine as Vanessa. And I don't want your damned charity. And your mother can be as superior as she likes, I'm not going on to my knees and imploring, but her——'

He was in a dreadful state. He had never loved her so much as at that moment. He had in fact (and this was true) never loved anyone before.

'Sally, my sweet, my pet. We'll be married when you like. To-morrow if you wish. Anything you say——' He caught her with his arms, carried her back to the sofa, and they lay there, close together, saying nothing, he kissing her mouth, her eyes, her hair.

And she thought: 'How terribly I love him. I'd give him anything. Why not be kind while one may?' As his body trembled in her arms she was infinitely touched. Oh, darling Arnold, darling, darling Arnold! Judith had loved a man outside marriage, and her own mother . . . She was herself illegitimate . . . and in these days, when everyone was free . . . He was right. . . . Who knew how long their happiness might last?

Why should she not be kind? Why should she not give anything she could that would make him happy? She sighed, touched his cheek.

'All right, Arnold darling,' she said. 'You can stay.'

MEN AT WAR

On this evening of May 3, 1926, Benjie took the dog Sam out for a little exercise. He had, only the day before, returned from Morocco and found that he was plunged into a world of turmoil. Tom, who was pale and tired and plainly overworked, said that by next morning we might find ourselves plunged into Revolution. 'Revolution,' said Benjie; 'how absurd!' But to himself, perhaps, more than to anyone else in London it did not seem absurd, for he carried, always present with him, that picture of a ragged mob crossing a bridge, of the skaters vanishing, of a sudden rifle-shot, of a square frozen and bare under a shining sun but quivering with danger, and, most tremendous of all, a multitude of people singing as though Paradise had come. And had Paradise come? Not at all. Murder, destruction, and the slow agonising beginning of a new world. . . . So here it might be also.

But what, he inquired, had been happening? Tom entered into a slow and tortuous explanation. The Secretary of the Miners' Federation, Arthur Cook, had made the trouble. After the Samuel Commission had recommended reduction in pay, Arthur Cook had replied: ' Not a cent off the pay, not a minute on the day,' and all the miners of England had repeated his words with emphasis. The Government had announced the withdrawal of the subsidy, and on April 23 the owners had delivered an ultimatum. Cook had not liked the terms of the ultimatum, his men had appealed for help to the Trades Union Congress, and that body, in its turn, had put the question of a General Strike to a ballot of its unions.

No one supposed that the Trades Union Congress really *wanted* a General Strike—of course they didn't—but they thought that mild Mr. Baldwin would capitulate. However, mild Mr. Baldwin gave a puff or two at his pipe and *didn't* capitulate. (It happened that the Government had been making their preparations ever since 1925.) Well, then, on this very Monday, members of the Association of Printers' Assistants working for the *Daily Mail* had demanded the withdrawal of a leading article entitled ' For King and Country,' and the men on the *Daily Mirror* had objected to a news article directing anti-strike volunteers to recruiting stations in the London area. The General Council Committee thought that they would go and have a talk with Mr. Baldwin, but when they went to see him he was not there. They were greatly surprised.

At midnight the General Strike was to begin. On the evening of the Monday, Benjie took Sam for a little walk. It was a fine night, and he went to Hyde Park, thinking that it would be a good occasion for himself and Sam (who was in excellent spirits) to listen to the Marble Arch orators.

They would surely be at their best at such a crisis
and most amusingly violent. But the gates at
Hyde Park Corner were closed. A cordon of
police was stationed there, and the policemen said,
quietly and coldly as though they were thinking
of something else: ' Move on there, please! '

He joined the crowd pressed against the railings, and in this crowd no one spoke—only they
gazed. Very odd, thought Benjie, on this fine
May evening, and the strike not yet declared, to
see Hyde Park a camp. Inside the railings there
were fleets of lorries and huts and tents rising. No
one spoke: only Sam barked at a chow tethered
by a blue cord to the arm of a lady. Benjie looked
at the lady and saw that she was fair. Her figure
was as slim as fashion dictated figures should be
(to Benjie's constant chagrin, for he liked figures
to be plump). She was wearing a little blue hat,
her hair was pale gold, and she had the face of an
innocent, rather bewildered child. Her chow
was aloof and dignified. Sam, at the end of
his lead, strained towards it. Benjie raised his
hat.

' The Government seems to have got in first,'
he said.

' Oh yes,' she answered in a voice that was all
music. ' Isn't it splendid of them? '

It had been difficult, with his one arm, to raise
his hat and control Sam at the same time. His
movement had for a moment jerked Sam on to
his hind feet. She smiled at that. After all he
was seventy-one, but no one would know it. He
was spare and tough as he had been at forty.

'What is going to happen, do you think?' she asked him.

They walked away together. Half an hour later she had given him her address. She had rooms, it appeared, on the Chelsea Embankment. Her name, it seemed, was Miss Grace Mortimer.

He took her, that same evening, out to supper.

When he reached his own place at three or four o'clock the following morning he was aware of a deep and bitter unhappiness. He sat on his bed in his shirt, staring at his own abasement. He was not abased because he had been friendly to Miss Mortimer. He had done no harm to the pretty lady, to whom sudden meetings with strange gentlemen were no novel affair. She had been charming, had talked of her father, a General, now deceased, had shrugged her bare shoulders at the way the world was going, had thanked him for his generous gift, had begged him to come and have tea with her on the following afternoon. He had not told her that he was over seventy, and he was certain that she had not supposed him a day more than fifty. He had been ashamed of nothing that he had done, and yet he was most utterly ashamed.

At that hour of the morning with the chilly room hostile and the town preparing in a ghastly silence for the coming day's warfare, he was as lonely an old man as the world contained. Sam was sleeping in his basket near the window, comfortable and indifferent.

'Vanessa! Vanessa! I want you, I want you!

Where are you? Why aren't you here to keep me company in this damnable world? '

Then he got off the bed, pulled his shirt over his head, did his exercises. Afterwards he lay sleepless, seeing the lorry, projecting rifles like a hedgehog, hearing the wild shouts beneath the window, starting at that sudden flame on the horizon of a burning building. . . . He had never loved London so dearly as in those hours.

When daylight came he was still ashamed and abashed. He was saying to himself, as he had said so often before, that he was finished with women, but that statement did not lessen his abasement. He lay in bed, his head resting on his arm, wondering what was happening to the world and hating and despising himself. Here was the country tumbling into ruin and he doing nothing about it, but worse than that, here was he himself a hale and hearty old man who did nothing but wander about the world, sigh for a woman long dead, and appease his appetites in any selfish easy way that appeared to him. He was not convicted of sin. He did not feel a sinner who must hurry to repentance; but he *was* convicted of waste, of sterility.

He had achieved some kind of relation with his son, it was true, but in spite of their greater friendliness Tom still bored him. Tom wanted to mother him, and oh, God! he hated to be mothered!

And then there was Sally. Before he had left for Morocco he had taken Sally to the theatre. He could see that she was unhappy, but she wouldn't tell him anything. Just like these modern children; got no confidence in their parents. There was a gulf fixed between his generation and theirs. She was unhappy. This young man of hers was no good. Benjie didn't like him, a weak backbone-less kind of fellow, the sort of man women wanted to help. He was making Sally miserable, and Benjie's heart ached for her. He wanted, in fact, to be allowed to love someone—yes, although he was past seventy. He was damnably lonely and no use to anyone. Perhaps after all there was something in what Vanessa said. There was somewhere another, a secret life, and if you didn't find it you were ' left ' when you were old. Oh, but he was not going to whine! He didn't care if he *was* alone. Everyone was alone if it came to that. He had better be up and doing, see what was happening to this crazy world.

While he was dressing Tom came in.

' Look here,' said Benjie. ' How can I make myself useful? '

' Oh, easily. They want volunteers for every kind of thing. You can take that car of yours and drive people to their offices. Everyone's walking. It's a sight, I can tell you. Outside the Foreign Office it's packed with people waiting to enrol. They've enlisted a hundred thousand in the Volunteer Service Corps already. They're going to supply two million gallons of milk a day from Hyde Park. It's marvellous! England's middle-class counts for something in a crisis.'

' Yes, that's what Russia hadn't got,' said Benjie. He added, smiling: ' Our family will be pleased. I bet they're all busy serving the country. Any fighting yet?' Benjie asked.

' No, I don't think so. But I dare say there will be. I've got to go down to Limehouse.'

Benjie looked out of window. Not a soul was to be seen. He went out. Everyone was walking. He came to Birdcage Walk and found it packed with cars, crawling along four abreast. He discovered that the gates of Charing Cross railway station were locked. No one seemed to know quite what to do. It was a new world, a new life, but beneath the uncertainty he was aware of a strong united determination. He seemed to feel it in the very stones of the street. ' The Strike hasn't got a chance,' he thought. He decided that he would get his car from the garage and be of some use. He climbed on to a pirate omnibus driven by a very bright but determined young man in knickerbockers. Two young men standing beside him were going down to Dover to assist in the unloading of the ships. He thought that he would ·offer to go with them, but an unwonted shyness stopped him. He saw an omnibus that had been in the wars, standing derelict surrounded by a large, gazing, meditative crowd. He noticed a big advertisement on its boards: ' Maurice Moscovitch: The Great Lover.'

The great lover! Well, he was done with women and all the silly, sterile, messy things in his life, and then he saw a girl near to him, swaying uncomfortably as the bus moved. A pretty girl looking defenceless and a little frightened. He wondered whether she would not like his assist-

ance. A fat, rather breathless man near him said:
' This bloody Strike's being helped by the bloody
Germans. Give you my word! Syndicate of
German financiers. I happen to know. They're
landing bullion on the East Coast from a small
ship.'

Instantly Benjie's temper, which was easily
moved, was up. Silly damned liar! He'd like
to tell him so. He nearly did, but got off at the
top of Knightsbridge instead. Yes, he got off
and walked straight into Gordon Newmark.

' Hullo! ' said Gordon. ' Why, it's Benjie! '

' Yes,' said Benjie. ' It is! '

' Isn't this splendid! ' said Gordon. ' We'll
show them, the dirty tykes. No one knew what
England was capable of until now.'

He was swelled with elation, triumph, pride
and satisfaction. His handsome face (Benjie always
thought that he looked like a horse that was one
of the best and smartest performers in the most
famous of circuses) was carved into a proper model
of all that the English ruling classes should be.

' Here! ' cried Gordon. ' What are you doing
to help? '

' What ought I to do? ' Benjie asked modestly.

' Go down to the Mansion House. They'll
soon enrol you there and tell you what to do.'

' I will,' said Benjie. ' Thanks very much.'

At the same moment his daughter Sally was
saying to her employer, Mr. Bimberg:

' No, thank you, Mr. Bimberg. I can get
home quite all right this afternoon.'

Mr. Bimberg was plump, bald and very neatly

dressed. She had been quite comfortable with
him for a long time now, but of late—within the
last few months—he had taken, it seemed, a new
interest in her. He put his soft round hand on
her arm, he patted her shoulder. A pity, because
the job suited her.

But this morning she was too deeply involved
in her own private history to consider the outside
world very deeply. She was fighting with all the
strength that she had to keep dreadful terror at
bay. As she sat taking down Mr. Bimberg's
letters her thoughts were wild. Arnold had not
kept his appointment last night. She had waited
and waited. He had arranged to take her to
The Best People that they might together admire
the fine art of Miss Olga Lindo. She had sat in
her evening frock (she had worn it only twice
before) for a whole hour. How horrible that
hour had been! Sally was tutored to conceal her
emotions, but after that agony of suspense she had
burst into tears, torn off her frock and lain on
her bed. He might come. Something had kept
him. Ten. Eleven. Midnight. But why had
he not telephoned? In the morning there would
be a letter. But there was no letter. Choking
her independence, she had telephoned. He had
left the house half an hour before. So, her head
up, looking gravely at Mr. Bimberg, she had taken
down his letters.

At lunch-time, alone in the room, she had
telephoned again. Arnold answered her. Her
heart hammering, her voice a little breathless in
spite of herself, she said:

'Arnold, whatever happened last night?'
(She would forgive him whatever his excuse
might be.)

'Oh, my dear, I'm too frightfully sorry.'

'No—but whatever was it? I waited and
waited.'

She knew that he hesitated.

'Darling, I'll explain everything. It wasn't
my fault. Really it wasn't.'

'But what *was* it?' Her knees were trembling. She steadied herself with her hand on a
chair.

'I can't explain here.'

'But why didn't you telephone?'

'I couldn't. It was impossible where I was.'

'But where were you?'

'Don't be so difficult, sweet. You know how
difficult it is on a telephone.'

'But we can't leave it like this. I waited and
waited. It was awful. How soon can I see
you?'

Again he hesitated. Then he said:

'All right. I'll come along to your place about
six.'

'You *will* come?'

'Of course I will.'

A little reassured she sat there, thinking. She
did not go out to lunch, but stayed there without
moving. She ought not to have told him that
she cared. It was the doctrine of her friends that
a girl never showed that she cared for a man. She
could hear Margaret saying: 'So of course I told
him that if he wanted to go he could. *I* didn't

mind. So off he went, and I rang up Archie and we had a grand time at Ciro's. *Of course* he came round the next day. . . .'

But she wasn't quite like that. She had been Arnold's mistress for nearly a year and that did make a difference, didn't it? It made a difference in every kind of way, because Arnold now had everything he wanted while she . . . she wanted more and more. Not physical things, but for him to *want* her and to need her, to depend on her. . . . The physical thing was nothing, and yet it was everything because, after it happened, Sally was his mother, his sister, his friend, his companion, while Arnold was still only Sally's lover and that not so warmly as once he had been. He should have married her. It was not perhaps very fine of him to fear so abjectly his mother, and yet Sally understood that too. *She* was not afraid of his mother, but it was natural that Arnold should be. For he was afraid of a great many things, which was partly the reason of Sally's love for him because she wanted to shelter and protect him.

As the afternoon went on her fears grew again. *Why* had he not come?

' Yes,' said Mr. Bimberg. ' You had really better let me drive you home.'

' Oh no, thank you, Mr. Bimberg.'

' You'll have to walk all the way, you know.'

' I'm not going very far.' (Which was untrue.)

He looked at her with his round eyes like rather damp marbles. She thought that he was going to touch her. She stood her ground. But he did not. He sighed and ambled away.

The streets were very strange. Crowds of people were walking, all rather quickly and rather silently. Was this Revolution, the kind of thing that had happened in Russia? She did not care in the least if it were. She only cared about Arnold. They all walked together like an army obeying orders. She began to be conscious of something corporate in this movement. She saw an omnibus, ran for it, stood packed in a confusion of legs and bodies, had her penny collected by a very pleasant red-faced man in a brown suit, jumped off again, stood in a side-street listening to the sudden silence as though she expected to hear a gun fired or to see a flare of light against the sky. *Was* this Revolution? Would there be fighting and barricades? Perhaps Arnold would need her more if there was fighting—and she had a curious quick picture of herself as a small child, looking up from her book in the Hill Street house, seeing Ellis in the doorway and hearing him say: ' Sally, do come and play soldiers. . . .' She looked at her wrist-watch and hurried on.

' I mustn't show him that I care,' she thought. ' I must be quite indifferent. I *know* that he wants me. He *can't* do without me.'

When she reached the flat Arnold was already there, standing in front of the fireplace. When she saw him she loved him so dreadfully that it was all she could do not to hurry into his arms. But she did not. She went into her room, took off her small brown hat, gave her cropped hair a shake, waited for a moment staring at, but not seeing, the photograph of her mother on the

mantelpiece. Then she came in, sat down, lit a
cigarette and said:

'Well, you're a beauty, Arnold. Whatever did
you let me down for like that last night?'

He did not move towards her, and there was a
constricted movement at her heart as though a
cold finger had touched it. But she looked at him
quietly, noticed his tie of blue and red stripes, his
pale long hands, his eager, easily startled eyes.
Yes, she knew him so very well.

'Look here, darling,' he began. 'I'm most
awfully sorry about last night.'

'No—but what *was* it? Of course I'd have
understood if something had kept you, but even
then you should have 'phoned, shouldn't you?'

She knew that her voice slipped into a sharper
pitch, not from anger but from fear.

'Oh yes, I should. I meant to. But you see
I was at home——'

'Well, you've *got* a telephone in your house,
haven't you?'

'Yes. Of course. Don't be facetious, Sally. . . .'
He came forward a few steps, hesitated, then
plunged.

('Why,' thought Sally to herself, 'he's just like
a piece of seaweed, yellow, and if you pressed any
part of him with your finger it would go "pop."'
At the same time she wanted to take him and
smooth his hair, calm his fears, give him a
present, offer him a drink, lie down on the outside of the bed with him, draw his head to her
breast and listen to a catalogue of his troubles.
At the same time she also wanted to throw the

book on the table—she even saw the title, *Jacob's Room*—at his head and stamp on his toes. She always said that he wore shoes with too shiny a toe.)

These things passed through her mind and like odds and ends caught up with a shower were drowned in the one and only insistent drumming consciousness:

'He's come to tell me something. He's not going to see me any more.'

'The fact is, Sally, I had an awful row with my mother last night.'

'Oh, did you? What about?' (But she knew quite well what about.)

'About you. She says that I have to choose.'

'Choose?'

'Yes. Between you and her.'

Sally stared at him and saw the seaweed, gold with dark brown fronds swaying in a sea-pool, swaying indeterminately while the breeze ruffled the water of the pool into little angry protests.

'Oh, I see. She's told you that before.'

He went back to the fireplace, hanging his head at the gritty little fire and kicking the fender with his shoe.

'Yes, I know.' He turned round and faced her. 'Look here, Sally. I'm no good. You've got to give me up. I can't stand it. I've had more than a year of it, facing mother. It's more than my being afraid of her. It's like being afraid of oneself. Oh! I can't explain these things, but I'm sort of inside her. Part of me thinks just as she does—I've loved you frightfully, I do love you frightfully now, but all the time I'm wanting to be right with mother again. I thought, perhaps, she'd get over it. I thought she'd get used to the idea. But she doesn't. She hates it more and more.'

' *Why* does she hate me?' Sally asked in a small sharp voice.

' Oh, it isn't *you* that she hates! I think she'd make a fuss about my marrying anyone. She doesn't want to lose me. Of course that's all wrong and very selfish, but in a way I understand it. I don't really want to lose her either. All the same she'd get over that—because she's really an awfully good sort—if you . . . if you——' He hesitated. ' You see, Sally, she's heard a lot about your father and she says that there's one side of your family that's mad and it always has been. Of course that's all rot——'

' It isn't all rot at all,' Sally interrupted. ' If you look at it from one point of view it's true, I suppose.'

' Mother isn't conventional exactly, but——'

' Does she know,' Sally interrupted, ' that I'm your mistress? '

' No, she doesn't.' He squared his shoulders. His face was so white and miserable that something in Sally cried: ' I hate both these women who are making you so unhappy. Pay no attention to either of them.' And something else in her cried: ' You're a wretched weak creature and I'm a fool to have bothered over you for a single moment.'

' To tell you the truth, Sally, I'd be afraid for

her to know.   She's old-fashioned about those things.   And it wouldn't make it better if she did know.'

' She'd see me as the designing siren, I suppose,' Sally said.   ' Well, perhaps I have been.' Then, after a pause, she asked: ' What exactly did happen last night? '

' I was dressed and just going out to you when she came into my room.   She asked me where I was going and I told her.   She made a most awful scene.   Oh, it went on for hours!   She cried.   She wouldn't let me telephone or anything.'

' I see,' said Sally.   ' And then? '

' Oh, then—at last——'

' You promised to give me up? '

He nodded his head.

He began a torrent of explanation.   She cut him short.

' All right, Arnold.   I understand perfectly.'

She went up to him, kissed him gently on the forehead, held out her hand.

' Good-bye, my dear.'

' No, but, Sally——' He tried to catch her in his arms.   Quietly she moved away from him, stood looking at him for a moment, then said:

' Now cut along.   We've had a lovely time and I don't blame you a little bit.'

He was going to speak again but, looking at her, decided not to.   He picked up his hat and coat and went out.

Into his small room at the Mansion House, Benjie was aware just as the clock struck seven of the intrusion of panic. A stout General with very bright red tabs on his shoulders was shouting down the telephone: ' Oh, but, look here, the thing's absurd! Give the feller a kick in the pants and tell him to clear out. What do you say? I can't hear . . . very bad at Camden Town? Well, tell Ritchie to cut along. . . . Hullo! hullo! are you there, Ward? Well, why couldn't you say so? Can you hear me? Hullo! hullo! '

Benjie, his gaze idly fixed on the General's large posterior, wondered for the first time whether after all the Herries would manage to hold the fort. Everyone seemed to him to be Herries down here, and he himself, in these few days, had become civilised Herries too. He had enrolled countless men and women, urging them to do their utmost for King and Country, and as, with serious and patient faces, they had promised him to do so, he had thought: ' By God, this country is all right. The heart of this old country is sound,' almost as though he had been Cynthia or Alfred or Gordon or Adrian or even old Horace, who, the night before at Cynthia's, had beamed sentimentally through his glasses and, like a bishop pronouncing the blessing, had said: ' This will go down in history. England has proved herself.' It *would* go down in history, but he was not sure whether it would be quite in the fashion that his family had desired. What was happening beyond this quiet and dignified room?

The Government in its *British Gazette* proclaimed that it was maintaining with complete success all the vital services of supply—light, food

and power. Communications were improving
every day. On the other hand, fifty London
General omnibuses had not returned to their
depot last night; at Middlesbrough some women
and boys had held up a train; a motor-bus had
been set on fire in East London; shops were being
looted in Edinburgh; and Mr. Saklatvala had been
sentenced to two months' imprisonment. On this
very morning the *British Gazette* announced that
they had discovered that the General Council had
issued a new order to ' paralyse and break down
the supply of food and the necessaries of life.'
How far would this spread? Every day increased
the danger. He did not know that at any moment
returning through Piccadilly he might not see the
appearance of the lorry bristling like a hedgehog,
the pieces of red cloth tied to the rifles, the
windows of the Ritz smashed with machine-gun
fire. ' They don't know. They haven't had the
experience, any of them. They are blind to everything. Their whole social order has crumbled to
pieces under their very eyes and they are not
aware of it. This machinery—the machinery
they've been used to so long—may vanish in a
moment's temper. . . . They don't know it.
They haven't seen it. . . .'

' By God! ' the General was shouting into the
telephone, ' tell them they've *got* to or it will be
worse for them. This isn't Russia, you know.'

No, it wasn't Russia. The Herries were here.
There had been no Herries in Russia. All the
same . . .

' Coming along, Herries? ' the General said,

his face beaming. ' I told the bastards where *they* got off. Coming my way? I'll drive you.'

So he sat in the back of the car with the General and discovered as, with throngs of pedestrians on every side of them, they pushed their way towards Trafalgar Square, that this fine stout kindly officer was happier than ever he had been in his life before.

' This is what I've been wanting, Herries. Teach the blighters a lesson. I'll be damned glad myself if it does come to real trouble. Give us an excuse to be rid of a few of them. That feller Saklatvala—I'd string him up on a lamp-post if I had *my* way. By God, I've never been so proud of my country as I am to-night.'

So the Herries were saying. They'd all like to string Saklatvala up on a lamp-post. Old Judith Paris, he remembered, had written in her book somewhere of seeing a boy hanged outside a butcher's shop. She hadn't liked it. But then she'd always been a queer one. And the Herries were right. Civilisation had got to be kept on its feet. But suppose the old world was gone. Gone for ever and ever? Suppose on that evening when the whole world had burst out singing (he had sung like the others) they had sung the old world out of existence? Why, then *where* would the Herries be?

The town seemed to him sinister to-night. It had started to rain and soon it was a downpour. Through the rain the town was walking home. In the heart of the crowd the motor-cars, loaded with people—shop-girls, secretaries, elderly women, old men like himself—ploughed their way. The

lights flared and the darkness stifled the lights.
The whole town seemed on the move as though
the order had been given to abandon it, and everyone was fleeing for safety. And yet they were not
fleeing. That was the very last thing that they
were doing. These people were defending the
town, nobly, gallantly, without a thought for themselves. But what about the enemy? *He* knew how
silent a thin street could be, and behind every
window a concealed rifle. *He* knew how men
could gather, in secret, in silence, and then, at a
spoken word, the familiar places—so old, so safe,
so complacent—would be filled with death. This
was no melodrama. Efficient, historical fact. One
machine-gun at the Oxford Circus end of Regent
Street, where they now were, and that crowd would
turn in upon itself, would scream, cry aloud, bodies
crushed into the mud, and the rain pouring down.
. . . Oh, he was an old man! What had happened to his nerve?

'And that, my dear feller,' the General was
saying, ' is the way *I'd* deal with them! '

At the top of Portland Place, where several
roads meet, there was a complete confusion.
Under torrential rain a mass of cars, coming from
different directions, faced one another like angry
herds of cattle. Horns hooted, men shouted,
nothing could move. A policeman, his black
cape shining in the rain, appeared as it seemed
from the bowels of the earth, waving his hand.
He came right up to the General's car, placing his
hand on the bonnet, and Benjie saw his face, his
blue eyes, his cheeks wet with the rain, and a clear,

unflinching, unhesitating power of direction and order in his every movement. He seemed a giant from some other planet, impersonal and inhuman. He called out, waved his hand, and at once the disorder was composed into order: the cars separated and divided. Benjie was reassured. 'That man wasn't in Russia,' he thought. But just before his own car moved on he saw a girl, almost slipping, recovering, placing her hand for an instant against the window. It was Sally.

'Here. Let me out. Good night, General. See you to-morrow.'

A moment later he had caught his girl's arm.

'Hi! Sally! What are you doing here?'

The rain was driving in their faces, and the collar of her waterproof was drawn up. He held on to her arm, but he could feel that she was resisting him. They had moved away from the roar and confusion and stopped under a lamp. She looked up at him.

'Hullo, Father!' she said. 'What a coincidence!'

'The lamplight,' he thought, 'is making her look like this, and the rain. By God! something has happened to her, though. She's as though she were walking in her sleep.' Then she woke up. He felt her arm tremble under his hand, and her small pale face under the light little hat from which the rain was dripping hardened into that look of angry determination that was often exactly his own.

'I must get on,' she said. 'I'm late.'

'Where are you going?'

' Oh—I've got an engagement with a friend.'

Then her lower lip began to tremble. He saw that she was on the edge of tears. He put his arm round her.

' You haven't any engagement, my dear,' he said. ' Nor have I. I'll take you home.'

She had ceased to resist.

' All right,' she said. ' I don't care.'

They walked back to Oxford Street and not a word was spoken. Then they found an omnibus that was driven by quite an elderly party with a white moustache and was crowded with rowdy young men who were going off on some job.

' They say there's been terrible fighting in Camberwell to-night,' an elderly lady said.

' We'll protect you, ma'am,' the young men shouted. ' Lenin shan't get you.'

When they were in Sally's room and had taken off their wet things they sat opposite one another on either side of the fire.

' Margaret coming in? ' Benjie asked.

' No, I don't think so,' Sally said. Then she added: ' I've nothing to give you to eat, Father. There isn't a scrap in the place.'

' That doesn't matter.' He pulled out his pipe, crossed his thin legs, leaned back. He was weary. This was a life, when all was said and done, for an old man of seventy-one, and, fit though he was, his back ached and his legs told him that they had done enough for one day.

' Look here, Sally—that was all my eye about your going anywhere. You didn't know where you were going.'

She didn't answer him.

' What's the matter? '

Still she didn't answer him, but sat up straight in her chair, her hands crossed over her knees.

' Why don't you let me take you out and give you a meal? '

' Oh, it's all right, thanks.'

He said at last: ' I wish to God Vanessa was here.' He went on to cover the silence:

' You know, Sally, we ought to see more of one another. I've been a bit shy, I dare say, but it's been my fault that I've never, all my life, been able to get on any very sound terms with anyone except your mother. Light come and light go. And now I'm paying for it. All the same,' he said, ' you and I and Tom—we've only got one another now. You've got your young man, I suppose.'

' He's gone,' she said.

' What do you mean—he's gone? '

' Oh, he left me three or four days ago. His mother didn't like me.'

' Oh, so that's it,' said Benjie softly.

There was a long silence.

' Well, my dear,' Benjie said at last, ' I shouldn't worry about him too much. You'll find someone much better.'

' Oh, I dare say,' said Sally.

' He was frightened of his mother, wasn't he? '

' He was very fond of her. He hoped for a long time that she would get used to me. But she didn't.'

' Was it partly,' Benjie asked, ' because you had a bad lot for a father? '

' It was all of us. You and I and Vanessa and Judith Paris and your father being shot. Right away back. She seemed to know all about us. Now if I had been Rosalind or Mary it would have been all right.'

' I see,' said Benjie. ' Sins of the fathers. Very unfair, I always think.'

' She didn't know I was sleeping with Arnold,' said Sally in a dull toneless voice. ' That would only have made it worse.'

' He was a bit of a cad, I should say,' Benjie remarked. ' All the same I'm glad he didn't marry you.'

' No, he wasn't a cad at all. I understand him perfectly.'

' You'll get over it, my dear. One gets over everything. (All the same, he thought, I've never got over being without Vanessa.) I've come to the conclusion there's a lot to be said for marriage. Oh, I know, your generation don't think so, and I know that Vanessa had the hell of a time with Ellis. All the same I can see now that it would have been very pleasant if your mother and I had been married. It's the best arrangement society's discovered yet.'

' I didn't care,' Sally said, ' whether I was married to Arnold or not. I wanted to look after him. I wanted—I wanted——'

Her voice broke. She tried to recover herself, beating her hand against her knee. Her mouth moved and quivered and shook. Then she began to cry.

Benjie went over to her.

'Here, Sally—don't cry. It's all right. You've got your life in front of you. Darling—Sally darling.'

He knelt down beside her, putting his arm round her.

'These days—I didn't know anything could be so bad. . . . I didn't know I could miss anyone so much. I thought I knew enough not to be hurt by anything. He was so sweet. . . . He loved me . . . he did really. . . .'

'There, Sally, it will be all right. Really it will. It's been my fault. I haven't been with you as I ought to be. We'll stick together now. You can tell me anything. I've been very lonely too. . . . Hellish. . . .'

He drew her with him to the other chair, a big roomy one. He sat back, and with his arm around her wrapped her into his embrace. She was folded up in his arm like a child. She was so small that he could hold her easily. Her hand was clenched inside his. She dried her eyes and with little convulsive sobs told him everything: how Arnold had not taken her to the theatre, of their last meeting, of how, next day, she had not known what she was doing, had wandered about in the crowds, had worked for Bimberg mechanically, had not slept at all for three nights—and to-night she had not known, she had thought that perhaps now that everything was over it would be better. . . .

He held her more tightly, feeling her quiver against his heart.

'I know. We all go through it. It doesn't

matter what generation we belong to, how much
we think we know. It doesn't make any difference. . . .'

He thought of that last talk with Vanessa in
his room, the agony and distress of letting her go.
He was ashamed of his casual life, his neglect of
his promise—' I swear, Vanessa, I'll never let her
go again.'

A long time after Sally got up from the chair,
went into her room and washed her face and hands.

She stood looking at him, and smiled.

' You're rather a pet,' she said. ' You've been
awfully nice to me.'

' What shall we do? ' he asked. ' Go out and
have a meal? '

' Oh no. I don't think I could eat anything.'

' Let's see how the Strike's going.' He went
to the wireless and turned it on. Someone was
speaking. ' Why, it's old Baldwin! ' Benjie said.

Mr. Baldwin was saying:

' The Government is not fighting to lower the
standard of living of the miners. That sugges-
tion is being spread abroad. It is not true. No
honest person can doubt that my whole desire is
to maintain the standard of living of every worker.'

Then after a while there were the sonorous
tones of Lord Oxford:

' The real victims of a general strike are what
is called the common people. We should have
lost all self-respect if we were to allow any section
of the community, at its own will and for whatever
motives, to bring to a standstill the industrial and
social life of the nation. That would be to

acquiesce in the substitution for Free Government
of a Dictatorship. This the British People will
never do.'

The voice died away. Sally's eyes were
closing.

' Go on. Go to bed,' said Benjie.

He went with her into her bedroom and, with
a little sigh, without taking off even her slippers,
she lay down on the bed. He lay down beside her,
taking her in his arm again. In a moment, her
head against his waistcoat, she was asleep, and he
lay there, looking with his sharp, ironical eyes at
the ceiling, happier than he had been for many a
year.

BELOVED MOUNTAIN

'AND now,' said Tom, ' as we cross the bridge you'll see how beautiful it is! '

'And I hope to God she will,' he thought, for he was convinced now that the visit, the visit to which he had looked forward with such eagerness, would prove a terrible failure. Sally had invited herself: he would never have dared, of himself, to ask her. He had taken his three weeks' holiday late this year—it was now early in November 1928 —and, as always, had come up to Cumberland. He wanted to be nowhere else. It was lovelier with every visit. He had taken rooms in a house, Bella Vista, on the road from Grange to Manesty, and settled in there, very happy with Mrs. Zanazzi, his hostess, and Miss Zanazzi her daughter, and his books, walking every day, some-times a long tramp, when he would be away in Eskdale, or by Esthwaite, or Patterdale for the night. He was forty-four now and used to being alone. His father was in Spain. He had friends in London, but no one whom he wished to have with him.

And then Sally had written, saying that she would come and stay with him for a week, Sally who had been so strange and hard for so long, who had scarcely seen him, who had had nothing to say to him when they were together.

He had been terribly excited. Mrs. Zanazzi had arranged that Sally should have the best bedroom in the house, the room with the view out over the shelving fields to Skiddaw and the Lake.

They would have a glorious week. He and Sally would recover one another again. He knew how unhappy she was and, if he were very careful and did not show her in any way that he wanted to help her, he might give her something that she needed. Oh yes! how *very* careful he would be!

So he had gone to the station full of eager expectation. She wouldn't think much of his small Austin, but he would explain to her that it was better to have a small car in this country; so often the bridges were narrow and the roads little more than lanes. . . .

When he saw her come from the train he had gone eagerly forward.

' Hullo, Tom! ' she had said, and, at once (so sensitive he was) he had known that there was no change, that she was hundreds of miles away from him, that she didn't care for him, that she didn't know why she had come.

And the drive in the Austin had been terrible. She had shown no interest in anything. When he had asked her about London and had she been to parties and how was old Bimberg and Cynthia and Maurice and Margaret, she had assured him, ' Oh yes ' and ' Oh no ' and ' Everything's just the same.'

' And now,' he said, ' as we cross the bridge
you'll see how beautiful it is! '

To himself it was exquisite. The brilliant
autumn colouring was gone. Everything was
silver-grey. There had been much rain and the
Lake had flooded; the stream ran under the
bridge in tumbling curves and circles, watched
gravely by the dark hills while the last pale leaves
clung to the trees; the fields were faintly green,
floating in the last light of the autumn day towards
the Lake like green smoke gently stirred by the
wind.

He did not know that as Sally looked out she
was caught by a quick apprehension. ' Something
awful is going to happen. Why did I come?
Whatever made me write and ask to come? '
Tom's kind and serious face, his short heavy body
bent a little forward at the wheel, his eagerness
to make her happy. . . . Oh, why was Tom
always the same, why was he not some heavenly
messenger who had swung down in a silver
aeroplane and whispered to her: ' You have had
enough of this. You have had more than two
years of it. I will catch you up and we will fly,
like the golden Eagle, into coloured clouds and
a foaming brilliant sea '? But Tom was no
heavenly messenger, and like green smoke those
sleepy fields rolled into the Lake.

A pale ivory twilight lay over the landscape
when Sally looked from her window. She could
distinguish no detail, only overhead above the
dark shadows of clustering trees the sky broke into
spaces of dim ghostly light as though a moon were

somewhere hiding. When she heard running water something caught at her heart. Since her babyhood she had never been in this country, but now it was as though something familiar were returning to her; the smell of wet leaves, the sky that revealed nothing and yet seemed a world of motion and movement, the queer windy whisper in the air, dark shapes on the horizon that were, she knew, the mountains, these things were all familiar to her and unique. No country of hill and field where she had been was like this one, and yet she could see nothing but shadow and, when a dog barked, it was a voice welcoming her, reproaching her for being so long away.

After supper when she sat opposite Tom in the sitting-room she smiled.

' I like being here, Tom,' she said. ' It's as though I'd been here before.'

' Well, you have. You were born not far away from here.'

' I know. In a farm, in a storm. Mother nearly died getting to the farm. She often told me.'

' The funny thing is,' Tom said, ' that we came into this country two hundred years ago—old Rogue Herries riding a horse with his small son in front of him. Then we grew and multiplied like the Israelites. We covered the country. And now we've died away again. There are none of us here any more. But it's caught one after another of us, set its seal on us, made us influence others. Perhaps, although we haven't any of us been very important, we've altered England's history by coming here. That's what a small piece of country can do.'

' You ought to write about it, Tom,' she said, laughing and thinking that he was nicer here, sitting back, smoking his pipe, than he was anywhere else.

' I can't. That's what's so damnable.' He picked up an orange-covered book on a table near him. ' Listen to this, Sally.'

He read:

' *So she let her book lie unburied and dishevelled on the ground, and watched the vast view, varied like an ocean floor this evening with the sun lightening it and the shadows darkening it. There was a village with a church tower among elm trees; a grey domed manor house in a park; a spark of light burning on some glasshouse; a farmyard with yellow corn stacks. The fields were marked with black tree clumps and beyond the fields stretched long woodlands, and there was the gleam of a river, and then hills again. In the far distance Snowdon's crags broke white among the clouds; she saw the far Scottish hills and the wild tides that swirl about the Hebrides. She listened for the sound of gun-firing out at sea. No—only the wind blew. There was no war to-day. Drake had gone; Nelson had gone. "And there," she thought, letting her eyes, which had been looking at these far distances, drop once more to the land beneath her, " was my land once; that Castle between the downs was mine; and all that moor running to the sea was mine." Here the landscape (it must have been some trick of the fading light) shook itself, heaped itself, let all this encumbrance of houses, castles, and woods*

slide off its tent-shaped sides. The bare mountains of
Turkey were before her. It was blazing noon. She
looked straight at the baked hillside. Goats cropped
the sandy tufts at her feet. An eagle soared above
her. The raucous voice of old Rustum, the gipsy,
croaked in her ears, " What is your antiquity and
your race, and your possessions compared with this?
What do you need with four hundred bedrooms and
silver lids on your dishes, and housemaids dusting? " '

' Whatever's that? ' asked Sally.

' It's *Orlando*, by Virginia Woolf. Just out.'

' I don't understand a word of it. What's it
mean? '

' It means what it says. You must forget
things like space and time.'

' How can you? '

' You can if you like to go far enough. Do
you remember in Judith's book, little Harcourt
Herries reciting Pope to Francis and David at
Ravenglass? Well, he's still reciting it. He's
still moved by the beauty of it as I'm moved now
by the beauty of this.'

' That's nonsense,' said Sally.

' Yes, if you like to think so.'

They sat in silence, quite happy, coming
closer to one another with every tick of the clock.

' I'm beginning,' said Tom, ' to see why we
are all so restless and unhappy. It's an awful
time really.   No one seems to be sure of anything
any more—religion, economics, politics. So many
people out of jobs.   Why, look at you and me and
Father. I lost Mary, you lost Arnold, Father lost
Vanessa.   And so in a way everyone we know

seems to have lost something. But then, as the
gipsy says in *Orlando*, " What do you need with
four hundred bedrooms and silver lids on your
dishes? " You don't need them if you discover
the other world. Do you think I'm talking
rot? '

'I don't understand a word that you're
saying.'

'Well, I'm a failure, a complete and absolute
failure. I wanted to be a good writer. I wanted
to marry Mary. I adored Vanessa and she died.
I wanted you and Father to need me—and you
don't. Nobody needs me. So I'm a good example of times like these. I've been unhappy and
restless for years. But lately I've been finding
out that there's a world that has nothing to do
with my needs, nothing to do with space and
time, a world that has been showing me points of
light for years like the sun flashing on a window,
but I haven't seen. . . . If I could *live* in that
world, Sally, it wouldn't matter how much a
failure I myself was because it's so beautiful, so
timeless and so alive that personal failure is of no
importance at all.'

'It all sounds very vague to me,' said Sally,
but looking at him with curiosity. It was so odd
to see Tom with his heavy body, thick shoulders,
quiet ways, bursting like this into fantasy.

'But I too can be fantastic,' she thought,
realising suddenly why it was that, through all
these years, she had never been really intimate with
Margaret. 'I too can be fantastic,' and, looking
into the fire, she let her mind wander back over

the past year, which had, in truth, been as nasty and spiteful a year as she had ever known. Later, lying in bed, unable to sleep, she reviewed it and discovered that it had already altered its colours under the influence of this place. Like the families in Genesis, Margaret led to Olive Stane and Olive Stane to Miss Bourchier and Miss Bourchier to Freddie Tallent and Freddie to Freda and Freda to William Blake and William Blake (so *very* unlike the poet!) to Mrs. Carslake-King and Mrs. Carslake-King to stout, solid and feminist Mrs. Brent. At the stopping-place of Mrs. Brent, Sally considered herself as a feminist. She had not been a very good one. Why? It had seemed, after the tragedy of Arnold, the natural thing to consider men feeble and conceited and exasperating creatures. There was, if you were to believe them, a regular war of the sexes. All the men stood up for one another and were most unfair about it, and all the women stood up for one another and were not unfair about it. Some of the women were grand—Olive Stane and Miss Bourchier for instance. They had wit, humour, generosity, courage. What did they lack? They lacked nothing perhaps, but spent their time altogether too much in London literary sets, never really meeting anyone but one another, although they thought they did.

And so, not one of them reached the first class. As writers they were clever and no more, as politicians they were not effective, as women they left men cold and frightened.

So Sally, who had never really been at home

with them because she was not clever enough, admired them and left them. She went for a while to parties, but this life she soon abandoned. She disliked to be made love to in an absent-minded way, which was what the young men did; she disliked to be drunk; she disliked not to know the name of the hostess who was entertaining her. She disliked to drink gin dressed (for it was, that night, an Infant Party) as a babe-in-arms. She disliked people to take it for granted that unless she was Lesbian she was uninteresting. Nevertheless she did not make the mistake of supposing that the whole of her generation were worthless. On the contrary, she found among them enough courage, honesty and common sense to save Europe were someone really worth-while to get hold of it. Only there was not, it appeared, anyone worthwhile. Lenin was dead and Mussolini was in Italy.

So, unable to be intellectual, and weary of parties, she fell back on the Family. There were not many just now, of her own generation. There were two distant cousins, Phyllis and Anstey Veasey. Their great-grandfather had been the younger brother of Anna Veasey, who had married Warren, Adam Paris' father. Their own father was a Judge and they lived, in considerable splendour, in Connaught Place. They were amusing, full of vitality and very sure of themselves. Then there were two girls, Mabel and Jessie Rossiter, relations of Adrian's, who lived with a widowed mother in Chelsea. They were nice girls but extremely serious, believing in

Bertrand Russell and determining, as soon as they had children, to encourage them in complete freedom of expression.

No, so far as Sally was concerned, her only friends in the Family were poor old Horace and Maurice.

Maurice's marriage was unhappy, but just now everything about him was unhappy. He could not forget the War. He could not translate his experience of it into indifference and a kind of shoulder-shrugging tolerance as did so many of his contemporaries. Sally did what she could for him and he loved her.

No, she decided, turning over restlessly on her bed (which was comfortable because Mrs. Zanazzi knew how to please her guests), everything for ages had been awful except her father. There the relationship begun on the week of the Strike had bloomed. They were friends now and always would be. They enjoyed their times together, they understood one another, they cared for one another. And it was Benjie who, just before he had gone away to Spain, had suggested that she should go up to Cumberland and stay with Tom.

' You'll find it's like going home,' he had said.

Two things still troubled her, though. One was that she could not forget Arnold. He had married a Miss Thurston. Their pictures had been in the papers. That was all that Sally knew. But surely by now she, a sensible modern girl who would stand no nonsense, would have rid herself of his presence. But she could not. He still haunted her at every turn. Little things that he had said, done, looked, been . . .

And the other ghost was Vanessa. It was, she supposed, because she had been so unhappy that she had thought of her mother so constantly. But it had been more than thought. In London she had been constantly expecting that her mother would appear. She had even at times run up the long dark staircase to her rooms, thinking—in spite of all common sense and practical wisdom—that Vanessa would be there, waiting for her. This was a ghost that had no sense in it at all.

So, lying restlessly on her comfortable bed, she decided that things in general had been altogether rotten. Was there something in what Tom had said that evening about finding another world? Was that what everyone was wanting? Was this other world . . . and, so wondering, she fell asleep.

In the days that followed, the country opened up on every side of her. Miss Zanazzi was a great walker and climber. What she said was: ' There's no end to all of this, Miss Herries. You can go to the same spot every day for a year and it's always different. The changing clouds and the light, I suppose.' She explained to her that every part of the country had its own personality: Wastwater and Wasdale were savage, Windermere polite, Ullswater a fortress, Buttermere a fairy-tale, and every hill a separate character. Of course Scotland was bigger and finer, but the charm of this country was that it was so close together. With every step the view changed

and the colours altered. ' It's mysterious, Miss
Herries. You'll never come to the end of it.'

She went with Tom to Rosthwaite and saw the
little hill where old Rogue Herries' house had
been. There was a sturdy little stone house there
now. They went to Uldale and saw the green
field, on the edge of the moor, next to the church
(that had not been there in the old days) where
David's house had been, where Judith had grown
up, where Adam had died. They climbed Ireby
hill and looked over the wall at the Fortress and
saw an old lady come to the dining-room window
and stare at them.

' Uhland still walks there. I'm sure he does,'
said Tom.

They walked up the road from Bella Vista and
looked at the cottage on Cat Bells.

' Who lives there now? ' Sally asked, and Tom
told her that it was a novelist, none of whose books
Sally had ever read.

' What a shame! ' said Sally.

' Oh, I don't know,' said Tom. ' If he's happy
—only I wish he hadn't painted his garage door
blue.'

So everything was gone and yet everything remained. They went up from Rosthwaite to
Watendlath and visited John Green's House where
Judith had lived with her French husband. The
sun was shining on a birch tree, and they noticed,
as Dorothy Wordsworth once had noticed before
them, how ' it glanced in the wind like a flying
sunshiny shower.' Tom found the place in the
Journal that evening and read from it:

' *It was yielding to the gusty wind with all its tender twigs. The sun shone upon it, and it glanced in the wind like a flying sunshiny shower. It was a tree in shape, with stem and branches, but it was like a Spirit of water. The sun went in, and it resumed its purplish appearance, the twigs still yielding to the wind. The other birch trees that were near it looked bright and cheerful, but it was a creature by its own self among them. . . . We went through the wood. It became fair. There was a rainbow which spanned the lake from the island-house to the foot of Bainriggs. The village looked populous and beautiful. Catkins are coming out; palm trees budding; the alder, with its plum-coloured buds.*'

' Now isn't that lovely? ' said Tom. ' As fine as any poem by her brother. But how does she do it? There's hardly a word of more than two syllables. I suppose it's partly that she was so honest—no humbug—and partly that she found everything beautiful from the village to the smallest twig of the birch.'

But Sally was thinking of Judith in Watendlath:

' Do you remember how she saw her husband coming down the path, after he had been away so long, with the bright bird in the cage? It's as though it happened while we were there.'

' Do you see? ' said Tom triumphantly. ' I told you that Time's a fallacy. Live here long enough and you'll see that that's true.'

She felt that the process going on within her was mysterious. It was, as Benjie had told her, that she felt as though she had come home. ' I belong here. All my friends are here—and Tom is really a darling.' For the first time she began to forget Arnold.

But the days were passing and soon she must return to Mr. Bimberg. They decided that they would do one grand expedition before she returned to London. But it was late in the year for grand expeditions, and Miss Zanazzi warned them: 'The weather can be funny this time of year. Mists, you know, and there might even be some snow. It's turning colder.'

It was. One night there was a furious gale and the wind tore up the valley, whipping the trees on the right of the house, lashing the windows with rain, screaming with an exultation that Sally found splendid as it galloped up the mountain side.

The streams began to beat like drums and, behind the uproar, it seemed to Sally that men were shouting, calling, crying aloud. Yet, next morning, a shining and placid peace lay over the country. A frost glittered on the chrysanthemums and a long stretch of purple lay above the faint browns and greens, staining the bare trees and spreading on the hillsides in a thin grape-coloured cloud.

'How lovely!' Sally thought. 'It is as still as a dream.'

So they decided to make their expedition next day. Tom would drive the Austin to Seathwaite, leave it there, and then they would go up Stye Head, climb Scafell and be back for supper.

Next morning the sky was flurried with little

white clouds and the air was sharply cold. Miss
Zanazzi told them that the glass was going down,
but she thought that they would be safe for the
day. They started out in splendid spirits.

As they began to walk from Seathwaite, Tom
said:

' You know, Sally, I think this has been the
happiest week of my life.'

Sally, who disliked very much to express her
feelings, said:

' Well, that's all right.' But she added, because she could not help herself: ' We'll come up
here together again, won't we?—just the two of
us. And perhaps Father.'

' Oh, Father knows every inch of it. He loves
it more than I do.'

Tom chattered away. He wasn't tiresome
any more and Sally realised that people who need
affection are natural and easy once they have got
it. They are embarrassing only because they
are starved. ' I don't believe I'll ever be annoyed
by him again,' she thought.

They crossed the little Stockley Bridge. They
had been hemmed in by Glaramara on the left and
Base Brown on the right, and now the sharp
precipices of Great End filled up the valley in
front. It was here that Sally had the first perception that she was moving into an uncertain world.

' You'd think,' Tom said, ' that you're looking
at the same hill all the time, Great End. Well,
you're not—half-way between Seathwaite and
Seatoller it's Lingmell you've been looking at.'

The tops did indeed appear to be different with

every step, and soon after leaving Seathwaite all the civilised state of man dropped out of existence. Sour Milk Gill was a raging torrent, and the wind that blew in between crevices of rock and boulder frothed it to a spume. They were shut in by a barricade of hills, Glaramara on the left and Base Brown on the right.

'Base Brown,' Sally said. 'What a horrid name!' She was conscious of a return of the apprehension that she had felt on her drive from the station the first day. It was as though a wall of grey menacing stone rose in front of her and on the other side of it was Margaret throwing a book on to the sofa and crying: 'Well, of all the tosh!' and Humphrey Bell, the novelist, who could not forget that the War had personally insulted him and was therefore most blameworthy (as though the War were an absconding solicitor!) . . . and the wooden barricades in Piccadilly Circus, and Olive Stane saying: 'Oh, I'll make it a Gin and It,' and poor old Horace leading her so proudly in to dinner at the Piccadilly Grill, and the shimmering rug with purple trees and dark green birds on Cynthia's dining-room floor, and Adrian giving her tea in his lovely flat with the Duncan Grant landscape that had a barn in it of so deep an amber-red, and the green Elk of Carl Milles, and Unamuno's *Quixote* open on the table, and the old blind man in Piccadilly with the cup and his fat body and patient, patient face.

'And now we climb,' said Tom. 'Not much of one. That's Taylor Gill on the right. I've never seen it so fierce.'

She was both frightened and exhilarated. Everything seemed fierce and angry. The wind rose as they rose. In an incredibly short time the Borrowdale valley was far below, and at the far end of it over Skiddaw and Blencathra a grim wall of grey cloud was mounting but, miraculously, from some unseen place, a tongue of sunlight struck the valley, quivering across it like a searchlight.

At the top they were on a long boggy flat through which a stream ran. Lingmell was in front of them and Scafell Pike to the left of it.

Now they were truly in no-man's-land. A bird flew slowly, mournfully over their heads, but otherwise there was no sign of life at all. Sally saw that Tom was now completely happy, and in his happiness he had a strong family likeness to Benjie and Vanessa when *they* were happy. The true Tom appeared as he never appeared in London. His body did not seem thick and clumsy now. Sally was surprised at the easy agility with which he moved. In London, when he was in a room, you always watched with anxiety lest he should knock something over. Every teacup was in peril from him, but now you felt that he could shoulder a mountain with safety. He began to sing slightly out of tune, and soon Sally began to sing too. Really this was a splendid day.

They reached Stye Head Tarn and, as they did so, a pale sun, dim and veiled, burst the grey paper tissue of the clouds and shivered with a queer iridescent shimmer on the black surface of the little Tarn.

It was very cold, but they found shelter behind
a rock on the slope of Green Gable, looked
down to the Tarn across the flat, and ate their
luncheon. This was the very wildest scenery that
Sally had ever beheld. There were of course
many places of far greater splendour and terror
in the world, but the intimacy and closeness of this
place made it personal, as though it had a quality
of fairy-tale—one of the old stories when the hero
reaches at last his perilous destiny, and from the
dark rock, the shaggy tree, the awful enemy
emerges. And yet, with this peril there was also
friendliness. Gable with its great rounded top
is the least hostile of all mountains, and the whole
plateau with its stream and tarn is kind because it
has been there for so long and is so sure of its
passive power.

' It was just above here,' Tom said, ' by the
other tarn that David fought his duel.' As he
spoke a ripple of light ran across the Tarn.
Everything sprang to life as though it answered
him, then fell into a waiting silence again.

It was too cold to remain long where they were
and, after they had eaten, they walked slowly up
the slope to Esk Hause. Here, when Sally looked
down into Eskdale, she gave a cry. The valley
was sombre to-day and for many an observer
would have seemed little more than a tumble of
rock and rough grass falling away to the sea, but
at that moment, more than at any other, Sally
felt that she had come home. On every side of
her the hills rose darkly to a dark sky and there
was a strength in all those uncouth forms, a

strength and patience, a wildness controlled, that seemed to her lovelier than anything that she had ever known. She caught Tom's arm and held it. ' I feel as though I could never be unhappy again,' she said.

Then they started slowly to climb the Scafell Pike track. The wind was rising, murmuring from top to top, and the faint illumination of the pale sun vanished suddenly as though at a word of command. The heavy sky seemed to move down in a lower band above their heads.

' I thought I felt a flake of snow on my cheek,' Sally said.

' Oh, that's all right. It won't come to anything. Not at this time of year,' Tom answered. ' We'll soon be at the top.'

They turned slightly to the right up a green slope which was not difficult, although beyond them the eastern buttress of the Pike had a grim look.

Tom glanced at his wrist-watch. It was later than he had supposed; you grew, through the summer, accustomed to Summer Time and fancied that the light would last for ever. There should, for a long while yet, be enough, but it was a dark day and, in the last half-hour, had grown very swiftly darker.

Instinctively he hurried his steps and Sally called out: ' It's all right, isn't it? We've got plenty of time, haven't we? ' She had to shout, for the wind whistled in the air.

' Quite all right,' Tom called cheerfully.

She wondered whether she should suggest that they should turn back. Something would have

frightened her had she not been determined
against any sort of fright. Where Tom could go
she could, and she knew that these were little hills
and that, in the summer, the slopes of Scafell were
like a picnic party. Nevertheless she had spent
her life in the town; this was the first day she
had ever had on the Tops and her feet ached: if
she stopped for a moment the wind cut her with
its cold, and again she felt some lingering
flakes of snow against her cheek. But more than
these things it was the changed aspect of the scene
that alarmed her. The hills appeared to have
doubled their size, and instead of that entire
intimacy they had drawn apart, lifting black
shoulders and ragged edges against a sky that
seemed now to be alive with dark motion, piles
of cloud with the dead whiteness of dried bones
running before grey unsubstantial vapour. Still,
where Tom could go she could.

He stopped for her and held out his hand.

' We'll go back if you like,' he said.

' Oh no—we're near the top, aren't we? '

' Very near—and then we can run down in
five minutes.'

When the Pillar and Steeple came into view
Tom, who had often climbed this before, although
always in fine weather, knew that the rest of the
way would be rough.

' Look here, Sally. Perhaps we'd better go
back.'

' Oh no. Let's do it now we're here.'

The path now was a confusion of rough stones
and the wind seemed to meet them from every

quarter. A scurry came up from the valley and with it a whirl of light wet snow.

Then, a moment later, from no quarter at all as it seemed, a blinding storm came upon them. There was snow in it and a wet mist, and it appeared to Tom that from below them on either side a boiling vapour of mist rushed, edging up.

They were near the top, he supposed, but he could see nothing. He caught Sally close to him. It was as though they both of them stood on air. If there was ground it rocked under their feet, and the gale lashed their faces like the sharp whip of stinging twigs.

With his arm round her he shouted: ' I say, this is awful. We must find shelter somewhere. This will soon be over.'

The trouble was that it had become suddenly unknown country. He knew that on the one side of the Pike it was easy descent but on the other it was rock and precipice. They moved forward together, step by step, stumbling over the stones. The wind was ferocious, and the sleet came in waves as though it were timed and obeyed a certain rhythm.

Sally stumbled, she caught his arm, then put her hand up to his wet cheek.

' I wanted to be sure you were there. It's the cold—it takes your breath.'

He must shelter her somewhere until this gust was over, but he feared the whirling dusk that was now so thick and clinging that he was like a blind man who, sightless, yet knows his room is

turning about him. He felt that all round them
was a world of rock; stones that would seem
minute enough in daylight now were gigantic. It
was as though one single rock moved with them,
maliciously keeping them company.

'Look here, Sally,' he said. 'What do you
think we had best do? I don't know where we're
going. If I could tell which way the wind's
blowing, but it seems to be coming in every direction at once. If we could touch grass we'd be all
right, but the fact is I'm afraid of striking the
rocks on the other side.'

She scarcely heard him. She was ready for
anything, but this icy wind was beyond any
experience that she had ever had. The cold
seemed to grip and shake her; she had never
known before what it was to lose faith in her own
power of resistance, but her knees were cut with
the cold, her head was buffeted and her hands
were gone.

She realised that they were beginning to
descend, and the wind now leapt up from below,
tugging at their feet.

They turned the edge of a rock and the gale
fell. Bending down Tom saw that the rock was
arched. He groped round it and found that within
the curve there was shelter.

He manœuvred her into its hollow. 'Look
here. Rest your back against the rock here. Now
bend your knees up. You can't feel the wind
now.'

The relief was blessed, for the roar had died,
her face was no longer torn with the cold, and

she could feel her hands again. He knelt in front of her.

'Thank God. You'll be all right there till the storm's over. I don't suppose it will last long. It doesn't as a rule when it gets up as suddenly as that.'

She pulled at his arm.

'Come in too.'

'No. There isn't room. I'll stay here for a moment. Any second the mist can blow away and I'll see where we are.'

She held on to his arm.

'Tom, you're grand—as though you'd been in storms all your life. You are a brick to look after me.'

She'd never before praised him for looking after her. Well, that was something. He had his back to the gale and it was as though a thudding door of ice beat upon it. He turned sideways, lying up partly against her. So they waited, her hand on his knee.

He thought: 'Now I can do something. I'll see that she's all right. We'll be laughing at this in half an hour.'

Then the sleet changed to snow. There was a thin bright whiteness in the air; in spite of its thinness the general scene was no clearer. Nothing was more visible, but now the touch of the storm was soft and clinging while the wind moaned through the web with a singing, whining cry.

They waited. Time passed.

A long time later Tom put his hand on Sally's. It was icily cold. He bent forward and touched her cheek. She whispered, in a voice strangely unlike hers: ' It's fearfully cold, Tom.'

He took off his waterproof and his coat, then his thick woollen jersey.

' Look here. You've got to put this on.'

She acquiesced, and he knew at once that she was already sleepy with the cold, for, in her own self, she would have eagerly resisted.

But, as he held her against himself, he felt her whole body slacken. He pulled the jersey over her head, then laid his coat over her, thrusting her hands into its pockets. Lastly he took the waterproof and wrapped it round her legs. He saw that she was curled up well within the shelter of the rock. Her head fell forward and he knew that she was asleep. . . .

He waited. His eyes stared into the dancing thickness that now had, it seemed, a rosy light at its heart. Then the cold bit him; he felt its teeth at his breast and a warm breath against his nostrils as though out of the storm an animal had crept to him for shelter. . . .

Circles, crimson at the edge with centres of dazzling white, floated, hung, fell slowly and rose like telephone wires seen from a train. With a terrific effort he rose to his feet, tottered, balanced himself against the rock.

' Sally!' he whispered. ' Are you all right, Sally?' But of course she was all right. He smiled. Then he moved. He must move or he would sleep.

He stumbled into the light. For now the world broke into a dazzling brightness. He stepped forward to greet it. Soft hands caressed his cheeks and someone stroked his eyes.

Oh! Beloved Mountain! This place of light and splendour for which all his life long he had been waiting. Beloved Mountain that took him now with the warm strong caressing grasp of a friend.

Everywhere about him, from the height and the depth, voices greeted him. A light, more splendid than any that he had ever known, dazzled his closing eyes. He ran forward and fell.

Later a shepherd, looking for his sheep, found Sally sleeping under the rock.

FAMILY DINNER

Two events of the first importance occurred during the spring of 1930 in the Herries' family: one was the marriage on April 3 at St. Margaret's, Westminster, of Miss Mary Worcester to the Marquis of Paignton, the other was Alfred's removal to a very fine and spacious house in Hampstead. The two events were celebrated by the dinner that Alfred gave in the second week of May.

Lord Paignton was thirty-eight years of age when he invited Mary to be his Marchioness, and Mary was thirty-seven, so there was, as Adrian said, ' nothing of the virginal about it.' All the same Paignton was a very ' virginal ' man. He had proposed to other ladies on other occasions and had twice been engaged, but none of these young women had been serious enough for him. He was himself intensely serious-minded as was right and proper in the future Duke of Wendover. He was famous for his conversational opening gambit: ' If you are at all interested in my opinion of the matter. . . .' He had excellent views on Tariffs, Russia, Unemployment, the Pound Sterling, Agriculture, and Why Our Churches are Empty To-day. But the interesting thing about him, Adrian thought, was that he was marrying Mary for her brains rather than her looks.

She still *had* looks of a statuary, marble kind and he would, Adrian thought, be just the man to admire her poise, her immobility and air of watching repose. But no, her brain was the lure. ' I'm marrying the most intelligent woman in England,' he told his friends at the Bendish, a little club in St. James's Street where gatherings were held of so solemn a character that it was said that a waiter there hung himself because he hadn't seen anyone smile for five years.

' Does he think her clever because she never says anything?' Adrian wondered. But it did not matter. The Herries were pleased, although by this time they were so firmly the backbone of England that nothing either here or there could make any difference. Cynthia was now entirely swallowed up in the waters of bridge, and was so weary with her long, long efforts to find a husband for Mary that, when at last Mary found a husband for herself, she had very little to say about it.

Rosalind had married a Major Brigstock, a good fellow who luckily believed the Herries the finest family in the world, and Peile had died two years ago from influenza, so Cynthia thought now of nothing at all but Contract, her two Pekinese— Tang and Ming—and her figure, which was by this time as thin and sharp as a needle.

Alfred bought the house in Hampstead because money was very uncertain and he thought it not a bad thing to have it in property. He also saw quite clearly that very soon now the West End would be nothing but shops, and anyone who had to live in London would be ashamed to be seen south of St. John's Wood. He had also a very charming house near Sunningdale and, although he was sixty-eight this year, played a good game of golf every week-end. He was a dry self-satisfied old man with supreme confidence in himself and a contempt for anyone who was not practical. But he could be generous and, when his liver was in good order, could tell a funny story. He was now deeply disappointed with his son, Maurice, who settled down to nothing, thought that he could write poetry, and led a cat-and-dog life with his wife. On the other hand his girl, Clara, had married a rich American, Borden Wadsworth, and entertained regally in Chicago.

His only trouble had been that he liked women around him. Men as companions were only useful for golf and an exchange of opinions about the money-market. Quite recently this lack in his life had been strangely supplied. A woman called Abigail Hill, a single lady of forty or so, occupied the position of his best friend. The true story of Abigail Hill was a most interesting one and her influence on the whole Herries family already promised to be remarkable. She was a tall, gaunt, extremely fashionable woman who had lived, it appeared, for many years at Eastbourne with an old invalid father. He, dying, had left her a large sum of money. She had come to London and had taken a large flat at the Marble Arch end of Park Lane. Here she entertained, and with excellent taste. She was, apparently,

cynical and plain-spoken. She won a reputation
for her caustic remarks. But, cynical or no, she
became attached to old Alfred and he to her.

No one suggested for a moment that there was
anything lyrical in their association. They were
quite simply good friends and, whenever he gave
a dinner-party, it became natural to find her there
as hostess. She furnished the Hampstead house
for him and did it magnificently. She was modern
and not too modern. This was a good time, because of the growing distress · in Europe and
America, for ' picking up ' things cheaply, and
Alfred's pictures and furniture were worth seeing.
He, like the other Herries before him, cared little
or nothing for property as such. It was beneath
a Herries' dignity to think that he or she was valuable because of possessions. All Alfred wanted
was that he should be suitably surrounded. Abigail Hill saw that it was so.

In a short time she had made her mark on
every member of the family. She played bridge
with Cynthia, talked cynically with Adrian, flattered Gordon, soothed Maurice and even bothered
to have tea with poor old Horace. The only
members of the family with whom she could do
nothing at all were Benjie and Sally. She complained of them to Alfred.

' They're too sentimental for anything. They
don't seem like your relations.'

' Benjie's always been a bad lot,' Alfred said,
' and his daughter takes after him.'

Nevertheless they were invited to the dinner-
party because Abigail said that what was needed

2 D

was a little variety. ' You're all a little monoton-
ous in the lump,' she said, ' and as a matter of fact
I rather like Benjie even though he detests *me*.'

Adrian was engaged and therefore a young
Frenchman and his sister, children of a French
financier of importance to Alfred, were invited.
They were the only two present who were not of
the family circle, and only at the last moment was it
discovered that the Frenchman, Raymond Herriot,
was blind—blinded in the War.

' That's uncomfortable,' Alfred said. ' I wish
we hadn't asked them.'

' I believe he's no trouble at all,' Abigail
answered. ' He goes about quite a lot.'

The dinner-party consisted of Alfred, Miss
Hill, Gordon, Maurice and his wife, Tim Bellairs
the painter, now living in London, Phyllis and
Anstey Veasey, Mary and Lord Paignton, Cynthia,
Rosalind (her husband the Major was away in
Ireland), Raymond and Mlle. Herriot, Sally and
Benjie.

Yes, quite a party.

Sally had given up her rooms and lived with
her father ever since Tom's death. They got on
splendidly. Now as she drove him up to Hampstead in her small bright-red Midget he thought
of her with most loving affection. Tom's death
had wrought a deep change in her. It was
strange, when you thought of it, that Tom had
longed all his life to do something for those he
loved, and in his death, which had seemed accidental, gratuitous, he had at last won his desire.

Well, perhaps nothing was gratuitous, accidental . . .

But with Sally it was the three great unhappinesses of her life—her mother's death, her misadventure with Arnold, and Tom's death—that made her what she now was, and Benjie, looking at her, knowing her courage, common sense, humour and kindness, wondered whether ever in England before there had been created a generation so fine and intelligent as this one of Sally's. "Only we can't tell yet. We can't tell for another twenty years.'

Assembled in Alfred's grand drawing-room, panelled, the splendid possessor of three lovely Canalettos, they found that they were the last of the party.

'Yes, this *is* the Family!' Benjie thought, sarcastically, for whenever he encountered them *en masse* he disliked them, felt that they disliked him and would be relieved if he left them for ever. He could never be with the Family without, at the same time, feeling rather ashamed of himself, and that made him both shy and angry. For they had succeeded. As a family (for they had only the slenderest connection with the Scottish Herries) in 1730 they had been nothing, in 1780 a little something, in 1820 people were aware of them, in 1850 they counted, in 1900 they were prominent, and now in 1930 they were everywhere. . . . And yet for him now as he looked at them, the romantic period of their history was closing. They no longer fought, struggled, were jealous, cruel. . . . Cynthia, Alfred, Mary, Gordon, Rosalind.

. . . They had become part of England, and future history would be made of struggles elsewhere and of another kind.

'We've been interesting for just two hundred years,' he thought. 'Sally and Maurice and the Veasey children may make history, but it will be a new chapter.'

For he was old enough now to be a philosopher and have a perspective. And, physically, he was in splendid condition for an old boy who had led a life, had only one arm and was seventy-five years of age.

They marched into the dining-room. The long shining table was lit by tall candles in high silver candlesticks. Over the mantelpiece was a fine picture by John of a peasant in a blue cloak standing against a background of dark hills.

Benjie threw his eye around him. He was himself sitting between Phyllis Veasey and a grave dark girl with charming intelligent eyes whose name he did not know.

'Who is it on the other side of me?' he asked Phyllis under cover of the opening babble of conversation.

'French,' said Phyllis. 'A Mademoiselle Herriot. That's her brother over there next to Sally. He's blind.'

He looked across and saw, next to Abigail Hill, a young man with black hair and a strong watchful face. He was watchful because he was blind. His brown eyes gazed with a steady absorbed look in front of him and, instead of appearing sightless, had a penetration that seemed to go beyond all things physical, to rest calmly in a world where everything was quiet, profound and real. . . .

'Vanessa's world,' Benjie thought.

Phyllis Veasey began at once to talk. She found it difficult to keep still. She was gay, bright, like a coloured bird who had just risen from the water and must shake the sparkling drops from its wings.

She had been reading a very long book called *Kristin Lavransdatter*.

'I'm afraid you don't read much, Cousin Benjie.'

'No, not very much. I never have. I'm an old man and want to see everything I can before my time's up. I like a man called Hudson who writes about birds.'

'Well, *Kristin Lavransdatter*'s miles long. I like long books, don't you? You go on and on and on. I got this one from the Book Society.'

'What's the Book Society?'

'Oh, five writers tell you what to read.'

'Why five?'

'Oh, I don't know. Five's better than one. Not so prejudiced.'

'I should have thought five times as prejudiced. Anyway what do you want anyone to tell you what to read for? Why don't you decide for yourself?'

'Oh, there isn't any time and one wants to read what other people are reading.'

'The girl's an idiot,' thought Benjie crossly. He found that his temper rose just as quickly as ever

it had done in spite of his seventy-five years. So
he turned to Mlle. Herriot and found, to his
relief, that she talked perfect English. For his
own French was nothing to be proud of.

'Don't we seem odd to you,' he asked her;
'an English family all dining together inside the
security of one's own fortress?'

'In what way—odd?' She had a most charming smile, gay and gentle. And, at that same
moment, he realised that young Herriot, turning
to Sally, had the same smile.

'Well, the French and English never really
understand one another, do they? And never will.
You are so realistic. We so sentimental. Now
we don't look sentimental, all of us in this room.
But I assure you that we are. We believe de-
voutly in our fairy-stories—the splendour of England, that hearts are more than coronets, although
we are the most snobbish people on earth, and that
the Herries family is unique in the world for its
qualities of good sense, patriotism and fine breeding.'

'But I think England *is* splendid—and France
too. You see, I also am romantic. I think, too, that
England has her faults, her stupidities, and France
too. Now is not that a safe answer?'

'Very safe,' he said, smiling. 'That is your
brother—on the other side to the left, sitting next
to my daughter?'

'Yes. Oh, is that your daughter? What an
amusing face she has! And how intelligent! She
is more alive than anyone else here.' Then she
hurried on lest he should think that she was paying

obvious compliments. ' My brother, Raymond,
was blinded in the War. He is the most splendid
man I know. His blindness hardly handicaps him
at all. He lives in Berlin. He is working with
a group of other young men for international
understanding.'

' Not an easy job,' said Benjie.

' No,' Mlle. Herriot said eagerly. ' But most
interesting. He gets on with the Germans
splendidly. His blindness seems to help him.
He says that people accept from him, because he
is blind, more than they would from others.'

' Perhaps it would be better if some more of
us were blind. We might see farther.'

Just then he caught Sally's eyes and they
smiled at one another. He could see that she was
very happy. She was. She had not looked forward
with great pleasure to this party. Big dinners were
out of fashion now, family groups were out of
fashion, and old Alfred and Abigail were not, in
Sally's view, an interesting pair.

She had left Bimberg long ago, and now
(because work she must) was helping the famous
Lady Connington in an effort to rouse the people
of England to an interest in the League of
Nations. Benjie was not rich, nor had she inherited anything from Ellis who, in a will
written shortly after Vanessa's flight, had left
his wealth first to the Miss Trents, and at
their death to charities. Lady Connington was
a fool, and the League was not, at times, very
encouraging. It attracted so many half-baked
nit-wits. Nevertheless, Sally was staunch to it.

It was, Mr. Rack-Bunden told her, ' the only thing
there is.' ' Without it our civilisation is ruined.
We go tottering into the abyss.' So Sally held on
to the League, went about the country in her M.G.
speaking for it, and explained to Sheffield and
Newark and Doncaster what Mr. Gandhi's theory
was and what was happening in China. . . .

She had felt, in fact, after Tom's death that
she must try and do some good somewhere. Do
something for him in return, as it were. She had
long ago understood that among her friends the
worst thing that anyone could say about anyone else
was that he or she was trying to do good. It was
simply too ' shy-making,' in the phrase of the
moment. At the same time she realised that many
of them did a great deal of good in a humorous,
cynical, and ' Don't you dare to remind me of it '
manner. She hid her motives; she tried to pretend that Lady Connington and the League satisfied her. She was exceedingly lonely. Here she
was, twenty-six years of age, and she had achieved
nothing whatever except to be considered, by a
stupid, ignorant woman, not good enough for a
weak, helpless young man. She had lost her
mother, her lover and her brother. She was beginning to wonder, in spite of her twentieth-century
materialism, whether there was not a curse on her
father and herself. They were, both of them, so
plainly isolated, by themselves, not wanted.

So she had not looked forward to the dinner.
Abigail Hill did not like her; Alfred thought that
she encouraged Maurice in his discontents; Gordon
disliked her; the Veaseys were afraid of her.

And then, when, after five minutes, a few words with Gordon, her neighbour on her left, had convinced her that their hatred of one another was entirely mutual, she turned to her other companion. He turned also with eyes that seemed to stare with a gentle, almost indecent obstinacy into her heart. They did, indeed, make her heart suddenly beat with a confusing rapidity. She did not know him. She had never seen him before. Why did he stare at her so? And then she saw that his hands moved round his plate, touched, very quickly, the knives and forks. Then that his duck had been cut into small pieces before it was brought to him. She knew now why his eyes so unwinkingly stared.

'You must forgive me,' she heard him say (his English was good, but it had a very pleasing accent). 'I am blind, and so am unable to be sure whether you want to talk with me or not. I don't even know whether you are looking my way.'

She touched his sleeve with her hand.

'I am looking your way and I want to talk.'

'*Bien.* Thank you very much. I don't often go to dinner-parties because I'm afraid of being tiresome. Or, rather, I did not. But now my life in Berlin includes a good deal of—what do you say?—sociability, so I am getting over my shyness.'

'Oh, do you live in Berlin?' asked Sally.

'Yes. I was blinded in the War. At Verdun. I was in hospital for two years and did not know

what to do with myself.   And then in '25 a very
brilliant man, a Swiss, a Monsieur Holthois,
formed an International Group with members
in all the principal cities in Europe—also in
America.   His purpose was no more than for
internationally-minded people of every country to
be in constant communication—see each other
often, you know.   We are all patriots, but inter-
nationalists as well—not so difficult as you suppose.
Our only rules are that we deliberately discuss
everything—are not afraid to—and that we see
one another's point of view and that we allow no
difference of opinion to separate us.   We are
growing very fast, and I am the principal French
representative in Berlin.   But, dear me, I talk
only of myself.   Tell me about *you*.   What are
you called?   Who are you?   Married or single?
What do you look like?   You see, you must help
me.'

   ' Yes,' said Sally, rather breathlessly.   ' I want
to.   My name is Sally Herries.   I'm twenty-six
years of age and not married.   I help Lady Connington about the League of Nations, or try to,
but I'm not much use, I'm afraid.   My father
is sitting on the other side of the table.   He and
I live together.   My mother died when I was
only nine, but I've never forgotten her.   She was
the finest person I've ever known.   Then my
only brother was killed in Cumberland in 1928
—we were caught in a storm on a mountain, and
he kept me warm by wrapping his clothes round
me, and he fell over a rock and was stunned and
died of the cold.'

'I'm very sorry,' said Raymond Herriot.

'Yes, so you see there's nothing very special about *me*.'

'Would you please tell me,' he asked, dropping his voice a little, 'if you do not think it impertinent, what you look like?'

'Of course.' She laughed. 'Shall I be honest? I'd better be, because other people would tell you the truth if I didn't. I'm short and small. I've got dark-brown hair—short, you know—a sallow complexion which I try to brighten up a bit, a snub nose and not a very pretty mouth. On the other hand, my eyes are nice. I've quite good hands and very small feet —only my legs are too short.'

'Thank you,' he said.

She did not know whether she had been impertinent or too familiar or too hasty. She had never had an experience like this before. She felt that she would tell him anything.

'One thing you have not said. You have a beautiful voice.'

'My voice isn't bad,' she answered recklessly, 'when I'm in a good mood. I have an awful temper. I get that from Father, and then, when I lose it, my temper I mean, my voice has a nasty edge to it.' She added, thinking that it was time to get away from the personal: 'What a wonderful thing to do! To work like that in Berlin! I do envy you.'

'Come and work there too,' he said earnestly.

'Oh, do you think I could?'

'Why not?' Then he added: 'I feel as

though we were meant to meet to-night.   Please
let this not be our last meeting.'

'Oh no!' Sally said.   'Oh no!   We'll meet
as often as you like!'

It was after that that her eyes met Benjie's and
they smiled.

By this time everyone was very gay.   Alfred's
wines were excellent, and that spirit of self-confidence that always developed when members of
the family were for a time together was now most
happily universal.

Dessert came and Alfred made a little speech
(he liked to make speeches).

'I welcome you all to my new house and I
hope you will be very often here.   It may seem
ostentatious for an old man like me to have a new
house, but it is intended for the Family as much as
for myself.   I don't know whether some of you
remember,' he went on.   'It is a long time ago
but it is very vivid to myself.   At the beginning
of the War, before Gordon and Maurice went to
the Front, some of you had dinner with me, and
Sally here, who was only a child then, lit a candle
which we passed from one to another.   I must
say that I think there has been something that
has held us all together through all the hard times,
and will, I am convinced, hold us together still.

'I would like to say how pleased I am that on
this occasion we should have with us two friends
from that splendid country so grandly our ally
then and now.   I drink to the health of glorious
France.'

Everyone stood up and drank.

Then young Herriot replied.   He said only a
few words:

'I must thank you very much on behalf of my
country and my sister and myself.   We are all
proud of the countries to which we belong: it is,
I think, that pride, one of the finest things in
human nature—but with it there must go something as fine—pride in the whole world, a desire
to see the whole world one, so that so dreadful a
thing as war can never return to the world again.'

Then there was a very regrettable episode—
one of those episodes for ever recurring in the
Herries history.   Young Anstey Veasey had been
drinking.   He was a nice young fellow.   Everyone agreed about that afterwards.   What he did
any one of his generation might have done.
Luckily the little affair was very soon over.   Fifty
years ago there would have been more lasting
consequences; a hundred years ago perhaps a
family feud as in the famous ancient story of poor
Christabel and the fan.   But now—well, now
in the twentieth century the Herries temper
had mellowed, the hysterical element in it had
been taught discipline.

What occurred was that young Veasey cried
out:

'It's all very well for you fellows who had all
the fun to say that there's to be no war—but what
about us?   Are we never to have any adventure
again?   Oh, I know what all you older people
say—that the last war was horrible and the next
one will be worse.   But how do we know?   You
had some pretty good times in the War.   I've

heard lots of fellows say it was the best time in
their lives. Of course men were killed and
wounded, but we've all got to die some time, and
after all it's the greatest adventure can happen to
anybody. I don't think another war would be
such a bad thing when all's said and done. It
would clear up some of the mess the world's in
anyway. After all, you can't stop men fighting.
It's their nature to fight, and I think a jolly old
scrap with the Russians or someone would do a
lot of good.'

He was, of course, only a boy who had had too
much to drink, and his silly nonsense should have
passed unnoticed.

But what happened was that before anyone
else could speak Maurice had sprung to his
feet.

' It's a damnable lie! ' he cried out. He stood
there, white-faced, his thin nervous body trembling, his voice pitched high. ' I say it's a lie!
My God, is this what we went through all that
hell for? Only a few years and already there are
fools daring to talk that blasphemy. We suffered
—we suffered, millions of us, men, women and
children suffered. We went through hell day
after day, month after month, year after year.
Our lives have been wrecked. We've lost everything, friends, faith, belief in God. . . . We've
been ruined, been damned. . . . The only hope
we've ever had is that at least what we suffered has
made it impossible for anyone to suffer that way
again. And now, now—already—it's coming
back, and men dare to say they want it back—and

all we've been through has been no good. Anyone, anyone—who helps another war is damned.
They're enemies of their fellow-men — the
cruellest——'

He stopped short and, to everyone's horror,
burst into tears. He stood there, his hand in front
of his face, sobbing. Then, with a gesture of his
hand, his head down, he turned and hurried from
the room.

There was a moment's silence then. Rosalind
got up and went after him.

'I say,' said young Anstey, 'I'm most awfully
sorry——'

Paignton broke in: 'If anyone cares to hear
what I think——'

Conversation became general. It was very
unpleasant, of course, and especially because there
were those present who were not English and
because Maurice was Alfred's son.

But all the concentrated common sense of the
Family rose like a calming breeze. They knew
nowadays—Alfred and Cynthia and Gordon and
Mary—how to deal with that sort of hysteria.
Poor Maurice! It was natural enough that he
should feel as he did, but at his age he should
really have learnt to control his emotions—one
of the first and most important lessons.

Soon everyone was easy again. Rosalind returned and said that Maurice had gone.

'He's been having his headaches,' she explained.

'Poor boy!' Alfred said. 'You'd think that
after all these years his nerves would be in better

control. I think of sending him to Vienna.
There's a doctor there . . .'

Later, in a corner of the drawing-room under
the enchanting Canaletto that showed the gon-
dolas like butterflies, the figures of rose and silver
in their masks crossing the bridge, Sally had some
last words with Raymond Herriot. His sister
was saying her farewells to Alfred.

They were partly concealed from the others
by the folds of a curtain of dark shadowed gold.
He put out his hand and touched her sleeve.
Then his hand rested firmly on her arm.

'It is,' he said, 'how do you say?—up to you,
our next meeting.'

'I will meet you whenever and wherever you
like,' she answered.

'Well, then—why not to-morrow? Would
you come and have tea, perhaps, with my sister
and me? We are at Brown's Hotel.'

'Yes. Of course I will.'

'*Bien.* And then one day perhaps you will
come to Berlin?'

'Yes, if you would like me to.'

'Yes, I would like you to.' His face broke
into a beautiful smile. 'I have a perfect picture
of you in my mind—already.'

'You must ask your sister,' Sally answered.

'I don't need to ask anyone.' Then very
abruptly he said: 'Now, how old do you suppose
I am?'

'Oh——' She moved a little closer to him.
'I should say—thirty-five.'

' Yes — thirty-six. And still a bachelor. Strange, is it not? '

' I don't know. I'm not married either.'

' Yes, that is very strange. But you are ten years younger.'

She said nothing.

With that quiet gentle voice that she found extremely charming he asked her: ' That is not too great a difference in years—between us? '

' No. Of course not.'

She could not help herself. She put out her hand and caught his. He held hers and then, raising it, kissed it.

She sat beside her father, driving the car, staring in front of her.

' Did you enjoy it? ' he asked her.

' Yes, Father—most awfully.'

' Pity Maurice had that outburst. I hate to see a man cry. Poor chap. If I had my way, I'd give young Anstey a good leathering. Rotten manners with Herriot there! '

' Lots of his generation think like that.'

' Do they? More fools they.' He looked at her. ' You seemed to get on well with that young Frenchman.'

' Yes. I'm going to tea with him and his sister to-morrow.'

Then she added:

' He thinks I might help him in their work in Berlin.'

' Oh, does he? Would you like to? '

' Yes, I think I would.'

He sighed, but so gently that Sally did not hear him. So that was Sally's destiny. Just what she wanted, someone with her own notions, someone for her to look after. But blind? And a Frenchman?

Sally would manage it. She'd found what she wanted. And so the last link was broken. He would be alone now—the last of the bad Herries. They were all good now. . . .

Cumberland.

It was as though the Derwent suddenly broke in a torrent across Piccadilly and Glaramara rose towering above the Ritz.

He put his hand on Sally's knee.

' He looks a fine fellow,' he said, ' if you want to know what I think about it. And when you're married I shall take the next train for Keswick.'

Sally laughed.

' Father, how ridiculous! I don't know that he even likes me.'

' No, but I do. Look out! You nearly had that taxi.'

When later she kissed him good-night she was quite especially affectionate, and, after she had gone to bed, he sat for a long while looking at Vanessa's photograph.

' Sentimental,' he said, knocking his pipe out on the fender. ' That's what I've become! All the same—Vanessa would have approved of that man. He's her sort.'

COUNTRY FAIR

SALLY HERRIES was engaged to Raymond Herriot just before Christmas 1930. They were married in London at a register office on the 14th of November 1931.

In February 1932 Benjie paid them a visit in Berlin. He stayed with them for a fortnight and had a grand time. The more he saw of young Herriot the better he liked him, and Sally's happiness was founded on excellent reason. The only thing that distressed him was that she might become *too* international. She had, in a few weeks, the troubles of Germany at her finger-tips. She knew what Schleicher wanted, what Hitler said, and what the German Princes were doing. She also knew why the middle-class German was starving. At the same time she understood to a marvel what were the difficulties of M. Herriot (no relation at all of her husband's). She understood the ambitions of Mussolini, the restlessness of the Japanese, the confusion of the Chinese, why America would be Democratic before the end of the year and just how far the Five Year Plan had collapsed.

'You know,' said Benjie when he had listened to a great deal of discussion, 'I'm so old now that none of these things seem to me of the least importance.' He patted Sally on the shoulder. ' When you are busy making the new world don't forget there's such a place as Cumberland.'

' There you are, you see,' Sally said. ' How can you say that the state of the world isn't important? How can Cumberland be happy if there isn't enough to eat?'

' Temporary questions, temporary questions,' Benjie murmured. ' There's something more important.'

' What is?' She put her arm around his neck. He was such a fine old man, so sturdy on his legs, so irascible and jolly and indignant and easily placated, so strong and healthy for his years.

' I don't know—and I don't care, as long as I know that *something* is——'

He kissed her. They were saying farewell. It was in the Kurfürstendamm on a Sunday evening. They had been seeing Jannings' new film *Tempest* with the new actress Anna Sten. She had excited Benjie and he would have given anything to be able to kiss her adorable and most mysterious almond eyes. ' But I don't kiss women any more,' he told Sally. ' Or hardly ever. Old men of my age should look and not touch.'

He was catching the night train to the Hook, and in the train he felt for a while very melancholy. The last link was gone. Not only was he alone now, but the romantic history of the Herries family was closed and finished. He would go back to Cumberland and never leave it till he died. He hated to feel lonely, so he thought of Vanessa. He

opened a novel that he had been told was good—
The Fountain, by Charles Morgan.   He was very
quickly interested in it although he seldom read
novels.   'Sort of book Vanessa would like,' he
thought.

In the summer he did a ridiculous thing.   He
bought a caravan.   He had been staying for some
days near Canterbury and he saw this thing.   It
looked very handsome, for it was painted a deep
crimson and the curtains of the little windows were
pink and white.   It contained, he discovered, every
possible requirement and was remarkably cheap
because its owner had just been declared bankrupt.
He found that his motor-car could be attached to
it very comfortably.   He bought it there and then.
Afterwards he had the difficult task of explaining
its advantages to John Holly.   Holly was his man,
chauffeur, cook, bottle-washer, general factotum,
friend and perpetual grumbler, who had been with
him now for several years.   He was a small spindle-
shanked man whose appearance was never as smart
as Benjie wished.   He had a passion for engines,
dogs and women.   He was sober and industrious,
but an abominable gossip and a Bolshevik in
politics.   He was no respecter of persons.

'Gor blimey!   What do you want a bloody
caravan for?'

'To live in.'

'To live in?   You can't live in a caravan in
London.'

'We aren't going to live in London any more,
John.   We shall probably never see it again.   We
are going up to Cumberland to stay.'

' Oh, well, you can take my notice. I'm not going to live in the country.'

' All right. You can go as soon as you like.'

' I damned well would go if it weren't for the dog.'

' There you are, you see. It's much better for Sam to live in the country. You're always saying he doesn't get enough exercise.'

Sam, although he was no longer young, behaved like a puppy still. Holly adored him.

' A caravan! My God! We *will* look a couple of pretties! '

Before his departure for Cumberland, Benjie went round and said good-bye to the Family. They were none of them sorry to see him go, as he very well knew. Only Horace perhaps regretted him, which was ironic, because Benjie had for so long detested Horace. However, Sally had cared for him, and now at the age of seventy-four he put up, on the whole, a very brave show.

He was as optimistic as ever and even quoted ' God's in His heaven: All's right with the world.'

' Everything possible is wrong with it,' said Benjie, ' and we're two old derelicts who ought to have been dead long ago.'

' I'm remarkably well,' Horace said, ' except for a twinge of rheumatism. I'll come up and visit you in Cumberland one day.'

' I'm damned if you will,' thought Benjie. However, he shook him warmly by the hand.

Cynthia's Pekinese barked at him until he was deafened (he detested toy dogs), Alfred showed him round the Hampstead garden, Gordon slapped him on the back, Adrian, who was now a weary dyspeptic pessimist, said to him:

' I'll be sorry not to see you about, Benjie. I've always admired you, you know.'

' Admired me? Good God—why? '

' You've always gone your way. I might have done once. And then you make me think of Vanessa, the only woman I ever really loved.'

They weren't so bad, he thought, when he'd said good-bye to all of them. He had fought them all his life and was glad to be rid of them, but he saw quite clearly their integrity, their wholesome common sense, their loyalty to their own beliefs.

' There have to be the imaginative and the unimaginative, but they'll never understand one another. And that's that.'

August this year was luckily a dry fine month. Everyone was astonished—as everyone in England always is when holidays are fine—astonished and a little indignant, as though England were posing slightly. The caravan was most amusing. Benjie, Holly, and Sam all slept in the little cupboard behind the general living-room unless the nights were dry, when Holly and Sam slept out of doors. But they got on very well. They were all quiet and unemotional sleepers.

There was a great deal of traffic and general holiday rejoicing. Holly, as was the way of his kind, was extremely proud of the caravan in the presence of strangers and very indignant about it to Benjie.

' Blasted old inculus ' (he meant ' incubus ').

' It wobbles like an old fat woman.' But he
talked to everyone—farmers, hotel girls, motor-
cyclists and the A.A. officials.

' Ought to have one,' Benjie heard him say.
' Everyone will be having them soon.   They say
we all got to economise.   Well, what about it?
Most economic thing going.'

When they were north of Doncaster, Benjie's
spirits rose higher and higher.   For one thing,
he'd never felt better in his life.

' What do you think of me for seventy-seven? '
he would ask John.   He would be doing his
exercises, half stripped on a sunny morning outside the caravan, while Sam sniffed for rabbits
under the hedge.

' Take care you don't catch no cold,' John
would say.   ' And another thing.   Don't let no
women see you.   They'll think we're nudists.'
Then, with a reluctant and cynical smile he would
add: ' You've got a fine brown skin—like the
gipsies.   I'm a gipsy now myself, I reckon, but
I can't get that brown colour.   Lived too much
in towns.'

On the whole they found that farmers, pro-
prietors of fields, publicans and sinners were all
very agreeable to them.   A very good thing, for
Benjie's temper was up in a minute.

' I give what I get—always have.   Give me
sauce and you'll know it.'

Then, when they came to Kendal, it was just
like going home.   There's a brow of the hill between Kendal and Windermere when the waters
of the Lake are suddenly revealed.   It is as though

a door were unlocked. Benjie caught Holly's shoulder. 'Look at that, John, and thank your Maker.'

'Here, look out—I'll be driving into the hedge.'

'Well, stop the damned thing.

All three of them got out and looked at the Promised Land.

'The only woman I ever loved lived with me there. I was born there. My children were born there.'

'What!' said Holly, astonished. 'Only loved one woman in your life? A gay old man like you? Glad I can't say the same.'

But Benjie didn't answer.

They came into Keswick on a fine summer's afternoon and attracted a good deal of attention, but they didn't stop there. They found that on the following day, September 3rd, were the Braithwaite Games, so Benjie said that they should pitch their caravan in a field near by. They found a nice green one under the beneficent shadow of Grisedale and Grasmoor. They found a farmer too, a little bouncing man with a red face.

At first he was very angry and then he was very friendly. He told them to clear out and Benjie spoke his mind. Holly, watching them, found it amusing to see two little men so furious.

'What I want to know,' Benjie remarked, ' is why you can't keep a civil tongue in your head. We aren't doing any harm to your blasted field. I'll pay you properly, if that's your trouble.'

' Aye,' said the farmer, ' but I don't want your money or your company either.'

Then he smiled. Benjie was standing, with his hat off, his blue eyes fiery as though he wanted nothing better than a hand-to-hand encounter.

' It's a nice day,' the farmer said. ' You can stay if you like—and I don't want your money either.'

They shook hands and finally sat down on the steps of the caravan and had a chat.

And next morning it came down a regular posh. Not only did it pour, but the wind blew, and not only did the wind blow, but it blew from every possible direction. The whole world was a turmoil of wind and water. But Braithwaite people are not easily discouraged. Have they not the finest village hall for entertainments in the County? No, they are not the people to be defeated. Benjie in a mackintosh and Sam with his stiff short hair blown sideways and one ear over one eye (all the work of the wind) went along to see how things were progressing. They discovered that the tea-tent had just been blown down for the third time. Everyone was in a state of mind. As the *Mid-Cumberland Herald* afterwards neatly put it: ' *All morning wind and rain conspired to make conditions as unpleasant as possible. While the caterers were manfully struggling to erect a marquee in which to feed the spectators, and had to give up after the third attempt, the would-be spectators were debating in their own minds whether to attend or not. The secretary and committee were wondering what the patrons would do.*'

Benjie and Sam assisted for a while and then, feeling that they were wet enough for anything, went back to the caravan. Here, for the rest of the morning, while the rain beat and the wind blew, Benjie wrote to Sally and entertained Sam.

Sam had never grown up. He had not changed in the slightest since Benjie first had him; the white and brown curls of his coat were as charming as ever, his brown eyes as alive and his body as packed with quivering and alert eagerness. A small rubber ball was everything that he needed to turn life from a dull sombre business into a matter of quicksilver daring and adventure.

The caravan apartment was small and loaded with cooking-things, clothes, a rifle, a broken-down armchair, a radio and a number of books. In and out of this confusion Benjie and Sam enjoyed an entertainment that had surprise for motive and confusion for its atmosphere. As the ball bounced man and dog rushed for it together. Benjie was, after many years of practice, up to every kind of guile, but Sam knew all the tricks. He stood, the stump of his tail erect and quivering, his eyes on fire, his nose twitching, his right foreleg trembling! Had you shouted in his ear that the Last Trump was at hand it would have been no matter. Benjie, his arm raised, held the ball: he feinted towards the cooking-stove and Sam's body swung in that direction but his eyes did not shift. He knew two of that. When the ball bounced his teeth snapped, he sprang and Benjie grabbed. Books fell, tins rattled, clothes swung

in mid-air.   Benjie was on his belly groping under
the chair while Sam, in no way deceived in this
manœuvre, knowing well that Benjie had the ball
set in his hand, stayed, his legs parted, his eyes
burning, his complete soul (for he had one) concentrated. . . .

Meanwhile the rain lashed the caravan, sweeping across the field in sheeted splendour.

' Not bad for seventy-seven! ' Benjie cried to
Holly, who, standing disdainful in his yellow
ulster, saw his master with his shirt open, on his
knees, and dust on his cheeks.

' Gawd, what weather! ' Holly said.

Nevertheless in the afternoon they ventured
and had their reward.   Cumberland people are not
to be shaken by the weather and there was a good
crowd.   The weather in fact shook its head and
decided to improve.   The rain when it did come
was a deluge, but in between the sun shone and
the colours came out like a picture-show.   The
clouds rushed like mad things across the sky.   The
sun fell, as though the light had been spilled from
a bucket, on to Skiddaw and at once the purple
glow of the heather on its flanks spread like a living
shadow from shoulder to shoulder while above and
below it the green turf almost hurt the eye with
its brightness.   Then, on the other side of the
valley you might see (if you had time to notice)
the dark clouds piling up over the tops and swinging through Coledale Pass like an army.   On the
clouds came and a minute later the rain poured
down.   The army marched on to invade Keswick

and out the sun came again. If you cared to
watch you could time the showers and run for
shelter.

In the heavens it was all life and movement
and on the ground the same stir and constant
change.

Benjie drew a deep breath of satisfaction.
When he saw Mr. Bowe, the secretary, who for
weeks past had been saying to all and sundry,
' Now, whatever you do you mustn't miss Braithwaite,' hastening hither and thither to see that
everything was up to time, his own excitement was
intense. He was home again; he was among
friends again; he was breathing the air that was,
by right of birth, his own. He knew exactly what
they were all feeling and wanting and hoping, and
he felt and wanted and hoped with them. The
clouds were his and the grass was his and the
surrounding watching hills.

In a noisy crowd the bookies shouted their
odds. In spite of the rain the booths with sweets
and apples and ginger-beer drove their trade.
Dogs were everywhere, and children and anxious
parents, farmers and Keswick citizens and men
from Cockermouth and Bassenthwaite, from
Under Skiddaw and Threlkeld and Grange and
Portinscale.

Soon everything was in motion. In the centre
of the field were the wrestlers, the twelve-stoners
and the ten-stoners, moving slowly round and
round one another with a heavy foot-treading
solemnity. Round and round they would go,
arms out, broad backs straining; they would seem

thus like nothing so much as dreamers who find
that meditation on the Deity, the character of the
soil they tread, the end of their mysterious
destinies, can be obtained best by this slow
motion and steady contemplation. Western
mystics with their proper sacred ceremonies—
and then suddenly there is a start, a jerk, they are
locked in one another's arms like lovers, a face
stares to the sky, a vast leg stiffens, there is a
fall.

'Aye, it will be Blakeney's for sartain,' a
farmer beside Benjie prophesied to him gravely.

'Why Blakeney?'

'Didn't ye know? Three times nine and
a half stone world champion — aye. He's a
lad. . . .'

Round the circle of the field the flat-racers
were already arranging themselves.

But it was the Puppy Trail that made Benjie's
heart beat. In his excitement he dragged Holly
by the arm, for that man of a mechanical world
was gazing about him with an urban civilised
scorn for these poor countrymen who knew nothing better than, on a wet day, to strip almost to
the buff and circle slowly round and round on a
sodden field.

Benjie might be seventy-seven, but he ran as
well as anyone, climbed the low wall and hurried
into the next field to see the start of the Trail.
At the sight of the men holding the hounds in
leash, at the sight of those same hounds straining,
yelping, pulling, he sniffed the air as though he
were an old hound himself. The last hound-

trail he had seen he had been with Vanessa over
Loweswater way. It had been a glorious day, he
remembered, so hot that they had sheltered together under a thick tree for the cool. Afterwards
they had had their tea there, and the shadows,
moving to the sound of the running beck at their
side, had slowly covered the slope of the hill.
Then the first stars had come out and, as they had
walked together to the road, they had heard from
the tent the softened buzzing of the band. . . .

Now, as he waited, the sun flashed between the
showers, the two trail-runners with their ' pads '
of old stockings and their aniseed bottles came
running in, someone dashed down the flag and
the hounds were off. Up the hill, over the wall,
across the field and they were lost to view.

After they were gone there was a strange
silence, a vacuum, a sense of ' How shall we fill
in the time until they're back again? ' Some with
field-glasses climbed the slope, others stood in
clusters discussing results—was it to be Starlight
or Saturn or Meg?

They turned back for a brief while to watch
the wrestling. As Benjie stopped before the wall
he felt his shoulder gripped. Against him, at his
shoulder, was a strong old man roughly dressed
in corduroys, black-haired, bent a little in the
back. It was George Endicott.

Benjie stared, feeling that now at this very
moment he was wrestling with George on that
parlour floor while on the staircase above the
woman stood with the candle, waiting, listening
. . . that moment that had twisted wrongly his

whole life.   He had not seen Endicott for ten years.

' George! '

' Funny to see you here.   Thought you were dead.'

' And you.'

' Come and have a drink.'   It was as though they had never parted.   It was his last struggle. He was old and Endicott was old, but there was time yet, old though they were, for the ancient shabbiness, wildness, waste, to return.   George had still his black eyes, his loose mouth, that animal lurch of his shoulders.   Benjie had never gone away with George yet but that one thing had led to another and so, step by step, into a craziness that ended in darkness.   Odd how, at the sight of George, that other world crowded in, all the women he had kissed, the silly toasts he had drunk, the fights he had fought, yes, and farther back through that, striking back to some old scene when a woman had been sold in a tent and on a starlit night swords had flashed, and on the Carlisle wall, befogged, he had seen the Devil. . . . Had he or had he not?   Was this the last touch of that wild hand on his shoulder?

It seemed that it was, for, smiling, he said:

' No, George, thank you.'

' What? ' said George.   ' Too old for drinking? '

' Oh, I'll drink with you sometime, but I'm waiting for the hounds to come back.'

George's dark eyes covered him.   They studied him from head to toe.

' You look fit.'

' Yes, very fit, thanks.   Only a stiffness in my right leg once and again.   Are you staying round here? '

' No.   I'm moving on to Carlisle to-night. Like to come? '

' What are you doing there? '

' Eh, I don't know.   Meeting a man about a dog, you know.'

There flamed up in him one final tempting impulse.   He was lonely.   He had thought, this morning, that it was happiness enough wandering the country with John and Sam.   But he didn't know. . . . It would be good to be with George again, to move, ancient though he was, into that old world without law, without order, without discipline.

Then he shook his head.

' Afraid I can't.'

' Sure? '

' Yes.   Can't get away.'

' So long then.   See you sometime.'

George vanished and Benjie turned back to see where Holly was, almost as though he needed protection.

He felt an intense relief as though a weight that had hampered him for years past were gone. A relief—and a loneliness—for he was old and, in the final stage of life, with every added year our fellows recede from us further.

He waited on the edge of the hill, watching for the first sight of the hounds.   To John at his side he explained the mysteries.   ' You must be careful laying your trail.   You've got to watch

2 E

out that it isn't too dangerous for the hounds, loose scree or falling boulders, and your curve mustn't have too small a radius because a clever hound will pick up the scent on the far side and cut off a troublesome corner. There are hounds who'll be half a mile ahead of the others again and again simply by cutting off corners. And you've got to watch out for men stopping them on the course, giving them meat or something. Once you have betting, men will do anything. All the same it's the prettiest thing in the world, this and sheep-dog trials. You've come to the right country, John.'

'Well—so you say——'

Then, suddenly, there was a shout. Over the top of Barrow the hounds had been sighted. Against the dark green slopes you could see the light-coloured bodies moving now in spots of colour, hidden by trees and then, in a moment, all in a line along the fell path.

'There they are!' 'I can see Starlight!' 'Meg's in front.' 'Nay, that's Saturn!'

Now they had all vanished behind a knoll. There was a breathless pause and then a great shout as two hounds appeared abreast.

' 'Tis Starlight!'

'Nay—Saturn! Saturn! Saturn!'

'Yes, 'tis Starlight all right!'

Then down, down the hill they came all together over the hedge on to the roadway. At the last fence Saturn was over first, Starlight just behind him.

'By God! a grand finish!' someone shouted. But the hullabaloo was now fearful, for all the trainers, with signals perfectly understood by their hounds, let them know, with plenty of time to spare, where the finishing-point may be. The shrieks, yells, howls, whistles can be heard a mile away, and some farmer driving his cart up a country lane catches the din on the breeze and will say:

'Yes. Yon's t'hound-trail at Braithwaite.'

Starlight and Saturn were up the field together, and had either slackened victory would have been to the other. Did they slacken? Not they. It was one of the best finishes for years—and Saturn has it, two lengths ahead of Starlight, and Granite close behind him.

The rain came, the rain cleared. A lovely mellow light covered the earth. It was the final of the twelve-stone wrestling—Bob Greatouse of Arradfoot had been beaten in the final of the twelve-stone by Blakeney the champion, but the other Greatouse of Arradfoot was in the final of the ten-stone. He was wrestling Pickthall of Cleator Moor. All men held their breath. The two figures went round and round. There was a clinch. Everyone said 'Ah!' Pickthall was thrown with a back-heel. . . . Round and round again. Another 'Ah!' Pickthall was thrown again, this time with a twist off the breast and a back-heel. Arradfoot could be proud that night.

Benjie was talking, he did not know to whom. Everyone was friendly. Someone asked him whence he had come.

'Oh, from the South.'

And where would he be going to?
' I'm going nowhere.   I'm staying here.'
' Aye.   Nowt t'matter wi' Coomberland.'
He turned back and looked up to Barrow.
Yes, he was staying.   He'd come home.

THE EAGLE

DURING the following weeks Benjie made a number of friends. He was of course quickly recognised, the wild young Herries who had grown up with his mother at Ireby, married beneath him, disappeared and then returned with a woman not his wife, shut himself up for years in Newlands.

In the old days you might have disapproved or not disapproved according to your own uprightness of character. But now he was no longer a danger. They called him ' an old rascal ' but his teeth were drawn now. He was a character with his one arm, his short-cropped grey curly hair, face like a russet apple, bright blue eyes. And he liked to wear blue shirts and dark-red ties. So he went about the district with his caravan and his man and his dog.

' Yes, he's a rascal,' they'd say, but he never did any harm to anyone. He had a fiery temper and knocked a man down in Cockermouth in spite of his seventy-seven years, but for the most part he was ready to be friendly.

Moreover he was a Herries, and the Herries, although they'd been queer, had been fond of the district for two hundred years. And Judith Paris was still remembered everywhere—Madame with her white hair and grand manner and walking-stick.

' Glad you've come back,' they said to Benjie, and they were.

There came a day in October at last when he thought he would pitch his caravan in a field by Rosthwaite. He had avoided this for weeks: some superstitious feeling had kept him away, as though that ride from Keswick to Rosthwaite and his sitting down there at the spot where the Herries house had once been under the shadow of Watend-lath, had some kind of deep spiritual significance for him. He didn't believe much in deep spiritual significances, but there came times when a man stopped, like Balaam's ass, at a shadow in the path. He had been everywhere else—Uldale and Ireby and Cat Bells and Newlands and Seascale and Gosforth and Ravenglass—all the places that kept anything of Vanessa in their atmosphere—but he had held back from Rosthwaite.

'When I get there I'm closing the chapter.' He didn't know, but he thought it likely that he would end his days in Borrowdale. ' And then that's the finish. No Herries here any more.'

But at last, on a lovely October day, he decided to move on to Rosthwaite. First he had luncheon at the Keswick Hotel, by invitation, with two Keswick residents—Mr. Glossop and Mr. Blane. Mr. Glossop was a bachelor, a large stout cheery man in very baggy knickerbockers. He lived in St. John's in the Vale and was reputed to be wealthy. Mr. Blane was married, had three children and a small income. He had been a

Civil Servant in India, had retired, and suffered from a very uncertain digestion. It was natural that Glossop should be an optimist and Blane a pessimist, but Benjie was interested to realise, as luncheon continued, how very much less certain he was of his opinions than were these two much younger men. He neither knew so certainly nor cared so deeply.

As they walked into the hotel Glossop was waving his arms and crying out cheerily: 'What a day! What a grand day! How are you, Mrs. Wivell? Pretty good? That's right. . . . No, Herries, as I was saying, this Government seems to me to be doing wonderfully well. Of course we know that people complain about the Means Test, but what I say is this . . .'

Later at luncheon Mr. Blane looked at Mr. Glossop with his rather dim yellow-shadowed eyes and remarked, nervously crumbling his bread:

'Really, Glossop, how you dare! Why, we're on the edge of the pit, the whole lot of us. Hasn't sterling gone down eight points this very week? Isn't France at her wits' end to balance her budget? Haven't those poor fellows from all parts of the country been marching through the rain all this week on London? Isn't Germany making ready to fight Poland and shan't we be compelled because of Locarno to join in? Really, Glossop, I'd be surprised if I didn't know you. Don't be taken in by him, Mr. Herries. His spirits go down to zero the minute he has the toothache——'

'Ha! Bah!' said Glossop. 'You're a defeatist, Blane, that's what you are! One would think that a little bit of discomfort means the ruin of the universe! Why, after the Napoleonic Wars they had thirty years of distress and a much worse distress than anything we're experiencing. You just wait until after the American election. You'll be surprised how quickly things settle themselves and trade's booming again! Why, Davis from America is over here consulting with MacDonald this very week, and I see that to-day's *Express* says . . .'

So it went on and Benjie's mind wandered. He pulled himself together to say once:

'I've got a girl in Berlin working on international affairs.'

'And what does she tell you?' said Glossop, beaming.

'Well, she doesn't tell me anything.'

And then a little later he remarked:

'Of course if they can teach Doyle to defend himself he'll make some of those Americans look silly. He's a natural fighter.'

But he couldn't really attend. Mr. Blane cried:

'Well, I simply can't understand you, Glossop. There you are, fiddling while Rome is burning.' He added, 'We're bewildered, that's what we all are. Don't feel safe any more.'

And Benjie thought: 'That's his generation— afraid. Sally's isn't.'

He remarked: 'Sam had a great fight yesterday in Penrith. One of those nasty Aberdeens some fat woman was carrying round with her. He just about bit its ear off.'

And after luncheon he could not fix his mind on serious matters. It was as though this going out to Rosthwaite were all-absorbing. They went with him through the town to where his caravan was pitched between the Art School and Crosthwaite Church. All the way along Mr. Glossop was heartily greeting his friends.

'How are you, Mrs. Fox?' and then in parenthesis, 'Mrs. Fox of Fawe Park—American— charming woman,' or 'Fine day, Mrs. Johnson. How's the boy getting on at Cambridge?' or 'How do, Todd,' or 'How are you, Lewin?' as a clergyman passed them on a bicycle. While on the other hand Mr. Blane recognised no one, nor did he see the charm of the old tower nor the break between the houses which showed the sunlit hills rolling through the mortar and brick, nor the white cloud like a gigantic bird's nest perched between the breasts of Skiddaw. He saw nothing, for, defeated once again by the malignant obstinacy of his greed, he had eaten Cumberland ham at luncheon, the richest ham in the world and for him the most destructive. Already he saw pain and discomfort approaching him down the road. . . .

Before Benjie sat with Holly in the front of the motor that pulled the caravan (and Sam on his knee) he shouted to Mr. Blane:

'Try five-minute exercises with your colon like that fellow I read about in a book the other day. Nothing like it for the digestion.' But Mr. Blane didn't think that funny. He assumed a rather sinister air.

As they sputtered off along Main Street, Benjie was cross.

'Having a joke with some men about their digestion is as serious as joking about their religion.'

'That's all right,' said Holly, 'if your stomach's behaving proper. You've got a stomach like an ostrich. I've always said so.'

As usual, they were a sensation in the town, and to-day, under the blue sky, the red caravan with all the handles to the doors highly polished was a fine sight. Benjie, his hat cocked on one side, a late rosebud in his buttonhole, was a throw-back, as he himself had observed, to Britannia seated on her throne in the old circus processions.

'You know, Holly,' he said, 'two hundred years ago on a dark night a very wicked ancestor of mine rode out into Borrowdale just as we're doing.'

He was thinking a lot about Francis Herries just then, for a fortnight ago he had read Judith's book once again right through. Times weren't so good, with investments down as they were. It is true that now that Sally was settled his needs were small, but he had wondered whether, after all, Judith's book mightn't be worth publishing. After reading it he decided that it would be sacrilege. But the whole world of that book was very present to him. When you were as old as he was time vanished and had no meaning.

Holly had no interest whatever in the Herries family, but he *was* interested in scandal.

'What way was he wicked?' he asked.

'Oh, the usual way.'

'Wine, women and song! Oh, boy!' said Holly.

'There's no need to be American, John,' Benjie remarked. 'They're fine people and their own language suits them, but you're English.'

'You bet,' Holly said. 'No damned foreigners for me.'

When they reached the Ashness gate Benjie made him pull up. He got out and looked across the Lake. There was not a ripple on the water, which was coloured so faintly blue that it was almost white, to the Manesty bank. Here the trees, the chestnuts, the maples, the larches flamed on the water's edge. They seemed in actual fact to be burning. You might fancy that, across the still water, you heard the branches crackle in the blaze. From the darkest crimson, through amber, orange, the rich yellow of a canary's wing, to the faint gold pallor of Chinese lacquer, they were massed against the red cloud of bracken that covered the fell. To the right the cloud that had been a bird's nest on Skiddaw had grown until it enveloped the peaks in a tumbled mass that glittered like frozen snow. There was no sound nor breath of stirring.

'It's a fine day,' he said, climbing back beside Holly.

'And it'll rain to-morrow, I bet you,' said Holly.

With every yard of ground—past the Lodore Hotel, the Borrowdale, Grange Bridge, the Bowder Stone, down the hill into the valley—

Benjie's spirits rose. The outer world slipped behind them. The old valley was still shut in even as in ancient days, when its citizens had, as the legend went, tried to build a wall to enclose the cuckoo. Glaramara and Grey Knotts and Brandreth were the advance guard; Gable, Scafell, Great End, Bowfell were still guardians at the close, as for so many hundreds of years they had been. The valley was as still as the Lake had been, and above the green fields, to the right at the side of the streams, the leaves in orange and crimson lifted their glory to the blue.

' Where are we going? ' asked Holly. ' Does this valley lead to anywhere? '

' No. It does not. We're stopping for the night near the place where that same ancestor of mine built a house.'

' Kind of lost sort of place, this valley,' said Holly.

Where the path leads off the high road up to Watendlath they halted. Here there was a little stone bridge that crossed a stream flecked now with the blue of the sky, and just above it was a solid little stone house.

' Is that the place your ancestor built? '

' No. That's not the house, but it's the spot. Two ladies lived there, but now it's sold. There's nobody in it, I fancy, just now.'

After some trouble they found a spot on the level below the house where the caravan could remain.

When they were settled Benjie lit a pipe, and, taking with him that day's *Times* which he had

procured in Keswick, Judith's book at which he
thought he would have another look, and Casson's
Wise Kings of Borrowdale (an old friend of his that
he had not seen for many a year but had found
to-day in Chaplin's shop), he seated himself comfortably on the step of the caravan while Sam
pursued idyllic scents on the border of the stream.

He had only to raise his eyes, he reflected, and
there was old Rogue Herries riding up the path
with the little boy in his arms. . . . The boy runs
forward and flings open the door . . .

He opened Judith's book at the beginning and
read:

'I, Judith Paris, was born at Rosthwaite in
the valley of Borrowdale, Cumberland, on the
28th of November in the Year of Our Lord
1774 . . .' He skipped a little, but old Aunt
Jane's feminine mid-Victorian hand was wonderfully clear. 'I have heard very much of what
happened in those long-ago times from my half-
brother David Herries. David Herries was my
father's son by his first wife, and he was fifty-five
when I was born, so that I could have been his
granddaughter. . . . He told me that he remembered exactly the night that he first arrived in
Keswick. He could remember every detail, and
so do I, even at this distance of time. How he
was in the inn at Keswick in a big canopied bed
with his sisters Mary and Deborah. The canopy
that ran round the top of the bed was a faded
green and had a gold thread in it. There were
fire-dogs by the fire with mouths like grinning
dragons. And he remembered that a woman

was sitting warming herself in front of the fire, a
woman he hated.   Then his father came in and
thought he was sleeping.   He remembered that
his father was wearing a beautiful coat of a claret
colour and a chestnut wig, and there were red
roses on his grey silk waistcoat. . . .'

Benjie skipped a page or two.   He came to
the ride through Borrowdale.   ' David was wide
awake now and knew that his father was happily
drunk.   He sang a song that was popular with
children then.   David had played it as a game:

> ' Lady Queen Anne who sits in her stand,
> And a pair of green gloves upon her hand.
> As white as a lily, as fair as a swan,
> The fairest lady in a' the land.

They rode on and suddenly the clouds broke and
a moon sailed out and the sky was covered with
stars.   Then they moved up the little hill and it
was all very quiet.   It all seemed very wonderful
to David, who had never seen mountains before,
and of course they were very large in the moonlight.

' Then they stopped and someone said:

' " That is the house on the left of us."

' They went on through a thick group of trees
and now they were outside a rough stone wall
guarding a courtyard where grass was growing.
David remembered that he was sadly disappointed
in his first view of the house, for it looked so small
under the hill.   Then some dogs ran out, barking,
and his father put him to the ground and he ran
forward and was first into the house.   In the hall,

which through the open door was moonlit, he saw
two shining suits of armour. . . .'

'It's all very vivid', thought Benjie; 'if I try
hard enough I can see it just as it was and the boy
running across the courtyard.' The air was so
still that it was not difficult to fancy that there
were figures standing listening, and that the old
house was still there with the moon shining in on
the suits of armour.

The fresh air made him feel sleepy. The past
was so much more real to him than the present,
as it is perhaps to all old people. The things that
the two men had discussed at luncheon were dim
and shadowy.

'It may be', he thought, 'that it is only when
you are old that you see things in their true perspective. The world seems to be crumbling but
it has crumbled so often before, changing into a
new shape that will appear as solid to another
generation as its earlier form seemed to the older
people. But I'm no philosopher. I've been better
at doing things than thinking them.' And his
life crowded up into his consciousness, all of it
moving at the same time. He was with Barney
and Ellis at the music-hall and a lady gave him
a white rose, he asked Vanessa to marry him
in the moonlight in the Fortress garden, he
wrestled with Endicott; once again, misery at his
heart, he told Vanessa that he was married, and
once again he stood by the Chinese clock while
Ellis shouted at them from below; he was in
Newlands and there came the most wonderful

moment of his life when Vanessa, brushing her hair, turned and looked at him. . . .

He would go no further. But how strange that all these things should be still so alive and other things that had nothing to do with his heart—Africa and Spain and (the greatest moment in his life apart from Vanessa) the sunlit day in Petrograd when they had marched, singing, into the new world. Why, he thought, were the only things that counted in a man's life, when you looked back, the things that touched his spirit— if he had one?

Was it true, as Vanessa believed, that there was a secret life, progressive, unceasing, all-important?

Holly had come to the caravan-door, a frying-pan in his hand.

' John, do you think there's a secret life? '

' Will you have your eggs scrambled or fried? ' John asked, disregarding, as he so often did, Benjie's mad way of asking questions that meant nothing.

Benjie turned back to the scene. It was growing cold. As fire dies into ash so the sky was fading into grey. He was very happy. His memories and this country made him so.

He opened Casson's thin green book, but could scarcely see to read.

I bid ye mourn not for the death of beauty.
For, though the Springtide fades from Cumberland,
Her streams and tarns, there is eternal spring
In heaven. And, on my island where I live,
I dream that heaven is very like this land,
Mountains and lakes and rivers undecaying,

And simple woodlands and wild cherry flowers.
At least I know no better. But weep not.
For, though this land is but the shadow of heaven,
It yet is heaven's shadow.

He was almost asleep. His pipe fell from his
hand. It was so small a country—this green valley,
up the Pass into the hollow guarded by Gable,
and the Scafells with dark Wastwater to one
side, lonely Ennerdale to another, Eskdale, and,
to the south the Pikes and Langdale, Esthwaite
and Windermere and Coniston. One turn of the
hand to the north, and in close company Grasmere
and Rydal, Ullswater, and so, towards the Border,
Derwentwater, Buttermere, Crummock . . . a
land that the sweep of a bird might in a flash of
the sun cover with its shadow. England itself,
from these little hills and lakes, through the dark
space of the Midlands, in a moment of time, over
field and stream and sloping hill to the sea. . . .
The Eagle's wing embraced it. The White
Horse, striking •upward from the dark water,
climbed the icy hill. The Eagle free, the White
Horse triumphant, the same Eagle, the same
Horse as in captivity, now lost themselves in a
larger liberty, in a purpose far grander than their
individual struggle. . . .
Was he asleep? He thought he heard Holly's
voice:
' You'll get cold out there. Supper's nearly
ready.'
But he rested his head against the upper step.
He sighed with happiness because all the struggle
was over. No one was afraid any longer. Vanessa

was all right. Tom was all right. Sally, who knew no fear, was building the new world. And he himself was at home where he had always wanted to be.

He turned his head, smiling, and sleepily murmured, as in the past he had so often done:

' Good night, Vanessa.'

Over this country, when the giant Eagle flings the shadow of his wing, the land is darkened. So compact is it that the wing covers all its extent in one pause of the flight. The sea breaks on the pale line of the shore; to the Eagle's proud glance waves run in to the foot of the hills that are like rocks planted in green water.

From Whinlatter to Black Combe the clouds are never still. The Tarns like black unwinking eyes watch their chase, and the colours are laid out in patterns on the rocks and are continually changed. The Eagle can see the shadows rise from their knees at the base of Scafell and Gable, he can see the black precipitous flanks of the Screes washed with rain and the dark purple hummocks of Borrowdale crags flash suddenly with gold.

So small is the extent of this country that the sweep of the Eagle's wing caresses all of it, but there is no ground in the world more mysterious, no land at once so bare in its nakedness and so rich in its luxury, so warm with sun and so cold in pitiless rain, so gentle and pastoral, so wild and lonely; with sea and lake and river there is always the sound of moving water, and its strong people have their feet in the soil and are independent of all men.

During the flight of the Eagle two hundred years are but as a day—and the life of a man, as against all odds he pushes towards immortality, is eternal. . . .

THE END

Edinburgh, *Christmas Eve,* 1931.
Brackenburn, *October 26,* 1932.

HERRIES

A CHRONICLE IN FOUR PARTS

J'ai la tête romanesque.
J'aime le pittoresque.

Begun EDINBURGH,
    Christmas Eve, 1927.
Ended BRACKENBURN,
    October 26, 1932.